EPIC

QUESTS & JOURNEYS MYTHS & TALES

ANTHOLOGY OF CLASSIC TALES

Foreword by Matt Cardin

FLAME TREE PUBLISHING

TALES

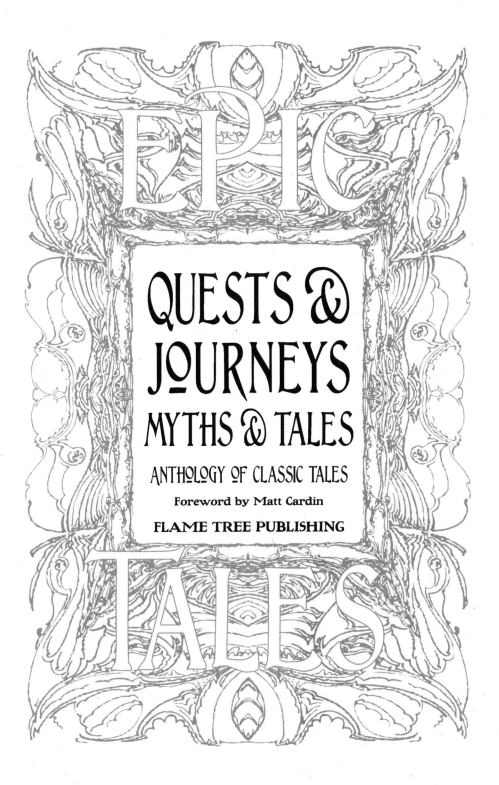

This is a FLAME TREE Book

Publisher & Creative Director: Nick Wells
Editorial Director: Catherine Taylor
Project Editors: Taylor Bentley and Jocelyn Pontes
Special thanks to Michael Kerrigan

FLAME TREE PUBLISHING
6 Melbray Mews, Fulham,
London SW6 3NS, United Kingdom
www.flametreepublishing.com

First published 2024

24 26 28 27 25
1 3 5 7 9 10 8 6 4 2

ISBN: 978-1-80417-801-0
Special ISBN: 978-1-80417-946-8

The cover image is created by Flame Tree Studio based on artwork by Bourbon-88. Internal decorations are courtesy Shutterstock.com and the following artists: Tribalium and xtock

A copy of the CIP data for this book is available from the British Library.

Printed and bound in China

EPIC TALES

QUESTS & JOURNEYS MYTHS & TALES

ANTHOLOGY OF CLASSIC TALES

Foreword by Matt Cardin

FLAME TREE PUBLISHING

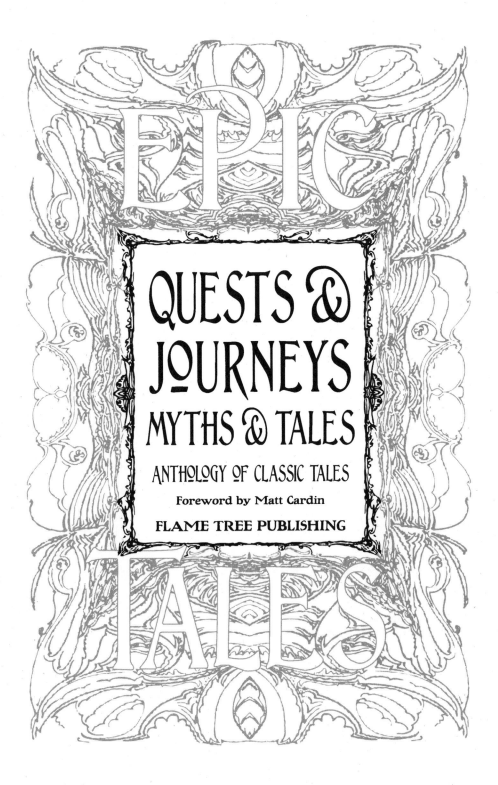

Contents

Foreword

THE IMPLICIT APPEAL of tales of quests and journeys – an appeal beyond their surface attraction as exciting stories – is that they operate on multiple levels. In doing so, they speak to the reader's or hearer's personal, existential concerns. Even as they entertain on one level, on another level they evoke some of the most profound and poignant emotions and intimations in all of human experience.

Such stories are always, ultimately, about more than just the events and characters they portray. They are not even *primarily* about these. Rather, they are about the reader. They are about the unchosen journey the reader was set upon by the sheer fact of being born, and they are about the quest the reader was assigned by the sheer fact of being born as a self-conscious creature that automatically, helplessly feels incomplete and therefore searches for the answer to the riddle of its existence, the mystery of its appearance as a separate presence, a singular subjectivity confronted by an outer, objective world into which it has been cast, and with which it often finds itself at odds, and within which it must find the reason for its existence. The primal, unchosen journey invoked by any tale in this vein is the journey from nothing to something and then back again – from birth, through the world, to death. The primal quest is to find out why this experience should have happened at all: the answer to who one actually is, and what the world is, and what one is supposed to be doing here, and how to locate the object of that implanted sense of numinous yearning, and even whether – dream of all dreams – it might be possible to forestall or eliminate the seemingly surefire end point of annihilation.

Again, this is what stories of quests and journeys invoke beyond their surface elements. They metaphorize the reader's life situation, both its subjective and objective aspects, and they depict its outworking and resolution in a multitude of different narratives, terms and cultural iterations.

There is also another division into levels or layers that likewise parallels the reader's life. It is one that skilled storytellers around the world have always known. Today it is the purview of novelists, screenwriters, and game writers, who have honed it to a fine point and deployed it *en masse* in the multitude of fictional narratives that now pervade our lives. The principle is simply this: All quests and journeys are both outer and inner. The quest for an external object is simultaneously a quest for an inner object. A story's outer events are always a mutual reflection of its protagonist's inner search. Importantly, this is not separate from, and in fact it is an aspect of, the first principle.

A journey through a world of adventure, conflict, loss, love and all the rest is a journey through the landscape of the protagonist's soul. The events and experiences that make up the story of a Ulysses struggling for ten years to return to Ithaca, or a Percival questing for the Holy Grail, or a Sindbad seeking adventure and riches on the high seas, are simultaneously the chronicle of an inner journey toward some altered state of being, some shift of personal character, some realization, some attainment of wisdom or insight, whether of the nominally positive or negative sort. In some classic tales, such as those of Gilgamesh and Maui, the quest is for immortality itself, and there is essentially no distinction between outer and inner, surface text and subtext. In all cases, the dual journey intertwines with the fact of the reader's involvement, as described above, to make such stories a chronicle of the reader's inner quest. When the alchemy of storytelling is activated at its highest pitch, this can result in a deeply moving sense of simultaneous revelation and confirmation. Contemporary storytellers with their narrative codification of this principle are simply continuing an ancient tradition, one as old as the art of telling stories at all.

These principles are important aspects of the powerful, perennial fascination we feel for tales of quests and journeys. But of course one does not have to think about them while reading the stories themselves, nor is it advisable to do so. On a much simpler level, there is the winsome attraction of the surface story itself, the sheer pleasure of adventure, romance and so on, the enjoyment of accompanying colourful characters on dramatic, dangerous, passionate, frightening, humorous, epic, entertaining trips. This is the basic level at which we approach any story, and unless we are scholars or philosophers who come bearing an explicitly analytical intent, it is the level at which we are best advised to read them.

In fact, those other, 'deeper' layers of meaning and engagement are most deeply felt, and are most powerfully effective, when we leave them to work on their own, beyond our peripheral vision, in the shadows of the unconscious mind, instead of straining to see and know them consciously. So, we read the story, hear the narrative, engage the adventure, let ourselves get swept up in the enjoyment and fascination of it all. Meanwhile, secret things are happening in our soul, in parallel with the protagonist's inner journey and the story's symbolic unfolding. This marriage of soul between the reader/listener and the story is an ancient meta-tale in itself: the tale of *telling ourselves*, of storytelling as a means and manifestation of our individual and collective quests. When we engage with the global tradition of such stories, we rehearse, and we mythically inform and enrich, the story of our own origin and destiny, of the journey we are each called upon to make, which we have *no choice* but to make, through an outer/inner world on a quest for the knowledge and happiness – ultimately inseparable, ultimately the same thing – that constitute the answer to the riddle of our lives.

Matt Cardin

Publisher's Note

QUESTS AND JOURNEYS LIE at the heart of myths and folktales around the world, serving as vehicles for transformation and growth, both spiritual and physical. In the following pages you will find stories of sacrifice, adventure, love and redemption, as heroes venture off in to the unknown. We have endeavoured to create a thoughtful collection of stories, drawing on legends and tales from across the globe. While it was a challenge to winnow them down, we hope this final selection showcases a vibrant, diverse range of timeless tales, that will inspire our readers as they have generations before.

The stories in this book come from a variety of sources, and as is the nature with stories rooted in an oral storytelling tradition, their exact narrative how they have been interpreted by those who have put them to paper. Each tale the influence of those who have transcribed and translated them, their original source, and the historical and cultural context of their time. More can be learned about them in the back of the book. In many instances, diacritical marks have been removed, particularly if their usage in original sources was inconsistent. We have also ask readers to keep in mind that opinions expressed regarding the nature of different cultures and peoples, spelling and writing styles, as well as factual information, stem from the era during which these stories were written.

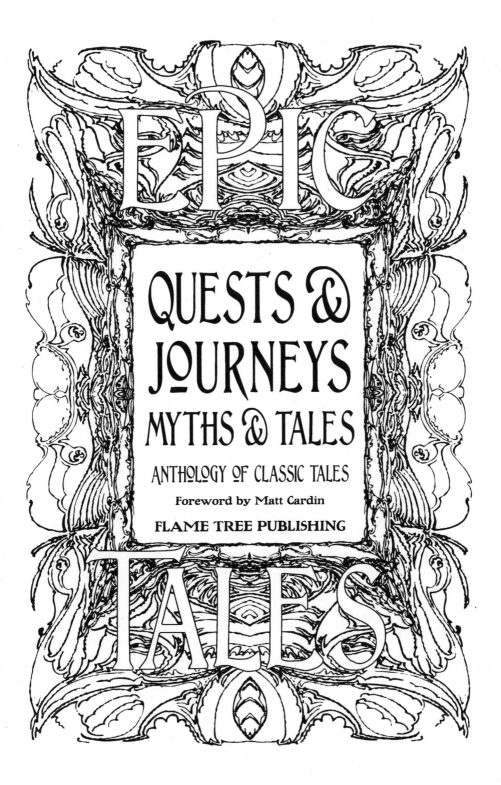

EPIC

QUESTS & JOURNEYS MYTHS & TALES

ANTHOLOGY OF CLASSIC TALES

Foreword by Matt Cardin

FLAME TREE PUBLISHING

TALES

Quests & Journeys

Introduction

THE IDEA OF LIFE as a journey appears to be just about as old as the human imagination, insofar as that is to be found recorded in poetry. David in Psalm 23 – written, it's believed, some time around 1000 BCE – describes himself walking 'through the valley of the shadow of death'. Homer's *Odyssey*, which was probably composed a couple of centuries after that, presents the hero's long and roundabout voyage home from the Trojan War as a sort of ordeal through which, whilst having lots of colourful adventures, he attains a certain growth.

Like the twenty-first-century celebrity who wants to tell us about his or her 'personal journey', these ancient poets saw the idea of movement in space as analogous to the way we all experience change and challenge. Life is never quite as static as it seems, however sedentary our personal existence seems to be. Simply living each day, we are in some sense moving through a changing scene. We talk of important dates as 'milestones'. Emotional ups and downs; family tensions; joyful events; setbacks and successes in the world of work … these things come and go as we continue in our routines, each apparently taking us – like travellers – to a new place.

Taking Charge

This being so, it doesn't seem so strange that someone finding him- or herself in a state of chaos or confusion should see a journey with a purpose as a way of taking charge, or decide, as the folktales so often put it, to 'go out and seek their fortune'. That decision at least gives the impression of changing us from an essentially passive person to whom things happen to one who is consciously shaping – or at least trying to – his or her own life.

The immediate stimulus may well be economic, and so apparently banal. Starvation lies in store for the girl in the Japanese story 'The Black Bowl' if she stays in her village tending her parents' graves. But when she sets off on her travels, she is not just giving herself a better chance of begging food and finding work: she is striking out alone psychologically as well, literally putting distance between herself and the life she's led so far. However lowly this 'beggar-maiden' may be, she will at least be her own woman, with responsibility for her own destiny; her own independent will. And, of course, she's opened herself up to new experiences – new narrative possibilities, from the storyteller's point of view.

Chivalric Values

The journey as assertion of individual will, as voyage of self-discovery, is most consciously embraced in the 'quest' of the mythic medieval knight. Stories with this charismatic figure at their centre seem first to have been told in the oral tradition, but these were written down as literary romances between the eleventh and fifteenth centuries. As composed by medieval writers from Chrétien de Troyes to Sir Thomas Malory, the Arthurian romances were designed to excite and entertain but also to move emotionally and, in many cases, stir with moral warmth.

The court of King Arthur was at the centre of this world. Its 'chivalric' milieu came fully furnished with a colourful backcloth of banquets and tournaments and with an elegant ethos of 'courtly love'. No longer quite the knockabout figure of the old heroic literature, the knight was expected to be gallant – a 'gentleman'; not just a warrior, tough and brave. Psychologically, he was supposed to be deeper, dedicating himself, his life, his soldierly prowess and all his deeds of valour to the lady for whom he languished in (stereotypically) unrequited love. Ladies were important – not least because they made up much of the romances' readership and didn't just want to be told about mindless macho thugs.

Arthur himself, in the mythic record, is marked out by the moral and spiritual purity that makes him the only man able to draw the sword from the stone in the famous tale. He makes his court at Camelot a centre for all the chivalric values.

The Road to Betterment

The knight's nobility rested in his readiness to defend the poor and weak, and all his warlike efforts were directed to the cause of good. The importance of self-sacrifice is clear, but so too, when we consider the romances more closely, is a broader emphasis on self-improvement. It was in this spirit that the knight – whether desirous to do service to his lady, obey an order from his king or honour some commitment he'd made personally – would set out on a journey to find some special place or attain some particular goal.

It is easy to see how such quests could become the narrative mainstay of these stories. First and most obviously, of course, the chivalric quest was an adventure: the knight would have to negotiate formidable obstacles along the way. Thick forests; rushing rivers; treacherous swamps; rocky mountains; deep ravines and barren moors. He would also have to fight off attackers, from common robbers to rival knights. This was before he even got to the miscellany of dragons, giants and other monsters he was liable to meet; often as not he had to free the fair maidens he found them holding captive.

Moral Heroism

Along with his geographical journey, however, went an inward, spiritual quest; the physical hazards he faced were matched by moral ones. Mostly, in the medieval romances, this dimension is implicit, but the assumption is nevertheless clearly there that the questing hero was testing his integrity as much as he was his skill with a sword or lance. And that his fearlessness in facing the dragon's flaming breath or the giant's flailing club could also be seen to suggest the courage he had of his more spiritual convictions.

This more high-flown aspect of the medieval romances was always going to appeal to a post-Romantic (with a capital 'R') sensibility that set a new and unprecedented value on the inner life, and which saw this deepened sense of psychological interiority resonating with the beauties – and the perils – of the outside world. Hence the rediscovery of the Arthurian mythos by Victorian poets like Alfred, Lord Tennyson and by pre-Raphaelite painters like Dante Gabriel Rossetti, John Everett Millais and William Holman Hunt. A century later, these romances would be read afresh and renewed with a slightly different mystic spin in the fiction of J.R.R. Tolkien and his followers.

An Elusive Emblem

The archetypal example of the chivalric 'quest' is that for the 'Holy Grail' – as made by (among others) Sir Perceval, Sir Galahad and Sir Gawain. That this was a case in which what mattered was the quest itself and not its apparent object is underlined by the fact that to this day we do not know what the 'Holy Grail' actually was. Depending on which author you read, it was either the dish the lamb had rested in when Christ and his Apostles ate their Last Supper together or the chalice from which they'd shared the wine. (The same cup, some said, was to be held up beside Christ's beaten, tattered body at the Crucifixion to catch the blood that came streaming down from his pierced side.)

Other medieval sources offered different suggestions as to what the Grail might have been. Whatever it was, in an age that saw a sacred talismanic value in 'Holy Relics' of every kind, it became the ultimate object of chivalric quest, and so, in modern popular parlance, a byword for what is universally sought – if never, perhaps, to be attained. Such allusions are of course for the most part flippant. Talk of 'my Holy Grail moisturizer …' makes self-mocking fun of the strenuousness with which we pursue the goal of perfect skin. The suggestion that 'a simple, reliable printer' might be 'the Holy Grail' reflects widespread exasperation with a besetting problem of our age. Even as jokes, though, they reference the seriousness of the aspiration the Grail represents.

Wanting More

Might aspiration itself not be the real subject of the quest-romance? Might not the geographical journey be just a way of representing our desire to transcend our circumstances, whether spiritual or worldly, establish ourselves in a different, better situation than we are? In the Japanese tale 'Horaizan', the quest is for the herb of Immortality, only to be found on the eastern island of that name. Sent by his tyrannical emperor to obtain it, Jofuku will suffer many tribulations on his voyage to what he'll finally learn is inevitable old age and death.

Arguably out-Grailing the Grail in obvious importance, Immortality is a frequent goal of heroic journeys. It features in what may well have been the first, indeed. Written in the second half of the second millennium BC, the Sumerian poem *The Epic of Gilgamesh* sees the hero making his way (with his travelling companion, the 'wild man' Enkidu) through the mountains and forests of the Middle East braving all manner of hardships and hazards. It perhaps goes without saying that Gilgamesh is no more successful than Jofuku was in finding the secret of eternal life. As its title suggests, the story 'Maui Seeking Immortality' describes the efforts of the Hawaiian deity to reach this goal, hoping to free his human subjects from the fear of death.

That the quest may be seen to some extent to dramatize our efforts to explore the limits of our existence, in life and death, is borne out by the number of journeys into the underworld made by mythic heroes – a trope to which the Greeks were even to give a name, *katabasis* ('going down'). The most famous descent of this sort is perhaps that by the divine minstrel Orpheus in the Greek legend, in the attempt to recover Euridice, his lost wife. (That he almost succeeds until, forgetting the warning he's been given, he looks back over his shoulder to see her following him, reminds us of how precarious a hold we have on life.)

But Orpheus is very much not the only one. Odysseus ventures down into the earth in *The Odyssey*; not to be outdone, Virgil's Aeneas does too (and even meets his late-lamented father Anchises there). On the strength of this, Virgil acts as guide to Hell for the Italian poet Dante when, reimagining the idea for the Christian era, he visited it as narrator in his *Divine Comedy* (*c*. 1321). But this idea isn't only to be found in the classic literature of the West. A similar journey made by the Mesopotamian hero Gilgamesh is thought very likely to have given the Greek poets the idea for Odysseus's *katabasis*. Great mythic minds were meanwhile thinking alike in far-off Japan, where we find the story of the deity Izanagi descending to the underworld in search of his sister Izanami in 'The Tale of Yomi'.

A twist on this tradition is to be found in the Native American story 'The Crane Who Crossed the River', in which a hunter and his sons are abandoned by his faithless wife. The recollection of her cruelty makes her absence haunt her husband and her growing boys like a baleful presence which they feel as they go about their daily lives. Eventually, they decide to leave and journey south in hopes of fleeing her. She follows, though, until they reach a river. A giant crane agrees to carry them across, one by one, on the condition that they don't try to touch his head's bald crown. Even now, it seems, they aren't to be safe of the wife's attention. She too tries to clamber on to the crane's back in her turn. Transgressive to the last, however, she tries to sneak a touch of the crane's crown and is carried away, once and for all, down the rushing stream.

Obviously, only in the sketchiest, most stylized way can adventures of this kind be seen as philosophical enquiries – let alone as investigations of a 'scientific' kind. They do, however, at very least lay down a marker, asserting our ambition as humans to try to reach some understanding of our universe, our life.

Worthy of the Prize

Often, though, the prize is more specific, the importance of the goal more arbitrary, its significance obviously talismanic, its splendour emblematic of the glory the hero has secured by winning it. When in the Greek legend, King Pelias of Iolcus sends Jason off to find, secure and bring back the Golden Fleece, it's to establish his fitness to succeed him on his throne. His heroic voyage with the 'Argonauts' has clearly demonstrated his determination, his courage and his cunning and firmly established his qualifications to be king.

A quest can be for love: in the Slavic tale 'The Dwarf with the Golden Beard', a prince is robbed of his princess bride when, on their wedding day, she's carried off by a swirling wind, whipped up, it seems, by a jealous former suitor, the Dwarf with the Golden Beard, who sweeps her away to his far-off castle. The Prince must brave an array of enchanted monsters and magic spells on his hazardous journey to rescue her. If the heroics performed for the Princess's sake underscore her value as a prize, it's undoubtedly the Prince whose worth is in the spotlight here. So it is again in the Persian story of 'The Three Silver Citrons'. Here, an old king, uncertain as to which of his three sons he should bequeath his kingdom to, makes their finding of a bride a more general test of character. Each must go out into the world and bring home the maiden of his choice. Whoever's bride is most beautiful will have his throne. In gratitude for the help of the youngest prince, a mysterious old woman gives him a magic pipe, which leads him to the loveliest young princess in the world. His challenges are only beginning, for he has to rescue her from the king of the trolls who's keeping her prisoner, but of course in saving her and bringing her home he makes clear his worthiness to reign.

The Long Road Home

Typically, the hero makes his journey and returns home, his purity proven, his wisdom reaffirmed. Tried in the fire, he has been seen to 'pass the test'. So it is with Odysseus, in Homer's *Odyssey* – his culminating triumph is to come back to Ithaca and reclaim his home and wife. Though she hasn't stirred from the house in which she's worked away at her never-ending tapestry, unpicking at night what she's produced by day, Penelope has made a 'journey' of her own. Beset by suitors who've tried to tempt and bully her into giving up on her long-absent husband, she has undergone trials of her own but remained true. As exotic as so many of its locations are, from Calypso's Cave to the island of the Cyclopes, the hero's home in Ithaca is the fixed point in his story.

That home base may be as important to the quest narrative as its apparent prize is underlined by what we find in the Chinese story 'Ta-Nan in Search of his Father'. Here the boy-hero's quest is clearly at some deeper level for recognition. 'In my end is my beginning,' T.S. Eliot was one day to say. But sometimes our beginnings have to be ratified, made right.

Bullied into leaving by his shrewish second wife Shên, Hsi Ch'eng-lieh abandons his concubine Ho Chua-jung as well. It's to her that a baby boy is subsequently born. While Ta-Nan, in his travels, rises in status and fortune, ending up a man of considerable wealth and influence, a catalogue of coincidences leads to Ho finding Hsi before he does himself. He's so overjoyed to see his sometime mistress that he marries her. By the time Ta-Nan turns up at his father's house, indeed, another coincidence has brought Shên to his door, but in a much more lowly situation. He takes her on as his concubine and she must now take orders from Ho Chua-jung. Whilst there's a hint of poetic justice in this reversal, there's no suggestion of vengeful anger on Ho's part or of any lasting humiliation for Shên. Under Tan-Nan's protection, the household thrives. The result of his quest overall has been to correct the moral and spiritual dysfunction in his home and produce an arrangement more in keeping with the way we as readers feel that they 'should' be.

Outward/Inward

Virgil's *Aeneid* became for the Romans what Homer's *Odyssey* had been for the Greeks: an epic which acquired the status of a founding myth for a whole civilization. Here the great quest of the hero is precisely to find a homeland. He doesn't know it, but he's really pursuing a quest in reverse, striving heroically not to venture out into the world but to reach his starting point. Aeneas is a prince of Troy, forced into exile after his city's sacking by the Greeks. His roundabout voyage to Italy, and his efforts to carve out a home there, will take many years.

So it was to be for the Maori, too, on the other side of the world in the Pacific. Their traditional stories of 'The Discovery of New Zealand' offer a mythologized view of what must have been something like their real history, describing the voyage of their ancestors from their first homeland, 'Haiwaki'. Their great voyage wasn't out into the world but into this, their New Zealand home.

In the story of 'King Gumbi and his Lost Daughter', traditionally told by the Manyema people of the Congo, the King's journey is made, not in quest, but in escape. Given the belief that a curse hangs over any king whose daughter makes ten mistakes, he gives the order that any girl-children his wives should have are to be put to death. He's forced to flee, at least for a while, by his women's rage. When his forsaken wives give birth and, of ten children, five do indeed turn out to be girls, four are duly murdered but no one can bear to kill the fifth, the beautiful Miami. She is reared in secret until, on reaching her maturity, it's time for her to embark on a real quest, journeying to find her father and her home. She goes drifting down the river in a canoe until she does.

Change and Change About

The importance of the quest as a moral trial, a test of character, can of course be overstated. We've already seen that the paradigm provided storytellers with a ready-made structure, endowing their narratives with a compelling drive. So central were these structural qualities that it was easy enough for writers and readers to imagine the moral tables being turned more or less completely. Even in the Arthurian stories, the campaign mounted against King Arthur by his scheming sister, the sorceress Morgan le Fay, in her determination to destroy him can be seen as a sort of evil anti-quest in which an out-and-out villainess takes on the hero's part.

Or, as in the Japanese story 'Green Willow', the part normally played by the monster may be performed by a beautiful and (genuinely, as far as we can tell) virtuous maiden. This is just one enchanting quirk in an extraordinary story which reminds us in multiple ways at once that the mythic 'quest' can come in many forms. It is hardly even a quest (in the sense of a 'search') at all in the case of the story's protagonist, the samurai Tomodata. His lord or *daimyo* sends him on a journey carrying a secret message – but his errand must still be carried out with complete dedication and the purest purpose. 'Ride and do not spare your beast,' says Lord Noto:

> *Ride straight, and fear not the mountains nor the enemies' country. Stay not for storm nor any other thing. Lose your life; but betray not your trust. Above all, do not look any maid between the eyes. Ride, and bring me word again quickly.*

But the hazards of the road can come in many forms as well. Waylaid at a roadside shrine by a beautiful young woman who it seems is universally known by the name of the Green

Willow, from the three weeping willow trees growing nearby, he doesn't take long to forget his daimyo's warning. Nor indeed, to forget Lord Noto's errand altogether. He's moved beyond measure when he realizes that this lovely creature cannot bear to see him leave.

He took her in his arms without a word, and soon he set her on his horse before him, and together they rode the livelong day. It was little they recked of the road they went, for all the while they looked into each other's eyes. The heat and the cold were nothing to them. They felt not the sun nor the rain; of truth or falsehood they thought nothing at all; nor of filial piety, nor of the Lord of Noto's quest, nor of honour nor plighted word. They knew but the one thing. Alas, for the ways of love!

A Benign Betrayal?

Alas, indeed. There is never so much as the slightest suggestion that the Green Willow is an agent of evil or indeed that she's anything other than the earthly angel she appears to be. But she nevertheless represents the neglect of the hero's higher purpose. His love for the Green Willow involves a retreat into oblivious disregard of what should be his duty.

At last they came to an unknown city, where they stayed. Tomodata carried gold and jewels in his girdle, so they found a house built of white wood, spread with sweet white mats. In every dim room there could be heard the sound of the garden waterfall, whilst the swallow flitted across and across the paper lattice.

It's a perfect life, but it's premised on the pushing away from consciousness of every other responsibility. 'Here they dwelt,' says the narrator, 'knowing but the one thing.' That one thing is love, of course, and, beguiling as it may be (the couple's years in the city will be 'like garlands of sweet flowers'), this isn't the life that the samurai, at any rate, is supposed to lead.

In the end, the Green Willow dies – or, rather, disappears before his eyes, leaving only a little heap of clothing. A reflection of the vanity of human passions or just a recognition that the greatest happiness must end? One thing we can clearly see is that it's only now, at this late stage in his own story, that Tomodata's real quest begins. A holy man now, he tramps from holy place to holy place. One day he finds himself by the humble shrine where he first met his love. Sadly, he sees that 'her' three willows have been cut down. We never do discover what Lord Noto's message was – like the Holy Grail it's something of a cipher, standing in for something of immense but undefined importance. Nor do we really get a ruling on whether in falling for Green Willow and abandoning his first quest Tomodata has earned our censure when in his second quest he in some ways seems so obviously to be leading his best life. That judgement, it appears, is left to us.

A Journey to Nowhere?

The idea that, like the Grail, the object of the quest may be what the film critics call a 'MacGuffin' – a pivotal but intrinsically unimportant plot device – is perhaps best illustrated by the Serbian story, 'The Trade that No One Knows'. Here a boy of humble birth shocks his parents by demanding that they ask the King for his permission for him to marry his daughter. The King allows the Princess to choose. She says she will marry him if he learns 'the trade that no one knows'. Off he goes, out into the world, to discover what he can of this oxymoronic occupation. A great many adventures and enchantments later, the young man – having shape-shifted into a church, a bouquet of flowers, a fox, a bag of millet-seed and sundry other forms – returns to claim his bride. Even now, we remain among those who don't know the trade that no one knows, but we've unquestionably been richly entertained. The journey, not the destination, as they say, matters.

Quests of Honour, Adventure, Love & Vengeance

Introduction

'BOKWEWA, THE HUMPBACK', in the Native American story, is an immortal in his wisdom, weak and handicapped as he might be in his outward form. So when his brother Kwasynd falls in love with a woman he sees lying dead upon a scaffold, he's able to raise her back to life so he can marry her. But he also understands, as Kwasynd can't, when she leaves him a few years later. Kwasynd's quest for her takes him, with a mighty throng, to a 'fair country', his true 'native land', where he's joyfully reunited with his spirit-wife. Travel takes us out of ourselves; breaks our routines; extends our horizons; brings us up against the limits of our normal lives – and often breaks them. Some make this the centre of their lives. Wise counsel warns against risking everything to go out into the world and seek adventure; still less does it recommend giving up all for romantic love. Revenge is not only condemned on moral grounds but on pragmatic ones as well. ('Before you embark on a journey of revenge, dig two graves,' said the Chinese sage Confucius.) Such advice is well and good, and in our real lives we may even heed it, but in the world of story anything goes, and we like to live more intensely.

The Odyssey: Books IX–XII (Extract)

Book IX

Ulysses Declares Himself and Begins His Story – The Cicons, Lotophagi, and Cyclopes

AND ULYSSES ANSWERED, "King Alcinous, it is a good thing to hear a bard with such a divine voice as this man has. There is nothing better or more delightful than when a whole people make merry together, with the guests sitting orderly to listen, while the table is loaded with bread and meats, and the cup-bearer draws wine and fills his cup for every man. This is indeed as fair a sight as a man can see. Now, however, since you are inclined to ask the story of my sorrows, and rekindle my own sad memories in respect of them, I do not know how to begin, nor yet how to continue and conclude my tale, for the hand of heaven has been laid heavily upon me.

"Firstly, then, I will tell you my name that you too may know it, and one day, if I outlive this time of sorrow, may become my guests though I live so far away from all of you. I am Ulysses son of Laertes, renowned among mankind for all manner of subtlety, so that my fame ascends to heaven. I live in Ithaca, where there is a high mountain called Neritum, covered with forests; and not far from it there is a group of islands very near to one another – Dulichium, Same, and the wooded island of Zacynthus. It lies squat on the horizon, all highest up in the sea towards the sunset, while the others lie away from it towards dawn. It is a rugged island, but it breeds brave men, and my eyes know none that they better love to look upon. The goddess Calypso kept me with her in her cave, and wanted me to marry her, as did also the cunning Aeaean goddess Circe; but they could neither of them persuade me, for there is nothing dearer to a man than his own country and his parents, and however splendid a home he may have in a foreign country, if it be far from father or mother, he does not care about it. Now, however, I will tell you of the many hazardous adventures which by Jove's will I met with on my return from Troy.

"When I had set sail thence the wind took me first to Ismarus, which is the city of the Cicons. There I sacked the town and put the people to the sword. We took their wives and also much booty, which we divided equitably amongst us, so that none might have reason to complain. I then said that we had better make off at once, but my men very foolishly would not obey me, so they staid there drinking much wine and killing great numbers of sheep and oxen on the sea shore. Meanwhile the Cicons cried out for help to other Cicons who lived inland. These were more in number, and stronger, and they were more skilled in the art of war, for they could fight, either from chariots or on foot as the occasion served; in the morning, therefore, they came as thick as leaves and bloom in summer, and the hand of heaven was against us, so that we were hard pressed. They set the battle in array near the ships, and the hosts aimed their bronze-shod spears at one another. So long as the day waxed and it was still morning, we held our own against them, though they were more in number than we; but as the sun went down, towards the time when men loose their oxen, the Cicons got the better of us, and we lost half a dozen men from every ship we had; so we got away with those that were left.

"Thence we sailed onward with sorrow in our hearts, but glad to have escaped death though we had lost our comrades, nor did we leave till we had thrice invoked each one of the poor fellows who had perished by the hands of the Cicons. Then Jove raised the North wind against us till it blew a hurricane, so that land and sky were hidden in thick clouds, and night sprang forth out of the heavens. We let the ships run before the gale, but the force of the wind tore our sails to tatters, so we took them down for fear of shipwreck, and rowed our hardest towards the land. There we lay two days and two nights suffering much alike from toil and distress of mind, but on the morning of the third day we again raised our masts, set sail, and took our places, letting the wind and steersmen direct our ship. I should have got home at that time unharmed had not the North wind and the currents been against me as I was doubling Cape Malea, and set me off my course hard by the island of Cythera.

"I was driven thence by foul winds for a space of nine days upon the sea, but on the tenth day we reached the land of the Lotus-eaters, who live on a food that comes from a kind of flower. Here we landed to take in fresh water, and our crews got their mid-day meal on the shore near the ships. When they had eaten and drunk I sent two of my company to see what manner of men the people of the place might be, and they had a third man under them. They started at once, and went about among the Lotus-eaters, who did them no hurt, but gave them to eat of the lotus, which was so delicious that those who ate of it left off caring about home, and did not even want to go back and say what had happened to them, but were for staying and munching lotus with the Lotus-eaters without thinking further of their return; nevertheless, though they wept bitterly I forced them back to the ships and made them fast under the benches. Then I told the rest to go on board at once, lest any of them should taste of the lotus and leave off wanting to get home, so they took their places and smote the grey sea with their oars.

"We sailed hence, always in much distress, till we came to the land of the lawless and inhuman Cyclopes. Now the Cyclopes neither plant nor plough, but trust in providence, and live on such wheat, barley, and grapes as grow wild without any kind of tillage, and their wild grapes yield them wine as the sun and the rain may grow them. They have no laws nor assemblies of the people, but live in caves on the tops of high mountains; each is lord and master in his family, and they take no account of their neighbours.

"Now off their harbour there lies a wooded and fertile island not quite close to the land of the Cyclopes, but still not far. It is over-run with wild goats, that breed there in great numbers and are never disturbed by foot of man; for sportsmen – who as a rule will suffer so much hardship in forest or among mountain precipices – do not go there, nor yet again is it ever ploughed or fed down, but it lies a wilderness untilled and unsown from year to year, and has no living thing upon it but only goats. For the Cyclopes have no ships, nor yet shipwrights who could make ships for them; they cannot therefore go from city to city, or sail over the sea to one another's country as people who have ships can do; if they had had these they would have colonized the island, for it is a very good one, and would yield everything in due season. There are meadows that in some places come right down to the sea shore, well watered and full of luscious grass; grapes would do there excellently; there is level land for ploughing, and it would always yield heavily at harvest time, for the soil is deep. There is a good harbour where no cables are wanted, nor yet anchors, nor need a ship be moored, but all one has to do is to beach one's vessel and stay there till the wind becomes fair for putting out to sea again.

At the head of the harbour there is a spring of clear water coming out of a cave, and there are poplars growing all round it.

"Here we entered, but so dark was the night that some god must have brought us in, for there was nothing whatever to be seen. A thick mist hung all round our ships; the moon was hidden behind a mass of clouds so that no one could have seen the island if he had looked for it, nor were there any breakers to tell us we were close in shore before we found ourselves upon the land itself; when, however, we had beached the ships, we took down the sails, went ashore and camped upon the beach till daybreak.

"When the child of morning, rosy-fingered Dawn appeared, we admired the island and wandered all over it, while the nymphs Jove's daughters roused the wild goats that we might get some meat for our dinner. On this we fetched our spears and bows and arrows from the ships, and dividing ourselves into three bands began to shoot the goats. Heaven sent us excellent sport; I had twelve ships with me, and each ship got nine goats, while my own ship had ten; thus through the livelong day to the going down of the sun we ate and drank our fill, and we had plenty of wine left, for each one of us had taken many jars full when we sacked the city of the Cicons, and this had not yet run out. While we were feasting we kept turning our eyes towards the land of the Cyclopes, which was hard by, and saw the smoke of their stubble fires. We could almost fancy we heard their voices and the bleating of their sheep and goats, but when the sun went down and it came on dark, we camped down upon the beach, and next morning I called a council.

"'Stay here, my brave fellows,' said I, 'all the rest of you, while I go with my ship and exploit these people myself: I want to see if they are uncivilized savages, or a hospitable and humane race.'

"I went on board, bidding my men to do so also and loose the hawsers; so they took their places and smote the grey sea with their oars. When we got to the land, which was not far, there, on the face of a cliff near the sea, we saw a great cave overhung with laurels. It was a station for a great many sheep and goats, and outside there was a large yard, with a high wall round it made of stones built into the ground and of trees both pine and oak. This was the abode of a huge monster who was then away from home shepherding his flocks. He would have nothing to do with other people, but led the life of an outlaw. He was a horrid creature, not like a human being at all, but resembling rather some crag that stands out boldly against the sky on the top of a high mountain.

"I told my men to draw the ship ashore, and stay where they were, all but the twelve best among them, who were to go along with myself. I also took a goatskin of sweet black wine which had been given me by Maron, son of Euanthes, who was priest of Apollo the patron god of Ismarus, and lived within the wooded precincts of the temple. When we were sacking the city we respected him, and spared his life, as also his wife and child; so he made me some presents of great value – seven talents of fine gold, and a bowl of silver, with twelve jars of sweet wine, unblended, and of the most exquisite flavour. Not a man nor maid in the house knew about it, but only himself, his wife, and one housekeeper: when he drank it he mixed twenty parts of water to one of wine, and yet the fragrance from the mixing-bowl was so exquisite that it was impossible to refrain from drinking. I filled a large skin with this wine, and took a wallet full of provisions with me, for my mind misgave me that I might have to deal with some savage who would be of great strength, and would respect neither right nor law.

"We soon reached his cave, but he was out shepherding, so we went inside and took stock of all that we could see. His cheese-racks were loaded with cheeses, and he had more lambs and kids than his pens could hold. They were kept in separate flocks; first there were the hoggets, then the oldest of the younger lambs and lastly the very young ones all kept apart from one another; as for his dairy, all the vessels, bowls, and milk pails into which he milked, were swimming with whey. When they saw all this, my men begged me to let them first steal some cheeses, and make off with them to the ship; they would then return, drive down the lambs and kids, put them on board and sail away with them. It would have been indeed better if we had done so but I would not listen to them, for I wanted to see the owner himself, in the hope that he might give me a present. When, however, we saw him my poor men found him ill to deal with.

"We lit a fire, offered some of the cheeses in sacrifice, ate others of them, and then sat waiting till the Cyclops should come in with his sheep. When he came, he brought in with him a huge load of dry firewood to light the fire for his supper, and this he flung with such a noise on to the floor of his cave that we hid ourselves for fear at the far end of the cavern. Meanwhile he drove all the ewes inside, as well as the she-goats that he was going to milk, leaving the males, both rams and he-goats, outside in the yards. Then he rolled a huge stone to the mouth of the cave – so huge that two and twenty strong four-wheeled waggons would not be enough to draw it from its place against the doorway. When he had so done he sat down and milked his ewes and goats, all in due course, and then let each of them have her own young. He curdled half the milk and set it aside in wicker strainers, but the other half he poured into bowls that he might drink it for his supper. When he had got through with all his work, he lit the fire, and then caught sight of us, whereon he said:

"'Strangers, who are you? Where do sail from? Are you traders, or do you sail the sea as rovers, with your hands against every man, and every man's hand against you?'

"We were frightened out of our senses by his loud voice and monstrous form, but I managed to say, 'We are Achaeans on our way home from Troy, but by the will of Jove, and stress of weather, we have been driven far out of our course. We are the people of Agamemnon, son of Atreus, who has won infinite renown throughout the whole world, by sacking so great a city and killing so many people. We therefore humbly pray you to show us some hospitality, and otherwise make us such presents as visitors may reasonably expect. May your excellency fear the wrath of heaven, for we are your suppliants, and Jove takes all respectable travellers under his protection, for he is the avenger of all suppliants and foreigners in distress.'

"To this he gave me but a pitiless answer, 'Stranger,' said he, 'you are a fool, or else you know nothing of this country. Talk to me, indeed, about fearing the gods or shunning their anger? We Cyclopes do not care about Jove or any of your blessed gods, for we are ever so much stronger than they. I shall not spare either yourself or your companions out of any regard for Jove, unless I am in the humour for doing so. And now tell me where you made your ship fast when you came on shore. Was it round the point, or is she lying straight off the land?'

"He said this to draw me out, but I was too cunning to be caught in that way, so I answered with a lie; 'Neptune,' said I, 'sent my ship on to the rocks at the far end of your country, and wrecked it. We were driven on to them from the open sea, but I and those who are with me escaped the jaws of death.'

"The cruel wretch vouchsafed me not one word of answer, but with a sudden clutch he gripped up two of my men at once and dashed them down upon the ground as though they had been puppies. Their brains were shed upon the ground, and the earth was wet with their blood. Then he tore them limb from limb and supped upon them. He gobbled them up like a lion in the wilderness, flesh, bones, marrow, and entrails, without leaving anything uneaten. As for us, we wept and lifted up our hands to heaven on seeing such a horrid sight, for we did not know what else to do; but when the Cyclops had filled his huge paunch, and had washed down his meal of human flesh with a drink of neat milk, he stretched himself full length upon the ground among his sheep, and went to sleep. I was at first inclined to seize my sword, draw it, and drive it into his vitals, but I reflected that if I did we should all certainly be lost, for we should never be able to shift the stone which the monster had put in front of the door. So we stayed sobbing and sighing where we were till morning came.

"When the child of morning, rosy-fingered dawn, appeared, he again lit his fire, milked his goats and ewes, all quite rightly, and then let each have her own young one; as soon as he had got through with all his work, he clutched up two more of my men, and began eating them for his morning's meal. Presently, with the utmost ease, he rolled the stone away from the door and drove out his sheep, but he at once put it back again – as easily as though he were merely clapping the lid on to a quiver full of arrows. As soon as he had done so he shouted, and cried 'Shoo, shoo,' after his sheep to drive them on to the mountain; so I was left to scheme some way of taking my revenge and covering myself with glory.

"In the end I deemed it would be the best plan to do as follows: The Cyclops had a great club which was lying near one of the sheep pens; it was of green olive wood, and he had cut it intending to use it for a staff as soon as it should be dry. It was so huge that we could only compare it to the mast of a twenty-oared merchant vessel of large burden, and able to venture out into open sea. I went up to this club and cut off about six feet of it; I then gave this piece to the men and told them to fine it evenly off at one end, which they proceeded to do, and lastly I brought it to a point myself, charring the end in the fire to make it harder. When I had done this I hid it under dung, which was lying about all over the cave, and told the men to cast lots which of them should venture along with myself to lift it and bore it into the monster's eye while he was asleep. The lot fell upon the very four whom I should have chosen, and I myself made five. In the evening the wretch came back from shepherding, and drove his flocks into the cave – this time driving them all inside, and not leaving any in the yards; I suppose some fancy must have taken him, or a god must have prompted him to do so. As soon as he had put the stone back to its place against the door, he sat down, milked his ewes and his goats all quite rightly, and then let each have her own young one; when he had got through with all this work, he gripped up two more of my men, and made his supper off them. So I went up to him with an ivy-wood bowl of black wine in my hands:

"'Look here, Cyclops,' said I, you have been eating a great deal of man's flesh, so take this and drink some wine, that you may see what kind of liquor we had on board my ship. I was bringing it to you as a drink-offering, in the hope that you would take compassion upon me and further me on my way home, whereas all you do is to go on ramping and raving most intolerably. You ought to be ashamed of yourself; how can you expect people to come see you any more if you treat them in this way?'

"He then took the cup and drank. He was so delighted with the taste of the wine that he begged me for another bowl full. 'Be so kind,' he said, 'as to give me some more, and tell me your name at once. I want to make you a present that you will be glad to have. We have wine even in this country, for our soil grows grapes and the sun ripens them, but this drinks like Nectar and Ambrosia all in one.'

"I then gave him some more; three times did I fill the bowl for him, and three times did he drain it without thought or heed; then, when I saw that the wine had got into his head, I said to him as plausibly as I could: 'Cyclops, you ask my name and I will tell it you; give me, therefore, the present you promised me; my name is Noman; this is what my father and mother and my friends have always called me.'

"But the cruel wretch said, 'Then I will eat all Noman's comrades before Noman himself, and will keep Noman for the last. This is the present that I will make him.'

"As he spoke he reeled, and fell sprawling face upwards on the ground. His great neck hung heavily backwards and a deep sleep took hold upon him. Presently he turned sick, and threw up both wine and the gobbets of human flesh on which he had been gorging, for he was very drunk. Then I thrust the beam of wood far into the embers to heat it, and encouraged my men lest any of them should turn faint-hearted. When the wood, green though it was, was about to blaze, I drew it out of the fire glowing with heat, and my men gathered round me, for heaven had filled their hearts with courage. We drove the sharp end of the beam into the monster's eye, and bearing upon it with all my weight I kept turning it round and round as though I were boring a hole in a ship's plank with an auger, which two men with a wheel and strap can keep on turning as long as they choose. Even thus did we bore the red hot beam into his eye, till the boiling blood bubbled all over it as we worked it round and round, so that the steam from the burning eyeball scalded his eyelids and eyebrows, and the roots of the eye sputtered in the fire. As a blacksmith plunges an axe or hatchet into cold water to temper it – for it is this that gives strength to the iron – and it makes a great hiss as he does so, even thus did the Cyclops' eye hiss round the beam of olive wood, and his hideous yells made the cave ring again. We ran away in a fright, but he plucked the beam all besmirched with gore from his eye, and hurled it from him in a frenzy of rage and pain, shouting as he did so to the other Cyclopes who lived on the bleak headlands near him; so they gathered from all quarters round his cave when they heard him crying, and asked what was the matter with him.

"'What ails you, Polyphemus,' said they, 'that you make such a noise, breaking the stillness of the night, and preventing us from being able to sleep? Surely no man is carrying off your sheep? Surely no man is trying to kill you either by fraud or by force?'

"But Polyphemus shouted to them from inside the cave, 'Noman is killing me by fraud; no man is killing me by force.'

"'Then,' said they, 'if no man is attacking you, you must be ill; when Jove makes people ill, there is no help for it, and you had better pray to your father Neptune.'

"Then they went away, and I laughed inwardly at the success of my clever stratagem, but the Cyclops, groaning and in an agony of pain, felt about with his hands till he found the stone and took it from the door; then he sat in the doorway and stretched his hands in front of it to catch anyone going out with the sheep, for he thought I might be foolish enough to attempt this.

"As for myself I kept on puzzling to think how I could best save my own life and those of my companions; I schemed and schemed, as one who knows that his life depends upon it, for the danger was very great. In the end I deemed that this plan would be the best; the male sheep were well grown, and carried a heavy black fleece, so I bound them noiselessly in threes together, with some of the withies on which the wicked monster used to sleep. There was to be a man under the middle sheep, and the two on either side were to cover him, so that there were three sheep to each man. As for myself there was a ram finer than any of the others, so I caught hold of him by the back, esconced myself in the thick wool under his belly, and hung on patiently to his fleece, face upwards, keeping a firm hold on it all the time.

"Thus, then, did we wait in great fear of mind till morning came, but when the child of morning, rosy-fingered Dawn, appeared, the male sheep hurried out to feed, while the ewes remained bleating about the pens waiting to be milked, for their udders were full to bursting; but their master in spite of all his pain felt the backs of all the sheep as they stood upright, without being sharp enough to find out that the men were underneath their bellies. As the ram was going out, last of all, heavy with its fleece and with the weight of my crafty self, Polyphemus laid hold of it and said:

"'My good ram, what is it that makes you the last to leave my cave this morning? You are not wont to let the ewes go before you, but lead the mob with a run whether to flowery mead or bubbling fountain, and are the first to come home again at night; but now you lag last of all. Is it because you know your master has lost his eye, and are sorry because that wicked Noman and his horrid crew has got him down in his drink and blinded him? But I will have his life yet. If you could understand and talk, you would tell me where the wretch is hiding, and I would dash his brains upon the ground till they flew all over the cave. I should thus have some satisfaction for the harm this no-good Noman has done me.'

"As he spoke he drove the ram outside, but when we were a little way out from the cave and yards, I first got from under the ram's belly, and then freed my comrades; as for the sheep, which were very fat, by constantly heading them in the right direction we managed to drive them down to the ship. The crew rejoiced greatly at seeing those of us who had escaped death, but wept for the others whom the Cyclops had killed. However, I made signs to them by nodding and frowning that they were to hush their crying, and told them to get all the sheep on board at once and put out to sea; so they went aboard, took their places, and smote the grey sea with their oars. Then, when I had got as far out as my voice would reach, I began to jeer at the Cyclops.

"'Cyclops,' said I, 'you should have taken better measure of your man before eating up his comrades in your cave. You wretch, eat up your visitors in your own house? You might have known that your sin would find you out, and now Jove and the other gods have punished you.'

"He got more and more furious as he heard me, so he tore the top from off a high mountain, and flung it just in front of my ship so that it was within a little of hitting the end of the rudder. The sea quaked as the rock fell into it, and the wash of the wave it raised carried us back towards the mainland, and forced us towards the shore. But I snatched up a long pole and kept the ship off, making signs to my men by nodding my head, that they must row for their lives, whereon they laid out with a will. When we had got twice as far as we were before, I was for jeering at the Cyclops again, but the men begged and prayed of me to hold my tongue.

"'Do not,' they exclaimed, 'be mad enough to provoke this savage creature further; he has thrown one rock at us already which drove us back again to the mainland, and we made sure it had been the death of us; if he had then heard any further sound of voices he would have pounded our heads and our ship's timbers into a jelly with the rugged rocks he would have heaved at us, for he can throw them a long way.'

"But I would not listen to them, and shouted out to him in my rage, 'Cyclops, if anyone asks you who it was that put your eye out and spoiled your beauty, say it was the valiant warrior Ulysses, son of Laertes, who lives in Ithaca.'

"On this he groaned, and cried out, 'Alas, alas, then the old prophecy about me is coming true. There was a prophet here, at one time, a man both brave and of great stature, Telemus son of Eurymus, who was an excellent seer, and did all the prophesying for the Cyclopes till he grew old; he told me that all this would happen to me some day, and said I should lose my sight by the hand of Ulysses. I have been all along expecting someone of imposing presence and superhuman strength, whereas he turns out to be a little insignificant weakling, who has managed to blind my eye by taking advantage of me in my drink; come here, then, Ulysses, that I may make you presents to show my hospitality, and urge Neptune to help you forward on your journey – for Neptune and I are father and son. He, if he so will, shall heal me, which no one else neither god nor man can do.'

"Then I said, 'I wish I could be as sure of killing you outright and sending you down to the house of Hades, as I am that it will take more than Neptune to cure that eye of yours.'

"On this he lifted up his hands to the firmament of heaven and prayed, saying, 'Hear me, great Neptune; if I am indeed your own true begotten son, grant that Ulysses may never reach his home alive; or if he must get back to his friends at last, let him do so late and in sore plight after losing all his men let him reach his home in another man's ship and find trouble in his house.'

"Thus did he pray, and Neptune heard his prayer. Then he picked up a rock much larger than the first, swung it aloft and hurled it with prodigious force. It fell just short of the ship, but was within a little of hitting the end of the rudder. The sea quaked as the rock fell into it, and the wash of the wave it raised drove us onwards on our way towards the shore of the island.

"When at last we got to the island where we had left the rest of our ships, we found our comrades lamenting us, and anxiously awaiting our return. We ran our vessel upon the sands and got out of her on to the sea shore; we also landed the Cyclops' sheep, and divided them equitably amongst us so that none might have reason to complain. As for the ram, my companions agreed that I should have it as an extra share; so I sacrificed it on the sea shore, and burned its thigh bones to Jove, who is the lord of all. But he heeded not my sacrifice, and only thought how he might destroy both my ships and my comrades.

"Thus through the livelong day to the going down of the sun we feasted our fill on meat and drink, but when the sun went down and it came on dark, we camped upon the beach. When the child of morning rosy-fingered Dawn appeared, I bade my men on board and loose the hawsers. Then they took their places and smote the grey sea with their oars; so we sailed on with sorrow in our hearts, but glad to have escaped death though we had lost our comrades.

Book X

Aeolus, The Laestrygones, Circe.

"Thence we went on to the Aeolian island where lives Aeolus son of Hippotas, dear to the immortal gods. It is an island that floats (as it were) upon the sea, iron bound with a wall that girds it. Now, Aeolus has six daughters and six lusty sons, so he made the sons marry the daughters, and they all live with their dear father and mother, feasting and enjoying every conceivable kind of luxury. All day long the atmosphere of the house is loaded with the savour of roasting meats till it groans again, yard and all; but by night they sleep on their well made bedsteads, each with his own wife between the blankets. These were the people among whom we had now come.

"Aeolus entertained me for a whole month asking me questions all the time about Troy, the Argive fleet, and the return of the Achaeans. I told him exactly how everything had happened, and when I said I must go, and asked him to further me on my way, he made no sort of difficulty, but set about doing so at once. Moreover, he flayed me a prime ox-hide to hold the ways of the roaring winds, which he shut up in the hide as in a sack – for Jove had made him captain over the winds, and he could stir or still each one of them according to his own pleasure. He put the sack in the ship and bound the mouth so tightly with a silver thread that not even a breath of a side-wind could blow from any quarter. The West wind which was fair for us did he alone let blow as it chose; but it all came to nothing, for we were lost through our own folly.

"Nine days and nine nights did we sail, and on the tenth day our native land showed on the horizon. We got so close in that we could see the stubble fires burning, and I, being then dead beat, fell into a light sleep, for I had never let the rudder out of my own hands, that we might get home the faster. On this the men fell to talking among themselves, and said I was bringing back gold and silver in the sack that Aeolus had given me. 'Bless my heart,' would one turn to his neighbour, saying, 'how this man gets honoured and makes friends to whatever city or country he may go. See what fine prizes he is taking home from Troy, while we, who have travelled just as far as he has, come back with hands as empty as we set out with – and now Aeolus has given him ever so much more. Quick – let us see what it all is, and how much gold and silver there is in the sack he gave him.'

"Thus they talked and evil counsels prevailed. They loosed the sack, whereupon the wind flew howling forth and raised a storm that carried us weeping out to sea and away from our own country. Then I awoke, and knew not whether to throw myself into the sea or to live on and make the best of it; but I bore it, covered myself up, and lay down in the ship, while the men lamented bitterly as the fierce winds bore our fleet back to the Aeolian island.

"When we reached it we went ashore to take in water, and dined hard by the ships. Immediately after dinner I took a herald and one of my men and went straight to the house of Aeolus, where I found him feasting with his wife and family; so we sat down as suppliants on the threshold. They were astounded when they saw us and said, 'Ulysses, what brings you here? What god has been ill-treating you? We took great pains to further you on your way home to Ithaca, or wherever it was that you wanted to go to.'

"Thus did they speak, but I answered sorrowfully, 'My men have undone me; they, and cruel sleep, have ruined me. My friends, mend me this mischief, for you can if you will.'

"I spoke as movingly as I could, but they said nothing, till their father answered, 'Vilest of mankind, get you gone at once out of the island; him whom heaven hates will I in no wise help. Be off, for you come here as one abhorred of heaven.' And with these words he sent me sorrowing from his door.

"Thence we sailed sadly on till the men were worn out with long and fruitless rowing, for there was no longer any wind to help them. Six days, night and day did we toil, and on the seventh day we reached the rocky stronghold of Lamus – Telepylus, the city of the Laestrygonians, where the shepherd who is driving in his sheep and goats (to be milked) salutes him who is driving out his flock (to feed) and this last answers the salute. In that country a man who could do without sleep might earn double wages, one as a herdsman of cattle, and another as a shepherd, for they work much the same by night as they do by day.

"When we reached the harbour we found it land-locked under steep cliffs, with a narrow entrance between two headlands. My captains took all their ships inside, and made them fast close to one another, for there was never so much as a breath of wind inside, but it was always dead calm. I kept my own ship outside, and moored it to a rock at the very end of the point; then I climbed a high rock to reconnoitre, but could see no sign neither of man nor cattle, only some smoke rising from the ground. So I sent two of my company with an attendant to find out what sort of people the inhabitants were.

"The men when they got on shore followed a level road by which the people draw their firewood from the mountains into the town, till presently they met a young woman who had come outside to fetch water, and who was daughter to a Laestrygonian named Antiphates. She was going to the fountain Artacia from which the people bring in their water, and when my men had come close up to her, they asked her who the king of that country might be, and over what kind of people he ruled; so she directed them to her father's house, but when they got there they found his wife to be a giantess as huge as a mountain, and they were horrified at the sight of her.

"She at once called her husband Antiphates from the place of assembly, and forthwith he set about killing my men. He snatched up one of them, and began to make his dinner off him then and there, whereon the other two ran back to the ships as fast as ever they could. But Antiphates raised a hue-and-cry after them, and thousands of sturdy Laestrygonians sprang up from every quarter – ogres, not men. They threw vast rocks at us from the cliffs as though they had been mere stones, and I heard the horrid sound of the ships crunching up against one another, and the death cries of my men, as the Laestrygonians speared them like fishes and took them home to eat them. While they were thus killing my men within the harbour I drew my sword, cut the cable of my own ship, and told my men to row with all their might if they too would not fare like the rest; so they laid out for their lives, and we were thankful enough when we got into open water out of reach of the rocks they hurled at us. As for the others there was not one of them left.

"Thence we sailed sadly on, glad to have escaped death, though we had lost our comrades, and came to the Aeaean island, where Circe lives – a great and cunning goddess who is own sister to the magician Aeetes – for they are both children of the sun by Perse, who is daughter to Oceanus. We brought our ship into a safe harbour without a word, for some god guided us thither, and having landed we lay there for two days and two nights, worn out in body and mind. When the morning of the third day came I took my spear and my sword, and went away from the ship to reconnoitre, and see if I could discover signs of human handiwork, or hear the sound of voices. Climbing to the top of a high look-out I espied the smoke of Circe's house rising upwards amid a dense forest of trees, and when I saw this I doubted whether, having seen the smoke, I would not go on at once and find out more, but in the end I deemed it best to go back to the ship, give the men their dinners, and send some of them instead of going myself.

"When I had nearly got back to the ship some god took pity upon my solitude, and sent a fine antlered stag right into the middle of my path. He was coming down his pasture in the forest to drink of the river, for the heat of the sun drove him, and as he passed I struck him in the middle of the back; the bronze point of the spear went clean through him, and he lay groaning in the dust until the life went out of him. Then I set my foot upon him, drew my spear from the wound, and laid it down; I also gathered rough grass and rushes and twisted them into a fathom or so of good stout rope, with which I bound the four feet of the noble creature together; having so done I hung him round my neck and walked back to the ship leaning upon my spear, for the stag was much too big for me to be able to carry him on my shoulder, steadying him with one hand. As I threw him down in front of the ship, I called the men and spoke cheeringly man by man to each of them. 'Look here my friends,' said I, 'we are not going to die so much before our time after all, and at any rate we will not starve so long as we have got something to eat and drink on board.' On this they uncovered their heads upon the sea shore and admired the stag, for he was indeed a splendid fellow. Then, when they had feasted their eyes upon him sufficiently, they washed their hands and began to cook him for dinner.

"Thus through the livelong day to the going down of the sun we stayed there eating and drinking our fill, but when the sun went down and it came on dark, we camped upon the sea shore. When the child of morning, rosy-fingered Dawn, appeared, I called a council and said, 'My friends, we are in very great difficulties; listen therefore to me. We have no idea where the sun either sets or rises, so that we do not even know East from West. I see no way out of it; nevertheless, we must try and find one. We are certainly on an island, for I went as high as I could this morning, and saw the sea reaching all round it to the horizon; it lies low, but towards the middle I saw smoke rising from out of a thick forest of trees.'

"Their hearts sank as they heard me, for they remembered how they had been treated by the Laestrygonian Antiphates, and by the savage ogre Polyphemus. They wept bitterly in their dismay, but there was nothing to be got by crying, so I divided them into two companies and set a captain over each; I gave one company to Eurylochus, while I took command of the other myself. Then we cast lots in a helmet, and the lot fell upon Eurylochus; so he set out with his twenty-two men, and they wept, as also did we who were left behind.

"When they reached Circe's house they found it built of cut stones, on a site that could be seen from far, in the middle of the forest. There were wild mountain wolves and lions prowling all round it – poor bewitched creatures whom she had tamed by her enchantments and drugged into subjection. They did not attack my men, but wagged their great tails, fawned upon them, and rubbed their noses lovingly against them. As hounds crowd round their master when they see him coming from dinner – for they know he will bring them something – even so did these wolves and lions with their great claws fawn upon my men, but the men were terribly frightened at seeing such strange creatures. Presently they reached the gates of the goddess's house, and as they stood there they could hear Circe within, singing most beautifully as she worked at her loom, making a web so fine, so soft, and of such dazzling colours as no one but a goddess could weave. On this Polites, whom I valued and trusted more than any other of my men, said, 'There is someone inside working at a loom and singing most beautifully; the whole place resounds with it, let us call her and see whether she is woman or goddess.'

"They called her and she came down, unfastened the door, and bade them enter. They, thinking no evil, followed her, all except Eurylochus, who suspected mischief and staid outside. When she had got them into her house, she set them upon benches and seats and mixed them a mess with cheese, honey, meal, and Pramnian wine, but she drugged it with wicked poisons to make them forget their homes, and when they had drunk she turned them into pigs by a stroke of her wand, and shut them up in her pig-styes. They were like pigs – head, hair, and all, and they grunted just as pigs do; but their senses were the same as before, and they remembered everything.

"Thus then were they shut up squealing, and Circe threw them some acorns and beech masts such as pigs eat, but Eurylochus hurried back to tell me about the sad fate of our comrades. He was so overcome with dismay that though he tried to speak he could find no words to do so; his eyes filled with tears and he could only sob and sigh, till at last we forced his story out of him, and he told us what had happened to the others.

"'We went,' said he, 'as you told us, through the forest, and in the middle of it there was a fine house built with cut stones in a place that could be seen from far. There we found a woman, or else she was a goddess, working at her loom and singing sweetly; so the men shouted to her and called her, whereon she at once came down, opened the door, and invited us in. The others did not suspect any mischief so they followed her into the house, but I staid where I was, for I thought there might be some treachery. From that moment I saw them no more, for not one of them ever came out, though I sat a long time watching for them.'

"Then I took my sword of bronze and slung it over my shoulders; I also took my bow, and told Eurylochus to come back with me and shew me the way. But he laid hold of me with both his hands and spoke piteously, saying, 'Sir, do not force me to go with you, but let me stay here, for I know you will not bring one of them back with you, nor even return alive yourself;

let us rather see if we cannot escape at any rate with the few that are left us, for we may still save our lives.'

"'Stay where you are, then,' answered I, 'eating and drinking at the ship, but I must go, for I am most urgently bound to do so.'

"With this I left the ship and went up inland. When I got through the charmed grove, and was near the great house of the enchantress Circe, I met Mercury with his golden wand, disguised as a young man in the hey-day of his youth and beauty with the down just coming upon his face. He came up to me and took my hand within his own, saying, 'My poor unhappy man, whither are you going over this mountain top, alone and without knowing the way? Your men are shut up in Circe's pigstyes, like so many wild boars in their lairs. You surely do not fancy that you can set them free? I can tell you that you will never get back and will have to stay there with the rest of them. But never mind, I will protect you and get you out of your difficulty. Take this herb, which is one of great virtue, and keep it about you when you go to Circe's house, it will be a talisman to you against every kind of mischief.

"'And I will tell you of all the wicked witchcraft that Circe will try to practice upon you. She will mix a mess for you to drink, and she will drug the meal with which she makes it, but she will not be able to charm you, for the virtue of the herb that I shall give you will prevent her spells from working. I will tell you all about it. When Circe strikes you with her wand, draw your sword and spring upon her as though you were going to kill her. She will then be frightened, and will desire you to go to bed with her; on this you must not point blank refuse her, for you want her to set your companions free, and to take good care also of yourself, but you must make her swear solemnly by all the blessed gods that she will plot no further mischief against you, or else when she has got you naked she will unman you and make you fit for nothing.'

"As he spoke he pulled the herb out of the ground and shewed me what it was like. The root was black, while the flower was as white as milk; the gods call it Moly, and mortal men cannot uproot it, but the gods can do whatever they like.

"Then Mercury went back to high Olympus passing over the wooded island; but I fared onward to the house of Circe, and my heart was clouded with care as I walked along. When I got to the gates I stood there and called the goddess, and as soon as she heard me she came down, opened the door, and asked me to come in; so I followed her – much troubled in my mind. She set me on a richly decorated seat inlaid with silver, there was a footstool also under my feet, and she mixed a mess in a golden goblet for me to drink; but she drugged it, for she meant me mischief. When she had given it me, and I had drunk it without its charming me, she struck me with her wand. 'There now,' she cried, 'be off to the pigstye, and make your lair with the rest of them.'

"But I rushed at her with my sword drawn as though I would kill her, whereon she fell with a loud scream, clasped my knees, and spoke piteously, saying, 'Who and whence are you? from what place and people have you come? How can it be that my drugs have no power to charm you? Never yet was any man able to stand so much as a taste of the herb I gave you; you must be spell-proof; surely you can be none other than the bold hero Ulysses, who Mercury always said would come here some day with his ship while on his way home from Troy; so be it then; sheathe your sword and let us go to bed, that we may make friends and learn to trust each other.'

"And I answered, 'Circe, how can you expect me to be friendly with you when you have just been turning all my men into pigs? And now that you have got me here myself, you mean me mischief when you ask me to go to bed with you, and will unman me and make me fit for nothing. I shall certainly not consent to go to bed with you unless you will first take your solemn oath to plot no further harm against me.'

"So she swore at once as I had told her, and when she had completed her oath then I went to bed with her.

"Meanwhile her four servants, who are her housemaids, set about their work. They are the children of the groves and fountains, and of the holy waters that run down into the sea. One of them spread a fair purple cloth over a seat, and laid a carpet underneath it. Another brought tables of silver up to the seats, and set them with baskets of gold. A third mixed some sweet wine with water in a silver bowl and put golden cups upon the tables, while the fourth brought in water and set it to boil in a large cauldron over a good fire which she had lighted. When the water in the cauldron was boiling, she poured cold into it till it was just as I liked it, and then she set me in a bath and began washing me from the cauldron about the head and shoulders, to take the tire and stiffness out of my limbs. As soon as she had done washing me and anointing me with oil, she arrayed me in a good cloak and shirt and led me to a richly decorated seat inlaid with silver; there was a footstool also under my feet. A maid servant then brought me water in a beautiful golden ewer and poured it into a silver basin for me to wash my hands, and she drew a clean table beside me; an upper servant brought me bread and offered me many things of what there was in the house, and then Circe bade me eat, but I would not, and sat without heeding what was before me, still moody and suspicious.

"When Circe saw me sitting there without eating, and in great grief, she came to me and said, 'Ulysses, why do you sit like that as though you were dumb, gnawing at your own heart, and refusing both meat and drink? Is it that you are still suspicious? You ought not to be, for I have already sworn solemnly that I will not hurt you.'

"And I said, 'Circe, no man with any sense of what is right can think of either eating or drinking in your house until you have set his friends free and let him see them. If you want me to eat and drink, you must free my men and bring them to me that I may see them with my own eyes.'

"When I had said this she went straight through the court with her wand in her hand and opened the pigstye doors. My men came out like so many prime hogs and stood looking at her, but she went about among them and anointed each with a second drug, whereon the bristles that the bad drug had given them fell off, and they became men again, younger than they were before, and much taller and better looking. They knew me at once, seized me each of them by the hand, and wept for joy till the whole house was filled with the sound of their halloa-ballooing, and Circe herself was so sorry for them that she came up to me and said, 'Ulysses, noble son of Laertes, go back at once to the sea where you have left your ship, and first draw it on to the land. Then, hide all your ship's gear and property in some cave, and come back here with your men.'

"I agreed to this, so I went back to the sea shore, and found the men at the ship weeping and wailing most piteously. When they saw me the silly blubbering fellows began frisking round me as calves break out and gambol round their mothers, when they see them coming home to be milked after they have been feeding all day, and the homestead resounds with their lowing. They seemed as glad to see me as though they had got back to their own rugged Ithaca, where they had been born and bred. 'Sir,' said the affectionate creatures, 'we are as glad to see you back as though we had got safe home to Ithaca; but tell us all about the fate of our comrades.'

"I spoke comfortingly to them and said, 'We must draw our ship on to the land, and hide the ship's gear with all our property in some cave; then come with me all of you as fast as you can to Circe's house, where you will find your comrades eating and drinking in the midst of great abundance.'

"On this the men would have come with me at once, but Eurylochus tried to hold them back and said, 'Alas, poor wretches that we are, what will become of us? Rush not on your ruin by going to the house of Circe, who will turn us all into pigs or wolves or lions, and we shall have to keep guard over her house. Remember how the Cyclops treated us when our comrades went inside his cave, and Ulysses with them. It was all through his sheer folly that those men lost their lives.'

"When I heard him I was in two minds whether or no to draw the keen blade that hung by my sturdy thigh and cut his head off in spite of his being a near relation of my own; but the men interceded for him and said, 'Sir, if it may so be, let this fellow stay here and mind the ship, but take the rest of us with you to Circe's house.'

"On this we all went inland, and Eurylochus was not left behind after all, but came on too, for he was frightened by the severe reprimand that I had given him.

"Meanwhile Circe had been seeing that the men who had been left behind were washed and anointed with olive oil; she had also given them woollen cloaks and shirts, and when we came we found them all comfortably at dinner in her house. As soon as the men saw each other face to face and knew one another, they wept for joy and cried aloud till the whole palace rang again. Thereon Circe came up to me and said, 'Ulysses, noble son of Laertes, tell your men to leave off crying; I know how much you have all of you suffered at sea, and how ill you have fared among cruel savages on the mainland, but that is over now, so stay here, and eat and drink till you are once more as strong and hearty as you were when you left Ithaca; for at present you are weakened both in body and mind; you keep all the time thinking of the hardships you have suffered during your travels, so that you have no more cheerfulness left in you.'

"Thus did she speak and we assented. We stayed with Circe for a whole twelvemonth feasting upon an untold quantity both of meat and wine. But when the year had passed in the waning of moons and the long days had come round, my men called me apart and said, 'Sir, it is time you began to think about going home, if so be you are to be spared to see your house and native country at all.'

"Thus did they speak and I assented. Thereon through the livelong day to the going down of the sun we feasted our fill on meat and wine, but when the sun went down and it came on dark the men laid themselves down to sleep in the covered cloisters. I, however, after I had got into bed with Circe, besought her by her knees, and the goddess listened to what I had got to say. 'Circe,' said I, 'please to keep the promise you made me about furthering me on my homeward voyage. I want to get back and so do my men, they are always pestering me with their complaints as soon as ever your back is turned.'

"And the goddess answered, 'Ulysses, noble son of Laertes, you shall none of you stay here any longer if you do not want to, but there is another journey which you have got to take before you can sail homewards. You must go to the house of Hades and of dread Proserpine to consult the ghost of the blind Theban prophet Teiresias, whose reason is still unshaken. To him alone has Proserpine left his understanding even in death, but the other ghosts flit about aimlessly.'

"I was dismayed when I heard this. I sat up in bed and wept, and would gladly have lived no longer to see the light of the sun, but presently when I was tired of weeping and tossing myself about, I said, 'And who shall guide me upon this voyage – for the house of Hades is a port that no ship can reach.'

"'You will want no guide,' she answered; 'raise your mast, set your white sails, sit quite still, and the North Wind will blow you there of itself. When your ship has traversed the waters of Oceanus, you will reach the fertile shore of Proserpine's country with its groves of tall poplars and willows that shed their fruit untimely; here beach your ship upon the shore of Oceanus, and go straight on to the dark abode of Hades. You will find it near the place where the rivers Pyriphlegethon and Cocytus (which is a branch of the river Styx) flow into Acheron, and you will see a rock near it, just where the two roaring rivers run into one another.

"'When you have reached this spot, as I now tell you, dig a trench a cubit or so in length, breadth, and depth, and pour into it as a drink-offering to all the dead, first, honey mixed with milk, then wine, and in the third place water – sprinkling white barley meal over the whole. Moreover you must offer many prayers to the poor feeble ghosts, and promise them that when you get back to Ithaca you will sacrifice a barren heifer to them, the best you have, and will load the pyre with good things. More particularly you must promise that Teiresias shall have a black sheep all to himself, the finest in all your flocks.

"'When you shall have thus besought the ghosts with your prayers, offer them a ram and a black ewe, bending their heads towards Erebus; but yourself turn away from them as though you would make towards the river. On this, many dead men's ghosts will come to you, and you must tell your men to skin the two sheep that you have just killed, and offer them as a burnt sacrifice with prayers to Hades and to Proserpine. Then draw your sword and sit there, so as to prevent any other poor ghost from coming near the spilt blood before Teiresias shall have answered your questions. The seer will presently come to you, and will tell you about your voyage – what stages you are to make, and how you are to sail the sea so as to reach your home.'

"It was day-break by the time she had done speaking, so she dressed me in my shirt and cloak. As for herself she threw a beautiful light gossamer fabric over her shoulders, fastening it with a golden girdle round her waist, and she covered her head with a mantle. Then I went about among the men everywhere all over the house, and spoke kindly to each of them man by man: 'You must not lie sleeping here any longer,' said I to them, 'we must be going, for Circe has told me all about it.' And on this they did as I bade them.

"Even so, however, I did not get them away without misadventure. We had with us a certain youth named Elpenor, not very remarkable for sense or courage, who had got drunk and was lying on the house-top away from the rest of the men, to sleep off his liquor in the cool. When he heard the noise of the men bustling about, he jumped up on a sudden and forgot all about coming down by the main staircase, so he tumbled right off the roof and broke his neck, and his soul went down to the house of Hades.

"When I had got the men together I said to them, 'You think you are about to start home again, but Circe has explained to me that instead of this, we have got to go to the house of Hades and Proserpine to consult the ghost of the Theban prophet Teiresias.'

"The men were broken-hearted as they heard me, and threw themselves on the ground groaning and tearing their hair, but they did not mend matters by crying. When we reached the sea shore, weeping and lamenting our fate, Circe brought the ram and the ewe, and we made them fast hard by the ship. She passed through the midst of us without our knowing it, for who can see the comings and goings of a god, if the god does not wish to be seen?

Book XI

The Visit to the Dead

"Then, when we had got down to the sea shore we drew our ship into the water and got her mast and sails into her; we also put the sheep on board and took our places, weeping and in great distress of mind. Circe, that great and cunning goddess, sent us a fair wind that blew dead aft and staid steadily with us keeping our sails all the time well filled; so we did whatever wanted doing to the ship's gear and let her go as the wind and helmsman headed her. All day long her sails were full as she held her course over the sea, but when the sun went down and darkness was over all the earth, we got into the deep waters of the river Oceanus, where lie the land and city of the Cimmerians who live enshrouded in mist and darkness which the rays of the sun never pierce neither at his rising nor as he goes down again out of the heavens, but the poor wretches live in one long melancholy night. When we got there we beached the ship, took the sheep out of her, and went along by the waters of Oceanus till we came to the place of which Circe had told us.

"Here Perimedes and Eurylochus held the victims, while I drew my sword and dug the trench a cubit each way. I made a drink-offering to all the dead, first with honey and milk, then with wine, and thirdly with water, and I sprinkled white barley meal over the whole, praying earnestly to the poor feckless ghosts, and promising them that when I got back to Ithaca I would sacrifice a barren heifer for them, the best I had, and would load the pyre with good things. I also particularly promised that Teiresias should have a black sheep to himself, the best in all my flocks. When I had prayed sufficiently to the dead, I cut the throats of the two sheep and let the blood run into the trench, whereon the ghosts came trooping up from Erebus – brides, young bachelors, old men worn out with toil, maids who had been crossed in love, and brave men who had been killed in battle, with their armour still smirched with blood; they came from every quarter and flitted round the trench with a strange kind of screaming sound that made me turn pale with fear. When I saw them coming I told the men to be quick and flay the carcasses of the two dead sheep and make burnt offerings of them, and at the same time to repeat prayers to Hades and to Proserpine; but I sat where I was with my sword drawn and would not let the poor feckless ghosts come near the blood till Teiresias should have answered my questions.

"The first ghost that came was that of my comrade Elpenor, for he had not yet been laid beneath the earth. We had left his body unwaked and unburied in Circe's house, for we had had too much else to do. I was very sorry for him, and cried when I saw him: 'Elpenor,' said I, 'how did you come down here into this gloom and darkness? You have got here on foot quicker than I have with my ship.'

"'Sir,' he answered with a groan, 'it was all bad luck, and my own unspeakable drunkenness. I was lying asleep on the top of Circe's house, and never thought of coming down again by the great staircase but fell right off the roof and broke my neck, so my soul came down to the house of Hades. And now I beseech you by all those whom you have left behind you, though they are not here, by your wife, by the father who brought you up when you were a child, and by Telemachus who is the one hope of your house, do what I shall now ask you. I know that when you leave this limbo you will again hold your ship for the Aeaean island. Do not go thence leaving me unwaked and unburied behind you, or I may bring heaven's anger upon you; but burn me with whatever armour I have, build a barrow for me on the sea shore, that may tell people in days to come what a poor unlucky fellow I was, and plant over my grave the oar I used to row with when I was yet alive and with my messmates.' And I said, 'My poor fellow, I will do all that you have asked of me.'

"Thus, then, did we sit and hold sad talk with one another, I on the one side of the trench with my sword held over the blood, and the ghost of my comrade saying all this to me from the other side. Then came the ghost of my dead mother Anticlea, daughter to Autolycus. I had left her alive when I set out for Troy and was moved to tears when I saw her, but even so, for all my sorrow I would not let her come near the blood till I had asked my questions of Teiresias.

"Then came also the ghost of Theban Teiresias, with his golden sceptre in his hand. He knew me and said, 'Ulysses, noble son of Laertes, why, poor man, have you left the light of day and come down to visit the dead in this sad place? Stand back from the trench and withdraw your sword that I may drink of the blood and answer your questions truly.'

"So I drew back, and sheathed my sword, whereon when he had drank of the blood he began with his prophecy.

"'You want to know,' said he, 'about your return home, but heaven will make this hard for you. I do not think that you will escape the eye of Neptune, who still nurses his bitter grudge against you for having blinded his son. Still, after much suffering you may get home if you can restrain yourself and your companions when your ship reaches the Thrinacian island, where you will find the sheep and cattle belonging to the sun, who sees and gives ear to everything. If you leave these flocks unharmed and think of nothing but of getting home, you may yet after much hardship reach Ithaca; but if you harm them, then I forewarn you of the destruction both of your ship and of your men. Even though you may yourself escape, you will return in bad plight after losing all your men, in another man's ship, and you will find trouble in your house, which will be overrun by high-handed people, who are devouring your substance under the pretext of paying court and making presents to your wife.

"'When you get home you will take your revenge on these suitors; and after you have killed them by force or fraud in your own house, you must take a well made oar and carry it on and on, till you come to a country where the people have never heard of the sea and do not even mix salt with their food, nor do they know anything about ships, and oars that are as the wings of a ship. I will give you this certain token which cannot escape your notice. A wayfarer will meet you and will say it must be a winnowing shovel that you have got upon your shoulder; on this you must fix the oar in the ground and sacrifice a ram, a bull, and a boar to Neptune. Then go home and offer hecatombs to all the gods in heaven one after the other. As for yourself, death shall come to you from the sea, and your life shall ebb away very gently when you are full of years and peace of mind, and your people shall bless you. All that I have said will come true.'

"'This,' I answered, 'must be as it may please heaven, but tell me and tell me and tell me true, I see my poor mother's ghost close by us; she is sitting by the blood without saying a word, and though I am her own son she does not remember me and speak to me; tell me, Sir, how I can make her know me.'

"'That,' said he, 'I can soon do. Any ghost that you let taste of the blood will talk with you like a reasonable being, but if you do not let them have any blood they will go away again.'

"On this the ghost of Teiresias went back to the house of Hades, for his prophecyings had now been spoken, but I sat still where I was until my mother came up and tasted the blood. Then she knew me at once and spoke fondly to me, saying, 'My son, how did you come down to this abode of darkness while you are still alive? It is a hard thing for the living to see these places, for between us and them there are great and terrible waters, and there is Oceanus, which no man can cross on foot, but he must have a good ship to take him. Are you all this time trying to find your way home from Troy, and have you never yet got back to Ithaca nor seen your wife in your own house?'

"'Mother,' said I, 'I was forced to come here to consult the ghost of the Theban prophet Teiresias. I have never yet been near the Achaean land nor set foot on my native country, and I have had nothing but one long series of misfortunes from the very first day that I set out with Agamemnon for Ilius, the land of noble steeds, to fight the Trojans. But tell me, and tell me true, in what way did you die? Did you have a long illness, or did heaven vouchsafe you a gentle easy passage to eternity? Tell me also about my father, and the son whom I left behind me, is my property still in their hands, or has someone else got hold of it, who thinks that I shall not return to claim it? Tell me again what my wife intends doing, and in what mind she is; does she live with my son and guard my estate securely, or has she made the best match she could and married again?'

"My mother answered, 'Your wife still remains in your house, but she is in great distress of mind and spends her whole time in tears both night and day. No one as yet has got possession of your fine property, and Telemachus still holds your lands undisturbed. He has to entertain largely, as of course he must, considering his position as a magistrate, and how every one invites him; your father remains at his old place in the country and never goes near the town. He has no comfortable bed nor bedding; in the winter he sleeps on the floor in front of the fire with the men and goes about all in rags, but in summer, when the warm weather comes on again, he lies out in the vineyard on a bed of vine leaves thrown any how upon the ground. He grieves continually about your never having come home, and suffers more and more as he grows older. As for my own end it was in this wise: heaven did not take me swiftly and painlessly in my own house, nor was I attacked by any illness such as those that generally wear people out and kill them, but my longing to know what you were doing and the force of my affection for you – this it was that was the death of me.'

"Then I tried to find some way of embracing my poor mother's ghost. Thrice I sprang towards her and tried to clasp her in my arms, but each time she flitted from my embrace as it were a dream or phantom, and being touched to the quick I said to her, 'Mother, why do you not stay still when I would embrace you? If we could throw our arms around one another we might find sad comfort in the sharing of our sorrows even in the house of Hades; does Proserpine want to lay a still further load of grief upon me by mocking me with a phantom only?'

"'My son,' she answered, 'most ill-fated of all mankind, it is not Proserpine that is beguiling you, but all people are like this when they are dead. The sinews no longer hold the flesh and bones together; these perish in the fierceness of consuming fire as soon as life has left the body, and the soul flits away as though it were a dream. Now, however, go back to the light of day as soon as you can, and note all these things that you may tell them to your wife hereafter.'

"Thus did we converse, and anon Proserpine sent up the ghosts of the wives and daughters of all the most famous men. They gathered in crowds about the blood, and I considered how I might question them severally. In the end I deemed that it would be best to draw the keen blade that hung by my sturdy thigh, and keep them from all drinking the blood at once. So they came up one after the other, and each one as I questioned her told me her race and lineage.

"The first I saw was Tyro. She was daughter of Salmoneus and wife of Cretheus the son of Aeolus. She fell in love with the river Enipeus who is much the most beautiful river in the whole world. Once when she was taking a walk by his side as usual, Neptune, disguised as her lover, lay with her at the mouth of the river, and a huge blue wave arched itself like a mountain over them to hide both woman and god, whereon he loosed her virgin girdle and laid her in a deep slumber. When the god had accomplished the deed of love, he took her hand in his own and said, 'Tyro, rejoice in all good will; the embraces of the gods are not fruitless, and you will have fine twins about this time twelve months. Take great care of them. I am Neptune, so now go home, but hold your tongue and do not tell anyone.'

"Then he dived under the sea, and she in due course bore Pelias and Neleus, who both of them served Jove with all their might. Pelias was a great breeder of sheep and lived in Iolcus, but the other lived in Pylos. The rest of her children were by Cretheus, namely, Aeson, Pheres, and Amythaon, who was a mighty warrior and charioteer.

"Next to her I saw Antiope, daughter to Asopus, who could boast of having slept in the arms of even Jove himself, and who bore him two sons Amphion and Zethus. These founded Thebes with its seven gates, and built a wall all round it; for strong though they were they could not hold Thebes till they had walled it.

"Then I saw Alcmena, the wife of Amphitryon, who also bore to Jove indomitable Hercules; and Megara who was daughter to great King Creon, and married the redoubtable son of Amphitryon.

"I also saw fair Epicaste mother of king Oedipodes whose awful lot it was to marry her own son without suspecting it. He married her after having killed his father, but the gods proclaimed the whole story to the world; whereon he remained king of Thebes, in great grief for the spite the gods had borne him; but Epicaste went to the house of the mighty jailor Hades, having hanged herself for grief, and the avenging spirits haunted him as for an outraged mother – to his ruing bitterly thereafter.

"Then I saw Chloris, whom Neleus married for her beauty, having given priceless presents for her. She was youngest daughter to Amphion son of Iasus and king of Minyan Orchomenus, and was Queen in Pylos. She bore Nestor, Chromius, and Periclymenus, and she also bore that marvellously lovely woman Pero, who was wooed by all the country round; but Neleus would only give her to him who should raid the cattle of Iphicles from the grazing grounds of Phylace, and this was a hard task. The only man who would undertake to raid them was a certain excellent seer, but the will of heaven was against him, for the rangers of the cattle caught him and put him in prison; nevertheless when a full year had passed and the same season came round again, Iphicles set him at liberty, after he had expounded all the oracles of heaven. Thus, then, was the will of Jove accomplished.

"And I saw Leda the wife of Tyndarus, who bore him two famous sons, Castor breaker of horses, and Pollux the mighty boxer. Both these heroes are lying under the earth, though they are still alive, for by a special dispensation of Jove, they die and come to life again, each one of them every other day throughout all time, and they have the rank of gods.

"After her I saw Iphimedeia wife of Aloeus who boasted the embrace of Neptune. She bore two sons Otus and Ephialtes, but both were short lived. They were the finest children that were ever born in this world, and the best looking, Orion only excepted; for at nine years old they were nine fathoms high, and measured nine cubits round the chest. They threatened to make war with the gods in Olympus, and tried to set Mount Ossa on the top of Mount Olympus, and Mount Pelion on the top of Ossa, that they might scale heaven itself, and they would have done it too if they had been grown up, but Apollo, son of Leto, killed both of them, before they had got so much as a sign of hair upon their cheeks or chin.

"Then I saw Phaedra, and Procris, and fair Ariadne daughter of the magician Minos, whom Theseus was carrying off from Crete to Athens, but he did not enjoy her, for before he could do so Diana killed her in the island of Dia on account of what Bacchus had said against her.

"I also saw Maera and Clymene and hateful Eriphyle, who sold her own husband for gold. But it would take me all night if I were to name every single one of the wives and daughters of heroes whom I saw, and it is time for me to go to bed, either on board ship with my crew, or here. As for my escort, heaven and yourselves will see to it."

Here he ended, and the guests sat all of them enthralled and speechless throughout the covered cloister. Then Arete said to them: –

"What do you think of this man, O Phaeacians? Is he not tall and good looking, and is he not clever? True, he is my own guest, but all of you share in the distinction. Do not be in a hurry to send him away, nor niggardly in the presents you make to one who is in such great need, for heaven has blessed all of you with great abundance."

Then spoke the aged hero Echeneus who was one of the oldest men among them, "My friends," said he, "what our august queen has just said to us is both reasonable and to the purpose, therefore be persuaded by it; but the decision whether in word or deed rests ultimately with King Alcinous."

"The thing shall be done," exclaimed Alcinous, "as surely as I still live and reign over the Phaeacians. Our guest is indeed very anxious to get home, still we must persuade him to remain with us until tomorrow, by which time I shall be able to get together the whole sum that I mean to give him. As regards his escort it will be a matter for you all, and mine above all others as the chief person among you."

And Ulysses answered, "King Alcinous, if you were to bid me to stay here for a whole twelve months, and then speed me on my way, loaded with your noble gifts, I should obey you gladly and it would redound greatly to my advantage, for I should return fuller-handed to my own people, and should thus be more respected and beloved by all who see me when I get back to Ithaca."

"Ulysses," replied Alcinous, "not one of us who sees you has any idea that you are a charlatan or a swindler. I know there are many people going about who tell such plausible stories that it is very hard to see through them, but there is a style about your language which assures me of your good disposition. Moreover you have told the story of your own misfortunes, and those of the Argives, as though you were a practiced bard; but tell me, and tell me true, whether you saw any of the mighty heroes who went to Troy at the same time with yourself, and perished there. The evenings are still at their longest, and it is not yet bed time – go on, therefore, with your divine story, for I could stay here listening till tomorrow morning, so long as you will continue to tell us of your adventures."

"Alcinous," answered Ulysses, "there is a time for making speeches, and a time for going to bed; nevertheless, since you so desire, I will not refrain from telling you the still sadder tale of those of my comrades who did not fall fighting with the Trojans, but perished on their return, through the treachery of a wicked woman.

"When Proserpine had dismissed the female ghosts in all directions, the ghost of Agamemnon son of Atreus came sadly up to me, surrounded by those who had perished with him in the house of Aegisthus. As soon as he had tasted the blood, he knew me, and weeping bitterly stretched out his arms towards me to embrace me; but he had no strength nor substance any more, and I too wept and pitied him as I beheld him. 'How did you come by your death,' said I, 'King Agamemnon? Did Neptune raise his winds and waves against you when you were at sea, or did your enemies make an end of you on the main land when you were cattle-lifting or sheep-stealing, or while they were fighting in defence of their wives and city?'

"'Ulysses,' he answered, 'noble son of Laertes, I was not lost at sea in any storm of Neptune's raising, nor did my foes despatch me upon the mainland, but Aegisthus and my wicked wife were the death of me between them. He asked me to his house, feasted me, and then butchered me most miserably as though I were a fat beast in a slaughter house, while all around me my comrades were slain like sheep or pigs for the wedding breakfast, or picnic, or gorgeous banquet of some great nobleman. You must have seen numbers of men killed either in a general engagement, or in single combat, but you never saw anything so truly pitiable as the way in which we fell in that cloister, with the mixing bowl and the loaded tables lying all about, and the ground reeking with our blood. I heard Priam's daughter Cassandra scream as Clytemnestra killed her close beside me. I lay dying upon the earth with the sword in my body, and raised my hands to kill the slut of a murderess, but she slipped away from me; she would not even close my lips nor my eyes when I was dying, for there is nothing in this world so cruel and so shameless as a woman when she has fallen into such guilt as hers was. Fancy murdering her own husband! I thought I was going to be welcomed home by my children and my servants, but her abominable crime has brought disgrace on herself and all women who shall come after – even on the good ones.'

"And I said, 'In truth Jove has hated the house of Atreus from first to last in the matter of their women's counsels. See how many of us fell for Helen's sake, and now it seems that Clytemnestra hatched mischief against you too during your absence.'

"'Be sure, therefore,' continued Agamemnon, 'and not be too friendly even with your own wife. Do not tell her all that you know perfectly well yourself. Tell her a part only, and keep your own counsel about the rest. Not that your wife, Ulysses, is likely to murder you, for Penelope is a very admirable woman, and has an excellent nature. We left her a young bride with an infant at her breast when we set out for Troy. This child no doubt is now grown up happily to man's estate, and he and his father will have a joyful meeting and embrace one another as it is right they should do, whereas my wicked wife did not even allow me the happiness of looking upon my son, but killed me ere I could do so. Furthermore I say – and lay my saying to your heart – do not tell people when you are bringing your ship to Ithaca, but steal a march upon them, for after all this there is no trusting women. But now tell me, and tell me true, can you give me any news of my son Orestes? Is he in Orchomenus, or at Pylos, or is he at Sparta with Menelaus – for I presume that he is still living.'

"And I said, 'Agamemnon, why do you ask me? I do not know whether your son is alive or dead, and it is not right to talk when one does not know.'

"As we two sat weeping and talking thus sadly with one another the ghost of Achilles came up to us with Patroclus, Antilochus, and Ajax who was the finest and goodliest man of all the Danaans after the son of Peleus. The fleet descendant of Aeacus knew me and spoke piteously, saying, 'Ulysses, noble son of Laertes, what deed of daring will you undertake next, that you venture down to the house of Hades among us silly dead, who are but the ghosts of them that can labour no more?'

"And I said, 'Achilles, son of Peleus, foremost champion of the Achaeans, I came to consult Teiresias, and see if he could advise me about my return home to Ithaca, for I have never yet been able to get near the Achaean land, nor to set foot in my own country, but have been in trouble all the time. As for you, Achilles, no one was ever yet so fortunate as you have been, nor ever will be, for you were adored by all us Argives as long as you were alive, and now that you are here you are a great prince among the dead. Do not, therefore, take it so much to heart even if you are dead.'

"'Say not a word,' he answered, 'in death's favour; I would rather be a paid servant in a poor man's house and be above ground than king of kings among the dead. But give me news about my son; is he gone to the wars and will he be a great soldier, or is this not so? Tell me also if you have heard anything about my father Peleus – does he still rule among the Myrmidons, or do they show him no respect throughout Hellas and Phthia now that he is old and his limbs fail him? Could I but stand by his side, in the light of day, with the same strength that I had when I killed the bravest of our foes upon the plain of Troy – could I but be as I then was and go even for a short time to my father's house, anyone who tried to do him violence or supersede him would soon rue it.'

"'I have heard nothing,' I answered, 'of Peleus, but I can tell you all about your son Neoptolemus, for I took him in my own ship from Scyros with the Achaeans. In our councils of war before Troy he was always first to speak, and his judgement was unerring. Nestor and I were the only two who could surpass him; and when it came to fighting on the plain of Troy, he would never remain with the body of his men, but would dash on far in front, foremost of them all in valour. Many a man did he kill in battle – I cannot name every single one of those whom he slew while fighting on the side of the Argives, but will only say how he killed that valiant hero Eurypylus son of Telephus, who was the handsomest man I ever saw except Memnon; many others also of the Ceteians fell around him by reason of a woman's bribes. Moreover, when all the bravest of the Argives went inside the horse that Epeus had made, and it was left to me to settle when we should either open the door of our ambuscade, or close it, though all the other leaders and chief men among the Danaans were drying their eyes and quaking in every limb, I never once saw him turn pale nor wipe a tear from his cheek; he was all the time urging me to break out from the horse – grasping the handle of his sword and his bronze-shod spear, and breathing fury against the foe. Yet when we had sacked the city of Priam he got his handsome share of the prize money and went on board (such is the fortune of war) without a wound upon him, neither from a thrown spear nor in close combat, for the rage of Mars is a matter of great chance.'

"When I had told him this, the ghost of Achilles strode off across a meadow full of asphodel, exulting over what I had said concerning the prowess of his son.

"The ghosts of other dead men stood near me and told me each his own melancholy tale; but that of Ajax son of Telamon alone held aloof – still angry with me for having won the cause in our dispute about the armour of Achilles. Thetis had offered it as a prize, but the Trojan prisoners and Minerva were the judges. Would that I had never gained the day in such a contest, for it cost the life of Ajax, who was foremost of all the Danaans after the son of Peleus, alike in stature and prowess.

"When I saw him I tried to pacify him and said, 'Ajax, will you not forget and forgive even in death, but must the judgement about that hateful armour still rankle with you? It cost us Argives dear enough to lose such a tower of strength as you were to us. We mourned you as much as we mourned Achilles son of Peleus himself, nor can the blame be laid on anything but on the spite which Jove bore against the Danaans, for it was this that made him counsel your destruction – come hither, therefore, bring your proud spirit into subjection, and hear what I can tell you.'

"He would not answer, but turned away to Erebus and to the other ghosts; nevertheless, I should have made him talk to me in spite of his being so angry, or I should have gone on talking to him, only that there were still others among the dead whom I desired to see.

"Then I saw Minos son of Jove with his golden sceptre in his hand sitting in judgement on the dead, and the ghosts were gathered sitting and standing round him in the spacious house of Hades, to learn his sentences upon them.

"After him I saw huge Orion in a meadow full of asphodel driving the ghosts of the wild beasts that he had killed upon the mountains, and he had a great bronze club in his hand, unbreakable for ever and ever.

"And I saw Tityus son of Gaia stretched upon the plain and covering some nine acres of ground. Two vultures on either side of him were digging their beaks into his liver, and he kept on trying to beat them off with his hands, but could not; for he had violated Jove's mistress Leto as she was going through Panopeus on her way to Pytho.

"I saw also the dreadful fate of Tantalus, who stood in a lake that reached his chin; he was dying to quench his thirst, but could never reach the water, for whenever the poor creature stooped to drink, it dried up and vanished, so that there was nothing but dry ground – parched by the spite of heaven. There were tall trees, moreover, that shed their fruit over his head – pears, pomegranates, apples, sweet figs and juicy olives, but whenever the poor creature stretched out his hand to take some, the wind tossed the branches back again to the clouds.

"And I saw Sisyphus at his endless task raising his prodigious stone with both his hands. With hands and feet he tried to roll it up to the top of the hill, but always, just before he could roll it over on to the other side, its weight would be too much for him, and the pitiless stone would come thundering down again on to the plain. Then he would begin trying to push it up hill again, and the sweat ran off him and the steam rose after him.

"After him I saw mighty Hercules, but it was his phantom only, for he is feasting ever with the immortal gods, and has lovely Hebe to wife, who is daughter of Jove and Juno. The ghosts were screaming round him like scared birds flying all whithers. He looked black as night with his bare bow in his hands and his arrow on the string, glaring around as though ever on the point of taking aim. About his breast there was a wondrous golden belt adorned in the most marvellous fashion with bears, wild boars, and lions with gleaming eyes; there was also war, battle, and death. The man who made that belt, do what he might, would never be able to make another like it. Hercules knew me at once when he saw me, and spoke piteously, saying, 'My poor Ulysses, noble son of Laertes, are you too leading the same sorry kind of life that I did when I was above ground? I was son of Jove, but I went through an infinity of suffering, for I became bondsman to one who was far beneath me – a low fellow who set me all manner of labours. He once sent me here to fetch the hell-hound – for he did not think he could find anything harder for me than this, but I got the hound out of Hades and brought him to him, for Mercury and Minerva helped me.'

"On this Hercules went down again into the house of Hades, but I stayed where I was in case some other of the mighty dead should come to me. And I should have seen still other of them that are gone before, whom I would fain have seen – Theseus and Pirithous – glorious children of the gods, but so many thousands of ghosts came round me and uttered such appalling cries, that I was panic stricken lest Proserpine should send up from the house of Hades the head of that awful monster Gorgon. On this I hastened back to my ship and ordered my men to go on board at once and loose the hawsers; so they embarked and took their places, whereon the ship went down the stream of the river Oceanus. We had to row at first, but presently a fair wind sprang up.

Book XII

The Sirens, Scylla and Charybdis, the Cattle of the Sun

"After we were clear of the river Oceanus, and had got out into the open sea, we went on till we reached the Aeaean island where there is dawn and sun-rise as in other places. We then drew our ship on to the sands and got out of her on to the shore, where we went to sleep and waited till day should break.

"Then, when the child of morning, rosy-fingered Dawn, appeared, I sent some men to Circe's house to fetch the body of Elpenor. We cut firewood from a wood where the headland jutted out into the sea, and after we had wept over him and lamented him we performed his funeral rites. When his body and armour had been burned to ashes, we raised a cairn, set a stone over it, and at the top of the cairn we fixed the oar that he had been used to row with.

"While we were doing all this, Circe, who knew that we had got back from the house of Hades, dressed herself and came to us as fast as she could; and her maid servants came with her bringing us bread, meat, and wine. Then she stood in the midst of us and said, 'You have done a bold thing in going down alive to the house of Hades, and you will have died twice, to other people's once; now, then, stay here for the rest of the day, feast your fill, and go on with your voyage at daybreak tomorrow morning. In the meantime I will tell Ulysses about your course, and will explain everything to him so as to prevent your suffering from misadventure either by land or sea.'

"We agreed to do as she had said, and feasted through the livelong day to the going down of the sun, but when the sun had set and it came on dark, the men laid themselves down to sleep by the stern cables of the ship. Then Circe took me by the hand and bade me be seated away from the others, while she reclined by my side and asked me all about our adventures.

"'So far so good,' said she, when I had ended my story, 'and now pay attention to what I am about to tell you – heaven itself, indeed, will recall it to your recollection. First you will come to the Sirens who enchant all who come near them. If anyone unwarily draws in too close and hears the singing of the Sirens, his wife and children will never welcome him home again, for they sit in a green field and warble him to death with the sweetness of their song. There is a great heap of dead men's bones lying all around, with the flesh still rotting off them. Therefore pass these Sirens by, and stop your men's ears with wax that none of them may hear; but if you like you can listen yourself, for you may get the men to bind you as you stand upright on a cross piece half way up the mast, and they must lash the rope's ends to the mast itself, that you may have the pleasure of listening. If you beg and pray the men to unloose you, then they must bind you faster.

"'When your crew have taken you past these Sirens, I cannot give you coherent directions as to which of two courses you are to take; I will lay the two alternatives before you, and you must consider them for yourself. On the one hand there are some overhanging rocks against which the deep blue waves of Amphitrite beat with terrific fury; the blessed gods call these rocks the Wanderers. Here not even a bird may pass, no, not even the timid doves that bring ambrosia to Father Jove, but the sheer rock always carries off one of them, and Father Jove has to send another to make up their number; no ship that ever yet came to these rocks has got away again, but the waves and whirlwinds of fire are freighted with wreckage and with the bodies of dead men. The only vessel that ever sailed and got through, was the famous Argo on her way from the house of Aetes, and she too would have gone against these great rocks, only that Juno piloted her past them for the love she bore to Jason.

"'Of these two rocks the one reaches heaven and its peak is lost in a dark cloud. This never leaves it, so that the top is never clear not even in summer and early autumn. No man though he had twenty hands and twenty feet could get a foothold on it and climb it, for it runs sheer up, as smooth as though it had been polished. In the middle of it there is a large cavern, looking West and turned towards Erebus; you must take your ship this way, but the cave is so high up that not even the stoutest archer could send an arrow into it. Inside it Scylla sits and yelps with a voice that you might take to be that of a young hound, but in truth she is a dreadful monster and no one – not even a god – could face her without being terror-struck.

She has twelve mis-shapen feet, and six necks of the most prodigious length; and at the end of each neck she has a frightful head with three rows of teeth in each, all set very close together, so that they would crunch anyone to death in a moment, and she sits deep within her shady cell thrusting out her heads and peering all round the rock, fishing for dolphins or dogfish or any larger monster that she can catch, of the thousands with which Amphitrite teems. No ship ever yet got past her without losing some men, for she shoots out all her heads at once, and carries off a man in each mouth.

"'You will find the other rock lie lower, but they are so close together that there is not more than a bow-shot between them. A large fig tree in full leaf grows upon it, and under it lies the sucking whirlpool of Charybdis. Three times in the day does she vomit forth her waters, and three times she sucks them down again; see that you be not there when she is sucking, for if you are, Neptune himself could not save you; you must hug the Scylla side and drive ship by as fast as you can, for you had better lose six men than your whole crew.'

"'Is there no way,' said I, 'of escaping Charybdis, and at the same time keeping Scylla off when she is trying to harm my men?'

"'You dare devil,' replied the goddess, 'you are always wanting to fight somebody or something; you will not let yourself be beaten even by the immortals. For Scylla is not mortal; moreover she is savage, extreme, rude, cruel and invincible. There is no help for it; your best chance will be to get by her as fast as ever you can, for if you dawdle about her rock while you are putting on your armour, she may catch you with a second cast of her six heads, and snap up another half dozen of your men; so drive your ship past her at full speed, and roar out lustily to Crataiis who is Scylla's dam, bad luck to her; she will then stop her from making a second raid upon you.'

"'You will now come to the Thrinacian island, and here you will see many herds of cattle and flocks of sheep belonging to the sun-god – seven herds of cattle and seven flocks of sheep, with fifty head in each flock. They do not breed, nor do they become fewer in number, and they are tended by the goddesses Phaethusa and Lampetie, who are children of the sun-god Hyperion by Neaera. Their mother when she had borne them and had done suckling them sent them to the Thrinacian island, which was a long way off, to live there and look after their father's flocks and herds. If you leave these flocks unharmed, and think of nothing but getting home, you may yet after much hardship reach Ithaca; but if you harm them, then I forewarn you of the destruction both of your ship and of your comrades; and even though you may yourself escape, you will return late, in bad plight, after losing all your men.'

"Here she ended, and dawn enthroned in gold began to show in heaven, whereon she returned inland. I then went on board and told my men to loose the ship from her moorings; so they at once got into her, took their places, and began to smite the grey sea with their oars. Presently the great and cunning goddess Circe befriended us with a fair wind that blew dead aft, and staid steadily with us, keeping our sails well filled, so we did whatever wanted doing to the ship's gear, and let her go as wind and helmsman headed her.

"Then, being much troubled in mind, I said to my men, 'My friends, it is not right that one or two of us alone should know the prophecies that Circe has made me, I will therefore tell you about them, so that whether we live or die we may do so with our eyes open. First she said we were to keep clear of the Sirens, who sit and sing most beautifully in a field of flowers; but she said I might hear them myself so long as no one else did. Therefore, take me and bind me to the crosspiece half way up the mast; bind me as I stand upright, with a bond so fast that I cannot possibly break away, and lash the rope's ends to the mast itself. If I beg and pray you to set me free, then bind me more tightly still.'

"I had hardly finished telling everything to the men before we reached the island of the two Sirens, for the wind had been very favourable. Then all of a sudden it fell dead calm; there was not a breath of wind nor a ripple upon the water, so the men furled the sails and stowed them; then taking to their oars they whitened the water with the foam they raised in rowing. Meanwhile I look a large wheel of wax and cut it up small with my sword. Then I kneaded the wax in my strong hands till it became soft, which it soon did between the kneading and the rays of the sun-god son of Hyperion. Then I stopped the ears of all my men, and they bound me hands and feet to the mast as I stood upright on the cross piece; but they went on rowing themselves. When we had got within earshot of the land, and the ship was going at a good rate, the Sirens saw that we were getting in shore and began with their singing.

"'Come here,' they sang, 'renowned Ulysses, honour to the Achaean name, and listen to our two voices. No one ever sailed past us without staying to hear the enchanting sweetness of our song – and he who listens will go on his way not only charmed, but wiser, for we know all the ills that the gods laid upon the Argives and Trojans before Troy, and can tell you everything that is going to happen over the whole world.'

"They sang these words most musically, and as I longed to hear them further I made signs by frowning to my men that they should set me free; but they quickened their stroke, and Eurylochus and Perimedes bound me with still stronger bonds till we had got out of hearing of the Sirens' voices. Then my men took the wax from their ears and unbound me.

"Immediately after we had got past the island I saw a great wave from which spray was rising, and I heard a loud roaring sound. The men were so frightened that they loosed hold of their oars, for the whole sea resounded with the rushing of the waters, but the ship stayed where it was, for the men had left off rowing. I went round, therefore, and exhorted them man by man not to lose heart.

"'My friends,' said I, 'this is not the first time that we have been in danger, and we are in nothing like so bad a case as when the Cyclops shut us up in his cave; nevertheless, my courage and wise counsel saved us then, and we shall live to look back on all this as well. Now, therefore, let us all do as I say, trust in Jove and row on with might and main. As for you, coxswain, these are your orders; attend to them, for the ship is in your hands; turn her head away from these steaming rapids and hug the rock, or she will give you the slip and be over yonder before you know where you are, and you will be the death of us.'

"So they did as I told them; but I said nothing about the awful monster Scylla, for I knew the men would not go on rowing if I did, but would huddle together in the hold. In one thing only did I disobey Circe's strict instructions – I put on my armour. Then seizing two strong spears I took my stand on the ship's bows, for it was there that I expected first to see the monster of the rock, who was to do my men so much harm; but I could not make her out anywhere, though I strained my eyes with looking the gloomy rock all over and over.

"Then we entered the Straits in great fear of mind, for on the one hand was Scylla, and on the other dread Charybdis kept sucking up the salt water. As she vomited it up, it was like the water in a cauldron when it is boiling over upon a great fire, and the spray reached the top of the rocks on either side. When she began to suck again, we could see the water all inside whirling round and round, and it made a deafening sound as it broke against the rocks. We could see the bottom of the whirlpool all black with sand and mud, and the men were at their wits ends for fear. While we were taken up with this, and were expecting each moment to be our last, Scylla pounced down suddenly upon us and snatched up my six best men. I was looking at once after both ship and men, and in a moment I saw their hands and feet ever so high above me, struggling in the air as Scylla was carrying them off, and I heard them call out my name in one last despairing cry. As a fisherman, seated, spear in hand, upon some jutting rock throws bait into the water to deceive the poor little fishes, and spears them with the ox's horn with which his spear is shod, throwing them gasping on to the land as he catches them one by one – even so did Scylla land these panting creatures on her rock and munch them up at the mouth of her den, while they screamed and stretched out their hands to me in their mortal agony. This was the most sickening sight that I saw throughout all my voyages.

"When we had passed the Wandering rocks, with Scylla and terrible Charybdis, we reached the noble island of the sun-god, where were the goodly cattle and sheep belonging to the sun Hyperion. While still at sea in my ship I could bear the cattle lowing as they came home to the yards, and the sheep bleating. Then I remembered what the blind Theban prophet Teiresias had told me, and how carefully Aeaean Circe had warned me to shun the island of the blessed sun-god. So being much troubled I said to the men, 'My men, I know you are hard pressed, but listen while I tell you the prophecy that Teiresias made me, and how carefully Aeaean Circe warned me to shun the island of the blessed sun-god, for it was here, she said, that our worst danger would lie. Head the ship, therefore, away from the island.'

"The men were in despair at this, and Eurylochus at once gave me an insolent answer. 'Ulysses,' said he, 'you are cruel; you are very strong yourself and never get worn out; you seem to be made of iron, and now, though your men are exhausted with toil and want of sleep, you will not let them land and cook themselves a good supper upon this island, but bid them put out to sea and go faring fruitlessly on through the watches of the flying night. It is by night that the winds blow hardest and do so much damage; how can we escape should one of those sudden squalls spring up from South West or West, which so often wreck a vessel when our lords the gods are unpropitious? Now, therefore, let us obey the behests of night and prepare our supper here hard by the ship; tomorrow morning we will go on board again and put out to sea.'

"Thus spoke Eurylochus, and the men approved his words. I saw that heaven meant us a mischief and said, 'You force me to yield, for you are many against one, but at any rate each one of you must take his solemn oath that if he meet with a herd of cattle or a large flock of sheep, he will not be so mad as to kill a single head of either, but will be satisfied with the food that Circe has given us.'

"They all swore as I bade them, and when they had completed their oath we made the ship fast in a harbour that was near a stream of fresh water, and the men went ashore and cooked their suppers. As soon as they had had enough to eat and drink, they began talking about their poor comrades whom Scylla had snatched up and eaten; this set them weeping and they went on crying till they fell off into a sound sleep.

"In the third watch of the night when the stars had shifted their places, Jove raised a great gale of wind that flew a hurricane so that land and sea were covered with thick clouds, and night sprang forth out of the heavens. When the child of morning, rosy-fingered Dawn, appeared, we brought the ship to land and drew her into a cave wherein the sea-nymphs hold their courts and dances, and I called the men together in council.

"'My friends,' said I, 'we have meat and drink in the ship, let us mind, therefore, and not touch the cattle, or we shall suffer for it; for these cattle and sheep belong to the mighty sun, who sees and gives ear to everything.' And again they promised that they would obey.

"For a whole month the wind blew steadily from the South, and there was no other wind, but only South and East. As long as corn and wine held out the men did not touch the cattle when they were hungry; when, however, they had eaten all there was in the ship, they were forced to go further afield, with hook and line, catching birds, and taking whatever they could lay their hands on; for they were starving. One day, therefore, I went up inland that I might pray heaven to show me some means of getting away. When I had gone far enough to be clear of all my men, and had found a place that was well sheltered from the wind, I washed my hands and prayed to all the gods in Olympus till by and by they sent me off into a sweet sleep.

"Meanwhile Eurylochus had been giving evil counsel to the men, 'Listen to me,' said he, 'my poor comrades. All deaths are bad enough but there is none so bad as famine. Why should not we drive in the best of these cows and offer them in sacrifice to the immortal gods? If we ever get back to Ithaca, we can build a fine temple to the sun-god and enrich it with every kind of ornament; if, however, he is determined to sink our ship out of revenge for these horned cattle, and the other gods are of the same mind, I for one would rather drink salt water once for all and have done with it, than be starved to death by inches in such a desert island as this is.'

"Thus spoke Eurylochus, and the men approved his words. Now the cattle, so fair and goodly, were feeding not far from the ship; the men, therefore, drove in the best of them, and they all stood round them saying their prayers, and using young oak-shoots instead of barley-meal, for there was no barley left. When they had done praying they killed the cows and dressed their carcasses; they cut out the thigh bones, wrapped them round in two layers of fat, and set some pieces of raw meat on top of them. They had no wine with which to make drink-offerings over the sacrifice while it was cooking, so they kept pouring on a little water from time to time while the inward meats were being grilled; then, when the thigh bones were burned and they had tasted the inward meats, they cut the rest up small and put the pieces upon the spits.

"By this time my deep sleep had left me, and I turned back to the ship and to the sea shore. As I drew near I began to smell hot roast meat, so I groaned out a prayer to the immortal gods. 'Father Jove,' I exclaimed, 'and all you other gods who live in everlasting bliss, you have done me a cruel mischief by the sleep into which you have sent me; see what fine work these men of mine have been making in my absence.'

"Meanwhile Lampetie went straight off to the sun and told him we had been killing his cows, whereon he flew into a great rage, and said to the immortals, 'Father Jove, and all you other gods who live in everlasting bliss, I must have vengeance on the crew of Ulysses' ship: they have had the insolence to kill my cows, which were the one thing I loved to look upon, whether I was going up heaven or down again. If they do not square accounts with me about my cows, I will go down to Hades and shine there among the dead.'

"'Sun,' said Jove, 'go on shining upon us gods and upon mankind over the fruitful earth. I will shiver their ship into little pieces with a bolt of white lightning as soon as they get out to sea.'

"I was told all this by Calypso, who said she had heard it from the mouth of Mercury.

"As soon as I got down to my ship and to the sea shore I rebuked each one of the men separately, but we could see no way out of it, for the cows were dead already. And indeed the gods began at once to show signs and wonders among us, for the hides of the cattle crawled about, and the joints upon the spits began to low like cows, and the meat, whether cooked or raw, kept on making a noise just as cows do.

"For six days my men kept driving in the best cows and feasting upon them, but when Jove the son of Saturn had added a seventh day, the fury of the gale abated; we therefore went on board, raised our masts, spread sail, and put out to sea. As soon as we were well away from the island, and could see nothing but sky and sea, the son of Saturn raised a black cloud over our ship, and the sea grew dark beneath it. We did not get on much further, for in another moment we were caught by a terrific squall from the West that snapped the forestays of the mast so that it fell aft, while all the ship's gear tumbled about at the bottom of the vessel. The mast fell upon the head of the helmsman in the ship's stern, so that the bones of his head were crushed to pieces, and he fell overboard as though he were diving, with no more life left in him.

"Then Jove let fly with his thunderbolts, and the ship went round and round, and was filled with fire and brimstone as the lightning struck it. The men all fell into the sea; they were carried about in the water round the ship, looking like so many sea-gulls, but the god presently deprived them of all chance of getting home again.

"I stuck to the ship till the sea knocked her sides from her keel (which drifted about by itself) and struck the mast out of her in the direction of the keel; but there was a backstay of stout ox-thong still hanging about it, and with this I lashed the mast and keel together, and getting astride of them was carried wherever the winds chose to take me.

"The gale from the West had now spent its force, and the wind got into the South again, which frightened me lest I should be taken back to the terrible whirlpool of Charybdis. This indeed was what actually happened, for I was borne along by the waves all night, and by sunrise had reached the rock of Scylla, and the whirlpool. She was then sucking down the salt sea water, but I was carried aloft toward the fig tree, which I caught hold of and clung on to like a bat. I could not plant my feet anywhere so as to stand securely, for the roots were a long way off and the boughs that overshadowed the whole pool were too high, too vast, and too far apart for me to reach them; so I hung patiently on, waiting till the pool should discharge my mast and raft again – and a very long while it seemed. A jury-man is not more glad to get home to supper, after having been long detained in court by troublesome cases, than I was to see my raft beginning to work its way out of the whirlpool again. At last I let go with my hands and feet, and fell heavily into the sea, hard by my raft on to which I then got, and began to row with my hands. As for Scylla, the father of gods and men would not let her get further sight of me – otherwise I should have certainly been lost.

"Hence I was carried along for nine days till on the tenth night the gods stranded me on the Ogygian island, where dwells the great and powerful goddess Calypso. She took me in and was kind to me, but I need say no more about this, for I told you and your noble wife all about it yesterday, and I hate saying the same thing over and over again."

The Winning of the Golden Fleece

In which the Jason, leader of the Argonauts and storied hero of Ancient Greece, wins the Golden Fleece after many trials and adventures.

THEY TOOK THE SHIP out of the backwater and they brought her to a wharf in the city. At a place that was called 'The Ram's Couch' they fastened the *Argo*. Then they marched to the field of Ares, where the king and the Colchian people were.

Jason, carrying his shield and spear, went before the king. From the king's hand he took the gleaming helmet that held the dragon's teeth. This he put into the hands of Theseus, who went with him. Then with the spear and shield in his hands, with his sword girt across his shoulders, and with his mantle stripped off, Jason looked across the field of Ares.

He saw the plough that he was to yoke to the bulls; he saw the yoke of bronze near it; he saw the tracks of the bulls' hooves. He followed the tracks until he came to the lair of the fire-breathing bulls. Out of that lair, which was underground, smoke and fire belched.

He set his feet firmly upon the ground and he held his shield before him. He awaited the onset of the bulls. They came clanging up with loud bellowing, breathing out fire. They lowered their heads, and with mighty, iron-tipped horns they came to gore and trample him.

Medea's charm had made him strong; Medea's charm had made his shield impregnable. The rush of the bulls did not overthrow him. His comrades shouted to see him standing firmly there, and in wonder the Colchians gazed upon him. All round him, as from a furnace, there came smoke and fire.

The bulls roared mightily. Grasping the horns of the bull that was upon his right hand, Jason dragged him until he had brought him beside the yoke of bronze. Striking the brazen knees of the bull suddenly with his foot he forced him down. Then he smote the other bull as it rushed upon him, and it too he forced down upon its knees.

Castor and Polydeuces held the yoke to him. Jason bound it upon the necks of the bulls. He fastened the plough to the yoke. Then he took his shield and set it upon his back, and grasping the handles of the plough he started to make the furrow.

With his long spear he drove the bulls before him as with a goad. Terribly they raged, furiously they breathed out fire. Beside Jason Theseus went holding the helmet that held the dragon's teeth. The hard ground was torn up by the plough of adamant, and the clods groaned as they were cast up. Jason flung the teeth between the open sods, often turning his head in fear that the deadly crop of the Earth-born Men were rising behind him.

By the time that a third of the day was finished the field of Ares had been ploughed and sown. As yet the furrows were free of the Earth-born Men. Jason went down to the river and filled his helmet full of water and drank deeply. And his knees that were stiffened with the ploughing he bent until they were made supple again.

He saw the field rising into mounds. It seemed that there were graves all over the field of Ares. Then he saw spears and shields and helmets rising up out of the earth. Then armed warriors sprang up, a fierce battle cry upon their lips.

Jason remembered the counsel of Medea. He raised a boulder that four men could hardly raise and with arms hardened by the ploughing he cast it. The Colchians shouted to see such a stone cast by the hands of one man. Right into the middle of the Earth-born Men the stone came. They leaped upon it like hounds, striking at one another as they came together. Shield crashed on shield, spear rang upon spear as they struck at each other. The Earth-born Men, as fast as they arose, went down before the weapons in the hands of their brethren.

Jason rushed upon them, his sword in his hand. He slew some who had risen out of the earth only as far as the shoulders; he slew others whose feet were still in the earth; he slew others who were ready to spring upon him. Soon all the Earth-born Men were slain, and the furrows ran with their dark blood as channels run with water in springtime.

The Argonauts shouted loudly for Jason's victory. King Æetes rose from his seat that was beside the river and he went back to the city. The Colchians followed him. Day faded, and Jason's contest was ended.

* * *

But it was not the will of Æetes that the strangers should be let depart peaceably with the Golden Fleece that Jason had won. In the assembly place, with his son Apsyrtus beside him, and with the furious Colchians all around him, the king stood: on his breast was the gleaming corselet that Ares had given him, and on his head was that golden helmet with its four plumes that made him look as if he were truly the son of Helios, the Sun. Lightnings flashed from his great eyes; he spoke fiercely to the Colchians, holding in his hand his bronze-topped spear.

He would have them attack the strangers and burn the *Argo*. He would have the sons of Phrixus slain for bringing them to Aea. There was a prophecy, he declared, that would have him be watchful of the treachery of his own offspring: this prophecy was being fulfilled by the children of Chalciope; he feared, too, that his daughter, Medea, had aided the strangers. So the king spoke, and the Colchians, hating all strangers, shouted around him.

Word of what her father had said was brought to Medea. She knew that she would have to go to the Argonauts and bid them flee hastily from Aea. They would not go, she knew, without the Golden Fleece; then she, Medea, would have to show them how to gain the Fleece.

Then she could never again go back to her father's palace, she could never again sit in this chamber and talk to her handmaidens, and be with Chalciope, her sister. Forever afterward she would be dependent on the kindness of strangers. Medea wept when she thought of all this. And then she cut off a tress of her hair and she left it in her chamber as a farewell from one who was going afar. Into the chamber where Chalciope was she whispered farewell.

The palace doors were all heavily bolted, but Medea did not have to pull back the bolts. As she chanted her Magic Song the bolts softly drew back, the doors softly opened. Swiftly she went along the ways that led to the river. She came to where fires were blazing and she knew that the Argonauts were there.

She called to them, and Phrontis, Chalciope's son, heard the cry and knew the voice. To Jason he spoke, and Jason quickly went to where Medea stood.

She clasped Jason's hand and she drew him with her. "The Golden Fleece," she said, "the time has come when you must pluck the Golden Fleece off the oak in the grove of Ares." When she said these words all Jason's being became taut like the string of a bow.

It was then the hour when huntsmen cast sleep from their eyes – huntsmen who never sleep away the end of the night, but who are ever ready to be up and away with their hounds before the beams of the sun efface the track and the scent of the quarry. Along a path that went from the river Medea drew Jason. They entered a grove. Then Jason saw something that was like a cloud filled with the light of the rising sun. It hung from a great oak tree. In awe he stood and looked upon it, knowing that at last he looked upon The Golden Fleece.

His hand let slip Medea's hand and he went to seize the Fleece. As he did he heard a dreadful hiss. And then he saw the guardian of the Golden Fleece. Coiled all around the tree, with outstretched neck and keen and sleepless eyes, was a deadly serpent. Its hiss ran all through the grove and the birds that were wakening up squawked in terror.

Like rings of smoke that rise one above the other, the coils of the serpent went around the tree – coils covered by hard and gleaming scales. It uncoiled, stretched itself, and lifted its head to strike. Then Medea dropped on her knees before it, and began to chant her Magic Song.

As she sang, the coils around the tree grew slack. Like a dark, noiseless wave the serpent sank down on the ground. But still its jaws were open, and those dreadful jaws threatened Jason. Medea, with a newly cut spray of juniper dipped in a mystic brew, touched its deadly eyes. And still she chanted her Magic Song. The serpent's jaws closed; its eyes became deadened; far through the grove its length was stretched out.

Then Jason took the Golden Fleece. As he raised his hands to it, its brightness was such as to make a flame on his face. Medea called to him. He strove to gather it all up in his arms; Medea was beside him, and they went swiftly on.

They came to the river and down to the place where the *Argo* was moored. The heroes who were aboard started up, astonished to see the Fleece that shone as with the lightning of Zeus. Over Medea Jason cast it, and he lifted her aboard the *Argo*.

"O friends," he cried, "the quest on which we dared the gulfs of the sea and the wrath of kings is accomplished, thanks to the help of this maiden. Now may we return to Greece; now have we the hope of looking upon our fathers and our friends once more. And in all honour will we bring this maiden with us, Medea, the daughter of King Æetes."

Then he drew his sword and cut the hawsers of the ship, calling upon the heroes to drive the *Argo* on. There was a din and a strain and a splash of oars, and away from Aea the *Argo* dashed. Beside the mast Medea stood; the Golden Fleece had fallen at her feet, and her head and face were covered by her silver veil.

The Seven Voyages of Sindbad the Sailor

IN THE TIMES of the Caliph Haroun-al-Raschid there lived in Bagdad a poor porter named Hindbad, who on a very hot day was sent to carry a heavy load from one end of the city to the other. Before he had accomplished half the distance he was so tired that, finding himself in a quiet street where the pavement was sprinkled with rose water, and a cool breeze was blowing, he set his burden upon the ground, and sat down to rest in the shade of a grand house. Very soon he decided that he could not have chosen a pleasanter place; a delicious perfume of aloes wood and pastilles came from the open windows and mingled with the scent of the rose water which steamed up from the hot pavement. Within the palace he heard some music, as of many instruments cunningly played, and the melodious warble of nightingales and other birds, and by this, and the appetizing smell of many dainty dishes of which he presently became aware, he judged that feasting and merry making were going on. He wondered who lived in this magnificent house which he had never seen before, the street in which it stood being one which he seldom had occasion to pass. To satisfy his curiosity he went up to some splendidly dressed servants who stood at the door, and asked one of them the name of the master of the mansion.

"What," replied he, "do you live in Bagdad, and not know that here lives the noble Sindbad the Sailor, that famous traveller who sailed over every sea upon which the sun shines?"

The porter, who had often heard people speak of the immense wealth of Sindbad, could not help feeling envious of one whose lot seemed to be as happy as his own was miserable. Casting his eyes up to the sky he exclaimed aloud,

"Consider, Mighty Creator of all things, the differences between Sindbad's life and mine. Every day I suffer a thousand hardships and misfortunes, and have hard work to get even enough bad barley bread to keep myself and my family alive, while the lucky Sindbad spends money right and left and lives upon the fat of the land! What has he done that you should give him this pleasant life – what have I done to deserve so hard a fate?"

So saying he stamped upon the ground like one beside himself with misery and despair. Just at this moment a servant came out of the palace, and taking him by the arm said, "Come with me, the noble Sindbad, my master, wishes to speak to you."

Hindbad was not a little surprised at this summons, and feared that his unguarded words might have drawn upon him the displeasure of Sindbad, so he tried to excuse himself upon the pretext that he could not leave the burden which had been entrusted to him in the street. However the lackey promised him that it should be taken care of, and urged him to obey the call so pressingly that at last the porter was obliged to yield.

He followed the servant into a vast room, where a great company was seated round a table covered with all sorts of delicacies. In the place of honour sat a tall, grave man whose long white beard gave him a venerable air. Behind his chair stood a crowd of attendants eager to minister to his wants. This was the famous Sindbad himself. The porter, more than ever alarmed at the sight of so much magnificence, tremblingly saluted the noble company. Sindbad, making a sign to him to approach, caused him to be seated at his right hand, and himself heaped choice morsels upon his plate, and poured out for him a draught of excellent wine, and presently, when the banquet drew to a close, spoke to him familiarly, asking his name and occupation.

"My lord," replied the porter, "I am called Hindbad."

"I am glad to see you here," continued Sindbad. "And I will answer for the rest of the company that they are equally pleased, but I wish you to tell me what it was that you said just now in the street." For Sindbad, passing by the open window before the feast began, had heard his complaint and therefore had sent for him.

At this question Hindbad was covered with confusion, and hanging down his head, replied, "My lord, I confess that, overcome by weariness and ill-humour, I uttered indiscreet words, which I pray you to pardon me."

"Oh!" replied Sindbad, "do not imagine that I am so unjust as to blame you. On the contrary, I understand your situation and can pity you. Only you appear to be mistaken about me, and I wish to set you right. You doubtless imagine that I have acquired all the wealth and luxury that you see me enjoy without difficulty or danger, but this is far indeed from being the case. I have only reached this happy state after having for years suffered every possible kind of toil and danger.

"Yes, my noble friends," he continued, addressing the company, "I assure you that my adventures have been strange enough to deter even the most avaricious men from seeking wealth by traversing the seas. Since you have, perhaps, heard but confused accounts of my seven voyages, and the dangers and wonders that I have met with by sea and land, I will now give you a full and true account of them, which I think you will be well pleased to hear."

As Sindbad was relating his adventures chiefly on account of the porter, he ordered, before beginning his tale, that the burden which had been left in the street should be carried by some of his own servants to the place for which Hindbad had set out at first, while he remained to listen to the story.

First Voyage

I had inherited considerable wealth from my parents, and being young and foolish I at first squandered it recklessly upon every kind of pleasure, but presently, finding that riches speedily take to themselves wings if managed as badly as I was managing mine, and remembering also that to be old and poor is misery indeed, I began to bethink me of how I could make the best of what still remained to me. I sold all my household goods by public auction, and joined a company of merchants who traded by sea, embarking with them at Balsora in a ship which we had fitted out between us.

We set sail and took our course towards the East Indies by the Persian Gulf, having the coast of Persia upon our left hand and upon our right the shores of Arabia Felix. I was at first much troubled by the uneasy motion of the vessel, but speedily recovered my health, and since that hour have been no more plagued by sea-sickness.

From time to time we landed at various islands, where we sold or exchanged our merchandise, and one day, when the wind dropped suddenly, we found ourselves becalmed close to a small island like a green meadow, which only rose slightly above the surface of the water. Our sails were furled, and the captain gave permission to all who wished to land for a while and amuse themselves. I was among the number, but when after strolling about for some time we lighted a fire and sat down to enjoy the repast which we had brought with us, we were startled by a sudden and violent trembling of the island, while at the same moment those left upon the ship set up an outcry bidding us come on board for our lives, since what we had taken for an island was nothing but the back of a sleeping whale. Those who were nearest to the boat threw themselves into it, others sprang into the sea, but before I could save myself the whale plunged suddenly into the depths of the ocean, leaving me clinging to a piece of the wood which we had brought to make our fire. Meanwhile a breeze had sprung up, and in the confusion that ensued on board our vessel in hoisting the sails and taking up those who were in the boat and clinging to its sides, no one missed me and I was left at the mercy of the waves. All that day I floated up and down, now beaten this way, now that, and when night fell I despaired for my life; but, weary and spent as I was, I clung to my frail support, and great was my joy when the morning light showed me that I had drifted against an island.

The cliffs were high and steep, but luckily for me some tree-roots protruded in places, and by their aid I climbed up at last, and stretched myself upon the turf at the top, where I lay, more dead than alive, till the sun was high in the heavens. By that time I was very hungry, but after some searching I came upon some eatable herbs, and a spring of clear water, and much refreshed I set out to explore the island. Presently I reached a great plain where a grazing horse was tethered, and as I stood looking at it I heard voices talking apparently underground, and in a moment a man appeared who asked me how I came upon the island. I told him my adventures, and heard in return that he was one of the grooms of Mihrage, the king of the island, and that each year they came to feed their master's horses in this plain. He took me to a cave where his companions were assembled, and when I had eaten of the food they set before me, they bade me think myself fortunate to have come upon them when I did, since they were going back to their master on the morrow, and without their aid I could certainly never have found my way to the inhabited part of the island.

Early the next morning we accordingly set out, and when we reached the capital I was graciously received by the king, to whom I related my adventures, upon which he ordered that I should be well cared for and provided with such things as I needed. Being a merchant I sought out men of my own profession, and particularly those who came from foreign countries, as I hoped in this way to hear news from Bagdad, and find out some means of returning thither, for the capital was situated upon the seashore, and visited by vessels from all parts of the world. In the meantime I heard many curious things, and answered many questions concerning my own country, for I talked willingly with all who came to me. Also to while away the time of waiting I explored a little island named Cassel, which belonged to King Mihrage, and which was supposed to be inhabited by a spirit named Deggial. Indeed, the sailors assured me that often at night the playing of timbals could be heard upon it. However, I saw nothing strange upon my voyage, saving some fish that were full two hundred cubits long, but were fortunately more in dread of us than even we were of them, and fled from us if we did but strike upon a board to frighten them. Other fishes there were only a cubit long which had heads like owls.

One day after my return, as I went down to the quay, I saw a ship which had just cast anchor, and was discharging her cargo, while the merchants to whom it belonged were busily directing the removal of it to their warehouses. Drawing nearer I presently noticed that my own name was marked upon some of the packages, and after having carefully examined them, I felt sure that they were indeed those which I had put on board our ship at Balsora. I then recognized the captain of the vessel, but as I was certain that he believed me to be dead, I went up to him and asked who owned the packages that I was looking at.

"There was on board my ship," he replied, "a merchant of Bagdad named Sindbad. One day he and several of my other passengers landed upon what we supposed to be an island, but which was really an enormous whale floating asleep upon the waves. No sooner did it feel upon its back the heat of the fire which had been kindled, than it plunged into the depths of the sea. Several of the people who were upon it perished in the waters, and among others this unlucky Sindbad. This merchandise is his, but I have resolved to dispose of it for the benefit of his family if I should ever chance to meet with them."

"Captain," said I, "I am that Sindbad whom you believe to be dead, and these are my possessions!"

When the captain heard these words he cried out in amazement, "Lackaday! and what is the world coming to? In these days there is not an honest man to be met with. Did I not with my own eyes see Sindbad drown, and now you have the audacity to tell me that you are he! I should have taken you to be a just man, and yet for the sake of obtaining that which does not belong to you, you are ready to invent this horrible falsehood."

"Have patience, and do me the favour to hear my story," said I.

"Speak then," replied the captain, "I'm all attention."

So I told him of my escape and of my fortunate meeting with the king's grooms, and how kindly I had been received at the palace. Very soon I began to see that I had made some impression upon him, and after the arrival of some of the other merchants, who showed great joy at once more seeing me alive, he declared that he also recognized me.

Throwing himself upon my neck he exclaimed, "Heaven be praised that you have escaped from so great a danger. As to your goods, I pray you take them, and dispose of them as you please." I thanked him, and praised his honesty, begging him to accept several bales of merchandise in token of my gratitude, but he would take nothing. Of the choicest of my goods I prepared a present for King Mihrage, who was at first amazed, having known that I had lost my all. However, when I had explained to him how my bales had been miraculously restored to me, he graciously accepted my gifts, and in return gave me many valuable things. I then took leave of him, and exchanging my merchandise for sandal and aloes wood, camphor, nutmegs, cloves, pepper, and ginger, I embarked upon the same vessel and traded so successfully upon our homeward voyage that I arrived in Balsora with about one hundred thousand sequins. My family received me with as much joy as I felt upon seeing them once more. I bought land and slaves, and built a great house in which I resolved to live happily, and in the enjoyment of all the pleasures of life to forget my past sufferings.

Here Sindbad paused, and commanded the musicians to play again, while the feasting continued until evening. When the time came for the porter to depart, Sindbad gave him a purse containing one hundred sequins, saying, "Take this, Hindbad, and go home, but tomorrow come again and you shall hear more of my adventures."

The porter retired quite overcome by so much generosity, and you may imagine that he was well received at home, where his wife and children thanked their lucky stars that he had found such a benefactor.

The next day Hindbad, dressed in his best, returned to the voyager's house, and was received with open arms. As soon as all the guests had arrived the banquet began as before, and when they had feasted long and merrily, Sindbad addressed them thus:

"My friends, I beg that you will give me your attention while I relate the adventures of my second voyage, which you will find even more astonishing than the first."

Second Voyage

I had resolved, as you know, on my return from my first voyage, to spend the rest of my days quietly in Bagdad, but very soon I grew tired of such an idle life and longed once more to find myself upon the sea.

I procured, therefore, such goods as were suitable for the places I intended to visit, and embarked for the second time in a good ship with other merchants whom I knew to be honourable men. We went from island to island, often making excellent bargains, until one day we landed at a spot which, though covered with fruit trees and abounding in springs of excellent water, appeared to possess neither houses nor people. While my companions wandered here and there gathering flowers and fruit I sat down in a shady place, and, having heartily enjoyed the provisions and the wine I had brought with me, I fell asleep, lulled by the murmur of a clear brook which flowed close by.

How long I slept I know not, but when I opened my eyes and started to my feet I perceived with horror that I was alone and that the ship was gone. I rushed to and fro like one distracted, uttering cries of despair, and when from the shore I saw the vessel under full sail just disappearing upon the horizon, I wished bitterly enough that I had been content to stay at home in safety. But since wishes could do me no good, I presently took courage and looked about me for a means of escape. When I had climbed a tall tree I first of all directed my anxious glances towards the sea; but, finding nothing hopeful there, I turned landward, and my curiosity was excited by a huge dazzling white object, so far off that I could not make out what it might be.

Descending from the tree I hastily collected what remained of my provisions and set off as fast as I could go towards it. As I drew near it seemed to me to be a white ball of immense size and height, and when I could touch it, I found it marvellously smooth and soft. As it was impossible to climb it – for it presented no foot-hold – I walked round about it seeking some opening, but there was none. I counted, however, that it was at least fifty paces round. By this time the sun was near setting, but quite suddenly it fell dark, something like a huge black cloud came swiftly over me, and I saw with amazement that it was a bird of extraordinary size which was hovering near. Then I remembered that I had often heard the sailors speak of a wonderful bird called a roc, and it occurred to me that the white object which had so puzzled me must be its egg.

Sure enough the bird settled slowly down upon it, covering it with its wings to keep it warm, and I cowered close beside the egg in such a position that one of the bird's feet, which was as large as the trunk of a tree, was just in front of me. Taking off my turban I bound myself securely to it with the linen in the hope that the roc, when it took flight next morning, would bear me away with it from the desolate island. And this was precisely what did happen. As soon as the dawn appeared the bird rose into the air carrying me up and up till I could no longer see the earth, and then suddenly it descended so swiftly that I almost lost consciousness. When I became aware that the roc had settled and that I was once again upon solid ground, I hastily unbound my turban from its foot and freed myself, and that not a moment too soon; for the bird, pouncing upon a huge snake, killed it with a few blows from its powerful beak, and seizing it up rose into the air once more and soon disappeared from my view. When I had looked about me I began to doubt if I had gained anything by quitting the desolate island.

The valley in which I found myself was deep and narrow, and surrounded by mountains which towered into the clouds, and were so steep and rocky that there was no way of climbing up their sides. As I wandered about, seeking anxiously for some means of escaping from this trap, I observed that the ground was strewed with diamonds, some of them of an astonishing size. This sight gave me great pleasure, but my delight was speedily damped when I saw also numbers of horrible snakes so long and so large that the smallest of them could have swallowed an elephant with ease. Fortunately for me they seemed to hide in caverns of the rocks by day, and only came out by night, probably because of their enemy the roc.

All day long I wandered up and down the valley, and when it grew dusk I crept into a little cave, and having blocked up the entrance to it with a stone, I ate part of my little store of food and lay down to sleep, but all through the night the serpents crawled to and fro, hissing horribly, so that I could scarcely close my eyes for terror. I was thankful when the morning light appeared, and when I judged by the silence that the serpents had retreated to their dens I came tremblingly out of my cave and wandered up and down the valley once more, kicking the diamonds contemptuously out of my path, for I felt that they were indeed vain things to a man in my situation. At last, overcome with weariness, I sat down upon a rock, but I had hardly closed my eyes when I was startled by something which fell to the ground with a thud close beside me.

It was a huge piece of fresh meat, and as I stared at it several more pieces rolled over the cliffs in different places. I had always thought that the stories the sailors told of the famous valley of diamonds, and of the cunning way which some merchants had devised for getting at the precious stones, were mere travellers' tales invented to give pleasure to the hearers, but now I perceived that they were surely true. These merchants came to the valley at the time when the eagles, which keep their eyries in the rocks, had hatched their young. The merchants then threw great lumps of meat into the valley. These, falling with so much force upon the diamonds, were sure to take up some of the precious stones with them, when the eagles pounced upon the meat and carried it off to their nests to feed their hungry broods. Then the merchants, scaring away the parent birds with shouts and outcries, would secure their treasures. Until this moment I had looked upon the valley as my grave, for I had seen no possibility of getting out of it alive, but now I took courage and began to devise a means of escape. I began by picking up all the largest diamonds I could find and storing them carefully in the leathern wallet which had held my provisions; this I tied securely to my belt. I then chose the piece of meat which seemed most suited to my purpose, and with the aid of my turban bound it firmly to my back; this done I laid down upon my face and awaited the coming of the eagles. I soon heard the flapping of their mighty wings above me, and had the satisfaction of feeling one of them seize upon my piece of meat, and me with it, and rise slowly towards his nest, into which he presently dropped me. Luckily for me the merchants were on the watch, and setting up their usual outcries they rushed to the nest scaring away the eagle. Their amazement was great when they discovered me, and also their disappointment, and with one accord they fell to abusing me for having robbed them of their usual profit. Addressing myself to the one who seemed most aggrieved, I said: "I am sure, if you knew all that I have suffered, you would show more kindness towards me, and as for diamonds, I have enough here of the very best for you and me and all your company." So saying I showed them to him. The others all crowded round me, wondering at my adventures and admiring the device by which I had escaped from the valley, and when they had led me to their camp and examined my diamonds, they assured me that in all the years that they had carried on their trade they had seen no stones to be compared with them for size and beauty.

I found that each merchant chose a particular nest, and took his chance of what he might find in it. So I begged the one who owned the nest to which I had been carried to take as much as he would of my treasure, but he contented himself with one stone, and that by no means the largest, assuring me that with such a gem his fortune was made, and he need toil no more. I stayed with the merchants several days, and then as they were journeying homewards I gladly accompanied them. Our way lay across high mountains infested with frightful serpents, but we had the good luck to escape them and came at last to the seashore. Thence we sailed to the isle of Rohat where the camphor trees grow to such a size that a hundred men could shelter under one of them with ease. The sap flows from an incision made high up in the tree into a vessel hung there to receive it, and soon hardens into the substance called camphor, but the tree itself withers up and dies when it has been so treated.

In this same island we saw the rhinoceros, an animal which is smaller than the elephant and larger than the buffalo. It has one horn about a cubit long which is solid, but has a furrow from the base to the tip. Upon it is traced in white lines the figure of a man. The rhinoceros fights with the elephant, and transfixing him with his horn carries him off upon his head, but becoming blinded with the blood of his enemy, he falls helpless to the ground, and then comes the roc, and clutches them both up in his talons and takes them to feed his young. This doubtless astonishes you, but if you do not believe my tale go to Rohat and see for yourself. For fear of wearying you I pass over in silence many other wonderful things which we saw in this island. Before we left I exchanged one of my diamonds for much goodly merchandise by which I profited greatly on our homeward way. At last we reached Balsora, whence I hastened to Bagdad, where my first action was to bestow large sums of money upon the poor, after which I settled down to enjoy tranquilly the riches I had gained with so much toil and pain.

Having thus related the adventures of his second voyage, Sindbad again bestowed a hundred sequins upon Hindbad, inviting him to come again on the following day and hear how he fared upon his third voyage. The other guests also departed to their homes, but all returned at the same hour next day, including the porter, whose former life of hard work and poverty had already begun to seem to him like a bad dream. Again after the feast was over did Sindbad claim the attention of his guests and began the account of his third voyage.

Third Voyage

After a very short time the pleasant easy life I led made me quite forget the perils of my two voyages. Moreover, as I was still in the prime of life, it pleased me better to be up and doing. So once more providing myself with the rarest and choicest merchandise of Bagdad, I conveyed it to Balsora, and set sail with other merchants of my acquaintance for distant lands. We had touched at many ports and made much profit, when one day upon the open sea we were caught by a terrible wind which blew us completely out of our reckoning, and lasting for several days finally drove us into harbour on a strange island.

"I would rather have come to anchor anywhere than here," quoth our captain. "This island and all adjoining it are inhabited by hairy savages, who are certain to attack us, and whatever these dwarfs may do we dare not resist, since they swarm like locusts, and if one of them is killed the rest will fall upon us, and speedily make an end of us."

These words caused great consternation among all the ship's company, and only too soon we were to find out that the captain spoke truly. There appeared a vast multitude of hideous savages, not more than two feet high and covered with reddish fur. Throwing themselves into the waves they surrounded our vessel. Chattering meanwhile in a language we could not understand, and clutching at ropes and gangways, they swarmed up the ship's side with such speed and agility that they almost seemed to fly.

You may imagine the rage and terror that seized us as we watched them, neither daring to hinder them nor able to speak a word to deter them from their purpose, whatever it might be. Of this we were not left long in doubt. Hoisting the sails, and cutting the cable of the anchor, they sailed our vessel to an island which lay a little further off, where they drove us ashore; then taking possession of her, they made off to the place from which they had come, leaving us helpless upon a shore avoided with horror by all mariners for a reason which you will soon learn.

Turning away from the sea we wandered miserably inland, finding as we went various herbs and fruits which we ate, feeling that we might as well live as long as possible though we had no hope of escape. Presently we saw in the far distance what seemed to us to be a splendid palace, towards which we turned our weary steps, but when we reached it we saw that it was a castle, lofty, and strongly built. Pushing back the heavy ebony doors we entered the courtyard, but upon the threshold of the great hall beyond it we paused, frozen with horror, at the sight which greeted us. On one side lay a huge pile of bones – human bones, and on the other numberless spits for roasting! Overcome with despair we sank trembling to the ground, and lay there without speech or motion. The sun was setting when a loud noise aroused us, the door of the hall was violently burst open and a horrible giant entered. He was as tall as a palm tree, and perfectly black, and had one eye, which flamed like a burning coal in the middle of his forehead. His teeth were long and sharp and grinned horribly, while his lower lip hung down upon his chest, and he had ears like elephant's ears, which covered his shoulders, and nails like the claws of some fierce bird.

At this terrible sight our senses left us and we lay like dead men. When at last we came to ourselves the giant sat examining us attentively with his fearful eye. Presently when he had looked at us enough he came towards us, and stretching out his hand took me by the back of the neck, turning me this way and that, but feeling that I was mere skin and bone he set me down again and went on to the next, whom he treated in the same fashion; at last he came to the captain, and finding him the fattest of us all, he took him up in one hand and stuck him upon a spit and proceeded to kindle a huge fire at which he presently roasted him. After the giant had supped he lay down to sleep, snoring like the loudest thunder, while we lay shivering with horror the whole night through, and when day broke he awoke and went out, leaving us in the castle.

When we believed him to be really gone we started up bemoaning our horrible fate, until the hall echoed with our despairing cries. Though we were many and our enemy was alone it did not occur to us to kill him, and indeed we should have found that a hard task, even if we had thought of it, and no plan could we devise to deliver ourselves. So at last, submitting to our sad fate, we spent the day in wandering up and down the island eating such fruits as we could find, and when night came we returned to the castle, having sought in vain for any other place of shelter. At sunset the giant returned, supped upon one of our unhappy comrades, slept and snored till dawn, and then left us as before. Our condition seemed to us so frightful that several of my companions thought it would be better to leap from the cliffs and perish in the waves at once, rather than await so miserable an end; but I had a plan of escape which I now unfolded to them, and which they at once agreed to attempt.

"Listen, my brothers," I added. "You know that plenty of driftwood lies along the shore. Let us make several rafts, and carry them to a suitable place. If our plot succeeds, we can wait patiently for the chance of some passing ship which would rescue us from this fatal island. If it fails, we must quickly take to our rafts; frail as they are, we have more chance of saving our lives with them than we have if we remain here."

All agreed with me, and we spent the day in building rafts, each capable of carrying three persons. At nightfall we returned to the castle, and very soon in came the giant, and one more of our number was sacrificed. But the time of our vengeance was at hand! As soon as he had finished his horrible repast he lay down to sleep as before, and when we heard him begin to snore I, and nine of the boldest of my comrades, rose softly, and took each a spit, which we made red-hot in the fire, and then at a given signal we plunged it with one accord into the giant's eye, completely blinding him. Uttering a terrible cry, he sprang to his feet clutching in all directions to try to seize one of us, but we had all fled different ways as soon as the deed was done, and thrown ourselves flat upon the ground in corners where he was not likely to touch us with his feet.

After a vain search he fumbled about till he found the door, and fled out of it howling frightfully. As for us, when he was gone we made haste to leave the fatal castle, and, stationing ourselves beside our rafts, we waited to see what would happen. Our idea was that if, when the sun rose, we saw nothing of the giant, and no longer heard his howls, which still came faintly through the darkness, growing more and more distant, we should conclude that he was dead, and that we might safely stay upon the island and need not risk our lives upon the frail rafts. But alas! morning light showed us our enemy approaching us, supported on either hand by two giants nearly as large and fearful as himself, while a crowd of others followed close upon their heels. Hesitating no longer we clambered upon our rafts and rowed with all our might out to sea. The giants, seeing their prey escaping them, seized up huge pieces of rock, and wading into the water hurled them after us with such good aim that all the rafts except the one I was upon were swamped, and their luckless crews drowned, without our being able to do anything to help them. Indeed I and my two companions had all we could do to keep our own raft beyond the reach of the giants, but by dint of hard rowing we at last gained the open sea. Here we were at the mercy of the winds and waves, which tossed us to and fro all that day and night, but the next morning we found ourselves near an island, upon which we gladly landed.

There we found delicious fruits, and having satisfied our hunger we presently lay down to rest upon the shore. Suddenly we were aroused by a loud rustling noise, and starting up, saw that it was caused by an immense snake which was gliding towards us over the sand. So swiftly it came that it had seized one of my comrades before he had time to fly, and in spite of his cries and struggles speedily crushed the life out of him in its mighty coils and proceeded to swallow him. By this time my other companion and I were running for our lives to some place where we might hope to be safe from this new horror, and seeing a tall tree we climbed up into it, having first provided ourselves with a store of fruit off the surrounding bushes. When night came I fell asleep, but only to be awakened once more by the terrible snake, which after hissing horribly round the tree at last reared itself up against it, and finding my sleeping comrade who was perched just below me, it swallowed him also, and crawled away leaving me half dead with terror.

When the sun rose I crept down from the tree with hardly a hope of escaping the dreadful fate which had over-taken my comrades; but life is sweet, and I determined to do all I could to save myself. All day long I toiled with frantic haste and collected quantities of dry brushwood, reeds and thorns, which I bound with faggots, and making a circle of them under my tree I piled them firmly one upon another until I had a kind of tent in which I crouched like a mouse in a hole when she sees the cat coming. You may imagine what a fearful night I passed, for the snake returned eager to devour me, and glided round and round my frail shelter seeking an entrance. Every moment I feared that it would succeed in pushing aside some of the faggots, but happily for me they held together, and when it grew light my enemy retired, baffled and hungry, to his den. As for me I was more dead than alive! Shaking with fright and half suffocated by the poisonous breath of the monster, I came out of my tent and crawled down to the sea, feeling that it would be better to plunge from the cliffs and end my life at once than pass such another night of horror. But to my joy and relief I saw a ship sailing by, and by shouting wildly and waving my turban I managed to attract the attention of her crew.

A boat was sent to rescue me, and very soon I found myself on board surrounded by a wondering crowd of sailors and merchants eager to know by what chance I found myself in that desolate island. After I had told my story they regaled me with the choicest food the ship afforded, and the captain, seeing that I was in rags, generously bestowed upon me one of his own coats. After sailing about for some time and touching at many ports we came at last to the island of Salahat, where sandal wood grows in great abundance. Here we anchored, and as I stood watching the merchants disembarking their goods and preparing to sell or exchange them, the captain came up to me and said,

"I have here, brother, some merchandise belonging to a passenger of mine who is dead. Will you do me the favour to trade with it, and when I meet with his heirs I shall be able to give them the money, though it will be only just that you shall have a portion for your trouble."

I consented gladly, for I did not like standing by idle. Whereupon he pointed the bales out to me, and sent for the person whose duty it was to keep a list of the goods that were upon the ship. When this man came he asked in what name the merchandise was to be registered.

"In the name of Sindbad the Sailor," replied the captain.

At this I was greatly surprised, but looking carefully at him I recognized him to be the captain of the ship upon which I had made my second voyage, though he had altered much since that time. As for him, believing me to be dead it was no wonder that he had not recognized me.

"So, captain," said I, "the merchant who owned those bales was called Sindbad?"

"Yes," he replied. "He was so named. He belonged to Bagdad, and joined my ship at Balsora, but by mischance he was left behind upon a desert island where we had landed to fill up our water-casks, and it was not until four hours later that he was missed. By that time the wind had freshened, and it was impossible to put back for him."

"You suppose him to have perished then?" said I.

"Alas! yes," he answered.

"Why, captain!" I cried, "look well at me. I am that Sindbad who fell asleep upon the island and awoke to find himself abandoned!"

The captain stared at me in amazement, but was presently convinced that I was indeed speaking the truth, and rejoiced greatly at my escape.

"I am glad to have that piece of carelessness off my conscience at any rate," said he. "Now take your goods, and the profit I have made for you upon them, and may you prosper in future."

I took them gratefully, and as we went from one island to another I laid in stores of cloves, cinnamon, and other spices. In one place I saw a tortoise which was twenty cubits long and as many broad, also a fish that was like a cow and had skin so thick that it was used to make shields. Another I saw that was like a camel in shape and colour. So by degrees we came back to Balsora, and I returned to Bagdad with so much money that I could not myself count it, besides treasures without end. I gave largely to the poor, and bought much land to add to what I already possessed, and thus ended my third voyage.

When Sindbad had finished his story he gave another hundred sequins to Hindbad, who then departed with the other guests, but next day when they had all reassembled, and the banquet was ended, their host continued his adventures.

Fourth Voyage

Rich and happy as I was after my third voyage, I could not make up my mind to stay at home altogether. My love of trading, and the pleasure I took in anything that was new and strange, made me set my affairs in order, and begin my journey through some of the Persian provinces, having first sent off stores of goods to await my coming in the different places I intended to visit. I took ship at a distant seaport, and for some time all went well, but at last, being caught in a violent hurricane, our vessel became a total wreck in spite of all our worthy captain could do to save her, and many of our company perished in the waves. I, with a few others, had the good fortune to be washed ashore clinging to pieces of the wreck, for the storm had driven us near an island, and scrambling up beyond the reach of the waves we threw ourselves down quite exhausted, to wait for morning.

At daylight we wandered inland, and soon saw some huts, to which we directed our steps. As we drew near their black inhabitants swarmed out in great numbers and surrounded us, and we were led to their houses, and as it were divided among our captors. I with five others was taken into a hut, where we were made to sit upon the ground, and certain herbs were given to us, which the blacks made signs to us to eat. Observing that they themselves did not touch them, I was careful only to pretend to taste my portion; but my companions, being very hungry, rashly ate up all that was set before them, and very soon I had the horror of seeing them become perfectly mad. Though they chattered incessantly I could not understand a word they said, nor did they heed when I spoke to them. The savages now produced large bowls full of rice prepared with cocoanut oil, of which my crazy comrades ate eagerly, but I only tasted a few grains, understanding clearly that the object of our captors was to fatten us speedily for their own eating, and this was exactly what happened. My unlucky companions having lost their reason, felt neither anxiety nor fear, and ate greedily all that was offered them. So they were soon fat and there was an end of them, but I grew leaner day by day, for I ate but little, and even that little did me no good by reason of my fear of what lay before me. However, as I was so far from being a tempting morsel, I was allowed to wander about freely, and one day, when all the blacks had gone off upon some expedition leaving only an old man to guard me, I managed to escape from him and plunged into the forest, running faster the more he cried to me to come back, until I had completely distanced him.

For seven days I hurried on, resting only when the darkness stopped me, and living chiefly upon cocoanuts, which afforded me both meat and drink, and on the eighth day I reached the seashore and saw a party of white men gathering pepper, which grew abundantly all about. Reassured by the nature of their occupation, I advanced towards them and they greeted me in Arabic, asking who I was and whence I came. My delight was great on hearing this familiar speech, and I willingly satisfied their curiosity, telling them how I had been shipwrecked, and captured by the blacks. "But these savages devour men!" said they. "How did you escape?" I repeated to them what I have just told you, at which they were mightily astonished. I stayed with them until they had collected as much pepper as they wished, and then they took me back to their own country and presented me to their king, by whom I was hospitably received. To him also I had to relate my adventures, which surprised him much, and when I had finished he ordered that I should be supplied with food and raiment and treated with consideration.

The island on which I found myself was full of people, and abounded in all sorts of desirable things, and a great deal of traffic went on in the capital, where I soon began to feel at home and contented. Moreover, the king treated me with special favour, and in consequence of this everyone, whether at the court or in the town, sought to make life pleasant to me. One thing I remarked which I thought very strange; this was that, from the greatest to the least, all men rode their horses without bridle or stirrups. I one day presumed to ask his majesty why he did not use them, to which he replied, "You speak to me of things of which I have never before heard!" This gave me an idea. I found a clever workman, and made him cut out under my direction the foundation of a saddle, which I wadded and covered with choice leather, adorning it with rich gold embroidery. I then got a lock-smith to make me a bit and a pair of spurs after a pattern that I drew for him, and when all these things were completed I presented them to the king and showed him how to use them. When I had saddled one of his horses he mounted it and rode about quite delighted with the novelty, and to show his gratitude he rewarded me with large gifts. After this I had to make saddles for all the principal officers of the king's household, and as they all gave me rich presents I soon became very wealthy and quite an important person in the city.

One day the king sent for me and said, "Sindbad, I am going to ask a favour of you. Both I and my subjects esteem you, and wish you to end your days amongst us. Therefore I desire that you will marry a rich and beautiful lady whom I will find for you, and think no more of your own country."

As the king's will was law I accepted the charming bride he presented to me, and lived happily with her. Nevertheless I had every intention of escaping at the first opportunity, and going back to Bagdad. Things were thus going prosperously with me when it happened that the wife of one of my neighbours, with whom I had struck up quite a friendship, fell ill, and presently died. I went to his house to offer my consolations, and found him in the depths of woe.

"Heaven preserve you," said I, "and send you a long life!"

"Alas!" he replied, "what is the good of saying that when I have but an hour left to live!"

"Come, come!" said I, "surely it is not so bad as all that. I trust that you may be spared to me for many years."

"I hope," answered he, "that your life may be long, but as for me, all is finished. I have set my house in order, and today I shall be buried with my wife. This has been the law upon our island from the earliest ages – the living husband goes to the grave with his dead wife, the living wife with her dead husband. So did our fathers, and so must we do. The law changes not, and all must submit to it!"

As he spoke the friends and relations of the unhappy pair began to assemble. The body, decked in rich robes and sparkling with jewels, was laid upon an open bier, and the procession started, taking its way to a high mountain at some distance from the city, the wretched husband, clothed from head to foot in a black mantle, following mournfully.

When the place of interment was reached the corpse was lowered, just as it was, into a deep pit. Then the husband, bidding farewell to all his friends, stretched himself upon another bier, upon which were laid seven little loaves of bread and a pitcher of water, and he also was let down-down-down to the depths of the horrible cavern, and then a stone was laid over the opening, and the melancholy company wended its way back to the city.

You may imagine that I was no unmoved spectator of these proceedings; to all the others it was a thing to which they had been accustomed from their youth up; but I was so horrified that I could not help telling the king how it struck me.

"Sire," I said, "I am more astonished than I can express to you at the strange custom which exists in your dominions of burying the living with the dead. In all my travels I have never before met with so cruel and horrible a law."

"What would you have, Sindbad?" he replied. "It is the law for everybody. I myself should be buried with the Queen if she were the first to die."

"But, your Majesty," said I, "dare I ask if this law applies to foreigners also?"

"Why, yes," replied the king smiling, in what I could but consider a very heartless manner, "they are no exception to the rule if they have married in the country."

When I heard this I went home much cast down, and from that time forward my mind was never easy. If only my wife's little finger ached I fancied she was going to die, and sure enough before very long she fell really ill and in a few days breathed her last. My dismay was great, for it seemed to me that to be buried alive was even a worse fate than to be devoured by cannibals, nevertheless there was no escape. The body of my wife, arrayed in her richest robes and decked with all her jewels, was laid upon the bier. I followed it, and after me came a great procession, headed by the king and all his nobles, and in this order we reached the fatal mountain, which was one of a lofty chain bordering the sea.

Here I made one more frantic effort to excite the pity of the king and those who stood by, hoping to save myself even at this last moment, but it was of no avail. No one spoke to me, they even appeared to hasten over their dreadful task, and I speedily found myself descending into the gloomy pit, with my seven loaves and pitcher of water beside me. Almost before I reached the bottom the stone was rolled into its place above my head, and I was left to my fate. A feeble ray of light shone into the cavern through some chink, and when I had the courage to look about me I could see that I was in a vast vault, bestrewn with bones and bodies of the dead. I even fancied that I heard the expiring sighs of those who, like myself, had come into this dismal place alive. All in vain did I shriek aloud with rage and despair, reproaching myself for the love of gain and adventure which had brought me to such a pass, but at length, growing calmer, I took up my bread and water, and wrapping my face in my mantle I groped my way towards the end of the cavern, where the air was fresher.

Here I lived in darkness and misery until my provisions were exhausted, but just as I was nearly dead from starvation the rock was rolled away overhead and I saw that a bier was being lowered into the cavern, and that the corpse upon it was a man. In a moment my mind was made up, the woman who followed had nothing to expect but a lingering death; I should be doing her a service if I shortened her misery. Therefore when she descended, already insensible from terror, I was ready armed with a huge bone, one blow from which left her dead, and I secured the bread and water which gave me a hope of life. Several times did I have recourse to this desperate expedient, and I know not how long I had been a prisoner when one day I fancied that I heard something near me, which breathed loudly. Turning to the place from which the sound came I dimly saw a shadowy form which fled at my movement, squeezing itself through a cranny in the wall. I pursued it as fast as I could, and found myself in a narrow crack among the rocks, along which I was just able to force my way. I followed it for what seemed to me many miles, and at last saw before me a glimmer of light which grew clearer every moment until I emerged upon the sea shore with a joy which I cannot describe. When I was sure that I was not dreaming, I realized that it was doubtless some little animal which had found its way into the cavern from the sea, and when disturbed had fled, showing me a means of escape which I could never have discovered for myself. I hastily surveyed my surroundings, and saw that I was safe from all pursuit from the town.

The mountains sloped sheer down to the sea, and there was no road across them. Being assured of this I returned to the cavern, and amassed a rich treasure of diamonds, rubies, emeralds, and jewels of all kinds which strewed the ground. These I made up into bales, and stored them into a safe place upon the beach, and then waited hopefully for the passing of a ship. I had looked out for two days, however, before a single sail appeared, so it was with much delight that I at last saw a vessel not very far from the shore, and by waving my arms and uttering loud cries succeeded in attracting the attention of her crew. A boat was sent off to me, and in answer to the questions of the sailors as to how I came to be in such a plight, I replied that I had been shipwrecked two days before, but had managed to scramble ashore with the bales which I pointed out to them. Luckily for me they believed my story, and without even looking at the place where they found me, took up my bundles, and rowed me back to the ship. Once on board, I soon saw that the captain was too much occupied with the difficulties of navigation to pay much heed to me, though he generously made me welcome, and would not even accept the jewels with which I offered to pay my passage. Our voyage was prosperous, and after visiting many lands, and collecting in each place great store of goodly merchandise, I found myself at last in Bagdad once more with unheard of riches of every description. Again I gave large sums of money to the poor, and enriched all the mosques in the city, after which I gave myself up to my friends and relations, with whom I passed my time in feasting and merriment.

Here Sindbad paused, and all his hearers declared that the adventures of his fourth voyage had pleased them better than anything they had heard before. hey then took their leave, followed by Hindbad, who had once more received a hundred sequins, and with the rest had been bidden to return next day for the story of the fifth voyage.

When the time came all were in their places, and when they had eaten and drunk of all that was set before them Sindbad began his tale.

Fifth Voyage

Not even all that I had gone through could make me contented with a quiet life. I soon wearied of its pleasures, and longed for change and adventure. Therefore I set out once more, but this time in a ship of my own, which I built and fitted out at the nearest seaport. I wished to be able to call at whatever port I chose, taking my own time; but as I did not intend carrying enough goods for a full cargo, I invited several merchants of different nations to join me. We set sail with the first favourable wind, and after a long voyage upon the open seas we landed upon an unknown island which proved to be uninhabited. We determined, however, to explore it, but had not gone far when we found a roc's egg, as large as the one I had seen before and evidently very nearly hatched, for the beak of the young bird had already pierced the shell. In spite of all I could say to deter them, the merchants who were with me fell upon it with their hatchets, breaking the shell, and killing the young roc. Then lighting a fire upon the ground they hacked morsels from the bird, and proceeded to roast them while I stood by aghast.

Scarcely had they finished their ill-omened repast, when the air above us was darkened by two mighty shadows. The captain of my ship, knowing by experience what this meant, cried out to us that the parent birds were coming, and urged us to get on board with all speed. This we did, and the sails were hoisted, but before we had made any way the rocs reached their despoiled nest and hovered about it, uttering frightful cries when they discovered the mangled remains of their young one. For a moment we lost sight of them, and were flattering ourselves that we had escaped, when they reappeared and soared into the air directly over our vessel, and we saw that each held in its claws an immense rock ready to crush us. There was a moment of breathless suspense, then one bird loosed its hold and the huge block of stone hurtled through the air, but thanks to the presence of mind of the helmsman, who turned our ship violently in another direction, it fell into the sea close beside us, cleaving it asunder till we could nearly see the bottom. We had hardly time to draw a breath of relief before the other rock fell with a mighty crash right in the midst of our luckless vessel, smashing it into a thousand fragments, and crushing, or hurling into the sea, passengers and crew. I myself went down with the rest, but had the good fortune to rise unhurt, and by holding on to a piece of driftwood with one hand and swimming with the other I kept myself afloat and was presently washed up by the tide on to an island. Its shores were steep and rocky, but I scrambled up safely and threw myself down to rest upon the green turf.

When I had somewhat recovered I began to examine the spot in which I found myself, and truly it seemed to me that I had reached a garden of delights. There were trees everywhere, and they were laden with flowers and fruit, while a crystal stream wandered in and out under their shadow. When night came I slept sweetly in a cosy nook, though the remembrance that I was alone in a strange land made me sometimes start up and look around me in alarm, and then I wished heartily that I had stayed at home at ease. However, the morning sunlight restored my courage, and I once more wandered among the trees, but always with some anxiety as to what I might see next. I had penetrated some distance into the island when I saw an old man bent and feeble sitting upon the river bank, and at first I took him to be some ship-wrecked mariner like myself. Going up to him I greeted him in a friendly way, but he only nodded his head at me in reply. I then asked what he did there, and he made signs to me that he wished to get across the river to gather some fruit, and seemed to beg me to carry him on my back. Pitying his age and feebleness, I took him up, and wading across the stream I bent down that he might more easily reach the bank, and bade him get down. But instead of allowing himself to be set upon his feet (even now it makes me laugh to think of it!), this creature who had seemed to me so decrepit leaped nimbly upon my shoulders, and hooking his legs round my neck gripped me so tightly that I was well-nigh choked, and so overcome with terror that I fell insensible to the ground. When I recovered my enemy was still in his place, though he had released his hold enough to allow me breathing space, and seeing me revive he prodded me adroitly first with one foot and then with the other, until I was forced to get up and stagger about with him under the trees while he gathered and ate the choicest fruits. This went on all day, and even at night, when I threw myself down half dead with weariness, the terrible old man held on tight to my neck, nor did he fail to greet the first glimmer of morning light by drumming upon me with his heels, until I perforce awoke and resumed my dreary march with rage and bitterness in my heart.

It happened one day that I passed a tree under which lay several dry gourds, and catching one up I amused myself with scooping out its contents and pressing into it the juice of several bunches of grapes which hung from every bush. When it was full I left it propped in the fork of a tree, and a few days later, carrying the hateful old man that way, I snatched at my gourd as I passed it and had the satisfaction of a draught of excellent wine so good and refreshing that I even forgot my detestable burden, and began to sing and caper.

The old monster was not slow to perceive the effect which my draught had produced and that I carried him more lightly than usual, so he stretched out his skinny hand and seizing the gourd first tasted its contents cautiously, then drained them to the very last drop. The wine was strong and the gourd capacious, so he also began to sing after a fashion, and soon I had the delight of feeling the iron grip of his goblin legs unclasp, and with one vigorous effort I threw him to the ground, from which he never moved again. I was so rejoiced to have at last got rid of this uncanny old man that I ran leaping and bounding down to the sea shore, where, by the greatest good luck, I met with some mariners who had anchored off the island to enjoy the delicious fruits, and to renew their supply of water.

They heard the story of my escape with amazement, saying, "You fell into the hands of the Old Man of the Sea, and it is a mercy that he did not strangle you as he has everyone else upon whose shoulders he has managed to perch himself. This island is well known as the scene of his evil deeds, and no merchant or sailor who lands upon it cares to stray far away from his comrades." After we had talked for a while they took me back with them on board their ship, where the captain received me kindly, and we soon set sail, and after several days reached a large and prosperous-looking town where all the houses were built of stone. Here we anchored, and one of the merchants, who had been very friendly to me on the way, took me ashore with him and showed me a lodging set apart for strange merchants. He then provided me with a large sack, and pointed out to me a party of others equipped in like manner.

"Go with them," said he, "and do as they do, but beware of losing sight of them, for if you strayed your life would be in danger."

With that he supplied me with provisions, and bade me farewell, and I set out with my new companions. I soon learnt that the object of our expedition was to fill our sacks with cocoanuts, but when at length I saw the trees and noted their immense height and the slippery smoothness of their slender trunks, I did not at all understand how we were to do it. The crowns of the cocoa-palms were all alive with monkeys, big and little, which skipped from one to the other with surprising agility, seeming to be curious about us and disturbed at our appearance, and I was at first surprised when my companions after collecting stones began to throw them at the lively creatures, which seemed to me quite harmless. But very soon I saw the reason of it and joined them heartily, for the monkeys, annoyed and wishing to pay us back in our own coin, began to tear the nuts from the trees and cast them at us with angry and spiteful gestures, so that after very little labour our sacks were filled with the fruit which we could not otherwise have obtained.

As soon as we had as many as we could carry we went back to the town, where my friend bought my share and advised me to continue the same occupation until I had earned money enough to carry me to my own country. This I did, and before long had amassed a considerable sum. Just then I heard that there was a trading ship ready to sail, and taking leave of my friend I went on board, carrying with me a goodly store of cocoanuts; and we sailed first to the islands where pepper grows, then to Comari where the best aloes wood is found, and where men drink no wine by an unalterable law. Here I exchanged my nuts for pepper and good aloes wood, and went a-fishing for pearls with some of the other merchants, and my divers were so lucky that very soon I had an immense number, and those very large and perfect. With all these treasures I came joyfully back to Bagdad, where I disposed of them for large sums of money, of which I did not fail as before to give the tenth part to the poor, and after that I rested from my labours and comforted myself with all the pleasures that my riches could give me.

Having thus ended his story, Sindbad ordered that one hundred sequins should be given to Hindbad, and the guests then withdrew; but after the next day's feast he began the account of his sixth voyage as follows.

Sixth Voyage

It must be a marvel to you how, after having five times met with shipwreck and unheard of perils, I could again tempt fortune and risk fresh trouble. I am even surprised myself when I look back, but evidently it was my fate to rove, and after a year of repose I prepared to make a sixth voyage, regardless of the entreaties of my friends and relations, who did all they could to keep me at home. Instead of going by the Persian Gulf, I travelled a considerable way overland, and finally embarked from a distant Indian port with a captain who meant to make a long voyage. And truly he did so, for we fell in with stormy weather which drove us completely out of our course, so that for many days neither captain nor pilot knew where we were, nor where we were going. When they did at last discover our position we had small ground for rejoicing, for the captain, casting his turban upon the deck and tearing his beard, declared that we were in the most dangerous spot upon the whole wide sea, and had been caught by a current which was at that minute sweeping us to destruction. It was too true! In spite of all the sailors could do we were driven with frightful rapidity towards the foot of a mountain, which rose sheer out of the sea, and our vessel was dashed to pieces upon the rocks at its base, not, however, until we had managed to scramble on shore, carrying with us the most precious of our possessions. When we had done this the captain said to us:

"Now we are here we may as well begin to dig our graves at once, since from this fatal spot no shipwrecked mariner has ever returned."

This speech discouraged us much, and we began to lament over our sad fate.

The mountain formed the seaward boundary of a large island, and the narrow strip of rocky shore upon which we stood was strewn with the wreckage of a thousand gallant ships, while the bones of the luckless mariners shone white in the sunshine, and we shuddered to think how soon our own would be added to the heap. All around, too, lay vast quantities of the costliest merchandise, and treasures were heaped in every cranny of the rocks, but all these things only added to the desolation of the scene. It struck me as a very strange thing that a river of clear fresh water, which gushed out from the mountain not far from where we stood, instead of flowing into the sea as rivers generally do, turned off sharply, and flowed out of sight under a natural archway of rock, and when I went to examine it more closely I found that inside the cave the walls were thick with diamonds, and rubies, and masses of crystal, and the floor was strewn with ambergris. Here, then, upon this desolate shore we abandoned ourselves to our fate, for there was no possibility of scaling the mountain, and if a ship had appeared it could only have shared our doom. The first thing our captain did was to divide equally amongst us all the food we possessed, and then the length of each man's life depended on the time he could make his portion last. I myself could live upon very little.

Nevertheless, by the time I had buried the last of my companions my stock of provisions was so small that I hardly thought I should live long enough to dig my own grave, which I set about doing, while I regretted bitterly the roving disposition which was always bringing me into such straits, and thought longingly of all the comfort and luxury that I had left. But luckily for me the fancy took me to stand once more beside the river where it plunged out of sight in the depths of the cavern, and as I did so an idea struck me. This river which hid itself underground doubtless emerged again at some distant spot. Why should I not build a raft and trust myself to its swiftly flowing waters? If I perished before I could reach the light of day once more I should be no worse off than I was now, for death stared me in the face, while there was always the possibility that, as I was born under a lucky star, I might find myself safe and sound in some desirable land. I decided at any rate to risk it, and speedily built myself a stout raft of driftwood with strong cords, of which enough and to spare lay strewn upon the beach. I then made up many packages of rubies, emeralds, rock crystal, ambergris, and precious stuffs, and bound them upon my raft, being careful to preserve the balance, and then I seated myself upon it, having two small oars that I had fashioned laid ready to my hand, and loosed the cord which held it to the bank. Once out in the current my raft flew swiftly under the gloomy archway, and I found myself in total darkness, carried smoothly forward by the rapid river. On I went as it seemed to me for many nights and days. Once the channel became so small that I had a narrow escape of being crushed against the rocky roof, and after that I took the precaution of lying flat upon my precious bales. Though I only ate what was absolutely necessary to keep myself alive, the inevitable moment came when, after swallowing my last morsel of food, I began to wonder if I must after all die of hunger. Then, worn out with anxiety and fatigue, I fell into a deep sleep, and when I again opened my eyes I was once more in the light of day; a beautiful country lay before me, and my raft, which was tied to the river bank, was surrounded by friendly looking black men. I rose and saluted them, and they spoke to me in return, but I could not understand a word of their language. Feeling perfectly bewildered by my sudden return to life and light, I murmured to myself in Arabic, "Close thine eyes, and while thou sleepest Heaven will change thy fortune from evil to good."

One of the natives, who understood this tongue, then came forward saying:

"My brother, be not surprised to see us; this is our land, and as we came to get water from the river we noticed your raft floating down it, and one of us swam out and brought you to the shore. We have waited for your awakening; tell us now whence you come and where you were going by that dangerous way?"

I replied that nothing would please me better than to tell them, but that I was starving, and would fain eat something first. I was soon supplied with all I needed, and having satisfied my hunger I told them faithfully all that had befallen me. They were lost in wonder at my tale when it was interpreted to them, and said that adventures so surprising must be related to their king only by the man to whom they had happened. So, procuring a horse, they mounted me upon it, and we set out, followed by several strong men carrying my raft just as it was upon their shoulders. In this order we marched into the city of Serendib, where the natives presented me to their king, whom I saluted in the Indian fashion, prostrating myself at his feet and kissing the ground; but the monarch bade me rise and sit beside him, asking first what was my name.

"I am Sindbad," I replied, "whom men call 'the Sailor,' for I have voyaged much upon many seas."

"And how come you here?" asked the king.

I told my story, concealing nothing, and his surprise and delight were so great that he ordered my adventures to be written in letters of gold and laid up in the archives of his kingdom.

Presently my raft was brought in and the bales opened in his presence, and the king declared that in all his treasury there were no such rubies and emeralds as those which lay in great heaps before him. Seeing that he looked at them with interest, I ventured to say that I myself and all that I had were at his disposal, but he answered me smiling:

"Nay, Sindbad. Heaven forbid that I should covet your riches; I will rather add to them, for I desire that you shall not leave my kingdom without some tokens of my good will." He then commanded his officers to provide me with a suitable lodging at his expense, and sent slaves to wait upon me and carry my raft and my bales to my new dwelling place. You may imagine that I praised his generosity and gave him grateful thanks, nor did I fail to present myself daily in his audience chamber, and for the rest of my time I amused myself in seeing all that was most worthy of attention in the city. The island of Serendib being situated on the equinoctial line, the days and nights there are of equal length. The chief city is placed at the end of a beautiful valley, formed by the highest mountain in the world, which is in the middle of the island. I had the curiosity to ascend to its very summit, for this was the place to which Adam was banished out of Paradise. Here are found rubies and many precious things, and rare plants grow abundantly, with cedar trees and cocoa palms. On the seashore and at the mouths of the rivers the divers seek for pearls, and in some valleys diamonds are plentiful. After many days I petitioned the king that I might return to my own country, to which he graciously consented. Moreover, he loaded me with rich gifts, and when I went to take leave of him he entrusted me with a royal present and a letter to the Commander of the Faithful, our sovereign lord, saying, "I pray you give these to the Caliph Haroun al Raschid, and assure him of my friendship."

I accepted the charge respectfully, and soon embarked upon the vessel which the king himself had chosen for me. The king's letter was written in blue characters upon a rare and precious skin of yellowish colour, and these were the words of it: "The King of the Indies, before whom walk a thousand elephants, who lives in a palace, of which the roof blazes with a hundred thousand rubies, and whose treasure house contains twenty thousand diamond crowns, to the Caliph Haroun al Raschid sends greeting. Though the offering we present to you is unworthy of your notice, we pray you to accept it as a mark of the esteem and friendship which we cherish for you, and of which we gladly send you this token, and we ask of you a like regard if you deem us worthy of it. Adieu, brother."

The present consisted of a vase carved from a single ruby, six inches high and as thick as my finger; this was filled with the choicest pearls, large, and of perfect shape and lustre; secondly, a huge snake skin, with scales as large as a sequin, which would preserve from sickness those who slept upon it. Then quantities of aloes wood, camphor, and pistachio-nuts; and lastly, a beautiful slave girl, whose robes glittered with precious stones.

After a long and prosperous voyage we landed at Balsora, and I made haste to reach Bagdad, and taking the king's letter I presented myself at the palace gate, followed by the beautiful slave, and various members of my own family, bearing the treasure.

As soon as I had declared my errand I was conducted into the presence of the Caliph, to whom, after I had made my obeisance, I gave the letter and the king's gift, and when he had examined them he demanded of me whether the Prince of Serendib was really as rich and powerful as he claimed to be.

"Commander of the Faithful," I replied, again bowing humbly before him, "I can assure your Majesty that he has in no way exaggerated his wealth and grandeur. Nothing can equal the magnificence of his palace. When he goes abroad his throne is prepared upon the back of an elephant, and on either side of him ride his ministers, his favourites, and courtiers. On his elephant's neck sits an officer, his golden lance in his hand, and behind him stands another bearing a pillar of gold, at the top of which is an emerald as long as my hand. A thousand men in cloth of gold, mounted upon richly caparisoned elephants, go before him, and as the procession moves onward the officer who guides his elephant cries aloud, 'Behold the mighty monarch, the powerful and valiant Sultan of the Indies, whose palace is covered with a hundred thousand rubies, who possesses twenty thousand diamond crowns. Behold a monarch greater than Solomon and Mihrage in all their glory!'"

"Then the one who stands behind the throne answers: 'This king, so great and powerful, must die, must die, must die!'"

"And the first takes up the chant again, 'All praise to Him who lives for evermore.'"

"Further, my lord, in Serendib no judge is needed, for to the king himself his people come for justice."

The Caliph was well satisfied with my report.

"From the king's letter," said he, "I judged that he was a wise man. It seems that he is worthy of his people, and his people of him."

So saying he dismissed me with rich presents, and I returned in peace to my own house.

When Sindbad had done speaking his guests withdrew, Hindbad having first received a hundred sequins, but all returned next day to hear the story of the seventh voyage, Sindbad thus began.

Seventh and Last Voyage

After my sixth voyage I was quite determined that I would go to sea no more. I was now of an age to appreciate a quiet life, and I had run risks enough. I only wished to end my days in peace. One day, however, when I was entertaining a number of my friends, I was told that an officer of the Caliph wished to speak to me, and when he was admitted he bade me follow him into the presence of Haroun al Raschid, which I accordingly did. After I had saluted him, the Caliph said:

"I have sent for you, Sindbad, because I need your services. I have chosen you to bear a letter and a gift to the King of Serendib in return for his message of friendship."

The Caliph's commandment fell upon me like a thunderbolt.

"Commander of the Faithful," I answered, "I am ready to do all that your Majesty commands, but I humbly pray you to remember that I am utterly disheartened by the unheard of sufferings I have undergone. Indeed, I have made a vow never again to leave Bagdad."

With this I gave him a long account of some of my strangest adventures, to which he listened patiently.

"I admit," said he, "that you have indeed had some extraordinary experiences, but I do not see why they should hinder you from doing as I wish. You have only to go straight to Serendib and give my message, then you are free to come back and do as you will. But go you must; my honour and dignity demand it."

Seeing that there was no help for it, I declared myself willing to obey; and the Caliph, delighted at having got his own way, gave me a thousand sequins for the expenses of the voyage. I was soon ready to start, and taking the letter and the present I embarked at Balsora, and sailed quickly and safely to Serendib. Here, when I had disclosed my errand, I was well received, and brought into the presence of the king, who greeted me with joy.

"Welcome, Sindbad," he cried. "I have thought of you often, and rejoice to see you once more."

After thanking him for the honour that he did me, I displayed the Caliph's gifts. First a bed with complete hangings all cloth of gold, which cost a thousand sequins, and another like to it of crimson stuff. Fifty robes of rich embroidery, a hundred of the finest white linen from Cairo, Suez, Cufa, and Alexandria. Then more beds of different fashion, and an agate vase carved with the figure of a man aiming an arrow at a lion, and finally a costly table, which had once belonged to King Solomon. The King of Serendib received with satisfaction the assurance of the Caliph's friendliness toward him, and now my task being accomplished I was anxious to depart, but it was some time before the king would think of letting me go. At last, however, he dismissed me with many presents, and I lost no time in going on board a ship, which sailed at once, and for four days all went well. On the fifth day we had the misfortune to fall in with pirates, who seized our vessel, killing all who resisted, and making prisoners of those who were prudent enough to submit at once, of whom I was one. When they had despoiled us of all we possessed, they forced us to put on vile raiment, and sailing to a distant island there sold us for slaves. I fell into the hands of a rich merchant, who took me home with him, and clothed and fed me well, and after some days sent for me and questioned me as to what I could do.

I answered that I was a rich merchant who had been captured by pirates, and therefore I knew no trade.

"Tell me," said he, "can you shoot with a bow?"

I replied that this had been one of the pastimes of my youth, and that doubtless with practice my skill would come back to me.

Upon this he provided me with a bow and arrows, and mounting me with him upon his own elephant took the way to a vast forest which lay far from the town. When we had reached the wildest part of it we stopped, and my master said to me: "This forest swarms with elephants. Hide yourself in this great tree, and shoot at all that pass you. When you have succeeded in killing one come and tell me."

So saying he gave me a supply of food, and returned to the town, and I perched myself high up in the tree and kept watch. That night I saw nothing, but just after sunrise the next morning a large herd of elephants came crashing and trampling by. I lost no time in letting fly several arrows, and at last one of the great animals fell to the ground dead, and the others retreated, leaving me free to come down from my hiding place and run back to tell my master of my success, for which I was praised and regaled with good things. Then we went back to the forest together and dug a mighty trench in which we buried the elephant I had killed, in order that when it became a skeleton my master might return and secure its tusks.

For two months I hunted thus, and no day passed without my securing, an elephant. Of course I did not always station myself in the same tree, but sometimes in one place, sometimes in another. One morning as I watched the coming of the elephants I was surprised to see that, instead of passing the tree I was in, as they usually did, they paused, and completely surrounded it, trumpeting horribly, and shaking the very ground with their heavy tread, and when I saw that their eyes were fixed upon me I was terrified, and my arrows dropped from my trembling hand. I had indeed good reason for my terror when, an instant later, the largest of the animals wound his trunk round the stem of my tree, and with one mighty effort tore it up by the roots, bringing me to the ground entangled in its branches. I thought now that my last hour was surely come; but the huge creature, picking me up gently enough, set me upon its back, where I clung more dead than alive, and followed by the whole herd turned and crashed off into the dense forest. It seemed to me a long time before I was once more set upon my feet by the elephant, and I stood as if in a dream watching the herd, which turned and trampled off in another direction, and were soon hidden in the dense underwood. Then, recovering myself, I looked about me, and found that I was standing upon the side of a great hill, strewn as far as I could see on either hand with bones and tusks of elephants. "This then must be the elephants' burying place," I said to myself, "and they must have brought me here that I might cease to persecute them, seeing that I want nothing but their tusks, and here lie more than I could carry away in a lifetime."

Whereupon I turned and made for the city as fast as I could go, not seeing a single elephant by the way, which convinced me that they had retired deeper into the forest to leave the way open to the Ivory Hill, and I did not know how sufficiently to admire their sagacity. After a day and a night I reached my master's house, and was received by him with joyful surprise.

"Ah! poor Sindbad," he cried, "I was wondering what could have become of you. When I went to the forest I found the tree newly uprooted, and the arrows lying beside it, and I feared I should never see you again. Pray tell me how you escaped death."

I soon satisfied his curiosity, and the next day we went together to the Ivory Hill, and he was overjoyed to find that I had told him nothing but the truth. When we had loaded our elephant with as many tusks as it could carry and were on our way back to the city, he said:

"My brother – since I can no longer treat as a slave one who has enriched me thus – take your liberty and may Heaven prosper you. I will no longer conceal from you that these wild elephants have killed numbers of our slaves every year. No matter what good advice we gave them, they were caught sooner or later. You alone have escaped the wiles of these animals, therefore you must be under the special protection of Heaven. Now through you the whole town will be enriched without further loss of life, therefore you shall not only receive your liberty, but I will also bestow a fortune upon you."

To which I replied, "Master, I thank you, and wish you all prosperity. For myself I only ask liberty to return to my own country."

"It is well," he answered, "the monsoon will soon bring the ivory ships hither, then I will send you on your way with somewhat to pay your passage."

So I stayed with him till the time of the monsoon, and every day we added to our store of ivory till all his ware-houses were overflowing with it. By this time the other merchants knew the secret, but there was enough and to spare for all. When the ships at last arrived my master himself chose the one in which I was to sail, and put on board for me a great store of choice provisions, also ivory in abundance, and all the costliest curiosities of the country, for which I could not thank him enough, and so we parted. I left the ship at the first port we came to, not feeling at ease upon the sea after all that had happened to me by reason of it, and having disposed of my ivory for much gold, and bought many rare and costly presents, I loaded my pack animals, and joined a caravan of merchants. Our journey was long and tedious, but I bore it patiently, reflecting that at least I had not to fear tempests, nor pirates, nor serpents, nor any of the other perils from which I had suffered before, and at length we reached Bagdad. My first care was to present myself before the Caliph, and give him an account of my embassy. He assured me that my long absence had disquieted him much, but he had nevertheless hoped for the best. As to my adventure among the elephants he heard it with amazement, declaring that he could not have believed it had not my truthfulness been well known to him.

By his orders this story and the others I had told him were written by his scribes in letters of gold, and laid up among his treasures. I took my leave of him, well satisfied with the honours and rewards he bestowed upon me; and since that time I have rested from my labours, and given myself up wholly to my family and my friends.

Thus Sindbad ended the story of his seventh and last voyage, and turning to Hindbad he added:

"Well, my friend, and what do you think now? Have you ever heard of anyone who has suffered more, or had more narrow escapes than I have? Is it not just that I should now enjoy a life of ease and tranquillity?"

Hindbad drew near, and kissing his hand respectfully, replied, "Sir, you have indeed known fearful perils; my troubles have been nothing compared to yours. Moreover, the generous use you make of your wealth proves that you deserve it. May you live long and happily in the enjoyment in it."

Sindbad then gave him a hundred sequins, and hence-forward counted him among his friends; also he caused him to give up his profession as a porter, and to eat daily at his table that he might all his life remember Sindbad the Sailor.

The Three Silver Citrons

THERE WAS ONCE A KING who had three sons, and he loved them all equally, one no more than the other.

When he had grown old and felt his strength leaving him, he called the three Princes before him.

"My sons," said he, "I am no longer young, and soon the time will come when I must leave you. I have it in mind to give the kingdom to one or the other of you now and not to leave it for you to quarrel over after I have gone. You have reached a time of life when you should marry. Go forth into the world and seek, each one of you, a bride for himself. He who brings home the most beautiful Princess shall have the kingdom."

The three Princes were well content with what their father said. At once the two elder ones made ready to set out; but the youngest one said he would wait a bit. "It is not right," said he, "that our father should be left alone in his old age. I will wait until my brothers return, and then I too will start out to try my fortune in the world."

That was good hearing for the older Princes, for they had always been a bit jealous of their younger brother and were just as well pleased not to have him with them.

Before they set out they packed a bag full of food to carry with them, for they had no wish to starve by the wayside. They took baked meats and boiled meats, and little cakes and big cakes, and fine white bread, and wine to drink.

Well, off they set, and on they went, a short way and a long way, until they came to the edge of a forest, and there they sat down in the shade to eat; and when they spread the food out before them it made a fine feast, I can tell you.

Just as they were about to begin an old woman came hobbling out of the forest. She was so old that her nose and her chin met and she was so bent that she could barely get along even with the help of the crutch she had.

"Good masters, give me a bite and a sup, I beg of you," she said. "It is a hundred years since I have tasted anything but black bread."

"If you have lived on black bread that long you can live on it a little longer," said one of the Princes, and then they both laughed. However, they bade the old crone come back there after they had gone, and it might be she would find some broken bits lying round, and those she might have if she cared to gather them up.

Then the Princes went on eating and drinking, and after they had finished they journeyed on again.

Presently they came to a crossroads, and there they separated; one went east and one went west. The eldest Prince took the east road, and soon it brought him to a castle, and in this castle lived a Princess who was as pretty as a picture. It was not long before the Prince won her to be his wife, for he was a stout and comely lad, and as soon as they were married he set out for home, taking his bride with him.

As it happened with the eldest Prince, so it did with the second brother. He also found a castle and a Princess, and won her to be his bride, and brought her home with him to his father's house; and when the two Princesses met it was hard to choose between them, they were both so pretty. It seemed as though the kingdom would have to be divided between the elder brothers and their pretty brides.

But first it was only right that the youngest Prince should have a chance, so now that his brothers had returned he was ready to set out into the wide world and see what sort of a beauty he could pick up. His brothers laughed at him, for they had never had much of an opinion of his wit, even though they were jealous of him.

"Only see that she has two eyes and a stout pair of hands," said they. "Our Princesses will find something for her to do about the palace, no doubt, and as for you, you shall always have a warm place in the chimney corner where you can sit."

The youngest Prince answered never a word, but he put some food in a scrip and off he set.

He journeyed on and on, a short way and a long way, and then he too came to the forest and sat down in the shade to eat, as his brothers had done before him.

Presently the old crone came hobbling out from the forest, and she was more bent and hideous than ever.

"Good youth, give me a bite and sup, I beg of you," she said. "It is a hundred years since I have tasted anything but black bread."

"Then it is high time you had something else to eat," said the Prince, and he gave her the best of all he had, both food and wine.

The old woman ate and drank, and by the time she finished there was little enough left for the Prince. Then she drew out from her sleeve a pretty little pipe and gave it to him. "Take this," she said, "and if there is anything you wish for play a tune upon the pipe, and it may help you to find it."

After that she disappeared into the forest again.

The Prince hung his scrip over his shoulder, and then he was ready to set out, but first he thought he might as well see what the pipe was good for. He set it to his lips and blew a tune.

Immediately a score of little black Trolls with long noses appeared before him. "Master, here we are!" they cried. "What would you have of us?"

"I did not know I was your master," thought the Prince, but what he said was, "What I want is the prettiest Princess in twelve kingdoms for a bride, and if you can get me such a one I'll thank you kindly."

"We know where to find such a Princess, and we can show you the way," said the oldest and blackest of the Trolls, "but we ourselves cannot touch her. You will have to win her for yourself."

Well, that suited the Prince, and if they would only show him the Princess he would do his best to get her. So off they set, and presently they came to a high mountain, and it belonged to the King of the Trolls. The Prince blew upon the pipe again, and the mountain opened before him. He went in, and there he was in a great chamber, where the Troll kept the three daughters of three Kings whom he had taken captive and brought there, and they were so beautiful that their beauty lighted the whole place so there was no need of lamps.

When the girls saw the Prince they were terrified and began to run about this way and that, looking for a place to hide; but they could find no place, for the chamber was quite smooth and bare. Then they changed themselves into three silver citrons and rolled about this way and that, all over the room.

The Prince was terribly distressed that the girls had changed into citrons, for they were so lovely that he would have been glad to have anyone of them for a wife.

However, he took up the citrons and hid them in his bosom, and then, as there seemed nothing better to do, he set out for home again, for after having seen three such beauties as that he would never be satisfied with anyone else.

After a while as he journeyed he came to the wood where he had seen the old crone before, and there she was, waiting for him.

"Well, and did you get what you set out to search for?" she asked.

"I did and I didn't," answered the Prince; – and then he told her the whole story and showed her the three citrons that he still carried in his bosom. "They are three beauties, I can tell you," said he, "but of what use are they as long as they remain as citrons?"

"I may be able to help you again," said the old hag. She then gave him a silver knife and a little golden cup. "Keep the citrons until you come to a running stream. Then take one, – whichever one you please, – and cut it open with this knife. At once one of the Princesses will appear. She will ask you for a drink of water. Give it to her immediately in this golden cup, and after that she will remain with you and you can have her for your wife."

The Prince was delighted. He took the knife and cup and thanked the old woman gratefully, and then she again disappeared in the shadow of the forest.

The Prince journeyed on until he came to a running stream, and it was not so very far from his father's palace. Then he got out the knife and the cup and one of the citrons. He cut the citron, and at once one of the Princesses appeared before him. If she had looked a beauty when he saw her in the mountain, she was ten times lovelier now that he saw her in the light of day. The Prince could only gape and gape at her.

"Give me a cup of water to drink," demanded the Princess; but the Prince was so busy staring at her that he did not move, and in a moment the Princess vanished from before him, and where she went he could not tell. He was filled with grief over the loss of her, but she was gone, and that was all of it.

Then the Prince took out the second citron. "This time I will be ready for her," he thought. He took his knife and cut the second citron. At once the second Princess appeared before him.

"Give me a cup of water to drink," she demanded. But again the Prince was so overcome by her beauty that he could no more move than if he had been rooted to the ground, and the next moment she too disappeared from before his eyes.

The Prince was in despair. He ran this way and that way, calling aloud and trying to find her, but she had vanished like the fading of a breath.

And now there was only one other citron left, and the Prince trembled at the thought of opening it, for he was afraid he would lose this third Princess as he had the others. At last he drew it from his bosom and prepared to cut it, but first he filled the golden cup and set it ready to his hand. Then he seized the knife and with one stroke divided the citron in two.

At once the third Princess stood before him, and though the others had been beautiful she exceeded them in beauty as the full moon exceeds the stars in splendour.

"Give me a cup of water," said she; and this time the Prince was ready. Almost before she could speak he had caught up the golden cup and presented it to her.

The Princess took the cup and drank, and then she smiled upon him so brightly that he was dazzled.

"Now I am yours, and you are mine," said she, "and where you go I will follow, for I have no one in all the wide world but you."

The Prince was almost wild with happiness. He kissed her hands and looked with joy upon her face.

But she was dressed only in a linen shift.

The Prince took off his cloak and wrapped it about her. "Climb up into a tree," said he, "and hide yourself among the branches, and I will go to the castle and bring you from thence robes and jewels and all things fitting for such a beautiful Princess to wear."

To this the Princess agreed. The Prince helped her to climb up among the branches of a tree that overhung the water, and then he hastened away to the castle.

The beauty sat there among the leaves waiting for his return, and the time of waiting was long, for when the Prince reached the castle he was obliged to stay and tell the whole story to his father before the King would permit him to return with the robes and jewels he had promised to bring to his bride.

Meanwhile an ugly kitchen wench who worked in the castle came to fetch water from the spring, for every day the Princesses required it for their baths. The girl had brought with her an earthen jar to hold the water.

As she leaned over the stream to fill the jar she looked down into the water and saw the face of the Princess reflected there, as she peered out from the leaves above.

The servant wench, whose name was Lucy, thought it was the reflection of her own face that she saw. She gazed upon it with wonder and joy. "Ah! Ah!" she cried. "What a beauty I am; why did no one ever tell me so? Not even the two Princesses are as beautiful as I." She knelt there, staring and staring at the reflection. Then in a rage she sprang to her feet.

"And they send me to draw water for them! Me, who ought to sit on a throne above them all. But I'll no longer be their slave. I'll break their water jar to pieces, and if they send me with others I'll break them too!"

With that she threw down the jar with such violence that it was broken into bits, and then she stamped about with rage.

The sight amused the Princess so that she laughed aloud. The servant wench looked up and saw the lovely face peering out at her from among the green leaves; it was the same beautiful face she had seen reflected in the water.

"Who are you? What are you doing up there among the leaves?" she asked in a thick voice.

"I am the promised bride of the Prince who has just gone up to the castle," answered the beauty. "He has gone to fetch fine robes and jewels that I may dress myself properly before I appear before his father."

When she said this an evil thought came into the servant wench's head.

"Come down," said she, "and I will dress your hair for you; I have often done this for the other Princesses, and I can arrange it so that you will look even more beautiful when the Prince returns."

The Princess was nothing loath. She had no thought of evil. She climbed down from the tree and sat herself upon a rock, while Lucy looped and pinned her hair in place and wove a crown of flowers to place upon it. "Come now, and see how beautiful you are," said the servant.

She led the Princess to the place where the stream was deepest, and then, when the beauty stooped to look at herself in the water, Lucy pushed her in. After that she stripped herself to her shift, and hid her clothes under a rock, and climbed up into the tree. There she sat among the leaves, peering out just as the Princess had done.

Presently the Prince returned, bringing with him all sorts of beautiful clothes and gifts for his Princess bride. What was his amazement to see, instead of the beauty he left in the tree, the ugly face of the servant wench smiling down at him from among the leaves.

"What are you doing there?" he cried. "And what have you done with the Princess?"

"Alas," said the servant maid, pretending to weep, "I am the Princess. After you left me a wicked enchantress came by this way and changed me into this shape."

The Prince was filled with grief and horror at these words. However, he believed her and could not find it in his heart to punish her for a misfortune she could not help. He showed her the robes and jewels he had brought, and the servant wench made haste to come down and dress herself in them. When she had done this she looked more hideous than ever. The Prince could hardly bear to look at her, his grief and shame were so great. Nevertheless he took her by the hand and led her back to the castle.

There the King was waiting full of impatience to see the bride of his youngest son, this most beautiful Princess in all of twelve kingdoms. But when the Prince brought the ugly servant wench before him he could hardly believe his eyes.

"This a beauty!" he cried. "Are you a fool or do you take me for one? It is an insult to bring me such a creature for a daughter-in-law."

The older Princes and their brides did not try to hide their scorn or laughter, but the servant sank on her knees, weeping, and repeated to the king the same story she had told the Prince. She assured him that she had been as beautiful as the day when she had climbed up into the tree and would be so still if the wicked enchantress had not passed by and bewitched her.

The King frowned and stroked his beard. "Yours is a sad case," said he, "and since the Prince has given his word to marry you, marry you he must. Perchance sometime your beauty may return."

He then gave orders that Lucy should be shown to the apartments prepared for the Princess and that she should be waited on and served just as though she were the beauty his son had promised him.

But the heart of the Prince was like a stone in his bosom, and he could not bear to look upon the ugly one who was to be his bride.

Now when the Princess had been pushed into the water she had not been drowned, as Lucy thought. Instead she changed into a beautiful silver fish that swam about in the stream or hid under a grassy bank.

Now there was another servant who came down to the stream for water instead of Lucy, and one day when this servant dipped the jar into the water the fish swam into it, and she carried it back to the castle with her.

It was so pretty that she showed it to the Prince, hoping it might cheer him for a moment.

No sooner had the Prince looked upon the fish than he grew quite light and happy. He would not let the servant take the fish away but kept it with him in a crystal bowl and now he no longer grieved so bitterly about his bride.

Lucy did not know why the Prince had grown happier. She thought perhaps he had begun to love her. But when she found that he scarcely ever came to see her, but spent all his time watching the fish, she became very angry.

She bribed a servant to steal the fish from the Prince's room and bring it to her. Then she had a fire built and threw the fish into it to burn.

No sooner did the flames touch the fish, however, than it changed into a beautiful silver bird and flew out of the window.

The false Princess was frightened. "There is some magic here," thought she, "and magic that will prove my ruin."

And now the silver bird sat on a branch outside the Princess's window and sang and sang. The Prince heard it, and his heart was filled with joy, he knew not why, and he forgot the fish that had disappeared from the bowl.

Lucy also heard it and was more frightened than ever. She sent for the servant who had stolen the fish and bribed him to set a net to catch the bird. This he did one day when the Prince was away, and then he brought the bird to the false Princess. But she shuddered at sight of it as though she were cold, and bade him take it outside and wring its neck.

This the servant was loath to do, but he dared not disobey her. He carried the bird outside and did as she commanded, and three drops of blood fell on the ground just below the Prince's window.

The next morning when the Prince awoke he saw with amazement that a beautiful citron tree was growing outside of his window. Its trunk was silver, and its leaves were silver, and on the branch nearest his window hung three silver citrons, and they were exactly like the silver citrons he had brought from the Troll's home under the mountain.

The Prince saw them hanging there, and his heart was filled with joy and hope as he looked at them. He reached out and plucked them and hid them in his bosom. Then he took the silver knife and the golden cup and hastened down to the stream where he had opened the citrons before.

He cut the first citron, and at once the first Princess appeared and asked him for a drink of water, but he scarcely looked at her, and she fled away.

He cut the second citron, and the second Princess appeared and demanded water, but he never stirred, and she too vanished.

Then he filled the golden cup with water and with a trembling hand cut the third citron.

Immediately the third Princess appeared. "Give me of the water to drink," said she.

At once the Prince handed her the golden cup. She drank deeply, and then she smiled upon him, and it was his own dear love who stood before him more beautiful than ever.

The Prince could hardly believe in his good fortune. But the Princess told him all that had happened to her – how Lucy had pushed her into the water, and how she had been changed first into a fish, and then into a bird, and then into a citron as she had been before. The Prince could not wonder and marvel enough. He took her by the hand and led her up to the castle, and her golden hair fell all about her so that she seemed to be clothed in a shimmering golden mantle.

When she appeared before the King he was amazed at the beauty of her, and when the Prince told him that this was his true bride and not the other, his happiness knew no bounds. The whole palace resounded with rejoicings. Only Lucy was so terrified that she ran and jumped out of a window and broke her neck.

But the kingdom was given to the youngest Prince, and he and the Princess reigned there in peace and happiness as long as they lived.

Mimir's Well

"Through our whole lives we strive towards the sun;
That burning forehead is the eye of Odin.
His second eye, the moon, shines not so bright;
It has he placed in pledge in Mimer's fountain,
That he may fetch the healing waters thence,
Each morning, for the strengthening of this eye."
—M. Howitt, Oehlenschläger

TO OBTAIN THE GREAT WISDOM for which he is so famous, Odin, in the morn of time, visited Mimir's (Memor, memory) spring, "the fountain of all wit and wisdom," in whose liquid depths even the future was clearly mirrored, and besought the old man who guarded it to let him have a draught. But Mimir, who well knew the value of such a favour (for his spring was considered the source or headwater of memory), refused the boon unless Odin would consent to give one of his eyes in exchange.

The god did not hesitate, so highly did he prize the draught, but immediately plucked out one of his eyes, which Mimir kept in pledge, sinking it deep down into his fountain, where it shone with mild lustre, leaving Odin with but one eye, which is considered emblematic of the sun.

Drinking deeply of Mimir's fount, Odin gained the knowledge he coveted, and he never regretted the sacrifice he had made, but as further memorial of that day broke off a branch of the sacred tree Yggdrasil, which overshadowed the spring, and fashioned from it his beloved spear Gungnir.

But although Odin was now all-wise, he was sad and oppressed, for he had gained an insight into futurity, and had become aware of the transitory nature of all things, and even of the fate of the gods, who were doomed to pass away. This knowledge so affected his spirits that he ever after wore a melancholy and contemplative expression.

To test the value of the wisdom he had thus obtained, Odin went to visit the most learned of all the giants, Vafthrudnir, and entered with him into a contest of wit, in which the stake was nothing less than the loser's head.

On this particular occasion Odin had disguised himself as a Wanderer, by Frigga's advice, and when asked his name declared it was Gangrad. The contest of wit immediately began, Vafthrudnir questioning his guest concerning the horses which carried Day and Night across the sky, the river Ifing separating Jötun-heim from Asgard, and also about Vigrid, the field where the last battle was to be fought.

All these questions were minutely answered by Odin, who, when Vafthrudnir had ended, began the interrogatory in his turn, and received equally explicit answers about the origin of heaven and earth, the creation of the gods, their quarrel with the Vanas, the occupations of the heroes in Valhalla, the offices of the Norns, and the rulers who were to replace the Aesir when they had all perished with the world they had created. But when, in conclusion, Odin bent near the giant and softly inquired what words Allfather whispered to his dead son Balder as he lay upon his funeral pyre, Vafthrudnir suddenly recognised his divine visitor. Starting back in dismay, he declared that no one but Odin himself could answer that question, and that it was now quite plain to him that he had madly striven in a contest of wisdom and wit with the king of the gods, and fully deserved the penalty of failure, the loss of his head.

As is the case with so many of the Northern myths, which are often fragmentary and obscure, this one ends here, and none of the scalds informs us whether Odin really slew his rival, nor what was the answer to his last question; but mythologists have hazarded the suggestion that the word whispered by Odin in Balder's ear, to console him for his untimely death, must have been "resurrection."

The Drawing of the Sword

LONG, LONG AGO, after Uther Pendragon died, there was no King in Britain, and every Knight hoped to seize the crown for himself. The country was like to fare ill when laws were broken on every side, and the corn which was to give the poor bread was trodden underfoot, and there was none to bring the evildoer to justice. Then, when things were at their worst, came forth Merlin the magician, and fast he rode to the place where the Archbishop of Canterbury had his dwelling. And they took counsel together, and agreed that all the lords and gentlemen of Britain should ride to London and meet on Christmas Day, now at hand, in the Great Church. So this was done. And on Christmas morning, as they left the church, they saw in the churchyard a large stone, and on it a bar of steel, and in the steel a naked sword was held, and about it was written in letters of gold, 'Whoso pulleth out this sword is by right of birth King of England.' They marvelled at these words, and called for the Archbishop, and brought him into the place where the stone stood. Then those Knights who fain would be King could not hold themselves back, and they tugged at the sword with all their might; but it never stirred. The Archbishop watched them in silence, but when they were faint from pulling he spoke: "The man is not here who shall lift out that sword, nor do I know where to find him. But this is my counsel – that two Knights be chosen, good and true men, to keep guard over the sword."

Thus it was done. But the lords and gentlemen-at-arms cried out that every man had a right to try to win the sword, and they decided that on New Year's Day a tournament should be held, and any Knight who would, might enter the lists.

So on New Year's Day, the Knights, as their custom was, went to hear service in the Great Church, and after it was over they met in the field to make ready for the tourney. Among them was a brave Knight called Sir Ector, who brought with him Sir Kay, his son, and Arthur, Kay's foster-brother. Now Kay had unbuckled his sword the evening before, and in his haste to be at the tourney had forgotten to put it on again, and he begged Arthur to ride back and fetch it for him. But when Arthur reached the house the door was locked, for the women had gone out to see the tourney, and though Arthur tried his best to get in he could not. Then he rode away in great anger, and said to himself, "Kay shall not be without a sword this day. I will take that sword in the churchyard, and give it to him"; and he galloped fast till he reached the gate of the churchyard. Here he jumped down and tied his horse tightly to a tree, then, running up to the stone, he seized the handle of the sword, and drew it easily out; afterwards he mounted his horse again, and delivered the sword to Sir Kay. The moment Sir Kay saw the sword he knew it was not his own, but the sword of the stone, and he sought out his father Sir Ector, and said to him, "Sir, this is the sword of the stone, therefore I am the rightful King." Sir Ector made no answer, but signed to Kay and Arthur to follow him, and they all three went back to the church. Leaving their horses outside, they entered the choir, and here Sir Ector took a holy book and bade Sir Kay swear how he came by that sword. "My brother Arthur gave it to me," replied Sir Kay. "How did you come by it?" asked Sir Ector, turning to Arthur. "Sir," said Arthur, "when I rode home for my brother's sword I found no one to deliver it to me, and as I resolved he should not be swordless I thought of the sword in this stone, and I pulled it out." "Were any Knights present when you did this?" asked Sir Ector. "No, none," said Arthur. "Then it is you," said Sir Ector, "who are the rightful King of this land." "But why am I the King?" inquired Arthur. "Because," answered Sir Ector, "this is an enchanted sword, and no man could draw it but he who was born a King. Therefore put the sword back into the stone, and let me see you take it out." "That is soon done," said Arthur replacing the sword, and Sir Ector himself tried to draw it, but he could not. "Now it is your turn," he said to Sir Kay, but Sir Kay fared no better than his father, though he tugged with all his might and main. "Now you, Arthur," and Arthur pulled it out as easily as if it had been lying in its sheath, and as he did so Sir Ector and Sir Kay sank on their knees before him. "Why do you, my father and brother, kneel to me?" asked Arthur in surprise. "Nay, nay, my lord," answered Sir Ector, "I was never your father, though till today I did not know who your father really was. You are the son of Uther Pendragon, and you were brought to me when you were born by Merlin himself, who promised that when the time came I should know from whom you sprang. And now it has been revealed to me." But when Arthur heard that Sir Ector was not his father, he wept bitterly. "If I am King," he said at last, "ask what you will, and I shall not fail you. For to you, and to my lady and mother, I owe more than to anyone in the world, for she loved me and treated me as her son." "Sir," replied Sir Ector, "I only ask that you will make your foster-brother, Sir Kay, Seneschal of all your lands." "That I will readily," answered Arthur, "and while he and I live no other shall fill that office."

Sir Ector then bade them seek out the Archbishop with him, and they told him all that had happened concerning the sword, which Arthur had left standing in the stone. And on the Twelfth Day the Knights and Barons came again, but none could draw it out but Arthur. When they saw this, many of the Barons became angry and cried out that they would never own a boy for King whose blood was no better than their own. So it was agreed to wait till Candlemas, when more Knights might be there, and meanwhile the same two men who had been chosen before watched the sword night and day; but at Candlemas it was the same thing, and at Easter. And when Pentecost came, the common people who were present, and saw Arthur pull out the sword, cried with one voice that he was their King, and they would kill any man who said differently. Then rich and poor fell on their knees before him, and Arthur took the sword and offered it upon the altar where the Archbishop stood, and the best man that was there made him Knight. After that the crown was put on his head, and he swore to his lords and commons that he would be a true King, and would do them justice all the days of his life.

The Questing Beast

BUT ARTHUR HAD MANY BATTLES TO FIGHT and many Kings to conquer before he was acknowledged lord of them all, and often he would have failed had he not listened to the wisdom of Merlin, and been helped by his sword Excalibur, which in obedience to Merlin's orders he never drew till things were going ill with him. Later it shall be told how the King got the sword Excalibur, which shone so bright in his enemies' eyes that they fell back, dazzled by the brightness. Many Knights came to his standard, and among them Sir Ban, King of Gaul beyond the sea, who was ever his faithful friend. And it was in one of these wars, when King Arthur and King Ban and King Bors went to the rescue of the King of Cameliard, that Arthur saw Guenevere, the King's daughter, whom he afterwards wedded. By and by King Ban and King Bors returned to their own country across the sea, and the King went to Carlion, a town on the River Usk, where a strange dream came to him.

He thought that the land was overrun with gryphons and serpents which burnt and slew his people, and he made war on the monsters, and was sorely wounded, though at last he killed them all. When he awoke the remembrance of his dream was heavy upon him, and to shake it off he summoned his Knights to hunt with him, and they rode fast till they reached a forest. Soon they spied a hart before them, which the King claimed as his game, and he spurred his horse and rode after him. But the hart ran fast and the King could not get near it, and the chase lasted so long that the King himself grew heavy and his horse fell dead under him. Then he sat under a tree and rested, till he heard the baying of hounds, and fancied he counted as many as thirty of them. He raised his head to look, and, coming towards him, saw a beast so strange that its like was not to be found throughout his kingdom. It went straight to the well and drank, making as it did so the noise of many hounds baying, and when it had drunk its fill the beast went its way.

While the King was wondering what sort of a beast this could be, a Knight rode by, who, seeing a man lying under a tree, stopped and said to him: "Knight full of thought and sleepy, tell me if a strange beast has passed this way?"

"Yes, truly," answered Arthur, "and by now it must be two miles distant. What do you want with it?"

"Oh sir, I have followed that beast from far," replied he, "and have ridden my horse to death. If only I could find another I would still go after it." As he spoke a squire came up leading a fresh horse for the King, and when the Knight saw it he prayed that it might be given to him, "for," said he, "I have followed this quest this twelvemonth, and either I shall slay him or he will slay me."

"Sir Knight," answered the King, "you have done your part; leave now your quest, and let me follow the beast for the same time that you have done." "Ah, fool!" replied the Knight, whose name was Pellinore, "it would be all in vain, for none may slay that beast but I or my next of kin"; and without more words he sprang into the saddle. "You may take my horse by force," said the King, "but I should like to prove first which of us two is the better horseman."

"Well," answered the Knight, "when you want me, come to this spring. Here you will always find me," and, spurring his horse, he galloped away. The King watched him till he was out of sight, then turned to his squire and bade him bring another horse as quickly as he could. While he was waiting for it the wizard Merlin came along in the likeness of a boy, and asked the King why he was so thoughtful.

"I may well be thoughtful," replied the King, "for I have seen the most wonderful sight in all the world."

"That I know well," said Merlin, "for I know all your thoughts. But it is folly to let your mind dwell on it, for thinking will mend nothing. I know, too, that Uther Pendragon was your father, and your mother was the Lady Igraine."

"How can a boy like you know that?" cried Arthur, growing angry; but Merlin only answered, "I know it better than any man living," and passed, returning soon after in the likeness of an old man of fourscore, and sitting down by the well to rest.

"What makes you so sad?" asked he.

"I may well be sad," replied Arthur, "there is plenty to make me so. And besides, there was a boy here who told me things that he had no business to know, and among them the names of my father and mother."

"He told you the truth," said the old man, "and if you would have listened he could have told you still more; how that your sister shall have a child who shall destroy you and all your Knights."

"Who are you?" asked Arthur, wondering.

"I am Merlin, and it was I who came to you in the likeness of a boy. I know all things; how that you shall die a noble death, being slain in battle, while my end will be shameful, for I shall be put alive into the earth."

There was no time to say more, for the man brought up the King's horse, and he mounted, and rode fast till he came to Carlion.

How Morgan le Fay Tried to Kill King Arthur

KING ARTHUR HAD A SISTER called Morgan le Fay, who was skilled in magic of all sorts, and hated her brother because he had slain in battle a Knight whom she loved. But to gain her own ends, and to revenge herself upon the King, she kept a smiling face, and let none guess the passion in her heart.

One day Morgan le Fay went to Queen Guenevere, and asked her leave to go into the country. The Queen wished her to wait till Arthur returned, but Morgan le Fay said she had had bad news and could not wait. Then the Queen let her depart without delay.

Early next morning at break of day Morgan le Fay mounted her horse and rode all day and all night, and at noon next day reached the Abbey of Nuns where King Arthur had gone to rest, for he had fought a hard battle, and for three nights had slept but little. "Do not wake him," said Morgan le Fay, who had come there knowing she would find him, "I will rouse him myself when I think he has had enough sleep," for she thought to steal his sword Excalibur from him. The nuns dared not disobey her, so Morgan le Fay went straight into the room where King Arthur was lying fast asleep in his bed, and in his right hand was grasped his sword Excalibur. When she beheld that sight, her heart fell, for she dared not touch the sword, knowing well that if Arthur waked and saw her she was a dead woman. So she took the scabbard, and went away on horseback.

When the King awoke and missed his scabbard, he was angry, and asked who had been there; and the nuns told him that it was his sister Morgan le Fay, who had gone away with a scabbard under her mantle. "Alas!" said Arthur, "you have watched me badly!"

"Sir," said they, "we dared not disobey your sister."

"Saddle the best horse that can be found," commanded the King, "and bid Sir Ontzlake take another and come with me." And they buckled on their armour and rode after Morgan le Fay.

They had not gone far before they met a cowherd, and they stopped to ask if he had seen any lady riding that way. "Yes," said the cowherd, "a lady passed by here, with forty horses behind her, and went into the forest yonder." Then they galloped hard till Arthur caught sight of Morgan le Fay, who looked back, and, seeing that it was Arthur who gave chase, pushed on faster than before. And when she saw she could not escape him, she rode into a lake that lay in the plain on the edge of the forest, and, crying out, "Whatever may befall me, my brother shall not have the scabbard," she threw the scabbard far into the water, and it sank, for it was heavy with gold and jewels. After that she fled into a valley full of great stones, and turned herself and her men and her horses into blocks of marble. Scarcely had she done this when the King rode up, but seeing her nowhere thought some evil must have befallen her in vengeance for her misdeeds. He then sought high and low for the scabbard, but could not find it, so he returned unto the Abbey. When Arthur was gone, Morgan le Fay turned herself and her horses and her men back into their former shapes and said, "Now, Sirs, we may go where we will." And she departed into the country of Gore, and made her towns and castles stronger than before, for she feared King Arthur greatly. Meanwhile King Arthur had rested himself at the Abbey, and afterwards he rode to Camelot, and was welcomed by his Queen and all his Knights. And when he told his adventures and how Morgan le Fay sought his death they longed to burn her for her treason.

The next morning there arrived a damsel at the Court with a message from Morgan le Fay, saying that she had sent the King her brother a rich mantle for a gift, covered with precious stones, and begged him to receive it and to forgive her in whatever she might have offended him. The King answered little, but the mantle pleased him, and he was about to throw it over his shoulders when the Lady of the Lake stepped forward, and begged that she might speak to him in private. "What is it?" asked the King. "Say on here, and fear nothing." "Sir," said the Lady, "do not put on this mantle, or suffer your Knights to put it on, till the bringer of it has worn it in your presence." "Your words are wise," answered the King, "I will do as you counsel me. Damsel, I desire you to put on this mantle that you have brought me, so that I may see it." "Sir," said she, "it does not become me to wear a King's garment." "By my head," cried Arthur, "you shall wear it before I put it on my back, or on the back of any of my Knights," and he signed to them to put it on her, and she fell down dead, burnt to ashes by the enchanted mantle. Then the King was filled with anger, more than he was before, that his sister should have dealt so wickedly by him.

The Quest of the Holy Graal

THIS IS A MYSTERIOUS PART of the adventures of King Arthur's Knights. We must remember that parts of these stories are very old; they were invented by the heathen Welsh, or by the ancient Britons, from whom the Welsh are descended, and by the old pagan Irish, who spoke Gaelic, a language not very unlike Welsh. Then these ancient stories were translated by French and other foreign writers, and Christian beliefs and chivalrous customs were added in the French romances, and, finally, the French was translated into English about the time of Edward IV by Sir Thomas Malory, who altered as he pleased. The Story of the Holy Graal, in this book, is mostly taken from Malory, but partly from *The High History of the Holy Graal*, translated by Dr. Sebastian Evans from an old French book.

What *was* the Holy Graal? In the stories it is the holy vessel used by our Lord, and brought to Britain by Joseph of Arimathea. But in the older heathen Irish stories there is a mysterious vessel of a magical sort, full of miraculous food, and probably the French writers of the romances confused this with the sacred vessel brought from the Holy Land. On account of the sins of men this relic was made invisible, but now and then it appeared, borne by angels or floating in a heavenly light. The Knights, against King Arthur's wish, made a vow to find it, and gave up their duties of redressing wrongs and keeping order, to pursue the beautiful vision. But most of them, for their sins, were unsuccessful, like Sir Lancelot, and the Round Table was scattered and the kingdom was weakened by the neglect of ordinary duties in the search for what could never be gained by mortal men. This appears to be the moral of the story, if it has any moral. But the stories are confused almost like a dream, though it is a beautiful dream.

I

How the King Went on Pilgrimage, and His Squire Was Slain in a Dream

Now the King was minded to go on a pilgrimage, and he agreed with the Queen that he would set forth to seek the holy chapel of St. Augustine, which is in the White Forest, and may only be found by adventure. Much he wished to undertake the quest alone, but this the Queen would not suffer, and to do her pleasure he consented that a youth, tall and strong of limb, should ride with him as his squire. Chaus was the youth's name, and he was son to Gwain li Aoutres. "Lie within tonight," commanded the King, "and take heed that my horse be saddled at break of day, and my arms ready." "At your pleasure, Sir," answered the youth, whose heart rejoiced because he was going alone with the King.

As night came on, all the Knights quitted the hall, but Chaus the squire stayed where he was, and would not take off his clothes or his shoes, lest sleep should fall on him and he might not be ready when the King called him. So he sat himself down by the great fire, but in spite of his will sleep fell heavily on him, and he dreamed a strange dream.

In his dream it seemed that the King had ridden away to the quest, and had left his squire behind him, which filled the young man with fear. And in his dream he set the saddle and bridle on his horse, and fastened his spurs, and girt on his sword, and galloped out of the castle after the King. He rode on a long space, till he entered a thick forest, and there before him lay traces of the King's horse, and he followed till the marks of the hoofs ceased suddenly at some open ground and he thought that the King had alighted there. On the right stood a chapel, and about it was a graveyard, and in the graveyard many coffins, and in his dream it seemed as if the King had entered the chapel, so the young man entered also. But no man did he behold save a Knight that lay dead upon a bier in the midst of the chapel, covered with a pall of rich silk, and four tapers in golden candlesticks were burning round him. The squire marvelled to see the body lying there so lonely, with no one near it, and likewise that the King was nowhere to be seen. Then he took out one of the tall tapers, and hid the candlestick under his cloak, and rode away until he should find the King.

On his journey through the forest he was stopped by a man black and ill-favoured, holding a large knife in his hand.

"Ho! You that stand there, have you seen King Arthur?" asked the squire.

'No, but I have met you, and I am glad thereof, for you have under your cloak one of the candlesticks of gold that was placed in honour of the Knight who lies dead in the chapel. Give it to me, and I will carry it back; and if you do not this of your own will, I will make you.'

"By my faith!" cried the squire, "I will never yield it to you! Rather, will I carry it off and make a present of it to King Arthur."

"You will pay for it dearly," answered the man, "if you yield it not up forthwith."

To this the squire did not make answer, but dashed forward, thinking to pass him by; but the man thrust at him with his knife, and it entered his body up to the hilt. And when the squire dreamed this, he cried, "Help! Help! For I am a dead man!"

As soon as the King and the Queen heard that cry they awoke from their sleep, and the Chamberlain said, "Sir, you must be moving, for it is day"; and the King rose and dressed himself, and put on his shoes. Then the cry came again: "Fetch me a priest, for I die!" and the King ran at great speed into the hall, while the Queen and the Chamberlain followed him with torches and candles. "What aileth you?" asked the King of his squire, and the squire told him of all that he had dreamed. "Ha," said the King, "is it, then, a dream?" "Yes, Sir," answered the squire, "but it is a right foul dream for me, for right foully it hath come true," and he lifted his left arm, and said, "Sir, look you here! Lo, here is the knife that was struck in my side up to the haft." After that, he drew forth the candlestick, and showed it to the King. "Sir, for this candlestick that I present to you was I wounded to the death!" The King took the candlestick in his hands and looked at it, and none so rich had he seen before, and he bade the Queen look also. "Sir," said the squire again, "draw not forth the knife out of my body till I be shriven of the priest." So the King commanded that a priest should be sent for, and when the squire had confessed his sins, the King drew the knife out of the body and the soul departed forthwith. Then the King grieved that the young man had come to his death in such strange wise, and ordered him a fair burial, and desired that the golden candlestick should be sent to the Church of Saint Paul in London, which at that time was newly built.

After this King Arthur would have none to go with him on his quest, and many strange adventures he achieved before he reached the chapel of St. Augustine, which was in the midst of the White Forest. There he alighted from his horse, and sought to enter, but though there was neither door nor bar he might not pass the threshold. But from without he heard wondrous voices singing, and saw a light shining brighter than any that he had seen before, and visions such as he scarcely dared to look upon. And he resolved greatly to amend his sins, and to bring peace and order into his kingdom. So he set forth, strengthened and comforted, and after divers more adventures returned to his Court.

II

The Coming of the Holy Graal

It was on the eve of Pentecost that all the Knights of the Table Round met together at Camelot, and a great feast was made ready for them. And as they sat at supper they heard a loud noise, as of the crashing of thunder, and it seemed as if the roof would fall on them. Then, in the midst of the thunder, there entered a sunbeam, brighter by seven times than the brightest day, and its brightness was not of this world. The Knights held their peace, but every man looked at his neighbour, and his countenance shone fairer than ever it had done before. As they sat dumb, for their tongues felt as if they could speak nothing, there floated in the hall the Holy Graal, and over it a veil of white samite, so that none might see it nor who bare it. But sweet odours filled the place, and every Knight had set before him the food he loved best; and after that the Holy Vessel departed suddenly, they wist not where. When it had gone their tongues were loosened, and the King gave thanks for the wonders that they had been permitted to see. After that he had finished, Sir Gawaine stood up and vowed to depart the next morning in quest of the Holy Graal, and not to return until he had seen it. "But if after a year and a day I may not speed in my quest," said he, "I shall come again, for I shall know that the sight of it is not for me." And many of the Knights there sitting swore a like vow.

But King Arthur, when he heard this, was sore displeased. "Alas!" cried he unto Sir Gawaine, "you have undone me by your vow. For through you is broken up the fairest fellowship, and the truest of knighthood, that ever the world saw, and when they have once departed they shall meet no more at the Table Round, for many shall die in the quest. It grieves me sore, for I have loved them as well as my own life." So he spoke, and paused, and tears came into his eyes. "Ah, Gawaine, Gawaine! You have set me in great sorrow."

"Comfort yourself," said Sir Lancelot, "for we shall win for ourselves great honour, and much more than if we had died in any other wise, since die we must." But the King would not be comforted, and the Queen and all the Court were troubled also for the love which they had to these Knights. Then the Queen came to Sir Galahad, who was sitting among those Knights though younger he was than any of them, and asked him whence he came, and of what country, and if he was son to Sir Lancelot. And King Arthur did him great honour, and he rested him in his own bed. And next morning the King and Queen went into the Minster, and the Knights followed them, dressed all in armour, save only their shields and their helmets. When the service was finished the King would know how many of the fellowship had sworn to undertake the quest of the Graal, and they were counted, and found to number a hundred and fifty. They bade farewell, and mounted their horses, and rode through the streets of Camelot, and there was weeping of both rich and poor, and the King could not speak for weeping. And at sunrise they all parted company with each other, and every Knight took the way he best liked.

III

The Adventure of Sir Galahad

Now Sir Galahad had as yet no shield, and he rode four days without meeting any adventure, till at last he came to a White Abbey, where he dismounted and asked if he might sleep there that night. The brethren received him with great reverence, and led him to a chamber, where he took off his armour, and then saw that he was in the presence of two Knights. "Sirs," said Sir Galahad, "what adventure brought you hither?" "Sir," replied they, "we heard that within this Abbey is a shield that no man may hang round his neck without being dead within three days, or some mischief befalling him. And if we fail in the adventure, you shall take it upon you." "Sirs," replied Sir Galahad, "I agree well thereto, for as yet I have no shield."

So on the morn they arose and heard Mass, and then a monk led them behind an altar where hung a shield white as snow, with a red cross in the middle of it. "Sirs," said the monk, "this shield cannot be hung round no Knight's neck, unless he be the worthiest Knight in the world, and therefore I counsel you to be well advised."

"Well," answered one of the Knights, whose name was King Bagdemagus, "I know truly that I am not the best Knight in the world, but yet shall I try to bear it," and he bare it out of the Abbey. Then he said to Sir Galahad, "I pray you abide here still, till you know how I shall speed," and he rode away, taking with him a squire to send tidings back to Sir Galahad.

After King Bagdemagus had ridden two miles he entered a fair valley, and there met him a goodly Knight seated on a white horse and clad in white armour. And they came together with their spears, and Sir Bagdemagus was borne from his horse, for the shield covered him not at all. Therewith the strange Knight alighted and took the white shield from him, and gave it to the squire, saying, "Bear this shield to the good Knight Sir Galahad that thou hast left in the Abbey, and greet him well from me."

"Sir," said the squire, "what is your name?"

"Take thou no heed of my name," answered the Knight, "for it is not for thee to know, nor for any earthly man."

"Now, fair Sir," said the squire, "tell me for what cause this shield may not be borne lest ill befalls him who bears it."

"Since you have asked me," answered the Knight, "know that no man shall bear this shield, save Sir Galahad only."

Then the squire turned to Bagdemagus, and asked him whether he were wounded or not. "Yes, truly," said he, "and I shall hardly escape from death"; and scarcely could he climb on to his horse's back when the squire brought it near him. But the squire led him to a monastery that lay in the valley, and there he was treated of his wounds, and after long lying came back to life. After the squire had given the Knight into the care of the monks, he rode back to the Abbey, bearing with him the shield. "Sir Galahad," said he, alighting before him, "the Knight that wounded Bagdemagus sends you greeting, and bids you bear this shield, which shall bring you many adventures."

"Now blessed be God and fortune," answered Sir Galahad, and called for his arms, and mounted his horse, hanging the shield about his neck. Then, followed by the squire, he set out. They rode straight to the hermitage, where they saw the White Knight who had sent the shield to Sir Galahad. The two Knights saluted each other courteously, and then the White Knight told Sir Galahad the story of the shield, and how it had been given into his charge. Afterwards they parted, and Sir Galahad and his squire returned unto the Abbey whence they came.

The monks made great joy at seeing Sir Galahad again, for they feared he was gone for ever; and as soon as he was alighted from his horse they brought him unto a tomb in the churchyard where there was night and day such a noise that any man who heard it should be driven nigh mad, or else lose his strength. "Sir," they said, "we deem it a fiend." Sir Galahad drew near, all armed save his helmet, and stood by the tomb. "Lift up the stone," said a monk, and Galahad lifted it, and a voice cried, "Come thou not nigh me, Sir Galahad, for thou shalt make me go again where I have been so long." But Galahad took no heed of him, and lifted the stone yet higher, and there rushed from the tomb a foul smoke, and in the midst of it leaped out the foulest figure that ever was seen in the likeness of a man. "Galahad," said the figure, "I see about thee so many angels that my power dare not touch thee." Then Galahad, stooping down, looked into the tomb, and he saw a body all armed lying there, with a sword by his side. "Fair brother," said Galahad, "let us remove this body, for he is not worthy to be in this churchyard, being a false Christian man."

This being done they all departed and returned unto the monastery, where they lay that night, and the next morning Sir Galahad knighted Melias his squire, as he had promised him aforetime. So Sir Galahad and Sir Melias departed thence, in quest of the Holy Graal, but they soon went their different ways and fell upon different adventures. In his first encounter Sir Melias was sore wounded, and Sir Galahad came to his help, and left him to an old monk who said that he would heal him of his wounds in the space of seven weeks, and that he was thus wounded because he had not come clean to the quest of the Graal, as Sir Galahad had done. Sir Galahad left him there, and rode on till he came to the Castle of Maidens, which he alone might enter who was free from sin. There he chased away the Knights who had seized the castle seven years agone, and restored all to the Duke's daughter, who owned it of right. Besides this he set free the maidens who were kept in prison, and summoned all those Knights in the country round who had held their lands of the Duke, bidding them do homage to his daughter. And in the morning one came to him and told him that as the seven Knights fled from the Castle of Maidens they fell upon the path of Sir Gawaine, Sir Gareth, and Sir Lewaine, who were seeking Sir Galahad, and they gave battle; and the seven Knights were slain by the three Knights. "It is well," said Galahad, and he took his armour and his horse and rode away.

So when Sir Galahad left the Castle of Maidens he rode till he came to a waste forest, and there he met with Sir Lancelot and Sir Percivale; but they knew him not, for he was now disguised. And they fought together, and the two Knights were smitten down out of the saddle. "God be with thee, thou best Knight in the world," cried a nun who dwelt in a hermitage close by; and she said it in a loud voice, so that Lancelot and Percivale might hear. But Sir Galahad feared that she would make known who he was, so he spurred his horse and struck deep into the forest before Sir Lancelot and Sir Percivale could mount again. They knew not which path he had taken, so Sir Percivale turned back to ask advice of the nun, and Sir Lancelot pressed forward.

IV

How Sir Lancelot Saw a Vision, and Repented of His Sins

He halted when he came to a stone cross, which had by it a block of marble, while nigh at hand stood an old chapel. He tied his horse to a tree, and hung his shield on a branch, and looked into the chapel, for the door was waste and broken. And he saw there a fair altar covered with a silken cloth, and a candlestick which had six branches, all of shining silver. A great light streamed from it, and at this sight Sir Lancelot would fain have entered in, but he could not. So he turned back sorrowful and dismayed, and took the saddle and bridle off his horse, and let him pasture where he would, while he himself unlaced his helm, and ungirded his sword, and lay down to sleep upon his shield, at the foot of the cross.

As he lay there, half waking and half sleeping, he saw two white palfreys come by, drawing a litter, wherein lay a sick Knight. When they reached the cross they paused, and Sir Lancelot heard the Knight say, "O sweet Lord, when shall this sorrow leave me, and when shall the Holy Vessel come by me, through which I shall be blessed? For I have endured long, though my ill deeds were few." Thus he spoke, and Sir Lancelot heard it, and of a sudden the great candlestick stood before the cross, though no man had brought it. And with it was a table of silver and the Holy Vessel of the Graal, which Lancelot had seen aforetime. Then the Knight rose up, and on his hands and knees he approached the Holy Vessel, and prayed, and was made whole of his sickness. After that the Graal went back into the chapel, and the light and the candlestick also, and Sir Lancelot would fain have followed, but could not, so heavy was the weight of his sins upon him. And the sick Knight arose and kissed the cross, and saw Sir Lancelot lying at the foot with his eyes shut. "I marvel greatly at this sleeping Knight," he said to his squire, "that he had no power to wake when the Holy Vessel was brought hither." "I dare right well say," answered the squire, "that he dwelleth in some deadly sin, whereof he was never confessed." "By my faith," said the Knight, "he is unhappy, whoever he is, for he is of the fellowship of the Round Table, which have undertaken the quest of the Graal." "Sir," replied the squire, "you have all your arms here, save only your sword and your helm. Take therefore those of this strange Knight, who has just put them off." And the Knight did as his squire said, and took Sir Lancelot's horse also, for it was better than his own.

After they had gone Sir Lancelot waked up wholly, and thought of what he had seen, wondering if he were in a dream or not. Suddenly a voice spoke to him, and it said, "Sir Lancelot, more hard than is the stone, more bitter than is the wood, more naked and barren than is the leaf of the fig tree, art thou; therefore go from hence and withdraw thee from this holy place." When Sir Lancelot heard this, his heart was passing heavy, and he wept, cursing the day when he had been born. But his helm and sword had gone from the spot where he had lain them at the foot of the cross, and his horse was gone also. And he smote himself and cried, "My sin and my wickedness have done me this dishonour; for when I sought worldly adventures for worldly desires I ever achieved them and had the better in every place, and never was I discomfited in any quarrel, were it right or wrong. And now I take upon me the adventures of holy things, I see and understand that my old sin hinders me, so that I could not move nor speak when the Holy Graal passed by." Thus he sorrowed till it was day, and he heard the birds sing, and at that he felt comforted. And as his horse was gone also, he departed on foot with a heavy heart.

V

The Adventure of Sir Percivale

All this while Sir Percivale had pursued adventures of his own, and came nigh unto losing his life, but he was saved from his enemies by the good Knight, Sir Galahad, whom he did not know, although he was seeking him, for Sir Galahad now bore a red shield, and not a white one. And at last the foes fled deep into the forest, and Sir Galahad followed; but Sir Percivale had no horse and was forced to stay behind. Then his eyes were opened, and he knew it was Sir Galahad who had come to his help, and he sat down under a tree and grieved sore.

While he was sitting there a Knight passed by riding a black horse, and when he was out of sight a yeoman came pricking after as fast as he might, and, seeing Sir Percivale, asked if he had seen a Knight mounted on a black horse. "Yes, Sir, forsooth," answered Sir Percivale, "why do you want to know?" "Ah, Sir, that is my steed which he has taken from me, and wherever my lord shall find me, he is sure to slay me." "Well," said Sir Percivale, "thou seest that I am on foot, but had I a good horse I would soon come up with him." "Take my hackney," said the yeoman, "and do the best you can, and I shall follow you on foot to watch how you speed." So Sir Percivale rode as fast as he might, and at last he saw that Knight, and he hailed him. The Knight turned and set his spear against Sir Percivale, and smote the hackney in the breast, so that he fell dead to the earth, and Sir Percivale fell with him; then the Knight rode away. But Sir Percivale was mad with wrath, and cried to the Knight to return and fight with him on foot, and the Knight answered not and went on his way. When Sir Percivale saw that he would not turn, he threw himself on the ground, and cast away his helm and sword, and bemoaned himself for the most unhappy of all Knights; and there he abode the whole day, and, being faint and weary, slept till it was midnight. And at midnight he waked and saw before him a woman, who said to him right fiercely, "Sir Percivale, what doest thou here?" "Neither good nor great ill," answered he. "If thou wilt promise to do my will when I call upon you," said she, "I will lend you my own horse, and he shall bear thee whither thou shalt choose." This Sir Percivale promised gladly, and the woman went and returned with a black horse, so large and well-apparelled that Sir Percivale marvelled. But he mounted him gladly, and drove in his spurs, and within an hour and less the horse bare him four days' journey hence, and would have borne him into a rough water that roared, had not Sir Percivale pulled at his bridle. The Knight stood doubting, for the water made a great noise, and he feared lest his horse could not get through it. Still, wishing greatly to pass over, he made himself ready, and signed the sign of the cross upon his forehead.

At that the fiend which had taken the shape of a horse shook off Sir Percivale and dashed into the water, crying and making great sorrow; and it seemed to him that the water burned. Then Sir Percivale knew that it was not a horse but a fiend, which would have brought him to perdition, and he gave thanks and prayed all that night long. As soon as it was day he looked about him, and saw he was in a wild mountain, girt round with the sea and filled with wild beasts. Then he rose and went into a valley, and there he saw a young serpent bring a young lion by the neck, and after that there passed a great lion, crying and roaring after the serpent, and a fierce battle began between them. Sir Percivale thought to help the lion, as he was the more natural beast of the twain, and he drew his sword and set his shield before him, and gave the serpent a deadly buffet. When the lion saw that, he made him all the cheer that a beast might make a man, and fawned about him like a spaniel, and stroked him with his paws. And about noon the lion took his little whelp, and placed him on his back, and bare him home again, and Sir Percivale, being left alone, prayed till he was comforted. But at eventide the lion returned, and couched down at his feet, and all night long he and the lion slept together.

VI

An Adventure of Sir Lancelot

As Lancelot went his way through the forest he met with many hermits who dwelled therein, and had adventure with the Knight who stole his horse and his helm, and got them back again. And he learned from one of the hermits that Sir Galahad was his son, and that it was he who at the Feast of Pentecost had sat in the Siege Perilous, which it was ordained by Merlin that none should sit in save the best Knight in the world. All that night Sir Lancelot abode with the hermit and laid him to rest, a hair shirt always on his body, and it pricked him sorely, but he bore it meekly and suffered the pain. When the day dawned he bade the hermit farewell. As he rode he came to a fair plain, in which was a great castle set about with tents and pavilions of divers hues. Here were full five hundred Knights riding on horseback, and those near the castle were mounted on black horses with black trappings, and they that were without were on white horses and their trappings white. And the two sides fought together, and Sir Lancelot looked on.

At last it seemed to him that the black Knights nearest the castle fared the worst, so, as he ever took the part of the weaker, he rode to their help and smote many of the white Knights to the earth and did marvellous deeds of arms. But always the white Knights held round Sir Lancelot to tire him out. And as no man may endure for ever, in the end Sir Lancelot waxed so faint of fighting that his arms would not lift themselves to deal a stroke; then they took him, and led him away into the forest and made him alight from his horse and rest, and when he was taken the fellowship of the castle were overcome for want of him. "Never ere now was I at tournament or jousts but I had the best," moaned Sir Lancelot to himself, as soon as the Knights had left him and he was alone. "But now am I shamed, and I am persuaded that I am more sinful than ever I was." Sorrowfully he rode on till he passed a chapel, where stood a nun, who called to him and asked him his name and what he was seeking.

So he told her who he was, and what had befallen him at the tournament, and the vision that had come to him in his sleep. "Ah, Lancelot," said she, "as long as you were a knight of earthly knighthood you were the most wonderful man in the world and the most adventurous. But now, since you are set among Knights of heavenly adventures, if you were worsted at that tournament it is no marvel. For the tournament was meant for a sign, and the earthly Knights were they who were clothed in black in token of the sins of which they were not yet purged. And the white Knights were they who had chosen the way of holiness, and in them the quest has already begun. Thus you beheld both the sinners and the good men, and when you saw the sinners overcome you went to their help, as they were your fellows in boasting and pride of the world, and all that must be left in that quest. And that caused your misadventure. Now that I have warned you of your vainglory and your pride, beware of everlasting pain, for of all earthly Knights I have pity of you, for I know well that among earthly sinful Knights you are without peer."

VII

An Adventure of Sir Gawaine

Sir Gawaine rode long without meeting any adventure, and from Pentecost to Michaelmas found none that pleased him. But at Michaelmas he met Sir Ector de Maris and rejoiced greatly.

As they sat talking there appeared before them a hand showing unto the elbow covered with red samite, and holding a great candle that burned right clear; and the hand passed into the chapel and vanished, they knew not where. Then they heard a voice which said, "Knights full of evil faith and poor belief, these two things have failed you, and therefore you may not come to the adventure of the Holy Graal." And this same told them a holy man to whom they confessed their sins, "for," said he, "you have failed in three things, charity, fasting, and truth, and have been great murderers. But sinful as Sir Lancelot was, since he went into the quest he never slew man, nor shall, till he come into Camelot again. For he has taken upon him to forsake sin. And were he not so unstable, he should be the next to achieve it, after Galahad his son. Yet shall he die an holy man, and in earthly sinful men he has no fellow."

"Sir," said Gawaine, "by your words it seems that our sins will not let us labour in that quest?" "Truly," answered the hermit, "there be an hundred such as you to whom it will bring naught but shame." So Gawaine departed and followed Sir Ector, who had ridden on before.

VIII

The Adventure of Sir Bors

When Sir Bors left Camelot on his quest he met a holy man riding on an ass, and Sir Bors saluted him. Then the good man knew him to be one of the Knights who were in quest of the Holy Graal. "What are you?" said he, and Sir Bors answered, "I am a Knight that fain would be counselled in the quest of the Graal, for he shall have much earthly worship that brings it to an end." "That is true," said the good man, "for he will be the best Knight in the world, but know well that there shall none attain it but by holiness and by confession of sin." So they rode together till they came to the hermitage, and the good man led Sir Bors into the chapel, where he made confession of his sins, and they ate bread and drank water together. "Now," said the hermit, "I pray you that you eat none other till you sit at the table where the Holy Graal shall be." "Sir," answered Sir Bors, "I agree thereto, but how know you that I shall sit there?" "That know I," said the holy man, "but there will be but few of your fellows with you. Also instead of a shirt you shall wear this garment until you have achieved your quest," and Sir Bors took off his clothes, and put on instead a scarlet coat. Then the good man questioned him, and marvelled to find him pure in life, and he armed him and bade him go. After this Sir Bors rode through many lands, and had many adventures, and was often sore tempted, but remembered the words of the holy man and kept his life clean of wrong. And once he had by mischance almost slain his own brother, but a voice cried, "Flee, Bors, and touch him not," and he hearkened and stayed his hand. And there fell between them a fiery cloud, which burned up both their shields, and they two fell to the earth in a great swoon; but when they awakened out of it Bors saw that his brother had no harm. With that the voice spoke to him saying, "Bors, go hence and bear your brother fellowship no longer; but take your way to the sea, where Sir Percivale abides till you come." Then Sir Bors prayed his brother to forgive him all he had unknowingly done, and rode straight to the sea. On the shore he found a vessel covered with white samite, and as soon as he stepped in the vessel it set sail so fast it might have been flying, and Sir Bors lay down and slept till it was day. When he waked he saw a Knight lying in the midst of the ship, all armed save for his helm, and he knew him for Sir Percivale, and welcomed him with great joy; and they told each other of their adventures and of their temptations, and had great happiness in each other's company. "We lack nothing but Galahad, the good Knight," Sir Percivale said.

IX

Adventure of Sir Galahad

Sir Galahad rested one evening at a hermitage. And while he was resting, there came a gentlewoman and asked leave of the hermit to speak with Sir Galahad, and would not be denied, though she was told he was weary and asleep. Then the hermit waked Sir Galahad and bade him rise, as a gentlewoman had great need of him, so Sir Galahad rose and asked her what she wished. "Galahad," said she, "I will that you arm yourself, and mount your horse and follow me, and I will show you the highest adventure that ever any Knight saw." And Sir Galahad bade her go, and he would follow wherever she led. In three days they reached the sea, where they found the ship where Sir Bors and Sir Percivale were lying. And the lady bade him leave his horse behind and said she would leave hers also, but their saddles and bridles they would take on board the ship. This they did, and were received with great joy by the two Knights; then the sails were spread, and the ship was driven before the wind at a marvellous pace till they reached the land of Logris, the entrance to which lies between two great rocks with a whirlpool in the middle.

Their own ship might not get safely through; but they left it and went into another ship that lay there, which had neither man nor woman in it. At the end of the ship was written these words: "Thou man which shalt enter this ship beware thou be in steadfast belief; if thou fail, I shall not help thee." Then the gentlewoman turned and said, "Percivale, do you know who I am?" "No, truly," answered he. "I am your sister, and therefore you are the man in the world that I most love. If you are without faith, or have any hidden sin, beware how you enter, else you will perish." "Fair sister," answered he, "I shall enter therein, for if I am an untrue Knight then shall I perish." So they entered the ship, and it was rich and well adorned, that they all marvelled.

In the midst of it was a fair bed, and Sir Galahad went thereto and found on it a crown of silk, and a sword drawn out of its sheath half a foot and more. The sword was of divers fashions, and the pommel of stone, wrought about with colours, and every colour with its own virtue, and the handle was of the ribs of two beasts. The one was the bone of a serpent, and no hand that handles it shall ever become weary or hurt; and the other is a bone of a fish that swims in Euphrates, and whoso handles it shall not think on joy or sorrow that he has had, but only on that which he beholds before him. And no man shall grip this sword but one that is better than other men. So first Sir Percivale stepped forward and set his hand to the sword, but he might not grasp it. Next Sir Bors tried to seize it, but he also failed. When Sir Galahad beheld the sword, he saw that there was written on it, in letters of blood, that he who tried to draw it should never fail of shame in his body or be wounded to the death. "By my faith," said Galahad, "I would draw this sword out of its sheath, but the offending is so great I shall not lay my hand thereto." "Sir," answered the gentlewoman, "know that no man can draw this sword save you alone"; and she told him many tales of the Knights who had set their hands to it, and of the evil things that had befallen them. And they all begged Sir Galahad to grip the sword, as it was ordained that he should. "I will grip it," said Galahad, "to give you courage, but it belongs no more to me than it does to you." Then he gripped it tight with his fingers, and the gentlewoman girt him about the middle with the sword, and after that they left that ship and went into another, which brought them to land, where they fell upon many strange adventures. And when they had wrought many great deeds, they departed from each other. But first Sir Percivale's sister died, being bled to death, so that another lady might live, and she prayed them to lay her body in a boat and leave the boat to go as the winds and waves carried it. And so it was done, and Sir Percivale wrote a letter telling how she had helped them in all their adventures; and he put it in her right hand, and laid her in a barge, and covered it with black silk. And the wind arose and drove it from their sight.

X

Sir Lancelot Meets Sir Galahad, and They Part For Ever

Now we must tell what happened to Sir Lancelot.

When he was come to a water called Mortoise he fell asleep, awaiting for the adventure that should be sent to him, and in his sleep a voice spoke to him, and bade him rise and take his armour, and enter the first ship he should find. So he started up and took his arms and made him ready, and on the strand he found a ship that was without sail or oar. As soon as he was within the ship, he felt himself wrapped round with a sweetness such as he had never known before, as if all that he could desire was fulfilled. And with this joy and peace about him he fell asleep. When he woke he found near him a fair bed, with a dead lady lying on it, whom he knew to be Sir Percivale's sister, and in her hand was the tale of her adventures, which Sir Lancelot took and read. For a month or more they dwelt in that ship together, and one day, when it had drifted near the shore, he heard a sound as of a horse; and when the steps came nearer he saw that a Knight was riding him. At the sight of the ship the Knight alighted and took the saddle and bridle, and entered the ship. "You are welcome," said Lancelot, and the Knight saluted him and said, "What is your name? for my heart goeth out to you."

"Truly," answered he, "my name is Sir Lancelot du Lake."

"Sir," said the new Knight, "you are welcome, for you were the beginner of me in the world."

"Ah," cried Sir Lancelot, "is it you, then, Galahad?"

"Yes, in sooth," said he, and kneeled down and asked Lancelot's blessing, and then took off his helm and kissed him. And there was great joy between them, and they told each other all that had befallen them since they left King Arthur's Court. Then Galahad saw the gentlewoman dead on the bed, and he knew her, and said he held her in great worship, and that she was the best maid in the world, and how it was great pity that she had come to her death. But when Lancelot heard that Galahad had won the marvellous sword he prayed that he might see it, and kissed the pommel and the hilt, and the scabbard. "In truth," he said, "never did I know of adventures so wonderful and strange." So dwelled Lancelot and Galahad in that ship for half a year, and served God daily and nightly with all their power. And after six months had gone it befell that on a Monday they drifted to the edge of the forest, where they saw a Knight with white armour bestriding one horse and holding another all white, by the bridle. And he came to the ship, and saluted the two Knights and said, "Galahad, you have been long enough with your father, therefore leave that ship and start upon this horse, and go on the quest of the Holy Graal." So Galahad went to his father and kissed him, saying,

"Fair sweet Father, I know not if I shall see you more till I have beheld the Holy Graal." Then they heard a voice which said, "The one shall never see the other till the day of doom." "Now, Galahad," said Lancelot, "since we are to bid farewell for ever now, I pray to the great Father to preserve me and you both." "Sir," answered Galahad, "no prayer availeth so much as yours."

The next day Sir Lancelot made his way back to Camelot, where he found King Arthur and Guenevere; but many of the Knights of the Round Table were slain and destroyed, more than the half. All the Court was passing glad to see Sir Lancelot, and the King asked many tidings of his son Sir Galahad.

XI

How Sir Galahad Found the Graal and Died of That Finding

Sir Galahad rode on till he met Sir Percivale and afterwards Sir Bors, whom they greeted most gladly, and they bare each other company. First they came to the Castle of Carbonek, where dwelled King Pelles, who welcomed them with joy, for he knew by their coming that they had fulfilled the quest of the Graal. They then departed on other adventures, and with the blood out of the Holy Lance Galahad anointed the maimed King and healed him. That same night at midnight a voice bade them arise and quit the castle, which they did, followed by three Knights of Gaul. Then Galahad prayed every one of them that if they reached King Arthur's Court they should salute Sir Lancelot his father, and those Knights of the Round Table that were present, and with that he left them, and Sir Bors and Sir Percivale with him. For three days they rode till they came to a shore, and found a ship awaiting them. And in the midst of it was the table of silver, and the Holy Graal which was covered with red samite. Then were their hearts right glad, and they made great reverence thereto, and Galahad prayed that at what time he asked, he might depart out of this world. So long he prayed that at length a voice said to him, "Galahad, thou shalt have thy desire, and when thou askest the death of the body thou shalt have it, and shalt find the life of the soul." Percivale likewise heard the voice, and besought Galahad to tell him why he asked such things. And Galahad answered, "The other day when we saw a part of the adventures of the Holy Graal, I was in such a joy of heart that never did man feel before, and I knew well that when my body is dead my soul shall be in joy of which the other was but a shadow."

Some time were the three Knights in that ship, till at length they saw before them the city of Sarras. Then they took from the ship the table of silver, and Sir Percivale and Sir Bors went first, and Sir Galahad followed after to the gate of the city, where sat an old man that was crooked. At the sight of the old man Sir Galahad called to him to help them carry the table, for it was heavy. "Truly," answered the old man, "it is ten years since I have gone without crutches." "Care not for that," said Galahad, "but rise up and show your good will." So he arose and found himself as whole as ever he was, and he ran to the table and held up the side next Galahad. And there was much noise in the city that a cripple was healed by three Knights newly entered in. This reached the ears of the King, who sent for the Knights and questioned them. And they told him the truth, and of the Holy Graal; but the King listened nothing to all they said, but put them into a deep hole in the prison. Even here they were not without comfort, for a vision of the Holy Graal sustained them. And at the end of a year the King lay sick and felt he should die, and he called the three Knights and asked forgiveness of the evil he had done to them, which they gave gladly. Then he died, and the whole city was afraid and knew not what to do, till while they were in counsel a voice came to them and bade them choose the youngest of the three strange Knights for their King. And they did so. After Galahad was proclaimed King, he ordered that a coffer of gold and precious stones should be made to encompass the table of silver, and every day he and the two Knights would kneel before it and make their prayers.

Now at the year's end, and on the selfsame day that Galahad had been crowned King, he arose up early and came with the two Knights to the Palace; and he saw a man in the likeness of a Bishop, encircled by a great crowd of angels, kneeling before the Holy Vessel. And he called to Galahad and said to him, "Come forth, thou servant of Christ, and thou shalt see what thou hast much desired to see." Then Galahad began to tremble right hard, when the flesh first beheld the things of the spirit, and he held up his hands to heaven and said, "Lord, I thank thee, for now I see that which hath been my desire for many a day. Now, blessed Lord, I would no longer live, if it might please Thee." Then Galahad went to Percivale and kissed him, and commended him to God; and he went to Sir Bors and kissed him, and commended him to God, and said, "Fair lord, salute me to my lord Sir Lancelot, my father, and bid him remember this unstable world." Therewith he kneeled down before the table and made his prayers, and while he was praying his soul suddenly left the body and was carried by angels up into heaven, which the two Knights right well beheld. Also they saw come from heaven a hand, but no body behind it, and it came unto the Vessel, and took it and the spear, and bare them back to heaven. And since then no man has dared to say that he has seen the Holy Graal.

When Percivale and Bors saw Galahad lying dead they made as much sorrow as ever two men did, and the people of the country and of the city were right heavy. And they buried him as befitted their King. As soon as Galahad was buried, Sir Percivale sought a hermitage outside the city, and put on the dress of a hermit, and Sir Bors was always with him, but kept the dress that he wore at Court. When a year and two months had passed Sir Percivale died also, and was buried by the side of Galahad; and Sir Bors left that land, and after long riding came to Camelot. Then was there great joy made of him in the Court, for they had held him as dead; and the King ordered great clerks to attend him, and to write down all his adventures and those of Sir Percivale and Sir Galahad. Next, Sir Lancelot told the adventures of the Graal which he had seen, and this likewise was written and placed with the other in almonries at Salisbury. And by and by Sir Bors said to Sir Lancelot, "Galahad your son saluteth you by me, and after you King Arthur and all the Court, and so did Sir Percivale; for I buried them with mine own hands in the City of Sarras. Also, Sir Lancelot, Galahad prayeth you to remember of this uncertain world, as you promised when you were together!" "That is true," said Sir Lancelot, "and I trust his prayer may avail me." But the prayer but little availed Sir Lancelot, for he fell to his old sins again. And now the Knights were few that survived the search for the Graal, and the evil days of Arthur began.

Princess Finola and the Dwarf

A LONG, LONG TIME AGO there lived in a little hut in the midst of a bare, brown, lonely moor an old woman and a young girl. The old woman was withered, sour-tempered, and dumb. The young girl was as sweet and as fresh as an opening rosebud, and her voice was as musical as the whisper of a stream in the woods in the hot days of summer. The little hut, made of branches woven closely together, was shaped like a beehive. In the centre of the hut a fire burned night and day from year's end to year's end, though it was never touched or tended by human hand. In the cold days and nights of winter it gave out light and heat that made the hut cosy and warm, but in the summer nights and days it gave out light only. With their heads to the wall of the hut and their feet towards the fire were two sleeping-couches – one of plain woodwork, in which slept the old woman; the other was Finola's. It was of bog-oak, polished as a looking-glass, and on it were carved flowers and birds of all kinds, that gleamed and shone in the light of the fire. This couch was fit for a princess, and a princess Finola was, though she did not know it herself.

Outside the hut the bare, brown, lonely moor stretched for miles on every side, but towards the east it was bounded by a range of mountains that looked to Finola blue in the daytime, but which put on a hundred changing colours as the sun went down. Nowhere was a house to be seen, nor a tree, nor a flower, nor sign of any living thing. From morning till night, nor hum of bee, nor song of bird, nor voice of man, nor any sound fell on Finola's ear. When the storm was in the air the great waves thundered on the shore beyond the mountains, and the wind shouted in the glens; but when it sped across the moor it lost its voice, and passed as silently as the dead. At first the silence frightened Finola, but she got used to it after a time, and often broke it by talking to herself and singing.

The only other person beside the old woman Finola ever saw was a dumb dwarf who, mounted on a broken-down horse, came once a month to the hut, bringing with him a sack of corn for the old woman and Finola. Although he couldn't speak to her, Finola was always glad to see the dwarf and his old horse, and she used to give them cake made with her own white hands. As for the dwarf he would have died for the little princess, he was so much in love with her, and often his heart was heavy and sad as he thought of her pining away in the lonely moor.

It chanced that he came one day, and she did not, as usual, come out to greet him. He made signs to the old woman, but she took up a stick and struck him, and beat his horse and drove him away; but as he was leaving he caught a glimpse of Finola at the door of the hut, and saw that she was crying. This sight made him so very miserable that he could think of nothing else but her sad face that he had always seen so bright, and he allowed the old horse to go on without minding where he was going. Suddenly he heard a voice saying: "It is time for you to come."

The dwarf looked, and right before him, at the foot of a green hill, was a little man not half as big as himself, dressed in a green jacket with brass buttons, and a red cap and tassel.

"It is time for you to come," he said the second time; "but you are welcome, anyhow. Get off your horse and come in with me, that I may touch your lips with the wand of speech, that we may have a talk together."

The dwarf got off his horse and followed the little man through a hole in the side of a green hill. The hole was so small that he had to go on his hands and knees to pass through it, and when he was able to stand he was only the same height as the little fairyman. After walking three or four steps they were in a splendid room, as bright as day. Diamonds sparkled in the roof as stars sparkle in the sky when the night is without a cloud. The roof rested on golden pillars, and between the pillars were silver lamps, but their light was dimmed by that of the diamonds. In the middle of the room was a table, on which were two golden plates and two silver knives and forks, and a brass bell as big as a hazelnut, and beside the table were two little chairs covered with blue silk and satin.

"Take a chair," said the fairy, "and I will ring for the wand of speech."

The dwarf sat down, and the fairyman rang the little brass bell, and in came a little weeny dwarf no bigger than your hand.

"Bring me the wand of speech," said the fairy, and the weeny dwarf bowed three times and walked out backwards, and in a minute he returned, carrying a little black wand with a red berry at the top of it, and, giving it to the fairy, he bowed three times and walked out backwards as he had done before.

The little man waved the rod three times over the dwarf, and struck him once on the right shoulder and once on the left shoulder, and then touched his lips with the red berry, and said: "Speak!"

The dwarf spoke, and he was so rejoiced at hearing the sound of his own voice that he danced about the room.

"Who are you at all, at all?" said he to the fairy.

"Who is yourself?" said the fairy. "But come, before we have any talk let us have something to eat, for I am sure you are hungry."

Then they sat down to table, and the fairy rang the little brass bell twice, and the weeny dwarf brought in two boiled snails in their shells, and when they had eaten the snails he brought in a dormouse, and when they had eaten the dormouse he brought in two wrens, and when they had eaten the wrens he brought in two nuts full of wine, and they became very merry, and the fairyman sang 'Cooleen dhas', and the dwarf sang 'The little blackbird of the glen'.

"Did you ever hear the 'Foggy Dew?'" said the fairy.

"No," said the dwarf.

"Well, then, I'll give it to you; but we must have some more wine."

And the wine was brought, and he sang the 'Foggy Dew', and the dwarf said it was the sweetest song he had ever heard, and that the fairyman's voice would coax the birds off the bushes.

"You asked me who I am?" said the fairy.

"I did," said the dwarf.

"And I asked you who is yourself?"

"You did," said the dwarf.

"And who are you, then?"

"Well, to tell the truth, I don't know," said the dwarf, and he blushed like a rose.

"Well, tell me what you know about yourself."

"I remember nothing at all," said the dwarf, "before the day I found myself going along with a crowd of all sorts of people to the great fair of the Liffey. We had to pass by the king's palace on our way, and as we were passing the king sent for a band of jugglers to come and show their tricks before him. I followed the jugglers to look on, and when the play was over the king called me to him, and asked me who I was and where I came from. I was dumb then, and couldn't answer; but even if I could speak I could not tell him what he wanted to know, for I remember nothing of myself before that day. Then the king asked the jugglers, but they knew nothing about me, and no one knew anything, and then the king said he would take me into his service; and the only work I have to do is to go once a month with a bag of corn to the hut in the lonely moor."

"And there you fell in love with the little princess," said the fairy, winking at the dwarf.

The poor dwarf blushed twice as much as he had done before.

"You need not blush," said the fairy; "it is a good man's case. And now tell me, truly, do you love the princess, and what would you give to free her from the spell of enchantment that is over her?"

"I would give my life," said the dwarf.

"Well, then, listen to me," said the fairy. "The Princess Finola was banished to the lonely moor by the king, your master. He killed her father, who was the rightful king, and would have killed Finola, only he was told by an old sorceress that if he killed her he would die himself on the same day, and she advised him to banish her to the lonely moor, and she said she would fling a spell of enchantment over it, and that until the spell was broken Finola could not leave the moor. And the sorceress also promised that she would send an old woman to watch over the princess by night and by day, so that no harm should come to her; but she told the king that he himself should select a messenger to take food to the hut, and that he should look out for someone who had never seen or heard of the princess, and whom he could trust never to tell anyone anything about her; and that is the reason he selected you."

"Since you know so much," said the dwarf, "can you tell me who I am, and where I came from?"

"You will know that time enough," said the fairy. "I have given you back your speech. It will depend solely on yourself whether you will get back your memory of who and what you were before the day you entered the king's service. But are you really willing to try and break the spell of enchantment and free the princess?"

"I am," said the dwarf.

"Whatever it will cost you?"

"Yes, if it cost me my life," said the dwarf; "but tell me, how can the spell be broken?"

"Oh, it is easy enough to break the spell if you have the weapons," said the fairy.

"And what are they, and where are they?" said the dwarf.

"The spear of the shining haft and the dark blue blade and the silver shield," said the fairy. "They are on the farther bank of the Mystic Lake in the Island of the Western Seas. They are there for the man who is bold enough to seek them. If you are the man who will bring them back to the lonely moor you will only have to strike the shield three times with the haft, and three times with the blade of the spear, and the silence of the moor will be broken for ever, the spell of enchantment will be removed, and the princess will be free."

"I will set out at once," said the dwarf, jumping from his chair.

"And whatever it cost you," said the fairy, "will you pay the price?"

"I will," said the dwarf.

"Well, then, mount your horse, give him his head, and he will take you to the shore opposite the Island of the Mystic Lake. You must cross to the island on his back, and make your way through the water-steeds that swim around the island night and day to guard it; but woe betide you if you attempt to cross without paying the price, for if you do the angry water-steeds will rend you and your horse to pieces. And when you come to the Mystic Lake you must wait until the waters are as red as wine, and then swim your horse across it, and on the farther side you will find the spear and shield; but woe betide you if you attempt to cross the lake before you pay the price, for if you do, the black Cormorants of the Western Seas will pick the flesh from your bones."

"What is the price?" said the dwarf.

"You will know that time enough," said the fairy; "but now go, and good luck go with you."

The dwarf thanked the fairy, and said goodbye! He then threw the reins on his horse's neck, and started up the hill, that seemed to grow bigger and bigger as he ascended, and the dwarf soon found that what he took for a hill was a great mountain. After travelling all the day, toiling up by steep crags and heathery passes, he reached the top as the sun was setting in the ocean, and he saw far below him out in the waters the island of the Mystic Lake.

He began his descent to the shore, but long before he reached it the sun had set, and darkness, unpierced by a single star, dropped upon the sea. The old horse, worn out by his long and painful journey, sank beneath him, and the dwarf was so tired that he rolled off his back and fell asleep by his side.

He awoke at the breaking of the morning, and saw that he was almost at the water's edge. He looked out to sea, and saw the island, but nowhere could he see the water-steeds, and he began to fear he must have taken a wrong course in the night, and that the island before him was not the one he was in search of. But even while he was so thinking he heard fierce and angry snortings, and, coming swiftly from the island to the shore, he saw the swimming and prancing steeds. Sometimes their heads and manes only were visible, and sometimes, rearing, they rose half out of the water, and, striking it with their hoofs, churned it into foam, and tossed the white spray to the skies. As they approached nearer and nearer their snortings became more terrible, and their nostrils shot forth clouds of vapour. The dwarf trembled at the sight and sound, and his old horse, quivering in every limb, moaned piteously, as if in pain. On came the steeds, until they almost touched the shore, then rearing, they seemed about to spring on to it. The frightened dwarf turned his head to fly, and as he did so he heard the twang of a golden harp, and right before him who should he see but the little man of the hills, holding a harp in one hand and striking the strings with the other.

"Are you ready to pay the price?" said he, nodding gaily to the dwarf.

As he asked the question, the listening water-steeds snorted more furiously than ever.

"Are you ready to pay the price?" said the little man a second time.

A shower of spray, tossed on shore by the angry steeds, drenched the dwarf to the skin, and sent a cold shiver to his bones, and he was so terrified that he could not answer.

"For the third and last time, are you ready to pay the price?" asked the fairy, as he flung the harp behind him and turned to depart.

When the dwarf saw him going he thought of the little princess in the lonely moor, and his courage came back, and he answered bravely:

"Yes, I am ready."

The water-steeds, hearing his answer, and snorting with rage, struck the shore with their pounding hoofs.

"Back to your waves!" cried the little harper; and as he ran his fingers across his lyre, the frightened steeds drew back into the waters.

"What is the price?" asked the dwarf.

"Your right eye," said the fairy; and before the dwarf could say a word, the fairy scooped out the eye with his finger, and put it into his pocket.

The dwarf suffered most terrible agony; but he resolved to bear it for the sake of the little princess. Then the fairy sat down on a rock at the edge of the sea, and, after striking a few notes, he began to play the 'Strains of Slumber'.

The sound crept along the waters, and the steeds, so ferocious a moment before, became perfectly still. They had no longer any motion of their own, and they floated on the top of the tide like foam before a breeze.

"Now," said the fairy, as he led the dwarf's horse to the edge of the tide.

The dwarf urged the horse into the water, and once out of his depth, the old horse struck out boldly for the island. The sleeping water-steeds drifted helplessly against him, and in a short time he reached the island safely, and he neighed joyously as his hoofs touched solid ground.

The dwarf rode on and on, until he came to a bridle-path, and following this, it led him up through winding lanes, bordered with golden furze that filled the air with fragrance, and brought him to the summit of the green hills that girdled and looked down on the Mystic Lake. Here the horse stopped of his own accord, and the dwarf's heart beat quickly as his eye rested on the lake, that, clipped round by the ring of hills, seemed in the breezeless and sunlit air –

"As still as death,
And as bright as life can be."

After gazing at it for a long time, he dismounted, and lay at his ease in the pleasant grass. Hour after hour passed, but no change came over the face of the waters, and when the night fell sleep closed the eyelids of the dwarf.

The song of the lark awoke him in the early morning, and, starting up, he looked at the lake, but its waters were as bright as they had been the day before.

Towards midday he beheld what he thought was a black cloud sailing across the sky from east to west. It seemed to grow larger as it came nearer and nearer, and when it was high above the lake he saw it was a huge bird, the shadow of whose outstretched wings darkened the waters of the lake; and the dwarf knew it was one of the Cormorants of the Western Seas. As it descended slowly, he saw that it held in one of its claws a branch of a tree larger than a full-grown oak, and laden with clusters of ripe red berries. It alighted at some distance from the dwarf, and, after resting for a time, it began to eat the berries and to throw the stones into the lake, and wherever a stone fell a bright red stain appeared in the water. As he looked more closely at the bird the dwarf saw that it had all the signs of old age, and he could not help wondering how it was able to carry such a heavy tree.

Later in the day, two other birds, as large as the first, but younger, came up from the west and settled down beside him. They also ate the berries, and throwing the stones into the lake it was soon as red as wine.

When they had eaten all the berries, the young birds began to pick the decayed feathers off the old bird and to smooth his plumage. As soon as they had completed their task, he rose slowly from the hill and sailed out over the lake, and dropping down on the waters, dived beneath them. In a moment he came to the surface, and shot up into the air with a joyous cry, and flew off to the west in all the vigour of renewed youth, followed by the other birds.

When they had gone so far that they were like specks in the sky, the dwarf mounted his horse and descended towards the lake.

He was almost at the margin, and in another minute would have plunged in, when he heard a fierce screaming in the air, and before he had time to look up, the three birds were hovering over the lake.

The dwarf drew back frightened.

The birds wheeled over his head, and then, swooping down, they flew close to the water, covering it with their wings, and uttering harsh cries.

Then, rising to a great height, they folded their wings and dropped headlong, like three rocks, on the lake, crashing its surface, and scattering a wine-red shower upon the hills.

Then the dwarf remembered what the fairy told him, that if he attempted to swim the lake, without paying the price, the three Cormorants of the Western Seas would pick the flesh off his bones. He knew not what to do, and was about to turn away, when he heard once more the twang of the golden harp, and the little fairy of the hills stood before him.

"Faint heart never won fair lady," said the little harper. "Are you ready to pay the price? The spear and shield are on the opposite bank, and the Princess Finola is crying this moment in the lonely moor."

At the mention of Finola's name the dwarf's heart grew strong.

"Yes," he said; "I am ready – win or die. What is the price?"

"Your left eye," said the fairy. And as soon as said he scooped out the eye, and put it in his pocket.

The poor blind dwarf almost fainted with pain.

"It's your last trial," said the fairy, "and now do what I tell you. Twist your horse's mane round your right hand, and I will lead him to the water. Plunge in, and fear not. I gave you back your speech. When you reach the opposite bank you will get back your memory, and you will know who and what you are."

Then the fairy led the horse to the margin of the lake.

"In with you now, and good luck go with you," said the fairy.

The dwarf urged the horse. He plunged into the lake, and went down and down until his feet struck the bottom. Then he began to ascend, and as he came near the surface of the water the dwarf thought he saw a glimmering light, and when he rose above the water he saw the bright sun shining and the green hills before him, and he shouted with joy at finding his sight restored.

But he saw more. Instead of the old horse he had ridden into the lake he was bestride a noble steed, and as the steed swam to the bank the dwarf felt a change coming over himself, and an unknown vigour in his limbs.

When the steed touched the shore he galloped up the hillside, and on the top of the hill was a silver shield, bright as the sun, resting against a spear standing upright in the ground.

The dwarf jumped off, and, running towards the shield, he saw himself as in a looking-glass.

He was no longer a dwarf, but a gallant knight. At that moment his memory came back to him, and he knew he was Conal, one of the Knights of the Red Branch, and he remembered now that the spell of dumbness and deformity had been cast upon him by the Witch of the Palace of the Quicken Trees.

Slinging his shield upon his left arm, he plucked the spear from the ground and leaped on to his horse. With a light heart he swam back over the lake, and nowhere could he see the black Cormorants of the Western Seas, but three white swans floating abreast followed him to the bank. When he reached the bank he galloped down to the sea, and crossed to the shore.

Then he flung the reins upon his horse's neck, and swifter than the wind the gallant horse swept on and on, and it was not long until he was bounding over the enchanted moor. Wherever his hoofs struck the ground, grass and flowers sprang up, and great trees with leafy branches rose on every side.

At last the knight reached the little hut. Three times he struck the shield with the haft and three times with the blade of his spear. At the last blow the hut disappeared, and standing before him was the little princess.

The knight took her in his arms and kissed her; then he lifted her on to the horse, and, leaping up before her, he turned towards the north, to the palace of the Red Branch Knights, and as they rode on beneath the leafy trees from every tree the birds sang out, for the spell of silence over the lonely moor was broken for ever.

The Dwarf with the Golden Beard

THE PRINCESS BEAUTIFUL was the daughter of the King of the Silver Mountains, and she was no less lovely than her name. Because of her beauty many heroes and princes came to her father's kingdom, all seeking her in marriage. The Princess cared for none of them, however, except the young Prince Dobrotek. Him she loved with all her heart, and her father was quite willing that she should choose him for a husband, for the Prince was rich and powerful as well as handsome.

The marriage between them was arranged, and the guests from far and near were invited to attend. Among those asked was a dwarf who had also been a suitor for the hand of the Princess.

This dwarf was a very powerful magician, and as he was very malicious as well as powerful, he was greatly feared by everyone. He was scarcely two feet high, and so ugly that it was enough to frighten one only to look at him. His great pride was his beard, which was seven feet long, and every hair of it was of pure gold. Because of its length he wore it twisted round and round his neck like a golden collar. Thus he avoided tripping over it at every step.

When this dwarf heard that the Princess was to marry Dobrotek he was filled with rage and chagrin. In spite of his hideousness he was so vain of his beard that he could not imagine why the Princess should have chosen another instead of himself. He swore that even still she should take him for a husband, and that if she did not do this then she should marry no one. However, he said nothing of this vow to anyone. He accepted the invitation to the wedding, and when the day came he was one of the first of the guests to arrive.

All went to the church and took their places, and when the Prince and Princess stood before the altar they were so handsome that everyone was filled with admiration.

The priest opened his book and was just about to make them man and wife when a frightful noise arose outside. It was a sound of whistling and roaring and rending. Then the doors were burst open, and a terrible hurricane swept into the church.

The guests were so frightened that they hid themselves under the seats, but the storm touched none of them. It swept up the aisle and caught up the Princess Beautiful as though she were a feather. The Prince threw his arms about her and tried to hold her. But he could do nothing against such a hurricane. She was torn from his grasp and swept out of the church and away, no one knew whither.

When the storm was over the people came out from under the seats and looked about them, but look as they might they could see no bride. Only the Prince was standing before the altar, tearing his hair with despair because the Princess was lost to him.

And well might he despair, for the hurricane that had carried the Princess away was no common storm. It had been raised by the wicked enchantments of the dwarf, and had swept Princess Beautiful far away, over plain and mountain, over sea and forest, to the very castle of the dwarf himself. There she was lying in an enchanted sleep, and it would be a bold man who could hope to rescue her.

When the King of the Silver Mountains found his daughter gone he was in a terrible rage. "It was for you to save her," cried he to the Prince. "She was your bride, and you should have lost your life before you allowed her to be torn from you."

To this the Prince answered nothing, for he thought the same himself. Yet who can stand against magic? Only enchantment, indeed, could have prevailed against him.

"Go!" cried the King, "find her and bring her back to me, or your life shall answer for it."

The Prince wished nothing better than to go in search of his bride. Life was worth nothing to him without her, and at once he made ready to depart. He was in such haste that he stopped for neither sword nor armour, but leaped upon his horse and rode forth as he was.

On and on he rode, many miles and many leagues, but the farther he rode the less he heard of the Princess, and the more he despaired of ever finding her. At last he entered a forest so dark and vast that it seemed to have no end. As he rode on through the shadows he suddenly heard a sharp and piteous cry. He looked about him to see whence it came, and presently he found a hare struggling in the clutch of a great grey owl.

The Prince had a kind heart. He seized a stick and quickly drove the owl away from its prey. For a while the hare lay stretched out and panting, but presently it recovered itself.

"Prince," it said to Dobrotek, "you have saved my life, and I am not ungrateful. I know why you are here and whom you seek. To rescue the Princess Beautiful will be no easy task. It was the Dwarf of the Golden Beard who raised the tempest that carried the Princess away. Even now he holds her a prisoner in his castle. Whoever would rescue her must first overcome the dwarf, and to do this one must be in possession of the Sword of Sharpness."

"And where is that sword to be found?" asked the Prince.

"On a mountain many leagues away. It is guarded by a dragon who keeps watch over it night and day. Only when the sun is at its highest does the dragon sleep, and then but for a few short minutes. To gain possession of the sword one must ride the wild horse that lives here in the forest and that moves faster than the wind."

"And can I find that horse and ride him?"

"It can be done. Under yonder rock lies a golden bridle. It has lain hidden there for over a hundred years. With it lies a golden whistle. The sound of that whistle will call the horse, wherever he is. But he is very terrible to look upon, for his eyes are like burning coals, and he breathes smoke and fire from his nostrils. He will come at you as though to tear you to pieces, but do not be afraid. Cast the bridle over his head, and he will at once become quite tame and gentle. Then you can ride him wheresoever you wish. He will bear you to the mountain where the dragon lies and will help you to gain possession of the sword."

The Prince thanked the hare for its advice. He lifted the rock from its place, and there beneath it lay the golden bridle and the golden whistle. The Prince took up the bridle, and at once the whole glade was filled with light; and no wonder, for the bridle was studded with precious stones and glittered like the sun. He raised the whistle to his lips and blew upon it loud and clear.

At once, from far away in the forest, came a loud sound of neighing, and of galloping hoofs. The wild horse was coming. On and on it came, nearer and nearer. Its eyes shone like coals of fire, and the leaves were withered on either side of it because of its fiery breath.

It rushed at the Prince as though it would tear him to pieces; but he was ready for it, and as soon as it was near enough he threw the bridle over its head. At once the fire faded from its eyes. Its breath grew quiet, and it stood there as gentle and harmless as a lamb.

"Master," it said to Dobrotek, "I am yours now. Whatsoever you wish me to do, I will do, and I will bear you wherever you wish to go."

"First, then," said the Prince, "I wish you to carry me to the mountain where I can find the Sword of Sharpness."

"Very well, Master, I will do so. But before we start on such a dangerous adventure as that you should be properly armed. Do you enter in at one of my ears and go on until you come out of the other."

At once it seemed to the Prince as though the horse's ear were a great cave opening out before him. He entered in and went on and on, though it was very dark there in the horse's head. Presently he saw another opening before him, and that was the horse's other ear. He came out through it and found himself in the forest again, but now he was clothed as a warrior prince should be, in shining armour, and he held a sword in his hand.

"That is right," said the horse. "Now mount and ride, for we have far to go."

So the Prince said goodbye to the friendly hare and thanked it again. He mounted upon the horse's back and away they went like the wind. Soon they were out of the forest, and the dark was left behind them. On they went and on they went, until they came within sight of a smoking mountain; there the horse stopped.

"Master," said he, "do you see that mountain in front of us and the smoke that rises over it?"

Yes, the Prince saw it.

"That smoke is the breath of the dragon that guards the Sword of Sharpness. Just now he is awake, and if we were to venture within reach he would soon scorch us to cinders with his breath. There are, as the hare told you, only a few short minutes at midday when he sleeps, and when we may approach him safely. To gain the sword I must, in those few minutes, cross the plain before us and climb the mountain. Only I, who go like the wind, could do such a thing, and even for me it will be difficult. We may both lose our lives in the attempt."

"Nevertheless, we must try it," said the Prince, "for unless I can gain the sword, and free the Princess from the dwarf, life is worth nothing to me."

"Very well," answered the horse. "Then we will attempt it, for you are my master."

So all the rest of that day the horse and the Prince lay hidden, for it was already afternoon. Through the night and the next morning they waited, and the Prince could see the flames and columns of smoke that the dragon breathed forth. But as the sun rose high in the heavens the dragon became sleepy, and the flames burned lower and with less smoke. At last the sun was at its height.

"And now, Master, is our time," cried the horse. With that he galloped out on to the plain and made for the mountain. On he flew as fast as the wind, and faster. The Prince could hardly breathe, and he could not see at all, so fast the horse went. The plain was crossed, the mountain climbed, but already the dragon was awakening. "Quick, quick! the sword. There it lies beside him!" cried the horse.

The Prince stooped and caught up the Sword of Sharpness, and in that instant the dragon awoke. It reared its head and seemed about to devour the Prince, but when it saw what he held in his hand it dropped its crest and fawned at his feet.

"You are my master," it said, "for you hold the Sword of Sharpness. But do not kill me. Spare my life, and I will give you advice that may save your own."

"What is the advice?" asked the Prince.

"When you reach the dwarf's castle (for I know that you are going there, and why), you may with this sword be able to overcome the dwarf. But after you have done that, you must cut off his beard and carry it away with you. It will serve as proof that you and you alone have slain him. You must also fill a flask with water from the fountain in the midst of the garden. It is the Water of Life, and you will need it. You will need the Cap of Invisibility too that the dwarf sometimes wears upon his head. All three of these things you must have. Do not neglect what I tell you, for if you do evil will certainly come upon you."

"It is well," said the Prince. "I will remember what you say, and if no good comes of it, no harm can either."

So saying, the Prince drew his own sword from its sheath and left it on the mountain, taking the Sword of Sharpness in its place. Then he rode down the mountain and away over the plain. Once he looked back, but he saw neither flame nor smoke behind him. The dragon lay there as harmless as any worm, for with the Sword of Sharpness all its power was gone.

On and on rode the Prince, so fast that the wind was left behind, and at last he and his horse came within sight of a castle all of iron. About it was a wall that was seven times the height of a man, and this also was of iron.

"Look, Prince," said the horse. "That is the dwarf's castle that we see before us."

Then on they went again and never stopped until they reached the castle gate. Beside the gate hung a great brazen war trumpet. The Prince lifted it to his lips and blew upon it such a blast that it was like to split the ears of those who heard it. Again he blew, and once again.

"And now, Master, take out the sword from its sheath and make ready, for the dwarf will soon be here," said the horse.

Meanwhile the Princess Beautiful had been living behind those iron walls, and she had been not unhappy, though she had often grieved because Prince Dobrotek was not with her.

When the dwarf had caused her to be swept away by the hurricane he had thrown her into an enchanted sleep, and in this sleep she lay until she was safely placed in a room that the dwarf had specially prepared for her. This room was made entirely of mirrors, only divided here and there by curtains of cloth of gold. These curtains were embroidered with scenes from the dwarf's own life and from the life of the Princess. In the mirrors Beautiful could see her own beauty repeated endlessly. The furniture of the room was all of gold, curiously carved, and the cushions were embroidered with gold and precious stones.

When the Princess opened her eyes and looked about her she did not know where she was. She had no remembrance of the storm that had brought her hither. She remembered only that she had stood beside Prince Dobrotek in the church, and that a great noise had arisen outside. After that she had known nothing until she awoke in this chamber.

She arose from the couch where she was lying and began to examine the room. All the light came from a dome overhead. She could find neither doors nor windows, and she wondered much how she had been brought into a room like this.

While she was looking about her she heard a noise behind her that made her turn quickly. At one side the mirrors had swung apart like doors, and through this opening came a procession of enormous slaves bearing a golden throne in their midst. Upon this throne sat the Dwarf with the Golden Beard. The slaves set the throne down in the middle of the room and at once withdrew, closing the mirrored doors behind them.

When the Princess saw the dwarf she was very much alarmed. She at once suspected that it was he who had brought her here, and that he meant to keep her a prisoner until she would consent to marry him.

The dwarf stepped down from the throne and approached her with a smiling air, but she shrank away from him into the farthest corner of the room.

The dwarf was magnificently dressed. His beard had been brushed till it shone like glass, and he had thrown it over one arm as though it were a mantle. But in his left hand he carried a cap of some coarse grey stuff that was in strange contrast with the rest of his dress.

"Most beautiful Princess," said he, "you are welcome indeed in my castle. None could be more so, and I hope to make you so happy that you will be more than content to spend your life here with me."

"Miserable dwarf!" cried the Princess, "do you really think you will be able to make me stay here with you? Do you not know that Prince Dobrotek will come in search of me soon? He will certainly find me! Then he will punish you as you deserve for your insolence."

The Princess was trembling now, but with rage rather than fear. The dwarf seemed not at all disturbed by her anger, however.

"Beautiful one," he said, still smiling, "you are even more beautiful when you are angry than when you are pleased. Let Prince Dobrotek come. I fear him not at all. But do not let us waste our time in talking of him. Instead let us talk of ourselves, and of how pleasantly we will pass our days together."

So saying, the dwarf came close to the Princess and attempted to take her hand. But instead of permitting this, the Princess gave him such a blow upon the ear that he fairly staggered under it. His beard slipped from his arm, and in trying to steady himself he tripped on it and fell his length upon the floor.

The Princess laughed maliciously. At the sound of her laughter the dwarf became filled with fury. His eyes flashed fire as he scrambled to his feet. "Miserable girl!" he cried. "Do you dare to laugh? The time will come when you will feel more like weeping, if not for me then for yourself. Some day you will be glad enough to receive my caresses. Now I will leave you, and when I come again it will be in a different manner." So saying, he gathered up his beard and rushed through the mirror door, closing it behind him.

His words, and his manner of going, frightened the Princess. She again began to look about her for some way of escape. Suddenly she saw upon the floor the grey cap that the dwarf had carried in his hand. He must have dropped it when he fell, and he had been too angry to notice that he was leaving it behind. She picked it up and stood turning it thoughtfully in her hands. Then, without considering why she did so, she placed it upon her head. She was standing directly in front of a mirror at the time. To her amazement, the moment she had the cap on her head every reflection of her vanished from every mirror in the room. The Princess could hardly believe her eyes. She might have been thin air for any impression she made upon the glass. She took the cap from her head, and immediately her reflections appeared again in the mirrors. She replaced it, and they vanished from sight. Then the Princess knew that she held the Cap of Invisibility – the cap that causes anyone who wears it to become invisible.

As she stood there with the cap still upon her head, the mirror door was burst open and the dwarf rushed into the room. His dress was disordered and his eyes glared wildly.

He looked hastily about him, but he could see neither the cap nor the Princess. At once he knew that she had found the cap and had put it on.

"Ah, ha!" he cried to the invisible Princess. "So you have found it! You have put it on, and hope so to escape me. But I know you are still here, even though I cannot see you. I will find you, never fear."

Spreading his arms wide, he rushed about the room, hoping to touch the Princess and seize her, but as he could not see her she was easily able to escape him. Now and then he stopped and listened, hoping the Princess would make some sound that would tell him where she was, but at these times Beautiful too stood still. She did not move, she scarcely breathed, lest he should hear her.

Suddenly the Princess saw something that gave her a hope of escape. The dwarf had neglected to fasten the swinging mirror behind him when he entered. She flew to it and pushed it open. Beyond lay a long corridor. Down this the Princess fled, not knowing where it would lead her.

But the dwarf saw the mirror move, and guessed she had passed out through it. With a cry of rage he sprang after her.

At the end of the corridor was a barred door. Beautiful had scarcely time to unfasten this door and run through before the dwarf reached it. But once outside the door she found herself in a wide and open garden. Here she could pause and take breath. The dwarf had no means of knowing in which direction she had gone. He could not hear her footsteps upon the soft grass, and the rustling of the wind among the leaves prevented his hearing the sound of her dress as she moved.

For a while the dwarf ran up and down the garden, hoping some accident might bring him to the Princess. But he grasped nothing except empty air. Discouraged, he turned back to the castle at last, muttering threats as he went.

After he had gone the Princess began to look about her. She found the garden very beautiful. There were winding paths and fountains and fruit trees and pergolas where she could rest when she was weary. She tasted the fruit and found it delicious. It seemed to her she could live there for ever very happily, if only her dear Prince Dobrotek were with her.

As for the dwarf, in the days that followed the Princess quite lost her fear of him, though he often came to the garden in search of her. After a time she even amused herself by teasing him. She would take off her cap and allow him to see her. Then, as he rushed toward her, she would put it on again and vanish from his sight. Or she would run just in front of him, singing as she went, that he might know where she was. The poor dwarf would chase madly after the sound. Then, when it seemed that he was just about to catch her, she would suddenly become silent and step aside on the grass, and laugh to herself to see him run past her, grasping at the air.

But this was a dangerous game for the Princess to play; she was not always to escape so easily. One day she was running before him, just out of reach, and calling to him to follow, when a low branch caught her cap and brushed it from her head. Immediately she became visible.

With a cry of triumph the dwarf caught the cap as it fell and thrust it in his bosom. Then he seized the Princess by the wrist.

"I have you now, my pretty bird. No use to struggle. You shall not escape again."

In despair the Princess tried to tear herself loose from his hold, but the dwarf's fingers were like iron.

At this moment from outside the gate sounded the loud blast of a war trumpet. At once the dwarf guessed that it was Prince Dobrotek who blew it, and that he had come in search of the Princess.

Suddenly, and before Beautiful could hinder him, he drew her to him and breathed upon her eyelids; at the same time he muttered the words of a magic charm.

At once the Princess felt her senses leaving her. In vain she strove to move or speak. In spite of herself her eyes closed, and she sank softly to the ground in a deep sleep.

As soon as the dwarf saw that his charm had worked he caused a dark cloud to gather about him, which entirely hid him from view. Rising in this cloud, he floated high above the iron walls and paused directly over Prince Dobrotek. He drew his sword and made ready to slay the bold Prince who had come against him.

Dobrotek looked up and wondered to see the dark cloud that had so suddenly gathered above him.

"Beware!" cried the wild horse loudly. "It is the dwarf. He is about to strike."

Scarcely had he spoken when the darkness drew down about them. Through this darkness shot a flash as bright as lightning. It was the dwarf's sword that had struck at the Prince. But swift as the stroke was, the horse was no less swift. He sprang aside, and the sword drove so deep into the earth that the dwarf was not able to draw it out again.

"Strike! Strike!" cried the horse to Dobrotek. "It is your chance!"

Dobrotek raised the Sword of Sharpness and struck into the cloud, and his blow was so sharp and true that the dwarf's head was cut from his body and fell at the Prince's feet.

Dobrotek alighted, and cutting off the dwarf's beard, he wound it about him like a glittering golden belt. Then, leaving the head where it lay, he opened the gate and went into the garden.

He had not far to go in his search for Beautiful, for she was lying asleep upon the grass close to the gate. Dobrotek was filled with joy at the sight.

"Princess, awake! Awake!" he cried. "It is I, Dobrotek. I have come to rescue you."

The Princess neither stirred nor woke. Her lashes rested on her cheeks, and she breathed so gently that her breast scarcely moved.

"Master," said the horse, "this is no natural sleep. It is some enchantment. Take up that cap that lies beside her. Then fill your flask at the fountain of the Water of Life and let us go. Do not try to wake her now. When it is time, you can do so by sprinkling upon her a few drops of the water. But first let us make haste to leave this place, for it is still full of evil magic."

Dobrotek was not slow to do as the horse bade him. He filled a flask with the Water of Life and hid the Cap of Invisibility in his bosom. Then, lifting the Princess in his arms, he mounted the horse and rode back with her the way they had come.

It was not long before they reached the place where the Prince had saved the hare from the owl in the forest. Here the Prince found his own horse. It had not wandered away, but had stayed there, browsing on the grass and leaves and drinking from a stream nearby.

"And now, Prince," said the wild steed, "it is time for us to part. Light down and take the bridle from my head. Put it back again where you found it, and cover it with the rock; but keep the whistle by you. If ever you need me, blow upon it, and I will come to your aid."

Dobrotek did as the steed bade him. He lighted down and took the bridle from its head. He put it in the hole where he had found it and rolled back the rock upon it. Then the horse bade him farewell, and tore away through the forest, neighing as it went and breathing flames of fire.

After it had gone the Prince felt very weary. He had not yet awakened the Princess, but had laid her, still asleep, upon the soft moss of the forest. Now he stretched himself at her feet, and at once fell into a deep slumber.

Now it so chanced that while he was asleep King Sarudine, the King of the Black Country, came riding through the forest. He too had been a suitor for the hand of the Princess, but he had been refused. When he heard that she had been spirited away, and that Prince Dobrotek had gone to seek for her, he also determined to set out on the same mission. He hoped that he might be the first to find her and so win her for his bride. For the King, her father, had sent out a proclamation that whoever could find the Princess Beautiful and rescue her should have her for his wife.

What was the amazement of Sarudine, as he came through the lonely wood, suddenly to see the Princess lying there asleep, with Dobrotek at her feet.

At first he drew his sword, thinking to kill the Prince; but after a moment's thought he put it back in its sheath. Then bending over Beautiful he very quietly lifted her in his arms, mounted his horse, and rode away with her.

Dobrotek was so wearied with his adventures that he slept on for some time, not knowing that the Princess had again been stolen from him.

But when at last he woke and found her gone, he was like one mad, so great was his despair. He rushed about hither and thither through the forest, calling her name aloud, and seeking her everywhere, but nowhere could he find her.

Suddenly he bethought him of his golden whistle, and putting it to his lips he blew so loud and shrill that the forest echoed to the sound. At once the great grey horse came galloping through the forest to him.

Dobrotek ran to meet it. "Tell me," he cried, "you who know all things, where is Beautiful? She has been stolen from me, and I cannot find her."

"She is no longer here in the forest," answered the horse. "She has been carried away by King Sarudine. He has taken her back to her father's castle, and now he claims her as his bride, for he says that he is the one who found and rescued her. But she still sleeps her enchanted sleep, and none can waken her. You alone can do this, for you have the Water of Life. Hasten back to the castle, therefore, but before you go to waken her, put on the Cap of Invisibility. King Sarudine fears you, and he has set guards about the castle with orders to slay you if you attempt to enter. All their watchfulness will be in vain, however, if you wear the cap upon your head."

The advice was wise, and Dobrotek at once did as the horse told him. He drew out the cap and put it upon his head. So he became invisible. Then he rode away in the direction of the country of the Silver Mountains.

He rode on and on, and after a while he came to where the first line of guards was set. They heard the galloping of a horse, and looked all about them, but they could see no one, so he passed in safety. Not long after he came to a second line of soldiers, and he went by them unseen also. Then he passed a third line of guards, and after that he was at the palace.

The Prince entered in, and went from one room to another, and presently he came to the great audience hall. There sat the King upon a golden throne. At his right hand sat King Sarudine, and at his left the Princess lay upon a golden couch, and so beautiful she looked as she lay asleep that the Prince's heart melted within him for love. He lifted the cap from his head, and there they all saw him standing before them.

The King of the Black Mountains turned pale and trembled at the sight of him, but the old King gave a loud cry of surprise. He had thought that Prince Dobrotek had met his death long ago, or that if he lived he would be afraid to return to the Silver Mountain Country without bringing the Princess with him.

"Rash Prince!" he cried; "what are you doing here? Do you not fear to appear before me, having failed in your search?"

"I did not fail," answered the Prince, "there lies the Princess, and were it not for me she would still be a prisoner in the castle of the Dwarf of the Golden Beard."

"How is that?" asked the King.

Then Dobrotek told them his story. He told of how he had become master of the wild horse in the forest, of how he had gained possession of the Sword of Sharpness, and then of how he had ridden to the dwarf's castle and slain him in battle. He also told how he had brought the Princess away with him, how he had fallen asleep in the forest, and of how the King of the Black Country had stolen Beautiful from him while he slept.

The old King listened attentively to all that Dobrotek told him. When the Prince had made an end to his story the old King turned to King Sarudine beside him.

"And what have you to say to this?" he asked. "Is this story true?"

"Much of it is true," answered Sarudine, hardily, "but still more of it is false. It is true that it was the dwarf who carried Beautiful away. It is true that he kept her a prisoner, and that he was slain by the Sword of Sharpness. But it was I who won the sword and slew the dwarf, and it was I who rescued the Princess. What better proof of this is needed than that it was I who brought her here?"

"That is only proof that you stole her from me," cried the Prince. "The proof that I can offer is better still. If you slew the dwarf, where is his beard?"

To this the King of the Black Country could answer nothing, for he did not know where the beard was.

"Then I can tell you," cried the Prince. With these words he threw aside his mantle, and there, wound about him like a glittering girdle, was the golden beard of the dwarf.

When the old King saw the beard he could doubt no longer as to which of the two had slain the dwarf and rescued the Princess. He turned such a terrible look upon Sarudine that the young King trembled.

"So you would have deceived me!" he cried. "You thought to win the Princess by a trick. Away! Away with you! Let me never see your face again; and if ever again you venture into my country, you shall be thrown into a dungeon and remain there as long as you live."

Then, as Sarudine was hurried away by the guards, the old King turned again to the Prince. "You have indeed rescued the Princess," he said, "but your task is still only half completed. She sleeps, and none can wake her. Until that is done, no man can have her for wife."

"That is not such a hard matter, either," said the Prince. With that he drew from his bosom the flask that held the Water of Life and scattered a few drops upon the Princess.

At once she drew a deep breath and slowly opened her eyes. As soon as she saw the Prince she sprang to her feet and threw herself into his arms. The enchantment was broken, and she had awakened at last.

Then throughout the palace there was the greatest happiness and rejoicing. There never had been anything like the favours the old King heaped upon Dobrotek. The marriage between him and the Princess was again prepared for, and this time all went well. Nothing happened to interfere with the wedding, and the Prince and Beautiful were made man and wife. They loved each other all the more tenderly for the dangers they had shared, and from that time on they lived in all the happiness that true love brings.

Long, Broad and Sharpsight

THERE WAS ONCE A KING who had one only son, and him he loved better than anything in the whole world – better even than his own life. The King's greatest desire was to see his son married, but though the Prince had travelled in many lands, and had seen many noble and beautiful ladies, there was not one among them all whom he wished to have for a wife.

One day the King called his son to him and said, "My son, for a long time now I have hoped to see you choose a bride, but you have desired no one. Take now this silver key. Go to the top of the castle, and there you will see a steel door. This key will unlock it. Open the door and enter. Look carefully at everything in the room, and then return and tell me what you have seen. But, whatever you do, do not touch nor draw aside the curtain that hangs at the right of the door. If you should disobey me and do this thing, you will suffer the greatest dangers, and may even pay for it with your life."

The Prince wondered greatly at his father's words, but he took the key and went to the top of the castle, and there he found the steel door his father had described. He unlocked it with the silver key, stepped inside, and looked about him. When he had done so, he was filled with amazement at what he saw. The room had twelve sides, and on eleven of these sides were pictures of eleven princesses more beautiful than any the Prince had ever seen in all his life before. Moreover, these pictures were as though they were alive. When the Prince looked at them, they moved and smiled and blushed and beckoned to him. He went from one to the other, and they were so beautiful that each one he looked upon seemed lovelier than the last. But lovely though they were, there was not one of them whom the Prince wished to have for a wife.

Last of all, the Prince came to the twelfth side of the room, and it was covered over with a curtain, and the curtain was of velvet richly embroidered with gold and precious stones. The Prince stood before it and looked at it and looked at it. He tried to peer under its edges, but he could see nothing; never in all his life had he longed for anything as he longed to lift that curtain and see what was behind it.

At last his longing grew so great that he could withstand it no longer. He laid his hand upon the folds and drew it aside, and when he had done so, his heart melted within him for love and joy. For there was the portrait of a maiden so fair and lovely that all the other eleven beauties were as nothing beside her.

The Prince stood and looked at her, and she looked back at him, and she did not blush or beckon to him as the others had done, but rather she grew pale.

"Yes," said the Prince at last, "you and you only shall be my bride, even though I should have to go to the ends of the world to find you."

When he said that, the picture bowed its head gravely.

Then the Prince dropped the curtain and left the room and went down to where the old King was waiting for him. As soon as he came before his father, the old man asked whether he had found the room and entered it.

"I did," answered the Prince.

"And what did you see in the room, my son?"

"I saw a picture of the maiden whom I wish to have for a wife."

"And which of the eleven was it?"

"It was none of the eleven; it was the twelfth – she whose portrait hangs behind the curtain."

When the old King heard this, he gave a cry of grief. "Alas, alas, my son! What have you done! Did I not warn you not to lift the curtain and not to look behind it?"

"You warned me, my father, and yet I could not but look, and now I have seen the only one whom I will ever marry. Tell me, I pray of you, who she is, that I may go in search of her."

"Well did I know that misfortune would come upon you if ever you entered that room. That Princess whom you have seen is indeed the most beautiful Princess in all the world, but she is also the most unfortunate. Because of her beauty, she was carried away by a wicked and powerful Magician who wished to marry her. To this, however, she would not consent. He still keeps her a prisoner in an iron castle far away beyond forest, plain, and mountain at the very end of the world. Many princes and heroes and brave men have tried to rescue her, but none has ever succeeded. They have lost their lives in the attempt, and the Magician has turned them all into stone statues to adorn his castle. And now you are determined to throw away your life also."

"That may be," said the Prince; "and yet it may also be that I shall succeed even though others have failed. At any rate, I must try, for I cannot live without her."

When the King found that his son was determined to go, and that nothing could stay him, he gave him a jewelled sword and the finest steed in his stable and bade him God-speed.

So the Prince set out with his father's blessing, and he rode along and rode along until at last he came to a forest that was so vast there seemed to be no end to it. In this forest he quite lost his way. He was therefore very glad when he saw someone trudging along in front of him.

The Prince rode on until he overtook the man, and then he reined in his horse and bade him good day.

"Good day," answered the man.

"Do you know the ways through this forest?" asked the Prince.

"No, I know nothing about them, but that never bothers me. If at any time I think I am going in the wrong direction, it is easy to right myself."

"How is that?" said the Prince.

"Oh, I have the power of stretching myself out to any length, and if I lose my way I have only to make myself tall enough to see over the tree-tops, and then I can easily tell where I am."

"That must be very curious. I should like to see that," said the Prince.

Well, that was easy enough, and the man would be glad enough to oblige him. So he began to stretch himself. He stretched and stretched and stretched until he was taller than the tallest tree in the forest. His head and body were quite lost to sight among the branches, and all that the Prince could see were his legs and feet.

"Is that enough?" the man called down to the Prince.

"Yes, that is enough," answered the Prince, and he had to shout to make himself heard, the man's head was so far away.

Then the man began to shrink. He shrank and shrank until he was no taller than the Prince himself.

"You are a wonderful fellow," said the Prince. "What is your name?"

The man's name was Long.

"And what did you see up there?"

"I saw a plain and great mountains beyond, and still beyond that an iron castle, and it was so far away that it must be at the very end of the world."

"It is that castle that I am seeking," said the Prince, "and now I see that you are the very man to guide me there. Tell me, Long, will you take service with me? If you will, I will pay you well."

Yes, Long would do that, and not for the sake of the money either, but because he had taken a fancy to the Prince.

So the Prince and his new servant travelled along together, and presently they came out of the forest on to a plain, and there, far in front of them, was another man also travelling along toward the mountains.

"Look, Master!" said Long. "Do you see that man? His name is Broad. You ought to have him for a servant too, for he is even more wonderful than I am."

"Call him, then," said the Prince, "and I will speak with him."

No, Long could not call him, for Broad was too far away to hear him, but he could soon overtake him. So Long stretched himself out until he was tall enough to go half a mile at every step. In this way he soon overtook Broad and stopped him, and then he and Broad waited until the Prince had caught up to them.

"Good day," said the Prince to Broad.

"Good day," answered Broad.

"My servant here tells me that you are a very wonderful person," said the Prince. "What can you do that is so wonderful?"

What Broad could do was to spread himself out until he was as broad across as he wished to be.

"I should like to see that," said the Prince.

Very well! Nothing was easier, and Broad was willing to show him. "But first," said Broad, "do you get behind those rocks over yonder. Otherwise you may get hurt. And now I will begin."

"Quick! Quick, Master!" cried Long, in a voice of fear. "We have not a moment to lose," and he ran at full speed and crouched down behind the rocks. The Prince followed him, and he also got behind the rocks, but he did not know why Long was in such a hurry, nor why he seemed so frightened. He soon saw, however, for when Broad began to spread, he spread so fast and with such force that unless the Prince and Long had been behind the rocks, they would certainly have been pushed against them and crushed.

"Is that enough?" cried Broad, after he had spread out so wide that the Prince could scarcely see across him.

"Yes, that is enough."

So Broad began to shrink, and soon he was no fatter than he had been before.

"Yes, you are certainly a very wonderful fellow, and I should like to have you for a servant," said the Prince. "Will you come with me also?"

Yes, Broad would come, for a master who was good enough for Long was good enough for him too. So now the Prince had two servants. He rode on across the plain toward the mountains, and the two followed him.

After a while they came to a man sitting by the way with a bandage over his eyes. The Prince stopped and spoke to him.

"Are you blind, my poor fellow, that you wear a bandage over your eyes?"

"No," answered the man, "I am not blind. I wear the bandage because I see too well without it. Even now, with this bandage, I can see as clearly as you ever can. If I take it off, I can see for hundreds of miles, and when I look at anything steadily my sight is so strong that the thing is riven to pieces, or bursts into flame and is burned."

"That is a very curious thing," said the Prince. "Could you break yonder rock to pieces merely by looking at it?"

"Yes, I could do that."

"I would like to see it done," said the Prince.

Well, the man was ready to oblige him. So he took the bandage from his eyes and fixed his gaze on the rock. First the rock grew hot, and then it smoked, and then, with a great noise, it exploded into tiny fragments, so that the pieces flew about through the air.

"Yes, you are even more wonderful than these other two," said the Prince, "and they are wonderful enough. How are you called?"

"My name is Sharpsight."

"Well, Sharpsight, will you take service with me, for I need just such a servant as you?"

Yes, Sharpsight would do that; so now the Prince had three servants, and they were such servants as no one in the world ever had before.

They travelled along over the plain, and at last they came to the foot of the mountain that lay between them and the iron castle.

"Now we must either go over it or round it," said the Prince; "and which shall it be?"

"No need for that, Master," answered Sharpsight. "Just let me unbandage my eyes, but be careful you are not struck by any of the flying pieces when the mountain begins to split."

So the Prince and Broad and Long took shelter behind a clump of trees, and then Sharpsight uncovered his eyes. He fixed his eyes on the mountain, and presently it began to groan and split and splinter. Pieces of sharp rock and stones flew through the air. It was not long before Sharpsight's gaze had bored a way straight through the mountain and out on the other side. Then he put back the bandage over his eyes and called to the Prince that the way was clear.

The Prince and his companions came out from their shelter, and when they saw the way that Sharpsight had made through the mountain they could not wonder enough. It was so broad and clear that ten men could have ridden through it abreast.

With such a way before them it did not take them long to go through the mountain, and then they found themselves in the country beyond, and a black and terrible land it was too. Nowhere was there any sound or sign of life. There were fields, but no grass. There were trees, but they bore neither leaves nor fruit. There was a river, but it did not flow, and there was light, and yet they saw no sun. But darker and gloomier than all the rest was the castle which rose before them. It was the iron castle where the Black Magician lived.

There was a moat round the castle and an iron bridge across it. The companions rode across the bridge, and no sooner were they over than the bridge rose behind them and they were prisoners.

They could not have turned back even if they had wished to, but none of them had any thought of such a thing.

The Prince struck with his sword upon the great door of the castle, and at once it opened before him, but when he entered he saw no one. Before him was a great hall, and on either side of it was a long row of stone figures. These statues were all figures of knights and kings and princes. The Prince looked at them and wondered, for they were so lifelike that it seemed scarcely possible to believe that they were of stone.

He and his companions went on farther into the castle, and everywhere they found rooms magnificently furnished, but silent and deserted. Nowhere was there any sign of life.

Last of all they entered what seemed to be a dining-hall. Here was a table set with the most delicious things to eat and drink. There were four places about the table, and one of them was somewhat higher than the others, as though intended for the Prince or King.

"One might think this table had been set for us," said the Prince. "We will wait for a while, and then, if no one comes, we will eat, at any rate."

They waited for some time and then took their places at the table. At once invisible hands filled the goblets and other invisible hands passed the dishes.

The Prince and his companions ate and drank all they wished, and then they rose from the table, meaning to look farther through the castle.

At this moment the door opened and a tall man with a long grey beard came into the room. From head to foot he was dressed entirely in black velvet, even to his cap and shoes, and round his waist his robe was fastened with three iron bands. In one hand was an ivory wand, curiously carved; with the other he led a lady so beautiful, and yet so pale and sad-looking, that the heart ached to look at her. The moment the Prince saw her he knew her as the one whose picture he had seen behind the golden curtain – the one whom he had said should be his bride.

The Magician, for it was he, spoke at once to the Prince. "I know why you have come here, and that you hope to win this Princess for your bride. Many others have come here with the same wish and have failed. Now you shall have your turn. For three nights you must watch here with her. If each morning I return and find her still with you, then you shall have her for a bride after the third morning. But if she is gone, you shall be turned into a stone statue, such as those you have already seen about my palace."

"That ought not to be a hard task," said the Prince. "Gladly will I watch with her for three nights; if in the morning you find her gone, I am willing to suffer whatever you will. But my three companions must also watch with me."

Yes, the Magician was willing to agree to that, so he left the lady there with the four, and then went away, closing the door behind him.

As soon as the Magician had gone the Prince and his followers made ready to guard the room so that no one could come in to take the lady away, nor could she herself leave without their knowing it.

Long lay down and stretched himself out until he encircled the whole room, and anyone who went in or out would have to step over him. Sharpsight sat down to watch, while Broad stood in the doorway and made himself so broad that no one could possibly have squeezed in past him. Meanwhile the Prince tried to talk to the lady, but she would not look at him nor answer him.

In this way some time passed, and then suddenly the Prince began to feel very drowsy. He tried to rouse himself, but in spite of his efforts his eyes closed, and he fell into a deep sleep.

It was not until the early morning that he woke. Then he roused himself and looked about him. His companions too were only just opening their eyes, for they, like himself, had been asleep, and the lady was gone from the room.

When the Prince saw this he began to groan and lament, but his companions told him not to despair.

"Wait until I see if I can tell you where she is," said Sharpsight. He leaned from the window and looked about.

"Yes, I see her," he said. "A hundred miles away from here is a forest. In that forest is an oak-tree. On the topmost bough of that oak-tree is an acorn, and in that acorn is the Princess hidden."

"But what good is it to know where she is unless we can get her back before the Magician comes?" cried the Prince. "It would take us days to journey there and to return."

"Not so long as that, Master," answered Long. "Have patience for a moment until I see what I can do." He then stepped outside and made himself so tall that he could go ten miles at a step. He set Sharpsight on his shoulder to show him the way, and away he went, and he made such good time that he was back in the castle again before the Prince could have walked three times round the room.

"Here, Master," he said, "here is the acorn. Take it and throw it upon the floor."

The Prince threw the acorn upon the floor, and at once it flew open, and there stood the Princess before him.

Hardly had this happened when the door opened and the Magician came into the room. When he saw the Princess he gave a cry of rage, and one of the iron bands about his middle broke with a loud noise.

He looked at the Prince, and his eyes flashed as if with red fire. "This time you have succeeded in keeping the Princess with you," he cried, "but do not be too sure that you can do the same thing again. Tonight you shall try once more."

So saying he went away, taking the Princess with him. In the evening he came again, and again he brought the Princess.

"Watch her well," said he to the Prince, with an evil smile. "Remember, if she is not still here tomorrow morning you will share the fate of the others who have tried to watch her and have failed."

"Very well," answered the Prince. "What must be must be, and I can only do my best."

The Magician then went away, leaving the Princess with them as before.

The Prince and his companions had determined that this night they would stay awake, whatever happened, but presently their eyelids grew as heavy as lead, and soon, in spite of themselves, they all fell into a deep sleep.

When they awoke the day was breaking, and the Princess had again disappeared. The Prince was ready to tear his hair with despair, but Sharpsight bade him take heart.

"Wait until I take a look about," he said. "If I cannot see her, then it will be time for you to despair."

He leaned from the window, and first he looked east, and then he looked west, and then he looked toward the north. "Yes, now I see her," he said, "but she is far enough away. Two hundred miles from here is a desert. In that desert is a rock, in that rock is a golden ring, and that ring is the Princess."

"That is far away indeed," groaned the Prince, "and at any moment the Magician may be here."

"Never mind, Master," cried Long. "Two hundred miles is not so far when one can go twenty miles at a step." He then made himself twice as tall as the day before, and taking Sharpsight on his shoulders he set out for the desert.

It was not long before he was back again, and in his hand he carried the golden ring. "If it had not been for Sharpsight," he said, "I would have been forced to bring back the whole rock with me, but he fixed his eyes upon it, and at once it split into a thousand pieces and the ring fell out. Here! Take the ring, Master, quick, and throw it upon the floor."

The Prince did so, and as soon as the ring touched the ground it was transformed into the Princess.

At this moment the Magician opened the door and came into the room. When he saw the Princess he stopped short, and his face turned black with rage and fear. At the same moment the second band about his middle flew apart.

"Ah, well!" he cried to the Prince, "no doubt you think you are very clever, but remember there is still another night, and next time you may not prove so lucky in keeping the Princess with you."

So saying he went away with the Princess, and the Prince saw him no more until evening. Then for the third time he came, and brought the Princess with him.

"Watch her well," said he, "for I promise you will not have so easy a task this time as you have had before."

Then he went away, and the four comrades set themselves to watch. But again all happened as it had before. In spite of themselves they could not stay awake. First they nodded and then they snored, and then they fell into such a deep sleep that if the walls had fallen about them they would not have known it. For this was an enchanted sleep that the Magician had thrown upon them in order to take away the Princess.

Not until day began to dawn did the four awake, and when they did there was nothing to be seen of the Princess.

"Well, she is not here in the room," said Sharpsight, "so methinks I'd better look outside."

Then he leaned from the window, and for a long time he looked about him. At last he spoke. "Master, I see the Princess, but to bring her back will not be such an easy task as it was before. Three hundred miles from here is a sea. At the bottom of the sea is a shell. In that shell is a pearl, and that pearl is the Princess. But to bring that pearl up from the sea is a task for Broad as well as Long."

"Very well," said the Prince, "then Long must take Broad with him on one shoulder. Only make haste and return again quickly, in heaven's name, or the Magician may be here before you are back, and we shall be turned into stone."

Well, the three servants were willing enough to be off. Long stretched himself out until he was three times as tall as he had been the first time, and that was the most he could stretch. Then he went away, thirty miles at a step. At that rate it was no time before he came to the sea. But the sea was fathoms deep, and the shell lay at the very bottom of it, and try as he might he could not reach it.

"Now it is my turn," said Broad. Then he lay down and put his mouth to the sea and began to drink. He drank and drank and swelled and swelled until it was wonderful to see him, and in the end he swallowed so much of the water that it was easy enough for Long to reach down and pick up the shell.

"And now we must make haste," cried Sharpsight, "for as I look back at the castle I see that the Magician is already waking."

At once Long took his companions on his shoulders and started back the way he had come. But Broad had drunk so much water and was so heavy that Long could not go as fast as he otherwise would. "Broad, you will have to wait here, and I will come back for you later," he cried, and with that he threw Broad down from his shoulder as though he had been a sack full of grain.

Broad had not been expecting such a fall and was not prepared for it. He gasped and choked, and then the sea he had swallowed rose all about them; it filled the valley and washed up over the foot of the mountains. Long was so tall that he was able to wade out of it, though the water was up to his waist, and Sharpsight too was safe, for he was on Long's shoulder; but Broad was like to have been drowned. He only saved himself by catching hold of Long's hand, and so he was drawn out of the water and up on dry land.

"That was a pretty trick to play upon me," he gasped and spluttered.

But Long had no time to answer him, for already Sharpsight was whispering in his ear that the Magician had awakened and was now on his way to the Prince. He caught Broad by the belt and swung him up on his shoulder, and this he could easily do, because now Broad was so shrunken that he was quite light.

In two more steps Long had reached the castle, but already the Magician was opening the door of the chamber where the Prince was.

"Quick! Quick!" cried Sharpsight. "Throw the pearl in at the window."

And indeed there was no time to be lost. Long threw the pearl in through the window, and the moment it touched the floor it turned into the Princess. She stood there before the Prince, no longer pale and sad, but smiling and as rosy as the dawn.

Already the Magician was in the room, with an evil smile upon his face. When he saw the Princess standing there he gave a cry so loud and terrible that the whole castle shook with it. And now the third iron band that was about his waist broke.

At once the black velvet robe that had been held about him by the bands rose and spread into two great black wings. His eyes shrank, his nose grew long and sharp, and instead of the Magician there was a great black raven in the room with them. Heavily flapping, it rose from the ground. Three times round the room it flew, croaking mournfully, and then out through the window.

And now through all the castle arose a stir and hum of life. The stone figures in the hall stirred and looked about them, and stepped down, no longer cold dead stone, but living, breathing people. They were those who had come to the castle to search for the Princess, and had been bewitched by the Magician and turned into statues; the evil charm was broken, and they were alive once more.

When they found that it was the Prince and his followers who had delivered them they did not know how to thank them enough. They could not even grudge the Princess to the Prince, for it was he who had brought them back to life. They all said they would return with the Prince to his own country, so as to be at the wedding when he was married to the Princess.

And what a wedding it was! There was enough cake and ale for all to feast to their hearts' content.

The old King was so happy that he at once made over the kingdom to his son, that he and his bride might reign.

As for the three companions, they ate and drank till they were full, and then they set out into the world again. The Prince begged and entreated them to stay with him, but they would not. They were too fond of travelling about the world, and for all I know they may be in some corner of it still.

The Trade that No One Knows

A LONG WHILE AGO there lived a poor old couple, who had an only son. The old man and his wife worked very hard to nourish their child well and bring him up properly, hoping that he, in return, would take care of them in their old age.

When, however, the boy had grown up, he said to his parents, "I am a man now, and I intend to marry, so I wish you to go at once to the king and ask him to give me his daughter for wife." The astonished parents rebuked him, saying, "What can you be thinking of? We have only this poor hut to shelter us, and hardly bread enough to eat, and we dare not presume to go into the king's presence, much less can we venture to ask for his daughter to be your wife."

The son, however, insisted that they should do as he said, threatening that if they did not comply with his wishes he would leave them, and go away into the world. Seeing that he was really in earnest in what he said, the unhappy parents promised him they would go and ask for the king's daughter. Then the old mother made a wedding cake in her son's presence, and, when it was ready, she put it in a bag, took her staff in her hand, and went straight to the palace where the king lived. There the king's servants bade her come in, and led her into the hall where his Majesty was accustomed to receive the poor people who came to ask alms or to present petitions.

The poor old woman stood in the hall, confused and ashamed at her worn-out, shabby clothes, and looking as if she were made of stone, until the king said to her kindly, "What do *you* want from me, old mother?"

She dared not, however, tell his Majesty why she had come, so she stammered out in her confusion, "Nothing, your Majesty."

Then the king smiled a little and said, "Perhaps you come to ask alms?"

Then the old woman, much abashed, replied, "Yes, your Majesty, if you please!"

Thereupon the king called his servants and ordered them to give the old woman ten crowns, which they did. Having received this money, she thanked his Majesty, and returned home, saying to herself, "I dare say when my son sees all this money he will not think any more of going away from us."

In this thought, however, she was quite mistaken, for no sooner had she entered the hut than the son came to her and asked impatiently, "Well, Mother, have you done as I asked you?"

At this she exclaimed, "Do give up, once for all, this silly fancy, my son. How could you expect me to ask the king for his daughter to be your wife? That would be a bold thing for a rich nobleman to do, how then can *we* think of such a thing? Anyhow, *I* dared not say one word to the king about it. But only look what a lot of money I have brought back. Now you can look for a wife suitable for you, and then you will forget the king's daughter."

When the young man heard his mother speak thus, he grew very angry, and said to her, "What do I want with the king's money? I don't want his money, but I *do* want his daughter! I see you are only playing with me, so I shall leave you. I will go away somewhere – anywhere – wherever my eyes lead me."

Then the poor old parents prayed and begged him not to go away from them, and leave them alone in their old age; but they could only quiet him by promising faithfully that the mother should go again next day to the king, and this time really ask him to give his daughter to her son for a wife.

In the morning, therefore, the old woman went again to the palace, and the servants showed her into the same hall she had been in before. The king, seeing her stand there, inquired, "What want you, my old woman, now?"

She was, however, so ashamed that she could hardly stammer, "Nothing, please, your Majesty."

The king, supposing that she came again to beg, ordered his servants to give her this time also ten crowns.

With this money the poor woman returned to her hut, where her son met her, asking, "Well, Mother, *this* time I hope you have done what I asked you?" But she replied, "Now, my dear son, do leave the king's daughter in peace. How can you really think of such a thing? Even if she would marry you, where is the house to bring her to? So be quiet, and take this money which I have brought you."

At these words the son was more angry than before, and said sharply, "As I see you will not let me marry the king's daughter, I will leave you this moment and never come back again"; and, rushing out of the hut, he ran away. His parents hurried after him, and at length prevailed on him to return, by swearing to him that his mother should go again to the king next morning and really and in truth ask his Majesty this time for his daughter.

So the young man agreed to go back home and wait until the next day.

On the morrow the old woman, with a heavy heart, went to the palace, and was shown as before into the king's presence. Seeing her there for the third time, his Majesty asked her impatiently, "What do you want this time, old woman?" And she, trembling all over, said, "Please, your Majesty – nothing." Then the king exclaimed, "But it cannot be nothing. Something you must want, so tell me the truth at once, if you value your life!" Thereupon the old woman was forced to tell all the story to the king; how her son had a great desire to marry the princess, and so had forced her to come and ask the king to give her to him for wife.

When the king had heard everything, he said, "Well, after all, *I* shall say nothing against it if my daughter will consent to it." He then told his servants to lead the princess into his presence. When she came he told her all about the affair, and asked her, "Are you willing to marry the son of this old woman?"

The princess answered, "Why not? If only he learns first the trade that no one knows!" Thereupon the king bade his attendants give money to the poor woman, who now went back to her hut with a light heart.

The moment she entered, her son asked her, "Have you engaged her?" And she returned, "Do let me get my breath a little! Well, *now* I have really asked the king; but it is of no use, for the princess declares she will not marry you until you have learnt the trade that no one knows!"

"Oh, that matters nothing!" exclaimed the son. "Now I only know the condition, it's all right!" The next morning the young man set out on his travels through the world in search of a man who could teach him the trade that no one knows. He wandered about a long time without being able to find out where he could learn such a trade. At length one day, being quite tired out with walking and very sad, he sat down on a fallen log by the wayside. After he had sat thus a little while, an old woman came up to him, and asked, "Why art thou so sad, my son?" And he answered, "What is the use of your asking, when you cannot help me?" But, she continued, "Only tell me what is the matter, and perhaps I can help you." Then he said, "Well, if you must know, the matter is this: I have been travelling about the world a long time to find a master who can teach me the trade which no one knows." "Oh, if it is only that," cried the old woman, "just listen to me! Don't be afraid, but go straight into the forest which lies before you, and there you will find what you want."

The young man was very glad to hear this, and got up at once and went to the forest. When he had gone pretty far in the wood, he saw a large castle, and, whilst he stood looking at it and wondering what it was, four giants came out of it and ran up to him, shouting, "Do you wish to learn the trade that no one knows?" He said, "Yes; that is just the reason why I come here." Whereupon they took him into the castle.

Next morning the giants prepared to go out hunting, and, before leaving, they said to him, "You must on no account go into the first room by the dining-hall." Hardly, however, were the giants well out of sight before the young man began to reason thus with himself: "I see very well that I have come into a place from which I shall never go out alive with my head, so I may as well see what is in the room, come what may afterwards." So he went and opened the door a little and peeped in. There stood a golden ass, bound to a golden manger. He looked at it a little, and was just going to shut the door when the ass said, "Come and take the halter from my head, and keep it hidden about you. It will serve you well if you only understand how to use it." So he took the halter, and, after fastening the room door, quickly concealed it under his clothes. He had not sat very long before the giants came home. They asked him at once if he had been in the first room, and he, much frightened, replied, "No, I have not been in." "But we know that you have been!" said the giants in great anger, and, seizing some large sticks, they beat him so severely that he could hardly stand on his feet. It was very lucky for him that he had the halter wound round his body under his clothes, or else he would certainly have been killed.

The next day the giants again prepared to go out hunting, but before leaving him they ordered him on no account to enter the second room.

Almost as soon as the giants had gone away he became so very curious to see what might be in the second room, that he could not resist going to the door. He stood there a little, thinking within himself, "Well, I am already more dead than alive, much worse cannot happen to me!" and so he opened the door and looked in. There he was surprised to see a very beautiful girl, dressed all in gold and silver, who sat combing her hair, and setting in every tress a large diamond. He stood admiring her a little while, and was just going to shut the door again, when she spoke: "Wait a minute, young man. Come and take this key, and mind you keep it safely. It will serve you some time, if you only know how to use it." So he went in and took the key from the girl, and then, going out, fastened the door and went and sat down in the same place he had sat before.

He had not remained there very long before the giants came home from hunting. The moment they entered the house they took up their large sticks to beat him, asking, at the same time, whether he had been in the second room.

Shaking all over with fear, he answered them, "No, I have not!"

"But we know that you have been," shouted the giants in great anger, and they then beat him worse than on the first day.

The next morning, as the giants went out as usual to hunt, they said to him, "Do not go into the third room, for anything in the world; for if you do go in we shall not forgive you as we did yesterday, and the day before! We shall kill you outright!" No sooner, however, had the giants gone out of sight, than the young man began to say to himself, "Most likely they will kill me, whether I go into the room or not. Besides, if they do not kill me, they have beaten me so badly already that I am sure I cannot live long, so, anyhow, I will go and see what is in the third room." Then he got up and went and opened the door.

He was quite shocked, however, when he saw that the room was full of human heads! These heads belonged to young men who had come, like himself, to learn the trade that no one knows, and who, not having obeyed faithfully and strictly the orders of the giants, had been killed by them.

The young man was turning quickly to go away, when one of the heads called out, "Don't be afraid, but come in!" Thereupon he went into the room. Then the head gave him an iron chain, and said, "Take care of this chain, for it will serve you some time if you know how to use it!" So he took the chain, and going out fastened the door.

He went and sat down in the usual place to wait for the coming home of the giants, and, as he waited, he grew quite frightened, for he fully expected that they would really kill him this time.

The instant the giants came home they took up their thick sticks and began to beat him without stopping to ask anything. They beat him so terribly that he was all but dead; then they threw him out of the house, saying to him, "Go away now, since you have learnt the trade that no one knows!" When he had lain a long time on the ground where they had thrown him, feeling very sore and miserable, at length he tried to move away, saying to himself, "Well, if they really have taught me the trade that no one knows, for the sake of the king's daughter I can suffer gladly all this pain, if I can only win her!"

After travelling for a long time, the young man came at last to the palace of the king whose daughter he wished to marry. When he saw the palace, he was exceedingly sad, and remembered the words of the princess; for, after all his wanderings and sufferings, he had learnt no trade, and had never been able to find what trade it was "that no one knows." Whilst considering what he had better do, he suddenly recollected the halter, the key, and the iron chain, which he had carried concealed about him ever since he left the castle of the four giants. He then said to himself, "Let me see what these things can do!" So he took the halter and struck the earth with it, and immediately a handsome horse, beautifully caparisoned, stood before him. Then he struck the ground with the iron chain, and instantly a hare and a greyhound appeared, and the hare began to run quickly and the greyhound to follow her. In a moment the young man hardly knew himself, for he found himself in a fine hunting-dress, riding on the horse after the hare, which took a path that passed immediately under the windows of the king's palace.

Now, it happened that the king stood at a window looking out, and noticed at once the beautiful greyhound which was chasing the hare, and the very handsome horse which a huntsman in a splendid dress was mounted on. The king was so pleased with the appearance of the horse and the greyhound, that he called instantly some of his servants, and, sending them after the strange rider, bade them invite him to come to the palace. The young man, however, hearing some people coming behind him calling and shouting, rode quickly behind a thick bush, and shook a little the halter and the iron chain. In a moment the horse, the greyhound, and the hare had vanished, and he found himself sitting on the ground under the trees dressed in his old shabby clothes. By this time the king's servants had come up, and, seeing him sitting there, they asked him whether he had seen a fine huntsman on a beautiful horse pass that way. But he answered them rudely, "No! I have not seen anyone pass, neither do I care to look to see who passes!"

Then the king's servants went on and searched the forest, calling and shouting as loudly as they could, but it was all in vain; they could neither see nor hear anything of the hunter. At length they went back to the king, and told him that the horse the huntsman rode was so exceedingly quick that they could not hear anything of him in the forest.

The young man now resolved to go to the hut where his old parents lived; and they were glad to see that he had come back to them once more.

Next morning, the son said to his father, "Now, father, I will show you what I have learned. I will change myself into a beautiful horse, and you must lead me into the city and sell me, but be very careful not to give away the halter, or else I shall remain always a horse!" Accordingly, in a moment he changed himself into a horse of extraordinary beauty, and the father took him to the market-place to sell him. Very soon a great number of people gathered round the horses wondering at his unusual beauty, and very high prices were offered for him; the old man, however, raised the price higher and higher at every offer.

The news spread quickly about the city that a wonderfully handsome horse was for sale in the market-place, and at length the king himself heard of it, and sent some servants to bring the horse, that he might see it. The old man led the horse at once before the palace, and the king, after looking at it for some time with great admiration, could not help exclaiming, "By my word, though I am a king, I never yet saw, much less rode, so handsome a horse!" Then he asked the old man if he would sell it him. "I will sell it to your Majesty, very willingly," said the old man; "but I will sell only the horse, and not the halter." Thereupon the king laughed, saying, "What should I want with your dirty halter? For such a horse I will have a halter of gold made!" So the horse was sold to the king for a very high price, and the old man returned home with the money.

Next morning, however, there was a great stir and much consternation in the royal stables, for the beautiful horse had vanished somehow during the night. And at the time when the horse disappeared, the young man returned to his parents' hut.

A day or two afterwards the young man said to his father, "Now I will turn myself into a fine church not far from the king's palace, and if the king wishes to buy it you may sell it him, only be sure not to part with the key or else I must remain always a church!"

When the king got up that morning and went to his window to look out, he saw a beautiful church which he had never noticed before. Then he sent his servants out to see what it was, and soon after they came back saying, that "the church belonged to an old pilgrim, who told them that he was willing to sell it if the king wished to buy it." Then the king sent to ask what price he would sell it for, and the pilgrim replied, "It is worth a great deal of money."

Whilst the servants were bargaining with the father an old woman came up. Now this was the same old woman who had sent the young man to the castle of the four giants, and she herself had been there and had learnt the trade that no one knew. As she understood at once all about the church, and had no mind to have a rival in the trade, she resolved to put an end to the young man. For this purpose she began to outbid the king, and offered, at last, so very large a sum of ready money, that the old man was quite astonished and confused at seeing the money which she showed him. He accordingly accepted her offer, but whilst he was counting the money, quite forgot about the key. Before long, however, he recollected what his son had said, and then, fearing some mischief, he ran after the old woman and demanded the key back. But the old woman could not be persuaded to give back the key, and said it belonged to the church which she had bought and paid for. Seeing she would not give up the key, the old man grew more and more alarmed, lest some ill should befall his son, so he took hold of the old woman by the neck and forced her to drop the key. She struggled very hard to get it back again, and, whilst the old man and she wrestled together, the key changed itself suddenly into a dove and flew away high in the air over the palace gardens.

When the old woman saw this, she changed herself into a hawk and chased the dove. Just, however, as the hawk was about to pounce upon it, the dove turned itself into a beautiful bouquet, and dropped down into the hand of the king's daughter who happened to be walking in the garden. Then the hawk changed again into the old woman, who went to the gate of the palace and begged very hard that the princess would give her that bouquet, or, at least, one single flower from it.

But the princess said, "No! Not for anything in the world. These flowers fell to me from heaven!" The old woman, however, was determined to get one flower from the bouquet, so, seeing the princess would not hear her, she went straight to the king, and begged piteously that he would order his daughter to give her one of the flowers from her bouquet. The king, thinking the old woman wanted one of the flowers to cure some disease, called his daughter to him, and told her to give one to the beggar.

But just as the king said this, the bouquet changed itself into a heap of millet-seed and scattered itself all over the ground. Then the old woman quickly changed herself into a hen and chickens, and began greedily to pick up the seeds. Suddenly, however, the millet vanished, and in its place appeared a fox, which sprang on the hen and killed her.

Then the fox changed into the young man, who explained to the astonished king and princess that he it was who had demanded the hand of the princess, and that, in order to obtain it, he had wandered all over the world in search of someone who could teach him "the trade that no one knows."

When the king and his daughter heard this, they gladly fulfilled their part of the bargain, seeing how well the young man had fulfilled his.

Then, shortly afterwards, the king's daughter married the son of the poor old couple; and the king built for the princess and her husband a palace close to his own. There they lived long and had plenty of children, and people say that some of their descendants are living at present, and that they go constantly to pray in the church, which is always open because the key of it turned itself into a young man who married the king's daughter after he had shown to her that he had done as she wished, and learnt, for her sake, "the trade that no one knows."

The Three Kingdoms: The Copper, the Silver and the Golden

IN A CERTAIN KINGDOM in a certain land lived a Tsar, – Bail Bailyanyin. He had a wife, Nastasya, Golden Tress, and three sons, – Pyotr Tsarevich, Vassili Tsarevich, and Ivan Tsarevich. The Tsaritsa went with her maidens and nurses to walk in the garden. All at once such a mighty Whirlwind rose that, God save us! it caught the Tsaritsa and bore her it was unknown whither.

The Tsar was grieved and distressed, and knew not what to do. His sons grew up, and he said to them: "My dear children, which of you will go to seek your mother?"

The two elder brothers made ready and went. After they had gone, the youngest begged permission of his father. "No," said the Tsar, "go not, my dear son; do not leave me an old man in loneliness."

"Let me go, father; I want awfully to wander over the white world and find my mother."

The Tsar dissuaded and dissuaded, but could not convince him. "Well, there is no help for it, go; God be with thee!"

Ivan saddled his good steed and set out. He rode and rode, whether it was long or short: a tale is soon told, but a deed is not soon done; he came to a forest. In that forest was the richest of castles. Ivan Tsarevich entered a broad court, saw an old man, and said, "Many years' health to thee!"

"We beg the favour of thy presence. Who art thou, gallant youth?"

"I am Ivan Tsarevich, the son of Tsar Bail Bailyanyin and of Tsaritsa Nastasya, Golden Tress."

"Oh, my own nephew! Whither is God bearing thee?"

"For this cause and that," said he, "I am in search of my mother. Canst thou not tell me, Uncle, where to find her?"

"No, nephew, I cannot; with what I am able, with that I do service. But here is a ball; throw it ahead, it will roll on before thee and lead thee to steep, rugged mountains. In those mountains is a cave, enter it; take there iron claws, put them on thy hands and thy feet, and climb up the mountains. Perhaps thou wilt find there thy mother, Nastasya, Golden Tress."

That was good aid. Ivan Tsarevich took leave of his uncle, and threw the ball before him; the ball rolled and rolled on, he rode behind it. Whether it was long or short, he saw his brothers, Pyotr Tsarevich and Vassili Tsarevich. They were encamped in the open field with thousands of troops. His brothers were surprised, and asked, "Where art thou going, Ivan Tsarevich?"

"Oh!" said he, "I grew weary at home, and I thought of going to look for my mother. Send your army home, and let us go on together."

They sent home the army, and the three went on together after the ball. While yet at a distance they saw the mountains, – such steep and lofty mountains that, God save us! they touched the heavens with their heads. The ball rolled straight to a cave. Ivan Tsarevich slipped down from his horse and said to his brothers, "Here, brothers, is my good steed; I will go up on the mountains to look for my mother, and ye remain here. Wait for me just three months. If I am not here in three months, there will be no use in waiting longer."

The brothers thought, but how could a man climb these mountains? He would break his head there.

"Well," said they, "go, with God; we will wait for thee here."

Ivan approached the cave; he saw that the door was of iron. He struck it with all his strength. It opened, he entered; iron claws went on to his feet and hands of themselves. He began to climb the mountains, – climb, climb; he toiled a whole month, reaching the top with difficulty. "Well," said he, "glory be to God!" He rested a little, and walked along on the mountain; walked and walked, walked and walked, saw a copper castle, at the gate terrible serpents fastened with copper chains, crowds of them; and right there was a well, and at the well a copper bucket hung by a copper chain. Ivan Tsarevich drew water and gave the serpents to drink. They became quiet, lay down, and he passed into the court.

The Tsaritsa of the Copper Kingdom ran out to meet him. "Who art thou, gallant youth?"

"I am Ivan Tsarevich."

"Well, hast thou come of thy own will, or against thy will?"

"Of my own will; I am in search of my mother, Nastasya, Golden Tress. A certain Whirlwind bore her away out of the garden. Dost thou know where she is?"

"No; but not far from here lives my second sister, the Tsaritsa of the Silver Kingdom, – maybe she will tell thee."

She gave him a copper ball and a copper ring. "The ball," said she, "will lead thee to my second sister, and in this ring is the whole Copper Kingdom. When thou overcomest Whirlwind, who keeps me here and flies to me once in three months, forget me not, poor woman, rescue me from this place, and take me with thee to the free world."

"I will," said Ivan Tsarevich. He threw the copper ball before him; the ball rolled ahead, and he followed after. He came to the Silver Kingdom and saw a castle finer than the first, all silver; at the gate were terrible serpents fastened to silver chains, and at the side of them was a well with a silver bucket. Ivan Tsarevich drew water and gave the serpents to drink. They lay down then, and let him enter the castle. The Tsaritsa of the Silver Kingdom came out.

"It will soon be three years," said she, "since mighty Whirlwind confined me here, and no Russian have I heard with hearing, or seen with sight; but now a Russian I see. Who art thou, good youth?"

"I am Ivan Tsarevich."

"How didst thou happen hither, – with thy own will, or against thy will?"

"With my own will; I am in search of my mother. She went in the green garden to walk, Whirlwind came and bore her away, it is unknown whither. Canst thou not tell me where to find her?"

"No, I cannot; but not far from here lives my eldest sister, the Tsaritsa of the Golden Kingdom, Yelena the Beautiful, – maybe she will tell thee. Here is a silver ball, roll it ahead and follow; it will lead thee to the Golden Kingdom. But see, when thou hast killed Whirlwind, forget me not, poor woman; rescue me from this place, and take me to the free world. Whirlwind holds me captive, and flies hither once in two months." Then she gave him a silver ring, saying, "In this ring is the whole Silver Kingdom."

Ivan rolled the ball; wherever it went he followed. Whether it was long or short, he saw a golden castle gleaming like fire; at the gate was a crowd of terrible serpents fastened to golden chains, and right there a well, at the well a golden bucket on a golden chain. Ivan

Tsarevich drew water, and gave the serpents to drink; they lay down and were soothed. He entered the palace; Yelena the Beautiful met him.

"Who art thou, gallant youth?"

"I am Ivan Tsarevich."

"How hast thou come hither, – of thy own will, or against thy will?"

"I came of my own will; I am in search of my mother, Nastasya, Golden Tress. Knowest thou not where to find her?"

"Why shouldn't I know? She lives not far from here, Whirlwind flies to her once a week, and to me once a month. Here is a golden ball for thee: throw it ahead and follow, – it will lead thee to thy mother. And take besides this golden ring; in this ring is the whole Golden Kingdom. And be careful when thou hast conquered Whirlwind. Forget me not, poor woman; take me with thee to the free world."

"I will take thee," said he.

Ivan Tsarevich rolled the ball and followed after; he went and went till he came to such a palace that, Lord save us! it was just blazing with diamonds and precious stones. At the gate six-headed serpents were hissing. Ivan Tsarevich gave them to drink; the serpents were soothed, and let him pass to the castle. He went through the great chambers, and in the most distant found his own mother. She was sitting on a lofty throne arrayed in Tsaritsa's robes and crowned with a costly crown. She looked at the stranger and cried: "Ah! Is that thou, my dear son? How hast thou come hither?"

"So and so," said Ivan; "I have come for thee."

"Well, dear son, 'twill be hard for thee. Here in these mountains reigns Whirlwind, the evil and mighty, all spirits obey him; he is the one that bore me away. Thou wilt have to fight him; come quickly to the cellar."

They went to the cellar; there were two tubs of water, one on the right, the other on the left hand. "Drink," said the Tsaritsa, "from the right-hand tub."

Ivan drank.

"Well, what strength is in thee?"

"I am so strong that I could turn the whole castle over with one hand."

"Then drink more."

Ivan drank again.

"What strength is in thee now?"

"If I wished, I could turn the whole world over."

"That is very great strength. Move these tubs from one place to the other: put that on the right to the left, that on the left take to the right."

Ivan interchanged the tubs.

"Thou seest, my dear son, in one tub is water of strength, in the other water of weakness. Whoso drinks from the first will be a strong, mighty hero; whoso drinks from the second will grow weak altogether. Whirlwind always drinks the water of strength and puts it on the right side; so we must deceive him, or thou canst never overcome him."

They returned to the castle.

"Soon Whirlwind will fly home," said the Tsaritsa to Ivan Tsarevich. "Sit under my purple robe, so that he may not see thee; and when he comes and runs to embrace and kiss me, do thou seize his club. He will rise high, high; he will bear thee over seas, over precipices: but see to it, let not the club go out of thy hand. Whirlwind will grow tired, will want to drink the water of strength, will come down to the cellar and rush to the tub placed on the right hand; but do thou drink from the tub on the left. Then he will grow weak; wrest his sword from him, and with one blow hew off his head. When his head is off, that moment there will be voices behind thee crying, 'Strike again, strike again.' Strike not, my son, but say in answer, 'A hero's hand strikes not twice, but always once.'"

Ivan Tsarevich had barely hidden under the robe when the court grew dark and everything trembled. Whirlwind flew home, struck the earth, became a brave hero, and entered the castle, in his hands a club.

"Tfu, tfu, tfu! Somehow it smells of Russia here. Was anyone visiting?"

"I don't know why it seems so to thee," said the Tsaritsa.

Whirlwind rushed to embrace her; but Ivan that moment seized the club.

"I'll eat thee!" shouted Whirlwind.

"Well, grandmother spoke double; either thou wilt eat, or thou wilt not."

Whirlwind tore out through the window and up to the sky; he bore Ivan Tsarevich away. Over mountains he said, "I will smash thee"; over seas he said, "I will drown thee." But Ivan did not let the club out of his hands. Whirlwind flew over the whole world, wearied himself out, and began to sink. He came down straight into the cellar, rushed to the tub on the right hand, and fell to drinking the water of weakness; but Ivan ran to the left, drank his fill of the water of strength, and became the first mighty hero in the whole world. He saw that Whirlwind had become utterly weak, wrested the sharp sword from him, and cut off his head with a blow. Voices cried behind, "Strike again, strike again, or he will come to life!" "No," said Ivan; "a hero's hand strikes not twice, but always finishes at a blow." Straightway he made a fire, burned the body and the head, scattered the ashes to the wind.

The mother of Ivan Tsarevich was glad. "Now, my dear son," said she, "let us rejoice. We will eat; and then for home with all speed, for it is wearisome here, – there are no people."

"But who serves thee?"

"Thou wilt see directly."

They had barely thought of eating, when a table set itself, and various meats and wines appeared on the table of themselves. The Tsaritsa and the Tsarevich dined. Meanwhile unseen musicians played wonderful songs for them. They ate and drank, and when they had rested, Ivan said, –

"Let us go, mother, it is time; for under the mountains my brothers are waiting. And on the road I must save three Tsaritsas who are living in Whirlwind's castles."

They took everything needful and set out on the journey. They went first to the Tsaritsa of the Golden Kingdom, then to her sisters of the Silver and Copper Kingdoms. They took them, and brought linen and all kinds of stuffs. In a short time they reached the place where they had to go down the mountain.

Ivan Tsarevich let his mother down first on the linen, then Yelena the Beautiful and her two sisters. The brothers were standing below waiting, and they thought to themselves, "Let us leave Ivan Tsarevich up there; we will take our mother and the three Tsaritsas to our father, and say that we found them." "I'll take Yelena the Beautiful for myself," said Pyotr Tsarevich; "thou, Vassili, wilt have the Tsaritsa of the Silver Kingdom; and we will give the Tsaritsa of the Copper Kingdom to some general."

When it was time for Ivan Tsarevich to come down from the mountain, his elder brothers seized the linen, pulled and tore it away. Ivan remained on the mountain. What could he do? He wept bitterly; then turned back, walked and walked over the Copper Kingdom, over the Silver Kingdom and the Golden Kingdom, – not a soul did he see. He came to the Diamond Kingdom, – no one there either. What was he to do alone, – deathly weariness! He looked around; on the window of the castle a whistle was lying. He took it in his hand. "Let me play from weariness," said he. He had barely blown when out sprang Lame and Crooked.

"What is thy pleasure?"

Said Ivan Tsarevich, "I want to eat." That moment, from wherever it came, a table was set, and on the table the very best food. Ivan Tsarevich ate and thought, "Now it would not be bad to rest." He blew on the whistle. Lame and Crooked appeared.

"What is thy pleasure, Ivan Tsarevich?"

"That a bed be ready." The word wasn't out of his mouth when the bed was ready. He lay down, slept splendidly, then whistled again.

"What is thy pleasure?" asked Lame and Crooked.

"Everything can be done, then?"

"Everything is possible, Ivan Tsarevich. Whoever blows that whistle, we will do everything for him. As we served Whirlwind before, so we are glad to serve thee now; it is only necessary to keep the whistle by thee at all times."

"Well," said Ivan, "let me be in my own kingdom this minute."

He had barely spoken when he appeared in his own kingdom, in the middle of the market square. He was walking along the square, when a shoemaker came toward him, – such a jolly fellow! The Tsarevich asked: "Whither art thou going, good man?"

"I am taking shoes to sell; I am a shoemaker."

"Take me into thy service," said Ivan.

"Dost thou know how to make shoes?"

"Yes, I can do everything. I can make not only shoes, but clothes."

"Well, come on."

They went to his house. The shoemaker said: "Go to work; here is leather for thee, – the best kind; I'll see what skill thou hast."

Ivan Tsarevich went to his own room, and took out the whistle. Lame and Crooked came. "What is thy pleasure, Ivan Tsarevich?"

"To have shoes ready by tomorrow."

"Oh, that is not work, that is play!"

"Here is the leather."

"What sort of leather is that? That's trash, nothing more; that should go out of the window."

Next morning Ivan Tsarevich woke up; on the table were beautiful shoes, the very best.

The shoemaker rose. "Well, young man, hast thou made the shoes?"

"They are finished."

"Well, show them." He looked at the shoes and was astonished. "See what a man I have got for myself, – not a shoemaker, but a wonder!" He took the shoes and carried them to the market to sell.

At that same time three weddings were in preparation at the palace. Pyotr Tsarevich was to marry Yelena the Beautiful, Vassili Tsarevich the Tsaritsa of the Silver Kingdom, and they were giving the Tsaritsa of the Copper Kingdom to a general. They were making dresses for those weddings. Yelena the Beautiful wanted shoes. Our shoemaker's shoes were better than all the others brought to the palace.

When Yelena looked at them she said, "What does this mean? They make shoes like these only in the mountains." She paid the shoemaker a large price and said, "Make me without measure another pair wonderfully sewed, ornamented with precious stones, and studded with diamonds. They must be ready by tomorrow; if not, to the gallows with thee."

The shoemaker took the precious stones and money and went home, – such a gloomy man! "Misery," said he, "what am I to do now? How can I make shoes by tomorrow, and besides without measure? It is clear that they will hang me tomorrow; let me have at least a last frolic with my friends."

He went to the inn. These friends of his were numerous; they asked, "Why art thou so gloomy, brother?"

"Oh, my dear friends," answered he, "they are going to hang me tomorrow!"

"Why so?"

The shoemaker told his trouble. "How think of work in such a position? Better I'll frolic tonight for the last time."

So they drank and drank, frolicked and frolicked; the shoemaker was staggering already.

"Well," said he, "I'll take home a keg of spirits, lie down to sleep; and tomorrow when they come to hang me, I'll drink a gallon and a half right away. Let them hang me without my senses."

He came home. "Well, thou reprobate!" said he to Ivan Tsarevich, "see what thy shoes have done … so and so.… When they come in the morning for me, wake me up."

In the night Ivan Tsarevich took out the whistle and blew. Lame and Crooked appeared. "What is thy pleasure, Ivan Tsarevich?"

"That shoes of such a kind be ready."

"We obey!"

Ivan lay down to sleep. Next morning he woke up; the shoes were on the table shining like fire. He went to rouse his master.

"It is time to rise, master."

"What! Have they come for me? Bring the keg quickly! Here is a cup, pour the spirits in; let them hang me drunk."

"But the shoes are made."

"How made? Where are they?"

The master ran and saw them. "But when did we make them?"

"In the night. Is it possible that thou dost not remember when we cut and sewed?"

"Oh, I've slept so long, brother! I barely, barely remember."

He took the shoes, wrapped them up, and ran to the palace.

Yelena the Beautiful saw the shoes and knew what had happened. "Surely," she thought, "the spirits made these for Ivan Tsarevich. – How didst thou make these?" asked she of the shoemaker.

"Oh! I know how to do everything."

"If that is the case, make me a wedding robe embroidered with gold, ornamented with diamonds and precious stones; let it be ready tomorrow morning: if not, off with thy head!"

The shoemaker went home again gloomy, and his friends were long waiting for him. "Well, what is it?"

"Nothing but cursedness. The destroyer of Christian people has come; she commanded me to make her a robe with gold and precious stones by tomorrow morning: and what sort of a tailor am I? They will take my head surely tomorrow."

"Ah! Brother, the morning is wiser than the evening; let us go and frolic."

They went to the inn, they drank and frolicked; the shoemaker got tipsy again, brought home a whole keg of spirits, and said to Ivan Tsarevich: "Now, young fellow, when thou wilt rouse me in the morning I'll toss off three gallons; let them cut the head off me drunk. I couldn't make such a robe in a lifetime." The shoemaker lay down to sleep and snored.

Ivan Tsarevich blew on the whistle, and Lame and Crooked appeared. "What is thy pleasure, Tsarevich?"

"That a robe be ready by tomorrow morning exactly such as Yelena the Beautiful wore in Whirlwind's house."

"We obey; it will be ready."

Ivan Tsarevich woke at daylight; the robe was on the table, shining like fire, so that the whole chamber was lighted up. Then he roused his master, who rubbed his eyes and asked, "What! Have they come to cut my head off? Give the spirits here this minute."

"But the robe is ready."

"Is that true? When did we make it?"

"In the night, of course; dost thou not remember cutting it thyself?"

"Ah, brother, I just remember, – see it as in a dream!"

The shoemaker took the robe and ran to the palace.

Yelena the Beautiful gave him much money and the command, "See that tomorrow by daylight the Golden Kingdom be on the sea, seven versts from shore, and from it to our palace let there be a golden bridge with costly velvet spread upon it, and at the railings on both sides let wonderful trees be growing, and let there be wonderful songbirds singing, with various voices. If thou wilt not have it done by morning, I'll give orders to quarter thee."

The shoemaker went from Yelena the Beautiful with drooping head. His friends met him. "Well, brother?"

"What well! I am lost; tomorrow I shall be quartered. She gave me such a task that no devil could do it."

"Oh, never mind! The morning is wiser than the evening; let us go to the inn."

"Well, let us go; at the last parting we must have a carousal at least."

They drank and drank; and towards evening the shoemaker drank so much they had to lead him home. "Farewell, young fellow," said he to Ivan; "tomorrow they will put me to death."

"But has a new task been given?"

"Yes, so and so, so and so." He lay down and snored; but Ivan Tsarevich went straight to his room, and blew on the whistle. Lame and Crooked appeared.

"What is thy pleasure, Ivan Tsarevich?"

"Can ye do me such a work as this?"

"Ivan Tsarevich, this is a work indeed. But there is no avoiding it; toward morning all will be ready."

When daylight began to come, Ivan woke up, looked out of the window. Fathers! Everything was ready as asked for. A golden castle was gleaming like fire. He roused his master, who sprang up. "Well, have they come for me? Give the keg here this minute!"

"But the palace is ready."

"What dost thou say?"

The shoemaker looked through the window and said, "Ah!" in astonishment, "how was that done?"

"Dost thou not remember how thou and I fixed it?"

"Yes, it is clear that I have slept too soundly; I barely, barely remember."

They ran to the golden castle; in it was wealth untold, unseen.

Said Ivan Tsarevich: "Here, master, is a wing, go and dust the railing of the bridge; and if they come and ask who lives in the palace, say thou nothing, but give this letter."

"Very well."

The shoemaker went to dust the railing of the bridge.

In the morning Yelena the Beautiful woke up; she saw the golden castle, and ran straight to the Tsar. "See what is done in our place! There is a golden palace on the sea, and from that palace a golden bridge seven versts long; and on both sides of the bridge wonderful trees are growing, and songbirds are singing in various voices."

The Tsar sent immediately to ask what that meant? Had not some hero come to his kingdom? The messengers came to the shoemaker, asked him. "I know not, but there is a letter to thy Tsar." In that letter Ivan Tsarevich related everything to his father as it was, – how he had liberated his mother, won Yelena the Beautiful, and how his elder brothers had deceived him. With the letter Ivan Tsarevich sent golden carriages, and begged the Tsar and Tsaritsa to come to him. Let Yelena the Beautiful and her sisters and his brothers be brought behind in simple wagons.

All assembled at once and started. Ivan Tsarevich met them with joy. The Tsar wished to put his elder sons to death for their untruths; but Ivan Tsarevich implored his father, and they were forgiven. Then began a mountain of a feast. Ivan Tsarevich married Yelena the Beautiful. They gave the Tsaritsa of the Silver Kingdom to Pyotr Tsarevich, the Tsaritsa of the Copper Kingdom to Vassili Tsarevich, and made the shoemaker a general.

Green Willow

TOMODATA, THE YOUNG *SAMURAI*, owed allegiance to the Lord of Noto. He was a soldier, a courtier, and a poet. He had a sweet voice and a beautiful face, a noble form and a very winning address. He was a graceful dancer, and excelled in every manly sport. He was wealthy and generous and kind. He was beloved by rich and by poor.

Now his *daimyo*, the Lord of Noto, wanted a man to undertake a mission of trust. He chose Tomodata, and called him to his presence.

"Are you loyal?" said the *daimyo*.

"My lord, you know it," answered Tomodata.

"Do you love me, then?" asked the *daimyo*.

"Ay, my good lord," said Tomodata, kneeling before him.

"Then carry my message," said the *daimyo*. "Ride and do not spare your beast. Ride straight, and fear not the mountains nor the enemies' country. Stay not for storm nor any other thing. Lose your life; but betray not your trust. Above all, do not look any maid between the eyes. Ride, and bring me word again quickly."

Thus spoke the Lord of Noto.

So Tomodata got him to horse, and away he rode upon his quest. Obedient to his lord's commands, he spared not his good beast. He rode straight, and was not afraid of the steep mountain passes nor of the enemies' country. Ere he had been three days upon the road the autumn tempest burst, for it was the ninth month. Down poured the rain in a torrent. Tomodata bowed his head and rode on. The wind howled in the pine-tree branches. It blew a typhoon. The good horse trembled and could scarcely keep its feet, but Tomodata spoke to it and urged it on. His own cloak he drew close about him and held it so that it might not blow away, and in this wise he rode on.

The fierce storm swept away many a familiar landmark of the road, and buffeted the *samurai* so that he became weary almost to fainting. Noontide was as dark as twilight, twilight was as dark as night, and when night fell it was as black as the night of Yomi, where lost souls wander and cry. By this time Tomodata had lost his way in a wild, lonely place, where, as it seemed to him, no human soul inhabited. His horse could carry him no longer, and he wandered on foot through bogs and marshes, through rocky and thorny tracks, until he fell into deep despair.

"Alack!" he cried, "must I die in this wilderness and the quest of the Lord of Noto be unfulfilled?"

At this moment the great winds blew away the clouds of the sky, so that the moon shone very brightly forth, and by the sudden light Tomodata saw a little hill on his right hand. Upon the hill was a small thatched cottage, and before the cottage grew three green weeping-willow trees.

"Now, indeed, the gods be thanked!" said Tomodata, and he climbed the hill in no time. Light shone from the chinks of the cottage door, and smoke curled out of a hole in the roof. The three willow trees swayed and flung out their green streamers in the wind. Tomodata threw his horse's rein over a branch of one of them, and called for admittance to the longed-for shelter.

At once the cottage door was opened by an old woman, very poorly but neatly clad.

"Who rides abroad upon such a night?" she asked, "and what wills he here?"

"I am a weary traveller, lost and benighted upon your lonely moor. My name is Tomodata. I am a *samurai* in the service of the Lord of Noto, upon whose business I ride. Show me hospitality for the love of the gods. I crave food and shelter for myself and my horse."

As the young man stood speaking the water streamed from his garments. He reeled a little, and put out a hand to hold on by the side-post of the door.

"Come in, come in, young sir!" cried the old woman, full of pity. "Come in to the warm fire. You are very welcome. We have but coarse fare to offer, but it shall be set before you with great goodwill. As to your horse, I see you have delivered him to my daughter; he is in good hands."

At this Tomodata turned sharply round. Just behind him, in the dim light, stood a very young girl with the horse's rein thrown over her arm. Her garments were blown about and her long loose hair streamed out upon the wind. The *samurai* wondered how she had come there. Then the old woman drew him into the cottage and shut the door. Before the fire sat the good man of the house, and the two old people did the very best they could for Tomodata. They gave him dry garments, comforted him with hot rice wine, and quickly prepared a good supper for him.

Presently the daughter of the house came in, and retired behind a screen to comb her hair and to dress afresh. Then she came forth to wait upon him. She wore a blue robe of homespun cotton. Her feet were bare. Her hair was not tied nor confined in any way, but lay along her smooth cheeks, and hung, straight and long and black, to her very knees. She was slender and graceful. Tomodata judged her to be about fifteen years old, and knew well that she was the fairest maiden he had ever seen.

At length she knelt at his side to pour wine into his cup. She held the wine-bottle in two hands and bent her head. Tomodata turned to look at her. When she had made an end of pouring the wine and had set down the bottle, their glances met, and Tomodata looked at her full between the eyes, for he forgot altogether the warning of his *daimyo*, the Lord of Noto.

"Maiden," he said, "what is your name?"

She answered: "They call me the Green Willow."

"The dearest name on earth," he said, and again he looked her between the eyes. And because he looked so long her face grew rosy red, from chin to forehead, and though she smiled her eyes filled with tears.

Ah me, for the Lord of Noto's quest!

Then Tomodata made this little song:

"Long-haired maiden, do you know
That with the red dawn I must go?
Do you wish me far away?
Cruel long-haired maiden, say –
Long-haired maiden, if you know
That with the red dawn I must go,
Why, oh why, do you blush so?"

And the maiden, the Green Willow, answered:

"The dawn comes if I will or no;
Never leave me, never go.
My sleeve shall hide the blush away.
The dawn comes if I will or no;
Never leave me, never go.
Lord, I lift my long sleeve so...."

"Oh, Green Willow, Green Willow..." sighed Tomodata.

That night he lay before the fire – still, but with wide eyes, for no sleep came to him though he was weary. He was sick for love of the Green Willow. Yet by the rules of his service he was bound in honour to think of no such thing. Moreover, he had the quest of the Lord of Noto that lay heavy on his heart, and he longed to keep truth and loyalty.

At the first peep of day he rose up. He looked upon the kind old man who had been his host, and left a purse of gold at his side as he slept. The maiden and her mother lay behind the screen.

Tomodata saddled and bridled his horse, and mounting, rode slowly away through the mist of the early morning. The storm was quite over and it was as still as Paradise. The green grass and the leaves shone with the wet. The sky was clear, and the path very bright with autumn flowers; but Tomodata was sad.

When the sunlight streamed across his saddlebow, "Ah, Green Willow, Green Willow," he sighed; and at noontide it was "Green Willow, Green Willow"; and "Green Willow, Green Willow," when the twilight fell. That night he lay in a deserted shrine, and the place was so holy that in spite of all he slept from midnight till the dawn. Then he rose, having it in his mind to wash himself in a cold stream that flowed nearby, so as to go refreshed upon his journey; but he was stopped upon the shrine's threshold. There lay the Green Willow, prone upon the ground. A slender thing she lay, face downwards, with her black hair flung about her. She lifted a hand and held Tomodata by the sleeve. "My lord, my lord," she said, and fell to sobbing piteously.

He took her in his arms without a word, and soon he set her on his horse before him, and together they rode the livelong day. It was little they recked of the road they went, for all the while they looked into each other's eyes. The heat and the cold were nothing to them. They felt not the sun nor the rain; of truth or falsehood they thought nothing at all; nor of filial piety, nor of the Lord of Noto's quest, nor of honour nor plighted word. They knew but the one thing. Alas, for the ways of love!

At last they came to an unknown city, where they stayed. Tomodata carried gold and jewels in his girdle, so they found a house built of white wood, spread with sweet white mats. In every dim room there could be heard the sound of the garden waterfall, whilst the swallow flitted across and across the paper lattice. Here they dwelt, knowing but the one thing. Here they dwelt three years of happy days, and for Tomodata and the Green Willow the years were like garlands of sweet flowers.

In the autumn of the third year it chanced that the two of them went forth into the garden at dusk, for they had a wish to see the round moon rise; and as they watched, the Green Willow began to shake and shiver.

"My dear," said Tomodata, "you shake and shiver; and it is no wonder, the night wind is chill. Come in." And he put his arm around her.

At this she gave a long and pitiful cry, very loud and full of agony, and when she had uttered the cry she failed, and dropped her head upon her love's breast.

"Tomodata," she whispered, "say a prayer for me; I die."

"Oh, say not so, my sweet, my sweet! You are but weary; you are faint."

He carried her to the stream's side, where the iris grew like swords, and the lotus-leaves like shields, and laved her forehead with water. He said: "What is it, my dear? Look up and live."

"The tree," she moaned, "the tree ... they have cut down my tree. Remember the Green Willow."

With that she slipped, as it seemed, from his arms to his feet; and he, casting himself upon the ground, found only silken garments, bright coloured, warm and sweet, and straw sandals, scarlet-thonged.

In after years, when Tomodata was a holy man, he travelled from shrine to shrine, painfully upon his feet, and acquired much merit.

Once, at nightfall, he found himself upon a lonely moor. On his right hand he beheld a little hill, and on it the sad ruins of a poor thatched cottage. The door swung to and fro with broken latch and creaking hinge. Before it stood three old stumps of willow trees that had long since been cut down. Tomodata stood for a long time still and silent. Then he sang gently to himself:

"Long-haired maiden, do you know
That with the red dawn I must go?
Do you wish me far away?
Cruel long-haired maiden, say –
Long-haired maiden, if you know
That with the red dawn I must go,
Why, oh why, do you blush so?"

"Ah, foolish song! The gods forgive me.... I should have recited the Holy Sutra for the Dead," said Tomodata.

Horaizan

JOFUKU WAS THE WISE MAN OF CHINA. Many books he read, and he never forgot what was in them. All the characters he knew as he knew the lines in the palm of his hand. He learned secrets from birds and beasts, and herbs and flowers and trees, and rocks and metals. He knew magic and poetry and philosophy. He grew full of years and wisdom. All the people honoured him; but he was not happy, for he had a word written upon his heart.

The word was *Mutability*. It was with him day and night, and sorely it troubled him. Moreover, in the days of Jofuku a tyrant ruled over China, and he made the Wise Man's life a burden.

"Jofuku," he said, "teach the nightingales of my wood to sing me the songs of the Chinese poets."

Jofuku could not do it for all his wisdom.

"Alas, liege," he said, "ask me another thing and I will give it you, though it cost me the blood of my heart."

"Have a care," said the Emperor, "look to your ways. Wise men are cheap in China; am I one to be dishonoured?"

"Ask me another thing," said the Wise Man.

"Well, then, scent me the peony with the scent of the jessamine. The peony is brilliant, imperial; the jessamine is small, pale, foolish. Nevertheless, its perfume is sweet. Scent me the peony with the scent of the jessamine."

But Jofuku stood silent and downcast.

"By the gods," cried the Emperor, "this wise man is a fool! Here, some of you, off with his head."

"Liege," said the Wise Man, "spare me my life and I will set sail for Horaizan where grows the herb Immortality. I will pluck this herb and bring it back to you again, that you may live and reign for ever."

The Emperor considered.

"Well, go," he said, "and linger not, or it will be the worse for you."

Jofuku went and found brave companions to go with him on the great adventure, and he manned a junk with the most famous mariners of China, and he took stores on board, and gold; and when he had made all things ready he set sail in the seventh month, about the time of the full moon.

The Emperor himself came down to the seashore.

"Speed, speed, Wise Man," he said; "fetch me the herb Immortality, and see that you do it presently. If you return without it, you and your companions shall die the death."

"Farewell, liege," called Jofuku from the junk. So they went with a fair wind for their white sails. The boards creaked, the ropes quivered, the water splashed against the junk's side, the sailors sang as they steered a course eastwards, the brave companions were merry. But the Wise Man of China looked forward and looked back, and was sad because of the word written upon his heart – *Mutability*.

The junk of Jofuku was for many days upon the wild sea, steering a course eastwards. He and the sailors and the brave companions suffered many things. The great heat burnt them, and the great cold froze them. Hungry and thirsty they were, and some of them fell sick and died. More were slain in a fight with pirates. Then came the dread typhoon, and mountain waves that swept the junk. The masts and the sails were washed away with the rich stores, and the gold was lost for ever. Drowned were the famous mariners, and the brave companions every one. Jofuku was left alone.

In the grey dawn he looked up. Far to the east he saw a mountain, very faint, the colour of pearl, and on the mountain top there grew a tree, tall, with spreading branches. The Wise Man murmured:

"The Island of Horaizan is east of the east, and there is Fusan, the Wonder Mountain. On the heights of Fusan there grows a tree whose branches hide the Mysteries of Life."

Jofuku lay weak and weary and could not lift a finger. Nevertheless, the junk glided nearer and nearer to the shore. Still and blue grew the waters of the sea, and Jofuku saw the bright green grass and the many-coloured flowers of the island. Soon there came troops of young men and maidens bearing garlands and singing songs of welcome; and they waded out into the water and drew the junk to land. Jofuku was aware of the sweet and spicy odours that clung to their garments and their hair. At their invitation he left the junk, which drifted away and was no more seen.

He said, "I have come to Horaizan the Blest." Looking up he saw that the trees were full of birds with blue and golden feathers. The birds filled the air with delightful melody. On all sides there hung the orange and the citron, the persimmon and the pomegranate, the peach and the plum and the loquat. The ground at his feet was as a rich brocade, embroidered with every flower that is. The happy dwellers in Horaizan took him by the hands and spoke lovingly to him.

"How strange it is," said Jofuku, "I do not feel my old age any more."

"What is old age?" they said.

"Neither do I feel any pain."

"Now what is pain?" they said.

"The word is no longer written on my heart."

"What word do you speak of, beloved?"

"*Mutability* is the word."

"And what may be its interpretation?"

"Tell me," said the Wise Man, "is this death?"

"We have never heard of death," said the inhabitants of Horaizan.

* * *

The Wise Man of Japan was Wasobiobe. He was full as wise as the Wise Man of China. He was not old but young. The people honoured him and loved him. Often he was happy enough.

It was his pleasure to venture alone in a frail boat out to sea, there to meditate in the wild and watery waste. Once as he did this it chanced that he fell asleep in his boat, and he slept all night long, while his boat drifted out to the eastward. So, when he awoke in the bright light of morning, he found himself beneath the shadow of Fusan, the Wonder Mountain. His boat lay in the waters of a river of Horaizan, and he steered her amongst the flowering iris and the lotus, and sprang on shore.

"The sweetest spot in the world!" he said. "I think I have come to Horaizan the Blest."

Soon came the youths and maidens of the island, and with them the Wise Man of China, as young and as happy as they.

"Welcome, welcome, dear brother," they cried, "welcome to the Island of Eternal Youth."

When they had given him to eat of the delicious fruit of the island, they laid them down upon a bank of flowers to hear sweet music. Afterwards they wandered in the woods and groves. They rode and hunted, or bathed in the warm seawater. They feasted and enjoyed every delightful pleasure. So the long day lingered, and there was no night, for there was no need of sleep, there was no weariness and no pain.

* * *

The Wise Man of Japan came to the Wise Man of China. He said:

"I cannot find my boat."

"What matter, brother?" said Jofuku. "You want no boat here."

"Indeed, my brother, I do. I want my boat to take me home. I am sick for home. There's the truth."

"Are you not happy in Horaizan?"

"No, for I have a word written upon my heart. The word is *Humanity*. Because of it I am troubled and have no peace."

"Strange," said the Wise Man of China. "Once I too had a word written on my heart. The word was *Mutability*, but I have forgotten what it means. Do you too forget."

"Nay, I can never forget," said the Wise Man of Japan.

He sought out the Crane, who is a great traveller, and besought her, "Take me home to my own land."

"Alas," the Crane said, "if I did so you would die. This is the Island of Eternal Youth; do you know you have been here for a hundred years? If you go away you will feel old age and weariness and pain, then you will die."

"No matter," said Wasobiobe, "take me home."

Then the Crane took him on her strong back and flew with him. Day and night she flew and never tarried and never tired. At last she said, "Do you see the shore?"

And he said, "I see it. Praise be to the gods."

She said, "Where shall I carry you? ... You have but a little time to live."

"Good Crane, upon the dear sand of my country, under the spreading pine, there sits a poor fisherman mending his net. Take me to him that I may die in his arms."

So the Crane laid Wasobiobe at the poor fisherman's feet. And the fisherman raised him in his arms. And Wasobiobe laid his head against the fisherman's humble breast.

"I might have lived for ever," he said, "but for the word that is written on my heart."

"What word?" said the fisherman.

"*Humanity* is the word," the Wise Man murmured. "I am grown old – hold me closer. Ah, the pain..." He gave a great cry.

Afterwards he smiled. Then his breath left him with a sigh, and he was dead.

"It is the way of all flesh," said the fisherman.

Ta-Nan in Search of His Father

HSI CH'ÊNG-LIEH WAS A CH'ÊNG-TU MAN. He had a wife and a concubine, the latter named Ho Chao-jung. His wife dying, he took a second by name Shên, who bullied the concubine dreadfully, and by her constant wrangling made his life perfectly unbearable, so that one day in a fit of anger he ran away and left them. Shortly afterwards Ho gave birth to a son, and called him Ta-nan; but as Hsi did not return, the wife Shên turned them out of the house, making them a daily allowance of food. By degrees Ta-nan became a big boy; and his mother, not daring to ask for an increase of victuals, was obliged to earn a little money by spinning. Meanwhile, Ta-nan, seeing all his companions go to school and learn to read, told his mother he should like to go too; and accordingly, as he was still very young, she sent him for a few days' probation. He turned out to be so clever that he soon beat the other boys; at which the master of the school was much pleased, and offered to teach him for nothing. His mother, therefore, sent him regularly, making what trifling presents she could to the master; and by the end of two or three years he had a first-rate knowledge of the Sacred Books.

One day he came home and asked his mother, saying, "All the fellows at our school get money from their fathers to buy cakes. Why don't I?" "Wait till you are grown up," replied his mother, "and I will explain it to you." "Why, mother," cried he, "I'm only seven or eight years old. What a time it will be before I'm grown up." "Whenever you pass the temple of the God of War on your way to school," said his mother, "you should go in and pray a while; that would make you grow faster." Ta-nan believed she was serious; and every day, going and coming, he went in and worshipped at that temple. When his mother found this out, she asked him how soon he was praying to be grown up; to which he replied that he only prayed that by the following year he might be as big as if he were fifteen or sixteen years old. His mother laughed; but Ta-nan went on, increasing in wisdom and stature alike, until by the time he was ten, he looked quite thirteen or fourteen, and his master was no longer able to correct his essays. Then he said to his mother, "You promised me that when I grew up you would tell me where my father is. Tell me now." "By-and-by, by-and-by," replied his mother; so he waited another year, and then pressed her so eagerly to tell him that she could no longer refuse, and related to him the whole story. He heard her recital with tears and lamentations, and expressed a wish to go in search of his father; but his mother objected that he was too young, and also that no one knew where his father was. Ta-nan said nothing; however, in the middle of the day he did not come home as usual, and his mother at once sent off to the school, where she found he had not shewn himself since breakfast. In great alarm, and thinking that he had been playing truant, she paid some people to go and hunt for him everywhere, but was unable to obtain the slightest clue to his whereabouts. As to Ta-nan himself, when he left the house he followed the road without knowing whither he was going, until at length he met a man who was on his way to K'uei-chou, and said his name was Ch'ien. Ta-nan begged of him something to eat, and went along with him; Mr. Ch'ien even procuring an animal for him to ride because he walked too slowly. The expenses of the journey were all defrayed by Ch'ien; and when they arrived at K'uei-chou they dined together, Ch'ien secretly putting some drug in Ta-nan's food which soon reduced him to a state of unconsciousness. Ch'ien then carried him off to a temple, and, pretending that Ta-nan was his son, offered him to the priests on the plea that he had no money to continue his journey. The priests, seeing what a nice-looking boy he was, were only too ready to buy him; and when Ch'ien had got his money he went away. They then gave Ta-nan a draught which brought him round; but as soon as the abbot heard of the affair and saw Ta-nan himself, he would not allow them to keep him, sending him away with a purse of money in his pocket. Ta-nan next met a gentleman named Chiang, from Lu-chou, who was returning home after having failed at the examination; and this Mr. Chiang was so pleased with the story of his filial piety that he took him to his own home at Lu-chou. There he remained for a month and more, asking everybody he saw for news of his father, until one day he was told that there was a man named Hsi among the Fokien traders. So he bade goodbye to Mr. Chiang, and set off for Fokien, his patron providing him with clothes and shoes, and the people of the place making up a subscription for him. On the road he met two traders in cotton cloth who were going to Fu-ch'ing, and he joined their party; but they had not travelled many stages before these men found out that he had money, and taking him to a lonely spot, bound him hand and foot and made off with all he had. Before long a Mr. Ch'ên, of Yung-fu, happened to pass by, and at once unbound him, and giving him a seat in one of his own vehicles, carried him off home. This Mr. Ch'ên was a wealthy man, and in his house Ta-nan had opportunities of meeting with traders from all quarters. He therefore begged them to aid him by making inquiries about his father, himself remaining as a fellow student with Mr. Ch'ên's sons, and roaming the country no more, neither hearing any news of his former and now distant home.

Meanwhile, his mother, Ho, had lived alone for three or four years, until the wife, Shên, wishing to reduce the expenses, tried to persuade her to find another husband. As Ho was now supporting herself, she steadfastly refused to do this; and then Shên sold her to a Chung-ch'ing trader, who took her away with him. However, she so frightened this man by hacking herself about with a knife, that when the wounds were healed he was only too happy to get rid of her to a trader from Yen-t'ing, who in his turn, after Ho had nearly disembowelled herself, readily listened to her repeated cries that she wished to become a nun. However, he persuaded her to hire herself out as housekeeper to a friend of his, as a means of reimbursing himself for his outlay in purchasing her; but no sooner had she set eyes on the gentleman in question than she found it was her own husband. For Hsi had given up the career of a scholar, and gone into business; and as he had no wife, he was consequently in want of a housekeeper. They were very glad to see each other again; and on relating their several adventures, Hsi knew for the first time that he had a son who had gone forth in search of his father. Hsi then asked all the traders and commercial travellers to keep a look out for Ta-nan, at the same time raising Ho from the status of concubine to that of wife. In consequence, however, of the many hardships Ho had gone through, her health was anything but good, and she was unable to do the work of the house; so she advised her husband to buy a concubine. This he was most unwilling to do, remembering too well the former squabbling he had to endure; but ultimately he yielded, asked a friend to buy for him an oldish woman – at any rate more than thirty years of age. A few months afterwards his friend arrived, bringing with him a person of about that age; and on looking closely at her, Hsi saw that she was no other than his own wife Shên!

Now this lady had lived by herself for a year and more when her brother Pao advised her to marry again, which she accordingly agreed to do. She was prevented, however, by the younger branches of the family from selling the landed property; but she disposed of everything else, and the proceeds passed into her brother's hands. About that time a Pao-ning trader, hearing that she had plenty of money, bribed her brother to marry her to himself; and afterwards, finding that she was a disagreeable woman, took possession of everything she had, and advertised her for sale. No one caring to buy a woman of her age, and her master being on the eve of starting for K'uei-chou, took her with him, finally getting rid of her to Hsi, who was in the same line of business as himself. When she stood before her former husband, she was overwhelmed with shame and fear, and had not a word to say; but Hsi gathered an outline of what had happened from the trader, and then said to her, "Your second marriage with this Pao-ning gentleman was doubtless contracted after you had given up all hope of seeing me again. It doesn't matter in the least, as now I am not in search of a wife but only of a concubine. So you had better begin by paying your respects to your mistress here, my wife Ho Chao-jung." Shên was ashamed to do this: but Hsi reminded her of the time when she had been in the wife's place, and in spite of all Ho's intercession insisted that she should do so, stimulating her to obedience by the smart application of a stick. Shên was therefore compelled to yield, but at the same time she never tried to gain Ho's favour, and kept away from her as much as possible. Ho, on the other hand, treated her with great consideration, and never took her to task on the performance of her duties; whilst Hsi himself, whenever he had a dinner-party, made her wait at table, though Ho often entreated him to hire a maid.

Now the magistrate at Yen-t'ing was named Ch'ên Tsung-ssŭ, and once when Hsi had some trifling difficulty with one of the neighbours he was further accused to this official of having forced his wife to assume the position of concubine. The magistrate, however, refused to take up the case, to the great satisfaction of Hsi and his wife, who lauded him to the skies as a virtuous mandarin. A few nights after, at rather a late hour, the servant knocked at the door, and called out, "The magistrate has come!" Hsi jumped up in a hurry, and began looking for his clothes and shoes; but the magistrate was already in the bedroom without either of them understanding what it all meant: when suddenly Ho, examining him closely, cried out, "It is my son!" She then burst into tears, and the magistrate, throwing himself on the ground, wept with his mother. It seemed he had taken the name of the gentleman with whom he had lived, and had since entered upon an official career. That on his way to the capital he had made a *détour* and visited his old home, where he heard to his infinite sorrow that both his mothers had married again; and that his relatives, finding him already a man of position, had restored to him the family property, of which he had left someone in charge in the hope that his father might return. That then he had been appointed to Yen-t'ing, but had wished to throw up the post and travel in search of his father, from which design he had been dissuaded by Mr. Ch'ên. Also that he had met a fortune-teller from whom he had obtained the following response to his inquiries: – "The lesser is the greater; the younger is the elder. Seeking the cock, you find the hen; seeking one, you get two. Your official life will be successfufl." Ch'ên then took up his appointment, but not finding his father he confined himself entirely to a vegetable diet, and gave up the use of wine. The above-mentioned case had subsequently come under his notice, and seeing the name Hsi, he quietly sent his private servant to find out, and thus discovered that this Hsi was his father. At night-fall he set off himself, and when he saw his mother he knew that the fortune-teller had told him true. Bidding them all say nothing to anybody about what had occurred, he provided money for the journey, and sent them back home. On arriving there, they found the place newly painted, and with their increased retinue of servants and horses, they were quite a wealthy family. As to Shên when she found what a great man Ta-nan had become, she put still more restraint upon herself; but her brother Pao brought an action for the purpose of reinstating her as wife. The presiding official happened to be a man of probity, and delivered the following judgement: – "Greedy of gain you urged your sister to re-marry. After she had driven Hsi away, she took two fresh husbands. How have you the face to talk about reinstating her as wife?" He thereupon ordered Pao to be severely bambooed, and from this time there was no longer any doubt about Shên's *status*. She was the lesser and Ho the greater; and yet in the matter of clothes and food Ho shewed herself by no means grasping. Shên was at first afraid that Ho would pay her out, and was consequently more than ever repentant; and Hsi himself, letting bygones be bygones, gave orders that Shên should be called *madam* by all alike, though of course she was excluded from any titles that might be gained for them by Ta-nan.

The Sky Bridge of Birds

NO BIRD IS MORE COMMON IN KOREA than the magpie. They are numbered by millions. Every day in the year, except the seventh day of the seventh month, the air is full of them. On that date, however, they have a standing engagement every year. They are all expected to be away from streets and houses, for every well-bred magpie is then far up in the sky building a bridge across the River of Stars, called the Milky Way. With their wings for the cables, and their heads to form the floor of the bridge, they make a pathway for lovers on either side of the Silver Stream.

Boys and girls are usually very kind to the magpies, but if a single one be found about the houses, on the roofs, or in the streets on the seventh of August, woe betide it! Every dirty-faced brat throws sticks or stones at the poor creature, for not being about its business of bridge-building across the Starry River. By evening time the magpies return to their usual places, for they are then supposed to have attended to their tasks and built the bridge.

To prove beyond a doubt that the bridge was made and walked over, you have only to look at the bare heads of the magpies at this time. Their feathers have been entirely worn off by the tramping of the crowd of retainers who follow the Prince of Star Land across the bridge to meet his bride.

If it be wet weather on the morning of this day of the Weaver Maiden and the Cattle Prince, the raindrops are the tears of joy shed by the lovers at their first meeting. If showers fall in the afternoon, they are the tears of sadness at saying farewell, when the prince and princess leave each other. If any thunder is heard, every boy and girl knows that this comes from the rumble of the wagons which carry the baggage of the prince and princess, as they move away, each from the other, homeward.

Now, this is the story which the Korean mothers tell to their children of the Bridge of Birds.

Long, long ago, in the Kingdom of the Stars, a king reigned who had a lovely daughter. Besides being the most beautiful to behold, she was a skilful weaver. There was no good thing to be done in the palace, but she could do it. She was not only highly accomplished, but of sweet temper and very willing. Being a model of all diligence, she was very greatly beloved of her parents and her influence over her father was very great. He would do almost anything to please his darling daughter.

In due time a young and very handsome prince, who lived in Star Land, came to her father's court and fell in love with the pretty princess. Her parents consenting, the wedding was celebrated with great splendour.

Now that she was a wife and had a home of her own to care for, she became all the more a model of lovely womanhood and an example to all the maidens of Korea forever. Besides showing diligence in the care of clothes and food and in setting her servants a good example of thrift, she thought much of their happiness. Her service to her husband was unremitting. Her chief ambition was to make his life one of constant joy.

But the prince, instead of following his bride's good example, and of appreciating what his beautiful and unselfish bride was doing for his happiness, gave himself up to waste and extravagance. He became lazy and dissipated. Neglecting his duties, he wasted his own fortune and his wife's dowry. He sold all his oxen and calves to get money only to lose it in gambling. He borrowed many and long ropes of coin from anyone who would lend him the brass and iron money. Finally he was so scandalously poor, being on his last string of cash, that he was in danger of being degraded from his rank as prince, and of having his name spoken with contempt.

The King of the Stars, having seen his son-in-law on the downward way, had more than once threatened to disinherit, or banish him, especially after the prince had parted with his cattle. Yet when his daughter, the young wife, interceded and begged pardon for her husband, the king relented, paid his son-in-law's debts and gave him another chance to do better. When, however, the worthless fellow fell back into his old ways, and grew worse and worse, the king resolved to separate the pair, one from the other. He banished the prince, far, far away, six months' distance from the north side of the River of Heaven, and exiled the princess a half year's measure of space from the south side of the Starry Stream.

Although the king in his wrath had hardened his heart, even against his own beloved child, and had driven her from court and palace, because of her worthless husband, yet, as a signal proof of his compassion, he ordained that on one night of the year, on the seventh night of the seventh moon, they might meet for a few hours.

The young people parted and took their sad journey to the edge of the starry heavens, but they loved each other so dearly that, as soon as they arrived at their place of banishment, they turned round to meet each other on August 7th.

So when the day came, after six months' weary journeying, they had reached the edge of the Starry River, and there they stood, catching glimpses and waving their hands, but unable to get closer to each other. There one may see them on summer nights shining on opposite sides of the broad Stream of Stars, loving each other but unable to cross.

Feeling that the great gulf of space could not be spanned, the loving couple burst into tears. The flood from their eyes, making the river overflow, deluged the earth below, threatening to float everything, houses, people, animals away. What could be done?

The four-footed creatures, fish and fowls, held a convention, but it was agreed that only those birds with strong wings and able to fly high could do anything. So the magpies, with many flattering speeches, were commended to the enterprise.

When these noisy and chattering creatures, that are nevertheless so kind and friendly to the sparrows, heard of the lovers' troubles aloft, they resolved to help the sorrowing pair over the River of Stars. Out of their big, ugly nests they flew gladly to the convention that voted to build the bridge. Sending out word all over the world, millions of magpies assembled in the air. Under the direction of their wisest chiefs, they began their work of making, with a mass of wings, a flying bridge that would reach from shore to shore of the Starry Stream. First, they put their heads together to furnish a floor, and, so closely, that the bridge looked as if it were paved with white granite. Then with their pinions they held up the great arch and highway, over which the prince crossed to his bride with all his baggage and train of followers. The tables were soon spread and the two royal lovers enjoyed a feast, with many tender words and caresses.

Every year, for ages past, on the seventh day of the seventh month, the magpies have done this. Indeed, although the star lovers meet only once a year, yet as they live on forever the wife has her husband and the husband his wife much longer than mortal couples who live on earth. It is law in the magpie kingdom that no bird can shirk this work.

Any magpie that tries to get out of the task and that is too bad or lazy to do its part in bridge building, is chased away by the Korean children, who want no such truant around. For does not every girl hope to be as diligent and accomplished as the Star Princess, so that when she grows up she may make as good a wife as the lovely lady that every year stands by the Starry River to meet her lord? As for the boys, it is hoped that they will become as faithful husbands as the penitent bridegroom, who every year, on the night of August 7th, awaits his bride on the shining shore of the River of Stars.

The Discovery of New Zealand

NOW PAY ATTENTION to the cause of the contention which arose between Poutini and Whaiapu, which led them to emigrate to New Zealand. For a long time they both rested in the same place, and Hine-tu–a-hoanga, to whom the stone Whaiapu belonged, became excessively enraged with Ngahue, and with his stone Poutini.

At last she drove Ngahue out and forced him to leave the place, and Ngahue departed and went to a strange land, taking his jasper. When Heni-tu-a-hoanga saw that he was departing with his precious stone, she followed after them, and Ngahue arrived at Tuhua with his stone, and Hine-tu-a-hoanga arrived and landed there at the same time with him, and began to drive him away again. Then Ngahue went to seek a place where his jasper stones might remain in peace, and he found in the sea this island Aotearoa (the northern island of New Zealand), and he thought he would land there.

Then he thought again, lest he and his enemy should be too close to one another, and should quarrel again, that it would be better for him to go farther off with his jasper, a very long way off. So he carried it off with him, and they coasted along, and at length arrived at Arahura (on the west coast of the middle island), and he made that an everlasting resting-piace for his jasper; then he broke off a portion of his jasper, and took it with him and returned, and as he coasted along he at length reached Wairere (believed to be upon the east coast of the northern island), and he visited Whangaparoa and Tauranga, and from thence he returned direct to Hawaiki, and reported that he had discovered a new country which produced the moa and jasper in abundance. He now manufactured sharp axes from his jasper; two axes were made from it, Tutauru and Hau-hau-te-rangi. He manufactured some portions of one piece of it into images for neck ornaments, and some portions into ear ornaments; the name of one of these ear ornaments was Kaukaumatua, which was recently in the possession of Te Heuheu, and was only lost in 1846, when he was killed with so many of his tribe by a landslip. The axe Tutauru was only lately lost by Purahokura and his brother Reretai, who were descended from Tama-ihu-toroa. When Ngahue returning, arrived again in Hawaiki, he found them all engaged in war, and when they heard his description of the beauty of this country of Aotea, some of them determined to come here.

Construction of Canoes to Emigrate to New Zealand

They then felled a totara tree in Rarotonga, which lies on the other side of Hawaiki, that they might build the Arawa from it. The tree was felled, and thus the canoe was hewn out from it and finished. The names of the men who built this canoe were, Rata, Wahie-roa, Ngahue, Parata, and some other skilful men, who helped to hew out the Arawa and to finish it.

A chief of the name of Hotu-roa, hearing that the Arawa was built, and wishing to accompany them, came to Tama-te-kapua and asked him to lend him his workmen to hew out some canoes for him too, and they went and built and finished the Tainui and some other canoes.

The workmen above mentioned are those who built the canoes in which our forefathers crossed the ocean to this island, to Aotea-roa. The names of the canoes were as follows: the Arawa was first completed, then Tainui, then Matatua, and Takitumu, and Kura-hau-po, and Toko-maru, and Matawhaorua. These are the names of the canoes in which our forefathers departed from Hawaiki, and crossed to this island. When they had lashed the topsides on to the Tainui, Rata slew the son of Manaia, and hid his body in the chips and shavings of the canoes. The names of the axes with which they hewed out these canoes were Hauhau-te-Rangi, and Tutauru. Tutauru was the axe with which they cut off the head of Uenuku.

All these axes were made from the block of green stone brought back by Ngahue to Hawaiki, which was called ' The fish of Ngahue.' He had previously come to these islands from Hawaiki, when he was driven out from thence by Hine-tu-a-hoanga, whose fish or stone was Obsidian. From that cause Ngahue came to these islands; the canoes which afterwards arrived here came in consequence of his discovery.

The Voyage to New Zealand

WHEN THE CANOES WERE BUILT and ready for sea, they were dragged afloat, the separate lading of each canoe was collected and put on board, with all the crews. Tama-te-kapua then remembered that he had no skilful priest on board his canoe, and he thought the best thing he could do was to outwit Ngatoro-i-rangi, the chief who had com–mand of the Tainui. So just as his canoe shoved off, he called out to Ngatoro: "I say, Ngatoro, just come on board my canoe, and perform the necessary religious rites for me." Then the priest Ngatoro came on board, and Tama-te-kapua said to him: "You had better also call your wife, Kearoa on board, that she may make the canoe clean or common, with an offering of sea-weed to be laid in the canoe instead of an offering of fish, for you know the second fish caught in a canoe, or seaweed, or some substitute, ought to be offered for the females, the first for the males; then my canoe will be quite common, for all the ceremonies will have been observed, which should be followed with canoes made by priests." Ngatoro assented to all this, and called his wife, and they both go into Tama's canoe. The very moment they were on board, Tama' called out to the men on board his canoe: "Heave up the anchors and make sail"; and he carried off with him Ngatoro and his wife, that he might have a priest and wise man on board his canoe. Then they up with the fore-sail, the main-sail, and the mizen, and away shot the canoe. Up then came Ngatoro from below, and said:

"Shorten sail, that we may go more slowly, lest I miss my own canoe." And Tama' replied: "Oh, no, no; wait a little, and your canoe will follow after us." For a short time it kept near them, but soon dropped more and more astern, and when darkness overtook them, on they sailed, each canoe proceeding on its own course.

Two thefts were upon this occasion perpetrated by Tama-te-kapua; he carried off the wife of Ruaeo, and Ngatoro and his wife, on board the Arawa. He made a fool of Ruaeo too, for he said to him: "Oh, Rua', you, like a good fellow, just run back to the village and fetch me my axe Tutauru, I pushed it in under the sill of the window of my house." And Rua' was foolish enough to run back to the house. Then off went Tama' with the canoe, and when Rua' came back again, the canoe was so far off that its sails did not look much bigger than little flies. So he fell to weeping for all his goods on board the canoe, and for his wife Whakaoti-rangi, whom Tama-te-kapua had carried off as a wife for himself. Tama-te-kapua committed these two great thefts when he sailed for these islands. Hence this proverb: 'A descendant of Tama-te-kapua will steal anything he can'.

When evening came on, Rua' threw himself into the water, as a preparation for his incantations to recover his wife, and he then changed the stars of evening into the stars of morning, and those of the morning into the stars of the evening, and this was accomplished. In the meantime the Arawa scudded away far out on the ocean, and Ngatoro thought to himself: "What a rate this canoe goes at – what a vast space we have already traversed. I know what I'll do, I'll climb up upon the roof of the house which is built on the platform joining the two canoes, and try to get a glimpse of the land in the horizon, and ascertain whether we are near it, or very far off." But in the first place he felt some suspicions about his wife, lest Tama-te-kapua should steal her too, for he had found out what a treacherous person he was. So ho took a string and tied one end of it to his wife's hair, and kept the other end of the string in his hand, and then he climbed up on the roof. He had hardly got on the top of the roof when Tama' laid hold of his wife, and he cunningly untied the end of the string which Ngatoro had fastened to her hair, and made it fast to one of the beams of the canoe, and Ngatoro feeling it tight thought his wife had not moved, and that it was still fast to her. At last Ngatoro came down again, and Tama-te-kapua heard the noise of his steps as he was coming, but he had not time to get the string tied fast to the hair of Kearoa's head again, but he jumped as fast as he could into his own berth, which was next to that of Ngatoro, and Ngatoro, to his surprise, found one end of the string tied fast to the beam of the canoe.

Then he knew that his wife had been disturbed by Tama', and he asked her, saying: "Oh, wife, has not someone disturbed you?" Then his wife replied to him: "Cannot you tell that from the string being fastened to the beam of the canoe?" And then he asked her: "Who was it?" And she said: "Who was it, indeed? Could it be anyone else but Tama-te-kapua?" Then her husband said to her: "You are a noble woman indeed thus to confess this; you have gladdened my heart by this confession; I thought after Tama' had carried us both off in this way, that he would have acted generously, and not loosely in this manner; but, since he has dealt in this way, I will now have my revenge on him."

Then that priest again went forth upon the roof of the house and stood there, and he called aloud to the heavens, in the same way that Rua' did, and he changed the stars of the evening into those of morning, and he raised the winds that they should blow upon the prow of the canoe, and drive it astern, and the crew of the canoe were at their wits' end, and quite forgot their skill as seamen, and the canoe drew straight into the whirlpool, called 'The throat of Te Parata', and dashed right into that whirlpool.

The canoe became engulphed by the whirlpool, and its prow disappeared in it. In a moment the waters reached the first bailing place in the bows, in another second they reached the second bailing place in the centre, and the canoe now appeared to be going down into the whirlpool head foremost; then up started Hei, but before he could rise they had already sunk far into the whirlpool. Next the rush of waters was heard by Ihenga, who slept forward, and he shouted out: "Oh, Ngatoro, oh, we are settling down head first. The pillow of your wife Kearoa has already fallen from under her head!" Ngatoro sat astern listening; the same cries of distress reached him a second time. Then up sprang Tama-te-kapua, and he in despair shouted out: "Oh, Ngatoro, Ngatoro, aloft there! Do you hear? The canoe is gone down so much by the bow, that Kearoa' s pillow has rolled from under her head." The priest heard them, but neither moved nor answered until he heard the goods rolling from the decks and splashing into the water; the crew meanwhile held on to the canoe with their hands with great difficulty, some of them having already fallen into the sea.

When these things all took place, the heart of Ngatoro was moved with pity, for he heard, too, the shrieks and cries of the men, and the weeping of the women and children. Then up stood that mighty man again, and by his incantations changed the aspect of the heavens, so that the storm ceased, and he repeated another incantation to draw the canoe back out of the whirlpool, that is, to lift it up again.

Lo, the canoe rose up from the whirlpool, floating rightly; but, although the canoe itself thus floated out of the whirlpool, a great part of its lading had been thrown out into the water, a few things only were saved, and remained in the canoe. A great part of their provisions were lost as the canoe was sinking into the whirlpool. Thence comes the native proverb, if they can give a stranger but little food, or only make a present of a small basket of food: 'Oh, it is the half-filled basket of Whakaoti-rangi, for she only managed to save a very small part of her provisions'. Then they sailed on, and landed at Whanga-Paraoa, in Aotea here. As they drew near to land, they saw with surprise some pohutukawa trees of the sea-coast, covered with beautiful red flowers, and the still water reflected back the redness of the trees.

Then one of the chiefs of the canoe cried out to his messmates: "See there, red ornaments for the head are much more plentiful in this country than in Hawaiki, so I'll throw my red head ornaments into the water"; and, so saying, he threw them into the sea. The name of that man was Tauninihi; the name of the red head ornament he threw into the sea was Taiwhakaea. The moment they got on shore they run to gather the pohutukawa flowers, but no sooner did they touch them than the flowers fell to pieces; then they found out that these red head ornaments were nothing but flowers. All the chiefs on board the Arawa were then troubled that they should have been so foolish as to throw away their red head ornaments into the sea. Very shortly afterwards the ornaments of Tauninihi were found by Mahina on the beach of Mabiti. As soon as Tauninihi heard they had been picked up, he ran to Mahina to get them again, but Mahina would not give them up to him; thence this proverb for anything which has been lost and is found by another person: 'I will not give it up, 'tis the red head ornament which Mahina found'.

As soon as the party landed at Whanga-Paraoa, they planted sweet potatoes, that they might grow there; and they are still to be found growing on the cliffs at that place.

Then the crew, wearied from the voyage, wandered idly along the shore, and there they found the fresh carcase of a sperm whale stranded upon the beach. The Tainui had already arrived in the same neighbourhood, although they did not at first see that canoe nor the people who had come in it; when, however, they met, they began to dispute as to who had landed first and first found the dead whale, and as to which canoe it consequently belonged; so, to settle the question, they agreed to examine the sacred place which each party had set up to return thanks in to the gods for their safe arrival, that they might see which had been longest built; and, doing so, they found that the posts of the sacred place put up by the Arawa were quite green, whilst the posts of the sacred place set up by the Tainui had evidently been carefully dried over the fire before they had been fixed in the ground. The people who had come in the Tainui also showed part of a rope which they had made fast to its jawbone. When these things were seen, it was admitted that the whale belonged to the people who came in the Tainui, and it was surrendered to them. And the people in the Arawa, determining to separate from those in the Tainui, selected some of their crew to explore the country in a north-west direction, following the coast line. The canoe then coasted along, the land party following it along the shore; this was made up of 140 men, whose chief was Taikehu, and these gave to a place the name of Te Ranga of Taikehu.

The Tainui left Whanga-Paraoa shortly after the Arawa, and, proceeding nearly in the same direction as the Arawa, made the Gulf of Hauraki, and then coasted along to Rakaumangamanga, or Cape Brett, and to the island with an arched passage through it, called Motukokako, which lies off the cape; thence they ran along the coast to Whiwhia, and to Te Aukanapanapa, and to Muri-whenua, or the country near the North Cape. Finding that the land ended there, they returned again along the coast until they reached the Tamaki, and landed there, and afterwards proceeded up the creek to Tau-oma, or the portage, where they were surprised to see flocks of sea-gulls and oyster-catchers passing over from the westward; so they went off to explore the country in that direction, and to their great surprise found a large sheet of water lying immediately behind them, so they determined to drag their canoes over the portage at a place they named Otahuhu, and to launch them again on the vast sheet of salt-water which they had found.

The first canoe which they hauled across was the Toko-maru – that they got across without difficulty. They next began to drag the Tainui over the isthmus; they hauled away at it in vain, they could not stir it; for one of the wives of Hoturoa, named Marama-kiko-hura, who was unwilling that the tired crews should proceed further on this new expedition, had by her enchantments fixed it so firmly to the earth that no human strength could stir it; so they hauled, they hauled, they excited themselves with cries and cheers, but they hauled in vain, they cried aloud in vain, they could not move it. When their strength was quite exhausted by these efforts, then another of the wives of Hoturoa, more learned in magic and incantations than Marama-kiko-hura, grieved at seeing the exhaustion and distress of her people, rose up, and chanted forth an incantation far more powerful than that of Marama-kiko-hura; then at once the canoe glided easily over the carefully-laid skids, and it soon floated securely upon the harbour of Manuka. The willing crews urged on the canoes with their paddles; they soon discovered the mouth of the harbour upon the west coast, and passed out through it into the open sea; they coasted along the western coast to the southwards, and discovering the small port of Kawhia, they entered it, and, hauling up their canoe, fixed themselves there for the time, whilst the Arawa was left at Maketu.

We now return to the Arawa. We left the people of it at Tauranga. That canoe next floated at Motiti; they named that place after a spot in Hawaiki (because there was no firewood there). Next Tia, to commemorate his name, called the place now known by the name of Rangiuru, Takapu-o-tapui-ika-nui-a-Tia. Then Hei stood up and called out: "I name that place Takapu-o-wai-tahanui-a-Hei"; the name of that place is now Otawa. Then stood up Tama-te-kapua, and pointing to the place now called the Heads of Maketu, he called out: "I name that place Te Kuraetanga-o-te-ihu-o-Tama-te-kapua." Next Kahu called a place, after his name, Motiti-nui-a-Kahu.

Ruaeo, who had already arrived at Maketu, started up. He was the first to arrive there in his canoe – the Pukeatea-wai-nui – for he had been left behind by the Arawa, and his wife Whakaoti-rangi had been carried off by Tama-te-kapua, and after the Arawa had left he had sailed in his own canoe for these islands, and landed at Maketu, and his canoe reached land the first; well, he started up, cast his line into the sea, with the hooks attached to it, and they got fast in one of the beams of the Arawa, and it was pulled ashore by him (whilst the crew were asleep), and the hundred and forty men who had accompanied him stood upon the beach of Maketu, with skids all ready laid, and the Arawa was by them dragged upon the shore in the night, and left there; and Ruaeo seated himself under the side of the Arawa, and played upon his flute, and the music woke his wife, and she said: "Dear me, that's Rua'!" – and when she looked, there he was sitting under the side of the canoe, and they passed the night together.

At last Rua' said: "O mother of my children, go back now to your new husband, and presently I'll play upon the flute and putorino, so that both you and Tama-te-kapua may hear. Then do you say to Tama-te-kapua 'O! la, I had a dream in the night that I heard Rua playing a tune upon his flute', and that will make him so jealous that he will give you a blow, and then you can run away from him again, as if you were in a rage and hurt, and you can come to me."

Then Whakaoti-rangi returned, and lay down by Tama-te-kapua, and she did everything exactly as Rua' had told her, and Tama' began to beat her (and she ran away from him). Early in the morning Rua' performed incantations, by which he kept all the people in the canoe in a profound sleep, and whilst they still slept from his enchantments, the sun rose, and mounted high up in the heavens. In the forenoon, Rua' gave the canoe a heavy blow with his club; they all started up; it was almost noon, and when they looked down over the edge of their canoe, there were the hundred and forty men of Rua' sitting under them, all beautifully dressed with feathers, as if they had been living on the Gannet Island, in the channel of Karewa, where feathers are so abundant; and when the crew of the Arawa heard this, they all rushed upon deck, and saw Rua' standing in the midst of his one hundred and forty warriors.

Then Rua' shouted out as he stood: "Come here, Tama-te-kapua; let us two fight the battle, you and I alone. If you are stronger than I am, well and good, let it be so; if I am stronger than you are, I'll dash you to the earth."

Up sprang then the hero Tama-te-kapua; he held a carved two-handed sword, a sword the handle of which was decked with red feathers. Rua' held a similar weapon. Tama' first struck a fierce blow at Rua'. Rua' parried it, and it glanced harmlessly off; then Rua' threw away his sword, and seized both the arms of Tama-te-kapua; he held his arms and his sword, and dashed him to the earth. Tama' half rose, and was again dashed down; once more he almost rose, and was thrown again. Still Tama' fiercely struggled to rise and renew the fight. For the fourth time he almost rose up, then Rua', overcome with rage, took a heap of vermin (this he had prepared for the purpose, to cover Tama' with insult and shame), and rubbed them on Tama-te-kapua's head and ear, and they adhered so fast that Tama' tried in vain to get them out.

Then Rua' said: "There, I've beaten you; now keep the woman, as a payment for the insults I've heaped upon you, and for having been beaten by me." But Tama' did not hear a word he said; he was almost driven mad with the pain and itching, and could do nothing but stand scratching and rubbing his head; whilst Rua' departed with his hundred and forty men to seek some other dweling-place for themselves; if they had turned against Tama' and his people to fight against them, they would have slain them all.

These men were giants – Tama-te-kapua was nine feet high, Rua' was eleven feet high; there have been no men since that time so tall as those heroes.

The only man of these later times who was as tall as these was Tu-hou-rangi: he was nine feet high; he was six feet up to the armpits. This generation have seen his bones, they used to be always set up by the priests in the sacred places when they were made high places for the sacred sacrifices of the natives, at the times the potatoes and sweet potatoes were dug up, and when the fishing season commenced, and when they attacked an enemy; then might be seen the people collecting, in their best garments, and with their ornaments, on the days when the priests exposed Tu-hou-rangi's bones to their view. At the time that the island Mokoia, in the lake of Roto-rua, was stormed and taken by the Nga-Puhi, they probably carried those bones off, for they have not since been seen.

After the dispute between Tama-te-kapua and Rua' took place, Tama' and his party dwelt at Maketu, and their descendants after a little time spread to other places. Ngatoro-i-rangi went, however, about the country, and where he found dry valleys, stamped on the earth, and brought forth springs of water; he also visited the mountains, and placed Patupaiarehe, or fairies, there, and then returned to Maketu and dwelt there.

After this a dispute arose between Tama-te-kapua and Kahu-mata-momoe, and in consequence of that disturbance, Tama' and Ngatoro removed to Tauranga, and found Taikehu living there, and collecting food for them (by fishing), and that place was called by them Te Bang a-a-Taikehu; it lies beyond Motu-hoa; then they departed from Tauranga, and stopped at Kati-kati, where they ate food. Tama's men devoured the food very fast, whilst he kept on only nibbling his, therefore they applied this circumstance as a name for the place, and called it: 'Kati-kati-o-Tama-te-kapua', the nibbling of Tama-te kapua; then they halted at Whakahau, so called because they here ordered food to be cooked, which they did not stop to eat, but went right on with Ngatoro, and this circumstance gave its name to the place; and they went on from place to place till they arrived at Whitianga, which they so called from their crossing the river there, and they continued going from one place to another till they came to Tangiaro, and Ngatoro stuck up a stone and left it there, and they dwelt in Moehau and Hau-raki.

They occupied those places as a permanent residence, and Tama-te-kapua died, and was buried there. When he was dying, he ordered his children to return to Maketu, to visit his relations; and they assented, and went back. If the children of Tama-te-kapua had remained at Hau-raki, that place would now have been left to them as a possession.

Tama-te-kapua, when dying, told his children where the precious ear-drop Kaukau-matua was, which he had hidden under the window of his house; and his children returned with Ngatoro to Maketu, and dwelt there; and as soon as Ngatoro arrived, he went to the waters to bathe himself, as he had come there in a state of tapu, upon account of his having buried Tama-te-kapua, and having bathed, he then became free from the tapu and clean.

Ngatoro then took the daughter of Ihenga to wife, and he went and searched for the precious ear-drop Kaukau-matua, and found it, as Tama-te-kapua had told him. After this the wife of Kahu-mata-momoe conceived a child.

At this time Ihenga, taking some dogs with him to catch kiwis with, went to Paritangi by way of Hakomiti, and kiwi was chased by one of his dogs, and caught in a lake, and the dog ate some of the fish and shellfish in the lake, after diving in the water to get them, and returned to its master carrying the captured kiwi in its mouth, and on reaching its master, it dropped the kiwi, and vomited up the raw fish and shell-fish which it had eaten.

When Ihenga saw his dog wet all over, and the fish it had vomited up, he knew there was a lake there, and was extremely glad, and returned joyfully to Maketu, and there he had the usual religious ceremonies which follow the birth of a child performed over his wife and the child she had given birth to; and when this had been done, he went to explore the coimtry which he had previously visited with his dog.

To his great surprise he discovered a lake; it was Lake Roto-iti; he left a mark there to show that he claimed it as his own. He went farther and discovered Lake Roto-rua; he saw that its waters were running; he left there also a mark to show that he claimed the lake as his own. As he went along the side of the lake; he found a man occupying the ground; then he thought to himself that he would endeavour to gain possession of it by craft, so he looked out for a spot fit for a sacred place, where men could offer up their prayers, and for another spot fit for a sacred place, where nets could be hung up, and he found fit spots; then he took suitable stones to surround the sacred place with, and old pieces of seaweed, looking as if they had years ago been employed as offerings, and he went into the middle of the shrubbery, thick with boughs of the taha shrub, of the koromuka, and of the karamu; there he stuck up the posts of the sacred place in the midst of the shrubs, and tied bunches of flax-leaves on the posts, and having done this, he went to visit the village of the people who lived there.

They saw someone approaching and cried out:

"A stranger, a stranger, is coming here!" As soon as Ihenga heard these cries, he sat down upon the ground, and then, without waiting for the people of the place to begin the speeches, he jumped up, and commenced to speak thus: "What theft is this, what theft is this of the people here, that they are taking away my land?" – for he saw that they had their store-houses full of prepared fern-roots and of dried fish, and shell-fish, and their heaps of fishing-nets, so as he spoke, he appeared to swell with rage, and his throat appeared to grow large from passion as he talked: "Who authorized you to come here, and take possession of my place? Be off, be off, be off! leave alone the place of the man who speaks to you, to whom it has belonged for a very long time, for a very long time indeed."

Then Maru-punga-nui, the son of Tua-Roto-rua, the man to whom the place really belonged, said to Ihenga: "It is not your place, it belongs to me; if it belongs to you, where is your village, where is your sacred place, where is your net, where are your cultivations and gardens?"

Ihenga answered him: "Come here and see them." So they went together, and ascended a hill, and Ihenga said: "See there, there is my net hanging up against the ricks"; but it was no such thing, it was only a mark like a net hanging up, caused by part of a cliff having slipped away; "and there are the posts of the pine round my village"; but there was really nothing but some old stumps of trees; "look there too at my sacred place a little beyond yours; and now come with me, and see my sacred place, if you are quite sure you see my village, and my fishing-net – come along." So they went together, and there he saw the sacred place standing in the shrubbery, until at last he believed Ihenga, and the place was all given up to Ihenga, and he took possession of it and lived there, and the descendants of Tua-Roto-rua departed from that place, and a portion of them, under the chiefs Kawa-arero and Mata-aho, occupied the island of Mokoia, in Lake Roto-rua.

At this time Ngatoro again went to stamp on the earth, and to bring forth springs in places where there was no water, and came out on the great central plains which surround Lake Taupo, where a piece of large cloak made of kiekie-leaves was stripped off by the bushes, and the strips took root, and became large trees, nearly as large as the Kahikatea tree (they are called Painanga, and many of them are growing there still).

Whenever he ascended a hill, he left marks there, to show that he claimed it; the marks he left were fairies. Some of the generation now living have seen these spirits; they are malicious spirits. If you take embers from an oven in which food has been cooked, and use them for a fire in a house, these spirits become offended; although there be many people sleeping in that house, not one of them could escape (the fairies would, whilst they slept, press the whole of them to death).

Ngatoro went straight on and rested at Taupo, and he beheld that the summit of Mount Tongariro was covered with snow, and he was seized with a longing to ascend it, and he climbed up, saying to his companions who remained below at their encampment: "Remember now, do not you, who I am going to leave behind, taste food from the time I leave you until I return, when we will all feast together." Then he began to ascend the mountain, but he had not quite got to the summit when those he had left behind began to eat food, and he therefore found the greatest difficulty in reacliing the summit of the mountain, and the hero nearly perished in the attempt.

At last he gathered strength, and thought he could save himself, if he prayed aloud to the gods of Hawaiki to send fire to him, and to produce a volcano upon the mountain; (and his prayer was answered,) and fire was given to him, and the mountain became a volcano, and it came by the way of Whakaari, or White Island, of Mau-tohora, of Okakaru, of Roto-ehu, of Roto-iti, of Roto-rua, of Tara-wera, of Pae-roa, of Orakeikorako, and of Taupo; it came right underneath the earth, spouting up at all the above-mentioned places, and ascended right up Tongariro, to him who was sitting upon the top of the mountain, and thence the hero was revived again, and descended, and returned to Maketu, and dwelt there.

The Arawa had been laid up by its crew at Maketu, where they landed, and the people who had arrived with the party in the Arawa spread themselves over the country, examining it, some penetrating to Roto-rua, some to Taupo, some to Whanganui, some to Ruatahuna, and no one was left at Maketu but Hei' and his son, and Tia and his son, and the usual place of residence of Ngatoro-i-rangi was on the island of Motiti. The people who came with the Tainui were still in Kawhia, where they had landed.

One of their chiefs, named Raumati, heard that the Arawa was laid up at Maketu, so he started with all his own immediate dependants, and reaching Tauranga, halted there, and in the evening again pressed on towards Maketu, and reached the bank of the river, opposite that on which the Arawa was lying, thatched over with reeds and dried branches and leaves; then he slung a dart, the point of which was bound round with combustible materials, over to the other side of the river; the point of the dart was lighted, and it stuck right in the dry thatch of the roof over the Arawa, and the shed of dry stuff taking fire, the canoe was entirely destroyed.

On the night that the Arawa was burnt by Raumati, there was not a person left at Maketu; they wore all scattered in the forests, at Tapu-ika, and at Waitaha, and Ngatoro-i-rangi was at that moment at his residence on the island of Motiti. The pa, or fortified village at Maketu, was left quite empty, without a soul in it. The canoe was lying alone, with none to watch it; they had all gone to collect food of different kinds – it happened to be a season in which food was very abundant, and from that cause the people were all scattered in small parties about the country, fishing, fowling, and collecting food.

As soon as the next morning dawned, Raumati could see that the fortified village of Maketu was empty, and not a person left in it, so he and his armed followers at once passed over the river and entered the village, which they found entirely deserted.

At night, as the Arawa burnt, the people, who were scattered about in the various parts of the country, saw the fire, for the bright glare of the gleaming flames was reflected in the sky, lighting up the heavens, and they all thought that it was the village at Maketu that had been burnt; but those persons who were near Waitaha and close to the seashore near where the Arawa was, at once said: "That must be the Arawa which is burning; it must have been accidentally set on fire by some of our friends who have come to visit us." The next day they went to see what had taken place, and when they reached the place where the Arawa had been lying, they found it had been burnt by an enemy, and that nothing but the ashes of it were left them. Then a messenger started to all the places where the people were scattered about, to warn them of what had taken place, and they then first heard the bad news.

The children of Hou, as they discussed in their house of assembly the burning of the Arawa, remembered the proverb of their father, which he spake to them as they were on the point of leaving Hawaiki, and when he bid them farewell.

He then said to them: "my children, Mako, O Tia, O Hei, hearken to these my words: There was but one great chief in Hawaiki, and that was Whakatauihu. Now do you, my dear children, depart in peace, and when you reach the place you are going to, do not follow after the deeds of Tu, the god of war; if you do you will perish, as if swept off by the winds, but rather follow quiet and useful occupations, then you will die tranquilly a natural death. Depart, and dwell in peace with all, leave war and strife behind you here. Depart, and dwell in peace. It is war and its evils which are driving you from hence; dwell in peace where you are going, conduct yourselves like men, let there be no quarrelling amongst you, but build up a great people."

These were the last words which Houmai-ta-whiti addressed to his children, and they ever kept these sayings of their father firmly fixed in their hearts. "Depart in peace to explore new homes for yourselves."

Uenuku perhaps gave no such parting words of advice to his children, when they left him for this country, because they brought war and its evils with them from the other side of the ocean to New Zealand. But, of course, when Raumati burnt the Arawa, the descendants of Houmai-ta-whiti could not help continually considering what they ought to do, whether they should declare war upon account of the destruction of their canoe, or whether they should let this act pass by without notice. They kept these thoughts always close in mind, and impatient feelings kept ever rising up in their hearts. They could not help saying to one another: "It was upon account of war and its consequences, that we deserted our own country, that we left our fathers, our homes, and our people, and war and evil are following after us here. Yet we cannot remain patient under such an injury, every feeling urges us to revenge this wrong."

At last they made an end of deliberation, and unanimously agreed that they would declare war, to obtain compensation for the evil act of Raumati in burning the Arawa; and then commenced the great war which was waged between those who arrived in the Arawa and those who arrived in the Tainui.

Luck, Fortune & Twists of Fate

Introduction

THE YOUNG PRINCE who helps an old woman out feels full of triumph when she rewards him with the bell she says will help him win the most beautiful woman in the world, the Flower Queen's daughter, in the Romanian folktale of that name. First, though, he has to find her and his rambling journey sees him riding through the world for years on end, undergoing all manner of strange experiences, meeting the King of Fishes, the King of the Foxes, the King of Eagles and the Dragon's Mother before he finds the girl he has been seeking. 'The mind of the man who dreams is fully satisfied by what happens to him,' André Breton, the founder of Surrealist art, observed. When we read folktales we feel as though we dream awake. The characters accept all sorts of weird coincidences and narrative non-sequiturs – why, we don't even bother to ask ourselves, wouldn't we? In this section's stories, travel is all about departure from the norm; taking leave of ordinary logic; abandoning everything that normally makes sense.

King Gumbi and His Lost Daughter

IT WAS BELIEVED IN THE OLDEN TIME that if a king's daughter had the misfortune to be guilty of ten mistakes, she should suffer for half of them, and her father would be punished for the rest. Now, King Gumbi had lately married ten wives, and all at once this old belief of the elders about troubles with daughters came into his head, and he issued a command, which was to be obeyed upon pain of death, that if any female children should be born to him they should be thrown into the Lualaba, and drowned, for, said he, "the dead are beyond temptation to err, and I shall escape mischief."

To avoid the reproaches of his wives, on account of the cruel order, the king thought he would absent himself, and he took a large following with him and went to visit other towns of his country. Within a few days after his departure there were born to him five sons and five daughters. Four of the female infants were at once disposed of according to the king's command; but when the fifth daughter was born, she was so beautiful, and had such great eyes, and her colour was mellow, so like a ripe banana, that the chief nurse hesitated, and when the mother pleaded so hard for her child's life, she made up her mind that the little infant should be saved. When the mother was able to rise, the nurse hastened her away secretly by night. In the morning the queen found herself in a dark forest, and, being alone, she began to talk to herself, as people generally do, and a grey parrot with a beautiful red tail came flying along, and asked, "What is it you are saying to yourself, O Miami?"

She answered and said, "Ah, beautiful little parrot, I am thinking what I ought to do to save the life of my little child. Tell me how I can save her, for Gumbi wishes to destroy all his female children."

The parrot replied, "I grieve for you greatly, but I do not know. Ask the next parrot you see," and he flew away.

A second parrot still more beautiful came flying towards her, whistling and screeching merrily, and the queen lifted her voice and cried –

"Ah, little parrot, stop a bit, and tell me how I can save my sweet child's life; for cruel Gumbi, her father, wants to kill it."

"Ah, mistress, I may not tell; but there is one comes behind me who knows; ask him," and he also flew to his day's haunts.

Then the third parrot was seen to fly towards her, and he made the forest ring with his happy whistling, and Miami cried out again –

"Oh, stay, little parrot, and tell me in what way I can save my sweet child, for Gumbi, her father, vows he will kill it."

"Deliver it to me," answered the parrot. "But first let me put a small banana stalk and two pieces of sugar-cane with it, and then I shall carry it safely to its grandmamma."

The parrot relieved the queen of her child, and flew through the air, screeching merrier than before, and in a short time had laid the little princess, her banana stalk, and two pieces of sugar-cane in the lap of the grandmamma, who was sitting at the door of her house, and said –

"This bundle contains a gift from your daughter, wife of Gumbi. She bids you be careful of it, and let none out of your own family see it, lest she should be slain by the king. And to remember this day, she requests you to plant the banana stalk in your garden at one end, and at the other end the two pieces of sugar-cane, for you may need both."

"Your words are good and wise," answered granny, as she received the babe.

On opening the bundle the old woman discovered a female child, exceedingly pretty, plump, and yellow as a ripe banana, with large black eyes, and such smiles on its bright face that the grandmother's heart glowed with affection for it.

Many seasons came and went by. No stranger came round to ask questions. The banana flourished and grew into a grove, and each sprout marked the passage of a season, and the sugar-cane likewise throve prodigiously as year after year passed and the infant grew into girlhood. When the princess had bloomed into a beautiful maiden, the grandmother had become so old that the events of long ago appeared to her to be like so many dreams, but she still worshipped her child's child, cooked for her, waited upon her, wove new grass mats for her bed, and fine grass-cloths for her dress, and every night before she retired she washed her dainty feet.

Then one day, before her ears were quite closed by age, and her limbs had become too weak to bear her about, the parrot who brought the child to her, came and rested upon a branch near her door, and after piping and whistling its greeting, cried out, "The time has come. Gumbi's daughter must depart, and seek her father. Furnish her with a little drum, teach her a song to sing while she beats it, and send her forth."

Then granny purchased for her a tiny drum, and taught her a song, and when she had been fully instructed she prepared a new canoe with food – from the bananas in the grove, and the plot of sugar-cane, and she made cushions from grass-cloth bags stuffed with silk-cotton floss for her to rest upon. When all was ready she embraced her grand-daughter, and with many tears sent her away down the river, with four women servants.

Granny stood for a long time by the river bank, watching the little canoe disappear with the current, then she turned and entered the doorway, and sitting down closed her eyes, and began to think of the pleasant life she had enjoyed while serving Miami's child; and while so doing she was so pleased that she smiled, and as she smiled she slept, and never woke again.

But the princess, as she floated down and bathed her eyes, which had smarted with her grief, began to think of all that granny had taught her, and began to sing in a fluty voice, as she beat her tiny drum –

"List, all you men,
To the song I sing.
I am Gumbi's child,
Brought up in the wild;
And home I return,
As you all will learn,
When this my little drum
Tells Gumbi I have come, come, come."

The sound of her drum attracted the attention of the fishermen who were engaged with their nets, and seeing a strange canoe with only five women aboard floating down the river, they drew near to it, and when they saw how beautiful the princess was, and noted her graceful, lithe figure clad in robes of fine grass-cloths, they were inclined to lay their hands upon her. But she sang again –

"I am Gumbi's child,
Make way for me;
I am homeward bound,
Make way for me."

Then the fishermen were afraid and did not molest her. But one desirous of being the first to carry the news to the king, and obtain favour and a reward for it, hastened away to tell him that his daughter was coming to visit him.

The news plunged King Gumbi into a state of wonder, for as he had taken such pains to destroy all female children, he could not imagine how he could be the father of a daughter.

Then he sent a quick-footed and confidential slave to inquire, who soon returned and assured him that the girl who was coming to him was his own true daughter.

Then he sent a man who had grown up with him, who knew all that had happened in his court; and he also returned and confirmed all that the slave had said.

Upon this he resolved to go himself, and when he met her he asked –

"Who art thou, child?"

And she replied, "I am the only daughter of Gumbi."

"And who is Gumbi?"

"He is the king of this country," she replied.

"Well, but I am Gumbi myself, and how canst thou be my daughter?" he asked.

"I am the child of thy wife, Miami, and after I was born she hid me that I might not be cast into the river. I have been living with grandmamma, who nursed me, and by the number of banana-stalks in her garden thou mayest tell the number of the seasons that have passed since my birth. One day she told me the time had come, and she sent me to seek my father; and I embarked in the canoe with four servants, and the river bore me to this land."

"Well," said Gumbi, "when I return home I shall question Miami, and I shall soon discover the truth of thy story; but meantime, what must I do for thee?"

"My grandmamma said that thou must sacrifice a goat to the meeting of the daughter with the father," she replied.

Then the king requested her to step on the shore, and when he saw the flash of her yellow feet, and the gleams of her body, which were like shining bright gum, and gazed on the clear, smooth features, and looked into the wondrous black eyes, Gumbi's heart melted and he was filled with pride that such a surpassingly beautiful creature should be his own daughter.

But she refused to set her feet on the shore until another goat had been sacrificed, for her grandmother had said ill-luck would befall her if these ceremonies were neglected.

Therefore the king commanded that two goats should be slain, one for the meeting with his daughter, and one to drive away ill-luck from before her in the land where she would first rest her feet.

When this had been done, she said, "Now, father, it is not meet that thy recovered daughter should soil her feet on the path to her father's house. Thou must lay a grass-cloth along the ground all the way to my mother's door."

The king thereupon ordered a grass-cloth to be spread along the path towards the women's quarters, but he did not mention to which doorway. His daughter then moved forward, the king by her side, until they came in view of all the king's wives, and then Gumbi cried out to them – "One of you, I am told, is the mother of this girl. Look on her, and be not ashamed to own her, for she is as perfect as the egg. At the first sight of her I felt like a man filled with pleasantness, so let the mother come forward and claim her, and let her not destroy herself with a lie."

Now all the women bent forward and longed to say, "She is mine, she is mine!" but Miami, who was ill and weak, sat at the door, and said –

"Continue the matting to my doorway, for as I feel my heart is connected with her as by a cord, she must be the child whom the parrot carried to my mother with a banana stalk and two pieces of sugar-cane."

"Yes, yes, thou must be my own mother," cried the princess; and when the grass-cloth was laid even to the inside of the house, she ran forward, and folded her arms around her.

When Gumbi saw them together he said, "Truly, equals always come together. I see now by many things that the princess must be right. But she will not long remain with me, I fear, for a king's daughter cannot remain many moons without suitors."

Now though Gumbi considered it a trifle to destroy children whom he had never seen, it never entered into his mind to hurt Miami or the princess. On the contrary, he was filled with a gladness which he was never tired of talking about. He was even prouder of his daughter, whose lovely shape and limpid eyes so charmed him, than of all his tall sons. He proved this by the feasts he caused to be provided for all the people. Goats were roasted and stewed, the fishermen brought fish without number, the peasants came loaded with weighty bunches of bananas, and baskets of yams, and manioc, and pots full of beans, and vetches, and millet and corn, and honey and palm-oil, and as for the fowls – who could count them? The people also had plenty to drink of the juice of the palm, and thus they were made to rejoice with the king in the return of the princess.

It was soon spread throughout Manyema that no woman was like unto Gumbi's daughter for beauty. Some said that she was of the colour of a ripe banana, others that she was like fossil gum, others like a reddish oil-nut, and others again that her face was more like the colour of the moon than anything else. The effect of this reputation was to bring nearly all the young chiefs in the land as suitors for her hand. Many of them would have been pleasing to the king, but the princess was averse to them, and she caused it to be made known that she would marry none save the young chief who could produce *matako* (brass rods) by polishing his teeth. The king was very much amused at this, but the chiefs stared in surprise as they heard it.

The king mustered the choicest young men of the land, and he told them it was useless for anyone to hope to be married to the princess unless he could drop brass rods by rubbing his teeth. Though they held it to be impossible that anyone could do such a thing, yet every one of them began to rub his teeth hard, and as they did so, lo! brass rods were seen to drop on the ground from the mouth of one of them, and the people gave a great shout for wonder at it.

The princess was then brought forward, and as the young chief rose to his feet he continued to rub his teeth, and the brass rods were heard to tinkle as they fell to the ground. The marriage was therefore duly proceeded with, and another round of feasts followed, for the king was rich in flocks of goats, and sheep, and in well-tilled fields and slaves.

But after the first moon had waned and gone, the husband said, "Come, now, let us depart, for Gumbi's land is no home for me."

And unknown to Gumbi they prepared for flight, and stowed their canoe with all things needful for a long journey, and one night soon after dark they embarked, and paddled down the river. One day the princess, while she was seated on her cushions, saw a curious nut floating near the canoe, upon which she sprang into the river to obtain it. It eluded her grasp. She swam after it, and the chief followed her as well as he was able, crying out to her to return to the canoe, as there were dangerous animals in the water. But she paid no heed to him, and continued to swim after the nut, until, when she had arrived opposite a village, the princess was hailed by an old woman, who cried, "Ho, princess, I have got what thou seekest. See." And she held the nut up in her hand. Then the princess stepped on shore, and her husband made fast his canoe to the bank.

"Give it to me," demanded the princess, holding out her hand.

"There is one thing thou must do for me before thou canst obtain it."

"What is that?" she asked.

"Thou must lay thy hands upon my bosom to cure me of my disease. Only thus canst thou have it," the old woman said.

The princess laid her hands upon her bosom, and as she did so the old woman was cured of her illness.

"Now thou mayest depart on thy journey, but remember what I tell thee. Thou and thy husband must cling close to this side of the river until thou comest abreast of an island which is in the middle of the entrance to a great lake. For the shore thou seekest is on this side. Once there thou wilt find peace and rest for many years. But if thou goest to the other side of the river thou wilt be lost, thou and thy husband."

Then they re-embarked, and the river ran straight and smooth before them. After some days they discovered that the side they were on was uninhabited, and that their provisions were exhausted, but the other side was cultivated, and possessed many villages and plantations. Forgetting the advice of the old woman, they crossed the river to the opposite shore, and they admired the beauty of the land, and joyed in the odours that came from the gardens and the plantations, and they dreamily listened to the winds that crumpled and tossed the great fronds of banana, and fancied that they had seen no sky so blue. And while they thus dreamed, lo! the river current was bearing them both swiftly along, and they saw the island which was at the entrance to the great lake, and in an instant the beauty of the land which had charmed them had died away, and they now heard the thunderous booming of waters, and saw them surging upward in great sweeps, and one great wave curved underneath them, and they were lifted up, up, up, and dropped down into the roaring abyss, and neither chief nor princess was ever seen again. They were both swallowed up in the deep.

Buttercup

THERE WAS ONCE A POOR WOMAN who I had one son, a little boy so fat and round, and with such bright yellow hair that he was called Buttercup. The house where they lived was upon the edge of a lonely forest, and upon the other side of this forest lived a wicked old witch.

One day when the woman was baking she heard Sharptooth, her dog, begin to bark. "Run, Buttercup, and see who is coming," she said.

Buttercup ran and looked out. "Oh, Mother, it is an old witch with her head under one arm and a bag under the other."

"Come, quick," cried the mother, "and hide yourself in the dough trough so that she may not see you."

Buttercup jumped into the dough trough and his mother shut the lid, so that no one would have known he was there.

Then in a moment there was a knock at the door, and the old witch opened it and looked in. She had put her head on where it belonged now, and she looked almost like any old woman.

"Good day, daughter," said she.

"Good day, mother," answered the woman.

"May I come in and rest my bones a bit?"

The woman did not want her to come in, but neither did she like to say no. "Come in, in heaven's name."

The old witch entered and sat down on the settle, and then she began to look and peer about the room.

"Have you no children?" she asked.

"Yes, I have one son."

"And how do you call him?"

"I call him Buttercup."

"Is he at home?"

"No; his father takes him out with him when he goes hunting."

The old witch looked greatly disappointed. "I am sorry Buttercup is not at home, for I have a sweet little knife – a beautiful silver knife, and it is so sharp that it will cut through anything. If he were only here I would give it to him."

When Buttercup in the dough trough heard this he opened the lid and looked out. "Peep! Peep! here I am!" he cried.

"That is a lucky thing," said she, and she looked well satisfied. "But the knife is at the bottom of my bag and I am so old and stiff that you will have to crawl in yourself and get it."

Buttercup was willing, so into the bag he crawled. Then the old witch closed it and flung it over her shoulder, and away she went so fast that the good mother could neither stop her nor follow her.

The old witch went on and on through the forest, but after a while she began to feel very tired.

"How far is it to Snoring?" she asked of Buttercup in the bag.

"A good two miles," answered Buttercup.

"Two miles! That is a long way. I'll just lie down and sleep a bit, and do you keep as still as a mouse in the bag, or it will be the worse for you."

She tied the mouth of the bag up tight, and then she fell fast asleep, and snored till the leaves shook overhead.

When he heard that, Buttercup took from his pocket a little dull old knife that his father had given him, and managed to cut a slit in the sack and crawl out. Then he found a gnarly stump of a fir tree and put that in the bag in his place and ran away home to his mother, and all this while the old witch never stirred.

After a time, however, she began to stretch her bones and look about her. "Eh! Eh!" she sighed, "that was a good sleep I had, but now we'll be journeying on again."

She slung the bag on her back, but the sharp points of the root kept sticking into her at every step. "That boy looked plump and soft enough," she muttered to herself, "but now he seems all elbows and knees." Then she cried to the stump, "Hey! There, you inside the bag, do not stick your bones into me like that. Do you think I am a pin cushion?"

The stump made no answer for it could not, and besides it had not heard, and the old witch hobbled on muttering and grumbling to herself.

When she reached her house her ugly, stupid witch daughter was watching for her from the window. "Have you brought home anything to eat?" she called.

"Yes, I have brought home a fine plump boy," said the witch, and she threw the bag down on the floor and began rubbing her bruises. "I'm half dead with carrying him, too."

"Let me see," cried the daughter, and she untied the mouth of the sack and looked in. "A boy!" she cried. "This is no boy, but only an old stump of a fir tree."

"Stupid you are, and stupid you will be," cried the witch. "I tell you it is a boy and a good fat boy at that."

"I tell you it is not," said the girl.

"I tell you it is." The old witch took up the sack and looked into it, and there, sure enough, was only an old stump that she had broken her back carrying home. Then she was in a fine rage. "How he got away I don't know, but never mind! I'll have him yet whether or no."

So the next morning while the good woman on the other side of the forest was making her beds she heard Sharptooth begin to bark.

"Run, Buttercup, and see who is coming," she called.

"Mother, it is the same old woman who was here yesterday."

"Quick! Jump into the clock case, and do not dare to so much as stir a finger until she has gone."

Buttercup ran and hid himself in the clock case, and presently there was a knock at the door and the old witch looked into the room.

"Good morning, daughter."

"Good morning, mother."

"May I come in and rest my poor old bones for a minute?"

"Come in, in heaven's name."

The old witch came in and sat down as near the dough trough as she dared.

"Daughter, I have journeyed far and I would be glad of a bit of bread to eat even if it is only the crust."

Well, she might have that and welcome, so the good woman went to the dough trough to get a piece, for that was where she kept it. No sooner had she opened the lid than the old witch was close behind her, looking over her shoulder, and she was disappointed enough when she found that no Buttercup was there.

However, she sat down again with the piece of bread in her hand and began to munch and mumble it, though she had no liking for such dry food as that.

"Is your little boy Buttercup at home today?" she asked.

"No. He has gone with his father to catch some trout for dinner."

"That is a pity," said the old witch, "for I brought a present for him in my bag. I brought him a silver fork, and it is such a dear little, pretty little fork that every bite it carries to your mouth tastes better than what the king himself has to eat."

When Buttercup heard that he could no longer keep still in the clock case. He must have that pretty little fork. "Peep! Peep!" he cried, "Here I am in the clock case." And he opened the door and jumped out.

"That is well," said the old witch, "but I am too old and stiff to bend over and you must crawl into the sack yourself to get the fork."

Before his mother could stop him Buttercup was in the sack, and the old woman had closed the mouth of it, had swung it over her shoulder and was out of the house and off. There was no use in running after her; she went so fast.

After while she was well in the forest, and then she did not hurry so.

"How far is it to Snoring now, you in the bag?" she asked.

"Oh, a mile and a half at least."

"That is a long way for old bones," said the witch. "I'll just sit down and rest a bit; but mind you, no tricks today, for I shall stay wide awake this time."

So she sat down by the road with her back against a tree. Then first she yawned, and next she nodded, and then she was asleep and snoring so that the very rocks around were shaken.

When Buttercup heard that, he whipped out his little knife and cut a slit in the sack and crawled out. Then he put a great heavy stone in the sack and ran away home as fast as his legs would carry him.

After while the old witch began to stretch and yawn. "Well, it's time to be journeying on if we would reach Snoring by daylight," she said, and she did not know she had been asleep at all. She picked up the bag, and whew! but it was heavy. "This boy is fat enough to break a body's back," said she. "He ought to make good eating." But at every step the stone bounced against her ribs till she was black and blue. "Hi! There, you inside the sack, can't you keep a little quieter?" she asked. But the stone made no answer, for it could not.

After a time the old witch reached her house, and her fat ugly daughter came running to meet her.

"Did you catch the same boy?" asked the girl.

"The very same, and fatter than ever," answered the witch, and she threw the bag down on the floor, bump!

"Oh, let me see him." And the witch girl put her hand on the bag.

"Let it alone!" screamed the witch mother. "If you go goggling at him again you'll turn him into a stick or a stone or something, as you did before. Put on a kettle of water, and as soon as it is hot I'll empty him into it."

The witch girl did as she was told, and every time she went past the sack she gave it a poke with her foot. "The boy may be fat," she said, "but he's tough enough to break a body's teeth in the eating."

When the water began to boil she called her mother, and the old witch picked up the sack intending to empty Buttercup into the pot, but instead the great stone rolled into it, ker-splash! and the boiling water flew all about. It flew on the old witch and burned her so that she stamped about the kitchen gnashing her teeth with rage. The fat daughter was so frightened she ran out and hid in the stable until all was quiet again. "Never mind!" said the old witch. "I'll have the boy tomorrow for sure." So the next day she took up the bag and started off for the third time through the forest.

The good mother was scrubbing her pans when Sharptooth began to bark outside. "Run, Buttercup, and see who is coming now."

"Mother, it is the same old witch who has been here twice before."

"Quick, quick! Hide in the cellar way, and try not to breathe until she has gone."

Buttercup ran and hid himself in the cellar way, and he was scarcely there before there was a knock at the door and the old witch pushed it open and looked in.

"May I come in and rest a bit?"

"Come in, in heaven's name."

The old witch stepped in and looked all about her.

"I would like to know what time it is."

"Well, look for yourself; there stands the clock."

The old witch went close to it and took the chance to peep inside the case, but no little boy was there. Then she sat down near the door.

"Is your little boy Buttercup at home today?"

The mother said, "No, he has gone to the mill with his father."

"That is a pity," said the old witch, "for I have a pretty little spoon in my bag that I meant to give to him, and it is such a smart little spoon that if you do but stir your porridge with it, it changes it into something so delicious that the princess herself would be glad to eat it."

When Buttercup in the cellar way heard that he wanted the spoon so badly that he could stay hidden no longer. "Peep! Peep! Here I am," said he.

"I am glad of that," said the witch, "for I had no wish to take the spoon home again; but you will have to crawl into the sack yourself to get it, for I am too old and stiff."

In a moment Buttercup was in the sack, and in another moment the old witch had swung it over her back and was making off as fast as her legs would carry her. This time she neither stayed nor stopped, but went straight on home, and flung the sack on the floor with Buttercup in it.

"Did you get him this time?" asked the girl.

"Yes, I did," said the old witch, "and there he is, as plump as any young chicken. Now I'll be off to ask the guests, and do you put him in the pot and make a nice stew of him."

As soon as she had gone the witch girl opened the sack and told Buttercup to come out. "Now put your head on the block, Buttercup," she said, "so that I may chop it off."

"But I do not know how," said Buttercup.

"Stupid! It is easy enough; anyone would know how to do that."

"Then show me how, and I will hold the axe for you."

The stupid witch girl put her head on the block, and as soon as she did that, Buttercup cut it off. He put the head on the pillow of the bed and drew the coverlid up about it and then it looked exactly as though the witch girl were lying there asleep, but the body of her he popped into the pot of boiling water. Then he climbed up on the roof and took the fir tree stump and the stone with him.

And now home came the old witch again and all her troll friends with her, and they were an ugly looking set all together.

They went stamping into the house and the old witch began to bawl for her daughter, but there was no answer. She looked about her and spied the head there on the pillow with the covers drawn up about it. "So there you are!" cried the old witch. "Well, if you are too lazy to get up and eat your dinner, you will have to be content with what we leave." Then she picked up a big spoon and tasted the broth.

"Good, by my troth,
Is Buttercup broth,"

said she, and smacked her lips.

"Good, by my troth,
Is witch daughter broth,"

sang Buttercup out on the roof.

"Who was that?" asked the witch.

"Oh, it was only a bird singing outside," said her husband, and he took the spoon himself and tasted the broth.

"Good, by my troth,
Is Buttercup broth,"

said he.

"Good, by my troth,
Is witch daughter broth,"

sang Buttercup on the roof.

"There certainly is someone outside there mocking at us," said the old witch, and she ran out to see.

As soon as she came out Buttercup threw the stump down on her and killed her, and that was the end of her.

The witch's husband waited for a time, and when she did not come back he went to call her, but as soon as he stepped outside Buttercup rolled the big stone down on him, and that was an end of him.

The friends who had come to share the broth waited and waited for the witch and her husband to come back, but after a time, as they did not, the guests grew impatient and came out to look for them. When they saw the two lying there dead they never stopped for the broth, but ran away as fast as they could go, and for all I know they may be running still.

But Buttercup climbed down from the roof, and hunted round in the house until he found where the witch kept her money chest all full of gold and silver money. Then he filled the sack with as much as he could carry, and started home again. When he reached there you may guess whether or not his mother was glad to see him. Then there was no more poverty for them, for the money in the sack was enough to make them rich for all their lives.

Esben and the Witch

THERE WAS ONCE A MAN who had twelve sons: the eleven eldest were both big and strong, but the twelfth, whose name was Esben, was only a little fellow. The eleven eldest went out with their father to field and forest, but Esben preferred to stay at home with his mother, and so he was never reckoned at all by the rest, but was a sort of outcast among them.

When the eleven had grown up to be men they decided to go out into the world to try their fortune, and they plagued their father to give them what they required for the journey. The father was not much in favour of this, for he was now old and weak, and could not well spare them from helping him with his work, but in the long run he had to give in. Each one of the eleven got a fine white horse and money for the journey, and so they said farewell to their father and their home, and rode away.

As for Esben, no one had ever thought about him; his brothers had not even said farewell to him.

After the eleven were gone Esben went to his father and said, "Father, give me also a horse and money; I should also like to see round about me in the world."

"You are a little fool," said his father. "If I could have let you go, and kept your eleven brothers at home, it would have been better for me in my old age."

"Well, you will soon be rid of me at any rate," said Esben.

As he could get no other horse, he went into the forest, broke off a branch, stripped the bark off it, so that it became still whiter than his brothers' horses, and, mounted on this, rode off after his eleven brothers.

The brothers rode on the whole day, and towards evening they came to a great forest, which they entered. Far within the wood they came to a little house, and knocked at the door. There came an old, ugly, bearded hag, and opened it, and they asked her whether all of them could get quarters for the night.

"Yes," said the old, bearded hag, "you shall all have quarters for the night, and, in addition, each of you shall have one of my daughters."

The eleven brothers thought that they had come to very hospitable people. They were well attended to, and when they went to bed, each of them got one of the hag's daughters.

Esben had been coming along behind them, and had followed the same way, and had also found the same house in the forest. He slipped into this, without either the witch or her daughters noticing him, and hid himself under one of the beds. A little before midnight he crept quietly out and wakened his brothers. He told these to change night-caps with the witch's daughters. The brothers saw no reason for this, but, to get rid of Esben's persistence, they made the exchange, and slept soundly again.

When midnight came Esben heard the old witch come creeping along. She had a broad-bladed axe in her hand, and went over all the eleven beds. It was so dark that she could not see a hand's breadth before her, but she felt her way, and hacked the heads off all the sleepers who had the men's night-caps on – and these were her own daughters. As soon as she had gone her way Esben wakened his brothers, and they hastily took their horses and rode off from the witch's house, glad that they had escaped so well. They quite forgot to thank Esben for what he had done for them.

When they had ridden onwards for some time they reached a king's palace, and inquired there whether they could be taken into service. Quite easily, they were told, if they would be stablemen, otherwise the king had no use for them. They were quite ready for this, and got the task of looking after all the king's horses.

Long after them came Esben riding on his stick, and he also wanted to get a place in the palace, but no one had any use for him, and he was told that he could just go back the way he had come. However, he stayed there and occupied himself as best he could. He got his food, but nothing more, and by night he lay just where he could.

At this time there was in the palace a knight who was called Sir Red. He was very well liked by the king, but hated by everyone else, for he was wicked both in will and deed. This Sir Red became angry with the eleven brothers, because they would not always stand at attention for him, so he determined to avenge himself on them.

One day, therefore, he went to the king, and said that the eleven brothers who had come to the palace a little while ago, and served as stablemen, could do a great deal more than they pretended. One day he had heard them say that if they liked they could get for the king a wonderful dove which had a feather of gold and a feather of silver time about. But they would not procure it unless they were threatened with death.

The king then had the eleven brothers called before him, and said to them, "You have said that you can get me a dove which has feathers of gold and silver time about."

All the eleven assured him that they had never said anything of the kind, and they did not believe that such a dove existed in the whole world.

"Take your own mind of it," said the king; "but if you don't get that dove within three days you shall lose your heads, the whole lot of you."

With that the king let them go, and there was great grief among them; some wept and others lamented.

At that moment Esben came along, and, seeing their sorrowful looks, said to them, "Hello, what's the matter with you?"

"What good would it do to tell you, you little fool? You can't help us."

"Oh, you don't know that," answered Esben. "I have helped you before."

In the end they told him how unreasonable the king was, and how he had ordered them to get for him a dove with feathers of gold and silver time about.

"Give me a bag of peas" said Esben, "and I shall see what I can do for you."

Esben got his bag of peas; then he took his white stick, and said,

Fly quick, my little stick, Carry me across the stream.

Straightway the stick carried him across the river and straight into the old witch's courtyard. Esben had noticed that she had such a dove; so when he arrived in the courtyard he shook the peas out of the bag, and the dove came fluttering down to pick them up. Esben caught it at once, put it into the bag, and hurried off before the witch caught sight of him; but the next moment she came running, and shouted after him, "Hey is that you, Esben?"

"Ye–e–s!"

"Is it you that has taken my dove?"

"Ye–e–s!"

"Was it you that made me kill my eleven daughters?"

"Ye–e–s!"

"Are you coming back again?"

"That may be," said Esben.

"Then you'll catch it," shouted the witch.

The stick carried Esben with the dove back to the king's palace, and his brothers were greatly delighted. The king thanked them many times for the dove, and gave them in return both silver and gold. At this Sir Red became still more embittered, and again thought of how to avenge himself on the brothers.

One day he went to the king and told him that the dove was by no means the best thing that the brothers could get for him; for one day he had heard them talking quietly among themselves, and they had said that they could procure a boar whose bristles were of gold and silver time about.

The king again summoned the brothers before him, and asked whether it was true that they had said that they could get for him a boar whose bristles were of gold and silver time about.

"No," said the brothers; they had never said nor thought such a thing, and they did not believe that there was such a boar in the whole world.

"You must get me that boar within three days," said the king, "or it will cost you your heads."

With that they had to go. This was still worse than before, they thought. Where could they get such a marvellous boar? They all went about hanging their heads; but when only one day remained of the three Esben came along. When he saw his brothers' sorrowful looks he cried, "Hallo, what's the matter now?"

"Oh, what's the use of telling you?" said his brothers. "You can't help us, at any rate."

"Ah, you don't know that," said Esben; "I've helped you before."

In the end they told him how Sir Red had stirred up the king against them, so that he had ordered them to get for him a boar with bristles of gold and silver time about.

"That's all right," said Esben; "give me a sack of malt, and it is not quite impossible that I may be able to help you."

Esben got his sack of malt; then he took his little white stick, set himself upon it, and said,

Fly quick, my little stick, Carry me across the stream.

Off went the stick with him, and very soon he was again in the witch's courtyard. There he emptied out the malt, and next moment came the boar, which had every second bristle of gold and of silver. Esben at once put it into his sack and hurried off before the witch should catch sight of him; but the next moment she came running, and shouted after him, "Hey! Is that you, Esben?"

"Ye–e–s!"

"Is it you that has taken my pretty boar?"

"Ye–e–s!"

"It was also you that took my dove?"

"Ye–e–s!"

"And it was you that made me kill my eleven daughters?"

"Ye–e–s!"

"Are you coming back again?"

"That may be," said Esben.

"Then you'll catch it," said the witch.

Esben was soon back at the palace with the boar, and his brothers scarcely knew which leg to stand on, so rejoiced were they that they were safe again. Not one of them, however, ever thought of thanking Esben for what he had done for them.

The king was still more rejoiced over the boar than he had been over the dove, and did not know what to give the brothers for it. At this Sir Red was again possessed with anger and envy, and again he went about and planned how to get the brothers into trouble.

One day he went again to the king and said, "These eleven brothers have now procured the dove and the boar, but they can do much more than that; I know they have said that if they liked they could get for the king a lamp that can shine over seven kingdoms."

"If they have said that," said the king, "they shall also be made to bring it to me. That would be a glorious lamp for me."

Again the king sent a message to the brothers to come up to the palace. They went accordingly, although very unwillingly, for they suspected that Sir Red had fallen on some new plan to bring them into trouble.

As soon as they came before the king he said to them,

"You brothers have said that you could, if you liked, get for me a lamp that can shine over seven kingdoms. That lamp must be mine within three days, or it will cost you your lives."

The brothers assured him that they had never said so, and they were sure that no such lamp existed, but their words were of no avail.

"The lamp!" said the king, "or it will cost you your heads."

The brothers were now in greater despair than ever. They did not know what to do, for such a lamp no one had ever heard of. But just as things looked their worst along came Esben.

"Something wrong again?" said he. "What's the matter with you now?"

"Oh, it's no use telling you," said they. "You can't help us, at any rate."

"Oh, you might at least tell me," said Esben; "I have helped you before."

In the end they told him that the king had ordered them to bring him a lamp which could shine over seven kingdoms, but such a lamp no one had ever heard tell of.

"Give me a bushel of salt," said Esben, "and we shall see how matters go."

He got his bushel of salt, and then mounted his little white stick, and said,

Fly quick, my little stick, Carry me across the stream.

With that both he and his bushel of salt were over beside the witch's courtyard. But now matters were less easy, for he could not get inside the yard, as it was evening and the gate was locked. Finally he hit upon a plan; he got up on the roof and crept down the chimney.

He searched all round for the lamp, but could find it nowhere, for the witch always had it safely guarded, as it was one of her most precious treasures. When he became tired of searching for it he crept into the baking-oven, intending to lie down there and sleep till morning; but just at that moment he heard the witch calling from her bed to one of her daughters, and telling her to make some porridge for her. She had grown hungry, and had taken such a fancy to some porridge. The daughter got out of bed, kindled the fire, and put on a pot with water in it.

"You mustn't put any salt in the porridge, though," cried the witch.

"No, neither will I," said the daughter; but while she was away getting the meal Esben slipped out of the oven and emptied the whole bushel of salt into the pot. The daughter came back then and put in the meal, and after it had boiled a little she took it in to her mother. The witch took a spoonful and tasted it.

"Uh!" said she; "didn't I tell you not to put any salt in it, and it's just as salt as the sea."

So the daughter had to go and make new porridge, and her mother warned her strictly not to put any salt in it. But now there was no water in the house, so she asked her mother to give her the lamp, so that she could go to the well for more.

"There you have it, then," said the witch; "but take good care of it."

The daughter took the lamp which shone over seven kingdoms, and went out to the well for water, while Esben slipped out after her. When she was going to draw the water from the well she set the lamp down on a stone beside her. Esben watched his chance, seized the lamp, and gave her a push from behind, so that she plumped head first into the well. Then he made off with the lamp. But the witch got out of her bed and ran after him, crying:

"Hey! is that you again, Esben?"

"Ye–e–s!"

"Was it you that took my dove?"

"Ye–e–s!"

"Was it also you that took my boar?"

"Ye–e–s!"

"And it was you that made me kill my eleven daughters?"

"Ye–e–s!"

"And now you have taken my lamp, and drowned my twelfth daughter in the well?"

"Ye–e–s!"

"Are you coming back again?"

"That may be," said Esben.

"Then you'll catch it," said the witch.

It was only a minute before the stick had again landed Esben at the king's palace, and the brothers were then freed from their distress. The king gave them many fine presents, but Esben did not get even so much as thanks from them.

Never had Sir Red been so eaten up with envy as he was now, and he racked his brain day and night to find something quite impossible to demand from the brothers.

One day he went to the king and told him that the lamp the brothers had procured was good enough, but they could still get for him something that was far better. The king asked what that was.

"It is," said Sir Red, "the most beautiful coverlet that any mortal ever heard tell of. It also has the property that, when anyone touches it, it sounds so that it can be heard over eight kingdoms."

"That must be a splendid coverlet," said the king, and he at once sent for the brothers.

"You have said that you know of a coverlet, the most beautiful in the whole world, and which sounds over eight kingdoms when anyone touches it. You shall procure it for me, or else lose your lives," said he.

The brothers answered him that they had never said a word about such a coverlet, did not believe it existed, and that it was quite impossible for them to procure it. But the king would not hear a word; he drove them away, telling them that if they did not get it very soon it would cost them their heads.

Things looked very black again for the brothers, for they were sure there was no escape for them. The youngest of them, indeed, asked where Esben was, but the others said that that little fool could scarcely keep himself in clothes, and it was not to be expected that he could help them. Not one of them thought it worthwhile to look for Esben, but he soon came along of himself.

"Well, what's the matter now?" said he.

"Oh, what's the use of telling you?" said the brothers. "You can't help us, at any rate."

"Ah! Who knows that?" said Esben. "I have helped you before."

In the end the brothers told him about the coverlet which, when one touched it, sounded so that it could be heard over eight kingdoms. Esben thought that this was the worst errand that he had had yet, but he could not do worse than fail, and so he would make the attempt.

He again took his little white stick, set himself on it, and said,

Fly quick, my little stick, Carry me across the stream.

Next moment he was across the river and beside the witch's house. It was evening, and the door was locked, but he knew the way down the chimney. When he had got into the house, however, the worst yet remained to do, for the coverlet was on the bed in which the witch lay and slept. He slipped into the room without either she or her daughter wakening; but as soon as he touched the coverlet to take it it sounded so that it could be heard over eight kingdoms. The witch awoke, sprang out of bed, and caught hold of Esben. He struggled with her, but could not free himself, and the witch called to her daughter, "Come and help me; we shall put him into the little dark room to be fattened. Ho, ho! Now I have him!"

Esben was now put into a little dark hole, where he neither saw sun nor moon, and there he was fed on sweet milk and nut-kernels. The daughter had enough to do cracking nuts for him, and at the end of fourteen days she had only one tooth left in her mouth; she had broken all the rest with the nuts. In this time however, she had taken a liking to Esben, and would willingly have set him free, but could not.

When some time had passed the witch told her daughter to go and cut a finger off Esben, so that she could see whether he was nearly fat enough yet. The daughter went and told Esben, and asked him what she should do. Esben told her to take an iron nail and wrap a piece of skin round it: she could then give her mother this to bite at.

The daughter did so, but when the witch bit it she cried, "Uh! No, no! This is nothing but skin and bone; he must be fattened much longer yet."

So Esben was fed for a while longer on sweet milk and nut-kernels, until one day the witch thought that now he must surely be fat enough, and told her daughter again to go and cut a finger off him. By this time Esben was tired of staying in the dark hole, so he told her to go and cut a teat off a cow, and give it to the witch to bite at. This the daughter did, and the witch cried, "Ah! now he is fat – so fat that one can scarcely feel the bone in him. Now he shall be killed."

Now this was just the very time that the witch had to go to Troms Church, where all the witches gather once every year, so she had no time to deal with Esben herself. She therefore told her daughter to heat up the big oven while she was away, take Esben out of his prison, and roast him in there before she came back. The daughter promised all this, and the witch went off on her journey.

The daughter then made the oven as hot as could be, and took Esben out of his prison in order to roast him. She brought the oven spade, and told Esben to seat himself on it, so that she could shoot him into the oven. Esben accordingly took his seat on it, but when she had got him to the mouth of the oven he spread his legs out wide, so that she could not get him pushed in.

"You mustn't sit like that," said she.

"How then?" said Esben.

"You must cross your legs," said the daughter; but Esben could not understand what she meant by this.

"Get out of the way," said she, "and I will show you how to place yourself."

She seated herself on the oven spade, but no sooner had she done so than Esben laid hold of it, shot her into the oven, and fastened the door of it. Then he ran and seized the coverlet, but as soon as he did so it sounded so that it could be heard over eight kingdoms, and the witch, who was at Troms Church, came flying home, and shouted, "Hey! is that you again, Esben?"

"Ye–e–s!"

"It was you that made me kill my eleven daughters?"

"Ye–e–s!"

"And took my dove?"

"Ye–e–s!"

"And my beautiful boar?"

"Ye–e–s!"

"And drowned my twelfth daughter in the well, and took my lamp?"

"Ye–e–s!"

"And now you have roasted my thirteenth and last daughter in the oven, and taken my coverlet?"

"Ye–e–s!"

"Are you coming back again?"

"No, never again," said Esben.

At this the witch became so furious that she sprang into numberless pieces of flint, and from this come all the flint stones that one finds about the country.

Esben had found again his little stick, which the witch had taken from him, so he said,

Fly quick, my little stick, Carry me across the stream.

Next moment he was back at the king's palace. Here things were in a bad way, for the king had thrown all the eleven brothers into prison, and they were to be executed very shortly because they had not brought him the coverlet. Esben now went up to the king and gave him the coverlet, with which the king was greatly delighted. When he touched it it could be heard over eight kingdoms, and all the other kings sat and were angry because they had not one like it.

Esben also told how everything had happened, and how Sir Red had done the brothers all the ill he could devise because he was envious of them. The brothers were at once set at liberty, while Sir Red, for his wickedness, was hanged on the highest tree that could be found, and so he got the reward he deserved.

Much was made of Esben and his brothers, and these now thanked him for all that he had done for them. The twelve of them received as much gold and silver as they could carry, and betook themselves home to their old father. When he saw again his twelve sons, whom he had never expected to see more, he was so glad that he wept for joy. The brothers told him how much Esben had done, and how he had saved their lives, and from that time forward he was no longer the butt of the rest at home.

The Isle of Udröst

ONCE UPON A TIME there lived at Vaerö, not far from Röst, a poor fisherman, named Isaac. He had nothing but a boat and a couple of goats, which his wife fed as well as she could with fish leavings, and with the grass she was able to gather on the surrounding hills; but his whole hut was full of hungry children. Yet he was always satisfied with what God sent him. The only thing that worried him was his inability to live at peace with his neighbour. The latter was a rich man, thought himself entitled to far more than such a beggarly fellow as Isaac, and wanted to get him out of the way, in order to take for himself the anchorage before Isaac's hut.

One day Isaac had put out a few miles to sea to fish, when suddenly a dark fog fell, and in a flash such a tremendous storm broke, that he had to throw all his fish overboard in order to lighten ship and save his life. Even then it was very hard to keep the boat afloat; but he steered a careful course between and across the mountainous waves, which seemed ready to swallow him from moment to moment. After he had kept on for five or six hours in this manner, he thought that he ought to touch land somewhere. But time went by, and the storm and fog grew worse and worse. Then he began to realize that either he was steering out to sea, or that the wind had veered, and at last he made sure the latter was the case; for he sailed on and on without a sight of land. Suddenly he heard a hideous cry from the stern of the boat, and felt certain that it was the *drang*, who was singing his death-song. Then he prayed God to guard his wife and children, for he thought his last hour had come. As he sat there and prayed, he made out something black; but when his boat drew nearer, he noticed that it was only three cormorants, sitting on a piece of driftwood and – swish! – he had passed them. Thus he sailed for a long time, and grew so hungry, so thirsty and so weary that he did not know what to do; for the most part he sat with the rudder in his hand and slept. But all of a sudden the boat ran up on a beach and stopped. Then Isaac opened his eyes. The sun broke through the fog, and shone on a beautiful land. Its hills and mountains were green to their very tops, fields and meadows lay among their slopes, and he seemed to breathe a fragrance of flowers and grass sweeter than any he had ever known before.

"God be praised, now I am safe, for this is Udröst!" said Isaac to himself. Directly ahead of him lay a field of barley, with ears so large and heavy that he had never seen their like, and through the barley-field a narrow path led to a green turf-roofed cottage of clay, that rose above the field, and on the roof of the cottage grazed a white goat with gilded horns, and an udder as large as that of the largest cow. Before the door sat a little man clad in blue, puffing away at a little pipe. He had a beard so long and so large that it hung far down upon his breast.

"Welcome to Udröst, Isaac!" said the man.

"Good day to you, father," said Isaac, "and do you know me?"

"It might be that I do," said the man. "I suppose you want to stay here overnight?"

"That would suit me very well, father," was Isaac's reply.

"The trouble is with my sons, for they cannot bear the smell of a Christian," answered the man. "Did you meet them?"

"No, I only met three cormorants, who were sitting on a piece of driftwood and croaking," was Isaac's reply.

"Well, those were my sons," said the man, and emptied his pipe, "and now come into the house, for I think you must be hungry and thirsty."

"I'll take that liberty, father," said Isaac.

When the man opened the door, everything within was so beautiful that Isaac could not get over his admiration. He had never seen anything like it. The table was covered with the finest dishes, bowls of cream, and salmon and game, and liver dumplings with syrup, and cheese as well, and there were whole piles of doughnuts, and there was mead, and everything else that is good. Isaac ate and drank bravely, and yet his plate was never empty; and no matter how much he drank, his glass was always full. The man neither ate much nor said much; but suddenly they heard a noise and clamour before the house, and the man went out. After a time he returned with his three sons, and Isaac trembled inwardly when they came through the door; but their father must have quieted them, for they were very friendly and amiable, and told Isaac he must use his guest-right, and sit down and drink with them; for Isaac had risen to leave the table, saying he had satisfied his hunger. But he gave in to them, and they drank mead together, and became good friends. And they said that Isaac must go fishing with them, so that he would have something to take with him when he went home.

The first time they put out a great storm was raging. One of the sons sat at the rudder, the second at the bow, and the third in the middle; and Isaac had to work with the bailing-can until he dripped perspiration. They sailed as though they were mad. They never reefed a sail, and when the boat was full of water, they danced on the crests of the waves, and slid down them so that the water in the stern spurted up like a fountain. After a time the storm subsided, and they began to fish. And the sea was so full of fish that they could not even put out an anchor, since mountains of fish were piled up beneath them. The sons of Udröst drew up one fish after another. Isaac knew his business; but he had taken along his own fishing-tackle, and as soon as a fish bit he let go again, and at last he had caught not a single one. When the boat was filled, they sailed home again to Udröst, and the sons cleaned the fish, and laid them on the stands. Meanwhile Isaac had complained to their father of his poor luck. The man promised that he should do better next time, and gave him a couple of hooks; and the next time they went out to fish, Isaac caught just as many as the others, and when they reached home, he was given three stands of fish as his share.

At length Isaac began to get homesick, and when he was about to leave, the man made him a present of a new fishing-boat, full of meal, and tackle and other useful things. Isaac thanked him repeatedly, and the man invited him to come back when the season opened again, since he himself was going to take a cargo to Bergen, in the second *stevne*, and Isaac could go along and sell his fish there himself. Isaac was more than willing, and asked him what course he should set when he again wanted to reach Udröst. "All you need do is to follow the cormorant when he heads for the open sea, then you will be on the right course," said the man. "Good luck on your way!"

But when Isaac got underway, and looked around, there was no Udröst in sight; far and wide, all around him, he saw no more than the ocean.

When the time came, Isaac sailed to join the man of Udröst's fishing-craft. But such a craft he had never seen before. It was two hails long, so that when the steersman, who was on look-out in the stern, wanted to call out something to the rower, the latter could not hear him. So they had stationed another man in the middle of the ship, close by the mast, who had to relay the steersman's call to the rower, and even he had to shout as loudly as he could in order to make himself heard.

Isaac's share was laid down in the forepart of the boat; and he himself took down the fish from the stands; yet he could not understand how it was that the stands were continually filled with fresh fish, no matter how many he took away, and when he sailed away they were still as full as ever. When he reached Bergen, he sold his fish, and got so much money for them that he was able to buy a new schooner, completely fitted out, and with a cargo to boot, as the man of Udröst had advised him. Late in the evening, when he was about to sail for home, the man came aboard and told him never to forget those who survived his neighbour, for his neighbour himself had died; and then he wished Isaac all possible success and good fortune for his schooner, in advance. "All is well, and all stands firm that towers in the air," said he, and what he meant was that there was one aboard whom none could see, but who would support the mast on his back, if need be.

Since that time fortune was Isaac's friend. And well he knew why this was so, and never forgot to prepare something good for whoever held the winter watch, when the schooner was drawn up on land in the fall. And every Christmas night there was the glow and shimmer of light, the sound of fiddles and music, of laughter and merriment, and of dancing on the deserted schooner.

The Dreamer

THERE ONCE LIVED A MAN AND HIS WIFE, named Peter and Kate, and they were so poor that they had scarcely enough bread to put in their mouths. They lived in a wretched, miserable hut, and in front of the hut was a river, and back of it a patch of ground and a gnarled old apple tree.

One night when Peter was sleeping he dreamed a dream, and in this dream a tall old man dressed in grey, and with a long grey beard, came to him and said, "Peter, I know that you have had a hard life, and have neither grumbled nor complained, and now I have a mind to help you. Follow down the river until you come to a bridge. On the other side of the river you will see a town. Take up your stand on the bridge and wait there patiently. It may be that nothing will happen the first day, and it may be that nothing will happen the second day either, but if you do not lose courage, but still wait patiently, some time during the third day someone will come to you, and tell you something that will make your fortune for you."

In the morning, when Peter awoke, he told his dream to Kate, his wife. "It would be a curious thing if I should do as the old man told me and really become rich," said he.

"Nonsense!" answered his wife. "Dreams are nothing but foolishness. Do you go over to Neighbour Goodkin and see whether he has not some wood to be cut, so you can earn a few pence to buy meal for tomorrow."

So Peter did as his wife told him, and went over to his neighbour's and worked there all day, and by evening he had almost forgotten his dream.

But that night, as soon as he fell asleep, the old man appeared before him again. "Why have you not done as I told you, Peter?" said he. "Remember, good luck will not wait forever. Tomorrow do you set out for the bridge and town I told you of, and believe, for it is the truth; if you wait there for three days and make the best of what will then be told you you will become a rich man."

When Peter awoke the next morning, his first thought was to set out in search of the bridge and town of which the old man had told him, but still his wife dissuaded him.

"Do not be so foolish," said she. "Sit down and eat your breakfast and be thankful that you have it. You earned a few pence yesterday, and who knows but what you may be lucky enough to earn even more today."

So Peter did not set out on his journey in search of fortune that day either.

But the next night for the third time the old man appeared before him, and now his look was stern and forbidding. "Thou fool!" said he. "Three times have I come to thee, and now I will come no more. Go to the bridge of which I have spoken and listen well to what is there said to thee. Otherwise want and poverty will still be thy portion, even as they have been heretofore."

With this the old man disappeared, and Peter awoke. And now it was of no use for his wife to scold and argue. As the old man had commanded so Peter would do. He only stopped to put some food in his stomach and more in his pockets, and off he set, one foot before another.

For a long time Peter journeyed on down the river till he was both footsore and weary, and then he came to a bridge that crossed the stream, and on the other side was a town, and Peter felt almost sure this was the place to which the old man of his dreams had told him to come.

So he took his stand on the bridge and stayed there all day. The passers-by stared at him, and some of them spoke to him, but none of them said to him anything that might, by any chance, lead him on to fortune. All that day he waited on the bridge, and all of the day after, and by the time the third day came, he had eaten all the food he had brought with him except one hard, dry crust of bread. Then he began to wonder whether he were not a simpleton to be loitering there day after day, all because of a dream, when he might, perhaps, be earning a few pennies at home in one way or another.

Now just beyond this bridge there was a tailor's shop, and the tailor who lived there was a very curious man. Ever since Peter had taken his stand on the bridge the tailor had been peeping out at him, and wondering why he was standing there, and what his business might be; and the longer Peter stayed the more curious the tailor became. He fussed and he fidgeted, and along toward the afternoon of the third day he could bear it no longer, and he put aside his work and went out to the bridge to find out what he could about Peter and what he was doing there.

When he came where Peter was he bade him good day.

"Good day," answered Peter.

"Are you waiting here on the bridge for someone?" asked the tailor.

"I am and I am not," replied Peter.

"Now what may be the meaning of that?" asked the tailor. "How can you be waiting and still not be waiting all at one and the same time?"

"I am waiting for someone – that is true"; said Peter, "but I know not who he is nor whence he will come, nor, for the matter of that, whether anyone will come at all." And then he related to the tailor his dream, and how he had been told that if he waited on the bridge for three days someone would come along and tell him something that would make him rich for life.

"Why, what a silly fellow you are," said the tailor. "I, too, have dreamed dreams, but I have too much sense to pay any attention to them. Only last week I dreamed three times that an old man came to me and told me to follow up along the bank of the river until I came to a hut where a man and his wife lived, – the man's name was Peter, and his wife's name was Kate. I was to go and dig among the roots of an apple tree back of this house, and there, buried among the roots of the tree, I would find a chest of golden money. That was what I dreamed. But did I go wandering off in search of such a place? No, indeed, I am not such a simpleton. I stick to my work, and I can manage to keep a warm roof over my head, and have plenty of food to eat, and when I am dressed in my best there is not one of the neighbours that looks half as fine as I do. No, no; go back to where you belong and set to work, my man, and maybe you can earn something better than those miserable rags you are wearing now."

So said the tailor, and then he went back to his tailor's bench and his sewing.

But Peter stood and scratched his head. "A man named Peter, and his wife named Kate! And an apple tree behind the house!" said he. "Now it's a strange thing if a fortune's been lying there under the roots of the apple tree all this while, and I had to come to this town and this bridge to hear about it!"

So said Peter as he stood there on the bridge. But then, after he had scratched his head and thought a bit longer, he pulled his hat down over his ears and off he set for home. The farther he went, the more of a hurry he was in, and at last, when he came within sight of his house again, he was all out of breath with the haste he had made.

He did not wait to go inside, but he bawled to his wife to fetch him a pick and shovel, and ran around the house to where the apple tree stood.

His wife did not know what had happened to him. She thought he must have lost his wits, but she brought him the pick and shovel, and he began digging around about the roots of the apple tree.

He had not dug for so very long when his pick struck something hard. He flung the pick aside and seized his spade, and presently he uncovered a great chest made of stout oak wood and bound about with iron.

The chest was so heavy that he could not lift it out of the hole himself, and his wife had to help him. The chest was locked, but that mattered little to Peter. He took his pick, and with a few blows he broke the hinges and fastenings, and lifted the lid from its place. At once he gave a loud cry, and fell on his knees beside the chest. He and his wife could scarce believe in their good fortune. It was brimming over with golden money, enough to make them rich for life.

They carried the chest into the house, and barred the door, and set about counting the money, and there was so much of it, they were all evening and part of the night counting it.

That was the way good fortune came to Peter, and all by way of a dream.

Now he and his wife built themselves a great house, and had fine food, and coaches, and horses, and handsome clothes, and they feasted the neighbours, and never a poor man came to the door but what they gave him as much food as he could eat and a piece of silver to put in his pocket.

One day Peter put on his finest clothes and made his wife dress herself in her best, and then they stepped into one of their coaches, and Peter bade the coachman drive to the town where he had stood on the bridge and listened to the tailor tell his dream of the chest of money buried under the apple tree.

Peter made the coachman drive up in front of the tailor's shop, and when the tailor saw the coach stopping at his door, and the fine people sitting in it, he thought it was some great nobleman and his wife, come perhaps to order a suit of clothes of him.

He came out, bowing and smiling and smirking, and Peter said to him, "Do you remember me?"

"No, your lordship," answered the tailor, still bowing and smiling, "I have not that honour, your lordship."

Then Peter told him he was the ragged fellow who had stood out there on the bridge waiting for good luck to come to him; and sure enough it had, for if it had not been for the dream the tailor told him, he would have known nothing about the gold buried under the apple tree and would never have become the rich man he was now.

When the tailor heard this tale, he was ready to tear his hair out, for if he had believed his dream he might have found the gold himself and have kept a share of it.

However, Peter gave him a hundred gold pieces to comfort him and ordered a fine suit. He also promised that after that he would buy all his clothes from the tailor and pay him a good price for them, so the tailor, too, got some good from all the dreaming.

The Stones of Plouvinec

IN THE LITTLE VILLAGE OF PLOUVINEC there once lived a poor stone-cutter named Bernet.

Bernet was an honest and industrious young man, and yet he never seemed to succeed in the world. Work as he might, he was always poor. This was a great grief to him, for he was in love with the beautiful Madeleine Pornec, and she was the daughter of the richest man in Plouvinec.

Madeleine had many suitors, but she cared for none of them except Bernet. She would gladly have married him in spite of his poverty, but her father was covetous as well as rich. He had no wish for a poor son-in-law, and Madeleine was so beautiful he expected her to marry some rich merchant, or a well-to-do farmer at least. But if Madeleine could not have Bernet for a husband, she was determined that she would have no one.

There came a winter when Bernet found himself poorer than he had ever been before. Scarcely anyone seemed to have any need for a stone-cutter, and even for such work as he did get he was poorly paid. He learned to know what it meant to go without a meal and to be cold as well as hungry.

As Christmas drew near, the landlord of the inn at Plouvinec decided to give a feast for all the good folk of the village, and Bernet was invited along with all the rest.

He was glad enough to go to the feast, for he knew that Madeleine was to be there, and even if he did not have a chance to talk to her, he could at least look at her, and that would be better than nothing.

The feast was a fine one. There was plenty to eat and drink, and all was of the best, and the more the guests feasted, the merrier they grew. If Bernet and Madeleine ate little and spoke less, no one noticed it. People were too busy filling their own stomachs and laughing at the jokes that were cracked. The fun was at its height when the door was pushed open, and a ragged, ill-looking beggar slipped into the room.

At the sight of him the laughter and merriment died away. This beggar was well known to all the people of the village, though none knew whence he came nor where he went when he was away on his wanderings. He was sly and crafty, and he was feared as well as disliked, for it was said that he had the evil eye. Whether he had or not, it was well known that no one had ever offended him without having some misfortune happen soon after.

"I heard there was a great feast here tonight," said the beggar in a humble voice, "and that all the village had been bidden to it. Perhaps, when all have eaten, there may be some scraps that I might pick up."

"Scraps there are in plenty," answered the landlord, "but it is not scraps that I am offering to anyone tonight. Draw up a chair to the table, and eat and drink what you will. There is more than enough for all." But the landlord looked none too well pleased as he spoke. It was a piece of ill-luck to have the beggar come to his house this night of all nights, to spoil the pleasure of the guests.

The beggar drew up to the table as the landlord bade him, but the fun and merriment were ended. Presently the guests began to leave the table, and after thanking their host, they went away to their own homes.

When the beggar had eaten and drunk to his heart's content, he pushed back his chair from the table.

"I have eaten well," said he to the landlord. "Is there not now some corner where I can spend the night?"

"There is the stable," answered the landlord grudgingly. "Every room in the house is full, but if you choose to sleep there among the clean hay, I am not the one to say you nay."

Well, the beggar was well content with that. He went out to the stable, and there he snuggled down among the soft hay, and soon he was fast asleep. He had slept for some hours, and it was midnight, when he suddenly awoke with a startled feeling that he was not alone in the stable. In the darkness two strange voices were talking together.

"Well, brother, how goes it since last Christmas?" asked one voice.

"Poorly, brother, but poorly," answered the other. "Methinks the work has been heavier these last twelve months than ever before."

The beggar, listening as he lay in the hay, wondered who could be talking there at this hour of the night. Then he discovered that the voices came from the stalls nearby; the ox and the donkey were talking together.

The beggar was so surprised that he almost exclaimed aloud, but he restrained himself. He remembered a story he had often heard, but had never before believed, that on every Christmas night it is given to the dumb beasts in the stalls to talk in human tones for a short time. It was said that those who had been lucky enough to hear them at such times had sometimes learned strange secrets from their talk. Now the beggar lay listening with all his ears, and scarcely daring to breathe lest he should disturb them.

"It has been a hard year for me too," said the ox, answering what the donkey had just said. "I would our master had some of the treasure that lies hidden under the stones of Plouvinec. Then he could buy more oxen and more donkeys, and the work would be easier for us."

"The treasure! What treasure is that?" asked the donkey.

The ox seemed very much surprised. "Have you never heard? I thought everyone knew of the hidden treasure under the stones."

"Tell me about it," said the donkey, "for I dearly love a tale."

The ox was not loath to do this. At once it began:

"You know the barren heath just outside of Plouvinec, and the great stones that lie there, each so large that it would take more than a team of oxen to drag it from its place?"

Yes, the donkey knew that heath, and the stones too. He had often passed by them on his journeys to the neighbouring town.

"It is said that under those stones lies hidden an enormous treasure of gold," said the ox. "That is the story; it is well known. But none has seen that treasure; jealously the stones guard it. Once in every hundred years, however, the stones go down to the river to drink. They are only away for a few minutes; then they come rolling back in mad haste to cover their gold again. But if anyone could be there on the heath for those few minutes, it is a wonderful sight that he would see while the stones are away. It is now a hundred years, all but a week, since the stones went down to drink."

"Then a week from tonight the treasure will be uncovered again?" asked the donkey.

"Yes, exactly a week from now, at midnight."

"Ah, if only our master knew this," and the donkey sighed heavily. "If only we could tell him! Then he might go to the heath and not only see the treasure, but gather a sack full of it for himself."

"Yes, but even if he did, he would never return with it alive. As I told you, the stones are very jealous of their treasure, and are away for only a few minutes. By the time he had gathered up the gold and was ready to escape, the stones would return and would crush him to powder."

The beggar, who had become very much excited at the story, felt a cold shiver creep over him at these words.

"No one could ever bring away any of it then?" asked the donkey.

"I did not say that. The stones are enchanted. If anyone could find a five-leaved clover, and carry it with him to the heath, the stones could not harm him, for the five-leaved clover is a magic plant that has power over all enchanted things, and those stones are enchanted."

"Then all he would need would be to have a five-leaved clover."

"If he carried that with him, the stones could not harm him. He might escape safely with the treasure, but it would do him little good. With the first rays of the sun the treasure would crumble away unless the life of a human being had been sacrificed to the stones there on the heath before sunrise."

"And who would sacrifice a human life for a treasure!" cried the donkey. "Not our master, I am sure."

The ox made no answer, and now the donkey too was silent. The hour had passed in which they could speak in human voices. For another year they would again be only dumb brutes.

As for the beggar, he lay among the hay, shaking all over with excitement. Visions of untold wealth shone before his eyes. The treasure of Plouvinec! Why, if he could only get it, he would be the richest man in the village. In the village? No, in the country – in the whole world! Only to see it and handle it for a few hours would be something. But before even that were possible and safe it would be necessary to find a five-leaved clover.

With the earliest peep of dawn the beggar rolled from the hay, and, wrapping his rags about him, stole out of the stable and away into the country. There he began looking about for bunches of clover. These were not hard to find; they were everywhere, though the most of them were withered now. He found and examined clump after clump. Here and there he found a stem that bore four leaves, but none had five. Night came on, and the darkness made him give up the search; but the next day he began anew. Again he was unsuccessful. So day after day passed by, and still he had not found the thing he sought so eagerly.

The beggar was in a fever of rage and disappointment. Six days slipped by. By the time the seventh dawned he was so discouraged that he hunted for only a few hours. Then, though it was still daylight, he determined to give up the search. With drooping head he turned back toward the village. As he was passing a heap of rocks he noticed a clump of clover growing in a crevice. Idly, and with no hope of success, he stooped and began to examine it leaf by leaf.

Suddenly he gave a cry of joy. His legs trembled under him so that he was obliged to sink to his knees. The last stem of all bore five leaves. He had found his five-leaved clover!

With the magic plant safely hidden away in his bosom the beggar hurried back toward the village. He would rest in the inn until night. Then he would go to the heath, and if the story the ox had told were true, he would see a sight such as no one living had ever seen before.

His way led him past the heath. Dusk was falling as he approached it. Suddenly the beggar paused and listened. From among the stones sounded a strange tap-tapping. Cautiously he drew nearer, peering about among the stones. Then he saw what seemed to him a curious sight for such a place and such a time. Before the largest stone of all stood Bernet, busily at work with hammer and chisel. He was cutting a cross upon the face of the rock.

The beggar drew near to him so quietly that Bernet did not notice him. He started as a voice suddenly spoke close to his ear.

"That is a strange thing for you to be doing," said the beggar. "Why should you waste your time in cutting a cross in such a lonely place as this?"

"The sign of the cross never comes amiss, wherever it may be," answered Bernet. "And as for wasting my time, no one seems to have any use for it at present. It is better for me to spend it in this way than to idle it away over nothing."

Suddenly a strange idea flashed into the beggar's mind – a thought so strange and terrible that it made him turn pale. He drew nearer to the stone-cutter and laid his hand upon his arm.

"Listen, Bernet," said he; "you are a clever workman and an honest one as well, and yet all your work scarcely brings you in enough to live on. Suppose I were to tell you that in one night you might become rich – richer than the richest man in the village – so that there would be no desire that you could not satisfy; what would you think of that?"

"I would think nothing of it, for I would know it was not true," answered Bernet carelessly.

"But it *is* true; it is *true*, I tell you," cried the beggar. "Listen, and I will tell you."

He drew still nearer to Bernet, so that his mouth almost touched the stone-cutter's ear, and in a whisper he repeated to him the story he had heard the ox telling the donkey – the story of the treasure that was buried under the stones of Plouvinec. But it was only a part of the story that he told after all, for he did not tell Bernet that anyone who was rash enough to seek the treasure would be crushed by the stones unless he carried a five-leaved clover; nor did he tell him that if the treasure were carried away from the heath it would turn to ashes unless a human life had been sacrificed to the stones. As Bernet listened to the story he became very grave. His eyes shone through the fading light as he stared at the beggar's face.

"Why do you tell me this?" he asked. "And why are you willing to share the treasure that might be all your own? If you make me rich, what do you expect me to do for you in return?"

"Do you not see?" answered the beggar. "You are much stronger than I. I, as you know, am a weak man and slow of movement. While the stones are away we two together could gather more than twice as much as I could gather myself. In return for telling you this secret, all I ask is that if we go there and gather all we can, and bring it away with us, you will make an even division with me – that you will give me half of all we get."

"That seems only just," said Bernet slowly. "It would be strange if this story of the hidden treasure proved to be true. At any rate, I will come with you to the heath tonight. We will bring with us some large bags, and if we manage to secure even a small part of the gold you talk of I shall never cease to be grateful to you."

The beggar could not answer. His teeth were chattering, half with fear and half with excitement. The honest stone-cutter little guessed that the beggar was planning to sacrifice him to the stones in order that he himself might become a rich man.

It was well on toward midnight when Bernet and the beggar returned to the heath with the bags. The moon shone clear and bright, and by its light they could see the stones towering up above them, solid and motionless. It seemed impossible to believe that they had ever stirred from their places, or ever would again. In the moonlight Bernet could clearly see the cross that he had carved upon the largest stone.

He and the beggar lay hidden behind a clump of bushes. All was still except for the faint sound of the river some short distance away. Suddenly a breath seemed to pass over the heath. Far off, in the village of Plouvinec, sounded the first stroke of twelve.

At that stroke the two men saw a strange and wonderful thing happen. The motionless stones rocked and stirred in their places. With a rending sound they tore themselves from the places where they had stood for so long. Then down the slope toward the river they rolled, bounding faster and faster, while there on the heath an immense treasure glittered in the moonlight.

"Quick! quick!" cried the beggar in a shrill voice. "They will return! We have not a moment to waste."

Greedily he threw himself upon the treasure. Gathering it up by handfuls he thrust it hurriedly into a sack. Bernet was not slow to follow his example. They worked with such frenzy that soon the two largest sacks were almost full. In their haste everything but the gold was forgotten.

Some sound, a rumbling and crashing, made Bernet look up. At once he sprang to his feet with a cry of fear.

"Look! look!" he cried. "The stones are returning. They are almost on us. We shall be crushed."

"You, perhaps; but not I," answered the beggar. "You should have provided yourself with a five-leaved clover. It is a magic herb, and the stones have no power to touch him who holds it."

Even as the beggar spoke the stones were almost upon them. Trembling, but secure, he held up the five-leaved clover before them. As he did so the ranks of stones divided, passing around him a rank on either side; then, closing together, they rolled on toward Bernet.

The poor stone-cutter felt that he was lost. He tried to murmur a prayer, but his tongue clove to the roof of his mouth with fear.

Suddenly the largest stone of all, the one upon which he had cut the cross, separated itself from the others. Rolling in front of them, it placed itself before him as a shield. Grey and immovable it towered above him. A moment the others paused as if irresolute, while Bernet cowered close against the protecting stone. Then they rolled by without touching him and settled sullenly into their places.

The beggar was already gathering up the sacks. He believed himself safe, but he wished to leave the heath as quickly as possible. He glanced fearfully over his shoulder. Then he gave a shriek, and, turning, he held up the five-leaved clover. The largest stone was rolling toward him. It was almost upon him.

But the magic herb had no power over a stone marked with a cross. On it rolled, over the miserable man, and into the place where it must rest again for still another hundred years.

* * *

It was morning, and the sun was high in the heavens when Bernet staggered into the inn at Plouvinec. A heavy, bulging sack was thrown over one shoulder; a second sack he dragged behind him. They were full of gold – the treasure from under the stones of Plouvinec.

From that time Bernet was the richest man in Plouvinec. Madeleine's father was glad enough to call him son-in-law and to welcome him into his family. He and Madeleine were married, and lived in the greatest comfort and happiness all their days. But for as long as he lived Bernet could never be induced to go near the heath nor to look upon the stones that had so nearly caused his death.

The Beautiful Maria di Legno

THERE WAS ONCE A MERCHANT who was so rich that no king could be richer. He and his wife had one daughter named Maria di Legno, and she was as dear to them as the apple of the eye. Now about the time when Maria was old enough to think of getting married, the merchant's wife fell ill, and feeling herself about to die she called her husband to her.

"My dear husband," she said, "I feel that I am near to death and it troubles me greatly to know that Maria is about to lose a mother's care. She is so beautiful and will be such an heiress that she will have many suitors. Promise me that she shall marry no one but the man whose finger fits this ring." She then took from her neck a little chain to which a ring was fastened, and laid it in her husband's hand.

Her husband could refuse her nothing. He gave her his word that it should be as she wished, and very soon afterward his wife died.

It was not long before the suitors began to come from far and near to ask for the hand of Maria di Legno in marriage. Some of them were very rich and powerful, and the merchant would have been very glad to have one of them for a son-in-law, but no man among them could wear the ring. For one it was too small, for another too large, and so they were all obliged to go away again with 'no' for the answer. It seemed as though the beautiful Maria would never be married at this rate, and the merchant began to repent him of his promise to his dead wife.

At last came a suitor richer and handsomer than any of the others. He said he was a prince, and he brought with him a long train of attendants, and gifts of great magnificence. The merchant took such a fancy to him that he felt that this was the man whom he would choose out of all the world for his daughter to marry.

Maria, however, was very unhappy, for she could feel nothing but fear and dislike for the stranger.

The prince was very courteous to everyone, and smiling and anxious to please; that was at first. But when he was told that before he could have Maria for a wife he must try on a certain ring and see if it fitted him, and that all depended upon that, he became very angry.

"This is a silly thing to ask of me," he said. "Is it not enough that I am rich and young and that I please you? I am not a child that I should play such a silly game as that."

He was so angry that it seemed at first as though he would ride away without even looking at the ring. However, after he had had a day to think it over he appeared as smiling and cheerful as ever, and seemed quite willing to submit to the test.

"After all, it was her mother's last wish," said he; "and besides that, I shall be very glad to prove to you beyond a doubt that I am the one out of all the world who ought to marry the beautiful Maria, for I am sure the ring will fit me."

Overjoyed, the merchant sent for the casket in which the ring was kept, but when he opened the lid what was his dismay to find that the ring was gone. And now he did not know what to do. He had promised his dead wife that Maria should not marry anyone who could not wear the ring, and now if it was lost it seemed she would never be able to marry anyone at all.

But when the prince found the merchant was reasoning in this way he flew into a fine rage. "What are you thinking of!" he cried. "First you tell me you will give me your daughter for a wife if I can wear a certain ring, and then when I am willing to stand the test, you tell me the ring can not be found. Is this a trick you are playing upon me? If it is it shall cost you dear."

The merchant tried to excuse himself, but the stranger would listen to nothing.

"Because you are so careless as to lose the ring, is that any reason your daughter should remain unmarried all her life?" he asked. "Set me three tasks to perform, no matter how difficult. If I fail in anyone of them I will ride away with no ill-feeling, and leave her to some more fortunate suitor; but if I perform them all to her satisfaction then I shall have her for a bride."

This seemed to the merchant only a fair and just proposal, and as he was very anxious for his daughter to marry the prince, he agreed to it. But when Maria heard all this she was in despair. She had depended upon the ring to protect her, for she did not believe it would fit the stranger, but now that it was gone she feared her father would force her into the marriage in spite of herself.

In her grief and dismay she bethought her of her godmother who was an old fairy and who lived in a forest over beyond the town. This fairy was very wise, and Maria knew that if anyone could help her in her trouble she could. So that evening she wrapped herself in a dark cloak so that no one should know her, and stole out of the palace and away to where the fairy lived.

She found her godmother at home, and after Maria bid her good evening, and presented to her some little cream cakes that she had brought with her as a gift, she began to tell her story. She told the fairy all about her suitor, and how she feared and detested him, and how, unless she could think of some task that he would be unable to perform, she would certainly be obliged to marry him.

The fairy listened attentively, and after Maria had ended, she sat silent for quite a while, thinking. At last she began, "Maria di Legno, this is a very difficult matter. You do well to fear this stranger, for he is a very wicked and a very powerful magician. He is indeed far more powerful than I, so that I can do nothing against him, and I fear that you will be obliged to marry him. Still, everything that I can do to help you I will, and you must follow my advice exactly. Tomorrow this evil one will come to inquire what is the first task that you wish him to perform. Try to appear smiling and cheerful, and ask him to bring you as a gift a dress woven of the stars of heaven. This will be a very difficult thing for him to get, and if he fails to bring it to you he can no longer insist on your marrying him."

Maria was more frightened than ever when she heard that her suitor was a wicked magician, and she promised to follow in every respect the advice that had been given her. Then she drew her hood over her head and made her way home again, and so well had she managed that no one there had any idea she had been away at all.

The next day when the suitor came to visit her he was delighted to find her cheerful and smiling as though she were no longer averse to him.

"Have you thought of what my first task shall be?" he asked.

"Yes," said Maria. "I wish you to bring me a dress woven of the stars of heaven."

As soon as the magician heard that, his brow grew black, and he gave her a suspicious look. "Someone must have told you to ask for that," he said. "You never would have thought of it yourself."

But he had agreed to do whatever she might ask of him, and he could not very well make any objections to this. He asked, however, to be allowed three days in which to procure the dress, and to this the merchant agreed.

For three days the stranger disappeared, and no one knew what had become of him, but when at the end of that time, he reappeared, he brought the dress with him. It was made entirely of the stars of heaven as Maria had demanded, and was so beautiful and shining that it was a joy to the eyes to see it.

Maria was dismayed to find he had so easily performed this first task, but she dissembled and tried to appear delighted with the gift; but she took the first opportunity she could find to steal away to the forest to visit her godmother. She told the fairy that her suitor had been able to perform the first task, and bring her the dress of stars, and when the fairy heard this she looked very grave.

"This is a bad business," said she. "Still there are two more tasks that you are to set him, and for the next one tell him he must bring you a dress woven entirely of moonbeams. This will be even more difficult for him to procure than the other, and it may be that he will fail to get it."

Maria promised to do as the fairy advised her, and then stole back to her home again.

The next day the suitor came to visit her again, and he looked as happy as though the marriage day were already set.

"What is the next task that I am to perform?" he asked. "You see however difficult the thing is I am not only willing but able to perform it."

"I would like," said Maria di Legno, "a dress woven entirely of moonbeams."

As soon as the magician heard that his look changed, and he cast upon her a terrible glance.

"Someone has told you to ask for that," he cried. "However, you shall have it, but you must give me three days in which to procure it, as you did before."

Maria would have refused this if she dared, but her father was very willing to allow it. For three days the magician disappeared, but at the end of that time he came again, and now it was a dress of woven moonbeams that he brought with him. If the other dress was beautiful this was ten times more so. The eyes could hardly bear to look at it, it was so bright.

Maria tried to pretend she was delighted, but as soon as she could she stole away to see her fairy godmother once more, and to tell her how the second trial had come out.

The fairy listened and shook her head. "My poor child, I fear this marriage must be. Still there is one more task you may set him, and this time tell him to bring you a dress woven entirely of sunbeams. This will be far more difficult for him to procure than either of the others, but if he should succeed in doing it there is no help for it, you will be obliged to marry him."

As soon as Maria heard this she burst into tears, but her godmother comforted her. "Listen," said she, "even though I cannot preserve you from this marriage, I may be able to save you in the end. As soon as the wedding is over the magician will take you away in a coach to carry you to his own country. Upon his head he will wear a velvet cap, and in this cap a long feather. Look well at the feather, for slipped over it is the magic ring. It is he who stole it from the casket, for he knew it would not fit him, and he feared to stand the test. After you are married to him, however, he will no longer be afraid to let you see he has it. You must manage in some way to get this ring from him, for if you succeed in escaping finally you will have need of it. And now listen further to what you must do." The fairy then told Maria that she would make a hollow wooden figure of an old woman for her. This she would hide in a certain spot in the forest near to which the magician's coach must pass. Just before they reached this place, Maria must make some excuse to leave the coach, and must hide herself in the wooden figure. She might then safely walk wherever she wished to go, for even if the magician met her he would certainly never guess that the figure of that ugly old woman contained his bride.

Maria thanked the fairy with tears of gratitude, and hastened home, and this time, too, nobody guessed that she had been away.

Soon the magician came to ask her what she would set him as a third task.

"I wish you to bring me another dress," said Maria, "and this time it is to be made entirely of sunbeams."

When the magician heard this the blood rushed to his face, and his eyes became like hot coals.

"You are not the one who thought of this," he cried. "You shall have it, but if I did but know who was back of this wish of yours he should suffer for it, whoever he is."

Maria was left trembling with fear, and for three days the magician was not seen by anyone. At the end of that time he reappeared, and this time it was the dress of sunbeams that he had brought back with him. If the others had been beautiful this was far beyond them, and it was so bright that the pages who carried it could hardly bear the light of it in their eyes.

And now Maria could make no further delay, she must marry the prince whether or no. A magnificent wedding was prepared for, and although Maria was very sad she looked so beautiful that the magician could hardly control his joy at the thought that he was to have her for a wife.

Immediately after they were married they entered a coach drawn by six coal-black horses and drove away toward the forest, for that was the direction in which lay the magician's country.

They rode along, and rode along, but all the while the bride kept looking out of the window instead of at her bridegroom.

"What are you looking at?" he asked at last, quite out of patience with her.

"I am looking at the beautiful flowers along the way. Do stop and gather some for me, and I will make a wreath for my hair, and another for your cap."

The magician was very anxious to please her, so he alighted immediately and gave his cap into the hands of Maria di Legno, and began to gather flowers for her along the way. She made a wreath for her hair and another for his cap, but before she handed it back to him she managed, without its being noticed, to slip the ring from the feather and hide it in her pocket.

Then they rode on again, and by the time they were well in the forest it was growing dark. Hundreds of fireflies flickered about among the trees, and Maria exclaimed how bright they were. Finally one passed so much larger and brighter than any of the others that it was like a star. "Look! Look!" cried Maria. "How beautiful that is. My dear husband, I do beg and entreat of you to catch that one for me if you can."

Again the prince, anxious to please her, stopped the coach, and alighting, ran away among the trees in pursuit of the firefly.

No sooner was he out of sight than Maria, too, sprang to the ground, and hastened to the spot where the fairy had told her she would find the wooden figure. She quickly discovered it behind some bushes, and opened the little hinged door in its back. The moment this was opened a soft light shone through the forest, for the fairy had put Maria's three beautiful dresses inside the figure, and they shone so that everything around was lighted up. The figure was hollowed out in such a way that there was room inside it for Maria and the dresses too.

Maria stepped inside and closed the door and immediately the forest grew dark again. Then she arranged a shawl about the figure so that the door would not show, took a staff in her hand and hobbled away through the forest, for the figure was made in such a way that it would move almost as easily as a real body.

All this time the magician had been pursuing the firefly. It led him this way and that but always away from the coach. It did not fly fast, and several times he thought he had it, but it always slipped through his fingers. The fact was the firefly was really the fairy who had taken this shape in order to lure him away through the forest and give Maria a chance to escape.

Suddenly a soft light shone through the forest and then died away. By that the fairy knew that Maria had found the figure and had stepped inside and closed the door. Then the firefly disappeared altogether, leaving the magician there alone in the darkness.

He made his way back to the coach in a very bad humour. "I could not catch the firefly," said he in a gruff voice; "I only succeeded in bruising myself against the trees." There was no answer. "Do you not hear?" cried he angrily. "I tell you I am black and blue with bruises, and all because you were silly enough to want a firefly." Still there was no answer, and the magician looked inside the coach. No one was there. Then he understood that he had been tricked, and he was in a fine rage. He ran about through the forest like a wild thing, peering and searching for his lost bride, and it would have been an ill thing for her if he had found her then. At last he came upon an old woman hobbling along with a staff in her hand, and a shawl about her shoulders.

"Tell me, old woman," he cried, "have you seen a beautiful young girl anywhere in the forest? A beautiful young girl dressed as a bride?"

"I have seen no one but you," mumbled the old crone. "Not a living soul but you," and she hobbled on still mumbling to herself.

The magician did not waste another glance upon her, for he never dreamed the beautiful young Maria was hidden inside that ugly old figure, but she was almost dead with fear lest he should guess it. He was filled with rage and despair, and rushing back to the coach he threw himself into it and was driven away like mad, and that was the last of him as far as Maria was concerned.

All that night Maria hobbled on, but toward morning she was so tired that she lay down under a tree and went to sleep. She had no fear, for robbers would never disturb one who looked as old and poor as she, and as for wild animals she was protected from them by the wooden figure in which she lay.

She slept then quietly for quite a while, but in the early morning she was awakened by the barking of dogs, and the sound of a horn. The prince of that country had come into the forest to hunt, and he and all his retinue were riding in her direction at full speed.

She struggled to her feet, but she was hardly up before the dogs burst through the bushes and threw her to the ground again. And now came the horses and riders; the young prince had almost ridden over Maria before he saw her and could stop his horse. However he managed to draw rein before she was touched, and then he said to his attendants, "Look at this poor old woman. Either the dogs have hurt her or else she has fainted from fear." And indeed Maria was so frightened that she could neither move nor speak.

The prince was very tender-hearted. He caused his attendants to lift her up and put her on the saddle in front of him. "There, there, mother," said he; "I believe you are more frightened than hurt. Tell me where you live and I will take you home, for you do not seem able to walk."

"Alas! I have no home to go to," answered Maria in a sorrowful voice.

"So old, and homeless, too," cried the prince. "If that is the case I will even carry you back with me to the palace, for you cannot be left here to die. There must be some work that you can do there in the kitchen or scullery, and you will at least be sure of food and shelter."

Maria was only too thankful to be taken with him, for she did not dare to brave her father's anger by returning to his house, and there seemed no other place for her to go. The prince still kept her on his horse in front of him, and rode back with her to the palace, and there she was handed over to the servants. They were ill-pleased enough to see her, too.

"Why is an old crone like this brought here," they muttered among themselves. "She is too old to work, and yet we will have to share what little we have with her."

"Never mind," said the steward. "It is the prince's pleasure that she should remain here, and we will find something for her to do. If nothing better she can help the scullery maid with the pots and pans."

So the beautiful Maria di Legno became the servant of servants, and cleaned pots and pans, and was scolded and sent upon errands. Sometimes the maids even struck her, but this they soon learned not to do, for it hurt their hands. "You are a very strange old woman," they would say. "In spite of your age your flesh is so hard that bone itself could not be harder."

Now after Maria had been at the palace for a few months the time of the carnival came round. The carnival was to be more magnificent this year than ever before, for the parents of the prince were anxious for him to choose a bride, and it might be that his choice would fall upon someone among the noble guests. Queens and princesses and ladies of rank came from far and near, and such magnificent clothes were hardly ever seen before. The prince was courteous to them all, but he did not seem to distinguish anyone above the others.

For the last three days of this carnival anyone was allowed to appear at it, even the palace servants if they chose. They did choose, and so when the first of these three days arrived there was a great stir and bustling and running to and fro in the kitchen. No one had any thought for the old woman who helped the scullery wench, and so no one noticed when she stole away by herself to the miserable loft where she slept. She took with her a jug of hot water, and after she had fastened the door and made sure she was alone she opened the figure and stepped out. First she washed herself and arranged her beautiful hair. Then she drew from the figure the dress of stars, and after she had put it on she was the most beautiful creature that was ever seen.

The ball was at its height when she appeared, and many beautiful ladies were there in silks and jewels, but Maria far outshone them all. Everyone stared and whispered, but she was at once so beautiful and so stately that no one dared to approach or question her. Only the prince felt privileged, by his high rank to speak to her and ask her hand for the dance.

When she answered him her voice was so soft, and her glance so modest, that the prince's heart went out to her, and he could think of no one else. When they danced together everyone said that such a handsome couple had never been seen before.

Before the ball ended Maria found an opportunity to slip away unseen. Hastening to her room she took off her beautiful dress and packed it away inside the figure. Then entering into it herself she closed it up and lay down to sleep.

The next day there was no talk all through the palace except about the beautiful stranger who had appeared at the ball the night before. Some thought she must be a fairy, and others that she was some great queen who had managed to arrive there unannounced; all were anxious to know whether she would reappear at the ball that evening.

The prince was not the least anxious person in the palace. He thought of his beautiful partner all day, and longed so to see her that he could neither eat nor rest.

That night the ball was again at its height before Maria di Legno arrived. She was clothed this time in her dress of moonbeams, and was so beautiful that when she entered there was a general sigh of wonder.

The prince who had been watching the door with impatience hurried to her side immediately and claimed her hand for the dance. That evening he tried in every way to find out who she was, but always she put him off with a smile and a word, and that night she managed to slip away, unperceived as before.

The last night of the carnival arrived, and with it appeared the beautiful Maria di Legno. This time she wore her dress made of sunlight, and was beautiful and bright beyond all words, so that the prince was beside himself with admiration. Again he begged her to tell him who she was and whence she came, but she would not. One thing however gave the prince some hope that she did not mean to forsake him entirely when the carnival should be over. She drew from her bosom a ring, and begged him to try it on, telling him that no one, so far, had ever been able to wear it. The prince slipped it on, and it fitted his finger exactly; it could not have fitted better if it had been made for him. Then the eyes of the beautiful stranger shone with joy, but she took the ring again and hid it in the bosom of her dress.

Maria meant to slip away unperceived this night as she had the two nights before, but the prince had determined that this should not be. He had told the palace guards to be on the watch, and not to let her escape without following her. He himself scarcely left her for a moment. However, toward the end of the evening he was obliged to turn away to acknowledge the greeting of some nobleman, and when he looked around again she was gone. She had slipped away the moment he had turned his head, and had hastened into a long gallery that seemed to be deserted, but looking behind she saw that the guards were following her. She hurried on but soon she found they did not mean to lose sight of her, and now she was almost in despair.

About her neck she wore a necklace of pearls which her father had given her, and as a last hope she broke the cord that held them and scattered them on the floor. When the guards saw the pearls rolling this way and that beneath their feet they could not resist stooping to pick them up and while they were doing this Maria managed to escape them and reach her room in safety. She quickly hid her shining dress and shut herself in the figure and then threw herself down on her hard and narrow bed to sleep. The next morning when the sleepy servants were busy with their work there was the old woman scrubbing pots and pans in the scullery as usual, and no one could possibly have dreamed that she was the beauty of the night before.

As for the young prince, when he found the beautiful stranger had disappeared and left no trace behind her he was so filled with grief and disappointment that he fell desperately ill. Doctors came from far and near to attend him, but they could do nothing for him. He remained sunk in melancholy, and at last the Queen Mother began to fear that unless some remedy was found he would die from sorrow.

All this was talked about in the kitchen, and when Maria heard how the prince was pining away for love of the beautiful stranger she made up her mind that it was time for her to make herself known. Therefore one day when the other servants were not looking she made a little cake, and in it she hid the magic ring that the prince had tried upon his finger that last night of the carnival. Then she caused word to be carried to the Queen Mother's ears that it was said by an old woman in the kitchen that she could cure the prince if they would only let her try.

At first the Queen Mother paid no attention to this talk but as day after day passed and her son grew no better, in despair she sent for the old woman to come to her.

Maria put the little cake upon a golden plate, and carrying it in her hand went to attend the queen.

She found her Majesty seated in a room with all her attendants around her, and as soon as she entered the queen began: "Old woman, it has been brought to my ears that you have said you can cure the prince. Is this true?"

"Yes, your majesty," answered Maria. "It certainly is true that I said it, and it is also true that I and I alone can do it."

"That is a brave boast for you to make," said the queen. "And what would you advise us to do for him?"

"Here is a cake which I have made myself," said Maria, "and in it is something which will surely cure him. That is, it will cure him if he eats the whole of the cake. If however even the smallest portion is thrown away all its virtue will be lost, and it will do him harm rather than good." This she said because she was afraid that if a part of the cake were thrown away the ring might be in it.

When the attendants heard the old woman say all this so gravely they began to laugh, for it sounded very silly. The Queen Mother however rebuked them and bade them be silent. "These old women," she said, "often know remedies that are unknown to the doctors. There may really be some virtue in this cake that will restore our son if he will but eat it."

She then bade the old woman leave the cake and presently she carried it in to the prince with her own hands.

She found him stretched on a couch before the window, gazing out at the sky with a melancholy air. She sat down by his side and asked him how he did, and then she showed him the little cake she had brought with her, and told him how the old woman had declared that if he would but eat it he would certainly be cured.

The prince heard her listlessly, and when she had ended he answered in a weak voice, "There is only one thing that can cure me, and that is to find some trace of the beautiful stranger, and indeed unless I can hope to see her again sometime, I do not care to live."

"Do but try the cake, however," said his mother persuasively. "See it is very small and light. I will break off a piece for you."

So saying she broke a piece from the cake to give to him, but what was her surprise to see there in the piece a golden ring.

"This is certainly a very strange thing," she cried. "Here is a ring in the cake."

"A ring!" the prince repeated. He raised himself on his elbow to look, and no sooner had he taken it in his hand than he started up with a loud cry of joy. "Where did you get the cake?" he cried. "Who brought it to you?" for he at once recognized the ring as the one the beautiful stranger had had.

"It was brought me by an old woman who works in the kitchen; Maria di Legno they call her."

"Let her be brought here at once," cried the prince.

An attendant was sent to summon Maria and while he waited the prince strode up and down the room holding the ring in his hand and unable to control his impatience.

Maria had been expecting this summons, and she had managed meanwhile to arrange her hair, and dress herself in her sunlight dress, and hide in the figure again; and so it was as the homely old woman that she appeared before the prince once more.

"Tell me, old woman," he cried, "was it you who put this ring in the cake?"

"It was," answered Maria.

"And do you know to whom it belongs?"

"I do."

"Then tell me instantly where she is," cried the prince, filled with hope.

"I am she," answered Maria.

When the prince heard this he thought the old woman must be mad, but Maria opened the door and stepped out from the figure in all her brightness and beauty. Then the heart of the prince seemed like to break with joy. He fell upon one knee and took Maria by the hand. "At last you have come," cried he. "And now you shall never leave me again, for you and you only out of all the world shall be my bride."

To this Maria gladly assented, for she had loved him from the first moment when he had found her in the wood.

She told her story, and after the king and queen found who she was they were very willing to have her for their daughter-in-law. She and the prince were married with great magnificence, and lived happily ever after, and the wooden figure they kept to show to their children and their children's children.

Catherine and Her Destiny

LONG AGO THERE LIVED A RICH MERCHANT who, besides possessing more treasures than any king in the world, had in his great hall three chairs, one of silver, one of gold, and one of diamonds. But his greatest treasure of all was his only daughter, who was called Catherine.

One day Catherine was sitting in her own room when suddenly the door flew open, and in came a tall and beautiful woman holding in her hands a little wheel.

"Catherine," she said, going up to the girl, "which would you rather have – a happy youth or a happy old age?"

Catherine was so taken by surprise that she did not know what to answer, and the lady repeated again, "Which would you rather have-a happy youth or a happy old age?"

Then Catherine thought to herself, "If I say a happy youth, then I shall have to suffer all the rest of my life. No, I would bear trouble now, and have something better to look forward to." So she looked up and replied, "Give me a happy old age."

"So be it," said the lady, and turned her wheel as she spoke, vanishing the next moment as suddenly as she had come.

Now this beautiful lady was the Destiny of poor Catherine.

Only a few days after this the merchant heard the news that all his finest ships, laden with the richest merchandise, had been sunk in a storm, and he was left a beggar. The shock was too much for him. He took to his bed, and in a short time he was dead of his disappointment.

So poor Catherine was left alone in the world without a penny or a creature to help her. But she was a brave girl and full of spirit, and soon made up her mind that the best thing she could do was to go to the nearest town and become a servant. She lost no time in getting herself ready, and did not take long over her journey; and as she was passing down the chief street of the town a noble lady saw her out of the window, and, struck by her sad face, said to her: "Where are you going all alone, my pretty girl?"

"Ah, my lady, I am very poor, and must go to service to earn my bread."

"I will take you into my service," said she; and Catherine served her well.

Some time after her mistress said to Catherine, "I am obliged to go out for a long while, and must lock the house door, so that no thieves shall get in."

So she went away, and Catherine took her work and sat down at the window. Suddenly the door burst open, and in came her Destiny.

"Oh! So here you are, Catherine! Did you really think I was going to leave you in peace?" And as she spoke she walked to the linen press where Catherine's mistress kept all her finest sheets and underclothes, tore everything in pieces, and flung them on the floor. Poor Catherine wrung her hands and wept, for she thought to herself, "When my lady comes back and sees all this ruin she will think it is my fault," and starting up, she fled through the open door. Then Destiny took all the pieces and made them whole again, and put them back in the press, and when everything was tidy she too left the house.

When the mistress reached home she called Catherine, but no Catherine was there. "Can she have robbed me?" thought the old lady, and looked hastily round the house; but nothing was missing. She wondered why Catherine should have disappeared like this, but she heard no more of her, and in a few days she filled her place.

Meanwhile Catherine wandered on and on, without knowing very well where she was going, till at last she came to another town. Just as before, a noble lady happened to see her passing her window, and called out to her, "Where are you going all alone, my pretty girl?"

And Catherine answered, "Ah, my lady, I am very poor, and must go to service to earn my bread."

"I will take you into my service," said the lady; and Catherine served her well, and hoped she might now be left in peace. But, exactly as before, one day that Catherine was left in the house alone her Destiny came again and spoke to her with hard words: "What! are you here now?" And in a passion she tore up everything she saw, till in sheer misery poor Catherine rushed out of the house. And so it befell for seven years, and directly Catherine found a fresh place her Destiny came and forced her to leave it.

After seven years, however, Destiny seemed to get tired of persecuting her, and a time of peace set in for Catherine. When she had been chased away from her last house by Destiny's wicked pranks she had taken service with another lady, who told her that it would be part of her daily work to walk to a mountain that overshadowed the town, and, climbing up to the top, she was to lay on the ground some loaves of freshly baked bread, and cry with a loud voice, "O Destiny, my mistress," three times. Then her lady's Destiny would come and take away the offering. "That will I gladly do," said Catherine.

So the years went by, and Catherine was still there, and every day she climbed the mountain with her basket of bread on her arm. She was happier than she had been, but sometimes, when no one saw her, she would weep as she thought over her old life, and how different it was to the one she was now leading. One day her lady saw her, and said, "Catherine, what is it? Why are you always weeping?" And then Catherine told her story.

"I have got an idea," exclaimed the lady. "Tomorrow, when you take the bread to the mountain, you shall pray my Destiny to speak to yours, and entreat her to leave you in peace. Perhaps something may come of it!"

At these words Catherine dried her eyes, and next morning, when she climbed the mountain, she told all she had suffered, and cried, "O Destiny, my mistress, pray, I entreat you, of my Destiny that she may leave me in peace."

And Destiny answered, "Oh, my poor girl, know you not your Destiny lies buried under seven coverlids, and can hear nothing? But if you will come tomorrow I will bring her with me."

And after Catherine had gone her way her lady's Destiny went to find her sister, and said to her, "Dear sister, has not Catherine suffered enough? It is surely time for her good days to begin?"

And the sister answered, "Tomorrow you shall bring her to me, and I will give her something that may help her out of her need."

The next morning Catherine set out earlier than usual for the mountain, and her lady's Destiny took the girl by the hand and led her to her sister, who lay under the seven coverlids. And her Destiny held out to Catherine a ball of silk, saying, "Keep this – it may be useful some day"; then pulled the coverings over her head again.

But Catherine walked sadly down the hill, and went straight to her lady and showed her the silken ball, which was the end of all her high hopes.

"What shall I do with it?" she asked. "It is not worth sixpence, and it is no good to me!"

"Take care of it," replied her mistress. "Who can tell how useful it may be?"

A little while after this grand preparations were made for the king's marriage, and all the tailors in the town were busy embroidering fine clothes. The wedding garment was so beautiful nothing like it had ever been seen before, but when it was almost finished the tailor found that he had no more silk. The colour was very rare, and none could be found like it, and the king made a proclamation that if anyone happened to possess any they should bring it to the court, and he would give them a large sum.

"Catherine!" exclaimed the lady, who had been to the tailors and seen the wedding garment, "your ball of silk is exactly the right colour. Bring it to the king, and you can ask what you like for it."

Then Catherine put on her best clothes and went to the court, and looked more beautiful than any woman there.

"May it please your Majesty," she said, "I have brought you a ball of silk of the colour you asked for, as no one else has any in the town."

"Your Majesty," asked one of the courtiers, "shall I give the maiden its weight in gold?"

The king agreed, and a pair of scales were brought; and a handful of gold was placed in one scale and the silken ball in the other. But lo! let the king lay in the scales as many gold pieces as he would, the silk was always heavier still. Then the king took some larger scales, and heaped up all his treasures on one side, but the silk on the other outweighed them all.

At last there was only one thing left that had not been put in, and that was his golden crown. And he took it from his head and set it on top of all, and at last the scale moved and the ball had founds its balance.

"Where got you this silk?" asked the king.

"It was given me, royal Majesty, by my mistress," replied Catherine.

"That is not true," said the king, "and if you do not tell me the truth I will have your head cut off this instant."

So Catherine told him the whole story, and how she had once been as rich as he.

Now there lived at the court a wise woman, and she said to Catherine, "You have suffered much, my poor girl, but at length your luck has turned, and I know by the weighing of the scales through the crown that you will die a queen."

"So she shall," cried the king, who overheard these words; "she shall die my queen, for she is more beautiful than all the ladies of the court, and I will marry no one else."

And so it fell out. The king sent back the bride he had promised to wed to her own country, and the same Catherine was queen at the marriage feast instead, and lived happy and contented to the end of her life.

The Flower Queen's Daughter

A YOUNG PRINCE was riding one day through a meadow that stretched for miles in front of him, when he came to a deep, open ditch. He was turning aside to avoid it, when he heard the sound of someone crying in the ditch. He dismounted from his horse, and stepped along in the direction the sound came from. To his astonishment he found an old woman, who begged him to help her out of the ditch. The Prince bent down and lifted her out of her living grave, asking her at the same time how she had managed to get there.

"My son," answered the old woman, "I am a very poor woman, and soon after midnight I set out for the neighbouring town in order to sell my eggs in the market on the following morning; but I lost my way in the dark, and fell into this deep ditch, where I might have remained for ever but for your kindness."

Then the Prince said to her, "You can hardly walk; I will put you on my horse and lead you home. Where do you live?"

"Over there, at the edge of the forest in the little hut you see in the distance," replied the old woman.

The Prince lifted her on to his horse, and soon they reached the hut, where the old woman got down, and turning to the Prince said, "Just wait a moment, and I will give you something." And she disappeared into her hut, but returned very soon and said, "You are a mighty Prince, but at the same time you have a kind heart, which deserves to be rewarded. Would you like to have the most beautiful woman in the world for your wife?"

"Most certainly I would," replied the Prince.

So the old woman continued, "The most beautiful woman in the whole world is the daughter of the Queen of the Flowers, who has been captured by a dragon. If you wish to marry her, you must first set her free, and this I will help you to do. I will give you this little bell: if you ring it once, the King of the Eagles will appear; if you ring it twice, the King of the Foxes will come to you; and if you ring it three times, you will see the King of the Fishes by your side. These will help you if you are in any difficulty. Now farewell, and heaven prosper your undertaking." She handed him the little bell, and there disappeared hut and all, as though the earth had swallowed her up.

Then it dawned on the Prince that he had been speaking to a good fairy, and putting the little bell carefully in his pocket, he rode home and told his father that he meant to set the daughter of the Flower Queen free, and intended setting out on the following day into the wide world in search of the maid.

So the next morning the Prince mounted his fine horse and left his home. He had roamed round the world for a whole year, and his horse had died of exhaustion, while he himself had suffered much from want and misery, but still he had come on no trace of her he was in search of. At last one day he came to a hut, in front of which sat a very old man. The Prince asked him, "Do you not know where the Dragon lives who keeps the daughter of the Flower Queen prisoner?"

"No, I do not," answered the old man. "But if you go straight along this road for a year, you will reach a hut where my father lives, and possibly he may be able to tell you."

The Prince thanked him for his information, and continued his journey for a whole year along the same road, and at the end of it came to the little hut, where he found a very old man. He asked him the same question, and the old man answered, "No, I do not know where the Dragon lives. But go straight along this road for another year, and you will come to a hut in which my father lives. I know he can tell you."

And so the Prince wandered on for another year, always on the same road, and at last reached the hut where he found the third old man. He put the same question to him as he had put to his son and grandson; but this time the old man answered, "The Dragon lives up there on the mountain, and he has just begun his year of sleep. For one whole year he is always awake, and the next he sleeps. But if you wish to see the Flower Queen's daughter go up the second mountain: the Dragon's old mother lives there, and she has a ball every night, to which the Flower Queen's daughter goes regularly."

So the Prince went up the second mountain, where he found a castle all made of gold with diamond windows. He opened the big gate leading into the courtyard, and was just going to walk in, when seven dragons rushed on him and asked him what he wanted.

The Prince replied, "I have heard so much of the beauty and kindness of the Dragon's Mother, and would like to enter her service."

This flattering speech pleased the dragons, and the eldest of them said, "Well, you may come with me, and I will take you to the Mother Dragon."

They entered the castle and walked through twelve splendid halls, all made of gold and diamonds. In the twelfth room they found the Mother Dragon seated on a diamond throne. She was the ugliest woman under the sun, and, added to it all, she had three heads. Her appearance was a great shock to the Prince, and so was her voice, which was like the croaking of many ravens. She asked him, "Why have you come here?"

The Prince answered at once, "I have heard so much of your beauty and kindness, that I would very much like to enter your service."

"Very well," said the Mother Dragon; "but if you wish to enter my service, you must first lead my mare out to the meadow and look after her for three days; but if you don't bring her home safely every evening, we will eat you up."

The Prince undertook the task and led the mare out to the meadow.

But no sooner had they reached the grass than she vanished. The Prince sought for her in vain, and at last in despair sat down on a big stone and contemplated his sad fate. As he sat thus lost in thought, he noticed an eagle flying over his head. Then he suddenly bethought him of his little bell, and taking it out of his pocket he rang it once. In a moment he heard a rustling sound in the air beside him, and the King of the Eagles sank at his feet.

"I know what you want of me," the bird said. "You are looking for the Mother Dragon's mare who is galloping about among the clouds. I will summon all the eagles of the air together, and order them to catch the mare and bring her to you." And with these words the King of the Eagles flew away. Towards evening the Prince heard a mighty rushing sound in the air, and when he looked up he saw thousands of eagles driving the mare before them. They sank at his feet on to the ground and gave the mare over to him. Then the Prince rode home to the old Mother Dragon, who was full of wonder when she saw him, and said, "You have succeeded today in looking after my mare, and as a reward you shall come to my ball tonight." She gave him at the same time a cloak made of copper, and led him to a big room where several young he-dragons and she-dragons were dancing together. Here, too, was the Flower Queen's beautiful daughter. Her dress was woven out of the most lovely flowers in the world, and her complexion was like lilies and roses. As the Prince was dancing with her he managed to whisper in her ear, "I have come to set you free!"

Then the beautiful girl said to him, "If you succeed in bringing the mare back safely the third day, ask the Mother Dragon to give you a foal of the mare as a reward."

The ball came to an end at midnight, and early next morning the Prince again led the Mother Dragon's mare out into the meadow. But again she vanished before his eyes. Then he took out his little bell and rang it twice.

In a moment the King of the Foxes stood before him and said: "I know already what you want, and will summon all the foxes of the world together to find the mare who has hidden herself in a hill."

With these words the King of the Foxes disappeared, and in the evening many thousand foxes brought the mare to the Prince.

Then he rode home to the Mother-Dragon, from whom he received this time a cloak made of silver, and again she led him to the ballroom.

The Flower Queen's daughter was delighted to see him safe and sound, and when they were dancing together she whispered in his ear: "If you succeed again tomorrow, wait for me with the foal in the meadow. After the ball we will fly away together."

On the third day the Prince led the mare to the meadow again; but once more she vanished before his eyes. Then the Prince took out his little bell and rang it three times.

In a moment the King of the Fishes appeared, and said to him: "I know quite well what you want me to do, and I will summon all the fishes of the sea together, and tell them to bring you back the mare, who is hiding herself in a river."

Towards evening the mare was returned to him, and when he led her home to the Mother Dragon she said to him:

"You are a brave youth, and I will make you my body-servant. But what shall I give you as a reward to begin with?"

The Prince begged for a foal of the mare, which the Mother Dragon at once gave him, and over and above, a cloak made of gold, for she had fallen in love with him because he had praised her beauty.

So in the evening he appeared at the ball in his golden cloak; but before the entertainment was over he slipped away, and went straight to the stables, where he mounted his foal and rode out into the meadow to wait for the Flower Queen's daughter. Towards midnight the beautiful girl appeared, and placing her in front of him on his horse, the Prince and she flew like the wind till they reached the Flower Queen's dwelling. But the dragons had noticed their flight, and woke their brother out of his year's sleep. He flew into a terrible rage when he heard what had happened, and determined to lay siege to the Flower Queen's palace; but the Queen caused a forest of flowers as high as the sky to grow up round her dwelling, through which no one could force a way.

When the Flower Queen heard that her daughter wanted to marry the Prince, she said to him: "I will give my consent to your marriage gladly, but my daughter can only stay with you in summer. In winter, when everything is dead and the ground covered with snow, she must come and live with me in my palace underground." The Prince consented to this, and led his beautiful bride home, where the wedding was held with great pomp and magnificence. The young couple lived happily together till winter came, when the Flower Queen's daughter departed and went home to her mother. In summer she returned to her husband, and their life of joy and happiness began again, and lasted till the approach of winter, when the Flower Queen's daughter went back again to her mother. This coming and going continued all her life long, and in spite of it they always lived happily together.

The Flying Ship

ONCE UPON A TIME there lived an old couple who had three sons; the two elder were clever, but the third was a regular dunce. The clever sons were very fond of their mother, gave her good clothes, and always spoke pleasantly to her; but the youngest was always getting in her way, and she had no patience with him. Now, one day it was announced in the village that the King had issued a decree, offering his daughter, the Princess, in marriage to whoever should build a ship that could fly. Immediately the two elder brothers determined to try their luck, and asked their parents' blessing. So the old mother smartened up their clothes, and gave them a store of provisions for their journey, not forgetting to add a bottle of brandy. When they had gone the poor simpleton began to tease his mother to smarten him up and let him start off.

"What would become of a dolt like you?" she answered. "Why, you would be eaten up by wolves."

But the foolish youth kept repeating, "I will go, I will go, I will go!"

Seeing that she could do nothing with him, the mother gave him a crust of bread and a bottle of water, and took no further heed of him.

So the Simpleton set off on his way. When he had gone a short distance he met a little old manikin. They greeted one another, and the manikin asked him where he was going.

"I am off to the King's Court," he answered. "He has promised to give his daughter to whoever can make a flying ship."

"And can you make such a ship?"

"Not I."

"Then why in the world are you going?"

"Can't tell," replied the Simpleton.

"Well, if that is the case," said the manikin, "sit down beside me; we can rest for a little and have something to eat. Give me what you have got in your satchel."

Now, the poor Simpleton was ashamed to show what was in it. However, he thought it best not to make a fuss, so he opened the satchel, and could scarcely believe his own eyes, for, instead of the hard crust, he saw two beautiful fresh rolls and some cold meat. He shared them with the manikin, who licked his lips and said:

"Now, go into that wood, and stop in front of the first tree, bow three times, and then strike the tree with your axe, fall on your knees on the ground, with your face on the earth, and remain there till you are raised up. You will then find a ship at your side, step into it and fly to the King's Palace. If you meet anyone on the way, take him with you."

The Simpleton thanked the manikin very kindly, bade him farewell, and went into the road. When he got to the first tree he stopped in front of it, did everything just as he had been told, and, kneeling on the ground with his face to the earth, fell asleep. After a little time he was aroused; he awoke and, rubbing his eyes, saw a ready-made ship at his side, and at once got into it.

And the ship rose and rose, and in another minute was flying through the air, when the Simpleton, who was on the look-out, cast his eyes down to the earth and saw a man beneath him on the road, who was kneeling with his ear upon the damp ground.

"Hallo!" he called out, "what are you doing down there?"

"I am listening to what is going on in the world," replied the man.

"Come with me in my ship," said the Simpleton.

So the man was only too glad, and got in beside him; and the ship flew, and flew, and flew through the air, till again from his outlook the Simpleton saw a man on the road below, who was hopping on one leg, while his other leg was tied up behind his ear. So he hailed him, calling out:

"Hallo! What are you doing, hopping on one leg?"

"I can't help it," replied the man. "I walk so fast that unless I tied up one leg I should be at the end of the earth in a bound."

"Come with us on my ship," he answered; and the man made no objections, but joined them; and the ship flew on, and on, and on, till suddenly the Simpleton, looking down on the road below, beheld a man aiming with a gun into the distance.

"Hallo!" he shouted to him, "what are you aiming at? As far as eye can see, there is no bird in sight."

"What would be the good of my taking a near shot?" replied the man; "I can hit beast or bird at a hundred miles' distance. That is the kind of shot I enjoy."

"Come into the ship with us," answered the Simpleton; and the man was only too glad to join them, and he got in; and the ship flew on, farther and farther, till again the Simpleton from his outlook saw a man on the road below, carrying on his back a basket full of bread. And he waved to him, calling out:

"Hallo! where are you going?"

"To fetch bread for my breakfast."

"Bread? Why, you have got a whole basket-load of it on your back."

"That's nothing," answered the man; "I should finish that in one mouthful."

"Come along with us in my ship, then."

And so the glutton joined the party, and the ship mounted again into the air, and flew up and onward, till the Simpleton from his outlook saw a man walking by the shore of a great lake, and evidently looking for something.

"Hallo!" he cried to him, "what are you seeking?"

"I want water to drink, I'm so thirsty," replied the man.

"Well, there's a whole lake in front of you; why don't you drink some of that?"

"Do you call that enough?" answered the other. "Why, I should drink it up in one gulp."

"Well, come with us in the ship."

And so the mighty drinker was added to the company; and the ship flew farther, and even farther, till again the Simpleton looked out, and this time he saw a man dragging a bundle of wood, walking through the forest beneath them.

"Hallo!" he shouted to him, "why are you carrying wood through a forest?"

"This is not common wood," answered the other.

"What sort of wood is it, then?" said the Simpleton.

"If you throw it upon the ground," said the man, "it will be changed into an army of soldiers."

"Come into the ship with us, then."

And so he too joined them; and away the ship flew on, and on, and on, and once more the Simpleton looked out, and this time he saw a man carrying straw upon his back.

"Hallo! Where are you carrying that straw to?"

"To the village," said the man.

"Do you mean to say there is no straw in the village?"

"Ah! But this is quite a peculiar straw. If you strew it about even in the hottest summer the air at once becomes cold, and snow falls, and the people freeze."

Then the Simpleton asked him also to join them.

At last the ship, with its strange crew, arrived at the King's Court. The King was having his dinner, but he at once despatched one of his courtiers to find out what the huge, strange new bird could be that had come flying through the air. The courtier peeped into the ship, and, seeing what it was, instantly went back to the King and told him that it was a flying ship, and that it was manned by a few peasants.

Then the King remembered his royal oath; but he made up his mind that he would never consent to let the Princess marry a poor peasant. So he thought and thought, and then said to himself:

"I will give him some impossible tasks to perform; that will be the best way of getting rid of him." And he there and then decided to despatch one of his courtiers to the Simpleton, with the command that he was to fetch the King the healing water from the world's end before he had finished his dinner.

But while the King was still instructing the courtier exactly what he was to say, the first man of the ship's company, the one with the miraculous power of hearing, had overheard the King's words, and hastily reported them to the poor Simpleton.

"Alas, alas!" he cried; "what am I to do now? It would take me quite a year, possibly my whole life, to find the water."

"Never fear," said his fleet-footed comrade, "I will fetch what the King wants."

Just then the courtier arrived, bearing the King's command.

"Tell his Majesty," said the Simpleton, "that his orders shall be obeyed"; and forthwith the swift runner unbound the foot that was strung up behind his ear and started off, and in less than no time had reached the world's end and drawn the healing water from the well.

"Dear me," he thought to himself, "that's rather tiring! I'll just rest for a few minutes; it will be some little time yet before the King has got to dessert." So he threw himself down on the grass, and, as the sun was very dazzling, he closed his eyes, and in a few seconds had fallen sound asleep.

In the meantime all the ship's crew were anxiously awaiting him; the King's dinner would soon be finished, and their comrade had not yet returned. So the man with the marvellous quick hearing lay down and, putting his ear to the ground, listened.

"That's a nice sort of fellow!" he suddenly exclaimed. "He's lying on the ground, snoring hard!"

At this the marksman seized his gun, took aim, and fired in the direction of the world's end, in order to awaken the sluggard. And a moment later the swift runner reappeared, and, stepping on board the ship, handed the healing water to the Simpleton. So while the King was still sitting at table finishing his dinner news was brought to him that his orders had been obeyed to the letter.

What was to be done now? The King determined to think of a still more impossible task. So he told another courtier to go to the Simpleton with the command that he and his comrades were instantly to eat up twelve oxen and twelve tons of bread. Once more the sharp-eared comrade overheard the King's words while he was still talking to the courtier, and reported them to the Simpleton.

"Alas, alas!" he sighed; "what in the world shall I do? Why, it would take us a year, possibly our whole lives, to eat up twelve oxen and twelve tons of bread."

"Never fear," said the glutton. "It will scarcely be enough for me, I'm so hungry."

So when the courtier arrived with the royal message he was told to take back word to the King that his orders should be obeyed. Then twelve roasted oxen and twelve tons of bread were brought alongside of the ship, and at one sitting the glutton had devoured it all.

"I call that a small meal," he said. "I wish they'd brought me some more."

Next, the King ordered that forty casks of wine, containing forty gallons each, were to be drunk up on the spot by the Simpleton and his party. When these words were overheard by the sharp-eared comrade and repeated to the Simpleton, he was in despair.

"Alas, alas!" he exclaimed; "what is to be done? It would take us a year, possibly our whole lives, to drink so much."

"Never fear," said his thirsty comrade. "I'll drink it all up at a gulp, see if I don't." And sure enough, when the forty casks of wine containing forty gallons each were brought alongside of the ship, they disappeared down the thirsty comrade's throat in no time; and when they were empty he remarked:

"Why, I'm still thirsty. I should have been glad of two more casks."

Then the King took counsel with himself and sent an order to the Simpleton that he was to have a bath, in a bathroom at the royal palace, and after that the betrothal should take place. Now the bathroom was built of iron, and the King gave orders that it was to be heated to such a pitch that it would suffocate the Simpleton. And so when the poor silly youth entered the room, he discovered that the iron walls were red hot. But, fortunately, his comrade with the straw on his back had entered behind him, and when the door was shut upon them he scattered the straw about, and suddenly the red-hot walls cooled down, and it became so very cold that the Simpleton could scarcely bear to take a bath, and all the water in the room froze. So the Simpleton climbed up upon the stove, and, wrapping himself up in the bath blankets, lay there the whole night. And in the morning when they opened the door there he lay sound and safe, singing cheerfully to himself.

Now when this strange tale was told to the King he became quite sad, not knowing what he should do to get rid of so undesirable a son-in-law, when suddenly a brilliant idea occurred to him.

"Tell the rascal to raise me an army, now at this instant!" he exclaimed to one of his courtiers. "Inform him at once of this, my royal will." And to himself he added, "I think I shall do for him this time."

As on former occasions, the quick-eared comrade had overheard the King's command and repeated it to the Simpleton.

"Alas, alas!" he groaned; "now I am quite done for."

"Not at all," replied one of his comrades (the one who had dragged the bundle of wood through the forest). "Have you quite forgotten me?"

In the meantime the courtier, who had run all the way from the palace, reached the ship panting and breathless, and delivered the King's message.

"Good!" remarked the Simpleton. "I will raise an army for the King," and he drew himself up. "But if, after that, the King refuses to accept me as his son-in-law, I will wage war against him, and carry the Princess off by force."

During the night the Simpleton and his comrade went, together into a big field, not forgetting to take the bundle of wood with them, which the man spread out in all directions – and in a moment a mighty army stood upon the spot, regiment on regiment of foot and horse soldiers; the bugles sounded and the drums beat, the chargers neighed, and their riders put their lances in rest, and the soldiers presented arms.

In the morning when the King awoke he was startled by these warlike sounds, the bugles and the drums, and the clatter of the horses, and the shouts of the soldiers. And, stepping to the window, he saw the lances gleam in the sunlight and the armour and weapons glitter. And the proud monarch said to himself, "I am powerless in comparison with this man." So he sent him royal robes and costly jewels, and commanded him to come to the palace to be married to the Princess. And his son-in-law put on the royal robes, and he looked so grand and stately that it was impossible to recognize the poor Simpleton, so changed was he; and the Princess fell in love with him as soon as ever she saw him.

Never before had so grand a wedding been seen, and there was so much food and wine that even the glutton and the thirsty comrade had enough to eat and drink.

The Triumph of Truth

THERE WAS ONCE A RAJAH who was both young and handsome, and yet he had never married. One time this Rajah, whose name was Chundun, found himself obliged to make a long journey. He took with him attendants and horsemen, and also his Wuzeer. This Wuzeer was a very wise man, – so wise that nothing was hid from him.

In a certain far-off part of the kingdom the Rajah saw a fine garden, and so beautiful was it that he stopped to admire it. He was surprised to see growing in the midst of it a small bengal tree that bore a number of fine figs, but not a single leaf.

"This is a very curious thing, and I do not understand it," said Chundun Rajah to his Wuzeer. "Why does this tree bear such fine and perfect fruit, and yet it has not a single leaf?"

"I could tell you the meaning," said the Wuzeer, "but I fear that if I did you would not believe me and would have me punished for telling a lie."

"That could never be," answered the Rajah; "I know you to be a very truthful man and wise above all others. Whatever you tell me I shall believe."

"Then this is the meaning of it," said the Wuzeer. "The gardener who has charge of this garden has one daughter; her name is Guzra Bai, and she is very beautiful. If you will count the bingals you will find there are twenty-and-one. Whosoever marries the gardener's daughter will have twenty and one children, – twenty boys and one girl."

Chundun Rajah was very much surprised at what his Wuzeer said. "I should like to see this Guzra Bai," said he.

"You can very easily see her," answered the Wuzeer. "Early every morning she comes into the garden to play among the flowers. If you come here early and hide you can see her without frightening her, as you would do if you went to her home."

The Rajah was pleased with this suggestion, and early the next morning he came to the garden and hid himself behind a flowering bush. It was not long before he saw the girl playing about among the flowers, and she was so very beautiful the Rajah at once fell in love with her. He determined to make her his Ranee, but he did not speak to her or show himself to her then for fear of frightening her. He determined to go to the gardener's house that evening and tell him he wished his daughter for a wife.

As he had determined, so he did. That very evening, accompanied only by his Wuzeer, he went to the gardener's house and knocked upon the door.

"Who is there?" asked the gardener from within.

"It is I, the Rajah," answered Chundun. "Open the door, for I wish to speak with you."

The gardener laughed. "That is a likely story," said he. "Why should the Rajah come to my poor hut? No, no; you are someone who wishes to play a trick on me, but you shall not succeed. I will not let you in."

"But it is indeed Chundun Rajah," called the Wuzeer. "Open the door that he may speak with you."

When the gardener heard the Wuzeer's voice he came and opened the door a crack, but still he only half believed what was told him. What was his amazement to see that it was indeed the Rajah who stood there in all his magnificence with his Wuzeer beside him. The poor man was terrified, fearing Chundun would be angry, but the Rajah spoke to him graciously.

"Do not be afraid," said he. "Call thy daughter that I may speak with her, for it is she whom I wish to see."

The girl was hiding (for she was afraid) and would not come until her father took her hand and drew her forward.

When the Rajah saw her now, this second time, she seemed to him even more beautiful than at first. He was filled with joy and wonder.

"Now I will tell you why I have come here," he said. "I wish to take Guzra Bai for my wife."

At first the gardener would not believe him, but when he found the Rajah did indeed mean what he said he turned to his daughter. "If the girl is willing you shall have her," said he, "but I will not force her to marry even a Rajah."

The girl was still afraid, yet she could not but love the Rajah, so handsome was he, and so kind and gracious was his manner. She gave her consent, and the gardener was overjoyed at the honour that had come to him and his daughter.

Chundun and the beautiful Guzra Bai were married soon after in the gardener's house, and then the Rajah and his new Ranee rode away together.

Now Chundun Rajah's mother, the old Ranee, was of a very proud and jealous nature. When she found her son had married a common girl, the daughter of a gardener, and that Chundun thought of nothing but his bride and her beauty, she was very angry. She determined to rid herself of Guzra Bai in some way or other. But Chundun watched over his young Ranee so carefully that for a long time the old Queen could find no chance to harm her.

But after a while the Rajah found it was again necessary for him to go on a long journey. Just before he set out he gave Guzra Bai a little golden bell. "If any danger should threaten or harm befall you, ring this bell," said he. "Wherever I am I shall hear it and be with you at once, even though I return from the farthest part of my kingdom."

No sooner had he gone than Guzra Bai began to wonder whether indeed it were possible that he could hear the bell at any distance and return to her. She wondered and wondered until at last her curiosity grew so great that she could not forbear from ringing it.

No sooner had it sounded than the Rajah stood before her. "What has happened?" he asked. "Why did you call me?"

"Nothing has happened," answered Guzra Bai, "but it did not seem to me possible that you could really hear the bell so far away, and I could not forbear from trying it."

"Very well," said the Rajah. "Now you know that it is true, so do not call me again unless you have need of me."

Again he went away, and Guzra Bai sat and thought and thought about the golden bell. At last she rang it again. At once the Rajah stood before her.

"Oh, my dear husband, please to forgive me," cried Guzra Bai. "It seemed so wonderful I thought I must have dreamed that the bell could bring you back."

"Guzra Bai, do not be so foolish," said her husband. "I will forgive you this time, but do not call me again unless you have need of me." And he went away.

Again and for the third time Guzra Bai rang the bell, and the Rajah appeared.

"Why do you call me again?" he asked. "Is it again for nothing, or has something happened to you?"

"Nothing has happened," answered Guzra Bai, "only somehow I felt so frightened that I wanted you near me."

"Guzra Bai, I am away on affairs of state," said the Rajah. "If you call me in this way when you have no need of me, I shall soon refuse to answer the bell. Remember this and do not call me again without reason."

And for the third time the Rajah went away and left her.

Soon after this the young Ranee had twenty-and-one beautiful children, twenty sons and one daughter.

When the old Queen heard of this she was more jealous than ever. "When the Rajah returns and sees all these children," she thought to herself, "he will be so delighted that he will love Guzra Bai more dearly than ever, and nothing I can do will ever separate them." She then began to plan within herself as to how she could get rid of the children before the Rajah's return.

She sent for the nurse who had charge of the babies, and who was as wicked as herself. "If you can rid me of these children, I will give you a lac of gold pieces," she said. "Only it must be done in such a way that the Rajah will lay all the blame on Guzra Bai."

"That can be done," answered the nurse. "I will throw the children out on the ash heaps, where they will soon perish, and I will put stones in their places. Then when the Rajah returns we will tell him Guzra Bai is a wicked sorceress, who has changed her children into stones."

The old Ranee was pleased with this plan and said that she herself would go with the nurse and see that it was carried out.

Guzra Bai looked from her window and saw the old Queen coming with the nurse, and at once she was afraid. She was sure they intended some harm to her or the children. She seized the golden bell and rang and rang it, but Chundun did not come. She had called him back so often for no reason at all that this time he did not believe she really needed him.

The nurse and the old Ranee carried away the children, as they had planned, and threw them on the ash heaps and brought twenty-one large stones that they put in their places.

When Chundun Rajah returned from his journey the old Ranee met him, weeping and tearing her hair. "Alas! Alas!" she cried. "Why did you marry a sorceress and bring such terrible misfortune upon us all!"

"What misfortune?" asked the Rajah. "What do you mean?"

His mother then told him that while he was away Guzra Bai had had twenty-one beautiful children, but she had turned them all into stones.

Chundun Rajah was thunderstruck. He called the wicked nurse and questioned her. She repeated what the old Ranee had already told him and also showed him the stones.

Then the Rajah believed them. He still loved Guzra Bai too much to put her to death, but he had her imprisoned in a high tower, and would not see her nor speak with her.

But meanwhile the little children who had been thrown out on the ash heap were being well taken care of. A large rat, of the kind called Bandicote, had heard them crying and had taken pity on them. She drew them down into her hole, which was close by and where they would be safe. She then called twenty of her friends together. She told them who the children were and where she had found them, and the twenty agreed to help her take care of the little ones. Each rat was to have the care of one of the little boys and to bring him suitable food, and the old Bandicote who had found them would care for the little girl.

This was done, and so well were the children fed that they grew rapidly. Before long they were large enough to leave the rat hole and go out to play among the ash heaps, but at night they always returned to the hole. The old Bandicote warned them that if they saw anyone coming they must at once hide in the hole, and under no circumstances must anyone see them.

The little boys were always careful to do this, but the little girl was very curious. Now it so happened that one day the wicked nurse came past the ash heaps. The little boys saw her coming and ran back into the hole to hide. But the little girl lingered until the nurse was quite close to her before she ran away.

The nurse went to the old Ranee, and said, "Do you know, I believe those children are still alive? I believe they are living in a rat hole near the ash heap, for I saw a pretty little girl playing there among the ashes, and when I came close to her she ran down into the largest rat hole and hid."

The Ranee was very much troubled when she heard this, for if it were true, as she thought it might be, she feared the Rajah would hear about it and inquire into the matter. "What shall I do?" she asked the nurse.

"Send out and have the ground dug over and filled in," the nurse replied. "In this way, if any of the children are hidden there, they will be covered over and smothered, and you will also kill the rats that have been harbouring them."

The Ranee at once sent for workmen and bade them go out to the rat holes and dig and fill them in, and the children and the rats would certainly have been smothered just as the nurse had planned, only luckily the old mother rat was hiding nearby and overheard what was said. She at once hastened home and told her friends what was going to happen, and they all made their escape before the workmen arrived. She also took the children out of the hole and hid them under the steps that led down into an old unused well. There were twenty-one steps, and she hid one child under each step. She told them not to utter a sound whatever happened, and then she and her friends ran away and left them.

Presently the workmen came with their tools and began to fill in the rat holes. The little daughter of the head workman had come with him, and while he and his fellows were at work the little girl amused herself by running up and down the steps into the well. Every time she trod upon a step it pinched the child who lay under it. The little boys made no sound when they were pinched, but lay as still as stones, but every time the child trod on the step under which the Princess lay she sighed, and the third time she felt the pinch she cried out, "Have pity on me and tread more lightly. I too am a little girl like you!"

The workman's daughter was very much frightened when she heard the voice. She ran to her father and told him the steps had spoken to her.

The workman thought this a strange thing. He at once went to the old Ranee and told her he dared no longer work near the well, for he believed a witch or a demon lived there under the steps; and he repeated what his little daughter had told him.

The wicked nurse was with the Ranee when the workman came to her. As soon as he had gone, the nurse said: "I am sure some of those children must still be alive. They must have escaped from the rat holes and be hiding under the steps. If we send out there we will probably find them."

The Ranee was frightened at the thought they might still be alive. She ordered some servants to come with her, and she and the nurse went out to look for the children.

But when the little girl had cried out the little boys were afraid some harm might follow, and prayed that they might be changed into trees, so that if anyone came to search for them they might not find them.

Their prayers were answered. The twenty little boys were changed into twenty little banyan trees that stood in a circle, and the little girl was changed into a rose bush that stood in the midst of the circle and was full of red and white roses.

The old Ranee and the nurse and the servants came to the well and searched under every step, but no one was there, so went away again.

All might now have been well, but the workman's mischievous little daughter chanced to come by that way again. At once she espied the banyan trees and the rose bush. "It is a curious thing that I never saw these trees before," she thought. "I will gather a bunch of roses."

She ran past the banyan trees without giving them a thought and began to break the flowers from the rose tree. At once a shiver ran through the tree, and it cried to her in a pitiful voice: "Oh! Oh! you are hurting me. Do not break my branches, I pray of you. I am a little girl, too, and can suffer just as you might."

The child ran back to her father and caught him by the hand. "Oh, I am frightened!" she cried. "I went to gather some roses from the rose-tree, and it spoke to me"; and she told him what the rose-tree had said.

At once the workman went off and repeated to the Ranee what his little daughter had told him, and the Queen gave him a piece of gold and sent him away, bidding him keep what he had heard a secret.

Then she called the wicked nurse to her and repeated the workman's story. "What had we better do now?" she asked.

"My advice is that you give orders to have all the trees cut down and burned," said the nurse. "In this way you will rid yourself of the children altogether."

This advice seemed good to the Ranee. She sent men and had the trees cut down and thrown in a heap to burn.

But heaven had pity on the children, and just as the men were about to set fire to the heap a heavy rain storm arose and put out the fire. Then the river rose over its banks, and swept the little trees down on its flood, far, far away to a jungle where no one lived. Here they were washed ashore and at once took on their real shapes again.

The children lived there in the jungle safely for twelve years, and the brothers grew up tall and straight and handsome, and the sister was like the new moon in her beauty, so slim and white and shining was she.

The brothers wove a hut of branches to shelter their sister, and every day ten of them went out hunting in the forest, and ten of them stayed at home to care for her. But one day it chanced they all wished to go hunting together, so they put their sister up in a high tree where she would be safe from the beasts of the forest, and then they went away and left her there alone.

The twenty brothers went on and on through the jungle, farther than they had ever gone before, and so came at last to an open space among the trees, and there was a hut.

"Who can be living here?" said one of the brothers.

"Let us knock and see," cried another.

The Princes knocked at the door and immediately it was opened to them by a great, wicked-looking Rakshas. She had only one red eye in the middle of her forehead; her grey hair hung in a tangled mat over her shoulders, and she was dressed in dirty rags.

When the Rakshasa saw the brothers she was filled with fury.

She considered all the jungle belonged to her, and she was not willing that anyone else should come there. Her one eye flashed fire, and she seized a stick and began beating the Princes, and each one, as she struck him, was turned into a crow. She then drove them away and went back into her hut and closed the door.

The twenty crows flew back through the forest, cawing mournfully. When they came to the tree where their sister sat they gathered about her, trying to make her understand that they were her brothers.

At first the Princess was frightened by the crows, but when she saw there were tears in their eyes, and when she counted them and found there were exactly twenty, she guessed what had happened, and that some wicked enchantment had changed her brothers into this shape. Then she wept over them and smoothed their feathers tenderly.

After this the sister lived up in the tree, and the crows brought her food every day and rested around her in the branches at night, so that no harm should come to her.

Some time after this a young Rajah came into that very jungle to hunt. In some way he became separated from his attendants and wandered deeper and deeper into the forest, until at length he came to the tree where the Princess sat. He threw himself down beneath the tree to rest. Hearing a sound of wings above him the Rajah looked up and was amazed to see a beautiful girl sitting there among the branches with a flock of crows about her.

The Rajah climbed the tree and brought the girl down, while the crows circled about his head, cawing hoarsely.

"Tell me, beautiful one, who are you? And how come you here in the depths of the jungle?" asked the Rajah.

Weeping, the Princess told him all her story except that the crows were her brothers; she let him believe that her brothers had gone off hunting and had never returned.

"Do not weep any more," said the Rajah. "You shall come home with me and be my Ranee, and I will have no other but you alone."

When the Princess heard this she smiled, for the Rajah was very handsome, and already she loved him.

She was very glad to go with him and be his wife. "But my crows must go with me," she said, "for they have fed me for many long days and have been my only companions."

To this the Rajah willingly consented, and he took her home with him to the palace; and the crows circled about above them, following closely all the way.

When the old Rajah and Ranee (the young Rajah's father and mother) saw what a very beautiful girl he had brought back with him from the jungle they gladly welcomed her as a daughter-in-law.

The young Ranee would have been very happy now in her new life, for she loved her husband dearly, but always the thought of her brothers was like a weight upon her heart. She had a number of trees planted outside her windows so that her brothers might rest there close to her. She cooked rice for them herself and fed them with her own hands, and often she sat under the trees and stroked them and talked to them while her tears fell upon their glossy feathers.

After a while the young Ranee had a son, and he was called Ramchundra. He grew up straight and tall, and he was the joy of his mother's eyes.

One day, when he was fourteen years old, and big and strong for his age, he sat in the garden with his mother. The crows flew down about them, and she began to caress and talk to them as usual. "Ah, my dear ones!" she cried, "how sad is your fate! If I could but release you, how happy I should be."

"Mother," said the boy, "I can plainly see that these crows are not ordinary birds. Tell me whence come they, and why you weep over them and talk to them as you do?"

At first his mother would not tell him, but in the end she related to him the whole story of who she was, and how she and her brothers had come to the jungle and had lived there happily enough until they were changed into crows; and then of how the Rajah had found her and brought her home with him to the palace.

"I can easily see," said Ramchundra, when she had ended the tale, "that my uncles must have met a Rakshasa somewhere in the forest and have been enchanted. Tell me exactly where the tree was – the tree where you lived – and what kind it was?"

The Ranee told him.

"And in which direction did your brothers go when they left you?"

This also his mother told him. "Why do you ask me these questions, my son?" she asked.

"I wish to know," said Ramchundra, "for sometime I intend to set out and find that Rakshasa and force her to free my uncles from her enchantment and change them back to their natural shapes again."

His mother was terrified when she heard this, but she said very little to him, hoping he would soon forget about it and not enter into such a dangerous adventure.

Not long afterward Ramchundra went to his father and said, "Father, I am no longer a child; give me your permission to ride out into the world and see it for myself."

The Rajah was willing for him to do this and asked what attendants his son would take with him.

"I wish for no attendants," answered Ramchundra. "Give me only a horse, and a groom to take care of it."

The Rajah gave his son the handsomest horse in his stables and also a well-mounted groom to ride with him. Ramchundra, however, only allowed the groom to go with him as far as the edge of the jungle, and then he sent him back home again with both the horses.

The Prince went on and on through the forest for a long distance until at last he came to a tree that he felt sure was the one his mother had told him of. From there he set forth in the same direction she told him his uncles had taken. He went on and on, ever deeper and deeper into the forest, until at last he came to a miserable-looking hut. The door was open, and he looked in. There lay an ugly old hag fast asleep. She had only one eye in the middle of her forehead, and her grey hair was tangled and matted and fell over her face. The Prince entered in very softly, and sitting down beside her, he began to rub her head. He suspected that this was the Rakshasa who had bewitched his uncles, and it was indeed she.

Presently the old woman awoke, "My pretty lad," said she, "you have a kind heart. Stay with me here and help me, for I am very old and feeble, as you see, and I cannot very well look out for myself."

This she said not because she really was old or feeble, but because she was lazy and wanted a servant to wait on her.

"Gladly will I stay," answered the lad, "and what I can do to serve you, that I will do."

So the Prince stayed there as the Rakshasa' servant. He served her hand and foot, and every day she made him sit down and rub her head.

One day, while he was rubbing her head and she was in a good humour he said to her, "Mother, why do you keep all those little jars of water standing along the wall? Let me throw out the water so that we may make some use of the jars."

"Do not touch them," cried the Rakshas. "That water is very powerful. One drop of it can break the strongest enchantment, and if anyone has been bewitched, that water has power to bring him back to his own shape again."

"And why do you keep that crooked stick behind the door? Tomorrow I shall break it up to build a fire."

"Do not touch it," cried the hag. "I have but to wave that stick, and I can conjure up a mountain, a forest, or a river just as I wish, and all in the twinkling of an eye."

The Prince said nothing to that, but went on rubbing her head. Presently he began to talk again. "Your hair is in a dreadful tangle, mother," he said. "Let me get a comb and comb it out."

"Do not dare!" screamed the Rakshas. "One hair of my head has the power to set the whole jungle in flames."

Ramchundra again was silent and went on rubbing her head, and after a while the old Rakshasa fell asleep and snored till the hut shook with her snoring.

Then, very quietly, the Prince arose. He plucked a hair from the old hag's head without awakening her, he took a flask of the magic water and the staff from behind the door, and set out as fast as he could go in the direction of the palace.

It was not long before he heard the Rakshasa coming through the jungle after him, for she had awakened and found him gone.

Nearer and nearer she came, and then the Prince turned and waved the crooked stick. At once a river rolled between him and the Rakshas.

Without pause the Rakshasa plunged into the river and struck out boldly, and soon she reached the other side.

On she came again close after Ramchundra. Again he turned and waved the staff. At once a thick screen of trees sprang up between him and the hag. The Rakshasa brushed them aside this way and that as though they had been nothing but twigs.

On she came, and again the Prince waved the staff. A high mountain arose, but the Rakshasa climbed it, and it did not take her long to do this.

Now she was so close that Ramchundra could hear her panting, but the edge of the jungle had been reached. He turned and cast the Rakshas' hair behind him. Immediately the whole jungle burst into fire, and the Rakshasa was burned up in the flames.

Soon after the Prince reached the palace and hastened out into the garden. There sat his mother weeping, with the crows gathered about her. When she saw Ramchundra she sprang to her feet with a scream of joy and ran to him and took him in her arms.

"My son! my son! I thought you had perished!" she cried. "Did you meet the Rakshas?"

"Not only did I meet her, but I have slain her and brought back with me that which will restore my uncles to their proper shapes," answered the Prince.

He then dipped his fingers into the jar he carried and sprinkled the magic water over the crows. At once the enchantment was broken, and the twenty Princes stood there, tall and handsome, in their own proper shapes.

The Ranee made haste to lead them to her husband and told him the whole story. The Rajah could not wonder enough when he understood that the Princes were his wife's brothers, and were the crows she had brought home with her.

He at once ordered a magnificent feast to be prepared and a day of rejoicing to be held throughout all the kingdom.

Many Rajahs from far and near were invited to the feast, and among those who came was the father of the Ranee and her brothers, but he never suspected, as he looked upon them, that they were his children.

Before they sat down to the feast the young Ranee said to him, "Where is your wife Guzra Bai? Why has she not come with you? We had expected to see her here?"

The Rajah was surprised that the young Ranee should know his wife's name, but he made some excuse as to why Guzra Bai was not there.

Then the young Rajah said, "Send for her, I beg of you, for the feast cannot begin till she is here."

The older Rajah was still more surprised at this. He could not think anyone was really concerned about Guzra Bai, and he feared the young Rajah wished, for some reason, to quarrel with him. But he agreed to send for his wife, and messengers were at once dispatched to bring Guzra Bai to the palace.

No sooner had she come than the young Ranee began to weep, and she and the Princes gathered about their mother. Then they told the Rajah the whole story of how his mother and the nurse had sought to destroy Guzra Bai and her children, and how they had been saved, and had now come to safety and great honour.

The Rajah was overcome with joy when he found that Guzra Bai was innocent. He prayed her to forgive him, and this she did, and all was joy and happiness.

As for the old Ranee, she was shut up in the tower where Guzra Bai had lived for so many years, but the old nurse was killed as befitted such a wicked woman.

The Boy With the Moon on His Forehead

THERE WAS A CERTAIN KING who had six queens, none of whom bore children. Physicians, holy sages, mendicants, were consulted, countless drugs were had recourse to, but all to no purpose. The king was disconsolate. His ministers told him to marry a seventh wife; and he was accordingly on the look-out.

In the royal city there lived a poor old woman who used to pick up cow-dung from the fields, make it into cakes, dry them in the sun, and sell them in the market for fuel. This was her only means of subsistence. This old woman had a daughter exquisitely beautiful. Her beauty excited the admiration of every one that saw her; and it was solely in consequence of her surpassing beauty that three young ladies, far above her in rank and station, contracted friendship with her. Those three young ladies were the daughter of the king's minister, the daughter of a wealthy merchant, and the daughter of the royal priest. These three young ladies, together with the daughter of the poor old woman, were one day bathing in a tank not far from the palace. As they were performing their ablutions, each dwelt on her own good qualities. "Look here, sister," said the minister's daughter, addressing the merchant's daughter, "the man that marries me will be a happy man, for he will not have to buy clothes for me. The cloth which I once put on never gets soiled, never gets old, never tears." The merchant's daughter said, "And my husband too will be a happy man, for the fuel which I use in cooking never gets turned into ashes. The same fuel serves from day to day, from year to year." "And my husband will also become a happy man," said the daughter of the royal chaplain, "for the rice which I cook one day never gets finished, and when we have all eaten, the same quantity which was first cooked remains always in the pot." The daughter of the poor old woman said in her turn, "And the man that marries me will also be happy, for I shall give birth to twin children, a son and a daughter. The daughter will be divinely fair, and the son will have the moon on his forehead and stars on the palms of his hands."

The above conversation was overheard by the king, who, as he was on the look-out for a seventh queen, used to skulk about in places where women met together. The king thus thought in his mind – "I don't care a straw for the girl whose clothes never tear and never get old; neither do I care for the other girl whose fuel is never consumed; nor for the third girl whose rice never fails in the pot. But the fourth girl is quite charming! She will give birth to twin children, a son and a daughter; the daughter will be divinely fair, and the son will have the moon on his forehead and stars on the palms of his hands. That is the girl I want. I'll make her my wife."

On making inquiries on the same day, the king found that the fourth girl was the daughter of a poor old woman who picked up cow-dung from the fields; but though there was thus an infinite disparity in rank, he determined to marry her. On the very same day he sent for the poor old woman. She, poor thing, was quite frightened when she saw a messenger of the king standing at the door of her hut. She thought that the king had sent for her to punish her, because, perhaps, she had some day unwittingly picked up the dung of the king's cattle. She went to the palace, and was admitted into the king's private chamber. The king asked her whether she had a very fair daughter, and whether that daughter was the friend of his own minister's and priest's daughters. When the woman answered in the affirmative, he said to her, "I will marry your daughter, and make her my queen." The woman hardly believed her own ears – the thing was so strange. He, however, solemnly declared to her that he had made up his mind, and was determined to marry her daughter. It was soon known in the capital that the king was going to marry the daughter of the old woman who picked up cow-dung in the fields. When the six queens heard the news, they would not believe it, till the king himself told them that the news was true. They thought that the king had somehow got mad. They reasoned with him thus – "What folly, what madness, to marry a girl who is not fit to be our maid-servant! And you expect us to treat her as our equal – a girl whose mother goes about picking up cow-dung in the fields! Surely, my lord, you are beside yourself!" The king's purpose, however, remained unshaken. The royal astrologer was called, and an auspicious day was fixed for the celebration of the king's marriage. On the appointed day the royal priest tied the marital knot, and the daughter of the poor old picker-up of cow-dung in the fields became the seventh and best beloved queen.

Some time after the celebration of the marriage, the king went for six months to another part of his dominions. Before setting out he called to him the seventh queen, and said to her, "I am going away to another part of my dominions for six months. Before the expiration of that period I expect you to be confined. But I should like to be present with you at the time, as your enemies may do mischief. Take this golden bell and hang it in your room. When the pains of childbirth come upon you, ring this bell, and I will be with you in a moment in whatever part of my dominions I may be at the time. Remember, you are to ring the bell only when you feel the pains of childbirth." After saying this the king started on his journey. The six queens, who had overheard the king, went on the next day to the apartments of the seventh queen, and said, "What a nice bell of gold you have got, sister! Where did you get it, and why have you hung it up?" The seventh queen, in her simplicity, said, "The king has given it to me, and if I were to ring it, the king would immediately come to me wherever he might be at the time." "Impossible!" said the six queens, "you must have misunderstood the king. Who can believe that this bell can be heard at the distance of hundreds of miles? Besides, if it could be heard, how would the king be able to travel a great distance in the twinkling of an eye? This must be a hoax. If you ring the bell, you will find that what the king said was pure nonsense." The six queens then told her to make a trial. At first she was unwilling, remembering what the king had told her; but at last she was prevailed upon to ring the bell. The king was at the moment halfway to the capital of his other dominions, but at the ringing of the bell he stopped short in his journey, turned back, and in no time stood in the queen's apartments. Finding the queen going about in her rooms, he asked why she had rung the bell though her hour had not come. She, without informing the king of the entreaty of the six queens, replied that she rang the bell only to see whether what he had said was true. The king was somewhat indignant, told her distinctly not to ring the bell again till the moment of the coming upon her of the pains of childbirth, and then went away. After the lapse of some weeks the six queens again begged of the seventh queen to make a second trial of the bell. They said to her, "The first time when you rang the bell, the king was only at a short distance from you, it was therefore easy for him to hear the bell and to come to you; but now he has long ago settled in his other capital, let us see if he will now hear the bell and come to you." She resisted for a long time, but was at last prevailed upon by them to ring the bell. When the sound of the bell reached the king he was in court dispensing justice, but when he heard the sound of the bell (and no one else heard it) he closed the court and in no time stood in the queen's apartments. Finding that the queen was not about to be confined, he asked her why she had again rung the bell before her hour. She, without saying anything of the importunities of the six queens, replied that she merely made a second trial of the bell. The king became very angry, and said to her, "Now listen, since you have called me twice for nothing, let it be known to you that when the throes of childbirth do really come upon you, and you ring the bell ever so lustily, I will not come to you. You must be left to your fate." The king then went away.

At last the day of the seventh queen's deliverance arrived. On first feeling the pains she rang the golden bell. She waited, but the king did not make his appearance. She rang again with all her might, still the king did not make his appearance. The king certainly did hear the sound of the bell; but he did not come as he was displeased with the queen. When the six queens saw that the king did not come, they went to the seventh queen and told her that it was not customary with the ladies of the palace to be confined in the king's apartments; she must go to a hut near the stables. They then sent for the midwife of the palace, and heavily bribed her to make away with the infant the moment it should be born into the world. The seventh queen gave birth to a son who had the moon on his forehead and stars on the palms of his hands, and also to an uncommonly beautiful girl. The midwife had come provided with a couple of newly born pups. She put the pups before the mother, saying – "You have given birth to these," and took away the twin children in an earthen vessel. The queen was quite insensible at the time, and did not notice the twins at the time they were carried away. The king, though he was angry with the seventh queen, yet remembering that she was destined to give birth to the heir of his throne, changed his mind, and came to see her the next morning. The pups were produced before the king as the offspring of the queen. The king's anger and vexation knew no bounds. He ordered that the seventh queen should be expelled from the palace, that she should be clothed in leather, and that she should be employed in the market-place to drive away crows and to keep off dogs. Though scarcely able to move she was driven away from the palace, stripped of her fine robes, clothed in leather, and set to drive away the crows of the market-place.

The midwife, when she put the twins in the earthen vessel, bethought herself of the best way to destroy them. She did not think it proper to throw them into a tank, lest they should be discovered the next day. Neither did she think of burying them in the ground, lest they should be dug up by a jackal and exposed to the gaze of people. The best way to make an end of them, she thought, would be to burn them, and reduce them to ashes, that no trace might be left of them. But how could she, at that dead hour of night, burn them without some other person helping her? A happy thought struck her. There was a potter on the outskirts of the city, who used during the day to mould vessels of clay on his wheel, and burn them during the latter part of the night. The midwife thought that the best plan would be to put the vessel with the twins along with the unburnt clay vessels which the potter had arranged in order and gone to sleep expecting to get up late at night and set them on fire; in this way, she thought, the twins would be reduced to ashes. She, accordingly, put the vessel with the twins along with the unburnt clay vessels of the potter, and went away.

Somehow or other, that night the potter and his wife overslept themselves. It was near the break of day when the potter's wife, awaking out of sleep, roused her husband, and said, "Oh, my good man, we have overslept ourselves; it is now near morning and I much fear it is now too late to set the pots on fire." Hastily unbolting the door of her cottage, she rushed out to the place where the pots were ranged in rows. She could scarcely believe her eyes when she saw that all the pots had been baked and were looking bright red, though neither she nor her husband had applied any fire to them. Wondering at her good luck, and not knowing what to make of it, she ran to her husband and said, "Just come and see!" The potter came, saw, and wondered. The pots had never before been so well baked. Who could have done this? This could have proceeded only from some god or goddess. Fumbling about the pots, he accidentally upturned one in which, lo and behold, were seen huddled up together two newly born infants of unearthly beauty. The potter said to his wife, "My dear, you must pretend to have given birth to these beautiful children." Accordingly all arrangements were made, and in due time it was given out that the twins had been born to her. And such lovely twins they were! On the same day many women of the neighbourhood came to see the potter's wife and the twins to which she had given birth, and to offer their congratulations on this unexpected good fortune. As for the potter's wife, she could not be too proud of her pretended children, and said to her admiring friends, "I had hardly hoped to have children at all. But now that the gods have given me these twins, may they receive the blessings of you all, and live for ever!"

The twins grew and were strengthened. The brother and sister, when they played about in the fields and lanes, were the admiration of everyone who saw them; and all wondered at the uncommonly good luck of the potter in being blessed with such angelic children. They were about twelve years old when the potter, their reputed father, became dangerously ill. It was evident to all that his sickness would end in death. The potter, perceiving his last end approaching, said to his wife, "My dear, I am going the way of all the earth; but I am leaving to you enough to live upon; live on and take care of these children." The woman said to her husband, "I am not going to survive you. Like all good and faithful wives, I am determined to die along with you. You and I will burn together on the same funeral pyre. As for the children, they are old enough to take care of themselves, and you are leaving them enough money." Her friends tried to dissuade her from her purpose, but in vain. The potter died; and as his remains were being burnt, his wife, now a widow, threw herself on the pyre, and burnt herself to death.

The boy with the moon on his forehead – by the way, he always kept his head covered with a turban lest the halo should attract notice – and his sister, now broke up the potter's establishment, sold the wheel and the pots and pans, and went to the bazaar in the king's city. The moment they entered, the bazaar was lit up on a sudden. The shopkeepers of the bazaar were greatly surprised. They thought some divine beings must have entered the place. They looked upon the beautiful boy and his sister with wonder. They begged of them to stay in the bazaar. They built a house for them. When they used to ramble about, they were always followed at a distance by the woman clothed in leather, who was appointed by the king to drive away the crows of the bazaar. By some unaccountable impulse she used also to hang about the house in which they lived. The boy in a short time bought a horse, and went a-hunting in the neighbouring forests. One day while he was hunting, the king was also hunting in the same forest, and seeing a brother huntsman the king drew near to him. The king was struck with the beauty of the lad and a yearning for him the moment he saw him. As a deer went past, the youth shot an arrow, and the reaction of the force necessary to shoot the arrow made the turban of his head fall off, on which a bright light, like that of the moon, was seen shining on his forehead. The king saw, and immediately thought of the son with the moon on his forehead and stars on the palms of his hands who was to have been born of his seventh queen. The youth on letting fly the arrow galloped off, in spite of the earnest entreaty of the king to wait and speak to him. The king went home a sadder man than he came out of it. He became very moody and melancholy. The six queens asked him why he was looking so sad. He told them that he had seen in the woods a lad with the moon on his forehead, which reminded him of the son who was to be born of the seventh queen. The six queens tried to comfort him in the best way they could; but they wondered who the youth could be. Was it possible that the twins were living? Did not the midwife say that she had burnt both the son and the daughter to ashes? Who, then, could this lad be? The midwife was sent for by the six queens and questioned. She swore that she had seen the twins burnt. As for the lad whom the king had met with, she would soon find out who he was. On making inquiries, the midwife soon found out that two strangers were living in the bazaar in a house which the shopkeepers had built for them. She entered the house and saw the girl only, as the lad had again gone out a-shooting. She pretended to be their aunt, who had gone away to another part of the country shortly after their birth; she had been searching after them for a long time, and was now glad to find them in the king's city near the palace. She greatly admired the beauty of the girl, and said to her, "My dear child, you are so beautiful, you require the *kataki* flower properly to set off your beauty. You should tell your brother to plant a row of that flower in this courtyard." "What flower is that, auntie? I never saw it." "How could you have seen it, my child? It is not found here; it grows on the other side of the ocean, guarded by seven hundred Rakshasas." "How, then," said the girl, "will my brother get it?" "He may try to get it, if you speak to him," replied the woman. The woman made this proposal in the hope that the boy with the moon on his forehead would perish in the attempt to get the flower.

When the youth with the moon on his forehead returned from hunting, his sister told him of the visit paid to her by their aunt, and requested him, if possible, to get for her the *kataki* flower. He was sceptical about the existence of any aunt of theirs in the world, but he was resolved that, to please his beloved sister, he would get the flower on which she had set her heart. Next morning, accordingly, he started on his journey, after bidding his sister not to stir out of the house till his return. He rode on his fleet steed, which was of the *Pakshiraj* tribe, and soon reached the outskirts of what seemed to him dense forests of interminable length. He descried some Rakshasas prowling about. He went to some distance, shot with his arrows some deer and rhinoceroses in the neighbouring thickets, and, approaching the place where the Rakshasas were prowling about, called out, "O auntie dear, O auntie dear, your nephew is here." A huge Rakshasi came towards him and said, "O, you are the youth with the moon on your forehead and stars on the palms of your hands. We were all expecting you, but as you have called me aunt, I will not eat you up. What is it you want? Have you brought any eatables for me?" The youth gave her the deer and rhinoceroses which he had killed. Her mouth watered at the sight of the dead animals, and she began eating them. After swallowing down all the carcases, she said, "Well, what do you want?" The youth said, "I want some *kataki* flowers for my sister." She then told him that it would be difficult for him to get the flower, as it was guarded by seven hundred Rakshasas; however, he might make the attempt, but in the first instance he must go to his uncle on the north side of that forest. While the youth was going to his uncle of the north, on the way he killed some deer and rhinoceroses, and seeing a gigantic Rakshasa at some distance, cried out, "Uncle dear, uncle dear, your nephew is here. Auntie has sent me to you." The Rakshasa came near and said, "You are the youth with the moon on your forehead and stars on the palms of your hands; I would have swallowed you outright, had you not called me uncle, and had you not said that your aunt had sent you to me. Now, what is it you want?" The savoury deer and rhinoceroses were then presented to him; he ate them all, and then listened to the petition of the youth. The youth wanted the *kataki* flower. The Rakshasa said, "You want the *kataki* flower! Very well, try and get it if you can. After passing through this forest, you will come to an impenetrable forest of *kachiri*. You will say to that forest, 'O mother *kachiri*! Please make way for me, or else I die.' On that the forest will open up a passage for you. You will next come to the ocean. You will say to the ocean, 'O mother ocean! Please make way for me, or else I die,' and the ocean will make way for you. After crossing the ocean, you enter the gardens where the *kataki* blooms. Goodbye; do as I have told you." The youth thanked his Rakshasa-uncle, and went on his way. After he had passed through the forest, he saw before him an impenetrable forest of *kachiri*. It was so close and thick, and withal so bristling with thorns, that not a mouse could go through it. Remembering the advice of his uncle, he stood before the forest with folded hands, and said, "O mother *kachiri*! Please make way for me, or else I die." On a sudden a clean path was opened up in the forest, and the youth gladly passed through it. The ocean now lay before him. He said to the ocean, "O mother ocean! make way for me, or else I die." Forthwith the waters of the ocean stood up on two sides like two walls, leaving an open passage between them, and the youth passed through dryshod.

Now, right before him were the gardens of the *kataki* flower. He entered the inclosure, and found himself in a spacious palace which seemed to be unoccupied. On going from apartment to apartment he found a young lady of more than earthly beauty sleeping on a bedstead of gold. He went near, and noticed two little sticks, one of gold and the other of silver, lying in the bedstead. The silver stick lay near the feet of the sleeping beauty, and the golden one near the head. He took up the sticks in his hands, and as he was examining them, the golden stick accidentally fell upon the feet of the lady. In a moment the lady woke and sat up, and said to the youth, "Stranger, how have you come to this dismal place? I know who you are, and I know your history. You are the youth with the moon on your forehead and stars on the palms of your hands. Flee, flee from this place! This is the residence of seven hundred Rakshasas who guard the gardens of the *kataki* flower. They have all gone a-hunting; they will return by sundown; and if they find you here you will be eaten up. One Rakshasi brought me from the earth where my father is king. She loves me very dearly, and will not let me go away. By means of these gold and silver sticks she kills me when she goes away in the morning, and by means of those sticks she revives me when she returns in the evening. Flee, flee hence, or you die!" The youth told the young lady how his sister wished very much to have the *kataki* flower, how he passed through the forest of *kachiri*, and how he crossed the ocean. He said also that he was determined not to go alone, he must take the young lady along with him. The remaining part of the day they spent together in rambling about the gardens. As the time was drawing near when the Rakshasas should return, the youth buried himself amid an enormous heap of *kataki* flower which lay in an adjoining apartment, after killing the young lady by touching her head with the golden stick. Just after sunset the youth heard the sound as of a mighty tempest: it was the return of the seven hundred Rakshasas into the gardens. One of them entered the apartment of the young lady, revived her, and said, "I smell a human being, I smell a human being." The young lady replied, "How can a human being come to this place? I am the only human being here." The Rakshasi then stretched herself on the floor, and told the young lady to shampoo her legs. As she was going on shampooing, she let fall a tearadrop on the Rakshasi's leg. "Why are you weeping, my dear child?" asked the raw-eater; "why are you weeping? Is anything troubling you?" "No, Mamma," answered the young lady, "nothing is troubling me. What can trouble me, when you have made me so comfortable? I was only thinking what will become of me when you die." "When I die, child?" said the Rakshasi; "shall I die? Yes, of course all creatures die; but the death of a Rakshasa or Rakshasi will never happen. You know, child, that deep tank in the middle part of these gardens. Well, at the bottom of that tank there is a wooden box, in which there are a male and a female bee. It is ordained by fate that if a human being who has the moon on his forehead and stars on the palms of his hands were to come here and dive into that tank, and get hold of the same wooden box, and crush to death the male and female bees without letting a drop of their blood fall to the ground, then we should die. But the accomplishment of this decree of fate is, I think, impossible. For, in the first place, there can be no such human being who will have the moon on his forehead and stars on the palms of his hands; and, in the second place, if there be such a man, he will find it impossible to come to this place, guarded as it is by seven hundred of us, encompassed by a deep ocean, and barricaded by an impervious forest of *kachiri* – not to speak of the outposts and sentinels that are stationed on the other side of the forest. And then, even if he succeeds in coming here, he will perhaps not know the secret of the wooden box; and even if he knows of the secret of the wooden box, he may not succeed in killing the bees without letting a drop of their blood fall on the ground. And woe be to him if a drop does fall on the ground, for in that case he will be torn up into seven hundred pieces by us. You see then, child, that we are almost immortal – not actually, but virtually so. You may, therefore, dismiss your fears."

On the next morning the Rakshasi got up, killed the young lady by means of the sticks, and went away in search of food along with other Rakshasas and Rakshasis. The lad, who had the moon on his forehead and stars on the palms of his hands, came out of the heap of flowers and revived the young lady. The young lady recited to the young man the whole of the conversation she had had with the Rakshasi. It was a perfect revelation to him. He, however, lost no time in beginning to act. He shut the heavy gates of the gardens. He dived into the tank and brought up the wooden box. He opened the wooden box, and caught hold of the male and female bees as they were about to escape. He crushed them on the palms of his hands, besmearing his body with every drop of their blood. The moment this was done, loud cries and groans were heard around about the inclosure of the gardens. Agreeably to the decree of fate all the Rakshasas approached the gardens and fell down dead. The youth with the moon on his forehead took as many *kataki* flowers as he could, together with their seeds, and left the palace, around which were lying in mountain heaps the carcases of the mighty dead, in company with the young and beautiful lady. The waters of the ocean retreated before the youth as before, and the forest of *kachiri* also opened up a passage through it; and the happy couple reached the house in the bazaar, where they were welcomed by the sister of the youth who had the moon on his forehead.

On the following morning the youth, as usual, went to hunt. The king was also there. A deer passed by, and the youth shot an arrow. As he shot, the turban as usual fell off his head, and a bright light issued from it. The king saw and wondered. He told the youth to stop, as he wished to contract friendship with him. The youth told him to come to his house, and gave him his address. The king went to the house of the youth in the middle of the day. Pushpavati – for that was the name of the young lady that had been brought from beyond the ocean – told the king – for she knew the whole history – how his seventh queen had been persuaded by the other six queens to ring the bell twice before her time, how she was delivered of a beautiful boy and girl, how pups were substituted in their room, how the twins were saved in a miraculous manner in the house of the potter, how they were well treated in the bazaar, and how the youth with the moon on his forehead rescued her from the clutches of the Rakshasas. The king, mightily incensed with the six queens, had them, on the following day, buried alive in the ground. The seventh queen was then brought from the market-place and reinstated in her position; and the youth with the moon on his forehead, and the lovely Pushpavati and their sister, lived happily together.

The Black Bowl

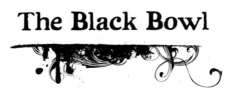

LONG AGO, IN A PART OF THE COUNTRY not very remote from Kyoto, the great gay city, there dwelt an honest couple. In a lonely place was their cottage, upon the outskirts of a deep wood of pine trees. Folks had it that the wood was haunted. They said it was full of deceiving foxes; they said that beneath the mossy ground the elves built their kitchens; they said that long-nosed *Tengu* had tea-parties in the forest thrice a month, and that the fairies' children played at hide-and-seek there every morning before seven. Over and above all this they didn't mind saying that the honest couple were queer in their ways, that the woman was a wise woman, and that the man was a warlock – which was as may be. But sure it was that they did no harm to living soul, that they lived as poor as poor, and that they had one fair daughter. She was as neat and pretty as a princess, and her manners were very fine; but for all that she worked as hard as a boy in the rice-fields, and within doors she was the housewife indeed, for she washed and cooked and drew water. She went barefoot in a grey homespun gown, and tied her black hair with a tough wisteria tendril. Brown she was and thin, but the sweetest beggar-maid that ever made shift with a bed of dry moss and no supper.

By-and-by the good man her father dies, and the wise woman her mother sickens within the year, and soon she lies in a corner of the cottage waiting for her end, with the maid near her crying bitter tears.

"Child," says the mother, "do you know you are as pretty as a princess?"

"Am I that?" says the maid, and goes on with her crying.

"Do you know that your manners are fine?" says the mother.

"Are they, then?" says the maid, and goes on with her crying.

"My own baby," says the mother, "could you stop your crying a minute and listen to me?"

So the maid stopped crying and put her head close by her mother's on the poor pillow.

"Now listen," says the mother, "and afterwards remember. It is a bad thing for a poor girl to be pretty. If she is pretty and lonely and innocent, none but the gods will help her. They will help you, my poor child, and I have thought of a way besides. Fetch me the great black rice-bowl from the shelf."

The girl fetched it.

"See, now, I put it on your head and all your beauty is hidden away."

"Alack, mother," said the poor child, "it is heavy."

"It will save you from what is heavier to bear," said the mother. "If you love me, promise me that you will not move it till the time comes."

"I promise! I promise! But how shall I know when the time comes?"

"That you shall know.... And now help me outside, for the sweet morning dawns and I've a fancy to see the fairies' children once again, as they run in the forest."

So the child, having the black bowl upon her head, held her mother in her arms in a grassy place near the great trees, and presently they saw the fairies' children threading their way between the dark trunks as they played at hide-and-seek. Their bright garments fluttered, and they laughed lightly as they went. The mother smiled to see them; before seven she died very sweetly as she smiled.

When her little store of rice was done, the maid with the wooden bowl knew well enough that she must starve or go and find more. So first she tended her father's and mother's graves and poured water for the dead, as is meet, and recited many a holy text. Then she bound on her sandals, kilted her grey skirts to show her scarlet petticoat, tied her household gods in a blue printed handkerchief, and set out all alone to seek her fortunes, the brave girl!

For all her slenderness and pretty feet she was a rarely odd sight, and soon she was to know it. The great black bowl covered her head and shadowed her face. As she went through a village two women looked up from washing in the stream, stared and laughed.

"It's a boggart come alive," says one.

"Out upon her," cries the other, "for a shameless wench! Out upon her false modesty to roam the country thus with her head in a black bowl, as who should cry aloud to every passing man, 'Come and see what is hidden!' It is enough to make a wholesome body sick."

On went the poor maid, and sometimes the children pelted her with mud and pebbles for sport. Sometimes she was handled roughly by village louts, who scoffed and caught at her dress as she went; they even laid hands upon the bowl itself and sought to drag it from her head by force. But they only played at that game once, for the bowl stung them as fiercely as if it had been a nettle, and the bullies ran away howling.

The beggar-maiden might seek her fortune, but it was very hard to find. She might ask for work; but see, would she get it? None were wishful to employ a girl with a black bowl on her head.

At last, on a fine day when she was tired out, she sat her upon a stone and began to cry as if her heart would break. Down rolled her tears from under the black bowl. They rolled down her cheeks and reached her white chin.

A wandering ballad-singer passed that way, with his *biwa* slung across his back. He had a sharp eye and marked the tears upon the maid's white chin. It was all he could see of her face, and, "Oh, girl with the black bowl on your head," quoth he, "why do you sit weeping by the roadside?"

"I weep," she answered, "because the world is hard. I am hungry and tired... No one will give me work or pay me money."

"Now that's unfortunate," said the ballad-singer, for he had a kind heart; "but I haven't a *rin* of my own, or it would be yours. Indeed I am sorry for you. In the circumstances the best I can do for you is to make you a little song." With that he whips his *biwa* round, thrums on it with his fingers and starts as easy as you please. "To the tears on your white chin," he says, and sings:

"The white cherry blooms by the roadside,
How black is the canopy of cloud!
The wild cherry droops by the roadside,
Beware of the black canopy of cloud.
Hark, hear the rain, hear the rainfall
From the black canopy of cloud.
Alas, the wild cherry, its sweet flowers are marred,
Marred are the sweet flowers, forlorn on the spray!"

"Sir, I do not understand your song," said the girl with the bowl on her head.

"Yet it is plain enough," said the ballad-singer, and went his way. He came to the house of a passing rich farmer. In he went, and they asked him to sing before the master of the house.

"With all the will in the world," says the ballad-singer. "I will sing him a new song that I have just made." So he sang of the wild cherry and the great black cloud.

When he had made an end, "Tell us the interpretation of your song," says the master of the house.

"With all the will in the world," quoth the ballad-singer. "The wild cherry is the face of a maiden whom I saw sitting by the wayside. She wore a great black wooden bowl upon her head, which is the great black cloud in my song, and from under it her tears flowed like rain, for I saw the drops upon her white chin. And she said that she wept for hunger, and because no one would give her work nor pay her money."

"Now I would I might help the poor girl with the bowl on her head," said the master of the house.

"That you may if you wish," quoth the ballad-singer. "She sits but a stone's throw from your gate."

The long and short of it was that the maid was put to labour in the rich farmer's harvest-fields. All the day long she worked in the waving rice, with her grey skirts kilted and her sleeves bound back with cords. All day long she plied the sickle, and the sun shone down upon the black bowl; but she had food to eat and good rest at night, and was well content.

She found favour in her master's eyes, and he kept her in the fields till all the harvest was gathered in. Then he took her into his house, where there was plenty for her to do, for his wife was but sickly. Now the maiden lived well and happily as a bird, and went singing about her labours. And every night she thanked the august gods for her good fortune. Still she wore the black bowl upon her head.

At the New Year time, "Bustle, bustle," says the farmer's wife; "scrub and cook and sew; put your best foot foremost, my dear, for we must have the house look at its very neatest."

"To be sure, and with all my heart," says the girl, and she put her back into the work; "but, mistress," she says, "if I may be so bold as to ask, are we having a party, or what?"

"Indeed we are, and many of them," says the farmer's wife. "My son that is in Kyoto, the great and gay, is coming home for a visit."

Presently home he comes, the handsome young man. Then the neighbours were called in, and great was the merry-making. They feasted and they danced, they jested and they sang, many a bowl of good red rice they ate, and many a cup of good *saké* they drank. All this time the girl, with bowl on her head, plied her work modestly in the kitchen, and well out of the way she was – the farmer's wife saw to that, good soul! All the same, one fine day the company called for more wine, and the wine was done, so the son of the house takes up the *saké* bottle and goes with it himself to the kitchen. What should he see there but the maiden sitting upon a pile of faggots, and fanning the kitchen fire with a split bamboo fan!

"My life, but I must see what is under that black bowl," says the handsome young man to himself. And sure enough he made it his daily care, and peeped as much as he could, which was not very much; but seemingly it was enough for him, for he thought no more of Kyoto, the great and gay, but stayed at home to do his courting.

His father laughed and his mother fretted, the neighbours held up their hands, all to no purpose.

"Oh, dear, dear maiden with the wooden bowl, she shall be my bride and no other. I must and will have her," cried the impetuous young man, and very soon he fixed the wedding-day himself.

When the time came, the young maidens of the village went to array the bride. They dressed her in a fair and costly robe of white brocade, and in trailing *hakama* of scarlet silk, and on her shoulders they hung a cloak of blue and purple and gold. They chattered, but as for the bride she said never a word. She was sad because she brought her bridegroom nothing, and because his parents were sore at his choice of a beggar-maid. She said nothing, but the tears glistened on her white chin.

"Now off with the ugly old bowl," cried the maidens; "it is time to dress the bride's hair and to do it with golden combs." So they laid hands to the bowl and would have lifted it away, but they could not move it.

"Try again," they said, and tugged at it with all their might. But it would not stir.

"There's witchcraft in it," they said; "try a third time." They tried a third time, and still the bowl stuck fast, but it gave out fearsome moans and cries.

"Ah! Let be, let be for pity's sake," said the poor bride, "for you make my head ache."

They were forced to lead her as she was to the bridegroom's presence.

"My dear, I am not afraid of the wooden bowl," said the young man.

So they poured the *saké* from the silver flagon, and from the silver cup the two of them drank the mystic 'Three Times Three' that made them man and wife.

Then the black bowl burst asunder with a loud noise, and fell to the ground in a thousand pieces. With it fell a shower of silver and gold, and pearls and rubies and emeralds, and every jewel of price. Great was the astonishment of the company as they gazed upon a dowry that for a princess would have been rich and rare.

But the bridegroom looked into the bride's face. "My dear," he said, "there are no jewels that shine like your eyes."

Tales of Animals & Mythical Creatures

Introduction

'THE CITY OF THE ELEPHANTS was a spacious and well-trodden glade... and the moment it was entered one saw how wisely the elephant families had arranged their manner of life.' So the storytellers of Basoko, in what is now the Democratic Republic of the Congo, said of the sight discovered by Dudu and Salimba, their ancestors, as they walked out into the forest in search of a special redwood tree. To travel the world is always to see new sights and to explore new horizons. In the world of folktale those sights and horizons have a way of being that much stranger. They certainly are in the Turkish story of 'The Horse-Devil and the Witch'. In this tale, a ruler so loves his horse that he marries his youngest daughter to him – fortunately for her he's really a handsome young man bewitched. Animals in folktales often come to the rescue of humans in adversity, as we see in the Lithuanian story 'The Prince and the Friendly Animals'. From Ireland comes the story of 'The Greek Princess and the Young Gardener', in which a magic fox helps the latter win the former's hand.

How the Dragon Was Tricked

ONCE UPON A TIME there lived a man who had two sons but they did not get on at all well together, for the younger was much handsomer than his elder brother who was very jealous of him. When they grew older, things became worse and worse, and at last one day as they were walking through a wood the elder youth seized hold of the other, tied him to a tree, and went on his way hoping that the boy might starve to death.

However, it happened that an old and humpbacked shepherd passed the tree with his flock, and seeing the prisoner, he stopped and said to him, "Tell me, my son why are you tied to that tree?"

"Because I was so crooked," answered the young man; "but it has quite cured me, and now my back is as straight as can be."

"I wish you would bind me to a tree," exclaimed the shepherd, "so that my back would get straight."

"With all the pleasure in life," replied the youth. "If you will loosen these cords I will tie you up with them as firmly as I can."

This was soon done, and then the young man drove off the sheep, leaving their real shepherd to repent of his folly; and before he had gone very far he met with a horse boy and a driver of oxen, and he persuaded them to turn with him and to seek for adventures.

By these and many other tricks he soon became so celebrated that his fame reached the king's ears, and his Majesty was filled with curiosity to see the man who had managed to outwit everybody. So he commanded his guards to capture the young man and bring him before him.

And when the young man stood before the king, the king spoke to him and said, "By your tricks and the pranks that you have played on other people, you have, in the eye of the law, forfeited your life. But on one condition I will spare you, and that is, if you will bring me the flying horse that belongs to the great dragon. Fail in this, and you shall be hewn in a thousand pieces."

"If that is all," said the youth, "you shall soon have it."

So he went out and made his way straight to the stable where the flying horse was tethered. He stretched his hand cautiously out to seize the bridle, when the horse suddenly began to neigh as loud as he could. Now the room in which the dragon slept was just above the stable, and at the sound of the neighing he woke and cried to the horse, "What is the matter, my treasure? is anything hurting you?" After waiting a little while the young man tried again to loose the horse, but a second time it neighed so loudly that the dragon woke up in a hurry and called out to know why the horse was making such a noise. But when the same thing happened the third time, the dragon lost his temper, and went down into the stable and took a whip and gave the horse a good beating. This offended the horse and made him angry, and when the young man stretched out his hand to untie his head, he made no further fuss, but suffered himself to be led quietly away. Once clear of the stable the young man sprang on his back and galloped off, calling over his shoulder, "Hi! dragon! dragon! if anyone asks you what has become of your horse, you can say that I have got him!"

But the king said, "The flying horse is all very well, but I want something more. You must bring me the covering with the little bells that lies on the bed of the dragon, or I will have you hewn into a thousand pieces."

"Is that all?" answered the youth. "That is easily done."

And when night came he went away to the dragon's house and climbed up on to the roof. Then he opened a little window in the roof and let down the chain from which the kettle usually hung, and tried to hook the bed covering and to draw it up. But the little bells all began to ring, and the dragon woke and said to his wife, "Wife, you have pulled off all the bed-clothes!" and drew the covering towards him, pulling, as he did so, the young man into the room. Then the dragon flung himself on the youth and bound him fast with cords saying as he tied the last knot, "Tomorrow when I go to church you must stay at home and kill him and cook him, and when I get back we will eat him together."

So the following morning the dragoness took hold of the young man and reached down from the shelf a sharp knife with which to kill him. But as she untied the cords the better to get hold of him, the prisoner caught her by the legs, threw her to the ground, seized her and speedily cut her throat, just as she had been about to do for him, and put her body in the oven. Then he snatched up the covering and carried it to the king.

The king was seated on his throne when the youth appeared before him and spread out the covering with a deep bow. "That is not enough," said his Majesty; "you must bring me the dragon himself, or I will have you hewn into a thousand pieces."

"It shall be done," answered the youth; "but you must give me two years to manage it, for my beard must grow so that he may not know me."

"So be it," said the king.

And the first thing the young man did when his beard was grown was to take the road to the dragon's house and on the way he met a beggar, whom he persuaded to change clothes with him, and in the beggar's garments he went fearlessly forth to the dragon.

He found his enemy before his house, very busy making a box, and addressed him politely, "Good morning, your worship. Have you a morsel of bread?"

"You must wait," replied the dragon, "till I have finished my box, and then I will see if I can find one."

"What will you do with the box when it is made?" inquired the beggar.

"It is for the young man who killed my wife, and stole my flying horse and my bed covering," said the dragon.

"He deserves nothing better," answered the beggar, "for it was an ill deed. Still that box is too small for him, for he is a big man."

"You are wrong," said the dragon. "The box is large enough even for me."

"Well, the rogue is nearly as tall as you," replied the beggar, "and, of course, if you can get in, he can. But I am sure you would find it a tight fit."

"No, there is plenty of room," said the dragon, tucking himself carefully inside.

But no sooner was he well in, than the young man clapped on the lid and called out, "Now press hard, just to see if he will be able to get out."

The dragon pressed as hard as he could, but the lid never moved.

"It is all right," he cried; "now you can open it."

But instead of opening it, the young man drove in long nails to make it tighter still; then he took the box on his back and brought it to the king. And when the king heard that the dragon was inside, he was so excited that he would not wait one moment, but broke the lock and lifted the lid just a little way to make sure he was really there. He was very careful not to leave enough space for the dragon to jump out, but unluckily there was just room for his great mouth, and with one snap the king vanished down his wide red jaws. Then the young man married the king's daughter and ruled over the land, but what he did with the dragon nobody knows.

The Horse-Devil and the Witch

THERE WAS ONCE UPON A TIME a Padishah who had three daughters. One day the old father made him ready for a journey, and calling to him his three daughters straightly charged them to feed and water his favourite horse, even though they neglected everything else. He loved the horse so much that he would not suffer any stranger to come near it.

So the Padishah went on his way, but when the eldest daughter brought the fodder into the stable the horse would not let her come near him. Then the middling daughter brought the forage, and he treated her likewise. Last of all the youngest daughter brought the forage, and when the horse saw her he never budged an inch, but let her feed him and then return to her sisters. The two elder sisters were content that the youngest should take care of the horse, so they troubled themselves about it no more.

The Padishah came home, and the first thing he asked was whether they had provided the horse with everything. "He wouldn't let us come near him," said the two elder sisters; "it was our youngest sister here who took care of him."

No sooner had the Padishah heard this than he gave his youngest daughter to the horse to wife, but his two other daughters he gave to the sons of his Chief Mufti and his Grand Vizier, and they celebrated the three marriages at a great banquet, which lasted forty days. Then the youngest daughter turned into the stable, but the two eldest dwelt in a splendid palace. In the daytime the youngest sister had only a horse for a husband and a stable for a dwelling; but in the night-time the stable became a garden of roses, the horse-husband a handsome hero, and they lived in a world of their own. Nobody knew of it but they two. They passed the day together as best they could, but eventide was the time of their impatient desires.

One day the Padishah held a tournament in the palace. Many gallant warriors entered the lists, but none strove so valiantly as the husbands of the Sultan's elder daughters.

"Only look now!" said the two elder daughters to their sister who dwelt in the stable, "only look now! how our husbands overthrow all the other warriors with their lances; our two lords are not so much lords as lions! Where is this horse-husband of thine, prythee?"

On hearing this from his wife, the horse-husband shivered all over, turned into a man, threw himself on horseback, told his wife not to betray him on any account, and in an instant appeared within the lists. He overthrew every one with his lance, unhorsed his two brothers-in-law, and re-appeared in the stable again as if he had never left it.

The next day, when the sports began again, the two elder sisters mocked as before, but then the unknown hero appeared again, conquered and vanished. On the third day the horse-husband said to his wife: "If ever I should come to grief or thou shouldst need my help, take these three wisps of hair, burn them, and it will help thee wherever thou art."

With that he hastened to the games again and triumphed over his brothers-in-law. Every one was amazed at his skill, the two elder sisters likewise, and again they said to their younger sister: "Look how these heroes excel in prowess! They are very different to thy dirty horse-husband!"

The girl could not endure standing there with nothing to say for herself, so she told her sisters that the handsome hero was no other than her horse-husband – and no sooner had she pointed at him than he vanished from before them as if he had never been. Then only did she call to mind her lord's command to her not to betray her secret, and away she hurried off to the stable. But 'twas all in vain, neither horse nor man came to her, and at midnight there was neither rose nor rose-garden.

"Alas!" wept the girl, "I have betrayed my lord, I have broken my word, what a crime is mine!" She never closed an eye all that night, but wept till morning. When the red dawn appeared she went to her father the Padishah, complained to him that she had lost her horse-husband, and begged that she might go to the ends of the earth to seek him. In vain her father tried to keep her back, in vain he pointed out to her that her husband was now most probably among devils, and she would never be able to find him – turn her from her resolution he could not. What could he do but let her go on her way?

With a great desire the damsel set out on her quest, she went on and on till her tender body was all aweary, and at last she sank down exhausted at the foot of a great mountain. Then she called to mind the three hairs, and she took out one and set fire to it – and lo! her lord and master was in her arms again, and they could not speak for joy.

"Did I not bid thee tell none of my secret?" cried the youth sorrowfully; "and now if my hag of a mother see thee she will instantly tear thee to pieces. This mountain is our dwelling-place. She will be here immediately, and woe to thee if she see thee!"

The poor Sultan's daughter was terribly frightened, and wept worse than ever at the thought of losing her lord again, after all her trouble in finding him. The heart of the devil's son was touched at her sorrow: he struck her once, changed her into an apple, and put her on the shelf. The hag flew down from the mountain with a terrible racket, and screeched out that she smelt the smell of a man, and her mouth watered for the taste of human flesh. In vain her son denied that there was any human flesh there, she would not believe him one bit.

"If thou wilt swear by the egg not to be offended, I'll show thee what I've hidden," said her son. The hag swore, and her son gave the apple a tap, and there before them stood the beautiful damsel. "Behold my wife!" said he to his mother. The old mother said never a word, what was done could not be undone. "I'll give the bride something to do all the same," thought she.

They lived a couple of days together in peace and quiet, but the hag was only waiting for her son to leave the house. At last one day the youth had work to do elsewhere, and scarcely had he put his foot out of doors when the hag said to the damsel: "Come, sweep and sweep not!" and with that she went out and said she should not be back till evening. The girl thought to herself again and again: "What am I to do now? What did she mean by 'sweep and sweep not?'" Then she thought of the hairs, and she took out and burned the second hair also. Immediately her lord stood before her and asked her what was the matter, and the girl told him of his mother's command: "Sweep and sweep not!" Then her lord explained to her that she was to sweep out the chamber, but not to sweep the ante-chamber.

The girl did as she was told, and when the hag came home in the evening she asked the girl whether she had accomplished her task. "Yes, little mother," replied the bride, "I have swept and I have not swept." – "Thou daughter of a dog," cried the old witch, "not thine own wit but my son's mouth hath told thee this thing."

The next morning when the hag got up she gave the damsel vases, and told her to fill them with tears. The moment the hag had gone the damsel placed the three vases before her, and wept and wept, but what could her few teardrops do to fill them? Then she took out and burned the third hair.

Again her lord appeared before her, and explained to her that she must fill the three vases with water, and then put a pinch of salt in each vase. The girl did so, and when the hag came home in the evening and demanded an account of her work, the girl showed her the three vases full of tears. "Thou daughter of a dog!" chided the old woman again, "that is not thy work; but I'll do for thee yet, and for my son too."

The next day she devised some other task for her to do; but her son guessed that his mother would vex the wench, so he hastened home to his bride. There the poor thing was worrying herself about it all alone, for the third hair was now burnt, and she did not know how to set about doing the task laid upon her. "Well, there is now nothing for it but to run away," said her lord, "for she won't rest now till she hath done thee a mischief." And with that he took his wife, and out into the wide world they went.

In the evening the hag came home, and saw neither her son nor his bride. "They have flown, the dogs!" cried the hag, with a threatening voice, and she called to her sister, who was also a witch, to make ready and go in pursuit of her son and his bride. So the witch jumped into a pitcher, snatched up a serpent for a whip, and went after them.

The demon-lover saw his aunt coming, and in an instant changed the girl into a bathing-house, and himself into a bath-man sitting down at the gate. The witch leaped from the pitcher, went to the bath-keeper, and asked him if he had not seen a young boy and girl pass by that way.

"I have only just warmed up my bath," said the youth, "there's nobody inside it; if thou dost not believe me, thou canst go and look for thyself." The witch thought: "'Tis impossible to get a sensible word out of a fellow of this sort," so she jumped into her pitcher, flew back, and told her sister that she couldn't find them. The other hag asked her whether she had exchanged words with anyone on the road. "Yes," replied the younger sister, "there was a bath-house by the roadside, and I asked the owner of it about them; but he was either a fool or deaf, so I took no notice of him."

"'Tis thou who wert the fool," snarled her elder sister. "Didst thou not recognize in him my son, and in the bath-house my daughter-in-law?" Then she called her second sister, and sent her after the fugitives.

The devil's son saw his second aunt flying along in her pitcher. Then he gave his wife a tap and turned her into a spring, but he himself sat down beside it, and began to draw water out of it with a pitcher. The witch went up to him, and asked him whether he had seen a girl and a boy pass by that way.

"There's drinkable water in this spring," replied he, with a vacant stare, "I am always drawing it." The witch thought she had to do with a fool, turned back, and told her sister that she had not met with them. Her sister asked her if she had not come across anyone by the way. "Yes, indeed," replied she, "a half-witted fellow was drawing water from a spring, but I couldn't get a single sensible word out of him."

"That half-witted fellow was my son, the spring was his wife, and a pretty wiseacre thou art," screeched her sister. "I shall have to go myself, I see," and with that she jumped into her pitcher, snatched up a serpent to serve her as a whip, and off she went.

Meanwhile the youth looked back again, and saw his mother coming after them. He gave the girl a tap and changed her into a tree, but he himself turned into a serpent, and coiled himself round the tree. The witch recognized them, and drew near to the tree to break it to pieces; but when she saw the serpent coiled round it, she was afraid to kill her own son along with it, so she said to her son: "Son, son! show me, at least, the girl's little finger, and then I'll leave you both in peace." The son saw that he could not free himself from her any other way, and that she must have at least a little morsel of the damsel to nibble at. So he showed her one of the girl's little fingers, and the old hag wrenched it off, and returned to her domains with it. Then the youth gave the girl a tap and himself another tap, put on human shape again, and away they went to the girl's father, the Padishah. The youth, since his talisman had been destroyed, remained a mortal man, but the diabolical part of him stayed at home with his witch-mother and her kindred. The Padishah rejoiced greatly in his children, gave them a wedding-banquet with a wave of his finger, and they inherited the realm after his death.

The City of the Elephants

A BUNGANDU MAN NAMED DUDU, and his wife Salimba, were one day seeking in the forest a long way from the town for a proper redwood-tree, out of which they could make a wooden mortar wherein they could pound their manioc. They saw several trees of this kind as they proceeded, but after examining one, and then another, they would appear to be dissatisfied, and say, "Perhaps if we went a little further we might find a still better tree for our purpose."

And so Dudu and Salimba proceeded further and further into the tall and thick woods, and ever before them there appeared to be still finer trees which would after all be unsuited for their purpose, being too soft, or too hard, or hollow, or too old, or of another kind than the useful redwood. They strayed in this manner very far. In the forest where there is no path or track, it is not easy to tell which direction one came from, and as they had walked round many trees, they were too confused to know which way they ought to turn homeward. When Dudu said he was sure that his course was the right one for home, Salimba was as sure that the opposite was the true way. They agreed to walk in the direction Dudu wished, and after a long time spent on it, they gave it up and tried another, but neither took them any nearer home.

The night overtook them and they slept at the foot of a tree. The next day they wandered still farther from their town, and they became anxious and hungry. As one cannot see many yards off on any side in the forest, an animal hears the coming step long before the hunter gets a chance to use his weapon. Therefore, though they heard the rustle of the flying antelope, or wild pig as it rushed away, it only served to make their anxiety greater. And the second day passed, and when night came upon them they were still hungrier.

Towards the middle of the third day, they came into an open place by a pool frequented by Kiboko (hippo), and there was a margin of grass round about it, and as they came in view of it, both, at the same time, sighted a grazing buffalo.

Dudu bade his wife stand behind a tree while he chose two of his best and sharpest arrows, and after a careful look at his bow-string, he crept up to the buffalo, and drove an arrow home as far as the guiding leaf, which nearly buried it in the body. While the beast looked around and started from the twinge within, Dudu shot his second arrow into his windpipe, and it fell to the ground quite choked. Now here was water to drink and food to eat, and after cutting a load of meat they chose a thick bush-clump a little distance from the pool, made a fire, and, after satisfying their hunger, slept in content. The fourth day they stopped and roasted a meat provision that would last many days, because they knew that luck is not constant in the woods.

On the fifth they travelled, and for three days more they wandered. They then met a young lion who, at the sight of them, boldly advanced, but Dudu sighted his bow, and sent an arrow into his chest which sickened him of the fight, and he turned and fled.

A few days afterwards, Dudu saw an elephant standing close to them behind a high bush, and whispered to his wife:

"Ah, now, we have a chance to get meat enough for a month."

"But," said Salimba, "why should you wish to kill him, when we have enough meat still with us? Do not hurt him. Ah, what a fine back he has, and how strong he is. Perhaps he would carry us home."

"How could an elephant understand our wishes?" asked Dudu.

"Talk to him anyhow, perhaps he will be clever enough to understand what we want."

Dudu laughed at his wife's simplicity, but to please her he said, "Elephant, we have lost our way; will you carry us and take us home, and we shall be your friends for ever."

The Elephant ceased waving his trunk, and nodding to himself, and turning to them said –

"If you come near to me and take hold of my ears, you may get on my back, and I will carry you safely."

When the Elephant spoke, Dudu fell back from surprise, and looked at him as though he had not heard aright, but Salimba advanced with all confidence, and laid hold of one of his ears, and pulled herself up on to his back. When she was seated, she cried out, "Come, Dudu, what are you looking at? Did you not hear him say he would carry you?"

Seeing his wife smiling and comfortable on the Elephant's back, Dudu became a little braver and moved forward slowly, when the Elephant spoke again, "Come, Dudu, be not afraid. Follow your wife, and do as she did, and then I will travel home with you quickly."

Dudu then put aside his fears, and his surprise, and seizing the Elephant's ear, he ascended and seated himself by his wife on the Elephant's back.

Without another word the Elephant moved on rapidly, and the motion seemed to Dudu and Salimba most delightful. Whenever any overhanging branch was in the way, the Elephant wrenched it off, or bent it and passed on. No creek, stream, gulley, or river, stopped him, he seemed to know exactly the way he should go, as if the road he was travelling was well known to him.

When it was getting dark he stopped and asked his friends if they would not like to rest for the night, and finding that they so wished it, he stopped at a nice place by the side of the river, and they slid to the ground, Dudu first, and Salimba last. He then broke dead branches for them, out of which they made a fire, and the Elephant stayed by them, as though he was their slave.

Hearing their talk, he understood that they would like to have something better than dried meat to eat, and he said to them, "I am glad to know your wishes, for I think I can help you. Bide here a little, and I will go and search."

About the middle of the night he returned to them with something white in his trunk, and a young antelope in front of him. The white thing was a great manioc root, which he dropped into Salimba's lap.

"There, Salimba," he said, "there is food for you, eat your fill and sleep in peace, for I will watch over you."

Dudu and Salimba had seen many strange things that day, but they were both still more astonished at the kindly and intelligent care which their friend the Elephant took of them. While they roasted their fresh meat over the flame, and the manioc root was baking under the heap of hot embers, the Elephant dug with his tusks for the juicy roots of his favourite trees round about their camp, and munched away contentedly.

The next morning, all three, after a bathe in the river, set out on their journey more familiar with one another, and in a happier mood.

About noon, while they were resting during the heat of the day, two lions came near to roar at them, but when Dudu was drawing his bow at one of them, the Elephant said:

"You leave them to me; I will make them run pretty quick," saying which he tore off a great bough of a tree, and nourishing this with his trunk, he trotted on the double quick towards them, and used it so heartily that they both skurried away with their bellies to the ground, and their hides shrinking and quivering out of fear of the great rod.

In the afternoon the Elephant and his human friends set off again, and some time after they came to a wide and deep river. He begged his friends to descend while he tried to find out the shallowest part. It took him some time to do this; but, having discovered a ford where the water was not quite over his back, he returned to them, and urged them to mount him as he wished to reach home before dark.

As the Elephant was about to enter the river, he said to Dudu, "I see some hunters of your own kind creeping up towards us. Perhaps they are your kinsmen. Talk to them, and let us see whether they be friends or foes."

Dudu hailed them, but they gave no answer, and, as they approached nearer, they were seen to prepare to cast their spears, so the Elephant said, "I see that they are not your friends; therefore, as I cross the river, do you look out for them, and keep them at a distance. If they come to the other side of the river, I shall know how to deal with them."

They got to the opposite bank safely; but, as they were landing, Dudu and Salimba noticed that their pursuers had discovered a canoe, and that they were pulling hard after them. But the Elephant soon after landing came to a broad path smoothed by much travel, over which he took them at a quick pace, so fast, indeed, that the pursuers had to run to be able to keep up with them. Dudu, every now and then let fly an arrow at the hunters, which kept them at a safe distance.

Towards night they came to the City of the Elephants, which was very large and fit to shelter such a multitude as they now saw. Their elephant did not linger, however, but took his friends at the same quick pace until they came to a mighty elephant that was much larger than any other, and his ivories were gleaming white and curled up, and exceedingly long. Before him Dudu and Salimba were told by their friend to descend and salaam, and he told his lord how he had found them lost in the woods, and how for the sake of the kindly words of the woman he had befriended them, and assisted them to the city of his tribe. When the King Elephant heard all this he was much pleased, and said to Dudu and Salimba that they were welcome to his city, and how they should not want for anything, as long as they would be pleased to stay with them, but as for the hunters who had dared to chase them, he would give orders at once. Accordingly he gave a signal, and ten active young elephants dashed out of the city, and in a short time not one of the hunters was left alive, though one of them had leaped into the river, thinking that he could escape in that manner. But then you know that an elephant is as much at home in a river, as a Kiboko (a hippopotamus), so that the last man was soon caught and was drowned.

Dudu and Salimba, however, on account of Salimba's kind heart in preventing her husband wounding the elephant, were made free of the place, and their friend took them with him to many families, and the big pa's and ma's told their little babies all about them and their habits, and said that, though most of the human kind were very stupid and wicked, Dudu and Salimba were very good, and putting their trunks into their ears they whispered that Salimba was the better of the two. Then the little elephants gathered about them and trotted by their side and around them and diverted them with their antics, their races, their wrestlings, and other trials of strength, but when they became familiar and somewhat rude in their rough play, their elephant friend would admonish them, and if that did not suffice, he would switch them soundly.

The City of the Elephants was a spacious and well-trodden glade in the midst of a thick forest, and as it was entered one saw how wisely the elephant families had arranged their manner of life. For without, the trees stood as thick as water-reeds, and the bush or underwood was like an old hedge of milkweed knitted together by thorny vines and snaky climbers into which the human hunter might not even poke his nose without hurt. Well, the burly elephants had, by much uprooting, created deep hollows, or recesses, wherein a family of two and more might snugly rest, and not even a dart of sunshine might reach them. Round about the great glade the dark leafy arches ran, and Dudu and his wife saw that the elephant families were numerous – for by one sweeping look they could tell that there were more elephants than there are human beings in a goodly village. In some of the recesses there was a row of six and more elephants; in another the parents stood head to head, and their children, big and little, clung close to their parents' sides; in another a family stood with heads turned towards the entrance, and so on all around – while under a big tree in the middle there was quite a gathering of big fellows, as though they were holding a serious palaver; under another tree one seemed to be on the outlook; another paced slowly from side to side; another plucked at this branch or at that; another appeared to be heaving a tree, or sharpening a blunted ivory; others seemed appointed to uproot the sprouts, lest the glade might become choked with underwood. Near the entrance on both sides were a brave company of them, faces turned outward, swinging their trunks, napping their ears, rubbing against each other, or who with pate against pate seemed to be drowsily considering something. There was a continual coming in and a going out, singly, or in small companies. The roads that ran through the glade were like a network, clean and smooth, while that which went towards the king's place was so wide that twenty men might walk abreast. At the far end the king stood under his own tree, with his family under the arches behind him.

This was the City of the Elephants as Dudu and Salimba saw it. I ought to say that the outlets of it were many. One went straight through the woods in a line up river, at the other end it ran in a line following the river downward; one went to a lakelet, where juicy plants and reeds throve like corn in a man's fields, and where the elephants rejoiced in its cool water, and washed themselves and infants; another went to an ancient clearing where the plantain and manioc grew wild, and wherein more than two human tribes might find food for countless seasons.

Then said their friend to Dudu and Salimba – "Now that I have shown you our manner of life, it is for you to ease your longing for awhile and rest with us. When you yearn for home, go tell our king, and he will send you with credit to your kindred."

Then Dudu and his wife resolved to stay, and eat, and they stayed a whole season, not only unhurt, but tenderly cared for, with never a hungry hour or uneasy night. But at last Salimba's heart remembered her children, and kinfolk, and her own warm house and village pleasures, and on hinting of these memories to her husband, he said that after all there was no place like Bungandu. He remembered his long pipe, and the talk-house, the stool-making, shaft-polishing, bow-fitting, and the little tinkering jobs, the wine-trough, and the merry drinking bouts, and he wept softly as he thought of them.

They thus agreed that it was time for them to travel homeward, and together they sought the elephant king, and frankly told him of their state.

"My friends," he replied, "be no longer sad, but haste to depart. With the morning's dawn guides shall take you to Bungandu with such gifts as shall make you welcome to your folk. And when you come to them, say to them that the elephant king desires lasting peace and friendship with them. On our side we shall not injure their plantations, neither a plantain, nor a manioc root belonging to them; and on your side dig no pits for our unwary youngsters, nor hang the barbed iron aloft, nor plant the poisoned stake in the path, so we shall escape hurt and be unprovoked." And Dudu put his hand on the king's trunk as the pledge of good faith.

In the morning, four elephants, as bearers of the gifts from the king – bales of bark-cloth, and showy mats, and soft hides and other things – and two fighting elephants besides their old friend, stood by the entrance to the city, and when the king elephant came up he lifted Salimba first on the back of her old companion, and then placed Dudu by her side, and at a parting wave the company moved on.

In ten days they reached the edge of the plantation of Bungandu, and the leader halted. The bales were set down on the ground, and then their friend asked of Dudu and his wife –

"Know you where you are?"

"We do," they answered.

"Is this Bungandu?" he asked.

"This is Bungandu," they replied.

"Then here we part, that we may not alarm your friends. Go now your way, and we go our way. Go tell your folk how the elephants treat their friends, and let there be peace for ever between us."

The elephants turned away, and Dudu and Salimba, after hiding their wealth in the underwood, went arm in arm into the village of Bungandu. When their friends saw them, they greeted them as we would greet our friends whom we have long believed to be dead, but who come back smiling and rejoicing to us. When the people heard their story they greatly wondered and doubted, but when Dudu and Salimba took them to the place of parting and showed them the hoof prints of seven elephants on the road, and the bales that they had hidden in the underwood, they believed their story. And they made it a rule from that day that no man of the tribe ever should lift a spear, or draw a bow, or dig a pit, or plant the poisoned stake in the path, or hang the barbed iron aloft, to do hurt to an elephant. And as a proof that I have but told the truth go ask the Bungandu, and they will say why none of their race will ever seek to hurt the elephant, and it will be the same as I have told you. That is my story.

Morongoe the Snake

MOKETE WAS A CHIEF'S DAUGHTER, but she was also beautiful beyond all the daughters of her father's house, and Morongoe the brave and Tau the lion both desired to possess her, but Tau found not favour in the eyes of her parents, neither desired she to be his wife, whereas Morongoe was rich and the son of a great chief, and upon him was Mokete bestowed in marriage.

But Tau swore by all the evil spirits that their happiness should not long continue, and he called to his aid the old witch doctor, whose power was greater than the tongue of man could tell; and one day Morongoe walked down to the water and was seen no more. Mokete wept and mourned for her brave young husband, to whom she had been wedded but ten short moons, but Tau rejoiced greatly.

When two more moons had waned, a son was born to Mokete, to whom she gave the name of Tsietse (sadness). The child grew and throve, and the years passed by, but brought no news of Morongoe.

One day, when Tsietse was nearly seven years old, he cried unto his mother, saying, "Mother, how is it that I have never seen my father? My companions see and know their fathers, and love them, but I alone know not the face of my father, I alone have not a father's protecting love."

"My son," replied his mother, "a father you have never known, for the evil spirits carried him from amongst us before ever you were born." She then related to him all that had happened.

From that day Tsietse played no more with the other boys, but wandered about from one pool of water to another, asking the frogs to tell him of his father.

Now the custom of the Basuto, when anyone falls into the water and is not found, is to drive cattle into the place where the person is supposed to have fallen, as they will bring him out. Many cattle had been driven into the different pools of water near Morongoe's village, but as they had failed to bring his father, Tsietse knew it was not much use looking near home. Accordingly, one day he went to a large pond a long distance off, and there he asked the frogs to help him in his search. One old frog hopped close to the child, and said, "You will find your father, my son, when you have walked to the edge of the world and taken a leap into the waters beneath; but he is no longer as you are, nor does he know of your existence."

This, at last, was the information Tsietse had longed for, now he could begin his search in real earnest. For many days he walked on, and ever on. At length, one day, just as the sun was setting, he saw before him a large sea of water of many beautiful colours. Stepping into it, he began to ask the same question; but at every word he uttered, the sea rose up, until at length it covered his head, and he began falling, falling through the deep sea. Suddenly he found himself upon dry ground, and upon looking round he saw flocks and herds, flowers and fruit, on every side. At first he was too much astonished to speak, but after a little while he went up to one of the herd boys and asked him if he had ever seen his (Tsietse's) father. The herd boy told him many strangers visited that place, and he had better see the chief, who would be able to answer his question.

When Tsietse had told his story to the chief, the old man knew at once that the great snake which dwelt in their midst must be the child's father; so, bidding the boy remain and rest, he went off to consult with the snake as to how they should tell Tsietse the truth without frightening him; but as they talked, Tsietse ran up to them, and, seeing the snake, at once embraced it, for he knew it was his father.

Then there was great joy in the heart of Morongoe, for he knew that by his son's aid he should be able to overcome his enemy, and return at length to his wife and home. So he told Tsietse how Tau had persuaded the old witch doctor to turn him into a snake, and banish him to this world below the earth. Soon afterwards Tsietse returned to his home, but he was no longer a child, but a noble youth, with a brave, straight look that made the wicked afraid. Very gently he told his mother all that had happened to him, and how eager his father was to return to his home. Mokete consulted an old doctor who lived in the mountain alone, and who told her she must get Tsietse to bring his father to the village in the brightness of the day-time, but that he must be so surrounded by his followers from the land beyond that none of his own people would be able to see him.

Quickly the news spread through the village that Morongoe had been found by his son and was returning to his people.

At length Tsietse was seen approaching with a great crowd of followers, while behind them came all the cattle which had been driven into the pools to seek Morongoe. As they approached Mokete's house the door opened and the old doctor stood upon the threshold.

Making a sign to command silence, he said: – "My children, many years ago your chief received a grievous wrong at the hand of his enemy, and was turned into a snake, but by the love and faithfulness of his son he is restored to you this day, and the wiles of his enemy are made of no account. Cover, then, your eyes, my children, lest the Evil Eye afflict you."

He then bade the snake, which was in the centre of the crowd, enter the hut, upon which he shut the door, and set fire to the hut. The people, when they saw the flames, cried out in horror, but the old doctor bade them be still, for that no harm would come to their chief, but rather a great good. When everything was completely burnt, the doctor took from the middle of the ruins a large burnt ball; this he threw into the pool nearby, and lo! from the water up rose Morongoe, clad in a kaross, the beauty of which was beyond all words, and carrying in his hand a stick of shining black, like none seen on this earth before, in beauty, or colour, or shape. Thus was the spell broken through the devotion of a true son, and peace and happiness restored, not only to Mokete's heart, but to the whole village.

The Tale of Murile

A MAN AND HIS WIFE living in the Chaga country had three sons, of whom Murile was the eldest. One day he went out with his mother to dig up *maduma*, and, noticing a particularly fine tuber among those which were to be put by for seed, he said, "Why, this one is as beautiful as my little brother!" His mother laughed at the notion of comparing a *taro* tuber with a baby; but he hid the root, and, later, when no one was looking, put it away in a hollow tree and sang a magic song over it. Next day he went to look, and found that the root had turned into a child. After that at every meal he secretly kept back some food, and, when he could do so without being seen, carried it to the tree and fed the baby, which grew and flourished from day to day. But Murile's mother became very anxious when she saw how thin the boy was growing, and she questioned him, but could get no satisfaction. Then one day his younger brothers noticed that when his portion of food was handed to him, instead of eating it at once, he put it aside. They told their mother, and she bade them follow him when he went away after dinner, and see what he did with it. They did so, and saw him feeding the baby in the hollow tree, and came back and told her. She went at once to the spot and strangled the child which was 'starving her son.'

When Murtle came back next day and found the child dead he was overcome with grief. He went home and sat down in the hut, crying bitterly. His mother asked him why he was crying, and he said it was because the smoke hurt his eyes. So she told him to go and sit on the other side of the fireplace. But, as he still wept and complained of the smoke when questioned, they said he had better take his father's stool and sit outside. He picked up the stool, went out into the courtyard, and sat down. Then he said, "Stool, go up on high, as my father's rope does when he hangs up his beehive in the forest!" And the stool rose up with him into the air and stuck fast in the branches of a tree. He repeated the words a second time, and again the stool moved upward. Just then his brothers happened to come out of the hut, and when they saw him they ran back and said to their mother, "Murile is going up into the sky!" She would not believe them. "Why do you tell me your eldest brother has gone up into the sky? Is there any road for him to go up by?" They told her to come and look, and when she saw him in the air she sang:

"Mrile, wuya na kunu!
Wuya na kunu, mwanako!
Wuya na kunu!"

["Murile, come back hither!
Come back hither, my child!
Come back hither!"]

But Murile answered, " I shall never come back, Mother! I shall never come back!"

Then his brothers called him, and received the same answer; his father called him – then his boy-friends, and, last of all, his uncle (*washidu*, his mother's brother, the nearest relation of all). They could just hear his answer, "I am not coming back, Uncle! I am never coming back!" Then he passed up out of sight.

The stool carried him up till he felt solid ground beneath his feet, and then he looked round and found himself in the Heaven country. He walked on till he came to some people gathering wood. He asked them the way to the Moon-chiefs kraal, and they said, "Just pick up some sticks for us, and then we will tell you." He collected a bundle of sticks, and they directed him to go on till he should come to some people cutting grass. He did so, and greeted the grass-cutters when he came to them. They answered his greeting, and when he asked them the way said they would show him if he would help them for a while with their work.

So he cut some grass, and they pointed out the road, telling him to go on till he came to some women hoeing. These, again, asked him to help them before they would show him the way, and, in succession, he met with some herd-boys, some women gathering beans, some people reaping millet, others gathering banana-leaves, and girls fetching water – all of them sending him forward with almost the same words. The water-carriers said, "Just go on in this direction till you come to a house where the people are eating." He found the house, and said, "Greeting, house-owners! Please show me the way to the Moon's kraal." They promised to do so if he would sit down and eat with them, which he did. At last by following their instructions he reached his destination, and found the people there eating their food raw. He asked them why they did not use fire to cook with, and found that they did not know what fire was. So he said, "If I prepare nice food for you by means of fire what will you give me?" The Moon-chief said, "We will give you cattle and goats and sheep." Murile told them to bring plenty of wood, and when they came with it he and the chief went behind the house, where the other people could not see them. Murile took his knife and cut two pieces of wood, one flat and the other pointed, and twirled the pointed stick till he got some sparks, with which he lit a bunch of dry grass and so kindled a fire. When it burned up he got the chief to send for some green plantains, which he roasted and offered to him. Then he cooked some meat and various other foods. The Moon-chief was delighted when he tasted them, and at once called all the people together, and said to them, "Here is a wonderful doctor come from a far country! We shall have to repay him for his fire." The people asked, "What must be paid to him?" He answered, "Let one man bring a cow, another a goat, another whatever he may have in his storehouse." So they went to fetch all these things. And Murile became a rich man, For he stayed some years at the Moon's great kraal and married wives and had children born to him, and his flocks and herds increased greatly. But in the end a longing for his home came over him. And he thought within himself: "How shall I go home again, unless I send a messenger before me? For I told them I was never coming back, and they must think that I am dead."

He called all the birds together and asked them one by one, "If I send you to my home what will you say?" The raven answered, "I shall say, *Kuruu! kuruu!*" and was rejected. So, in turn, were the hornbill, the hawk, the buzzard, and all the rest, till he came to Njorovi, the mocking-bird, who sang:

"Mrile etsha kilalawu
Tira ngama.
Mrile etsha kilalawu
Mdeye mafuda na kiliko!"

[Murile is coming the day after tomorrow,
Missing our tomorrow.
Murile is coming the day after tomorrow.
Keep some fat in the ladle for him!"]

Murile was pleased with this, and told her to go. So she flew down to earth and perched on the gate-post of his father's courtyard and sang her song. His father came out and said,

"What thing is crying out there, saying that Murile is coming the day after tomorrow? Why, Murile was lost long ago, and will never come back!" And he drove the bird away. She flew back and told Murile where she had been. But he would not believe her; he told her to go again and bring back his father's stick as a token that she had really gone to his home. So she flew down again, came to the house, and picked up the stick, which was leaning in the doorway. The children in the house saw her, and tried to snatch it from her, but she was too quick for them, and took it back to Murile. Then he said, "Now I will start for home." He took leave of his friends and of his wives, who were to stay with their own people, but his cattle and his boys came with him. It was a long march to the place of descent, and Murile began to grow very tired. There was a very fine bull in the herd, who walked beside Murile all the way. Suddenly he spoke and said, "As you are so weary, what will you do for me if I let you ride me?" If I take you on my back will you eat my flesh when they kill me?" Murile answered, "No! I will never eat you!" So the bull let him get on his back and carried him home. And Murile sang, as he rode along:

"Not a hoof nor a horn is wanting!
Mine are the cattle – hey!
Nought of the goods is wanting;
Mine are the bairns today.
Not a kid of the goats is wanting;
My flocks are on the way.
Nothing of mine is wanting;
Murile comes today
With his bairns and his cattle – hey!"

So he came home. And his father and mother ran out to meet him and anointed him with mutton-fat, as is the custom when a loved one comes home from distant parts. And his brothers and every one rejoiced and wondered greatly when they saw the cattle. But he showed his father the great bull that had carried him, and said, "This bull must be fed and cared for till he is old. And even if you kill him when he is old I will never eat of his flesh." So they lived quite happily for a time.

But when the bull had become very old Murile's father slaughtered him. The mother foolishly thought it such a pity that her son, who had always taken so much trouble over the beast, should have none of the beef when every one else was eating it. So she took a piece of fat and hid it in a pot. When she knew that all the meat was finished she ground some grain and cooked the fat with the meal and gave it to her son. As soon as he had tasted it the fat spoke and said to him, "Do you dare to eat me, who carried you on my back? You shall be eaten, as you are eating me!"

Then Murile sang: "O my mother, I said to you, 'Do not give me to eat of the bull's flesh!'" He took a second taste, and his foot sank into the ground. He sang the same words again, and then ate up the food his mother had given him. As soon as he had swallowed it he sank down and disappeared.

Other people who tell the story simply say, "He died." Be that as it may, that was the end of him.

Haamdaanee and the Wise Gazelle

THERE WAS ONCE UPON A TIME a man named Haamdaanee, who was very poor. He had no clothes but rags, and nothing to eat but the food that was given him in charity.

One day when he was searching about in the dust heap for stray grains of millet, he found a small piece of money. It seemed a fortune to the poor man, and he carefully tied it up in one corner of his rags that he might not lose it.

For a long time he could not decide what to buy with it, but one day when he was again scratching in the dust heap, a man came by with a cage full of gazelles which he wished to sell.

"Merchant," called Haamdaanee, "how much do you ask for your gazelles?"

"They are different prices," answered the merchant. "Some are very large and fine, and for those I ask a good price, but one is a weakling, and it I would sell for almost nothing."

Some men were passing by and they began to laugh. "Have you come into a fortune, Haamdaanee," they cried out, "and are you trying to spend it?" Then they said to the merchant, "Do not waste your time on that man. He is so poor that he has to scratch about in the dust heaps to find enough to keep him alive."

Haamdaanee untied the corner of his rags and held out the piece of money. "Here, merchant," he said, "take this and give me one of your gazelles."

The men were very much surprised to see the money. Then they said, "You are very foolish, Haamdaanee. You get a piece of money nobody knows how nor where, and then instead of buying for yourself a good meal you spend it for a gazelle which will also need food."

Haamdaanee, however, paid no attention to their jeers. He took the gazelle, and the merchant took his money, glad to have sold an animal that was so weak and small it seemed as though it would die at any rate.

Haamdaanee carried the little animal home with him to the hovel where he lived, and made a bed for it in one corner, but there was little he could give it to eat. If there had not been enough for one there was still less for two. However, he was not sorry he had bought it. It was company for him and he loved it as though it were his daughter.

One day when Haamdaanee was preparing to go out to the dust heap, the gazelle said to him, "Master, why do you not open the door and let me run out in the forest to find food for myself? If you will do this I will return to you in the evening, and you will only have had one to feed instead of two."

Haamdaanee was wonder-struck at hearing the gazelle speaking. "How is this?" he cried. "You can talk, and yet you are only a little animal I bought with a piece of money from the dust heap."

"That is true," said the gazelle, "but I am not an ordinary animal. I am very wise. Let me out every day so that I may run about, and I may find some way of helping your fortunes. I will always come back to you, for you bought me and you are my master."

The little gazelle spoke so sweetly that Haamdaanee opened the door as it wished, and immediately it ran away and into the deep forest, and was lost to sight. Then Haamdaanee was very sad. He thought, "That was a foolish thing to do. I will never see my gazelle again, and it was such a pretty, gentle little thing."

However, when he returned to his hovel that evening he found the little animal already there. "Master," it said, "I feasted well in the forest today, but I saw and heard nothing that would help your fortunes. But courage! Tomorrow I will go out again, and who knows what may happen?"

So the next morning Haamdaanee again opened the door for the gazelle, and after this he let it out every day, and it remained away until evening, when it came running home again.

But one day when the gazelle went into the forest the food it liked was very scarce, and it wandered on further than it had ever gone before. After a while it began to dig up roots with its sharp little hoofs. Presently it struck something hard, and when it turned it out from the earth it proved to be an enormous diamond.

The gazelle was delighted. It rolled the diamond up in leaves and took it in its mouth to carry it home to Haamdaanee. But then it began to think: "What could my master do with a diamond like this? No one would ever believe I had found it in the forest; if he showed it to people they would certainly think he had stolen it, and he would be beaten or taken before the judges. No, I must do something better than that with the stone."

The wise little animal thought for a while, and then with the diamond still in its mouth, it bounded away through the forest.

It ran on and on for three days and nights without stopping, until it came to a city where a great king lived. This king had a daughter who was so beautiful that the fame of her had spread everywhere; even Haamdaanee and his gazelle had heard of her.

The little animal went straight into the city and through the streets to the palace, and up the steps and into the room where the king was sitting with all his councillors about him. There it bent its fore knees and touched its forehead to the ground three times in token of respect.

"What is this animal, and where does it come from?" asked the king.

No one could tell him anything about it, but the gazelle itself answered.

"Oh, great king, I am a messenger from my master the Prince Daaraaee," it said, "and I have come from far away, a three days and three nights' journey through the forest."

"And what is the message your master sends?" asked the king.

"He wishes you to give him your beautiful daughter for a wife, and he sends you a small gift. It is but a poor thing, and scarce worth the sending, but it was as much as I could carry."

The gazelle then unwrapped the leaves from the diamond and presented it to the king. All were wonder-struck when they saw the size and brightness of the diamond. It was worth a kingdom.

"Your master must be very rich and powerful," said the king. "Has he many more jewels like this?"

"That is nothing to what he has in his treasure house," answered the gazelle.

"And he wishes the hand of my daughter?"

"Yes, your Majesty."

The king was delighted at the idea of having such a rich man for a son-in-law, and promised that Prince Daaraaee should have the hand of the princess.

The gazelle then made ready to leave, but first the king fed it with rice and milk, and hung a golden collar about its neck.

"In ten days' time I will return with my master. Be ready to receive him and his escort at that time," said the gazelle, and then it bounded away and was lost to sight in the forest.

Now all this time Haamdaanee had been mourning his gazelle as lost. Five days had passed without its returning. The sixth day he was sitting very mournfully on the dust heap when he felt something brush against him. He looked around, and what was his joy to see his little gazelle beside him. He stroked and caressed it, and then he saw the golden collar around its neck.

"What means this golden collar? And where have you been?" asked Haamdaanee.

"I have been far away at the palace of a king," exclaimed the gazelle. "It was he who gave me this collar, and more than that, he promised that you should have his beautiful daughter for a wife."

At first Haamdaanee could not believe what the gazelle told him, but when he had heard the whole story he was filled with terror. "You told the king I was a great prince," he said, "and when he sees me in my rags and filth I will be beaten and driven out into the forest to die."

"Do not be afraid, master," answered the gazelle. "Only do as I tell you and you will be received with great honour, and have a princess as your wife."

At last he persuaded Haamdaanee to come with him, and they set out together through the forest. They went on and on until they were within a day's journey of the king's palace, and then the gazelle stopped. "Master," said he, "do you now strip off your rags and hide them. Bathe in the stream, and as you bathe be careful to knock yourself against the stones so that you will show bruises. Then lie down beside the stream, and when I return from the city with an escort do nothing but groan and cry, 'Oh, those robbers! Those cruel and wicked robbers.'"

Haamdaanee stripped off his rags and stepped into the stream, and while he was still bathing and bruising himself the gazelle bounded away to the palace of the king. It rushed into the room where the king was and fell before him, breathless and apparently exhausted. "Oh, my master! My poor master!" it cried.

The king in great anxiety asked what had happened to the prince.

The gazelle told him that he and his master had come a long way through the forest in safety, and were within a day's journey of the city when they had been set upon by robbers. The robbers had stolen everything; they had stripped the Prince Daaraaee of all his magnificent clothes and jewels, and had beaten him and left him for dead on the banks of a stream. The Prince's escort had been carried away captive. "And I alone escaped," said the gazelle, "for I am so small they did not notice me. But oh, my poor master! If he is not already dead he must soon perish unless help is sent to him."

The king immediately commanded that a strong escort should set out to help the prince. He himself went with them, and a horse was loaded with magnificent robes for Prince Daaraaee to put on. They started out, and the gazelle ran along to show them the way.

When they reached the banks of the stream there lay Haamdaanee groaning, and bruised black and blue as though he had been beaten. They raised him up and clothed him in the magnificent robes they had brought, but all he would say was, "Oh, those robbers! Those cruel, wicked robbers!"

They put him on a great black horse and took him back to the palace of the king, and when so dressed and mounted he appeared a very handsome man indeed. The king was delighted with him, and the princess was no less so, and soon the marriage was celebrated with great feasting and rejoicing.

For a while Haamdaanee lived with his wife at the palace of the king, and he was so happy, and everything was so fine, that he could hardly believe in his good fortune. But after a time the princess began to ask her husband when they were to return to his own country. She longed to see his magnificent palace and all the treasures it contained.

Haamdaanee took the gazelle aside and said to it, "What are we to do now? I am surely ruined. The princess wishes to see the palace I have told her of, and I have no place to take her but the wretched hovel that will not even shelter us from the weather."

"Do not be afraid, master," answered the gazelle. "I will manage everything for you. Only let me go, and do you tell the princess you have sent me home to prepare for your reception. I will get a palace for you, and when I have it I will return and let you know."

Haamdaanee did as the gazelle bade him. The princess was told that the little animal was to set out immediately and would put all in order at the palace, so she was willing to wait a while longer before seeing her husband's treasures.

The gazelle at once started out on its journeyings. It ran on and on for several days, and then it came to another city even handsomer than that of the king, but when it entered the streets everything was silent and deserted. There was not a soul to be seen. The little animal went through one street after another and at last it came to a palace, and that too was silent and deserted. It knocked with its hard hoof, and after a long time the door opened a crack and an old, old woman looked out. As soon as she saw the gazelle she seemed frightened to death.

"How have you come here?" she cried. "Do you not know that this city belongs to a terrible snake with three heads, and that he eats every living thing? He has eaten all the people of the city except myself and he only left me alive that I might cook his meals and sweep his house. If he finds you here he will surely kill you."

"I am too tired to go farther," said the gazelle, "and I am so small that I can easily hide in a corner where the snake will not find me. Do but let me in to rest for a while. The snake need never know it."

For a time the old woman refused but the gazelle talked so sweetly that after a time she consented and allowed the little animal to slip through the crack of the door and into the house.

When it was inside it began to look about it. "This place would just do for my master if I could but get rid of the snake," it thought. Presently it saw a bright sword that hung on the wall. "What sword is that?" it asked of the old woman.

"It belongs to the snake," she answered, "and it is so sharp that it will cut anything at one stroke."

"That is the sword for me," said the gazelle, and it took it down from the wall in spite of all the old woman could say.

And now a great rushing noise was heard outside, and the old woman began to quake and tremble. "That is the snake," she cried, "and when he finds you here he will surely kill us both."

"Do not be afraid," said the gazelle. "I will tell you what to say and do, and who knows but what we may rid ourselves of him for good and all."

Now the snake was at the door and it began to sniff about. "What is this I smell?" it cried. "Some living thing has entered the city."

"Nonsense," answered the old woman. "A bird flying over the house dropped a piece of meat down the chimney, and I am cooking it for your dinner."

Then the snake said, "Open the door that I may come in."

"I cannot do that or the meat will burn," answered the old woman. "Come in through the window."

Then the snake stuck one of its heads in through the window. The gazelle was ready, and the moment the head appeared it cut it off with the sword, and the sword was so very sharp and keen that the snake did not feel the blow. "How dark it is in the house," it said. "I can see nothing," and it stuck its other head in. Quick as a flash the gazelle cut off that head too. "Oh! I think a hair fell on my neck," said the snake, and it stuck its third head in through the window. Then the gazelle cut off that head too, and the snake was dead.

The old woman rejoiced to know she was now free from the snake, and she could not make enough of the little animal that had killed him.

"I must go and get my master," said the gazelle, "for now that I have killed the snake, this city and all that is in it belongs to him; and if anyone asks you must say, This is the palace of Prince Daardaaee."

When Haamdaanee heard from the gazelle all that he had done, and how the palace and the treasures of the snake now belonged to him, he did not know what to do with himself for joy.

He and the princess soon set out together, and with them a number of people from the city, to whom Haamdaanee promised houses and wealth when they should reach his city.

The gazelle ran along beside them pointing out the way, and when they reached the palace it was more magnificent than anything the princess had dreamed of.

So they lived there very happily, and the little gazelle had soft cushions to lie on, and all the milk and rice that it could eat, so it did not have to run off into the forest any more, but could stay in the palace and take its ease.

The Great White Bear and the Trolls

THERE WAS ONCE A MAN IN FINMARK NAMED HALVOR, who had a great white bear, and this great white bear knew many tricks. One day the man thought to himself, "This bear is very wonderful. I will take it as a present to the King of Denmark, and perhaps he will give me in return a whole bag of money." So he set out along the road to Denmark, leading the bear behind him.

He journeyed on and journeyed on, and after a while he came to a deep, dark forest. There was no house in sight, and as it was almost night Halvor began to be afraid he would have to sleep on the ground, with only the trees overhead for a shelter.

Presently, however, he heard the sound of a woodcutter's axe. He followed the sound, and soon he came to an opening in the forest. There, sure enough, was a man hard at work cutting down trees. "And wherever there's a man," thought Halvor to himself, "there must be a house for him to live in."

"Good day," said Halvor.

"Good day!" answered the man, staring with all his eyes at the great white bear.

"Will you give us shelter for the night, my bear and me?" asked Halvor. "And will you give us a bit of food too? I will pay you well if you will."

"Gladly would I give you both food and shelter," answered the man, "but tonight, of all nights in the year, no one may stop in my home except at the risk of his life."

"How is that?" asked Halvor; and he was very much surprised.

"Why, it is this way. This is the eve of St John, and on every St John's Eve all the trolls in the forest come to my house. I am obliged to spread a feast for them, and there they stay all night, eating and drinking. If they found anyone in the house at that time, they would surely tear him to pieces. Even I and my wife dare not stay. We are obliged to spend the night in the forest."

"This is a strange business," said Halvor. "Nevertheless, I have a mind to stop there and see what these same trolls look like. As to their hurting me, as long as I have my bear with me there is nothing in the world that I am afraid of."

The woodcutter was alarmed at these words. "No, no; do not risk it, I beg of you!" he cried. "Do you spend the night with us out under the trees, and tomorrow we can safely return to our home."

But Halvor would not listen to this. He was determined to sleep in a house that night, and, moreover, he had a great curiosity to see what trolls looked like.

"Very well," said the woodcutter at last, "since you are determined to risk your life, do you follow yonder path, and it will soon bring you to my house."

Halvor thanked him and went on his way, and it was not long before he and his bear reached the woodcutter's home. He opened the door and went in, and when he saw the feast the woodcutter had spread for the trolls his mouth fairly watered to taste of it. There were sausages and ale and fish and cakes and rice porridge and all sorts of good things. He tasted a bit here and there and gave his bear some, and then he sat down to wait for the coming of the trolls. As for the bear, he lay down beside his master and went to sleep.

They had not been there long when a great noise arose in the forest outside. It was a sound of moaning and groaning and whistling and shrieking. So loud and terrible it grew that Halvor was frightened in spite of himself. The cold crept up and down his back and the hair rose on his head. The sound came nearer and nearer, and by the time it reached the door Halvor was so frightened that he could bear it no longer. He jumped up and ran to the stove. Quickly he opened the oven door and hid himself inside, pulling the door to behind him. The great white bear paid no attention, however, but only snored in his sleep.

Scarcely was Halvor inside the oven when the door of the house was burst open and all the trolls of the forest came pouring into the room.

There were big trolls and little trolls, fat trolls and thin. Some had long tails and some had short tails and some had no tails at all. Some had two eyes and some had three, and some had only one set in the middle of the forehead. One there was, and the others called him Long Nose, who had a nose as long and as thin as a poker.

The trolls banged the door behind them, and then they gathered round the table where the feast was spread.

"What is this?" cried the biggest troll in a terrible voice (and Halvor's heart trembled within him). "Someone has been here before us. The food has been tasted and ale has been spilled."

At once Long Nose began snuffing about. "Whoever has been here is here still," he cried. "Let us find him and tear him to pieces."

"Here is his pussy-cat, anyway," cried the smallest troll of all, pointing to the white bear. "Oh, what a pretty cat it is! Pussy! Pussy! Pussy!" And the little troll put a piece of sausage on a fork and stuck it against the white bear's nose.

At that the great white bear gave a roar and rose to its feet. It gave the troll a blow with its paw that sent him spinning across the room. He of the long nose had it almost broken off, and the big troll's ears rang with the box he got. This way and that the trolls were knocked and beaten by the bear, until at last they tore the door open and fled away into the forest, howling.

When they had all gone Halvor crawled out and closed the door, and then he and the white bear sat down and feasted to their hearts' content. After that the two of them lay down and slept quietly for the rest of the night.

In the morning the woodcutter and his family stole back to the house and peeped in at the window. What was their surprise to see Halvor and his bear sitting there and eating their breakfasts as though nothing in the world had happened to them.

"How is this?" cried the woodcutter. "Did the trolls not come?"

"Oh, yes, they came," answered Halvor, "but we drove them away, and I do not think they will trouble you again." He then told the woodcutter all that had happened in the night. "After the beating they received, they will be in no hurry to visit you again," he said.

The woodcutter was filled with joy and gratitude when he heard this. He and his wife entreated Halvor to stay there in the forest and make his home with them, but this he refused to do. He was on his way to Denmark to sell his bear to the King, and to Denmark he would go. So off he set, after saying goodbye, and the good wishes of the woodcutter and his wife went with him.

Now the very next year, on St John's Eve, the woodcutter was out in the forest cutting wood, when a great ugly troll stuck his head out of a tree nearby.

"Woodcutter! Woodcutter!" he cried.

"Well," said the woodcutter, "what is it?"

"Tell me, have you that great white cat with you still?"

"Yes, I have; and, moreover, now she has five kittens, and each one of them is larger and stronger than she is."

"Is that so?" cried the troll, in a great fright. "Then goodbye, woodcutter, for we will never come to your house again."

Then he drew in his head and the tree closed together, and that was the last the woodcutter heard or saw of the trolls. After that he and his family lived undisturbed and unafraid.

As for Halvor, he had already reached Denmark, and the King had been so pleased with the bear that he paid a whole bag of money for it, just as Halvor had hoped, and with that bag of money Halvor set up in trade so successfully that he became one of the richest men in Denmark.

East of the Sun and West of the Moon

ONCE UPON A TIME there was a poor tenant farmer who had a number of children whom he could feed but poorly, and had to clothe in the scantiest way. They were all handsome; but the most beautiful, after all, was the youngest daughter, for she was beautiful beyond all telling.

Now it happened that one Thursday evening late in the fall there was a terrible storm raging outside. It was pitch dark, and it rained and stormed so that the house shook in every joint. The whole family sat around the hearth, and each was busy with some work or other. Suddenly there were three loud knocks on the window-pane. The man went out to see who was there, and when he stepped outside, there stood a great white bear.

"Good evening," said the white bear.

"Good evening," returned the man.

"If you'll give me your youngest daughter, I will make you just as rich as now you are poor," said the bear.

The man was not ill-pleased that he was to become so rich; yet he did think that first he ought to speak to his daughter about it. So he went in again, and said that there was a white bear outside, who had promised to make him just as rich as he was poor now, if he could only have the youngest daughter for his bride. But the girl said no, and would not hear of it. Then the man went back to the bear again, and they both agreed that the white bear should return again the following Thursday and get his answer. In the meantime, however, the parents worked upon their daughter, and talked at length about all the riches they would gain, and how well she herself would fare. So at last she agreed, washed and mended the few poor clothes she had, adorned herself as well as she could, and made ready to travel. And what she was given to take along with her is not worth mentioning, either.

The following Thursday the white bear came to fetch his bride. The girl seated herself on his back with her bundle, and then he trotted off. After they had gone a good way, the white bear asked: "Are you afraid?"

"No, not at all," she answered.

"Just keep a tight hold on my fur, and then you will be in no danger," said the bear. So she rode on the bear's back, far, far away, until at last they came to a great rock. There the bear knocked, and at once a door opened through which they entered a great castle, with many brilliantly lighted rooms, where everything gleamed with gold and silver. Then they came into a great hall, and there stood a table completely covered with the most splendid dishes. Here the white bear gave the maiden a silver bell, and said that if there were anything she wanted, she need only ring the bell, and she should have it at once. And after the maiden had eaten, and evening came on, she felt like lying down and going to sleep. So she rang her bell; and at its very first peal she found herself transported to a room in which stood the most beautiful bed one might wish to have, with silken cushions and curtains with golden tassels; and all that was in the room was of gold and silver. Yet when she had lain down and put out the light, she saw a man come in and cast himself down in a corner. It was the white bear, who was allowed to throw off his fur at night; yet the maiden never actually saw him, for he never came until she had put out the light, and before dawn brightened he had disappeared again.

For a time all went well; but gradually the maiden grew sad and silent; for she had not a soul to keep her company the live-long day, and she felt very homesick for her parents and sisters. When the white bear asked her what troubled her, she told him she was always alone, and that she wanted so very much to see her parents and sisters again, and felt very sad because she could not do so. "O that can be managed," said the white bear. "But first you must promise me that you will never speak to your mother alone; but only when others are present. Very likely she will take you by the hand, and want to lead you into her room, so that she can speak to you alone. But this you must not allow, otherwise you will make us both unhappy."

And then, one Sunday, the white bear actually came and told her that now she might make the trip to her parents'. So she seated herself on the bear's back, and the bear set out. After they had gone a very long distance, they at length came to a fine, large, white house, before which her brothers and sisters were running about and playing, and all was so rich and splendid that it was a real pleasure merely to look at it.

"This is where your parents live," said the white bear. "Only do not forget what I told you, or you will make us both unhappy." "Heaven forbid that she should forget it", said the maiden; and when she had come to the house, she got down, and the bear turned back.

When the daughter entered her parents' home, they were more than happy; they told her that they could not thank her enough for what she had done, and that now all of them were doing splendidly. Then they asked her how she herself fared. The maiden answered that all was well with her, also, and that she had all that heart could desire. I do not know exactly all the other things she told them; but I do not believe she told them every last thing there was to tell. So in the afternoon, when the family had eaten dinner, it happened as the white bear had foretold; the mother wanted to talk to her daughter alone, in her room; but she thought of what the white bear had told her, and did not want to go with her mother, but said:

"All we have to say to each other can just as well be said here." Yet – she herself did not know exactly how it happened – her mother finally did persuade her, and then she had to tell just how things were. So she informed her that as soon as she put out the light at night, a man came and cast himself down in the corner of the room. She had never yet seen him, for he always went away before the dawn brightened. And this grieved her, for she did want to see him so very much, and she was alone through the day, and it was very dreary and lonely.

"Alas, perhaps he is a troll, after all," said the mother. "But I can give you some good advice as to how you can see him. Here is a candle-end, which you must hide under your wimple. When the troll is sleeping, light the light and look at him. But be careful not to let a drop of tallow fall on him."

The daughter took the candle-end and hid it in her wimple, and in the evening the white bear came to fetch her.

After they had gone a way the white bear asked whether everything had not happened just as he had said. Yes, such had been the case, and the maiden could not deny it.

"If you have listened to your mother's advice, then you will make us both unhappy, and all will be over between us," said the bear. "O, no, she had not done so," replied the maiden, indeed she had not.

When they reached home, and the maiden had gone to bed, all went as usual: a man came in and cast himself down in a corner of the room. But in the night, when she heard him sleeping soundly, she stood up and lighted the candle. She threw the light on him, and saw the handsomest prince one might wish to see. And she liked him so exceedingly well that she thought she would be unable to keep on living if she could not kiss him that very minute. She did so, but by mistake she let three hot drops of tallow fall on him, and he awoke.

"Alas, what have you done!" cried he. "Now you have made both of us unhappy. If you had only held out until the end of the year, I would have been delivered. I have a step-mother who has cast a spell on me, so that by day I am a bear, and at night a human being. But now all is over between us, and I must return to my step-mother. She lives in a castle that is east of the sun and west of the moon, where there is a princess with a nose three yards long, whom I must now marry."

The maiden wept and wailed; but to no avail, for the prince said he must journey away. Then she asked him whether she might not go with him. No, said he, that could not be.

"But can you not at least tell me the road, so that I can search for you? For surely that will be permitted me?"

"Yes, that you may do," said he. "But there is no road that leads there. The castle lies east of the sun and west of the moon, and neither now nor at any other time will you find the road to it!"

When the maiden awoke the next morning, the prince as well as the castle had disappeared. She lay in a green opening in the midst of a thick, dark wood, and beside her lay the bundle of poor belongings she had brought from home. And when she had rubbed the sleep out of her eyes, and had cried her fill, she set out and wandered many, many days, until at last she came to a great hill. And before the hill sat an old woman who was playing with a golden apple. The maiden asked the woman whether she did not know which road led to the prince who lived in the castle that was east of the sun and west of the moon, and who was to marry a princess with a nose three yards long.

"How do you come to know him?" asked the woman. "Are you, perhaps, the maiden he wanted to marry?"

"Yes, I am that maiden," she replied.

"So you are that girl," said the woman. "Well, my child, I am sorry to say that all I know of him is that he lives in the castle that is east of the sun and west of the moon, and that you will probably never get there. But I will loan you my horse, on which you may ride to my neighbour, and perhaps she can tell you. And when you get there just give the horse a blow back of his left ear, and order him to go home. And here, take this golden apple along!"

The maiden mounted the horse, and rode a long, long time. At length she again came to a hill, before which sat an old woman with a golden reel. The maiden asked whether she could not tell her the road which led to the castle that lay east of the sun and west of the moon. This woman said just what the other had, no, she knew no more of the castle than that it lay east of the sun and west of the moon. "And," said she, "you will probably never get there. But I will loan you my horse to ride to the nearest neighbour; perhaps she can tell you. And when you have reached her just give the horse a blow back of his left ear, and order him to go home again." And finally she gave the maiden the golden reel, for, said the old woman, it might be useful to her.

The maiden then mounted the horse, and again rode a long, long time. At length she once more came to a great hill, before which sat an old woman spinning at a golden spindle. Then the maiden once more asked after the prince, and the castle that lay east of the sun and west of the moon. And everything happened exactly as on the two previous occasions.

"Do you happen to be the maiden the prince wanted to marry?" asked the old woman.

"Yes, I am that maiden," answered the maiden.

But this old woman knew no more about the road than the two others. "Yes, the castle lies east of the sun and west of the moon, that I know," said she. "And you will probably never get there. But I will loan you my horse, and you may ride on it to the East Wind and ask him. Perhaps he is acquainted there, and can blow you thither. And when you reach him, just give my horse a blow back of the left ear, and then he will return here of his own accord." Finally the old woman gave her her golden spindle. "Perhaps it may be useful to you," said she.

The maiden now rode for many days and weeks, and it took a long, long time before she came to the East Wind. But at last she did find him, and then she asked the East Wind whether he could show her the road that led to the prince who lived in the castle that was east of the sun and west of the moon.

O, yes, he had heard tell of the prince, and of the castle as well, said the East Wind, but he did not know the road that led to it, for he had never blown so far. "But if you wish, I will take you to my brother, the West Wind, and perhaps he can tell you, for he is much stronger than I am. Just sit down on my back, and I will carry you to him."

The maiden did as he told her, and then they moved swiftly away. When they came to the West Wind, the East Wind said that here he was bringing the maiden whom the prince who lived in the castle that lay east of the sun and west of the moon had wanted to marry, that she was journeying on her way to him, and looking for him everywhere, and that he had accompanied her in order to find out whether the West Wind knew where this castle might be.

"No," said the West Wind to the maiden, "I have never blown so far, but if you wish I will take you to the South Wind, who is much stronger than both of us, and has travelled far and wide, and perhaps he can tell you. Seat yourself on my back, and I will carry you to him."

The maiden did so, and then they flew quickly off to the South Wind. When they found him, the West Wind asked whether the South Wind could show them the road that led to the castle that lay east of the sun and west of the moon; and that this was the maiden who was to have the prince.

"Well, well, so this is the girl?" cried the South Wind. "Yes, it is true that I have gone about a good deal during my life," said he, "yet I have never blown so far. But if you wish, I will take you to my brother, the North Wind. He is the oldest and strongest of us all. If he does not know where the castle lies, then no one in the whole world can tell you. Seat yourself on my back, and I will carry you to him."

The maiden seated herself on the back of the South Wind, and he flew away with a roar and a rush. The journey did not take long.

When they had reached the dwelling of the North Wind, the latter was so wild and unmannerly that he blew a cold blast at them while they were still a good way off. "What do you want?" cried he, as soon as he caught sight of them, so that a cold shiver ran down their backs.

"You should not greet us so rudely," said the South Wind. "It is I, the South Wind. And this is the maiden who wanted to marry the prince who lives in the castle that lies east of the sun and west of the moon. She wishes to ask you whether you have ever been there, and if you can show her the road that leads to it; for she would like to find the prince again."

"O, yes, I know very well where the castle lies," said the North Wind. "I blew an aspen leaf there just once, and then I was so weary that I could not blow at all for many a long day. But if you want to get there above all things, and are not afraid of me, I will take you on my back, and see whether I can blow you there."

The maiden said that she must and would get to the castle, if it were by any means possible, and that she was not afraid, no matter how hard the journey might be. "Very well, then you must stay here overnight," said the North Wind. "For if we are to get there tomorrow, we must have the whole day before us."

Early the next morning the North Wind awakened the maiden. Then he blew himself up, and made himself so large and thick that he was quite horrible to look at, and thereupon they rushed along through the air as though they meant to reach the end of the world at once. And everywhere beneath them raged such a storm that forests were pulled out by the roots, and houses torn down, and as they rushed across the sea, ships foundered by the hundreds. Further and further they went, so far that no one could even imagine it, and still they were flying across the sea; but gradually the North Wind grew weary, and became weaker and weaker. Finally he could hardly keep going, and sank lower and lower, and at last he flew so low that the waves washed his ankles.

"Are you afraid?" asked the North Wind.

"No, not at all," answered the maiden. By now they were not far distant from the land, and the North Wind had just enough strength left to be able to set down the maiden on the strand, beneath the windows of the castle that lay east of the sun and west of the moon. And then he was so wearied and wretched that he had to rest many a long day before he could set out for home again.

The next morning the maiden seated herself beneath the windows of the castle and played with the golden apple, and the first person who showed herself was the monster with the nose, whom the prince was to marry.

"What do you want for your golden apple?" asked the princess with the nose, as she opened the window.

"I will not sell it at all, either for gold or for money," answered the maiden.

"Well, what do you want for it, if you will not sell it either for gold or for money?" asked the princess. "Ask what you will!"

"I only want to speak tonight to the prince who lives here, then I will give you the apple," said the maiden who had come with the North Wind.

The princess replied that this could be arranged, and then she received the golden apple. But when the maiden came into the prince's room in the evening, he was sleeping soundly. She called and shook him, wept and wailed; but she could not wake him, and in the morning, as soon as it dawned, the princess with the long nose came and drove her out.

That day the maiden again sat beneath the windows of the castle, and wound her golden reel. And all went as on the preceding day. The princess asked what she wanted for the reel, and the maiden answered that she would sell it neither for gold nor for money; but if she might speak that night to the prince, then she would give the reel to the princess. Yet when the maiden came to the prince, he was again fast asleep, and no matter how much she wept and wailed, and cried and shook, she could not wake him. But as soon as day dawned, and it grew bright, the princess with the long nose came and drove her out. And that day the maiden again seated herself beneath the windows of the castle, and spun with her golden spindle; and, of course, the princess with the long nose wanted to have that, too. She opened the window, and asked what she wanted for the golden spindle. The maiden replied, as she had twice before, that she would sell the spindle neither for gold nor money; but that the princess could have it if she might speak to the prince again that night. Yes, that she was welcome to do, said the princess, and took the golden spindle. Now it happened that some Christians, who were captives in the castle, and quartered in a room beside that of the prince, had heard a woman weeping and wailing pitifully in the prince's room for the past two nights. So they told the prince. And that evening when the princess came to him with his night-cap, the prince pretended to drink it; but instead poured it out behind his back, for he could well imagine that she had put a sleeping-powder into the cup. Then, when the maiden came in, the prince was awake, and she had to tell him just how she had found the castle.

"You have come just in the nick of time," said he, "for tomorrow I am to marry the princess; but I do not want the monster with the nose at all, and you are the only person who can save me. I will say that first I wish to see whether my bride is a capable housewife, and demand that she wash the three drops of tallow from my shirt. She will naturally agree to this, for she does not know that you made the spots, for only Christian hands can wash them out again, but not the hands of this pack of trolls. Then I will say I will marry none other than the maiden who can wash out the spots, and ask you to do so," said the prince. And then both rejoiced and were happy beyond measure.

But on the following day, when the wedding was to take place, the prince said: "First I would like to see what my bride can do!" Yes, that was no more than right, said his mother-in-law. "I have a very handsome shirt," continued the prince, "which I would like to wear at the wedding. But there are three tallow-spots on it, and they must first be washed out. And I have made a vow to marry none other than the woman who can do this. So if my bride cannot manage to do it, then she is worthless."

Well, that would not be much of a task, said the woman, and agreed to the proposal. And the princess with the long nose at once began to wash. She washed with all her might and main, and took the greatest pains, but the longer she washed and rubbed, the larger grew the spots.

"O, you don't know how to wash!" said her mother, the old troll-wife. "Just give it to me!" But no sooner had she taken the shirt in her hand, than it began to look worse, and the more she washed and rubbed, the larger and blacker grew the spots. Then the other troll-women had to come and wash; but the longer they washed the shirt the uglier it grew, and finally it looked as though it had been hanging in the smokestack.

"Why, all of you are worthless!" said the prince. "Outside the window sits a beggar-girl. I'm sure she is a better washer-woman than all of you put together. You, girl, come in here!" he cried out of the window; and when the maiden came in he said: "Do you think you can wash this shirt clean for me?"

"I do not know," answered the maiden, "but I will try." And no more had she dipped the shirt in the water than it turned as white as newly fallen snow, yes, even whiter.

"Indeed, and you are the one I want!" said the prince.

Then the old troll-woman grew so angry that she burst in two, and the princess with the long nose and the rest of the troll-pack probably burst in two as well, for I never heard anything more of them. The prince and his bride then freed all the Christians who had been kept captive in the castle, and packed up as much gold and silver as they could possibly take with them, and went far away from the castle that lies east of the sun and west of the moon.

Faithful and Unfaithful

ONCE UPON A TIME there was a couple of humble cottagers who had no children until, at last, the man's wife was blessed with a boy, which made both of them very happy. They named him Faithful and when he was christened a *huldra* came to the hut, seated herself beside the child's cradle, and foretold that he would meet with good fortune. "What is more," she said, "when he is fifteen years of age, I will make him a present of a horse with many rare qualities, a horse that has the gift of speech!" And with that the *huldra* turned and went away.

The boy grew up and became strong and powerful. And when he had passed his fifteenth year, a strange old man came up to their hut one day, knocked, and said that the horse he was leading had been sent by his queen, and that henceforward it was to belong to Faithful, as she had promised. Then the ancient man departed; but the beautiful horse was admired by all, and Faithful learned to love it more with every passing day.

At length he grew weary of home. "I must away and try my fortune in the world," said he, and his parents did not like to object; for there was not much to wish for at home. So he led his dear horse from the stable, swung himself into the saddle, and rode hurriedly into the wood. He rode on and on, and had already covered a good bit of ground, when he saw two lions engaged in a struggle with a tiger, and they were well-nigh overcome. "Make haste to take your bow," said the horse, "shoot the tiger and deliver the two lions!" "Yes, that's what I will do," said the youth, fitted an arrow to the bow-string, and in a moment the tiger lay prone on the ground. The two lions drew nearer, nuzzled their preserver in a friendly and grateful manner, and then hastened back to their cave.

Faithful now rode along for a long time among the great trees until he suddenly spied two terrified white doves fleeing from a hawk who was on the point of catching them. "Make haste to take your bow," said the horse, "shoot the hawk and save the two doves!" "Yes, that's what I'll do," said the youth. He fitted an arrow to the bow-string, and in a moment the hawk lay prone on the ground. But the two doves flew nearer, fluttered about their deliverer in a tame and grateful manner, and then hurried back to their nest.

The youth pressed on through the wood and by now was far, far from home. But his horse did not tire easily, and ran on with him until they came to a great lake. There he saw a gull rise up from the water, holding a pike in its claws. "Make haste to take your bow," said the horse, "shoot the gull and save the pike!" "Yes, that's what I'll do," answered the youth, fitted an arrow to his bow-string, and in a moment the gull was threshing the ground with its wings, mortally wounded. But the pike who had been saved swam nearer, gave his deliverer a friendly, grateful glance, and then dove down to join his fellows beneath the waves.

Faithful rode on again, and before evening came to a great castle. He at once had himself announced to the king, and begged that the latter would take him into his service. "What kind of a place do you want?" asked the king, who was inclined to look with favour on the bold horseman.

"I should like to be a groom," was Faithful's answer, "but first of all I must have stable-room and fodder for my horse." "That you shall have," said the king, and the youth was taken on as a groom, and served so long and so well, that every one in the castle liked him, and the king in particular praised him highly.

But among the other servitors was one named Unfaithful who was jealous of Faithful, and did what he could to harm him; for he thought to himself:

"Then I would be rid of him, and need not see him continue to rise in my lord's favour." Now it happened that the king was very sad, for he had lost his queen, whom a troll had stolen from the castle. It is true that the queen had not taken pleasure in the king's society, and that she did not love him. Still the king longed for her greatly, and often spoke of it to Unfaithful his servant. So one day Unfaithful said: "My lord need distress himself no longer, for Faithful has been boasting to me that he could rescue your beautiful queen from the hands of the troll." "If he has done so," replied the king, "then he must keep his word."

He straightway ordered Faithful to be brought before him, and threatened him with death if he did not at once hurry into the hill and bring back the wife of whom he had been robbed. If he were successful great honour should be his reward. In vain Faithful denied what Unfaithful had said of him, the king stuck to his demand, and the youth withdrew, convinced that he had not long to live. Then he went to the stable to bid farewell to his beautiful horse, and stood beside him and wept. "What grieves you so?" asked the horse. Then the youth told him of all that had happened, and said that this was probably the last time he would be able to visit him. "If it be no more than that," said the horse, "there is a way to help you. Up in the garret of the castle there is an old fiddle, take it with you and play it when you come to the place where the queen is kept. And fashion for yourself armour of steel wire, and set knives into it everywhere, and then, when you see the troll open his jaws, descend into his maw, and thus slay him. But you must have no fear, and must trust me to show you the way." These words filled the youth with fresh courage. He went to the king and received permission to leave, secretly fashioned his steel armour, took the old fiddle from the garret of the castle, led his dear horse out of the stable, and without delay set forth for the troll's hill.

Before long he saw it, and rode directly to the troll's abode. When he came near, he saw the troll, who had crept out of his castle, lying stretched out at the entrance to his cave, fast asleep, and snoring so powerfully that the whole hill shook. But his mouth was wide open, and his maw was so tremendous that it was easy for the youth to crawl into it. He did so, for he was not afraid, and made his way into the troll's innards where he was so active that the troll was soon killed. Then Faithful crept out again, laid aside his armour, and entered the troll's castle. Within the great golden hall sat the captive queen, fettered with seven strong chains of gold. Faithful could not break the strong chains; but he took up his fiddle and played such tender music on it, that the golden chains were moved, and one after another, fell from the queen, until she was able to rise and was free once more. She looked at the courageous youth with joy and gratitude, and felt very kindly toward him, because he was so handsome and courteous. And the queen was perfectly willing to return with him to the king's castle.

The return of the queen gave rise to great joy, and Faithful received the promised reward from the king. But now the queen treated her husband with even less consideration than before. She would not exchange a word with him, she did not laugh, and locked herself up in her room with her gloomy thoughts. This greatly vexed the king, and one day he asked the queen why she was so sad: "Well," said she, "I cannot be happy unless I have the beautiful golden hall which I had in the hill at the troll's; for a hall like that is to be found nowhere else."

"It will be no easy matter to obtain it for you," said the king, "and I cannot promise you that anyone will be able to do it." But when he complained of his difficulty to his servant Unfaithful, the latter answered: "The chances of success are not so bad, for Faithful said he could easily bring the troll's golden hall to the castle." Faithful was at once sent for, and the king commanded him, as he loved his life, to make good his word and bring the golden hall from the troll's hill. It was in vain that Faithful denied Unfaithful's assertions: go he must, and bring back the golden hall.

Inconsolable, he went to his beautiful horse, wept and wanted to say farewell to him forever. "What troubles you?" asked the horse. And the youth replied: "Unfaithful has again been telling lies about me, and if I do not bring the troll's golden hall to the queen, my life will be forfeited." "Is it nothing more serious than that?" said the horse. "See that you obtain a great ship, take your fiddle with you and play the golden hall out of the hill, then hitch the troll's horses before it, and you will be able to bring the glistening hall here without trouble."

Then Faithful felt somewhat better, did as the horse had told him, and was successful in reaching the great hill. And as he stood there playing the fiddle, the golden hall heard him, and was drawn to the sounding music, and it moved slowly, slowly, until it stood outside the hill. It was built of virgin gold, like a house by itself, and under it were many wheels. Then the youth took the troll's horses, put them to the golden hall, and thus brought it aboard his ship. Soon he had crossed the lake, and brought it along safely so that it reached the castle without damage, to the great joy of the queen. Yet despite the fact, she was as weary of everything as she had been before, never spoke to her husband, the king, and no one ever saw her laugh.

Now the king grew even more vexed than he had been, and again asked her why she seemed so sad. "Ah, how can I be happy unless I have the two colts that used to belong to me, when I stayed at the troll's! Such handsome steeds are to be seen nowhere else!" "It will be anything but easy to obtain for you what you want," declared the king, "for they were untamed, and long ago must have run far away into the wild-wood." Then he left her, sadly, and did not know what to do. But Unfaithful said: "Let my lord give himself no concern, for Faithful has declared he could easily secure both of the troll's colts." Faithful was at once sent for, and the king threatened him with death, if he did not show his powers in the matter of the colts. But should he succeed in catching them, then he would be rewarded.

Now Faithful knew quite well that he could not hope to catch the troll's wild colts, and he once more turned to the stable in order to bid farewell to the *huldra*'s gift. "Why do you weep over such a trifle?" said the horse. "Hurry to the wood, play your fiddle, and all will be well!" Faithful did as he was told, and after a while the two lions whom he had rescued came leaping toward him, listened to his playing and asked him whether he was in distress. "Yes, indeed," said Faithful, and told them what he had to do. They at once ran back into the wood, one to one side and the other to the other, and returned quickly, driving the two colts before them. Then Faithful played his fiddle and the colts followed him, so that he soon reached the king's castle in safety, and could deliver the steeds to the queen.

The king now expected that his wife would be gay and happy. But she did not change, never addressed a word to him, and only seemed a little less sad when she happened to speak to the daring youth.

Then the king asked her to tell him what she lacked, and why she was so discontented. She answered: "I have secured the colts of the troll, and I often sit in the glittering hall of gold; but I can open none of the handsome chests that are filled to the brim with my valuables, because I have no keys. And if I do not get the keys again, how can I be happy?" "And where may the keys be?" asked the king. "In the lake by the troll's hill," said the queen, "for that is where I threw them when Faithful brought me here." "This is a ticklish affair, this business of those keys you want!" said the king. "And I can scarcely promise that you will ever see them again." In spite of this, however, he was willing to make an attempt, and talked it over with his servant Unfaithful. "Why, that is easily done," said the latter, "for Faithful boasted to me that he could get the queen's keys without any difficulty if he wished." "Then I shall compel him to keep his word," said the king. And he at once ordered Faithful, on pain of death, to get the queen's keys out of the lake by the troll's hill without delay.

This time the youth was not so depressed, for he thought to himself: "My wise horse will be able to help me." And so he was, for he advised him to go along playing his fiddle, and to wait for what might happen. After the youth had played for a while, the pike he had saved thrust his head out of the water, recognized him, and asked whether he could be of any service to him. "Yes, indeed!" said the youth, and told him what it was he wanted. The pike at once dived, quickly rose to the surface of the water with the golden keys in his mouth, and gave them to his deliverer. The latter hastened back with them, and now the queen could open the great chests in the golden hall to her heart's content.

Notwithstanding, the king's wife was as sorrowful as ever, and when the king complained about it to Unfaithful, the latter said: "No doubt it is because she loves Faithful. I would therefore advise that my lord have him beheaded. Then there will be a change." This advice suited the king well, and he determined to carry it out shortly. But one day Faithful's horse said to him: "The king is going to have your head chopped off. So hurry to the wood, play your fiddle, and beg the two doves to bring you a bottle of the water of life. Then go to the queen and ask her to set your head on your body and to sprinkle you with the water when you have been beheaded." Faithful did so. He went to the wood that very day with his fiddle, and before long the two doves were fluttering around him, and shortly after brought back the bottle filled with the water of life. He took it back home with him and gave it to the queen, so that she might sprinkle him with it after he had been beheaded. She did so, and at once Faithful rose again, as full of life as ever; but far better looking. The king was astonished at what he had seen, and told the queen to cut off his own head and then sprinkle him with the water. She at once seized the sword, and in a moment the king's head rolled to the ground. But she sprinkled none of the water of life upon it, and the king's body was quickly carried out and buried. Then the queen and Faithful celebrated their wedding with great pomp; but Unfaithful was banished from the land and went away in disgrace. The wise horse dwelt contentedly in a wonderful chamber, and the king and queen kept the magic fiddle, the golden hall, and the troll's other valuables, and lived in peace and happiness day after day.

Silverwhite and Lillwacker

ONCE UPON A TIME THERE WAS A KING, who had a queen whom he loved with a great love. But after a time the queen died, and all he had left was an only daughter. And now that the king was a widower, his whole heart went out to the little princess, whom he cherished as the apple of his eye. And the king's young daughter grew up into the most lovely maiden ever known.

When the princess had seen the snows of fifteen winters, it happened that a great war broke out, and that her father had to march against the foe.

But there was no one to whom the king could entrust his daughter while he was away at war; so he had a great tower built out in the forest, provided it with a plenteous store of supplies, and in it shut up his daughter and a maid. And he had it proclaimed that every man, no matter who he might be, was forbidden to approach the tower in which he had placed his daughter and the maid, under pain of death.

Now the king thought he had taken every precaution to protect his daughter, and went off to war. In the meantime the princess and her maid sat in the tower. But in the city there were a number of brave young sons of kings, as well as other young men, who would have liked to have talked to the beautiful maiden. And when they found that this was forbidden them, they conceived a great hatred for the king. At length they took counsel with an old woman who was wiser than most folk, and told her to arrange matters in such wise that the king's daughter and her maid might come into disrepute, without their having anything to do with it. The old hag promised to help them, enchanted some apples, laid them in a basket, and went to the lonely tower in which the maidens lived.

When the king's daughter and her maid saw the old woman, who was sitting beneath the window, they felt a great longing to try the beautiful apples.

So they called out and asked how much she wanted for her precious apples; but the old woman said they were not for sale. Yet as the girls kept on pleading with her, the old woman said she would make each of them a present of an apple; they only need let down a little basket from the tower. The princess and her maid, in all innocence, did as the troll-woman told them, and each received an apple. But the enchanted fruit had a strange effect, for in due course of time heaven sent them each a child. The king's daughter called her son Silverwhite, and the son of her maid received the name of Lillwacker.

The two boys grew up larger and stronger than other children, and were very handsome as well. They looked as much alike as one cherry-pit does to another, and one could easily see that they were related.

Seven years had passed, and the king was expected home from the war. Then both girls were terrified, and they took counsel together as to how they might hide their children. When at length they could find no other way out of the difficulty, they very sorrowfully bade their children farewell, and let them down from the tower at night, to seek their fortune in the wide, wide world. At parting the king's daughter gave Silverwhite a costly knife; but the maid had nothing to give her son.

The two foster-brethren now wandered out into the world. After they had been gone a while, they came to a dark forest. And in this forest they met a man, strange-looking and very tall. He wore two swords at his side, and was accompanied by six great dogs. He gave them a friendly greeting:

"Good day, little fellows, whence do you come and whither do you go?" The boys told him they came from a high tower, and were going out into the world to seek their fortune. The man replied:

"If such be the case, I know more about your origin than anyone else. And that you may have something by which to remember your father, I will give each of you a sword and three dogs. But you must promise me one thing, that you will never part from your dogs; but take them with you wherever you go." The boys thanked the man for his kind gifts, and promised to do as he had told them. Then they bade him farewell and went their way.

When they had travelled for some time they reached a crossroad. Then Silverwhite said:

"It seems to me that it would be the best for us to try our luck singly, so let us part." Lillwacker answered: "Your advice is good; but how am I to know whether or not you are doing well out in the world?"

"I will give you a token by which you may tell," said Silverwhite, "so long as the water runs clear in this spring you will know that I am alive; but if it turns red and roiled, it will mean that I am dead." Silverwhite then drew runes in the water of the spring, said farewell to his brother, and each of them went on alone. Lillwacker soon came to a king's court, and took service there; but every morning he would go to the spring to see how his brother fared.

Silverwhite continued to wander over hill and dale, until he reached a great city. But the whole city was in mourning, the houses were hung in black, and all the inhabitants went about full of grief and care, as though some great misfortune had occurred.

Silverwhite went though the city and inquired as to the cause of all the unhappiness he saw. They answered: "You must have come from far away, since you do not know that the king and queen were in danger of being drowned at sea, and he had to promise to give up their three daughters in order to escape. Tomorrow morning the sea-troll is coming to carry off the oldest princess." This news pleased Silverwhite; for he saw a fine opportunity to wealth and fame, should fortune favour him.

The next morning Silverwhite hung his sword at his side, called his dogs to him, and wandered down to the seashore alone. And as he sat on the strand he saw the king's daughter led out of the city, and with her went a courtier, who had promised to rescue her. But the princess was very sad and cried bitterly. Then Silverwhite stepped up to her with a polite greeting. When the king's daughter and her escort saw the fearless youth, they were much frightened, because they thought he was the sea-troll. The courtier was so alarmed that he ran away and took refuge in a tree. When Silverwhite saw how frightened the princess was, he said: "Lovely maiden, do not fear me, for I will do you no harm." The king's daughter answered:

"Are you the troll who is coming to carry me away?" "No," said Silverwhite, "I have come to rescue you." Then the princess was glad to think that such a brave hero was going to defend her, and they had a long, friendly talk. At the same time Silverwhite begged the king's daughter to comb his hair. She complied with his request, and Silverwhite laid his head in her lap; but when he did so the princess drew a golden ring from her finger and, unbeknown to him, wound it into his locks.

Suddenly the sea-troll rose from the deeps, setting the waves whirling and foaming far and near. When the troll saw Silverwhite, he grew angry and said: "Why do you sit there beside my princess?" The youth replied: "It seems to me that she is my princess, not yours." The sea-troll answered: "Time enough to see which of us is right; but first our dogs shall fight." Silverwhite was nothing loath, and set his dogs at the dogs of the troll, and there was a fierce struggle. But at last the youth's dogs got the upper hand and bit the dogs of the sea-troll to death. Then Silverwhite drew his sword with a great sweep, rushed upon the sea-troll, and gave him such a tremendous blow that the monster's head rolled on the sand. The troll gave a fearsome cry, and flung himself back into the sea, so that the water spurted to the very skies. Thereupon the youth drew out his silver-mounted knife, cut out the troll's eyes and put them in his pocket. Then he saluted the lovely princess and went away.

Now when the battle was over and the youth had disappeared, the courtier crawled down from his tree, and threatened to kill the princess if she did not say before all the people that he, and none other, had rescued her. The king's daughter did not dare refuse, since she feared for her life. So she returned to her father's castle with the courtier, where they were received with great distinction.

And joy reigned throughout the land when the news spread that the oldest princess had been rescued from the troll.

On the following day everything repeated itself. Silverwhite went down to the strand and met the second princess, just as she was to be delivered to the troll.

And when the king's daughter and her escort saw him, they were very much frightened, thinking he was the sea-troll. And the courtier climbed a tree, just as he had before; but the princess granted the youth's petition, combed his hair as her sister had done, and also wound her gold ring into his long curls.

After a time there was a great tumult out at sea, and a sea-troll rose from the waves. He had three heads and three dogs. But Silverwhite's dogs overcame those of the troll, and the youth killed the troll himself with his sword. Thereupon he took out his silver-mounted knife, cut out the troll's eyes, and went his way. But the courtier lost no time. He climbed down from his tree and forced the princess to promise to say that he, and none other, had rescued her. Then they returned to the castle, where the courtier was acclaimed as the greatest of heroes.

On the third day Silverwhite hung his sword at his side, called his three dogs to him, and again wandered down to the seashore. As he was sitting by the strand, he saw the youngest princess led out of the city, and with her the daring courtier who claimed to have rescued her sisters. But the princess was very sad and cried bitterly. Then Silverwhite stepped up and greeted the lovely maiden politely. Now when the king's daughter and her escort saw the handsome youth, they were very much frightened, for they believed him to be the sea-troll, and the courtier ran away and hid in a high tree that grew near the strand. When Silverwhite noticed the maiden's terror, he said:

"Lovely maiden, do not fear me, for I will do you no harm." The king's daughter answered: "Are you the troll who is coming to carry me away?" "No," said Silverwhite, "I have come to rescue you." Then the princess was very glad to have such a brave hero fight for her, and they had a long, friendly talk with each other. At the same time Silverwhite begged the lovely maiden to do him a favour and comb his hair. This the king's daughter was most willing to do, and Silverwhite laid his head in her lap. But when the princess saw the gold rings her sisters had wound in his locks, she was much surprised, and added her own to the others.

Suddenly the sea-troll came shooting up out of the deep with a terrific noise, so that waves and foam spurted to the very skies. This time the monster had six heads and nine dogs. When the troll saw Silverwhite sitting with the king's daughter, he fell into a rage and cried: "What are you doing with my princess?" The youth answered: "It seems to me that she is my princess rather than yours." Thereupon the troll said: "Time enough to see which of us is right; but first our dogs shall fight each other." Silverwhite did not delay, but set his dogs at the sea-dogs, and they had a battle royal. But in the end the youth's dogs got the upper hand and bit all nine of the sea-dogs to death. Finally Silverwhite drew out his bare sword, flung himself upon the sea-troll, and stretched all six of his heads on the sand with a single blow. The monster uttered a terrible cry, and rushed back into the sea so that the water spurted to the heavens. Then the youth drew his silver-mounted knife, cut out all twelve of the troll's eyes, saluted the king's young daughter, and hastily went away.

Now that the battle was over, and the youth had disappeared, the courtier climbed down from his tree, drew his sword and threatened to kill the princess unless she promised to say that he had rescued her from the troll, as he had her sisters.

The king's daughter did not dare refuse, since she feared for her life. So they went back to the castle together, and when the king saw that they had returned in safety, without so much as a scratch, he and the whole court were full of joy, and they were accorded great honours. And at court the courtier was quite another fellow from the one who had hid away in the tree. The king had a splendid banquet prepared, with amusements and games, and the sound of string music and dancing, and bestowed the hand of his youngest daughter on the courtier in reward for his bravery.

In the midst of the wedding festivities, when the king and his whole court were seated at table, the door opened, and in came Silverwhite with his dogs.

The youth stepped boldly into the hall of state and greeted the king. And when the three princesses saw who it was, they were full of joy, leaped up from their places, and ran over to him, much to the king's surprise, who asked what it all meant. Then the youngest princess told him all that had happened, from beginning to end, and that Silverwhite had rescued them, while the courtier sat in a tree. To prove it beyond any chance of doubt, each of the king's daughters showed her father the ring she had wound in Silverwhite's locks. But the king still did not know quite what to think of it all, until Silverwhite said: "My lord king! In order that you need not doubt what your daughters have told you, I will show you the eyes of the sea-trolls whom I slew." Then the king and all the rest saw that the princesses had told the truth. The traitorous courtier received his just punishment; but Silverwhite was paid every honour, and was given the youngest daughter and half of the kingdom with her.

After the wedding Silverwhite established himself with his young bride in a large castle belonging to the king, and there they lived quietly and happily.

One night, when all were sleeping, it chanced that he heard a knocking at the window, and a voice which said: "Come, Silverwhite, I have to talk to you!" The king, who did not want to wake his young wife, rose hastily, girded on his sword, called his dogs and went out. When he reached the open air, there stood a huge and savage-looking troll. The troll said: "Silverwhite, you have slain my three brothers, and I have come to bid you go down to the seashore with me, that we may fight with one another." This proposal suited the youth, and he followed the troll without protest. When they reached the seashore, there lay three great dogs belonging to the troll. Silverwhite at once set his dogs at the troll-dogs, and after a hard struggle the latter had to give in. The young king drew his sword, bravely attacked the troll and dealt him many a mighty blow. It was a tremendous battle. But when the troll noticed he was getting the worst of it, he grew frightened, quickly ran to a high tree, and clambered into it. Silverwhite and the dogs ran after him, the dogs barking as loudly as they could. Then the troll begged for his life and said: "Dear Silverwhite, I will take wergild for my brothers, only bid your dogs be still, so that we may talk." The king bade his dogs be still, but in vain, they only barked the more loudly. Then the troll tore three hairs from his head, handed them to Silverwhite and said: "Lay a hair on each of the dogs, and then they will be as quiet as can be." The king did so and at once the dogs fell silent, and lay motionless as though they had grown fast to the ground. Now Silverwhite realized that he had been deceived; but it was too late. The troll was already descending from the tree, and he drew his sword and again began to fight. But they had exchanged no more than a few blows, before Silverwhite received a mortal wound, and lay on the earth in a pool of blood.

But now we must tell about Lillwacker. The next morning he went to the spring by the cross-road and found it red with blood. Then he knew that Silverwhite was dead. He called his dogs, hung his sword at his side, and went on until he came to a great city. And the city was in festal array, the streets were crowded with people, and the houses were hung with scarlet cloths and splendid rugs. Lillwacker asked why everybody was so happy, and they said: "You must hail from distant parts, since you do not know that a famous hero has come here by the name of Silverwhite, who has rescued our three princesses, and is now the king's son-in-law." Lillwacker then inquired how it had all come about, and then went his way, reaching the royal castle in which Silverwhite dwelt with his beautiful queen in the evening.

When Lillwacker entered the castle gate, all greeted him as though he had been the king. For he resembled his foster-brother so closely that none could tell one from the other. When the youth came to the queen's room, she also took him for Silverwhite. She went up to him and said: "My lord king, where have you been so long? I have been awaiting you with great anxiety." Lillwacker said little, and was very taciturn. Then he lay down on a couch in a corner of the queen's room.

The young woman did not know what to think of his actions; for her husband did not act queerly at other times. But she thought: "One should not try to discover the secrets of others," and said nothing.

In the night, when all were sleeping, there was a knocking at the window, and a voice cried: "Come, Lillwacker, I have to talk to you!" The youth rose hastily, took his good sword, called his dogs and went. When he reached the open air, there stood the same troll who had slain Silverwhite. He said: "Come with me, Lillwacker, and then you shall see your foster-brother!" To this Lillwacker at once agreed, and the troll led the way. When they came to the seashore, there lay the three great dogs whom the troll had brought with him. Somewhat further away, where they had fought, lay Silverwhite in a pool of blood, and beside him his dogs were stretched out on the ground as though they had taken root in it. Then Lillwacker saw how everything had happened, and thought that he would gladly venture his life, if he might in some way call his brother back from the dead. He at once set his dogs at the troll-dogs, and they had a hard struggle, in which Lillwacker's dogs won the victory. Then the youth drew his sword, and attacked the troll with mighty blows. But when the troll saw that he was getting the worst of it, he took refuge in a lofty tree. Lillwacker and his dogs ran after him and the dogs barked loudly.

Then the troll humbly begged for his life, and said: "Dear Lillwacker, I will give you wergild for your brother, only bid your dogs be still, so that we may talk." At the same time the troll handed him three hairs from his head and added: "Lay one of these hairs on each of your dogs, and then they will soon be quiet." But Lillwacker saw through his cunning scheme, took the three hairs and laid them on the troll-dogs, which at once fell on the ground and lay like dead.

When the troll saw that his attempt had failed, he was much alarmed and said: "Dearest Lillwacker, I will give you wergild for your brother, if you will only leave me alone." But the youth answered:

"What is there you can give me that will compensate for my brother's life?" The troll replied: "Here are two flasks. In one is a liquid which, if you anoint a dead man with it, it will restore him to life; but as to the liquid in the other flask, if you moisten anything with it, and someone touches the place you have moistened, he will be unable to move from the spot. I think it would be hard to find anything more precious than the liquid in these flasks." Lillwacker said: "Your proposal suits me, and I will accept it. But there is something else you must promise to do: that you will release my brother's dogs." The troll agreed, climbed down from the tree, breathed on the dogs and thus freed them. Then Lillwacker took the two flasks and went away from the seashore with the troll. After they had gone a while they came to a great flat stone, lying near the highway. Lillwacker hastened on in advance and moistened it with liquid from the second flask. Then, as he was going by, Lillwacker suddenly set all six of his dogs at the troll, who stepped back and touched the stone. There he stuck, and could move neither forward nor backward. After a time the sun rose and shone on the stone. And when the troll saw the sun he burst – and was as dead as a doornail!

Lillwacker now ran back to his brother and sprinkled him with the liquid in the other flask, so that he came to life again, and they were both very happy, as may well be imagined. The two foster-brothers then returned to the castle, recounting the story of their experiences and adventures on the way. Lillwacker told how he had been taken for his brother. He even mentioned that he had lain down on a couch in a corner of the queen's room, and that she had never suspected that he was not her rightful husband. But when Silverwhite heard that, he thought that Lillwacker had offended against the queen's dignity, and he grew angry and fell into such a rage that he drew his sword, and thrust it into his brother's breast. Lillwacker fell to earth dead, and Silverwhite went home to the castle alone. But Lillwacker's dogs would not leave their master, and lay around him, whining and licking his wound.

In the evening, when the young king and his wife retired, the queen asked him why he had been so taciturn and serious the evening before. Then the queen said: "I am very curious to know what has befallen you during the last few days, but what I would like to know most of all, is why you lay down on a couch in a corner of my room the other night?" Now it was clear to Silverwhite that the brother he had slain was innocent of all offence, and he felt bitter regret at having repaid his faithfulness so badly. So King Silverwhite at once rose and went to the place where his brother was lying. He poured the water of life from his flask and anointed his brother's wound, and in a moment Lillwacker was alive again, and the two brother's went joyfully back to the castle.

When they got there, Silverwhite told his queen how Lillwacker had rescued him from death, and all the rest of their adventures, and all were happy at the royal court, and they paid the youth the greatest honours and compliments. After he had stayed there a time he sued for the hand of the second princess and obtained it. Thereupon the wedding was celebrated with great pomp, and Silverwhite divided his half of the kingdom with his foster-brother. The two brothers continued to live together in peace and unity, and if they have not died, they are living still.

The Little White Cat

A LONG, LONG TIME AGO, in a valley far away, the giant Trencoss lived in a great castle, surrounded by trees that were always green. The castle had a hundred doors, and every door was guarded by a huge, shaggy hound, with tongue of fire and claws of iron, who tore to pieces anyone who went to the castle without the giant's leave. Trencoss had made war on the King of the Torrents, and, having killed the king, and slain his people, and burned his palace, he carried off his only daughter, the Princess Eileen, to the castle in the valley. Here he provided her with beautiful rooms, and appointed a hundred dwarfs, dressed in blue and yellow satin, to wait upon her, and harpers to play sweet music for her, and he gave her diamonds without number, brighter than the sun; but he would not allow her to go outside the castle, and told her if she went one step beyond its doors, the hounds, with tongues of fire and claws of iron, would tear her to pieces. A week after her arrival, war broke out between the giant and the king of the islands, and before he set out for battle, the giant sent for the princess, and informed her that on his return he would make her his wife. When the princess heard this she began to cry, for she would rather die than marry the giant who had slain her father.

"Crying will only spoil your bright eyes, my little princess," said Trencoss, "and you will have to marry me whether you like it or no."

He then bade her go back to her room, and he ordered the dwarfs to give her everything she asked for while he was away, and the harpers to play the sweetest music for her. When the princess gained her room she cried as if her heart would break. The long day passed slowly, and the night came, but brought no sleep to Eileen, and in the grey light of the morning she rose and opened the window, and looked about in every direction to see if there were any chance of escape. But the window was ever so high above the ground, and below were the hungry and ever watchful hounds. With a heavy heart she was about to close the window when she thought she saw the branches of the tree that was nearest to it moving. She looked again, and she saw a little white cat creeping along one of the branches.

"Mew!" cried the cat.

"Poor little pussy," said the princess. "Come to me, pussy."

"Stand back from the window," said the cat, "and I will."

The princess stepped back, and the little white cat jumped into the room. The princess took the little cat on her lap and stroked him with her hand, and the cat raised up its back and began to purr.

"Where do you come from, and what is your name?" asked the princess.

"No matter where I come from or what's my name," said the cat, "I am a friend of yours, and I come to help you."

"I never wanted help worse," said the princess.

"I know that," said the cat; "and now listen to me. When the giant comes back from battle and asks you to marry him, say to him you will marry him."

"But I will never marry him," said the princess.

"Do what I tell you," said the cat. "When he asks you to marry him, say to him you will if his dwarfs will wind for you three balls from the fairy dew that lies on the bushes on a misty morning as big as these," said the cat, putting his right forefoot into his ear and taking out three balls – one yellow, one red, and one blue.

"They are very small," said the princess. "They are not much bigger than peas, and the dwarfs will not be long at their work."

"Won't they," said the cat. "It will take them a month and a day to make one, so that it will take three months and three days before the balls are wound; but the giant, like you, will think they can be made in a few days, and so he will readily promise to do what you ask. He will soon find out his mistake, but he will keep his word, and will not press you to marry him until the balls are wound."

"When will the giant come back?" asked Eileen.

"He will return tomorrow afternoon," said the cat.

"Will you stay with me until then?" said the princess. "I am very lonely."

"I cannot stay," said the cat. "I have to go away to my palace on the island on which no man ever placed his foot, and where no man but one shall ever come."

"And where is that island?" asked the princess, "and who is the man?"

"The island is in the far-off seas where vessel never sailed; the man you will see before many days are over; and if all goes well, he will one day slay the giant Trencoss, and free you from his power."

"Ah!" sighed the princess, "that can never be, for no weapon can wound the hundred hounds that guard the castle, and no sword can kill the giant Trencoss."

"There is a sword that will kill him," said the cat; "but I must go now. Remember what you are to say to the giant when he comes home, and every morning watch the tree on which you saw me, and if you see in the branches anyone you like better than yourself," said the cat, winking at the princess, "throw him these three balls and leave the rest to me; but take care not to speak a single word to him, for if you do all will be lost."

"Shall I ever see you again?" asked the princess.

"Time will tell," answered the cat, and, without saying so much as goodbye, he jumped through the window on to the tree, and in a second was out of sight.

The morrow afternoon came, and the giant Trencoss returned from battle. Eileen knew of his coming by the furious barking of the hounds, and her heart sank, for she knew that in a few moments she would be summoned to his presence. Indeed, he had hardly entered the castle when he sent for her, and told her to get ready for the wedding. The princess tried to look cheerful, as she answered:

"I will be ready as soon as you wish; but you must first promise me something."

"Ask anything you like, little princess," said Trencoss.

"Well, then," said Eileen, "before I marry you, you must make your dwarfs wind three balls as big as these from the fairy dew that lies on the bushes on a misty morning in summer."

"Is that all?" said Trencoss, laughing. "I shall give the dwarfs orders at once, and by this time tomorrow the balls will be wound, and our wedding can take place in the evening."

"And will you leave me to myself until then?"

"I will," said Trencoss.

"On your honour as a giant?" said Eileen.

"On my honour as a giant," replied Trencoss.

The princess returned to her rooms, and the giant summoned all his dwarfs, and he ordered them to go forth in the dawning of the morn and to gather all the fairy dew lying on the bushes, and to wind three balls – one yellow, one red, and one blue. The next morning, and the next, and the next, the dwarfs went out into the fields and searched all the hedgerows, but they could gather only as much fairy dew as would make a thread as long as a wee girl's eyelash; and so they had to go out morning after morning, and the giant fumed and threatened, but all to no purpose. He was very angry with the princess, and he was vexed with himself that she was so much cleverer than he was, and, moreover, he saw now that the wedding could not take place as soon as he expected.

When the little white cat went away from the castle he ran as fast as he could up hill and down dale, and never stopped until he came to the Prince of the Silver River. The prince was alone, and very sad and sorrowful he was, for he was thinking of the Princess Eileen, and wondering where she could be.

"Mew," said the cat, as he sprang softly into the room; but the prince did not heed him. "Mew," again said the cat; but again the prince did not heed him. "Mew," said the cat the third time, and he jumped up on the prince's knee.

"Where do you come from, and what do you want?" asked the prince.

"I come from where you would like to be," said the cat.

"And where is that?" said the prince.

"Oh, where is that, indeed! As if I didn't know what you are thinking of, and of whom you are thinking," said the cat; "and it would be far better for you to try and save her."

"I would give my life a thousand times over for her," said the prince.

"For whom?" said the cat, with a wink. "I named no name, your highness," said he.

"You know very well who she is," said the prince, "if you knew what I was thinking of; but do you know where she is?"

"She is in danger," said the cat. "She is in the castle of the giant Trencoss, in the valley beyond the mountains."

"I will set out there at once," said the prince "and I will challenge the giant to battle, and will slay him."

"Easier said than done," said the cat. "There is no sword made by the hands of man can kill him, and even if you could kill him, his hundred hounds, with tongues of fire and claws of iron, would tear you to pieces."

"Then, what am I to do?" asked the prince.

"Be said by me," said the cat. "Go to the wood that surrounds the giant's castle, and climb the high tree that's nearest to the window that looks towards the sunset, and shake the branches, and you will see what you will see. Then hold out your hat with the silver plumes, and three balls – one yellow, one red, and one blue – will be thrown into it. And then come back here as fast as you can; but speak no word, for if you utter a single word the hounds will hear you, and you shall be torn to pieces."

Well, the prince set off at once, and after two days' journey he came to the wood around the castle, and he climbed the tree that was nearest to the window that looked towards the sunset, and he shook the branches. As soon as he did so, the window opened and he saw the Princess Eileen, looking lovelier than ever. He was going to call out her name, but she placed her fingers on her lips, and he remembered what the cat had told him, that he was to speak no word. In silence he held out the hat with the silver plumes, and the princess threw into it the three balls, one after another, and, blowing him a kiss, she shut the window. And well it was she did so, for at that very moment she heard the voice of the giant, who was coming back from hunting.

The prince waited until the giant had entered the castle before he descended the tree. He set off as fast as he could. He went up hill and down dale, and never stopped until he arrived at his own palace, and there waiting for him was the little white cat.

"Have you brought the three balls?" said he.

"I have," said the prince.

"Then follow me," said the cat.

On they went until they left the palace far behind and came to the edge of the sea.

"Now," said the cat, "unravel a thread of the red ball, hold the thread in your right hand, drop the ball into the water, and you shall see what you shall see."

The prince did as he was told, and the ball floated out to sea, unravelling as it went, and it went on until it was out of sight.

"Pull now," said the cat.

The prince pulled, and, as he did, he saw far away something on the sea shining like silver. It came nearer and nearer, and he saw it was a little silver boat. At last it touched the strand.

"Now," said the cat, "step into this boat and it will bear you to the palace on the island on which no man has ever placed his foot – the island in the unknown seas that were never sailed by vessels made of human hands. In that palace there is a sword with a diamond hilt, and by that sword alone the giant Trencoss can be killed. There also are a hundred cakes, and it is only on eating these the hundred hounds can die. But mind what I say to you: if you eat or drink until you reach the palace of the little cat in the island in the unknown seas, you will forget the Princess Eileen."

"I will forget myself first," said the prince, as he stepped into the silver boat, which floated away so quickly that it was soon out of sight of land.

The day passed and the night fell, and the stars shone down upon the waters, but the boat never stopped. On she went for two whole days and nights, and on the third morning the prince saw an island in the distance, and very glad he was; for he thought it was his journey's end, and he was almost fainting with thirst and hunger. But the day passed and the island was still before him.

At long last, on the following day, he saw by the first light of the morning that he was quite close to it, and that trees laden with fruit of every kind were bending down over the water. The boat sailed round and round the island, going closer and closer every round, until, at last, the drooping branches almost touched it. The sight of the fruit within his reach made the prince hungrier and thirstier than he was before, and forgetting his promise to the little cat – not to eat anything until he entered the palace in the unknown seas – he caught one of the branches, and, in a moment, was in the tree eating the delicious fruit. While he was doing so the boat floated out to sea and soon was lost to sight; but the prince, having eaten, forgot all about it, and, worse still, forgot all about the princess in the giant's castle. When he had eaten enough he descended the tree, and, turning his back on the sea, set out straight before him. He had not gone far when he heard the sound of music, and soon after he saw a number of maidens playing on silver harps coming towards him. When they saw him they ceased playing, and cried out:

"Welcome! Welcome! Prince of the Silver River, welcome to the island of fruits and flowers. Our king and queen saw you coming over the sea, and they sent us to bring you to the palace."

The prince went with them, and at the palace gates the king and queen and their daughter Kathleen received him, and gave him welcome. He hardly saw the king and queen, for his eyes were fixed on the princess Kathleen, who looked more beautiful than a flower. He thought he had never seen anyone so lovely, for, of course, he had forgotten all about poor Eileen pining away in her castle prison in the lonely valley. When the king and queen had given welcome to the prince a great feast was spread, and all the lords and ladies of the court sat down to it, and the prince sat between the queen and the princess Kathleen, and long before the feast was finished he was over head and ears in love with her. When the feast was ended the queen ordered the ballroom to be made ready, and when night fell the dancing began, and was kept up until the morning star, and the prince danced all night with the princess, falling deeper and deeper in love with her every minute. Between dancing by night and feasting by day weeks went by. All the time poor Eileen in the giant's castle was counting the hours, and all this time the dwarfs were winding the balls, and a ball and a half were already wound. At last the prince asked the king and queen for their daughter in marriage, and they were delighted to be able to say yes, and the day was fixed for the wedding. But on the evening before the day on which it was to take place the prince was in his room, getting ready for a dance, when he felt something rubbing against his leg, and, looking down, who should he see but the little white cat. At the sight of him the prince remembered everything, and sad and sorry he was when he thought of Eileen watching and waiting and counting the days until he returned to save her. But he was very fond of the princess Kathleen, and so he did not know what to do.

"You can't do anything tonight," said the cat, for he knew what the prince was thinking of, "but when morning comes go down to the sea, and look not to the right or the left, and let no living thing touch you, for if you do you shall never leave the island. Drop the second ball into the water, as you did the first, and when the boat comes step in at once. Then you may look behind you, and you shall see what you shall see, and you'll know which you love best, the Princess Eileen or the Princess Kathleen, and you can either go or stay."

The prince didn't sleep a wink that night, and at the first glimpse of the morning he stole from the palace. When he reached the sea he threw out the ball, and when it had floated out of sight, he saw the little boat sparkling on the horizon like a newly-risen star. The prince had scarcely passed through the palace doors when he was missed, and the king and queen and the princess, and all the lords and ladies of the court, went in search of him, taking the quickest way to the sea. While the maidens with the silver harps played sweetest music, the princess, whose voice was sweeter than any music, called on the prince by his name, and so moved his heart that he was about to look behind, when he remembered how the cat had told him he should not do so until he was in the boat. Just as it touched the shore the princess put out her hand and almost caught the prince's arm, but he stepped into the boat in time to save himself, and it sped away like a receding wave. A loud scream caused the prince to look round suddenly, and when he did he saw no sign of king or queen, or princess, or lords or ladies, but only big green serpents, with red eyes and tongues, that hissed out fire and poison as they writhed in a hundred horrible coils.

The prince, having escaped from the enchanted island, sailed away for three days and three nights, and every night he hoped the coming morning would show him the island he was in search of. He was faint with hunger and beginning to despair, when on the fourth morning he saw in the distance an island that, in the first rays of the sun, gleamed like fire. On coming closer to it he saw that it was clad with trees, so covered with bright red berries that hardly a leaf was to be seen. Soon the boat was almost within a stone's cast of the island, and it began to sail round and round until it was well under the bending branches. The scent of the berries was so sweet that it sharpened the prince's hunger, and he longed to pluck them; but, remembering what had happened to him on the enchanted island, he was afraid to touch them. But the boat kept on sailing round and round, and at last a great wind rose from the sea and shook the branches, and the bright, sweet berries fell into the boat until it was filled with them, and they fell upon the prince's hands, and he took up some to look at them, and as he looked the desire to eat them grew stronger, and he said to himself it would be no harm to taste one; but when he tasted it the flavour was so delicious he swallowed it, and, of course, at once he forgot all about Eileen, and the boat drifted away from him and left him standing in the water.

He climbed on to the island, and having eaten enough of the berries, he set out to see what might be before him, and it was not long until he heard a great noise, and a huge iron ball knocked down one of the trees in front of him, and before he knew where he was a hundred giants came running after it. When they saw the prince they turned towards him, and one of them caught him up in his hand and held him up that all might see him. The prince was nearly squeezed to death, and seeing this the giant put him on the ground again.

"Who are you, my little man?" asked the giant.

"I am a prince," replied the prince.

"Oh, you are a prince, are you?" said the giant. "And what are you good for?" said he.

The prince did not know, for nobody had asked him that question before.

"I know what he's good for," said an old giantess, with one eye in her forehead and one in her chin. "I know what he's good for. He's good to eat."

When the giants heard this they laughed so loud that the prince was frightened almost to death.

"Why," said one, "he wouldn't make a mouthful."

"Oh, leave him to me," said the giantess, "and I'll fatten him up; and when he is cooked and dressed he will be a nice dainty dish for the king."

The giants, on this, gave the prince into the hands of the old giantess. She took him home with her to the kitchen, and fed him on sugar and spice and all things nice, so that he should be a sweet morsel for the king of the giants when he returned to the island. The poor prince would not eat anything at first, but the giantess held him over the fire until his feet were scorched, and then he said to himself it was better to eat than to be burnt alive.

Well, day after day passed, and the prince grew sadder and sadder, thinking that he would soon be cooked and dressed for the king; but sad as the prince was, he was not half as sad as the Princess Eileen in the giant's castle, watching and waiting for the prince to return and save her.

And the dwarfs had wound two balls, and were winding a third.

At last the prince heard from the old giantess that the king of the giants was to return on the following day, and she said to him:

"As this is the last night you have to live, tell me if you wish for anything, for if you do your wish will be granted."

"I don't wish for anything," said the prince, whose heart was dead within him.

"Well, I'll come back again," said the giantess, and she went away.

The prince sat down in a corner, thinking and thinking, until he heard close to his ear a sound like "purr, purr!" He looked around, and there before him was the little white cat.

"I ought not to come to you," said the cat; "but, indeed, it is not for your sake I come. I come for the sake of the Princess Eileen. Of course, you forgot all about her, and, of course, she is always thinking of you. It's always the way –

"Favoured lovers may forget,
Slighted lovers never yet."

The prince blushed with shame when he heard the name of the princess.

"'Tis you that ought to blush," said the cat; "but listen to me now, and remember, if you don't obey my directions this time you'll never see me again, and you'll never set your eyes on the Princess Eileen. When the old giantess comes back tell her you wish, when the morning comes, to go down to the sea to look at it for the last time. When you reach the sea you will know what to do. But I must go now, as I hear the giantess coming." And the cat jumped out of the window and disappeared.

"Well," said the giantess, when she came in, "is there anything you wish?"

"Is it true I must die tomorrow?" asked the prince.

"It is."

"Then," said he, "I should like to go down to the sea to look at it for the last time."

"You may do that," said the giantess, "if you get up early."

"I'll be up with the lark in the light of the morning," said the prince.

"Very well," said the giantess, and, saying "goodnight", she went away.

The prince thought the night would never pass, but at last it faded away before the grey light of the dawn, and he sped down to the sea. He threw out the third ball, and before long he saw the little boat coming towards him swifter than the wind. He threw himself into it the moment it touched the shore. Swifter than the wind it bore him out to sea, and before he had time to look behind him the island of the giantess was like a faint red speck in the distance. The day passed and the night fell, and the stars looked down, and the boat sailed on, and just as the sun rose above the sea it pushed its silver prow on the golden strand of an island greener than the leaves in summer. The prince jumped out, and went on and on until he entered a pleasant valley, at the head of which he saw a palace white as snow.

As he approached the central door it opened for him. On entering the hall he passed into several rooms without meeting with anyone; but, when he reached the principal apartment, he found himself in a circular room, in which were a thousand pillars, and every pillar was of marble, and on every pillar save one, which stood in the centre of the room, was a little white cat with black eyes. Ranged round the wall, from one door-jamb to the other, were three rows of precious jewels. The first was a row of brooches of gold and silver, with their pins fixed in the wall and their heads outwards; the second a row of torques of gold and silver; and the third a row of great swords, with hilts of gold and silver. And on many tables was food of all kinds, and drinking horns filled with foaming ale.

While the prince was looking about him the cats kept on jumping from pillar to pillar; but seeing that none of them jumped on to the pillar in the centre of the room, he began to wonder why this was so, when, all of a sudden, and before he could guess how it came about, there right before him on the centre pillar was the little white cat.

"Don't you know me?" said he.

"I do," said the prince.

"Ah, but you don't know who I am. This is the palace of the Little White Cat, and I am the King of the Cats. But you must be hungry, and the feast is spread."

Well, when the feast was ended, the king of the cats called for the sword that would kill the giant Trencoss, and the hundred cakes for the hundred watch-dogs.

The cats brought the sword and the cakes and laid them before the king.

"Now," said the king, "take these; you have no time to lose. Tomorrow the dwarfs will wind the last ball, and tomorrow the giant will claim the princess for his bride. So you should go at once; but before you go take this from me to your little girl."

And the king gave him a brooch lovelier than any on the palace walls.

The king and the prince, followed by the cats, went down to the strand, and when the prince stepped into the boat all the cats 'mewed' three times for good luck, and the prince waved his hat three times, and the little boat sped over the waters all through the night as brightly and as swiftly as a shooting star. In the first flush of the morning it touched the strand. The prince jumped out and went on and on, up hill and down dale, until he came to the giant's castle. When the hounds saw him they barked furiously, and bounded towards him to tear him to pieces. The prince flung the cakes to them, and as each hound swallowed his cake he fell dead. The prince then struck his shield three times with the sword which he had brought from the palace of the little white cat.

When the giant heard the sound he cried out: "Who comes to challenge me on my wedding day?"

The dwarfs went out to see, and, returning, told him it was a prince who challenged him to battle.

The giant, foaming with rage, seized his heaviest iron club, and rushed out to the fight. The fight lasted the whole day, and when the sun went down the giant said:

"We have had enough of fighting for the day. We can begin at sunrise tomorrow."

"Not so," said the prince. "Now or never; win or die."

"Then take this," cried the giant, as he aimed a blow with all his force at the prince's head; but the prince, darting forward like a flash of lightning, drove his sword into the giant's heart, and, with a groan, he fell over the bodies of the poisoned hounds.

When the dwarfs saw the giant dead they began to cry and tear their hair. But the prince told them they had nothing to fear, and he bade them go and tell the princess Eileen he wished to speak with her. But the princess had watched the battle from her window, and when she saw the giant fall she rushed out to greet the prince, and that very night he and she and all the dwarfs and harpers set out for the Palace of the Silver River, which they reached the next morning, and from that day to this there never has been a gayer wedding than the wedding of the Prince of the Silver River and the Princess Eileen; and though she had diamonds and pearls to spare, the only jewel she wore on her wedding day was the brooch which the prince had brought her from the Palace of the Little White Cat in the far-off seas.

The Greek Princess and the Young Gardener

THERE WAS ONCE A KING, but I didn't hear what country he was over, and he had one very beautiful daughter. Well, he was getting old and sickly, and the doctors found out that the finest medicine in the world for him was the apples of a tree that grew in the orchard just under his window. So you may be sure he had the tree well minded, and used to get the apples counted from the time they were the size of small marbles.

One harvest, just as they were beginning to turn ripe, the king was awakened one night by the flapping of wings outside in the orchard; and when he looked out, what did he see but a bird among the branches of his tree. Its feathers were so bright that they made a light all round them, and the minute it saw the king in his night-cap and night-shirt it picked off an apple, and flew away. "Oh, botheration to that thief of a gardener!" says the king, "this is a nice way he's watching my precious fruit."

He didn't sleep a wink the rest of the night; and as soon as anyone was stirring in the palace, he sent for the gardener, and abused him for his neglect.

"Please your Majesty!" says he, "not another apple you shall lose. My three sons are the best shots at the bow and arrow in the kingdom, and they and myself will watch in turn every night."

When the night came, the gardener's eldest son took his post in the garden, with his bow strung and his arrow between his fingers, and watched, and watched. But at the dead hour, the king, that was wide awake, heard the flapping of wings, and ran to the window. There was the bright bird in the tree, and the boy fast asleep, sitting with his back to the wall, and his bow on his lap.

"Rise, you lazy thief!" says the king, "there's the bird again, botheration to her!"

Up jumped the poor fellow; but while he was fumbling with the arrow and the string, away was the bird with the nicest apple on the tree. Well, to be sure, how the king fumed and fretted, and how he abused the gardener and the boy, and what a twenty-four hours he spent till midnight came again!

He had his eye this time on the second son of the gardener; but though he was up and lively enough when the clock began to strike twelve, it wasn't done with the last bang when he saw him stretched like one dead on the long grass, and saw the bright bird again, and heard the flap of her wings, and saw her carry away the third apple. The poor fellow woke with the roar the king let at him, and even was in time enough to let fly an arrow after the bird. He did not hit her, you may depend; and though the king was mad enough, he saw the poor fellows were under *pishtrogues*, and could not help it.

Well, he had some hopes out of the youngest, for he was a brave, active young fellow, that had everybody's good word. There he was ready, and there was the king watching him, and talking to him at the first stroke of twelve. At the last clang, the brightness coming before the bird lighted up the wall and the trees, and the rushing of the wings was heard as it flew into the branches; but at the same instant the crack of the arrow on her side might be heard a quarter of a mile off. Down came the arrow and a large bright feather along with it, and away was the bird, with a screech that was enough to break the drum of your ear. She hadn't time to carry off an apple; and bedad, when the feather was thrown up into the king's room it was heavier than lead, and turned out to be the finest beaten gold.

Well, there was great *cooramuch* made about the youngest boy next day, and he watched night after night for a week, but not a mite of a bird or bird's feather was to be seen, and then the king told him to go home and sleep. Everyone admired the beauty of the gold feather beyond anything, but the king was fairly bewitched. He was turning it round and round, and rubbing it against his forehead and his nose the live-long day; and at last he proclaimed that he'd give his daughter and half his kingdom to whoever would bring him the bird with the gold feathers, dead or alive.

The gardener's eldest son had great conceit of himself, and away he went to look for the bird. In the afternoon he sat down under a tree to rest himself, and eat a bit of bread and cold meat that he had in his wallet, when up comes as fine a looking fox as you'd see in the burrow of Munfin. "Musha, sir," says he, "would you spare a bit of that meat to a poor body that's hungry?"

"Well," says the other, "you must have the divil's own assurance, you common robber, to ask me such a question. Here's the answer," and he let fly at the *moddhereen rua*.

The arrow scraped from his side up over his back, as if he was made of hammered iron, and stuck in a tree a couple of perches off.

"Foul play," says the fox; "but I respect your young brother, and will give a bit of advice. At nightfall you'll come into a village. One side of the street you'll see a large room lighted up, and filled with young men and women, dancing and drinking. The other side you'll see a house with no light, only from the fire in the front room, and no one near it but a man and his wife, and their child. Take a fool's advice, and get lodging there." With that he curled his tail over his crupper, and trotted off.

The boy found things as the fox said, but *begonies* he chose the dancing and drinking, and there we'll leave him. In a week's time, when they got tired at home waiting for him, the second son said he'd try his fortune, and off he set. He was just as ill-natured and foolish as his brother, and the same thing happened to him. Well, when a week was over, away went the youngest of all, and as sure as the hearth-money, he sat under the same tree, and pulled out his bread and meat, and the same fox came up and saluted him. Well, the young fellow shared his dinner with the *moddhereen*, and he wasn't long beating about the bush, but told the other he knew all about his business.

"I'll help you," says he, "if I find you're biddable. So just at nightfall you'll come into a village.…Goodbye till tomorrow."

It was just as the fox said, but the boy took care not to go near dancer, drinker, fiddler, or piper. He got welcome in the quiet house to supper and bed, and was on his journey next morning before the sun was the height of the trees.

He wasn't gone a quarter of a mile when he saw the fox coming out of a wood that was by the roadside.

"Good morrow, fox," says one.

"Good morrow, sir," says the other.

"Have you any notion how far you have to travel till you find the golden bird?"

"Dickens a notion have I – how could I?"

"Well, I have. She's in the King of Spain's palace, and that's a good two hundred miles off."

"Oh, dear! We'll be a week going."

"No, we won't. Sit down on my tail, and we'll soon make the road short."

"Tail, indeed! That 'ud be the droll saddle, my poor *moddhereen*."

"Do as I tell you, or I'll leave you to yourself."

Well, rather than vex him he sat down on the tail that was spread out level like a wing, and away they went like thought. They overtook the wind that was before them, and the wind that came after didn't overtake them. In the afternoon, they stopped in a wood near the King of Spain's palace, and there they stayed till nightfall.

"Now," says the fox, "I'll go before you to make the minds of the guards easy, and you'll have nothing to do but go from lighted hall to another lighted hall till you find the golden bird in the last. If you have a head on you, you'll bring himself and his cage outside the door, and no one then can lay hands on him or you. If you haven't a head I can't help you, nor no one else." So he went over to the gates.

In a quarter of an hour the boy followed, and in the first hall he passed he saw a score of armed guards standing upright, but all dead asleep. In the next he saw a dozen, and in the next half a dozen, and in the next three, and in the room beyond that there was no guard at all, nor lamp, nor candle, but it was as bright as day; for there was the golden bird in a common wood and wire cage, and on the table were the three apples turned into solid gold.

On the same table was the most lovely golden cage eye ever beheld, and it entered the boy's head that it would be a thousand pities not to put the precious bird into it, the common cage was so unfit for her. Maybe he thought of the money it was worth; anyhow he made the exchange, and he had soon good reason to be sorry for it. The instant the shoulder of the bird's wing touched the golden wires, he let such a squawk out of him as was enough to break all the panes of glass in the windows, and at the same minute the three men, and the half-dozen, and the dozen, and the score men, woke up and clattered their swords and spears, and surrounded the poor boy, and jibed, and cursed, and swore at home, till he didn't know whether it's his foot or head he was standing on. They called the king, and told him what happened, and he put on a very grim face. "It's on a gibbet you ought to be this moment," says he, "but I'll give you a chance of your life, and of the golden bird, too. I lay you under prohibitions, and restrictions, and death, and destruction, to go and bring me the King of Morōco's bay filly that outruns the wind, and leaps over the walls of castle-bawns. When you fetch her into the bawn of this palace, you must get the golden bird, and liberty to go where you please."

Out passed the boy, very down-hearted, but as he went along, who should come out of a brake but the fox again.

"Ah, my friend," says he, "I was right when I suspected you hadn't a head on you; but I won't rub your hair again' the grain. Get on my tail again, and when we come to the King of Morōco's palace, we'll see what we can do."

So away they went like thought. The wind that was before them they would overtake; the wind that was behind them would not overtake them.

Well, the nightfall came on them in a wood near the palace, and says the fox, "I'll go and make things easy for you at the stables, and when you are leading out the filly, don't let her touch the door, nor doorposts, nor anything but the ground, and that with her hoofs; and if you haven't a head on you once you are in the stable, you'll be worse off than before."

So the boy delayed for a quarter of an hour, and then he went into the big bawn of the palace. There were two rows of armed men reaching from the gate to the stable, and every man was in the depth of deep sleep, and through them went the boy till he got into the stable. There was the filly, as handsome a beast as ever stretched leg, and there was one stable-boy with a currycomb in his hand, and another with a bridle, and another with a sieve of oats, and another with an armful of hay, and all as if they were cut out of stone. The filly was the only live thing in the place except himself. She had a common wood and leather saddle on her back, but a golden saddle with the nicest work on it was hung from the post, and he thought it the greatest pity not to put it in place of the other. Well, I believe there was some *pishrogues* over it for a saddle; anyhow, he took off the other, and put the gold one in its place.

Out came a squeal from the filly's throat when she felt the strange article, that might be heard from Tombrick to Bunclody, and all as ready were the armed men and the stable-boys to run and surround the *omadhan* of a boy, and the King of Morōco was soon there along with the rest, with a face on him as black as the sole of your foot. After he stood enjoying the abuse the poor boy got from everybody for some time, he says to him, "You deserve high hanging for your impudence, but I'll give you a chance for your life and the filly, too. I lay on you all sorts of prohibitions, and restrictions, and death, and destruction to go bring me Princess Golden Locks, the King of Greek's daughter. When you deliver her into my hand, you may have the 'daughter of the wind', and welcome. Come in and take your supper and your rest, and be off at the flight of night."

The poor boy was down in the mouth, you may suppose, as he was walking away next morning, and very much ashamed when the fox looked up in his face after coming out of the wood.

"What a thing it is," says he, "not to have a head when a body wants it worst; and here we have a fine long journey before us to the King of Greek's palace. The worse luck now, the same always. Here, get on my tail, and we'll be making the road shorter."

So he sat on the fox's tail, and swift as thought they went. The wind that was before them they would overtake it, the wind that was behind them would not overtake them, and in the evening they were eating their bread and cold meat in the wood near the castle.

"Now," says the fox, when they were done, "I'll go before you to make things easy. Follow me in a quarter of an hour. Don't let Princess Golden Locks touch the jambs of the doors with her hands, or hair, or clothes, and if you're asked any favour, mind how you answer. Once she's outside the door, no one can take her from you."

Into the palace walked the boy at the proper time, and there were the score, and the dozen, and the half-dozen, and the three guards all standing up or leaning on their arms, and all dead asleep, and in the farthest room of all was the Princess Golden Locks, as lovely as Venus herself. She was asleep in one chair, and her father, the King of Greek, in another. He stood before her for ever so long with the love sinking deeper into his heart every minute, till at last he went down on one knee, and took her darling white hand in his hand, and kissed it.

When she opened her eyes, she was a little frightened, but I believe not very angry, for the boy, as I call him, was a fine handsome young fellow, and all the respect and love that ever you could think of was in his face. She asked him what he wanted, and he stammered, and blushed, and began his story six times, before she understood it.

"And would you give me up to that ugly black King of Morōco?" says she.

"I am obliged to do so," says he, "by prohibitions, and restrictions, and death, and destruction, but I'll have his life and free you, or lose my own. If I can't get you for my wife, my days on the earth will be short."

"Well," says she, "let me take leave of my father at any rate."

"Ah, I can't do that," says he, "or they'd all waken, and myself would be put to death, or sent to some task worse than any I got yet."

But she asked leave at any rate to kiss the old man; that wouldn't waken him, and then she'd go. How could he refuse her, and his heart tied up in every curl of her hair? But, bedad, the moment her lips touched her father's, he let a cry, and every one of the score, the dozen guards woke up, and clashed their arms, and were going to make *gibbets* of the foolish boy.

But the king ordered them to hold their hands, till he'd be *insensed* of what it was all about, and when he heard the boy's story he gave him a chance for his life.

"There is," says he, "a great heap of clay in front of the palace, that won't let the sun shine on the walls in the middle of summer. Everyone that ever worked at it found two shovelfuls added to it for every one they threw away. Remove it, and I'll let my daughter go with you. If you're the man I suspect you to be, I think she'll be in no danger of being wife to that yellow *Molott*."

Early next morning was the boy tackled to his work, and for every shovelful he flung away two came back on him, and at last he could hardly get out of the heap that gathered round him. Well, the poor fellow scrambled out some way, and sat down on a sod, and he'd have cried only for the shame of it. He began at it in ever so many places, and one was still worse than the other, and in the heel of the evening, when he was sitting with his head between his hands, who should be standing before him but the fox.

"Well, my poor fellow," says he, "you're low enough. Go in: I won't say anything to add to your trouble. Take your supper and your rest: tomorrow will be a new day."

"How is the work going off?" says the king, when they were at supper.

"Faith, your Majesty," says the poor boy, "it's not going off, but coming on it is. I suppose you'll have the trouble of digging me out at sunset tomorrow, and waking me."

"I hope not," says the princess, with a smile on her kind face; and the boy was as happy as anything the rest of the evening.

He was wakened up next morning with voices shouting, and bugles blowing, and drums beating, and such a hullibulloo he never heard in his life before. He ran out to see what was the matter, and there, where the heap of clay was the evening before, were soldiers, and servants, and lords, and ladies, dancing like mad for joy that it was gone.

"Ah, my poor fox!" says he to himself, "this is your work."

Well, there was little delay about his return. The king was going to send a great retinue with the princess and himself, but he wouldn't let him take the trouble.

"I have a friend," says he, "that will bring us both to the King of Morōco's palace in a day, d— fly away with him!"

There was great crying when she was parting from her father.

"Ah!" says he, "what a lonesome life I'll have now! Your poor brother in the power of that wicked witch, and kept away from us, and now you taken from me in my old age!"

Well, they both were walking on through the wood, and he telling her how much he loved her; out walked the fox from behind a brake, and in a short time he and she were sitting on the brush, and holding one another fast for fear of slipping off, and away they went like thought. The wind that was before them they would overtake it, and in the evening he and she were in the big bawn of the King of Morōco's castle.

"Well," says he to the boy, "you've done your duty well; bring out the bay filly. I'd give the full of the bawn of such fillies, if I had them, for this handsome princess. Get on your steed, and here is a good purse of guineas for the road."

"Thank you," says he. "I suppose you'll let me shake hands with the princess before I start."

"Yes, indeed, and welcome."

Well, he was some little time about the hand-shaking, and before it was over he had her fixed snug behind him; and while you could count three, he, and she, and the filly were through all the guards, and a hundred perches away. On they went, and next morning they were in the wood near the King of Spain's palace, and there was the fox before them.

"Leave your princess here with me," says he, "and go get the golden bird and the three apples. If you don't bring us back the filly along with the bird, I must carry you both home myself."

Well, when the King of Spain saw the boy and the filly in the bawn, he made the golden bird, and the golden cage, and the golden apples be brought out and handed to him, and was very thankful and very glad of his prize. But the boy could not part with the nice beast without petting it and rubbing it; and while no one was expecting such a thing, he was up on its back, and through the guards, and a hundred perches away, and he wasn't long till he came to where he left his princess and the fox.

They hurried away till they were safe out of the King of Spain's land, and then they went on easier; and if I was to tell you all the loving things they said to one another, the story wouldn't be over till morning. When they were passing the village of the dance house, they found his two brothers begging, and they brought them along. When they came to where the fox appeared first, he begged the young man to cut off his head and his tail. He would not do it for him; he shivered at the very thought, but the eldest brother was ready enough. The head and tail vanished with the blows, and the body changed into the finest young man you could see, and who was he but the princess's brother that was bewitched. Whatever joy they had before, they had twice as much now, and when they arrived at the palace bonfires were set blazing, oxes roasting, and puncheons of wine put out in the lawn. The young Prince of Greece was married to the king's daughter, and the prince's sister to the gardener's son. He and she went a shorter way back to her father's house, with many attendants, and the king was so glad of the golden bird and the golden apples, that he had sent a waggon full of gold and a waggon full of silver along with them.

The Feather of the Zhar Bird

THERE WERE ONCE A MAN AND HIS WIFE who had one son named Tremsin, and they were all poor together, as poor as could be.

One day the man said to Tremsin, "Listen, my son. We have but enough meal left in the house for thy mother and myself, and we can shelter thee here no longer. Take the grey steed that stands in the stall and ride out into the world to seek thy fortune, and my blessing shall go with thee."

So Tremsin took the grey steed from the stall and mounted it, and rode out into the green world, seeking his fortune, and his father's blessing went with him.

He rode along and rode along, and afterwhile he came to the wide steppes. He heard a rushing of wings overhead, and a light shone about him, and when he looked up he saw a great bird crossing the heavens. It was pure white and shone like silver, and it flew over him as swift as the wind.

"Now in all the green earth never did I see such a bird before," said Tremsin. "I wonder what it may be."

"Master," said the grey steed, "that is the Zhar bird. Presently we will find one of its feathers lying beside our road; but whatever you do, master, do not pick it up, for if you do, evil as well as good will come upon you."

Tremsin made no answer, but he rode along and rode along, and presently he saw something bright lying beside the road. He came up to it and it was a feather. It was as white as silver, and so bright that no words can tell how it shone.

"Good or ill, that feather I must have," said Tremsin; so in spite of the good steed's warning he picked it up and laid it in his bosom.

After a while they came to a great city and in this city lived a nobleman. He was a very rich nobleman, and very powerful.

Tremsin rode to his house and asked if he might take service with him.

The nobleman looked at him up and down and saw that he was a good stout lad. "Why not?" said he. "I have need of servants to curry my horses, for I have more than fifty in my stalls."

So Tremsin was set to work in the stables, and the nobleman's own favourite steed was given him to take care of. Every day Tremsin curried it and rubbed it down, and after he had rubbed it its coat shone like glass. There never was anything like it. The nobleman was very much pleased, and made such a favourite of Tremsin that all his fellow servants grew jealous. They rubbed and curried their steeds, but they could not make them shine as Tremsin did. Then they set a little stable boy to watch Tremsin and see what he did to make the horse's coat so bright.

The stable boy hid in the manger, and after a while Tremsin came in and began to clean the horse. He rubbed it and curried it, but he did that no better than the other grooms. Lastly he looked about him, and seeing nobody, he drew from his breast the feather of the Zhar bird and stroked the horse with it. Immediately the steed shone like silver, so that all the stall was filled with light. Then he hid the feather in his bosom again, and led the horse out for the nobleman to ride him.

The little stable boy climbed out of the manger, and ran and told the other servants what he had seen, and as soon as they heard about the feather they knew it must be a feather of the Zhar bird. Then they were more envious than ever, and they laid a plot to rid themselves of Tremsin.

They went to the nobleman, and said to him, "Tremsin has a feather of the Zhar bird, and it is so bright that there never was anything like it. Moreover, he boasts that if he chose he could go out and catch the Zhar bird as easily as not, and bring it to you for a present."

The nobleman sent for Tremsin, and said him, "Your fellow servants tell me you have boasted thus and so. Now go you out and get the Zhar bird for me, for I can neither eat nor sleep until I have it."

It was in vain Tremsin swore and protested that never had he said such a thing. He must go and get the Zhar bird for the nobleman, or have his head cut off from his shoulders.

Tremsin went out to the stall where the grey steed stood and wept bitterly. "Yours was a wise warning, my good steed," he said. "Good came to me from the Zhar bird's feather, but now evil has come of it, and such evil that I must lose my head for it."

"How is that, my master?" asked the steed.

Then Tremsin told him all that the nobleman had said, and that as he could by no means bring the Zhar bird to his master he must surely die.

"There is no need to grieve over such a task as that," said the steed. "That is an easy trick. Do you get a strong net and ride me out to the steppe where we first saw the bird. There I will stretch myself out as though I were dead, and you must hide yourself beside me. Presently the Zhar bird will come and light upon me. Do not stir nor touch it until it hops upon my head and is about to peck my eyes. Then throw the net over it and you will have it safe."

Tremsin did as the grey steed bade him. He bought a great strong net and then he rode out to the place he had first seen the Zhar bird. There on the lonely steppes the steed laid himself out as though he were dead, and Tremsin hid beside him.

Presently there was a great rushing of wings overhead, and a white light shone and here came the Zhar bird.

He flew down and lighted on the grey steed's flank but Tremsin did not move. He lighted on the shoulder, but Tremsin never stirred. Lastly he went to the grey steed's head and stooped to peck his eyes. Then, quick as a flash, Tremsin threw the net over the bird, and there he had it safe, struggle as it might.

If Tremsin had been a favourite before it was nothing to the way it was now. The other servants were so jealous that they could hardly bear it. They got together and laid another plot to rid themselves of him. They went to the nobleman and told him: "Tremsin boasts that it was nothing to bring you the Zhar bird as a gift; that if he wished he could bring you the thrice-lovely Nastasia of the sea for a bride just as easily as not."

Now the thrice-lovely Nastasia was the most beautiful woman in the world, so that nobody could equal her, and after the nobleman had heard what they had to say he sent for Tremsin to come to him.

"Tremsin," he said, "I hear that you have boasted that if you wish you can bring me the thrice-lovely Nastasia of the sea for a bride. Go now and bring her to me, for if you do not, as surely as my sword hangs by my side, your head shall leave your shoulders."

It was in vain that Tremsin begged and protested, the nobleman would not listen to him and he went out to the grey steed's stall and wept bitterly.

"Why are you so sad, my master?" asked the grey steed.

"I am sad because of the evil the Zhar bird's feather has brought upon me. The nobleman has bidden me bring him the thrice-lovely Nastasia for a bride, and as I cannot do it I must die."

"Do not be troubled over that task," said the grey steed. "There are harder things than that in the world, and if you do as I say all may yet be well."

The steed then told Tremsin to go into the town and get for himself a snow-white tent, and all manner of silken scarfs and gold and silver ornaments. He was to purchase besides a golden pitcher of rare wine and a sleeping potion.

"When you have all these things," said the steed, "take them down to the seashore and spread the tent, and arrange in it all the things you have bought as though you were a merchant. Put the sleeping potion in the golden pitcher of wine, and do you lie down beside the tent as though you were asleep, and whatever you do, do not stir nor open your eyes until I neigh thrice."

Tremsin did all that the steed bade him; he bought the tent and the wares, the golden pitcher of wine and the sleeping potion, and carried them down to the seashore. He arranged them as a merchant would his wares. He put the sleeping potion in the wine, and then he lay down and pretended to be asleep.

After a while the thrice-lovely Nastasia came sailing past in her rose-red boat. She saw the shining white tent and landed to see what was in it. When she came to the door of it she saw all the silken scarfs and the gold and silver ornaments, and lying by the tent apparently fast asleep was a handsome youth, with a grey steed standing beside him.

"Merchant, merchant, waken and show me your wares," said the thrice-lovely Nastasia; but Tremsin did not stir.

"Up, merchant, for I have come to purchase of you."

Tremsin kept his eyes closed and only breathed the deeper.

Then Nastasia began to go about through the tent and look at the things. She slipped the bracelets on her arms, the rings upon her fingers, she wrapped the silken scarfs about her, and presently she found the golden pitcher of wine. She lifted it in her hands and tasted it. Then she drank deep of it and presently there was none left. Almost immediately she sank down in a deep sleep.

Then the grey steed neighed three times. "Up, up, my master," he cried. "Yonder lies the thrice-lovely Nastasia. Take her up in your arms and mount upon my back, and we will carry her to the house of the nobleman before she wakens."

Then Tremsin lifted her in his arms and mounted his steed, and away they went, swift as the wind, so that Nastasia's hair flew out behind them like a cloak.

After a while they came to the palace of the nobleman, and when he saw that Tremsin had brought him the thrice-lovely Nastasia for a bride he could not do enough for him. There was nothing Tremsin could ask of his master that he might not have had.

But the thrice-lovely Nastasia sat in her chamber and wept and wept. "Never will I marry any man," she cried, "until he can bring me my shining necklace of pearls that I left at the bottom of the sea."

Then the nobleman called Tremsin to him again. "Tremsin," he said, "you must still do something more for me. You have brought me the thrice-lovely Nastasia of the sea, but you left her necklace of shining pearls behind. Go and get it for me, or by the sword that hangs at my side, you shall surely die."

Tremsin went out to the stall of the grey steed and wept bitterly. "Surely the evil that comes to me will never end. I caught the Zhar bird in a net, the thrice-lovely Nastasia I brought my master for a bride and now I must bring the necklace of pearls from the bottom of the sea or I will lose my head from my shoulders."

"Master, do not let that grieve you," said the grey steed. "Do as I bid you and you may get the necklace. Go down to the seashore and hide yourself behind the rocks close to where the tent was spread. Presently you will see some crabs crawl up out of the water. Do not stir nor touch them until one comes larger than the rest and wearing a golden crown upon his head. He is the king of them all. Throw your cap over him. Hold it tight and do not let him go until he promises to bring you the pearl necklace of the thrice-lovely Nastasia from the bottom of the sea."

Tremsin was quick to do as the steed bade him. He went down to the seashore and hid behind some rocks. There he lay quiet; he hardly breathed.

Presently the crabs began to crawl up out of the water. They came one after another. Tremsin had never seen so many. Last of all came a crab larger than any of the rest, and on his head he wore a golden crown. Tremsin waited until this one came close by the rocks, and then, quick as a flash he threw his cap over it, and held it tight.

The crab struggled but it could not get free.

"Let me go, Tremsin," it cried, "and I will bring you such treasures that you will be a rich man forever."

"I will not let you go," said Tremsin, "until you promise to bring me the pearl necklace of the thrice-lovely Nastasia from the bottom of the sea."

Well, the crab did not want to promise, but there was nothing else for it. He had to say he would do it, and then Tremsin lifted his cap and let him go.

The crab sidled off and disappeared in the water and he was gone three hours. When he came back he held the necklace in his claws.

Tremsin took the necklace and thanked him, and hurried away to the palace of the nobleman.

When his master saw that he had brought the pearl necklace he could not do enough to show his gratitude.

But the thrice-lovely Nastasia sat in her chamber, and would do nothing but weep and weep.

"I will never marry any man," she said, "until I can ride to the church on my own fierce wild charger of the sea."

Well, there was nothing else for it; the nobleman sent for Tremsin again. "This one more thing you must do for me," he said. "You must bring me the thrice-lovely Nastasia's wild fierce charger from the sea. Bring me that and I will make you rich for all your life, but fail and your head shall surely be parted from your shoulders."

Out went Tremsin to the grey steed's stall.

"This is the last," he said. "If I can do thus and so I will be a rich man for life, but if I cannot I must surely die."

"Master," said the grey steed, "this is the hardest task that has been set you yet. Whether we can bring that fierce, wild charger from the sea I do not know. We can but try, but there is great danger in it."

Then the grey steed bade Tremsin go to the town and buy twenty hides, twenty poods of tar and twenty poods of horse-hair. "Load them upon my back," he said, "and drive me down to the seashore."

Tremsin went to the town and bought the twenty hides; he bought the twenty poods of tar and the twenty poods of horse-hair. He loaded them on the grey horse and drove him down to the sea.

"Master," said the grey steed, "do now exactly as I bid you, for if you do not I will surely perish. First of all, lay one of the hides upon me and bind it so it will not possibly come off. Over this spread a pood of tar, and fasten upon it another hide. Then another pood of tar and another hide, and so on until all have been used. Then I will plunge into the ocean, and as soon as the fierce strong charger of the thrice-lovely Nastasia sees me he will come at me and try to tear me to pieces, but if all goes well the hides will protect me. I will swim to the shore and he will follow me, and as soon as he comes out from the water do you be standing ready and strike him upon the head with the twenty poods of horse-hair. Immediately he will become so gentle that you may easily mount and ride him, but if you fail in anyone of these things I will be torn to pieces, and you with me."

Tremsin promised to obey the grey steed in everything. He fastened the hides upon the horse's back with the tar, just as he had been directed to do, and when it was all finished the grey steed plunged into the sea. Tremsin stood at the edge of the shore holding the twenty poods of horse-hair ready in his hands.

Presently all the surface of the sea became disturbed. It was churned into foam; great waves arose. There was a sound of neighing, and Tremsin knew the grey steed and the fierce wild charger of Nastasia were fighting terribly. The wild charger would soon have torn the grey steed to pieces, but he could not get at him on account of the hides.

Presently the horse of Tremsin swam to the shore, and it was so exhausted it could hardly drag itself from the water. The fierce wild charger was close after it, still biting and tearing, and it had torn all the hides from the grey steed but one. But Tremsin was ready. He swung the twenty poods of horse-hair on high and struck the charger with it.

Immediately the charger became perfectly gentle and quiet. It stood trembling, and the sweat poured from its sides like water. Tremsin mounted on its back and rode away to the house of the nobleman, and it was so gentle that he had no need of either bit or bridle.

When the nobleman saw him coming on the charger he was so delighted that he called him brother, and said that the half of all he had should be his.

Now the thrice-lovely Nastasia could find no excuse for putting off her marriage with the nobleman. He had restored to her her pearl necklace; her fierce wild charger had been brought to her from the sea. One last request she made, however, and then she would marry him.

"Have filled, I pray you," she said, "three large vats. Let the first be filled with cold milk, the second with warm milk, and the third with milk that is boiling hot."

The nobleman could refuse her nothing, so he had the vats prepared as she wished, the first with cold milk, the second with warm, the third with milk that was boiling.

When all was ready the thrice-lovely Nastasia stepped into the first vat, and when she came out she had changed to an old, old woman. She stepped into the second vat, and she became a blooming young girl. She stepped into the third vat, and when she came out from that she was the most beautiful woman that ever was seen. She shone like the moon, and all the people could look at no one else.

When Tremsin saw that, he too stepped into the first vat, and came out an old man. He stepped into the second vat and became young again. He stepped into the third vat and when he came out from that he was the handsomest youth in all the world. There never was anything like it, he was so handsome.

But the nobleman was filled with envy and jealousy, and he too wished to become the handsomest man in all the world. However, he was not willing to step into the first vat, for he did not wish to become an old man; he saw no reason for stepping into the second vat, for he was already young. He sprang straight into the third vat, and immediately the boiling milk scalded him to death, and he never came out again.

But Tremsin married the thrice-lovely Nastasia of the sea, and they were the handsomest couple that ever were seen, so that people have not done talking of them even yet.

The Eagles

THERE WAS ONCE A KING who had lost his wife. They had a family of thirteen – twelve gallant sons, and one daughter, who was exquisitely beautiful.

For twelve years after his wife's death the king grieved very much; he used to go daily to her tomb, and there weep, and pray, and give away alms to the poor. He thought never to marry again; for he had promised his dying wife never to give her children a stepmother.

One day, when visiting his dead wife's grave as usual, he saw beside him a maiden so entrancingly fair, that he fell in love with her, and soon made her his second queen. But before long he found out that he had made a great mistake. Though she was so beautiful she turned out to be a wicked sorceress, and not only made the king himself unhappy, but proved most unkind to his children, whom she wished out of the way, so that her own little son might inherit the kingdom.

One day, when the king was far away, at war against his enemies, the queen went into her stepchildren's apartments, and pronounced some magical words – on which every one of the twelve princes flew away in the shape of an eagle, and the princess was changed into a dove.

The queen looked out of the window, to see in what direction they would fly, when she saw right under the window an old man, with a beard as white as snow.

"What are you here for, old man?" she asked.

"To be witness of your deed," he answered.

"Then you saw it?"

"I saw it."

"Then be what I command!"

She whispered some magical words. The old man disappeared in a blaze of sunshine; and the queen, as she stood there, dumb with terror, was changed into a basilisk.

The basilisk ran off in fright; trying to hide herself underground. But her glance was so deadly, that it killed everyone she looked at, so that all the people in the palace were soon dead, including her own son, whom she slew by merely looking at him. And this once populous and happy royal residence quickly became an uninhabited ruin, which no one dared approach, for fear of the basilisk lurking in its underground vaults.

Meanwhile the princess, who had been changed into a dove, flew after her brothers the eagles, but not being able to overtake them, she rested under a wayside cross, and began cooing mournfully.

"What are you grieving for, pretty dove?" asked an old man, with a snow-white beard, who just then came by.

"I am grieving for my poor dear father, who is fighting in the wars far away; for my loved brothers, who have flown away from me into the clouds. I am grieving also for myself. Not long ago I was a happy princess; and now I must wander over the world as a dove, to hide from the birds of prey – and be parted for ever from my dear father and brothers!"

"You may grieve and weep, little dove; but do not lose hope," said the old man. "Sorrow is only for a time, and all will come right in the end."

So saying he stroked the little dove, and she at once regained her natural shape. She kissed the old man's hand in her gratitude, saying:

"How can I ever thank you enough! But since you are so kind, will you not tell me how to rescue my brothers?"

The old man gave her an ever-growing loaf, and said:

"This loaf is enough to sustain, not only you, but a thousand people for a thousand years, without ever diminishing. Go towards the sunset, and weep your tears into this little bottle. And when it is full…"

And the old man told her what else to do, blessed her, and disappeared.

The princess travelled on towards the sunset; and in about a year she reached the boundary of the next world, and stood before an iron door, where Death was keeping guard with his scythe.

"Stop, princess!" he said; "You can proceed no further, for you are not yet parted by death from your own world."

"But what am I to do?" she asked. "Must I go back without my poor brothers?"

"Your brothers," said Death, "fly here every day in the guise of eagles. They want to reach the other side of this door, which leads into the other world; for they hate the one they live in; nevertheless they, and you also, must remain there, until your time be come. Therefore every day I must compel them to go back, which they can do, because they are eagles. But how are you going to get back yourself? – Look there!"

The princess looked around her, and wept bitterly. For though she had not perceived this before, nor seen how she got there, she saw now that she was in a deep abyss, shut in on all sides by such high precipices, that she wondered how her brothers, even with eagle wings, could fly to the top.

But remembering what the mysterious old man had said she took courage, and began to pray and weep, till she had filled the little bottle with her tears. Soon she heard the sound of wings over her head, and saw twelve eagles flying.

The eagles dashed themselves against the iron portal, beating their wings upon it, and imploring Death to open it to them. But Death only threatened them with his scythe, saying:

"Hence! Ye enchanted princes! You must fulfil your penance on earth, till I come for you myself."

The eagles were about to turn and fly, when all at once they perceived their sister. They came round her, and caressed her hands lovingly with their beaks.

She at once began to sprinkle them with her tears from the lachrymatory; and in one moment the twelve eagles were changed back into the twelve princes, and joyfully embraced their sister.

The princess then fed them all round from her ever-growing loaf; but when their hunger was appeased they began to be troubled as to how they were to ascend from the abyss, since they had no longer eagles' wings to fly up.

But the princess knelt down and prayed:

"Bird of heavenly pity here,
By each labour, prayer and tear,
Come in thine unvanquished power,
Come and aid us in this hour!"

And all at once there shot down from heaven to the depth of the abyss a ray of sunshine, on which descended a gigantic bird, with rainbow wings, a bright sparkling crest, and peacock's eyes all over his body, a golden tail, and silvery breast.

"What are your commands, princess?" asked the bird.

"Carry us from this threshold of eternity to our own world."

"I will, but you must know, princess, that before I can reach the top of this precipice with you on my back, three days and nights must pass; and I must have food on the way, or my strength will fail me, and I shall fall down with you to the bottom, and we shall all perish."

"I have an ever-growing loaf, which will suffice both for you and ourselves," replied the princess.

"Then climb upon my back, and whenever I look round, give me some bread to eat."

The bird was so large that all the princes, and the princess in the midst of them, could easily find place on his back, and he began to fly upwards.

He flew higher and higher, and whenever he looked round at her, she gave him bits of the loaf, and he flew on, and upwards.

So they went on steadily for two nights and days; but upon the third day, when they were hoping in a short time to view the summit of the precipice, and to land upon the borders of this world, the bird looked round as usual for a piece of the loaf.

The princess was just going to break off some to give him, when a sudden violent gust of wind from the bottom of the abyss snatched the loaf from her hand, and sent it whistling downwards.

Not having received his usual meal the bird became sensibly weaker, and looked round once more.

The princess trembled with fear; she had nothing more to give him, and she felt that he was becoming exhausted. In utter desperation she cut off a piece of her flesh, and gave it to him.

Having eaten this the bird recovered strength, and flew upwards faster than before; but after an hour or two he looked round once more.

So she cut off another piece of her flesh; the bird seized it greedily, and flew on so fast that in a few minutes he reached the ground at the top of the precipice. When they alighted, and he asked her:

"Princess, what were those two delicious morsels you gave me last? I never ate anything so good before."

"They were part of my flesh, I had nothing else for you," replied the princess in a faint voice, for she was swooning away with pain and loss of blood.

The bird breathed upon her wounds; and the flesh at once healed over, and grew again as before. Then he flew up again to heaven, and was lost in the clouds.

The princess and her brothers resumed their journey, this time towards the sunrise, and at last arrived in their own country, where they met their father, returning from the wars.

The king was coming back victorious over his enemies, and on his way home had first heard of the sudden disappearance of his children and of the queen, and how his palace was tenanted only by a basilisk with a death-dealing glance.

He was therefore most surprised and overjoyed to meet his dear children once more, and on the way his daughter told him all that had come to pass.

When they got back to the palace the king sent one of his nobles with a looking-glass down into the underground vaults. The basilisk saw herself reflected in this mirror, and her own glance slew her immediately.

They gathered up the remains of the basilisk, and burnt them in a great fire in the courtyard, afterwards scattering the ashes to the four winds. When this was done the king, his sons, and his daughter, returned to live in their former home and were all as happy as could be ever after.

The Princes and the Friendly Animals

THERE WAS ONCE A KING WHO HAD THREE SONS, and he had also a stepdaughter. They all lived together in peace and happiness and had everything their hearts could desire. But after a time an enemy of the King came against him with a great army, and slew him, and took the kingdom and drove forth the Princes into the world, and their stepsister with them.

The three and the one journeyed on and on together until they came to a deep forest, and there they saw a mother bear, and her three cubs were with her.

The eldest Prince was about to shoot at her, but the bear cried out, "Do not shoot, Prince, and I will give you my three cubs for servants, one for you, and one for each of your brothers."

To this the Prince agreed. He let the bear go away unharmed, and the three cubs followed after the three Princes, each one behind his own master.

After they had gone a bit farther into the forest, they saw a lioness, and she also had three young ones with her.

Now it was the second Prince who was about to shoot, but the lioness called to him, "Do not slay me, Prince, and I will give my three cubs to you and your brothers, one to each of you."

Thereupon the Prince allowed her to go unharmed and the three young lions followed after the Princes with the bear cubs.

Soon after that they saw a mother fox, and three little ones were with her. This time it was the youngest Prince who would have shot, but the fox called to him, imploring him to spare her life and offering instead her three young ones to the Princes.

She too was allowed to escape, and now each Prince had a young fox, a young lion and a young bear to follow him.

After that the Princes met a hare and a boar, and these animals were also allowed to go unharmed because they each gave a young one to each one of the Princes to follow after and serve him.

And now the Princes came to a place where the road divided.

"I," said the youngest, "shall take the road toward the East, where the sun rises each morning."

"And I," said the second, "shall journey toward the West, where it is golden at sunset."

But the eldest Prince would take neither of these roads. "My way shall be neither toward the East nor toward the West," said he, "but straight ahead, and when I come to a place to dwell in, there will I stop."

The three brothers then asked their stepsister which of them she would follow, and she said she would go with the eldest Prince, for she too wished nothing better than a place to dwell in, where she could live in peace and safety.

So the three brothers parted, but first the eldest Prince cut three notches in a tree that stood at the parting of the ways. He cut one at the East, and one at the West, and one in the centre between them, one for each of his brothers, and one for himself.

He told them the notch to the East was for the youngest brother, the notch to the West was for the second brother, and the one in the centre belonged to himself.

"When any one of us returns to this spot," said he, "let him place his finger first upon one notch, and then upon the other. If milk flows forth from the notch, then all is well with the one to whom it belongs, but if blood flows forth, then it means death or misfortune to that one."

After that they bade each other farewell and set forth, each on his own way, and each with his animals following after him, and the stepsister went with the eldest brother, as she had chosen.

For a long time the eldest Prince and his sister journeyed on without seeing anyone, but toward evening they came to a house and there was a red light shining out from the window. When they looked inside they saw a band of robbers sitting there, counting the gold they had taken from the people they had killed.

The stepsister was so frightened that her teeth chattered in her head, and she was for going farther, but the Prince said no. "Hither we have come, and here we shall stop," said he.

Then he called his animals to him and threw open the door of the house.

When the robbers saw him, they started up and seized their weapons to slay him, but they had no time, for the faithful animals flew at them and tore them almost to pieces, so that they were dead, all except one; and he lay there with the others as though he had been killed also.

Then the Prince threw them down into the cellar and locked the door, and he and his stepsister got out food and drink and feasted to their hearts' content, and the animals feasted also.

The next morning the Prince went out hunting and he told his stepsister she might go all over the house and look at everything in it; only into the cellar she must not look, for there the robbers were lying, and that door must remain fastened.

After he had gone, the girl went about through the house and looked at everything. After she had seen all there was to be seen in the house, she began to think about the cellar, and more and more she wished to open the door and look at the robbers lying there.

At last she could resist no longer. She unfastened the door and looked down into the cellar. As soon as she did so, the robber who was only wounded lifted his head and spoke to her.

The girl was terribly frightened, and was for shutting the door at once, but the robber called to her so piteously that she could but stay and listen to him.

"Do not fear me," cried the robber. "Even if I desired it, I am too weak to harm you, but I wish you only good."

The robber then told her that if she would do as he said, he would soon be well and strong again. Then they would rid themselves of her brother and would be married, and the house and all the wealth that had been gathered would belong to their own two selves alone, and they would be very happy together.

The girl listened; and the longer she listened, the more the plan of the robber pleased her. She asked him what she must do to heal him.

"You must go into the kitchen and look in the cupboard," said the robber. "There you will find three flasks. Make haste and bring them here. In the first is an ointment. Rub it upon my wounds, and at once they will heal themselves. Hold the second flask to my lips, and all pain will leave me. Give me to drink from the third, and I will be perfectly well again and stronger than ever."

The girl did as the robber told her, and all happened as he had said. Then, after his wounds were healed and he was well again, he and the girl consulted as to how they could get rid of her brother.

"This is how it can be managed," said the robber. "You shall ask your brother how strong he is, and then, as a test of his strength you shall say you will tie his thumbs behind him with a cord, and he shall try if he can break it. If he cannot break it, then he will be helpless, and you must call to me, and I will come and slay him."

This plan pleased the girl, and at once she agreed to it.

That evening, when her brother came home, they sat at the table and ate and drank together, but the animals were left outside in the courtyard with the door locked and barred against them.

After supper, the stepsister began to talk to her brother and to question him as to how strong he was.

"I am so strong," replied the Prince, "that there are few bonds that could hold me."

"Suppose, I were to tie your thumbs together behind your back with a silken cord, could you break it?" asked the sister.

The Prince bade her try, and he put his hands behind him, and she tied his thumbs together with a silken cord the robber had given her. But no sooner did the Prince strain with his thumbs against the cord than it snapped in two and dropped from him.

"Sister, you must bind me with something stouter than the cord if you would hold me," said the brother.

The next day the Prince went hunting again, and as soon as he had gone, the girl went down to the cellar to talk to the robber. "You must give me something stronger than that to bind him with," said the stepsister. "He broke the cord as though it were no more than a spider's web."

The robber gave her a cord twice as strong.

"Now see if that will hold him," said he.

When the Prince came home that evening and he and the girl sat together at supper, she again began to talk of his strength.

"Here is a cord that is twice as strong as the other. If I tied your thumbs together behind your back, could you break this also?" she asked of him.

The brother told her to try. She tied his thumbs together as before with the second cord the robber had given her, but he snapped this also in two the moment he strained against it.

"Sister, you will need a stronger cord than that if you would hold me," said he.

The next day, as soon as the brother had left the house, the stepsister hastened down to talk again with the robber.

"It is of no use," said she. "He snaps the cords as easily as though there were nothing to them. Tonight I will tie his thumbs together with my girdle, and if he can break that, as he did the cords, then there is nothing that will hold him."

To this the robber agreed, so the next day, when the Prince came home, the girl asked him to let her once more tie his thumbs behind his back. "And this time," said she, "I will tie them with my girdle."

The lad put his hands behind him and the girl tied the thumbs together with her girdle. And now, though the Prince strained against it with all his power, he could not break it.

"Sister," said he, laughing. "You will have to untie it, for now indeed I am held prisoner."

"Then it is as I would have it," cried the girl, and she threw open the cellar door and called to the robber to come forth and slay him.

No sooner did the Prince see the robber than he knew the trick that had been played against him.

"I am indeed helpless," said he, "and if I must die, I must. But one little favour I would ask of you before I perish. Give me leave to blow three blasts upon my hunting-horn, and I will ask nothing else of you."

That seemed a harmless favour for the Prince to ask, and neither the robber nor the girl refused him. Still they would not untie the girdle. The stepsister held the horn to his mouth, and the Prince blew upon it so strong and loud that the girl and the robber were like to have been deafened by it. Three times he blew. The first blast woke the animals where they lay sleeping, and they raised their heads and listened. At the second blast they aroused themselves and gathered at the door of the house; and at the third blast they threw themselves against the door so that locks and bars were broken, and the wood itself was splintered. Then in a moment they rushed into the room and sprang upon the robber and tore him into shreds.

They would have torn the stepsister to pieces, too, but this the Prince would not permit. "I will not kill you," said he to the girl, "but you shall be punished."

He then took a chain and fastened it around her waist and to a staple in the wall. He placed food and drink within reach and an empty bowl before her. "When you have filled this bowl full of tears of repentance, the chain will drop from you," he said, "and you will be free; but until that time you shall remain a prisoner."

He then went away and left her, and the animals followed at his heels.

He went on and on until he came to another country, and there he stopped at an inn for food and rest. But there was little feasting at the inn, or resting either. Everyone was weeping and lamenting. The food had burned on the fire, and the malt had all run out of the barrels and was wasted.

The Prince called to the landlord and asked him the cause of all this sorrow.

"A sad and grievous cause, indeed," replied the landlord. "This day the King's daughter is to be sacrificed to a mighty dragon that is to come up out of the water. She must be left on the seashore over beyond the cliffs you see yonder, for him to devour her; and unless this is done, the dragon will ravage the whole country."

"But is there no one strong enough and brave enough to destroy this dragon?" asked the Prince.

"There is no one. Many have come hither to try it, for the King has promised that if anyone will do battle with the dragon and destroy him, he shall have the hand of the Princess in marriage, and she is so beautiful, that any man might well risk death to gain her. But everyeone who has seen the dragon as he lies out in the sea has been so filled with terror that he has fled away. Not one has stayed even to look upon him twice."

When the Prince heard this he made up his mind that he would at least have a look at the dragon, so he asked the landlord how he must go to reach the place where the monster lay. As soon as he had been told, off he set in that direction, and the animals were not far behind him.

It did not take him long to reach the seashore and when he looked off across the water he could see the dragon lying there. He was so long that his back looked like an island, and from his nostrils rose up streams of smoke that were full of fiery cinders.

The Prince hid himself behind a heap of rocks and lay there watching, and presently he heard a great noise. It was made by a procession of people who were bringing the Princess down to the seashore. She was very beautiful, but so sad looking that the Prince's heart melted within him for pity of her.

They brought her to the seashore and left her there, and everyone went away except two nobles of the Court. One of them was driving the coach that brought the Princess, and the other one sat beside him as footman. They were to wait until all was over, and then they were to take the news back to the King, but they kept the coach high up on top of the cliff where they would be out of danger.

The Prince waited until all the others had left her, and then he came out from behind the rocks and went to speak to the Princess; but when she saw him she was frightened, for she did not know who he was nor whence he came.

"Do not fear me," the Prince said to her. "I mean you no harm, but instead I have come hither to do battle with the dragon, and if it may be, to save you."

When the Princess heard this, she begged and implored him to leave her. "Why should you perish also? None can ever do battle with yonder monster and come out alive."

But the Prince would not listen to her.

And now the dragon bestirred itself and turned and came slowly toward the shore, and as it came they could smell the smoke of its breathing.

The Prince drew his sword and stood waiting for it. Then as it came still nearer, the fox sprang out on a rock, dipped his tail in the salty water and slashed it across the eyes of the monster so that it was almost blinded. The lion and the bear also splashed up the water; the boar ripped at the dragon with his sharp tusks; the hare sprang upon its head and struck with its paws; and the Prince drew his sword and plunged it into the monster's heart, so that the life blood ran out from it into the sea, and it was dead.

Then he went to the Princess, and they kissed each other on the lips, and she gave him the half of her handkerchief and the half of her ring to show that they were true lovers. He also took the tongue and the ears of the dragon, and then they went back to the coach where it was waiting on the cliff, and the Princess bade the nobleman drive them to the palace of the King, that she and the Prince might be married as her father had promised.

But on the way, the two noblemen talked together.

"Why should we drive this stranger to the palace?" said they. "No one knows who he is or whence he comes. Let us slay him, and then we will draw lots as to which of us shall claim the Princess."

So that was what they did. They made the Prince step down from the coach and slew him, and they made the Princess swear that she would tell no one that it was not they who had killed the dragon. Then they drew lots as to which should marry her, and the lot fell to the coachman.

But after they had driven on and left the Prince lying there, the faithful animals did not desert him. They stayed beside him and mourned over him, and the lion licked his face and hands, but it could not revive him.

Then the fox, which was very clever, reminded the animals of the flasks of ointment and healing water in the robbers' house.

The hare, which was very swift, said it would go and fetch the flasks, and it sped away to get them.

Now the stepsister had wept the bowl full of tears of repentance and was free again; and when the hare came to the door and told her what it wanted, she gladly gave it the flasks and hung them about its neck in a little wicker basket.

Then the hare fled back again to where the animals were waiting beside the Prince. With its tusks the boar broke the flask that held the ointment, and the bear rubbed it on the Prince's wounds so that they were healed. Then they poured some drops from the second bottle between his lips, and the colour came back to his cheeks and the light to his eyes. When they gave him to drink from the third bottle, he became quite well again and stronger than ever.

After that he rose and set out to follow the Princess. But the way was long, and before he reached the palace, night overtook him, and he had no place to sleep. He was about to make a bed among the grasses when he saw, not far in front of him, the light of a fire. He went on toward it, and as he came nearer, he saw an old, old woman standing beside it and cooking her supper in a pot. She was so old that her chin and nose almost met, and so skinny she was scarcely more than bones, and the eyes under her brows were red and evil.

"Good evening, mother," said the Prince.

"Good evening, son," replied the woman.

"May I and my animals warm ourselves beside the fire?" asked the Prince.

"As for yourself, you're welcome," said the old woman; "but as for your animals, I am afraid of them. Just let me give each one of them a little blow with my staff to show them I'm mistress, and then they may rest by the fire also."

The Prince did not say no, so the old woman took up her staff and with it she quickly touched one animal after the other, beginning with the lion and ending with the hare, and as soon as she touched them, each one was turned into a stone figure, for the old woman was a witch and as wicked as she was ugly. Then she touched the Prince with her staff, and he also became a stone image without life or motion.

Then the old hag laughed with glee and counted them over. They were not the only ones she had either. All about were other stones that had once been living beings.

Now some time after this, the second Prince, who had travelled far and was weary of journeying, came back to the branching road where the tree stood with its notches, and he wished to see how his brothers were faring.

He touched the notch that belonged to the youngest Prince, and milk flowed out from it. So he knew all was well with his youngest brother. Then he touched the notch that belonged to the eldest Prince, and forth from that flowed blood. Then he was grieved to the heart because he knew death or disaster must have come upon his brother.

"Now will I set forth in search of him," said he, "and never will I stop nor stay until I find what has become of him and whether I can give him succour."

So the second Prince journeyed on and on, along the road his eldest brother had gone before him, and it was not long until he came to the place where the old woman was tending her fire. All about in the shadows stood figures of stone, some big and some little, but the Prince did not think to look at them.

He asked if he and his animals might rest a bit beside the fire and warm themselves.

"You yourself are welcome," said the old woman, "but I fear that your animals, may tear at me or eat me." She then asked the Prince's permission to touch each animal with her rod, that it might know her as its mistress. "Then I will no longer fear them," said she.

The Prince was willing, so she took the rod that leaned against a tree nearby and struck the animals lightly, first one and then another, and as she touched them, they were turned to stone. Last of all she touched the Prince, and he too became a stone image.

Then the old hag laughed aloud for joy of her wickedness, and put aside her rod once more, and went on with her cooking.

Now it happened that not so very long after this the youngest Prince, who had journeyed far and wide in his wanderings, began to think of his two brothers and to wonder how it had gone with them in the world.

So he came back to the place where the three roads parted, and the tree stood with the three notches in it.

He put his finger on the notch that was his eldest brother's, and blood ran down from it; and his heart was heavy within him, for he knew that harm must have come to his brother. Then he put his finger upon the notch of the second brother, and from that, too, trickled down the blood. Then the young Prince cried aloud in his sorrow. "Never will I rest or stay," cried he, "until I know what has happened to my brothers and whether or no I can do aught to aid them."

So he set out the way the second brother had gone, and before long he, too, came to where the old woman was tending her fire.

The old hag laughed in her heart, when she saw him, for she thought, "here will be more stone images to be set round me." She spoke to the Prince and made him welcome, and bade him sit beside the fire to rest himself. But she said she feared his animals, and she took her staff in her hand and asked the Prince's leave to touch them each one with it. "Then," said she, "they will know me as their mistress and will not touch or harm me."

But the Prince replied, "Not so! No one but I must strike my faithful servants, no matter how lightly. Give me the rod, and then if needs be I will touch them."

So he took the rod from the old woman, though she indeed was loth to yield it, and first he touched the fox with it, for it was growling.

As soon as he did this, the fox was turned to stone, and then the Prince knew that here was evil magic. He looked about him and saw the stone images of his brothers and their animals, and many other stones as well, that had once been living, breathing people.

Then the Prince's heart was hot within him and he demanded of the hag that she should bring these people back to life, living and breathing as they had been before, and he threatened that unless she did this, his animals should tear her limb from limb and scatter the pieces of her through the forest.

The old woman was terrified, and she bade the Prince turn the staff that he held end for end and touch the people with it; then they would return to life.

This the Prince did, and at once, as she had promised, the cold dead stones became living flesh once more, all the people and all the animals.

Then they all rejoiced greatly, and they gathered about the Prince and thanked him, but none rejoiced more greatly than the brothers.

Then the others all went away to their own homes, and the youngest Prince broke the rod to pieces that the witch might no more use it for harm to others.

The three brothers talked together, and the eldest told them all about the Princess, and how he had saved her from the dragon. And he told them, too, how the noblemen had slain him and stolen the Princess from him, and how the faithful animals had brought him back to life.

After he had made an end of the story the youngest Prince said, "Now we must set out for the palace of the King at once, for it may be it is not yet too late for you to claim the Princess." So the three brothers set forth, with all the animals following behind them.

When they reached the palace, none dared to hinder them from entering, because of the animals, and the three went on through one room after another till they came to where the King was, and his daughter and the nobleman were with him.

The nobleman was very merry, for the wedding feast was even then preparing, and that night he was to be married to the lovely Princess. The King, too, was happy, for he was pleased at the thought of having such a brave hero for a son-in-law. Only the Princess was sad and would do nothing but weep and bemoan herself, but she could not tell her father the cause of her grief because of the oath she had sworn to the nobleman.

Now when the Prince and his two brothers entered the room where the King was sitting, the Princess gave a shriek of joy, but the nobleman turned pale and trembled, for he knew the Prince at once as the true hero who had saved the Princess from the dragon, and whom he and his companion had slain by the roadside.

Then the Prince began and told the King the whole story, and as the King listened, he wondered. When the Prince had made an end of the tale, the King turned to the nobleman. "And what answer have you to make to all this?" he asked him.

"That it is false and doubly false," cried the nobleman. "'Tis I and I alone who saved the Princess."

Then the Prince asked him what proof he had of the truth of his story, and when the nobleman could give no proof, the lad drew out a handkerchief and opened it, and there were the ears and the tongue of the dragon. He also showed the half of the handkerchief and the half of the ring the Princess had given him, and then it was clear to everyone that it was he and he alone who had slain the dragon.

Then the nobleman was punished as he deserved, but the Prince was married to the Princess, and his two brothers were married to the King's two younger daughters, and they all lived together in great joy and happiness forever.

The Dragon of the North

VERY LONG AGO, as old people have told me, there lived a terrible monster, who came out of the North, and laid waste whole tracts of country, devouring both men and beasts; and this monster was so destructive that it was feared that unless help came no living creature would be left on the face of the earth. It had a body like an ox, and legs like a frog, two short forelegs, and two long ones behind, and besides that it had a tail like a serpent, ten fathoms in length. When it moved it jumped like a frog, and with every spring it covered half a mile of ground. Fortunately its habit, was to remain for several years in the same place, and not to move on till the whole neighbourhood was eaten up. Nothing could hunt it, because its whole body was covered with scales, which were harder than stone or metal; its two great eyes shone by night, and even by day, like the brightest lamps, and anyone who had the ill luck to look into those eyes became as it were bewitched, and was obliged to rush of his own accord into the monster's jaws. In this way the Dragon was able to feed upon both men and beasts without the least trouble to itself, as it needed not to move from the spot where it was lying. All the neighbouring kings had offered rich rewards to anyone who should be able to destroy the monster, either by force or enchantment, and many had tried their luck, but all had miserably failed. Once a great forest in which the Dragon lay had been set on fire; the forest was burnt down, but the fire did not do the monster the least harm. However, there was a tradition amongst the wise men of the country that the Dragon might be overcome by one who possessed King Solomon's signet-ring, upon which a secret writing was engraved. This inscription would enable anyone who was wise enough to interpret it to find out how the Dragon could be destroyed. Only no one knew where the ring was hidden, nor was there any sorcerer or learned man to be found who would be able to explain the inscription.

At last a young man, with a good heart and plenty of courage, set out to search for the ring. He took his way towards the sunrising, because he knew that all the wisdom of old time comes from the East. After some years he met with a famous Eastern magician, and asked for his advice in the matter. The magician answered:

"Mortal men have but little wisdom, and can give you no help, but the birds of the air would be better guides to you if you could learn their language. I can help you to understand it if you will stay with me a few days."

The youth thankfully accepted the magician's offer, and said, "I cannot now offer you any reward for your kindness, but should my undertaking succeed your trouble shall be richly repaid."

Then the magician brewed a powerful potion out of nine sorts of herbs which he had gathered himself all alone by moonlight, and he gave the youth nine spoonfuls of it daily for three days, which made him able to understand the language of birds.

At parting the magician said to him. "If you ever find Solomon's ring and get possession of it, then come back to me, that I may explain the inscription on the ring to you, for there is no one else in the world who can do this."

From that time the youth never felt lonely as he walked along; he always had company, because he understood the language of birds; and in this way he learned many things which mere human knowledge could never have taught him. But time went on, and he heard nothing about the ring. It happened one evening, when he was hot and tired with walking, and had sat down under a tree in a forest to eat his supper, that he saw two gaily plumaged birds, that were strange to him, sitting at the top of the tree talking to one another about him. The first bird said:

"I know that wandering fool under the tree there, who has come so far without finding what he seeks. He is trying to find King Solomon's lost ring."

The other bird answered, "He will have to seek help from the Witch-maiden, who will doubtless be able to put him on the right track. If she has not got the ring herself, she knows well enough who has it."

"But where is he to find the Witch-maiden?" said the first bird. "She has no settled dwelling, but is here today and gone tomorrow. He might as well try to catch the wind."

The other replied, "I do not know, certainly, where she is at present, but in three nights from now she will come to the spring to wash her face, as she does every month when the moon is full, in order that she may never grow old nor wrinkled, but may always keep the bloom of youth."

"Well," said the first bird, "the spring is not far from here. Shall we go and see how it is she does it?"

"Willingly, if you like," said the other.

The youth immediately resolved to follow the birds to the spring, only two things made him uneasy: first, lest he might be asleep when the birds went, and secondly, lest he might lose sight of them, since he had not wings to carry him along so swiftly. He was too tired to keep awake all night, yet his anxiety prevented him from sleeping soundly, and when with the earliest dawn he looked up to the tree-top, he was glad to see his feathered companions still asleep with their heads under their wings. He ate his breakfast, and waited until the birds should start, but they did not leave the place all day. They hopped about from one tree to another looking for food, all day long until the evening, when they went back to their old perch to sleep. The next day the same thing happened, but on the third morning one bird said to the other, "Today we must go to the spring to see the Witch-maiden wash her face." They remained on the tree till noon; then they flew away and went towards the south. The young man's heart beat with anxiety lest he should lose sight of his guides, but he managed to keep the birds in view until they again perched upon a tree. The young man ran after them until he was quite exhausted and out of breath, and after three short rests the birds at length reached a small open space in the forest, on the edge of which they placed themselves on the top of a high tree. When the youth had overtaken them, he saw that there was a clear spring in the middle of the space. He sat down at the foot of the tree upon which the birds were perched, and listened attentively to what they were saying to each other.

"The sun is not down yet," said the first bird; "we must wait yet a while till the moon rises and the maiden comes to the spring. Do you think she will see that young man sitting under the tree?"

"Nothing is likely to escape her eyes, certainly not a young man," said the other bird. "Will the youth have the sense not to let himself be caught in her toils?"

"We will wait," said the first bird, "and see how they get on together."

The evening light had quite faded, and the full moon was already shining down upon the forest, when the young man heard a slight rustling sound. After a few moments there came out of the forest a maiden, gliding over the grass so lightly that her feet seemed scarcely to touch the ground, and stood beside the spring. The youth could not turn away his eyes from the maiden, for he had never in his life seen a woman so beautiful. Without seeming to notice anything, she went to the spring, looked up to the full moon, then knelt down and bathed her face nine times, then looked up to the moon again and walked nine times round the well, and as she walked she sang this song:

"Full-faced moon with light unshaded,
Let my beauty ne'er be faded.
Never let my cheek grow pale!
While the moon is waning nightly,
May the maiden bloom more brightly,
May her freshness never fail!"

Then she dried her face with her long hair, and was about to go away, when her eye suddenly fell upon the spot where the young man was sitting, and she turned towards the tree. The youth rose and stood waiting. Then the maiden said, "You ought to have a heavy punishment because you have presumed to watch my secret doings in the moonlight. But I will forgive you this time, because you are a stranger and knew no better. But you must tell me truly who you are and how you came to this place, where no mortal has ever set foot before."

The youth answered humbly: "Forgive me, beautiful maiden, if I have unintentionally offended you. I chanced to come here after long wandering, and found a good place to sleep under this tree. At your coming I did not know what to do, but stayed where I was, because I thought my silent watching could not offend you."

The maiden answered kindly, "Come and spend this night with us. You will sleep better on a pillow than on damp moss."

The youth hesitated for a little, but presently he heard the birds saying from the top of the tree, "Go where she calls you, but take care to give no blood, or you will sell your soul." So the youth went with her, and soon they reached a beautiful garden, where stood a splendid house, which glittered in the moonlight as if it was all built out of gold and silver. When the youth entered he found many splendid chambers, each one finer than the last. Hundreds of tapers burnt upon golden candlesticks, and shed a light like the brightest day. At length they reached a chamber where a table was spread with the most costly dishes. At the table were placed two chairs, one of silver, the other of gold. The maiden seated herself upon the golden chair, and offered the silver one to her companion. They were served by maidens dressed in white, whose feet made no sound as they moved about, and not a word was spoken during the meal. Afterwards the youth and the Witch-maiden conversed pleasantly together, until a woman, dressed in red, came in to remind them that it was bedtime. The youth was now shown into another room, containing a silken bed with down cushions, where he slept delightfully, yet he seemed to hear a voice near his bed which repeated to him, "Remember to give no blood!"

The next morning the maiden asked him whether he would not like to stay with her always in this beautiful place, and as he did not answer immediately, she continued: "You see how I always remain young and beautiful, and I am under no one's orders, but can do just what I like, so that I have never thought of marrying before. But from the moment I saw you I took a fancy to you, so if you agree, we might be married and might live together like princes, because I have great riches."

The youth could not but be tempted with the beautiful maiden's offer, but he remembered how the birds had called her the witch, and their warning always sounded in his ears. Therefore he answered cautiously, "Do not be angry, dear maiden, if I do not decide immediately on this important matter. Give me a few days to consider before we come to an understanding."

"Why not?" answered the maiden. "Take some weeks to consider if you like, and take counsel with your own heart." And to make the time pass pleasantly, she took the youth over every part of her beautiful dwelling, and showed him all her splendid treasures. But these treasures were all produced by enchantment, for the maiden could make anything she wished appear by the help of King Solomon's signet ring; only none of these things remained fixed; they passed away like the wind without leaving a trace behind. But the youth did not know this; he thought they were all real.

One day the maiden took him into a secret chamber, where a little gold box was standing on a silver table. Pointing to the box, she said, "Here is my greatest treasure, whose like is not to be found in the whole world. It is a precious gold ring. When you marry me, I will give you this ring as a marriage gift, and it will make you the happiest of mortal men. But in order that our love may last for ever, you must give me for the ring three drops of blood from the little finger of your left hand."

When the youth heard these words a cold shudder ran over him, for he remembered that his soul was at stake. He was cunning enough, however, to conceal his feelings and to make no direct answer, but he only asked the maiden, as if carelessly, what was remarkable about the ring?

She answered, "No mortal is able entirely to understand the power of this ring, because no one thoroughly understands the secret signs engraved upon it. But even with my half-knowledge I can work great wonders. If I put the ring upon the little finger of my left hand, then I can fly like a bird through the air wherever I wish to go. If I put it on the third finger of my left hand I am invisible, and I can see everything that passes around me, though no one can see me. If I put the ring upon the middle finger of my left hand, then neither fire nor water nor any sharp weapon can hurt me. If I put it on the forefinger of my left hand, then I can with its help produce whatever I wish. I can in a single moment build houses or anything I desire. Finally, as long as I wear the ring on the thumb of my left hand, that hand is so strong that it can break down rocks and walls. Besides these, the ring has other secret signs which, as I said, no one can understand. No doubt it contains secrets of great importance. The ring formerly belonged to King Solomon, the wisest of kings, during whose reign the wisest men lived. But it is not known whether this ring was ever made by mortal hands: it is supposed that an angel gave it to the wise King."

When the youth heard all this he determined to try and get possession of the ring, though he did not quite believe in all its wonderful gifts. He wished the maiden would let him have it in his hand, but he did not quite like to ask her to do so, and after a while she put it back into the box. A few days after they were again speaking of the magic ring, and the youth said, "I do not think it possible that the ring can have all the power you say it has."

Then the maiden opened the box and took the ring out, and it glittered as she held it like the clearest sunbeam. She put it on the middle finger of her left hand, and told the youth to take a knife and try as hard as he could to cut her with it, for he would not be able to hurt her. He was unwilling at first, but the maiden insisted. Then he tried, at first only in play, and then seriously, to strike her with the knife, but an invisible wall of iron seemed to be between them, and the maiden stood before him laughing and unhurt. Then she put the ring on her third finger, and in an instant she had vanished from his eyes. Presently she was beside him again laughing, and holding the ring between her fingers.

"Do let me try," said the youth, "whether I can do these wonderful things."

The maiden, suspecting no treachery, gave him the magic ring.

The youth pretended to have forgotten what to do, and asked what finger he must put the ring on so that no sharp weapon could hurt him.'

"Oh, the middle finger of your left hand," the maiden answered, laughing.

She took the knife and tried to strike the youth, and he even tried to cut himself with it, but found it impossible. Then he asked the maiden to show him how to split stones and rocks with the help of the ring. So she led him into a courtyard where stood a great boulder-stone. "Now," she said, "put the ring upon the thumb of your left hand, and you will see how strong that hand has become." The youth did so, and found to his astonishment that with a single blow of his fist the stone flew into a thousand pieces. Then the youth bethought him that he who does not use his luck when he has it is a fool, and that this was a chance which once lost might never return. So while they stood laughing at the shattered stone he placed the ring, as if in play, upon the third finger of his left hand.

"Now," said the maiden, "you are invisible to me until you take the ring off again."

But the youth had no mind to do that; on the contrary, he went farther off, then put the ring on the little finger of his left hand, and soared into the air like a bird.

When the maiden saw him flying away she thought at first that he was still in play, and cried, "Come back, friend, for now you see I have told you the truth." But the young man never came back.

Then the maiden saw she was deceived, and bitterly repented that she had ever trusted him with the ring.

The young man never halted in his flight until he reached the dwelling of the wise magician who had taught him the speech of birds. The magician was delighted to find that his search had been successful, and at once set to work to interpret the secret signs engraved upon the ring, but it took him seven weeks to make them out clearly. Then he gave the youth the following instructions how to overcome the Dragon of the North: "You must have an iron horse cast, which must have little wheels under each foot. You must also be armed with a spear two fathoms long, which you will be able to wield by means of the magic ring upon your left thumb. The spear must be as thick in the middle as a large tree, and both its ends must be sharp. In the middle of the spear you must have two strong chains ten fathoms in length. As soon as the Dragon has made himself fast to the spear, which you must thrust through his jaws, you must spring quickly from the iron horse and fasten the ends of the chains firmly to the ground with iron stakes, so that he cannot get away from them. After two or three days the monster's strength will be so far exhausted that you will be able to come near him. Then you can put Solomon's ring upon your left thumb and give him the finishing stroke, but keep the ring on your third finger until you have come close to him, so that the monster cannot see you, else he might strike you dead with his long tail. But when all is done, take care you do not lose the ring, and that no one takes it from you by cunning."

The young man thanked the magician for his directions, and promised, should they succeed, to reward him. But the magician answered, "I have profited so much by the wisdom the ring has taught me that I desire no other reward." Then they parted, and the youth quickly flew home through the air. After remaining in his own home for some weeks, he heard people say that the terrible Dragon of the North was not far off, and might shortly be expected in the country. The King announced publicly that he would give his daughter in marriage, as well as a large part of his kingdom, to whosoever should free the country from the monster. The youth then went to the King and told him that he had good hopes of subduing the Dragon, if the King would grant him all he desired for the purpose. The King willingly agreed, and the iron horse, the great spear, and the chains were all prepared as the youth requested. When all was ready, it was found that the iron horse was so heavy that a hundred men could not move it from the spot, so the youth found there was nothing for it but to move it with his own strength by means of the magic ring. The Dragon was now so near that in a couple of springs he would be over the frontier. The youth now began to consider how he should act, for if he had to push the iron horse from behind he could not ride upon it as the sorcerer had said he must. But a raven unexpectedly gave him this advice: "Ride upon the horse, and push the spear against the ground, as if you were pushing off a boat from the land." The youth did so, and found that in this way he could easily move forwards. The Dragon had his monstrous jaws wide open, all ready for his expected prey. A few paces nearer, and man and horse would have been swallowed up by them! The youth trembled with horror, and his blood ran cold, yet he did not lose his courage; but, holding the iron spear upright in his hand, he brought it down with all his might right through the monster's lower jaw. Then quick as lightning he sprang from his horse before the Dragon had time to shut his mouth. A fearful clap like thunder, which could be heard for miles around, now warned him that the Dragon's jaws had closed upon the spear. When the youth turned round he saw the point of the spear sticking up high above the Dragon's upper jaw, and knew that the other end must be fastened firmly to the ground; but the Dragon had got his teeth fixed in the iron horse, which was now useless. The youth now hastened to fasten down the chains to the ground by means of the enormous iron pegs which he had provided. The death struggle of the monster lasted three days and three nights; in his writhing he beat his tail so violently against the ground, that at ten miles' distance the earth trembled as if with an earthquake. When he at length lost power to move his tail, the youth with the help of the ring took up a stone which twenty ordinary men could not have moved, and beat the Dragon so hard about the head with it that very soon the monster lay lifeless before him.

You can fancy how great was the rejoicing when the news was spread abroad that the terrible monster was dead. His conqueror was received into the city with as much pomp as if he had been the mightiest of kings. The old King did not need to urge his daughter to marry the slayer of the Dragon; he found her already willing to bestow her hand upon this hero, who had done all alone what whole armies had tried in vain to do. In a few days a magnificent wedding was celebrated, at which the rejoicings lasted four whole weeks, for all the neighbouring kings had met together to thank the man who had freed the world from their common enemy. But everyone forgot amid the general joy that they ought to have buried the Dragon's monstrous body, for it began now to have such a bad smell that no one could live in the neighbourhood, and before long the whole air was poisoned, and a pestilence broke out which destroyed many hundreds of people. In this distress, the King's son-in-law resolved to seek help once more from the Eastern magician, to whom he at once travelled through the air like a bird by the help of the ring. But there is a proverb which says that ill-gotten gains never prosper, and the Prince found that the stolen ring brought him ill-luck after all. The Witch-maiden had never rested night nor day until she had found out where the ring was. As soon as she had discovered by means of magical arts that the Prince in the form of a bird was on his way to the Eastern magician, she changed herself into an eagle and watched in the air until the bird she was waiting for came in sight, for she knew him at once by the ring which was hung round his neck by a ribbon. Then the eagle pounced upon the bird, and the moment she seized him in her talons she tore the ring from his neck before the man in bird's shape had time to prevent her. Then the eagle flew down to the earth with her prey, and the two stood face to face once more in human form.

"Now, villain, you are in my power!" cried the Witch-maiden. "I favoured you with my love, and you repaid me with treachery and theft. You stole my most precious jewel from me, and do you expect to live happily as the King's son-in-law? Now the tables are turned; you are in my power, and I will be revenged on you for your crimes."

"Forgive me! Forgive me!" cried the Prince; "I know too well how deeply I have wronged you, and most heartily do I repent it."

The maiden answered, "Your prayers and your repentance come too late, and if I were to spare you everyone would think me a fool. You have doubly wronged me; first you scorned my love, and then you stole my ring, and you must bear the punishment."

With these words she put the ring upon her left thumb, lifted the young man with one hand, and walked away with him under her arm. This time she did not take him to a splendid palace, but to a deep cave in a rock, where there were chains hanging from the wall. The maiden now chained the young man's hands and feet so that he could not escape; then she said in an angry voice, "Here you shall remain chained up until you die. I will bring you every day enough food to prevent you dying of hunger, but you need never hope for freedom any more." With these words she left him.

The old King and his daughter waited anxiously for many weeks for the Prince's return, but no news of him arrived. The King's daughter often dreamed that her husband was going through some great suffering: she therefore begged her father to summon all the enchanters and magicians, that they might try to find out where the Prince was and how he could be set free. But the magicians, with all their arts, could find out nothing, except that he was still living and undergoing great suffering; but none could tell where he was to be found. At last a celebrated magician from Finland was brought before the King, who had found out that the King's son-in-law was imprisoned in the East, not by men, but by some more powerful being. The King now sent messengers to the East to look for his son-in-law, and they by good luck met with the old magician who had interpreted the signs on King Solomon's ring, and thus was possessed of more wisdom than anyone else in the world. The magician soon found out what he wished to know, and pointed out the place where the Prince was imprisoned, but said: "He is kept there by enchantment, and cannot be set free without my help. I will therefore go with you myself."

So they all set out, guided by birds, and after some days came to the cave where the unfortunate Prince had been chained up for nearly seven years. He recognized the magician immediately, but the old man did not know him, he had grown so thin. However, he undid the chains by the help of magic, and took care of the Prince until he recovered and became strong enough to travel. When he reached home he found that the old King had died that morning, so that he was now raised to the throne. And now after his long suffering came prosperity, which lasted to the end of his life; but he never got back the magic ring, nor has it ever again been seen by mortal eyes.

Now, if *you* had been the Prince, would you not rather have stayed with the pretty witch-maiden?

The Enchanted Princess

IN A CERTAIN KINGDOM a soldier served in the mounted guard of the king. He served twenty-five years in faithfulness and truth; and for his good conduct the king gave orders to discharge him with honour, and give him as reward the same horse on which he had ridden in the regiment, with all the caparison.

The soldier took farewell of his comrades and set out for his native place. He travelled a day, a second, and a third. Behold, a whole week had gone; a second and third week! The soldier had no money; he had nothing to eat himself, nothing to give his horse, and his home was far, far away. He saw that the affair was a very bad one; he wanted terribly to eat, began to look in one direction and another, and saw on one side a great castle. "Well," thought he, "better go there; maybe they will take me even for a time to serve. I'll earn something."

He turned to the castle, rode into the court, put his horse in the stable, gave him hay, and entered the castle. In the castle a table was set with food and wine, with everything that the soul could wish for.

The soldier ate and drank. "Now," thought he, "I may sleep."

All at once a bear came in. "Fear me not, brave hero; thou hast come in good time. I am not a savage bear, but a fair maiden, an enchanted princess. If thou canst endure and pass three nights in this place, the enchantment will be broken, I shall be a princess as before, and will marry thee."

The soldier consented. Now, there fell upon him such a sadness that he could not look on the world, and every moment the sadness increased; if there had been no wine he could not have held out a single night, as it seemed. The second night it went so far that the soldier resolved to leave everything and run away; but no matter how he struggled, no matter how he tried, he found no way out of the castle. There was no help for it, he had to stay in spite of himself.

He passed the third night. In the morning there stood before him a princess of unspeakable beauty. She thanked him for his service, and told him to make ready for the crown (marriage). Straightway they had the wedding, and began to live together without care or trouble. After a time the soldier remembered his native place; he wanted to spend some time there. The princess tried to dissuade him.

"Remain, stay here, my friend, go not away. What is lacking to thee?"

No, she could not dissuade him. She took farewell of her husband, gave him a sack filled with seeds, and said: "On whatever road thou mayest travel, throw these seeds on both sides. Wherever they fall, that moment trees will spring up; on the trees precious fruit will be hanging in beauty, various birds will sing songs, and tom cats from over the sea will tell tales."

The good hero sat on his horse of service and went his way. Wherever he journeyed he cast seeds on both sides, and after him forests were rising, just creeping out of the damp earth. He rode one day, he rode a second, a third, and saw in the open field a caravan. On the grass merchants were sitting playing cards, near them a great kettle was hanging, and, though there was no fire under the kettle, it was boiling like a fountain within the pot. "What a wonder!" thought the soldier; "there is no fire to be seen, and in the kettle it is boiling like a fountain, – let me look at it more closely." He turned his horse to the place and rode up to the merchants.

"Hail, honourable gentlemen!" He had no suspicion that these were not merchants, but all unclean. "That is a good trick of yours, – a kettle boiling without fire; but I have a better one."

He took out a seed and threw it on the ground, – that moment a full-grown tree came up; on the tree were precious fruits in their beauty, various birds were singing songs, and tom cats from over the sea were telling tales. From this boast the unclean knew him.

"Ah," said they among themselves, "this is the man who liberated the princess! Come, brothers, let us drug him with a weed, and let him sleep half a year."

They went to entertaining him, and drugged him with the magic weed. The soldier dropped on the grass and fell into deep sleep from which he could not be roused. The merchants, the caravan, and the kettle vanished in a twinkle.

Soon after the princess went out in her garden and saw that the tops of all the trees had begun to wither. "This is not for good," thought she; "it is evident that evil has come to my husband."

Three months passed. It was time for his return, and there was nothing of him, nothing. The princess made ready and went to search for him. She went by that road along which he had travelled, – on both sides forests were growing, birds were singing, and tom cats from over the sea were purring their tales. She reached the spot where there were no more trees, the road wound out into the open field; she thought, "Where has he gone to? Of course he has not sunk through the earth."

She looked. Aside by itself was one of the wonderful trees, and under it her dear husband. She ran to him, pushed, and tried to rouse him. No, he did not wake. She pinched him, stuck pins in his side, pricked and pricked him. He did not feel even the pain, – lay like a corpse without motion. The princess grew angry, and in her anger pronounced the spell: "Mayest thou be caught by the stormy whirlwind, thou good-for-nothing sleepy head, and be borne to places unknown!"

She had barely uttered these words when the wind began to whistle, to sound, and in one flash the soldier was caught up by a boisterous whirlwind and borne away from the eyes of the princess. She saw too late that she had spoken an evil speech. She shed bitter tears, went home, lived alone and lonely.

The poor soldier was borne by the whirlwind far, far away beyond the thrice-ninth land, to the thirtieth kingdom, and thrown on a point between two seas; he fell on the very narrowest little wedge. If the sleeping man were to turn to the right, or roll to the left, that moment he would tumble into the sea, and then remember his name.

The good hero slept out his half year, – moved not a finger; and when he woke he sprang straight to his feet, looked on both sides. The waves are rolling; no end can be seen to the broad sea. He stands in doubt, asking himself, "By what miracle have I come to this place? Who dragged me hither?" He turned back from the point and came out on an island; on that island was a mountain steep and lofty, touching the clouds with its peak, and on the mountain a great stone. He came near this mountain and saw three devils fighting; blood was just flowing from them, and bits of flesh flying.

"Stop, ye outcasts! What are ye fighting for?"

"But seest thou our father died three days ago and left three wonderful things: a flying carpet, swift-moving boots, and a cap of invisibility; and we cannot divide them."

"Oh, ye cursed fellows, to fight for such trifles! If ye wish I'll divide them between you, and ye shall be satisfied; I'll offend no one."

"Well then, countryman, divide between us if it please thee."

"Very good. Run quickly through the pine woods and gather one hundred poods of pitch, and bring it here."

The devils rushed through the pine woods, collected three hundred poods of pitch, and brought it to the soldier.

"Now bring me from your own kingdom the very largest kettle that is in it." The devils brought the very largest kettle, – one holding forty barrels, – and put the pitch into it. The soldier made a fire, and when the pitch was boiling he ordered the devils to take it on the mountain and pour it out from the top to the bottom. The devils did this in a flash. "Now," said the soldier, "push that stone there; let it roll from the mountain, and follow it. Whoever comes up with it first may take any of the three things; whoever comes up second will choose from the two remaining ones whichever he likes; and the last wonder will go to the third." The devils pushed the stone, and it rolled from the mountain quickly, quickly. One devil caught up, seized the stone, the stone turned, and in a flash put him under it, crushed him into the pitch. The second devil caught up, and then the third; and with them it happened as with the first, – they were driven firmly into the pitch.

The soldier took under his arm the swift boots and the cap of invisibility, sat on the flying carpet, and flew off to look for his own country. Whether it was long or short, he came to a hut, went in. In the hut was sitting a Baba-Yaga, boneleg, old and toothless. "Greetings to thee, grandmother! Tell how I am to find my fair princess."

"I have not seen her with sight, I have not heard of her with hearing; but pass over so many seas and so many lands, and there lives my second sister. She knows more than I do; mayhap she can tell thee."

The soldier sat on his carpet and flew away. He had to wander long over the white world. Whenever he wanted to eat or drink, he put on the cap of invisibility, let himself down, entered a shop, and took what his heart desired; then to the carpet and off on his journey. He came to the second hut, entered; inside was sitting Baba-Yaga, boneleg, old and toothless. "Greetings to thee, grandmother! Dost thou know how I can find my fair princess?"

"No, my dove, I do not know."

"Ah, thou old hag! How many years art thou living in the world? All thy teeth are out, and thou knowest no good."

He sat on the flying carpet and flew toward the eldest sister. Long did he wander, many seas and many lands did he see. At last he flew to the end of the world, where there was a hut and no road beyond, – nothing but outer darkness, nothing to be seen.

"Well," thought he, "if I can get no account here, there is nowhere else to fly to." He went into the hut; there a Baba-Yaga was sitting, grey, toothless.

"Greetings to thee, grandmother! Tell me where must I seek my princess."

"Wait a little; I will call all my winds together and ask them. They blow over all the world, so they must know where she is living at present."

The old woman went out on the porch, cried with a loud voice, whistled with a hero's whistle. Straightway the stormy winds rose and blew from every side; the hut just quivered.

"Quieter, quieter!" cried Baba-Yaga; and as soon as the winds had assembled, she said: "My stormy winds, ye blow through all the world. Have ye seen the beautiful princess anywhere?"

"We have not seen her anywhere," answered the winds in one voice.

"But are ye all here?"

"All but South Wind."

After waiting a little, South Wind flew up. The old woman asked: "Where hast thou been lost to this moment? I could hardly wait for thee."

"Pardon, grandmother; I went into a new kingdom, where the beautiful princess is living. Her husband has vanished without tidings, so now various Tsars and Tsars' sons, kings and kings' sons are paying court to her."

"And how far is it to the new kingdom?"

"For a man on foot thirty-five years, ten years on wings; but if I blow I can put a man there in three hours."

The soldier implored South Wind tearfully to take him and bear him to the new kingdom.

"I will, if it please thee," said South Wind, "provided thou wilt let me run around in thy kingdom three days and three nights as I like."

"Frolic three weeks if thou choosest."

"Well, I will rest for two or three days, collect my forces and my strength, and then for the road!"

South Wind rested, collected his strength, and said to the soldier: "Well, brother, make ready, we'll go straightway; but look out, have no fear, thou wilt arrive in safety."

All at once a mighty whirlwind whistled and roared, caught the soldier into the air, and bore him over mountains and seas up to the very clouds; and in three hours exactly he was in the new kingdom, where his beautiful princess was living. South Wind said, –

"Farewell, good hero; out of compassion for thee I will not frolic in thy kingdom."

"Why is that?"

"Because if I frolic, not one house will be standing in the town, not one tree in the gardens; I should put everything bottom upward."

"Farewell then; God save thee!" said the soldier, who put on his cap of invisibility and went to the white-walled castle. Behold, while he was absent from the kingdom all the trees in the garden had stood with withered tops, and the moment he appeared they came to life and began to bloom. He entered the great hall; there were sitting at the table various Tsars and Tsars' sons, kings and kings' sons who had come to pay court to the beautiful princess. They were sitting and entertaining themselves with sweet wines. Whoever filled a glass and raised it to his lips, the soldier that moment struck it with his fist and knocked it from his hand. All the gusts wondered at this; but the beautiful princess understood in a moment the reason.

"Surely," thought she, "my friend is here." She looked through the window; all the tree-tops in the garden had come to life, and she gave a riddle to the guests. "I had a home-made casket with a golden key; I lost this key, and did not think to find it: but now this key has found itself. Who guesses the riddle, him will I marry."

The Tsars and Tsars' sons, the kings and kings' sons were long breaking their wise heads over this riddle, and could not solve it in any way.

The princess said: "Show thyself, dear friend."

The soldier removed his cap of invisibility, took her by the white hand, and began to kiss her on the sweet mouth.

"Here is the riddle for you," said the fair princess: "I am the home-made casket, and the golden key is my faithful husband."

The wooers had to turn their wagon-shafts around. They all drove home, and the princess began to live with her husband, to live and win wealth.

Schippeitaro

THERE WAS ONCE A BRAVE JAPANESE LAD who wished to go out into the world and prove his courage in some great adventure. His father and mother did not say no to this. Instead they gave him their blessing, and allowed him to set forth.

For a long time he travelled along, crossing streams and passing through villages, but nowhere did he meet with any adventures.

One evening, as dusk drew on, he found himself in a dark forest, and he did not know which way to turn in order to get out of it. He wandered this way and that, and always the night grew darker and the way rougher, and then suddenly, between the tree trunks, he saw a red light shine out; sometimes it shone brighter and sometimes dimmer, but never with a steady shining.

He went toward the light, and before long he found himself near an old ruined temple. Within a fire was burning, and the temple was full of demon cats. They were leaping and whirling and dancing around the fire, and as they danced they sang. The song had words and they sang them over and over again, always the same thing.

At first the lad could not make out what the words were, but after he had listened carefully for a while he understood; and this was what they sang:

"Tonight we dance, tonight we sing;
Tomorrow the maiden they will bring."

They would sing this over and over and over, and then suddenly they would cease their bounding and whirling, and would stand still and all cry together, –

"But Schippeitaro must not know!
But Schippeitaro must not know!"

The lad stayed there for a long time watching them, and the longer he watched, the more he wondered.

After a while the fire burned low, they bounded less wildly, and their songs were still. Then the fire died out, and soon afterward the lad fell into a deep sleep.

When he awoke the next morning, he was both cold and stiff, and as he rubbed his eyes and looked about him, he thought that all he had seen the night before must have been only a dream, for the temple lay silent and deserted, and there were no signs of the demon cats or their revels, except a heap of burned-out ashes on the temple floor.

The lad arose from where he lay and went on his way wondering. Not long after he came to the edge of the forest and saw before him a village. He entered the village and looked about him, and everything was in mourning and all the people seemed very sad. In front of one of the principal houses a great crowd had gathered, and from within came a sound of weeping and lamenting.

The lad joined the crowd, and looked in through the door of the house. There he saw a maiden dressed as though for a festival, but she was very pale, and tears were running down her face; an old man and an old woman, who seemed to be her father and mother, sat one each side of her, holding her hands, and they also were weeping, with the tears running down their wrinkled faces. Two men were busy over a great chest bound around with iron, and with iron hasps, and every time the old man and woman looked at the chest, they shuddered and wept more bitterly than ever.

This sight made the youth very curious, and he turned to a man beside him and asked why the village was all in mourning, and why the beautiful young girl and her parents were weeping so bitterly.

"Are you a stranger in these parts that you ask such questions?" inquired the man.

"I come from beyond the other side of the forest, from far away," replied the youth, "and I know nothing of this village or what has happened here."

"Then I will tell you," said the man. "Over in the forest yonder there dwells a terrible demon. Every year he requires that a maiden shall be offered up to him as a sacrifice. Many of our most beautiful maidens have already been sacrificed to him, and today it is the turn of the one you see within there, and she is the fairest of them all."

"But why do not your men go into the forest and try to destroy this demon?" asked the youth.

"It would be useless, for we have been told and know that no mortal arm can prevail against him. He comes, as a cat, to the ruined temple over yonder in the forest, and with him comes a great company of seeming cats – but they also are demons and are his servants."

When the youth heard this, he remembered the cats he had seen dancing in the temple the night before and the song they had sung; and presently he asked, "Who is Schippeitaro?"

When he asked this, those around who heard him began to laugh. "You speak as though Schippeitaro were a man," said they. "Schippeitaro is a great dog that belongs to the Prince of this country. The Prince values him highly, for he is as big as a lion and twice as fierce. Never before was his like seen for strength and bigness, nor ever will be again."

The youth asked where the Prince kept the hound, and as soon as he had learned this, he set off walking very rapidly in the direction the man pointed out to him.

After a while he came to a house with a walled garden back of it. In this house lived the man who had charge of Schippeitaro, and the walled garden was for the dog to roam about in.

The youth knocked at the door, and presently the keeper of the dog opened it and asked him what he wanted.

"I want to borrow your great hound, Schippeitaro, for the night, and I will pay you well for lending him to me," said the lad.

"That you will not do," replied the keeper, "for I will not lend him to you. He is the favourite dog of the Prince of this country, and it would be as much as my life is worth to lend him to anyone."

Then the lad began to bargain with him. First he offered the man a third of all his money if he might have the dog just until morning; then he offered him the half of all his money, and then he offered him all of it.

That was more than the man could withstand. "Very well", said he, "you may take the dog; but remember it is only for this one night, and you must bring him back the first thing in the morning, and you need never ask to borrow him again for I shall not lend him to you."

A collar was then put around Schippeitaro's neck, and a chain fastened to it, and the lad took the chain in his hand and led the great dog back to the village he had just come from.

When he came to the house where he had seen the maiden, they were just about to put her in the chest, for that was always the way the maidens who were to be sacrificed were carried to the temple.

But the youth bade them stay their hands. "Listen to me," said he, "for I know whereof I speak. I have seen these demons, and I have a plan by which you may rid yourselves of them forever. Instead of the maiden, do you put Schippeitaro into the chest, carry him to the temple and leave him there. I myself will accompany you, and after you have gone, I will stay there and watch. Believe me, no harm shall come from this, but instead it will put an end to your having to offer up sacrifices to the demon."

At first the people would not listen to him, but afterward they agreed to do as he wished, though they were very much frightened. The great hound was put into the chest, the lid was fastened, and he was carried away and placed in the temple instead of the maiden. After that the men hastened back to the village, but the lad hid himself nearby to wait and watch for the demons as he had promised.

After a while it grew dark, and then, toward midnight, a dull red fire shone in the temple, and the lad saw that it was full of demon cats whirling and bounding and singing as they had before, but this time there was with them a great fierce black cat, larger than any of them, and he was the king of them all, and he leaped higher and sang louder than any of them. This time their song was of how a maiden had been brought to them as a sacrifice, and of what a tender morsel she would be. Then they all shouted together:

"And Schippeitaro does not know!
And Schippeitaro does not know!"

Nearer and nearer they came to the chest. Almost they brushed against it as they whirled about it. Then, with a cry, they bounded at it, and tore it open.

At once, out from the box leaped Schippeitaro. The demons shrieked at the sight of him and the great hound rushed at them and tore them. He seized the King Demon by the throat and shook him till the life was quite shaken out of him. Then he flew at the other cats, and when they tried to escape out through the doors or windows, the youth stood there with his sword and drove them back.

Many of the demons did Schippeitaro destroy that night; many of them he scattered over the floor in pieces, and those who escaped fled so far away that they were never seen in that neighbourhood again.

But the youth returned to the house of the parents of the maiden and asked them for her hand in marriage, for he had loved her from the first moment he had seen her, because of her beauty, and her gentle air. Gladly her parents agreed to give her to him, and the Prince himself came to the marriage, bringing with him gifts both rich and rare, for he had heard of the bravery and wit the youth had shown in ridding his people of the demons who had distressed them, and he brought Schippeitaro with him as a welcome guest.

After that the youth and his young wife returned to his own home, and there they lived happy forever after, honoured and admired by all who knew them.

The Cat's Elopement

ONCE UPON A TIME there lived a cat of marvellous beauty, with a skin as soft and shining as silk, and wise green eyes, that could see even in the dark. His name was Gon, and he belonged to a music teacher, who was so fond and proud of him that he would not have parted with him for anything in the world.

Now not far from the music master's house there dwelt a lady who possessed a most lovely little pussy cat called Koma. She was such a little dear altogether, and blinked her eyes so daintily, and ate her supper so tidily, and when she had finished she licked her pink nose so delicately with her little tongue, that her mistress was never tired of saying, "Koma, Koma, what should I do without you?"

Well, it happened one day that these two, when out for an evening stroll, met under a cherry tree, and in one moment fell madly in love with each other. Gon had long felt that it was time for him to find a wife, for all the ladies in the neighbourhood paid him so much attention that it made him quite shy; but he was not easy to please, and did not care about any of them. Now, before he had time to think, Cupid had entangled him in his net, and he was filled with love towards Koma. She fully returned his passion, but, like a woman, she saw the difficulties in the way, and consulted sadly with Gon as to the means of overcoming them. Gon entreated his master to set matters right by buying Koma, but her mistress would not part from her. Then the music master was asked to sell Gon to the lady, but he declined to listen to any such suggestion, so everything remained as before.

At length the love of the couple grew to such a pitch that they determined to please themselves, and to seek their fortunes together. So one moonlight night they stole away, and ventured out into an unknown world. All day long they marched bravely on through the sunshine, till they had left their homes far behind them, and towards evening they found themselves in a large park. The wanderers by this time were very hot and tired, and the grass looked very soft and inviting, and the trees cast cool deep shadows, when suddenly an ogre appeared in this Paradise, in the shape of a big, big dog! He came springing towards them showing all his teeth, and Koma shrieked, and rushed up a cherry tree. Gon, however, stood his ground boldly, and prepared to give battle, for he felt that Koma's eyes were upon him, and that he must not run away. But, alas! His courage would have availed him nothing had his enemy once touched him, for he was large and powerful, and very fierce. From her perch in the tree Koma saw it all, and screamed with all her might, hoping that someone would hear, and come to help. Luckily a servant of the princess to whom the park belonged was walking by, and he drove off the dog, and picking up the trembling Gon in his arms, carried him to his mistress.

So poor little Koma was left alone, while Gon was borne away full of trouble, not in the least knowing what to do. Even the attention paid him by the princess, who was delighted with his beauty and pretty ways, did not console him, but there was no use in fighting against fate, and he could only wait and see what would turn up.

The princess, Gon's new mistress, was so good and kind that everybody loved her, and she would have led a happy life, had it not been for a serpent who had fallen in love with her, and was constantly annoying her by his presence. Her servants had orders to drive him away as often as he appeared; but as they were careless, and the serpent very sly, it sometimes happened that he was able to slip past them, and to frighten the princess by appearing before her. One day she was seated in her room, playing on her favourite musical instrument, when she felt something gliding up her sash, and saw her enemy making his way to kiss her cheek. She shrieked and threw herself backwards, and Gon, who had been curled up on a stool at her feet, understood her terror, and with one bound seized the snake by his neck. He gave him one bite and one shake, and flung him on the ground, where he lay, never to worry the princess any more. Then she took Gon in her arms, and praised and caressed him, and saw that he had the nicest bits to eat, and the softest mats to lie on; and he would have had nothing in the world to wish for if only he could have seen Koma again.

Time passed on, and one morning Gon lay before the house door, basking in the sun. He looked lazily at the world stretched out before him, and saw in the distance a big ruffian of a cat teasing and ill-treating quite a little one. He jumped up, full of rage, and chased away the big cat, and then he turned to comfort the little one, when his heart nearly burst with joy to find that it was Koma. At first Koma did not know him again, he had grown so large and stately; but when it dawned upon her who it was, her happiness knew no bounds. And they rubbed their heads and their noses again and again, while their purring might have been heard a mile off.

Paw in paw they appeared before the princess, and told her the story of their life and its sorrows. The princess wept for sympathy, and promised that they should never more be parted, but should live with her to the end of their days. By-and-by the princess herself got married, and brought a prince to dwell in the palace in the park. And she told him all about her two cats, and how brave Gon had been, and how he had delivered her from her enemy the serpent.

And when the prince heard, he swore they should never leave them, but should go with the princess wherever she went. So it all fell out as the princess wished; and Gon and Koma had many children, and so had the princess, and they all played together, and were friends to the end of their lives.

Gray Eagle and His Five Brothers

THERE WERE SIX FALCONS living in a nest, five of whom were still too young to fly, when it so happened that both the parent birds were shot in one day. The young brood waited anxiously for their return; but night came, and they were left without parents and without food.

Gray Eagle, the eldest, and the only one whose feathers had become stout enough to enable him to leave the nest, took his place at the head of the family, and assumed the duty of stifling their cries and providing the little household with food, in which he was very successful. But, after a short time had passed, by an unlucky mischance, while out on a foraging excursion, he got one of his wings broken. This was the more to be regretted, as the season had arrived when they were soon to go to a southern country to pass the winter, and the children were only waiting to become a little stronger and more expert on the wing to set out on the journey.

Finding that their elder brother did not return, they resolved to go in search of him. After beating up and down the country for the better part of a whole day, they at last found him, sorely wounded and unable to fly, lodged in the upper branches of a sycamore-tree.

"Brothers," said Gray Eagle, as soon as they were gathered around, and questioned him as to the extent of his injuries, "an accident has befallen me, but let not this prevent your going to a warmer climate. Winter is rapidly approaching, and you can not remain here. It is better that I alone should die, than for you all to suffer on my account."

"No, no," they replied, with one voice. "We will not forsake you. We will share your sufferings; we will abandon our journey, and take care of you as you did of us before we were able to take care of ourselves. If the chill climate kills you, it shall kill us. Do you think we can so soon forget your brotherly care, which has equalled a father's, and even a mother's kindness? Whether you live or die, we will live or die with you."

They sought out a hollow tree to winter in, and contrived to carry their wounded nest-mate thither; and before the rigour of the season had set in, they had, by diligence and economy, stored up food enough to carry them through the winter months.

To make the provisions they had laid in last the better, it was agreed among them that two of their number should go south; leaving the other three to watch over, feed, and protect their wounded brother. The travellers set forth, sorry to leave home, but resolved that the first promise of spring should bring them back again. At the close of day, the three brothers who remained, mounting to the very peak of the tree, and bearing Gray Eagle in their arms, watched them, as they vanished away southward, till their forms blended with the air and were wholly lost to sight.

Their next business was to set the household in order, and this, with the judicious direction of Gray Eagle, who was propped up in a snug fork, with soft cushions of dry moss, they speedily accomplished. One of the sisters, for there were two of these, took upon herself the charge of nursing Gray Eagle, preparing his food, bringing him water, and changing his pillows when he grew tired of one position. She also looked to it that the house itself was kept in a tidy condition, and that the pantry was supplied with food. The second brother was assigned the duty of physician, and he was to prescribe such herbs and other medicines as the state of the health of Gray Eagle seemed to require. As the second brother had no other invalid on his visiting-list, he devoted the time not given to the cure of his patient, to the killing of game wherewith to stock the housekeeper's larder; so that, whatever he did, he was always busy in the line of professional duty – killing or curing. On his hunting excursions, Doctor Falcon carried with him his youngest brother, who, being a foolish young fellow, and inexperienced in the ways of the world, it was not thought safe to trust alone.

In due time, what with good nursing, and good feeding, and good air, Gray Eagle recovered from his wound, and he repaid the kindness of his brothers by giving them such advice and instruction in the art of hunting as his age and experience qualified him to impart. As spring advanced, they began to look about for the means of replenishing their store-house, whose supplies were running low; and they were all quite successful in their quest except the youngest, whose name was Peepi, or the Pigeon-Hawk, and who had of late begun to set up for himself. Being small and foolish, and feather-headed, flying hither and yonder without any set purpose, it so happened that Peepi always came home, so to phrase it, with an empty game-bag, and his pinions terribly rumpled.

At last Gray Eagle spoke to him, and demanded the cause of his ill-luck.

"It is not my smallness nor weakness of body," Peepi answered, "that prevents my bringing home provender as well as my brothers. I am all the time on the wing, hither and thither. I kill ducks and other birds every time I go out; but just as I get to the woods, on my way home, I am met by a large ko-ko-ho, who robs me of my prey; and," added Peepi, with great energy, "it's my settled opinion that the villain lies in wait for the very purpose of doing so."

"I have no doubt you are right, Brother Peepi," rejoined Gray Eagle. "I know this pirate – his name is White Owl; and now that I feel my strength fully recovered, I will go out with you tomorrow and help you look after this greedy bush-ranger."

The next day they went forth in company, and arrived at a fine freshwater lake. Gray Eagle seated himself hard by, while Peepi started out, and soon pounced upon a duck.

"Well done!" thought his brother, who saw his success; but just as little Peepi was getting to land with his prize, up sailed a large white owl from a tree where he, too, had been watching, and laid claim to it. He was on the point of wresting it from Peepi, when Gray

Eagle, calling out to the intruder to desist, rushed up, and, fixing his talons in both sides of the owl, without further introduction or ceremony, flew away with him.

The little Pigeon-Hawk followed closely, with the duck under his wing, rejoiced and happy to think that he had something to carry home at last. He was naturally much vexed with the owl, and had no sooner delivered over the duck to his sister, the housekeeper, than he flew in the owl's face, and, venting an abundance of reproachful terms, would, in his passion, have torn the very eyes out of the White Owl's head.

"Softly, Peepi," said the Gray Eagle, stepping in between them. "Don't be in such a huff, my little brother, nor exhibit so revengeful a temper. Do you not know that we are to forgive our enemies? White Owl, you may go; but let this be a lesson to you, not to play the tyrant over those who may chance to be weaker than yourself."

So, after adding to this much more good advice, and telling him what kind of herbs would cure his wounds, Gray Eagle dismissed White Owl, and the four brothers and sisters sat down to supper.

The next day, betimes, in the morning, before the household had fairly rubbed the cobwebs out of the corners of their eyes, there came a knock at the front door – which was a dry branch that lay down before the hollow of the tree in which they lodged – and being called to come in, who should make their appearance but the two nest-mates, who had just returned from the South, where they had been wintering. There was great rejoicing over their return, and now that they were all happily reunited, each one soon chose a mate and began to keep house in the woods for himself.

Spring had now revisited the North. The cold winds had all blown themselves away, the ice had melted, the streams were open, and smiled as they looked at the blue sky once more; and the forests, far and wide, in their green mantle, echoed every cheerful sound.

But it is in vain that spring returns, and that the heart of Nature is opened in bounty, if we are not thankful to the Master of Life, who has preserved us through the winter. Nor does that man answer the end for which he was made who does not show a kind and charitable feeling to all who are in want or sickness, especially to his blood relations.

The love and harmony of Gray Eagle and his brothers continued. They never forgot each other. Every week, on the fourth afternoon of the week (for that was the time when they had found their wounded elder brother), they had a meeting in the hollow of the old sycamore-tree, when they talked over family matters, and advised with each other, as brothers should, about their affairs.

The Magical & the Supernatural

Introduction

'CHERRY', IN THE ENGLISH tale, isn't allowed to go out into the world to seek her fortune as her older sisters have. She's too precious to her father; too protected. And so she slips off one fine morning, gets a job as a nurse to a wealthy gentleman's son and before she knows it finds she's working in Fairyland. In folktales, the boundary between the mundane and the magical has always been blurred at best and spirits – and even people – flit back and forth across it. Not always for the best, as far as a suffering humanity is concerned. Sribatsa, the wise man who in the Bengali tale 'The Evil Eye of Sani', tries to mediate between the goddess Lakshmi and the god Sani over who ranks higher, finds himself with a curse on him when he rashly rules for Lakshmi. Still less fortunate is Auchin, the Japanese monk in 'The Bell of Dōjōji', who falls in love with a nature-spirit, Kiohimé, Magic Lady of the Mere. Repenting of his sinful passion, he tries to escape her clutches, only to be burned alive in a great bronze bell. In a lighter vein, a Scottish story tells of the adventures of a magic oat cake which flees the table to avoid being eaten and takes itself off travelling, having all sorts of adventures along the way. In 'The Seven Golden Peahens', a Serbian story, a prince finds that the pests that are taking the apples from his father's tree are actually princesses in disguise.

How Orpheus the Minstrel Went Down to the World of the Dead

MANY WERE THE MINSTRELS who, in the early days, went through the world, telling to men the stories of the gods, telling of their wars and their births. Of all these minstrels none was so famous as Orpheus who had gone with the Argonauts; none could tell truer things about the gods, for he himself was half divine.

But a great grief came to Orpheus, a grief that stopped his singing and his playing upon the lyre. His young wife Eurydice was taken from him. One day, walking in the garden, she was bitten on the heel by a serpent, and straightway she went down to the world of the dead.

Then everything in this world was dark and bitter for the minstrel Orpheus; sleep would not come to him, and for him food had no taste. Then Orpheus said: "I will do that which no mortal has ever done before; I will do that which even the immortals might shrink from doing: I will go down into the world of the dead, and I will bring back to the living and to the light my bride Eurydice."

Then Orpheus went on his way to the valley of Acherusia which goes down, down into the world of the dead. He would never have found his way to that valley if the trees had not shown him the way. For as he went along Orpheus played upon his lyre and sang, and the trees heard his song and they were moved by his grief, and with their arms and their heads they showed him the way to the deep, deep valley of Acherusia.

Down, down by winding paths through that deepest and most shadowy of all valleys Orpheus went. He came at last to the great gate that opens upon the world of the dead. And the silent guards who keep watch there for the rulers of the dead were affrighted when they saw a living being, and they would not let Orpheus approach the gate.

But the minstrel, knowing the reason for their fear, said: "I am not Heracles come again to drag up from the world of the dead your three-headed dog Cerberus. I am Orpheus, and all that my hands can do is to make music upon my lyre."

And then he took the lyre in his hands and played upon it. As he played, the silent watchers gathered around him, leaving the gate unguarded. And as he played the rulers of the dead came forth, Aidoneus and Persephone, and listened to the words of the living man.

"The cause of my coming through the dark and fearful ways," sang Orpheus, "is to strive to gain a fairer fate for Eurydice, my bride. All that is above must come down to you at last, O rulers of the most lasting world. But before her time has Eurydice been brought here. I have desired strength to endure her loss, but I cannot endure it. And I come before you, Aidoneus and Persephone, brought here by Love."

When Orpheus said the name of Love, Persephone, the queen of the dead, bowed her young head, and bearded Aidoneus, the king, bowed his head also. Persephone remembered how Demeter, her mother, had sought her all through the world, and she remembered the touch of her mother's tears upon her face. And Aidoneus remembered how his love for Persephone had led him to carry her away from the valley in the upper world where she had been gathering flowers. He and Persephone bowed their heads and stood aside, and Orpheus went through the gate and came amongst the dead.

Still upon his lyre he played. Tantalus – who, for his crimes, had been condemned to stand up to his neck in water and yet never be able to assuage his thirst – Tantalus heard, and for a while did not strive to put his lips toward the water that ever flowed away from him; Sisyphus – who had been condemned to roll up a hill a stone that ever rolled back – Sisyphus heard the music that Orpheus played, and for a while he sat still upon his stone. And even those dread ones who bring to the dead the memories of all their crimes and all their faults, even the Eumenides had their cheeks wet with tears.

In the throng of the newly come dead Orpheus saw Eurydice. She looked upon her husband, but she had not the power to come near him. But slowly she came when Aidoneus called her. Then with joy Orpheus took her hands.

It would be granted them – no mortal ever gained such privilege before – to leave, both together, the world of the dead, and to abide for another space in the world of the living. One condition there would be – that on their way up through the valley of Acherusia neither Orpheus nor Eurydice should look back.

They went through the gate and came amongst the watchers that are around the portals. These showed them the path that went up through the valley of Acherusia. That way they went, Orpheus and Eurydice, he going before her.

Up and up through the darkened ways they went, Orpheus knowing that Eurydice was behind him, but never looking back upon her. But as he went, his heart was filled with things to tell – how the trees were blossoming in the garden she had left; how the water was sparkling in the fountain; how the doors of the house stood open, and how they, sitting together, would watch the sunlight on the laurel bushes. All these things were in his heart to tell her, to tell her who came behind him, silent and unseen.

And now they were nearing the place where the valley of Acherusia opened on the world of the living. Orpheus looked on the blue of the sky. A white-winged bird flew by. Orpheus turned around and cried, "O Eurydice, look upon the world that I have won you back to!"

He turned to say this to her. He saw her with her long dark hair and pale face. He held out his arms to clasp her. But in that instant she slipped back into the depths of the valley. And all he heard spoken was a single word, "Farewell!" Long, long had it taken Eurydice to climb so far, but in the moment of his turning around she had fallen back to her place amongst the dead.

Down through the valley of Acherusia Orpheus went again. Again he came before the watchers of the gate. But now he was not looked at nor listened to, and, hopeless, he had to return to the world of the living.

The birds were his friends now, and the trees and the stones. The birds flew around him and mourned with him; the trees and stones often followed him, moved by the music of his lyre. But a savage band slew Orpheus and threw his severed head and his lyre into the River Hebrus. It is said by the poets that while they floated in midstream the lyre gave out some mournful notes and the head of Orpheus answered the notes with song.

And now that he was no longer to be counted with the living, Orpheus went down to the world of the dead, not going now by that steep descent through the valley of Acherusia, but going down straightway. The silent watchers let him pass, and he went amongst the dead and saw his Eurydice in the throng. Again they were together, Orpheus and Eurydice, and as they went through the place that King Aidoneus ruled over, they had no fear of looking back, one upon the other.

The Quest of Gilgamesh

In which Gilgamesh, the hero of ancient Mesopotamia, ventures to the Underworld in search of immortality.

ON THE HEART OF GILGAMESH the fear of death had taken hold, and he determined to go in search of his ancestor, Ut-Napishtim, who might be able to show him a way of escape. Straightway putting his determination into effect, Gilgamesh set out for the abode of Ut-Napishtim. On the way he had to pass through mountain gorges, made terrible by the presence of wild beasts. From the power of these he was delivered by Sin, the moon-god, who enabled him to traverse the mountain passes in safety.

At length he came to a mountain higher than the rest, the entrance to which was guarded by scorpion-men. This was Mashu, the Mountain of the Sunset, which lies on the western horizon, between the earth and the underworld. "Then he came to the mountain of Mashu, the portals of which are guarded every day by monsters; their backs mount up to the ramparts of heaven, and their foreparts reach down beneath Aralu. Scorpion-men guard the gate (of Mashu); they strike terror into men, and it is death to behold them. Their splendour is great, for it overwhelms the mountains; from sunrise to sunset they guard the sun. Gilgamesh beheld them, and his face grew dark with fear and terror, and the wildness of their aspect robbed him of his senses." On approaching the entrance to the mountain Gilgamesh found his way barred by these scorpion-men, who, perceiving the strain of divinity in him, did not blast him with their glance, but questioned him regarding his purpose in drawing near the mountain of Mashu. When Gilgamesh had replied to their queries, telling them how he wished to reach the abode of his ancestor, Ut-Napishtim, and there learn the secret of perpetual life and youthfulness, the scorpion-men advised him to turn back. Before him, they said, lay the region of thick darkness; for twelve *kasbu* (twenty-four hours) he would have to journey through the thick darkness ere he again emerged into the light of day. And so they refused to let him pass. But Gilgamesh implored, "with tears," says the narrative, and at length the monsters consented to admit him. Having passed the gate of the Mountain of the Sunset (by virtue of his character as a solar deity) Gilgamesh traversed the region of thick darkness during the space of twelve *kasbu*. Toward the end of that period the darkness became ever less pronounced; finally it was broad day, and Gilgamesh found himself in a beautiful garden or park studded with trees, among which was the tree of the gods, thus charmingly depicted in the text – "Precious stones it bore as fruit, branches hung from it which were beautiful to behold. The top of the tree was lapis-lazuli, and it was laden with fruit which dazzled the eye of him that beheld." Having paused to admire the beauty of the scene, Gilgamesh bent his steps shoreward.

The tenth tablet describes the hero's encounter with the sea-goddess Sabitu, who, on the approach of one "who had the appearance of a god, in whose body was grief, and who looked as though he had made a long journey," retired into her palace and fastened the door. But Gilgamesh, knowing that her help was necessary to bring him to the dwelling of Ut-Napishtim, told her of his quest, and in despair threatened to break down the door unless she opened to him. At last Sabitu consented to listen to him whilst he asked the way to Ut-Napishtim.

Like the scorpion-men, the sea-goddess perceived that Gilgamesh was not to be turned aside from his quest, so at last she bade him go to Adad-Ea, Ut-Napishtim's ferryman, without whose aid, she said, it would be futile to persist further in his mission. Adad-Ea, likewise, being consulted by Gilgamesh, advised him to desist, but the hero, pursuing his plan of intimidation, began to smash the ferryman's boat with his axe, whereupon Adad-Ea was obliged to yield. He sent his would-be passenger into the forest for a new rudder, and after that the two sailed away.

The Magic Turban, the Magic Whip, and the Magic Carpet

ONCE UPON A TIME that was no time there were two brothers. Their father and mother had died and divided all their property between them. The elder brother opened a shop, but the younger brother, who was but a feather-brain, idled about and did nothing; so that at last, what with eating and drinking and gadding abroad, the day came when he had no more money left. Then he went to his elder brother and begged a copper or two of him, and when that all was spent he came to him again, and so he continued to live upon him.

At last the elder brother began to grow tired of this waste, but seeing that he could not be quit of his younger brother, he turned all his possessions into sequins, and embarked on a ship in order to go into another kingdom. The younger brother, however, had got wind of it, and before the ship started he managed to creep on board and conceal himself without anyone observing him. The elder brother suspected that if the younger one heard of his departure he would be sure to follow after, so he took good care not to show himself on deck. But scarcely had they unfurled the sails when the two brothers came face to face, and the elder brother found himself saddled with his younger brother again.

The elder brother was not a little angry, but what was the use of that! – for the ship did not stop till it came to Egypt. There the elder brother said to the younger brother: "Thou stay here, and I will go and get two mules that we may go on further." The youth sat down on the shore and waited for his brother, and waited, but waited in vain. "I think I had better look for him," thought he, and up he got and went after his elder brother.

He went on and on and on, he went a short distance and he went a long distance, six months was he crossing a field; but once as he looked over his shoulder, he saw that for all his walking he walked no further than a barley-stalk reaches. Then he strode still more, he strode still further, he strode for half a year continuously; he kept plucking violets as he went along, and as he went striding, striding, his feet struck upon a hill, and there he saw three youths quarrelling with one another about something. He soon made a fourth, and asked them what they were tussling about.

"We are the children of one father," said the youngest of them, "and our father has just died and left us, by way of inheritance, a turban, a whip, and a carpet. Whoever puts the turban on his head is hidden from mortal eyes. Whoever extends himself on the carpet and strikes it once with the whip can fly far away, after the manner of birds; and we are eternally quarrelling among ourselves as to whose shall be the turban, whose the whip, and whose the carpet."

"All three of them must belong to one of us," cried they all. "They are mine, because I am the biggest," said one. – "They are mine by right, because I am the middling-sized brother," cried the second. – "They are mine, because I am the smallest," cried the third. From words they speedily came to blows, so that it was as much as the youth could do to keep them apart.

"You can't settle it like that," said he; "I'll tell you what we'll do. I'll make an arrow from this little piece of wood, and shoot it off. You run after it, and he who brings it to me here soonest shall have all three things." Away flew the dart, and after it pelted the three brothers, helter-skelter; but the wise youth knew a trick worth two of that, for he stuck the turban on his head, sat down on the carpet, tapped it once with the whip, and cried: "Hipp – hopp! let me be where my elder brother is!" and when he awoke a large city lay before him.

He had scarce taken more than a couple of steps through the street, when the Padishah's herald came along, and proclaimed to the inhabitants of the town that the Sultan's daughter disappeared every night from the palace. Whoever could find out what became of her should receive the damsel and half the kingdom. "Here am I!" cried the youth, "lead me to the Padishah, and if I don't find out, let them take my head!"

So they brought the fool into the palace, and in the evening there lay the Sultan's daughter watching, with her eyes half-closed, all that was going on. The damsel was only waiting for him to go to sleep, and presently she stuck a needle into her heel, took the candle with her, lest the youth should awake, and went out by a side door.

The youth had his turban on his head in a trice, and no sooner had he popped out of the same door than he saw a black efrit standing there with a golden buckler on his head, and on the buckler sat the Sultan's daughter, and they were just on the point of starting off. The lad was not such a fool as to fancy that he could keep up with them by himself, so he also leaped on to the buckler, and very nearly upset the pair of them in consequence. The efrit was alarmed, and asked the damsel in Allah's name what she was about, as they were within a hair's-breadth of falling. "I never moved," said the damsel; "I am sitting on the buckler just as you put me there."

The black efrit had scarcely taken a couple of steps, when he felt that the buckler was unusually heavy. The youth's turban naturally made him invisible, so the efrit turned to the damsel and said: "My Sultana, thou art so heavy today that I all but break down beneath thee!" – "Darling Lala!" replied the girl, "thou art very odd tonight, for I am neither bigger nor smaller than I was yesterday."

Shaking his head the black efrit pursued his way, and they went on and on till they came to a wondrously beautiful garden, where the trees were made of nothing but silver and diamonds. The youth broke off a twig and put it in his pocket, when straightway the trees began to sigh and weep and say: "There's a child of man here who tortures us! there's a child of man here who tortures us!"

The efrit and the damsel looked at each other. "They sent a youth in to me today," said the damsel, "maybe his soul is pursuing us."

Then they went on still further, till they came to another garden, where every tree was sparkling with gold and precious stones. Here too the youth broke off a twig and shoved it into his pocket, and immediately the earth and the sky shook, and the rustling of the trees said: "There's a child of man here torturing us, there's a child of man here torturing us," so that both he and the damsel very nearly fell from the buckler in their fright. Not even the efrit knew what to make of it.

After that they came to a bridge, and beyond the bridge was a fairy palace, and there an army of slaves awaited the damsel, and with their hands straight down by their sides they bowed down before her till their foreheads touched the ground. The Sultan's daughter dismounted from the efrit's head, the youth also leaped down; and when they brought the princess a pair of slippers covered with diamonds and precious stones, the youth snatched one of them away, and put it in his pocket. The girl put on one of the slippers, but being unable to find the other, sent for another pair, when, presto! one of these also disappeared. At this the damsel was so annoyed that she walked on without slippers; but the youth, with the turban on his head and the whip and the carpet in his hand, followed her everywhere like her shadow. So the damsel went on before, and he followed her into a room, and there he saw the black Peri, one of whose lips touched the sky, while the other lip swept the ground. He angrily asked the damsel where she had been all the time, and why she hadn't come sooner. The damsel told him about the youth who had arrived the evening before, and about what had happened on the way, but the Peri comforted her by saying that the whole thing was fancy, and she was not to trouble herself about it any more. After that he sat down with the damsel, and ordered a slave to bring them sherbet. A black slave brought the noble drink in a lovely diamond cup, but just as he was handing it to the Sultan's daughter the invisible youth gave the hand of the slave such a wrench that he dropped and broke the cup to pieces. A piece of this also the youth concealed in his pocket.

"Now didn't I say that something was wrong?" cried the Sultan's daughter. "I want no sherbet nor anything else, and I think I had better get back again as soon as possible." – "Tush! tush!" said the efrit, and he ordered other slaves to bring them something to eat. So they brought a little table covered with many dishes, and they began to eat together; whereupon the hungry youth also set to work, and the viands disappeared as if three were eating instead of two.

And the black Peri himself began to be a little impatient, when not only the food but also the forks and spoons began to disappear, and he said to his sweetheart, the Sultan's daughter, that perhaps it would be as well if she did make haste home again. First of all the black efrit wanted to kiss the girl, but the youth slipped in between them, pulled them asunder, and one of them fell to the right and the other to the left. They both turned pale, called the Lala with his buckler, the damsel sat upon it, and away they went. But the youth took down a sword from the wall, bared his arm, and with one blow he chopped off the head of the black Peri. No sooner had his head rolled from his shoulders than the heavens roared so terribly, and the earth groaned so horribly, and a voice cried so mightily: "Woe to us, a child of man hath slain our king!" that the terrified youth knew not whether he stood on his head or his heels.

He seized his carpet, sat upon it, gave it one blow with his whip, and when the Sultan's daughter returned to the palace, there she found the youth snoring in his room. "Oh, thou wretched bald-pate," cried the damsel viciously, "what a night I've had of it. So much the worse for thee!" Then she took out a needle and pricked the youth in the heel, and because he never stirred she fancied he was asleep, and lay down to sleep herself also.

Next morning when she awoke she bade the youth prepare for death, as his last hour had come. "Nay," replied he, "not to thee do I owe an account of myself; let us both come before the Padishah."

Then they led him before the father of the damsel, but he said he would only tell them what had happened in the night if they called all the people of the town together. "In that way I shall find my brother, perhaps," thought he. So the town-crier called all the people together, and the youth stood on a high daïs beside the Padishah and the Sultana, and began to tell them the whole story, from the efrit's buckler to the Peri king. "Believe him not, my lord Padishah and father; he lies, my lord father and Padishah!" stammered the damsel; whereupon the youth drew from his pocket the diamond twig, the twig of gems, the golden slipper, the precious spoons and forks. Then he went on to tell them of the death of the black Peri, when all at once he caught sight of his elder brother, whom he had been searching for so long. He had now neither eyes nor ears for anything else, but leaping off the daïs, he forced his way on and on through the crowd to his brother, till they both came together.

Then the elder brother told *their* story, while the younger brother begged the Padishah to give his daughter and half the kingdom to his elder brother. He was quite content, he said, with the magic turban and the magic whip and carpet to the day of his death, if only he might live close to his elder brother.

But the Sultan's daughter rejoiced most of all when she heard of the death of the Peri king. He had carried her off by force from her room one day, and so enchanted her with his power that she had been unable to set herself free. In her joy she agreed that the youth's elder brother should be her lord; and they made a great banquet, at which they feasted forty days and forty nights with one another. I also was there, and I begged so much pilaw from the cook, and I got so much in the palm of my hand, that I limp to this day.

The Poor Man and the King of the Crows

THERE WAS ONCE A VERY POOR MAN, and he had two lean cows. The two cows were to the poor man as their mother's breast to children; for not only did they give milk and butter, for which he got a few coppers to buy salt, but he tilled his patch of land with them.

Now, he was ploughing one day at the edge of the woods with the two cows, when, from wherever it came, a six-horse coach stood before him, and in it sat no other than the King of the Crows, who found this to say to the poor man, –

"Listen, poor man; I will tell thee one thing, and two will come of it. Sell me those lean cows; I'll give thee good money for them. I'll pay double price. My army hasn't tasted a morsel for three days, and the soldiers will die of hunger and thirst unless thou wilt save them."

"If that's the case," said the poor man to the King of the Crows, "if it be that thy Highness's army hasn't eaten anything for three days, I don't mind the difficulty. I'll let thee have the cows, not for money; let thy Highness return a cow for a cow."

"Very good, poor man, let it be as thou sayest. I will give thee a cow for a cow; more than that, for two thou wilt get four cows. For that purpose find me in my kingdom, for I am the

King of the Crows. Thou hast but to look in the north for the black castle; thou'lt be sure to find it."

With that the King of the Crows vanished as if he had never been there, – as if the earth had swallowed him. The poor man kept on ploughing with the two lean cows, till, all at once, the army of the King of the Crows appeared like a black cloud approaching through the air, with mighty cawing, and seizing the two cows tore them bit from bit. When they had finished, the dark legions with tumultuous cawing moved on their way like a cloud. The poor man watched the direction in which they flew so that he might know the way.

Now he strolled home in great sadness, took leave of his two handsome sons and his dear wife, in the midst of bitter tears, and set out into the world to find the black castle. He travelled and journeyed over forty-nine kingdoms, beyond the Operentsia Sea and the glass mountains, and beyond that, where the little short-tailed pig roots, and beyond that, and still farther on, till he came to an ocean-great sand-plain.

Nowhere for gold was a town, a village, or a cabin to be seen where he might recline his head for a night's rest, or beg a morsel of bread or a cup of water. Food had long since left his bag, and he might have struck fire in the gourd which hung at his side. What was he to do? Where could he save his life? Here he must perish of hunger and thirst in the midst of this ocean-great desert, and then at home let them wait for him till the Day of Judgement. Here the poor man's power of walking decreased, and he floundered about like a dazed fish, like a man struck on the head. While stumbling along he sees on a sudden a shepherd's fire.

He moves towards the light, creeping on all fours. At last he arrives there with great difficulty, and sees that three or four men are lying around the fire, boiling kasha in a pot. He salutes them with, "God give you a good evening."

"God receive thee, poor man; how is it that thou art journeying in this strange land where even a bird does not go?"

"I am looking for the black castle in the north. Have ye heard nothing of it in your world-beautiful lives?"

"How not? Of course we have. Are we not the shepherds of that king, who rigorously and mercilessly enjoined that, if such and such a man, who sold him the two lean cows for his army, should find us, to treat him well with meat and drink, and then to show him the right road? Maybe thou art the man!"

"I am indeed."

"Is it possible?"

"I am no one else."

"In that case sit here on the sheepskin; eat, drink, and enjoy thyself, for the kasha will be ready this minute."

As they said, he did. The poor man sat by the fire, ate, drank, and satisfied himself, then lay down and fell asleep. When he rose in the morning they gave him a round cheese, and drove the air out of his bottle; then they let him go his way, showing him the right road.

The poor man travelled and journeyed along the right road; and now, when he was hungry and dry, he had his bag, and his bottle too. Towards evening he sees again a shepherd's fire. He draws near the great fire, and sees the shepherds of the King of the Crows sitting around it cooking a meat stew. He wishes them, "God give you a good day, my lords, the horseherds."

"God guard thee, poor man," said the chief herdsman; "where art thou going here in this strange land?"

"I am looking for the black castle of the King of the Crows. Hast thou never heard of it, brother, in thy world-beautiful life?"

"How not heard of it? Of course I have. Are we not the servants of him who commanded rigorously and unflinchingly that if such and such a poor man, who sold him two lean cows for his army, should wander along, to receive him kindly? Therefore, this is my word and speech to thee. Art thou, perchance, that man?"

"Of course I am."

"Is it possible?"

"I'm no one else."

"In that case sit down here by the fire, drink, and be filled."

The poor man sat down by the fire, ate, drank, and satisfied himself; then lying on the sheepskin, he fell asleep. When he rose in the morning the horseherds entertained the poor man again, wished him happiness, and showing the right road let him go his way; but they left neither his bag nor his bottle empty. Then he went along the right road. But why multiply words? – for there is an end even to a hundred words; it is enough to know that towards evening he came to the ground of the swineherds of the King of the Crows. He saluted them with, "God give you a good evening."

"God guard thee," said the reckoning swineherd. "How is it thou art journeying in this strange land, where even a bird does not go?"

"I am looking for the black castle of the King of the Crows. Has my lord elder brother never heard of it in his world-beautiful life?"

"Haho, poor man! How not heard of it? Are we not the servants of the lord of that castle? But art not thou the poor man who sold his Highness the two lean cows?"

"Well, what's the use in delay or denial? I am, indeed, he."

"Art thou in truth?"

"I am no one else."

"But how wilt thou enter the black castle, since it is covered all around with a stone wall, and whirls unceasingly on a golden cock's foot? But make no account of that. Here is a shining axe. Just strike the wall with it so that sparks will fly, and thou wilt come upon the door, which will spring open. Then jump in. Have a care, though; for if thou slip and fall, neither God nor man can save thee. When thou art once inside, the King of the Crows will come forward and receive thee kindly. He won't put his soul on the palm of his hand at once; but when his Highness inquires what thy wish is, ask for nothing else but the salt-mill which stands in the corner."

Well, the talk ended there. In the morning the poor man moves on towards the black castle. When he arrives there, he saw that it whirled of itself on a golden cock's foot, like some infernal spindle; and nowhere can he see either window or door upon it, – nothing but the naked wall. He took the swineherd's axe and struck the wall, and sparks flew from the axe in such style that it couldn't be better. After a time he came upon the door; it flew open, and he jumped in. If he had delayed but one flash of an eye the stone wall door would have crushed him; as it was, the edge of his trousers was carried off.

As soon as the poor man got in, he saw that the castle turned only on the outside. At this moment the King of the Crows was standing by the window, and saw the poor man coming for the price of the cows. He went to meet him, shook his hand, treated him as tenderly as an egg; then he led him into the most beautiful chamber, and seated him at his side on a golden couch. The poor man saw not a soul anywhere, although it was midday, the time of eating. All at once the table began to spread, and was soon bending under its load, so much food was on it. The poor man shook his head, – for, as I say, though no one was to be seen anywhere, neither cook nor kitchen-boy nor servant, still, wasn't the table spread? It was surely witchcraft, surely some infernal art, but not the work of a good spirit, – maybe the salt-mill had something to do with it. That, however, did not come into the poor man's mind, though the mill stood there in the corner.

He was there three days, the guest of the King of the Crows, who received him with every kindness he could offer, so that no man's son could raise a complaint against his Highness. Morning, noon, and night the poor man's food appeared in proper form, but the roast and the wine had no taste for him; for it came to his mind that while he was feasting there, most likely his wife and children had not bread enough. I say it came to his mind; he began to be restless and uneasy. The King of the Crows noticed this, and said to him: "Well, poor man, I see that thou dost not wish to stay longer with me, because thy heart is at home, therefore I ask what dost thou wish for the two lean cows? – believe me, brother, thou didst save me from great trouble that time; if thou hadst not taken pity on me I should have lost my whole army from famine."

"I want nothing else," said the poor man, "but that salt-mill standing there in the corner."

"Oh, poor man, hast thou lost thy wits? Tell me, what good couldst thou get of the mill?"

"Oh, I could grind corn or a little wheat from time to time; if I did not someone else might, so there would be something to take to the kitchen."

"Ask for something else; ask for all the cattle which in coming hither thou didst see."

"What should I do with such a tremendous lot of cattle? If I should drive them home, people would think evil of me; besides, I have neither stable nor pasture."

"But I'll give thee money. How much dost thou wish? Wouldst be content with three bags of it?"

"What could I do with such an ocean-great lot of money? My evil fate would use it to kill me; people would think that I stole the coin, or murdered some man for it; besides, I might be stopped with it on the road."

"But I'll give thee a soldier as a guard."

"What good is one of thy Highness's soldiers?" asked the poor man, smiling; "a hen, I think, would drive him away."

"What! One of my soldiers?"

Here the King of the Crows blew a small whistle; straightway a crow appeared which shook itself, and became such a gallant young fellow that he was not only so, but just so. "That's the kind of soldiers I have," said the king and commanded the young man out of the room. The soldier shook himself, became a crow, and flew away.

"It's all the same to me what kind of soldiers thy Highness has. Thy Highness promised to give me what I want, and I ask for nothing else but the salt-mill."

"I will not give it. Ask for all my herds, but not for that."

"I need not herds; all I want is the mill."

"Well, poor man, I have refused thee three times, and three times thou hast asked for the mill; now, whether I will or not, I must give it. But know that thou art not to grind corn or wheat with the mill; for it has this virtue, – that it accomplishes all wishes. Here it is, take it, though my heart bleeds after it. Thou didst me a good deed, therefore let it be thine."

The poor man put the mill on his back, took farewell of the King of the Crows, thanking him for his hospitality, and trudged home at his leisure. On the way back he entertained the swineherds, the horseherds, and the cowherds. All he did was to say, "Grind, my dear mill," and what food was dear to the eye, the mouth, and the taste appeared of itself; and if he said, "Draw up, my dear mill," all the food was as if the ground had swallowed it, – it vanished. Then he took leave of the good shepherds and continued his way.

As he travelled and journeyed, he came to a great wild wood; and having grown hungry, he said: "Grind, my dear mill." Straightway the table was spread, not for one, but for two persons. The mill knew at once that the poor man would have a guest; for that moment, wherever he came from, a great fat man appeared, who without saying a word, took his seat at the table. When they had enjoyed God's blessing, the great fat man spoke, and said:

"Listen, poor man. Give me that mill for this knotty club; for if thy mill has the power of accomplishing all thy desires (the fat man knew this already), my knotty club has this power, that thou hast need but to say, 'Strike, my club,' and the man thou hast in mind is the son of Death."

What was the poor man to do? Thinking if he did not give it of his free will the fat man would take it by force, he exchanged the mill for the knotty club; but when he had it once in his hand, he said in a low voice, for he was commanding the knotty club, "Strike, my dear club." And it so struck the fat man behind the ears that he gave forth not a sound; he didn't move his little finger. Then the poor man continued his journey homeward at his ease; and when seven years had passed he was able to say: "Here we are!"

His wife who was weeping by the hearth, mourning over her dear lost lord and the two lean cows, scarcely knew the poor man, but still she knew him. His two sons had become large, and had grown out of their long clothes. When the poor man put his foot in his own house he set the mill down in the chimney-corner, loosed his mantle from his neck, hung it up on a nail, and only then did they know him.

"Well, Father," said his wife, "thou hast come; God knows 'tis time. I never expected to see thee again; but what didst thou get for Bimbo and Csako?"

"This mill," answered he with many "see here's" and "see there's."

"If that's the case, the palsy strike thy work," cried the woman; "better for thee to have stayed at home these seven years, and swung thy feet around here, than to have dragged that good-for-nothing mill from such a distant land, just as if thou hadst eaten the crazy-weed!"

"Oh, my sweet wife, something is better than nothing; if we have no grain to grind for ourselves, we can grind for other people, if not in streams at least in drops."

"May a cancer eat thy mill! I haven't a thing to put between my teeth, and still—"

"Well, my sweet wife, if thou hast nothing to put between thy teeth thou'lt soon have. Grind, my dear mill."

At these words, so much meat and drink appeared on the poor man's table that half of it would have been enough. It was only then that the woman regretted her tongue rattling. But a woman is a woman; beat her with a stone, only let her talk.

The poor man, his wife, and two sons sat down at the table, looking at the food like an army of locusts. They ate and drank to their hearts' content. Whether from wine or some other cause, a desire to dance came to the two sons; and they jumped up and danced, so it was pure delight to look at them. "Oh," said the elder one, "if we only had a gypsy!" That moment a band of gypsies by the chimney struck up their music, and played away with such variations that the poor man too wished to dance, and so whirled his wife around that better could not be asked for. The neighbours knew not what to think of the affair. How was it that music was sounding in the poor man's house?

"What is this?" said they one to another, coming nearer and nearer, till they came up to the door and the windows. Only then did they see that a band of gypsies were fiddling away with might and main, and the old man, his wife, and their two sons were dancing, while the table was bending under loads of rich meat and drink.

"Come in cousin! Come in friend! Come in brother-in-law, bring thy wife! Come in brother!" and there was no end to the invitations of the poor man. Guests collected unceasingly, and still the table was spread. "'Pon my soul," said the poor man, "it's a pity my house isn't larger; for all these guests could scarcely find room in a palace." At these words, instead of the poor man's cabin, such a magnificent palace appeared, with chambers, twelve in a row, that the king himself hadn't the like of it.

A multitude of grand people with the king in the midst of them were out walking just at that time. "What's this? What's this?" asked they of one another. "There has always been a poor man's cabin here, now there's a king's palace, and besides, music is sounding, and gypsies are fiddling. Let's go and have a look."

The king went in front, and after him all the grand people, – counts, dukes, barons, and so on. The poor man came out and received the king with the great personages very kindly, and conducted them all to the head of the table as their fitting place. They ate, drank, and caroused, so that it was like a small wedding.

While they were enjoying themselves at the best, a great sealed letter came to the king. When he had read it, he turned yellow and blue, because it was written therein that the Turk-Tartar was nearing his kingdom with a great army, destroying everything with fire and sword, and sparing not the property of innocent, weeping people, whom he puts to the point of the sword; that the earth is drinking their blood; their flesh is devoured by dogs.

From great joy there was great sorrow.

Then the poor man stood forth and asked the king: "If 'tis no offence, may I ask a question?"

"What may it be, poor man?"

"Would thy Highness tell me the contents of that great letter received just now?"

"Why ask, poor man? Thou couldst not mend the affair."

"But if I can?"

"Well, know then, and let the whole kingdom know, that the Turk-Tartar is moving on our country with a great army, with cruel intent; that he spares not the property of innocent, weeping people, puts them to the sword, so that the earth drinks their blood, and their flesh is devoured by dogs."

"And what will be the reward of him who drives the enemy out of the country?" asked the poor man.

"In truth," said the king, "great reward and honour await him; for if he should have two sons, I would give them my two daughters in marriage, with half the kingdom. After my death they would inherit the whole kingdom."

"Well, I'll drive out the enemy all alone."

But the king did not place much confidence in the poor man's promise; he hurried together all his soldiers, and marched with them against the enemy. The two armies were looking at each other with wolves' eyes, when the poor man went between the camps and commanded the club: "Strike, my dear club." And the club pommelled the Turk-Tartar army so that only one man was left to carry home the tidings.

The poor man gained half the kingdom and the two beautiful princesses, whom he married to his two stalwart sons. They celebrated a wedding which spoke to the seven worlds; and they are living now if they are not dead.

Kiss Miklos and the Green Daughter of the Green King

THERE WAS ONCE A POOR MAN, and he had three sons. When the poor man was on his death-bed, he called his three sons, and this was his word and speech to them: "My dear sons, if I do not tell, still mayhap ye know why our kingdom is in mourning, in unbroken darkness, such that a spoon might stand up in it; but if ye know not, then I will tell. My sons, this unbroken darkness is here because they have stolen the sun and the moon from our bright heavens. But I will tell one thing, and two will come of it; a wizard foretold that among my three sons was one (which one I with firm trust cannot say) who would bring back the sun and the moon. Therefore, my sons, I leave you this: that after my death ye will go out to seek the sun and the moon, and not come home till ye bring back the sources of light."

With that the poor man turned to the wall, wandered forth from this world of shadows, and was buried with honour.

But here, my lord's son, what comes of the affair or what does not, I saw it as I see now; I was in the place where they were talking. The report ran through the whole kingdom of what the poor man had left in his will to his three sons, so that even the king heard it, and he summoned straightway to his presence the three brothers. And when the three brothers appeared before the king, he said: "My dear young men, I hear that your father – may God give him rest – on his death-bed left this to you: that after his death ye would go out into the wide, great world to look for the sun and the moon. Therefore, my sons, this is my word and speech to you: that whoso brings back the sun and the moon will be king after my death, and whoso will assist him in everything, this one I will make viceroy. Now go to my stable and to my armoury and choose for yourselves horses and swords; I will give in a sealed letter to you the order that wherever ye go men shall give you in all places, hay, oats, food, and drink free of cost."

Here the three young men entered the king's stable, and the two elder chose the most beautiful golden-haired steeds; but the youngest, somewhere off by the wall in a hidden corner, among cobwebs and dirt, picked out for himself a wretched, shaggy haired, plucked colt. The two elder brothers laughed at the youngest because he intended to go on that ragged, nasty colt that was hardly able to stand on its feet; but the youngest brother thought nothing of this, and did not give ear to the talk of his brothers.

Now they went to the king's armoury, where the elder brothers chose for themselves two beautiful gold-mounted swords; but the youngest brother, who had more wit, picked out a rusty steel sword. This rusty sword now jumped out of the sheath, now sprang in again, – played unceasingly. The two elder brothers laughed at the youngest again, but he put this as well as their former ridicule quietly in his pocket, thinking to himself that he laughs truly who laughs last; for the nasty colt, as surely as I live and as ye live – I was present where they were talking, I saw as I do now, and I was looking as I am now – was a magic six-legged steed, conceived of the Wind, and eating live coals; and the rusty sword had this kind of virtue that a man had only to say, "Cut, my dear sword," and it cut down whatever he wished. But the two elder brothers knew nothing of all this, for they did not understand woodwork.

Now the three brothers moved on their way through the kingdom, to look for the sun and the moon. They travelled and journeyed over forty-nine kingdoms, beyond the Operentsia Sea, beyond the glass mountains, and beyond that, to where the little short-tailed pig roots, and farther than that, and still farther, till they came to the silver bridge. When they came to the silver bridge the youngest brother, speaking a word, said to his two brothers: "My dear brothers, let us go under the bridge, for soon the steed of the moon will be here, and the twelve-headed dragon, from whose saddle-bow the bright moon is dangling."

Now, the two brothers had barely hidden when the steed of the moon was on the bridge, and on the steed the twelve-headed dragon, from whose saddle-bow the bright moon was dangling. The milk-white steed of the moon stumbled on the bridge. Then the twelve-headed dragon was enraged, and said this to the steed of the moon, –

"Ah, may the crow eat thy eye, may the dog eat thy flesh, may the earth drink thy blood! From forest to forest I have ridden thee, from mountain to mountain I have sprung with thee, and thou hast never stumbled, but now on the even road thou hast stumbled. Well, in my world-beautiful life I have always heard the fame of Kiss Miklos; if he were here now, I would like to have a struggle with him."

At this word our Kiss Miklos – for let it be said, meanwhile, this was the name of the youngest brother – sprang out from beneath to the silver bridge on his golden-haired magic steed, and closed with the twelve-headed dragon. Long did they struggle, the one with the other, but Kiss Miklos said to the rusty sword: "Cut, my dear sword!" and with that it cut three heads off the dragon, and in the same order till all the twelve heads were hewn off, so that the twelve-headed dragon drew his shortest breath. Then Kiss Miklos took by the halter the milk-white haired, black-maned steed of the moon, on whose saddle-bow was dangling the bright moon, and gave him to the care of his second brother. Then they passed over the silver bridge, which sounded like most beautiful music from the golden shoes of the magic steed.

They travelled and journeyed then through forty-nine kingdoms, beyond the Operentsia Sea and the glass mountains, beyond that, where the little short-tailed pig roots, beyond that, and farther, till they came to the golden bridge.

Then Kiss Miklos spoke, and said this to his two brothers, speaking speech: "My dear brothers, let us hide under the bridge, for soon will the steed of the sun be here, and on him the twenty-four-headed dragon, from whose saddle-bow the shining sun is dangling. He will call me out at once to the keen sword, and I will measure with him strength with strength. He will not be able to conquer me, nor I him; then he and I will turn into flames. He will be a red and I a blue flame, but even then we shall not be able to conquer one the other, for we shall be of equal strength. But here is a sulphur stone; when the red flame springs highest toward the sky to press down the blue flame, that is me, strike the sulphur stone on the red flame."

Our Kiss Miklos had barely finished his speech when the steed of the sun was on the bridge, bearing the twenty-four-headed dragon and the shining sun. The steed of the sun stumbled on the golden bridge. The twenty-four-headed dragon was enraged at him, and said, –

"Ah, may the crow eat thy eye, may the dog eat thy flesh, may the earth drink thy blood! I have ridden from forest to forest on thee, I have leaped thee from mountain to mountain, and never hast thou stumbled; but now on the even road thou hast stumbled. In my world-beautiful life I have heard always the fame of Kiss Miklos – may the dog devour him! – and if he were here now I would like to have a struggle with him."

At this word our Kiss Miklos sprang out on to the golden bridge, and closed with the twenty-four-headed dragon. But Kiss Miklos commanded, saying: "Cut, my dear sword!" and that instant it cut the twenty-four heads off the dragon; but, wonder of the world! when all the twenty-four heads were off, in the twinkle of an eye new ones grew out which the leaping sword could not cut. In vain Kiss Miklos said: "Cut, my dear sword!" for it could not cut these heads. Well, Kiss Miklos took the sword in his hand and whirled it like lightning; but he did nothing with it, for the dragon had power of the same kind as he.

When the dragon saw that he could not succeed against Kiss Miklos, he spoke in this way: "Listen to me, Kiss Miklos! I wish thou hadst perished with thy mother, for I see that I can do nothing with thee, nor thou with me. Let us make one trial. Turn thou into a blue flame, and I will turn into a red one, and whichever can put the other out, his will be the steed of the sun and the shining sun upon him."

That is what was done. Kiss Miklos turned to a blue flame, and the twenty-four-headed dragon to a red one. The two flames fought the one with the other, but neither was able to put out the other. Happily the two brothers threw the sulphur stone on the red flame, and then the blue flame put out the red one; and when it was quenched altogether, the twenty-four-headed dragon ceased to live.

Kiss Miklos gave the steed of the sun to his elder brother, and told his two brothers to go home quietly, for he had work of his own; and with that he took farewell of them. Miklos then shook himself, turned into a little grey cat, ran along the highroad, and all at once sprang into a cabin. In the cabin was the mother of the dragons and their two wives.

The younger dragon's wife saw the little grey cat; she took it on her lap, stroked it, and found this to say to the mother of the dragons: "Well, if I knew that that cursed Kiss Miklos had killed my lord, I would turn into such a spring of water that if he and his two brothers were to drink not more than one drop of it, they would die a fearful death on the spot."

With this the little grey cat sprang from the lap of the younger dragon's wife, and rubbed up to the skirt of the wife of the elder dragon, who took it on to her lap, stroked it, and found this to say: "Ah! If I knew that that cursed Kiss Miklos had killed my lord, I would change into such a pear-tree that if he and his two brothers were to eat no more than one morsel of a pear of mine, they would die a fearful death."

With this the little grey cat sprang from the lap of the elder dragon's wife, and rubbed on the skirt of the old woman, who took it on her lap, fondled it, and found this to say to her two daughters-in-law: "My dear girls, just prop up my two eyes with that iron bar, which weighs twelve hundred pounds, so that I may look around."

Her two daughters-in-law then took the twelve-hundred-pound iron bar and opened the old woman's eyes; then she spoke thuswise: "If that cursed Kiss Miklos has killed my two sons, I will turn into a mouth, one jaw of which will be on the earth and the other I will throw to the sky, so as to catch that cursed villain and his two brothers, and grind them as millstones grind wheat."

When the little grey cat had heard all this exactly, it shot away in a flash out of the cabin, sprang along, and never stopped till it came to the good magic steed. The old woman threw the twelve-hundred-pound bar after the cat, but she failed in her cast, for that moment her eyelids fell; she was not able to keep them open unless they were propped, for she was old. So Kiss Miklos escaped the twelve-hundred-pound bar, – certain death. I say that he escaped, for he came to his good magic steed, shook himself, and from a little grey cat became a young man as before. Then he sat on the good steed, which sprang once, jumped twice, and straightway Miklos was with his two brothers; then they fared homeward in quiet comfort.

The second brother grew thirsty, and found this to say: "Oh, but I am dry! My throat is burning!"

"If that is thy only trouble," said Miklos, "I will soon bring thee water. Out there a spring is bubbling up."

With that Kiss Miklos put spurs to his good magic steed, which sprang once, jumped twice, and was at the spring; but here, instead of filling the gourd that hung at his side, he drew his sharp sword, and thrust it three times into the bubbling water. In a moment from the spring blood gushed forth, and a word of bitter pain was heard. That was the blood of the younger dragon's wife, and the word of pain was her death-groan. The blood made all the water red, and when the two brothers came up they had no wish to drink a drop from the spring.

Well, they travelled and journeyed till the elder brother said: "Oh, but I am hungry!"

"If that is thy trouble," said Kiss Miklos, "we can easily cure it, for there near the dam is a pear-tree, and on it so much ripe fruit that the limbs are breaking. Wait, I will bring thee a pear directly; but lead thou the steed of the sun there."

Here Kiss Miklos put spurs to his steed, which sprang once, jumped twice, and stood before the pear-tree. Miklos drew his sharp sword and stabbed the pear-tree in the trunk three times; from the trunk blood gushed forth, and a bitter word of pain was heard. The red blood was the blood of the elder dragon's wife, and the bitter word of pain was her death-groan. With that the pears fell, so that when the two elder brothers reached the tree, not only would they not eat the pears, but the desire of eating had gone from them.

Now they journeyed and travelled through forty-nine kingdoms, till at last Miklos saw from a distance that an unmercifully great mouth, one jaw of which was on earth and the other thrown up to the heavens, was nearing them like the swiftest storm, so that they had barely time left to run into the door of the Lead Friend's house. And a thousand-fold was their luck that they got in; for the unmercifully great mouth stood before the threshold of the Lead Friend, so that whoever should go out would fall into it, and be swallowed that minute.

"Hei! Good Lead-Melting Friend," said Miklos, "hast thou much molten lead? I will pay thee for it in honest coin."

"Haho! My friend Kiss Miklos, I know thee; in my world-beautiful life I have ever heard thy fame. Long have I been waiting for thee. It is well that thou art here, – that thou hast entered my door, – for thou wilt never go a step farther from me."

"Oh! For God's sake," said Kiss Miklos, "do not pass thy own threshold, for straightway the mother of the dragons will swallow thee with her great mouth."

The Lead-Melting Friend went out of his chamber, saw the great mouth of the mother of the dragons, and went back in terror to his chamber, where he said this to Kiss Miklos: "Oh, my good friend Kiss Miklos, give counsel. What are we to do?"

"Hast thou much molten lead?"

"Not much, only eighteen tons; it is out there in the cauldron boiling."

"Knowest thou what? I will say one thing and two will come of it. Let us take the handles of that great cauldron and pour its contents into the great mouth of the mother of the dragons."

Here, 'pon my soul! the Lead-Melting Friend put one handle on his shoulder, Kiss Miklos the other on his, brought the unmercifully great cauldron to the threshold, and poured the eighteen tons of boiling lead into the old witch's mouth. The boiling lead burned up the stomach of the mother of the dragons, and straightway she breathed out her cursed soul.

So Kiss Miklos was freed from the mother of the dragons; but, poor fellow, he was like one that goes from the pail into the barrel, for the Lead-Melting Friend caught his Grace by the neck and took him, as he would a straw, to the chamber, where he found this to say, –

"Look here, my good friend Kiss Miklos, in my world-beautiful life I have ever heard thy fame; therefore let us struggle now and see who is stronger, thou or I." With that the Lead Friend put only his little finger on Kiss Miklos; from that he began to sink, and went down through the lead floor of the chamber the distance of an ell.

"Kiss Miklos, my friend, dost thou wish to fight with me?" asked the Lead Friend. "Thou sayest nothing, so I see that thou dost not; therefore this is my word and speech: I will keep thee in endless slavery unless thou bring me the Green Daughter of the Green King. But ye," and he turned to the two brothers, "ye may go home in gentle quietness, and take with you the steeds of the moon and the sun, on which are the bright moon and the shining sun, for of them I have no need."

Here our Miklos, in the midst of bitter tear-shedding, took farewell of his dear brothers. They held on their way homeward, and arrived there in health. Great was the rejoicing in the kingdom that the poor man's sons, as their father had bequeathed them on his deathbed, brought home the bright moon and the shining sun. Therefore the king assembled all that were in his dominions of dukes, counts, barons, lords, lord's sons, chosen gypsies, and broad-brimmed, country-dressed Slovaks; of these he sought council and asked, "What do brothers deserve who have brought home the bright moon and the shining sun?"

To this question then they answered, "Our high lord, the one who has brought back the steed of the sun, and on it the bright shining sun, deserves to be king of the country, and he who has brought home the steed of the bright moon, and on it the fair moon, to be viceroy; and each one of them should receive as wife a daughter of thy Highness."

So it was done. The poor man's eldest son became king, and the second son viceroy; and each one of them got a maiden princess as wife. Then they let out the steed of the bright moon and the steed of the shining sun on the highway of the heavens, but both the moon and the sun shone sadly. For this reason they shone sadly: that he was without merited reward who had really freed them from the dragons, for Kiss Miklos was now in never-ending slavery to the Lead Friend.

Once the Lead Friend called Miklos and found this to tell him: "Well, Miklos, if thou wilt bring me the Green Daughter of the Green King, I will let thee go free, and I will strike from thee the three-hundred-pound ring and the twelve-hundred-pound chain. Therefore, good friend Miklos, I advise thee to start in the morning with the bright shining sun, and bring to me my heart's desire."

Now our Miklos moved on the road again, and a long one too; whether there will be an end to it, only the good God knows. And as he travelled and journeyed across forty-nine kingdoms, and beyond that, and still farther, at the foot of a great mountain was a little hill, and as a shot arrow, as the swiftest whirlwind, ran towards him a man who was always crying, "Out of my way! Out of my way!" This was Swift Runner, who stood still in a moment, like a pillar, before Miklos, and asked, "Whither, whither, Kiss Miklos? For in my world-beautiful life I have ever heard thy fame."

"Haho! Swift Runner, better thou hadst not asked. I am going for the Green Daughter of the Green King. Hast thou ever heard of her?"

"I have not heard. I speak not of that, but of this: take me with thee, for thou wilt get good of me somewhere."

"Well, come on thy own legs, if it please thee."

They travelled and journeyed after that, two of them, till they came to the seashore, and saw a man who was drinking the sea to the last drop, just as I would drink a cup of water; and then he cried out unceasingly: "Oh, I'm thirsty! Oh, I'm thirsty!" This was Great Drinker who, when he saw Miklos, went to him and said: "God's good day, famous Kiss Miklos; for in my world-beautiful life I have ever heard thy fame."

"God keep thee, Great Drinker!"

"On what journey art thou, renowned Kiss Miklos?"

"On what journey? Haho! Better thou hadst not asked. I am going for the Green Daughter of the Green King. Hast thou heard of her?"

"I have not, in truth," answered Great Drinker; "I speak not of that, but of this: take me with thee, for mayhap thou'lt get good of me."

"Well, come on thy own legs, if it please thee."

So there were three of them, and they travelled and journeyed after that till they saw a man running on the plain towards cattle, and he thrust the beautiful bullocks one by one into his mouth as I would a piece of bread, and swallowed them, hide and horns, one after the other; and even when he had swallowed all the standing herd of three hundred and sixty-six bullocks, he called out unceasingly: "Oh, I am hungry! Oh, I am hungry!" This was Great Eater who, when he saw Miklos, went to him and said: "God give thee a good day, renowned Kiss Miklos; for in my world-beautiful life I have ever heard thy fame."

"God keep thee, Great Eater!"

"What journey art thou on, renowned Kiss Miklos?"

"Better thou hadst not asked. I am going for the Green Daughter of the Green King. Hast thou heard of her?"

"I have not heard, in truth," answered Great Eater; "but take me with thee, mayhap thou'lt get good of me."

"Well, come on thy own legs, if it please thee."

Now there were four of them, and they travelled and journeyed till one day they struck upon a man whose bolster was the glowing coals, whose pillow was the burning fire, and whose blanket was the flaming blaze; he had nine pairs of boots on his feet, nine pairs of drawers and nine shirts on his body, nine neckcloths on his neck, nine sheepskin caps on his head, nine pairs of trousers, nine vests on his body, and nine sheepskin overcoats hung from his shoulders, but even then he did nothing but cry out unceasingly: "Oh, I'm freezing! Oh, I'm freezing!" When he saw Kiss Miklos, he stood before him and said: "God give thee a good day, renowned Kiss Miklos; for in my world-beautiful life I have ever heard thy fame."

"God guard thee, Great Freezer!"

"What journey art thou on, renowned Kiss Miklos?"

"Ah, comrade, thou shouldst not have asked. Hast thou heard of the fame of the Green Daughter of the Green King?"

"I have not heard of it."

"Well, if thou hast not, hear now; for I am going to her as a wooer."

"Take me with thee, mayhap thou wilt get good of me."

"Well, come on thy own legs, if it please thee."

There were five of them now. They journeyed and travelled after that till they came upon a man who was looking around unceasingly. In one twinkle, in the turn of an eye, he saw the round earth, and in another turn of the eye he looked through the deep sea; and he saw Miklos and his comrades thirty-five miles off.

This was Far Seer, who stood before Miklos and said: "God give thee a good day, renowned Kiss Miklos."

"God keep thee, Far Seer!"

"On what journey art thou, renowned Kiss Miklos?"

"Haho! Good friend Far Seer, perhaps thou hast heard of the Green Daughter of the Green King."

"I have not."

"Well then, hear now, for I am going to woo her."

"Take me with thee, mayhap thou'lt get good of me."

Now there were six of them, and they journeyed and travelled after that, across forty-nine kingdoms and farther, till they came upon a man who threw a seven-hundred-pound iron club thirty-five miles as easily as I could throw a small stone a few yards. This was Far Caster, who, when he saw Kiss Miklos and his comrades, came and said: "God give thee a good day, renowned Kiss Miklos; for in my world-beautiful life I have ever heard thy fame."

"God guard thee, Far Caster!"

"What journey art thou on?"

"Better thou hadst not asked. Hast thou heard of the Green King?"

"I have not."

"Well, I am going to woo his daughter."

"Take me with thee, mayhap thou'lt get good of me."

"Come on thy own legs, if it please thee."

Like the seven deadly sins, they were seven now. They journeyed and travelled till they came to the castle of the Green King. Kiss Miklos stood before the king and said: "God give a good day to thy Highness."

"God keep thee, renowned Kiss Miklos; for in my world-beautiful life I have ever heard thy fame. What journey art thou on?"

"In my journeys and travels I have heard that thy Highness has a charming, love-pervaded, beautiful flower-stalk. What is the use in delay and denial? I have come for her."

"Haho! My good friend, the Green Daughter of the Green King is not so easily taken, for there are three tests before thee; if thou stand these tests, I will give thee my most beloved, my truly one and only daughter. The first test will be this: Thou hast a swift runner and so have I. They are making for my daughter at present a wedding dress at Pluto's, or perhaps it's ready this moment. If thy swift runner will bring that dress here, all right, – I care not: let the Green Daughter of the Green King be thine. My swift runner and thine will start tomorrow about four o'clock in the morning. But if I have not told thee, know now the thick end of the business, I will bring you all to the stake, if thy swift runner comes second."

But the Green King deceived; for that evening after sunset he sent off his swift runner, who was no other than his own old mother, who, let it be said meanwhile, was a witch, and a big one at that. Next morning at four o'clock, as had been agreed, Miklos started his own swift runner on the road so as to bring the wedding dress.

Swift Runner moved on, and he saw that the old mother of the Green King was a good way ahead, for she was just on the point of going in at Pluto's gate. Nothing more was needed. He rushed at her and she saw trouble soon, for he came up just as she had taken hold of the key; Swift Runner was not slow. He caught her by the jacket, hurled her back, ran in at the gate himself, and did not stop till he stood before his Highness, Pluto, told why he had come, and asked for the wedding dress. The dainty dress was nicely packed already in a box, and they gave it to him. Swift Runner hurried homeward, but the old mother of the Green King waited for him, and said: "Hear me, Swift Runner! Now thou art the victor, run not so fast; let us go home in pleasant quiet together."

Swift Runner stopped at the old woman's words, and they went on together, – went on till they came to a nice shady place, where the old woman found this to say: "Let us sit down in this shady place; let us rest. It is all the same. Thou art the winner. I will look in thy head."

Here Swift Runner sat down in the shady place; the old woman bent his head to her lap and began to search in it, and she searched and searched till Swift Runner fell asleep and was sunk in slumber. When Swift Runner was snoring away at his best, the old woman put a horse-skull under his head, – from that he would not have waked till the day of judgement; then she took the box from him and raced off as if she had been shot from a gun.

It was near four o'clock in the afternoon and Swift Runner had not come yet, though he said he ought to be there at three o'clock. Miklos therefore began to be uneasy, – his nose was itching, it was ringing in his right ear and jumping in his right eye, therefore he found this to say to his Far Seer: "Just look, canst thou see Swift Runner coming?"

Far Seer did not let this be repeated; in an instant he ran up on a hill, looked around, saw that Swift Runner was in a shady place, sleeping like a pumpkin, under a tree, with a horse-skull under his head.

"Oh, my good friend Kiss Miklos, the dog is in the garden! Swift Runner is sleeping in a nice shady place with a horse-skull under his head; the old woman is right here near the garden, and she has the wedding dress in a box."

"Here, good friend Far Caster," said Kiss Miklos, "stand forth and throw thy twelve-hundred-pound club at that cursed horse-skull under the head of Swift Runner; for as God is true, all seven of us will see shame, and die a fearful death."

Far Caster was not slow; in an instant he hurled the twelve-hundred-pound club and struck out luckily the horse-skull from under Swift Runner's head.

Then, 'pon my soul! Swift Runner sprang up, rubbed his eyes, looked around, saw that the old woman was running near the garden, and bearing the wedding robe. He was not slow. He rushed at her, but in truth it hung from a hair that he did not see disgrace, for the old woman had just taken the key of the Green King's door when Swift Runner reached her. He caught her by the jacket, took the box, and hurled the old woman back to Pluto's in such fashion that not her foot, nor even her little toe, touched ground on the way. Then he gave the wedding dress to Miklos, who took it that moment to the Green King, and putting it on the boxwood table said: "High lord, thy desire is accomplished; here is the dainty wedding dress."

"Haho! Renowned Kiss Miklos, this is but one trial in which thou art the winner, there are two behind. The Green Daughter of the Green King will not be thine till all of you, as many as there are, spend one night in my iron furnace, which I have heated with three hundred and sixty-six cords of wood; if ye can endure that terrible heat, all right; if not, ye will be roasted alive."

Here, 'pon my soul! what came of the affair or what did not, the Green King, as he had said, heated the iron furnace with three hundred and sixty-six cords of wood. The whole furnace was nothing but glowing fire, so that it was impossible to go near it. Now the question was, who should enter first, – who but Great Freezer? He was delighted with the pleasant amusement; he was shivering terribly because God's cold had then caught him, though he had nine pairs of boots on his feet, nine shirts and drawers on his body, nine neckcloths on his neck, nine sheepskin caps on his head, nine sheepskin overcoats on his back. I say, Great Freezer went first into the fiery furnace. He walked around in it, and straightway it became as cold as an ice-house; therefore he called out at the entrance: "Oh, I'm freezing! Oh, I'm freezing!" Then the others and Kiss Miklos went in, and they felt that the furnace was as cold as an ice-house, so that their teeth chattered. Kiss Miklos cried out at the entrance, saying, "Wood this way, or we shall freeze!"

The servants of the Green King threw an extra cord of wood into the furnace. With this Miklos and his companions made a fire, and gave earth no trouble. Next morning the Green King himself went to see the seven roasts, thinking they were burnt into dust. He opened the mouth of the furnace. He will fall on his back with horror, perhaps. Nothing of the sort; the seven good birds were sitting there alive in the furnace at the side of a fire, and not a dog's trouble had happened to a man of them.

Straightway the Green King called up Kiss Miklos and said to him: "Well, Renowned Kiss Miklos, thou hast stood two trials, but the third still remains. If ye pass that unharmed, then I don't care; my daughter will be thine, for I shall see that thou art not inferior to thy fame. The third trial is not other than this: In the yard is a herd of cattle not less than three hundred and sixty-six in number, and also there are three hundred and sixty-six kegs of wine, and if ye do not eat the three hundred and sixty-six heads of cattle and drink the three hundred and sixty-six kegs of wine by tomorrow, then I will have you all at the stake; but if ye eat and drink all, then as I say, I care not. Let my one and only most beloved daughter be thine."

In the evening after bedtime Miklos went with his comrades to the other yard where were the three hundred and sixty-six heads of cattle and the three hundred and sixty-six kegs of wine; but now the question was who should eat that ocean-great lot of cattle and drink that thundering lot of wine. No one would take more delight in the cattle than Great Eater, and with the thundering lot of wine no one felt better than Great Drinker; they would take care of them if they were twice as great. Miklos and his comrades, except Great Eater, knocked one of the bullocks on the head, pulled off his jacket, cut up his flesh and roasted it. That was enough for them, but it was not enough for Great Eater; for he would not spoil the taste of his mouth with it. He ate that herd of beasts, one after another, as if the earth had swallowed them, – ate hair, hide, bones, and horns, so that he didn't leave a single thing as a novelty; and even then he cried out nothing but, "Oh, I'm hungry! Oh, I'm hungry!" Then he went to his comrades, ate what they had left of the roast, and pressed it down with the ox-hide for a dessert. Even then he cried without ceasing, "Oh, I'm hungry! Oh, I'm hungry!"

Then they began at the wine. Miklos and his comrades, except Great Drinker, rolled forth one keg of wine, knocked the bottom out, and went to drinking. That keg was enough for them, but not enough for Great Drinker; for him it was as much as one drop would be for me. He would not spoil the taste of his mouth with it, but fell to drinking from the rest in such Magyar-Mishka style that when he looked around he saw that the three hundred and sixty-five kegs were empty. Then he cried unceasingly, "Oh, I'm thirsty! Oh, I'm thirsty!" After that he came to his comrades, and what they had left he drank to the last drop; and cried: "Oh, I'm thirsty! Oh, I'm thirsty!"

Next morning the Green King went himself to the yard to see if Kiss Miklos and his comrades had endured the third trial, – had they eaten the cattle and drunk the wine. It is a wonder that he didn't turn into a pillar of salt he was so frightened when he saw that there was not a horned beast left, nor a drop of wine. Then he complained: "They have eaten three hundred and sixty-six bullocks. Plague take it! Let them eat the cattle, but they might have left the hides; those could at least have been sold to a Jew for good money. – Well, renowned Kiss Miklos, thou hast stood the three tests, now my only and most dearly beloved daughter is thine; take her." With that the Green King seated his Green Daughter in a coach drawn by six black horses, and they drove towards the dominions of the Lead Friend.

On the road the Green Daughter of the Green King beckoned Miklos to her and asked him: "Hei! My heart's beautiful love, renowned Kiss Miklos, tell me, on thy true soul, art thou taking me for thyself or for another? If thou art not taking me for thyself, I will play tricks with thee."

"I am taking thee for myself; I am taking thee for another," answered Kiss Miklos.

Well, no more was said. Once, when turning and winding, they look in the coach; it is empty. The beautiful girl is gone. In a moment they stop, search the coach, but find her nowhere.

"Here, good friend Far Seer," said Kiss Miklos, "look around! Whither has our beautiful bird flown?"

Far Seer didn't let that be said twice. In the turn of an eye he surveyed the round earth, but he saw not the beautiful maiden.

"She is not on the dry earth," said Far Seer.

"Look into the sea," said Kiss Miklos.

Far Seer surveyed the deep sea, and saw her hidden in the belly of a three-pound whale, near the opposite shore of the sea.

"Ah, I see where she is!"

"Where?" asked Miklos.

"Hidden in the belly of a three-pound whale."

"Here, good friend Great Drinker," said Miklos, "come hither, and drink up the water of this deep sea!"

Great Drinker was not slow. He lay face under by the sea, and with three draughts drank up all the water. The three-pound whale was lying then in a bay near the opposite shore.

"Now, good brother Swift Runner," said Kiss Miklos, "step out and bring me that three-pound whale which is lying near the opposite shore."

Swift Runner rushed in a moment across the bottom of the sea, and brought back the three-pound whale. Miklos opened the whale, took out its stomach, cut it carefully, and out fell the Green Daughter of the Green King. Then he seated her in the coach, and they drove on.

They travelled and journeyed, and once the princess beckoned to Miklos, and asked: "My heart's beautiful love, renowned Kiss Miklos, tell me, on thy true soul, art thou taking me for thyself, or for another? If for thyself, very well; if not, I'll play tricks with thee."

"I am taking thee for myself; I am taking thee for another," answered Miklos.

No more was said. Once while turning and winding, the beautiful maiden is gone, the coach is empty. "Oh, the dog is in the garden!" They stop, search the six-horse coach, but find no beautiful princess.

"Here, good friend Far Seer," said Miklos, "stand forth, look around! Where is our beautiful bird?"

Far Seer surveyed the deep sea, but got no sight of the princess. "She is not in the sea."

"If she is not in the sea, look on dry land."

Far Seer looked around again, and he saw that the princess was at home, in the very middle of her father's garden, on the highest top of a blooming apple-tree, hidden in a ripe red apple. "I have found her!" said Far Seer.

"Where is she?"

"At home, in the very centre of the garden, hidden on the highest top of an apple-tree, in the middle of a ripe red apple."

"Here, Swift Runner, come forth!"

Swift Runner came forth, and stood like a pillar before Miklos, waiting for command.

"Run in a twinkle to the garden of the Green King, in the very middle of which is blooming an apple-tree; climb the tree, and bring me the ripe red apple which is on its highest top."

Swift Runner rushed as a whirlwind, at horse-death speed, found the tree, climbed it, plucked the red apple, and then, as if shot from a cannon, came back to Miklos, and gave him the apple. Miklos cut the apple in two; the Green Daughter of the Green King fell out. He seated her again in the coach, and they fared farther.

They travelled and journeyed, and again the princess beckoned to Miklos, and said: "My heart's heart, renowned Kiss Miklos, tell me, on thy true soul, art thou taking me for thyself, or for another? If for thyself, very well; if not, I'll play tricks with thee."

"I am taking thee for myself; I am taking thee for another."

Well, they said no more. Once, while turning and winding, they look in the coach the maiden is gone; the coach is empty. "Oh, the dog is in the garden!" They stop, search the six-horse coach, but find not the maiden.

"Friend Far Seer," said Miklos, "look around! Where is our beautiful bird?"

Far Seer was not slow; in the turn of an eye he surveyed the round earth, but saw nowhere the Green Daughter of the Green King. "She is not on the round earth," said he.

"Well, look in the deep sea."

Far Seer looked again; in the turn of an eye he surveyed the deep sea, but saw not the princess. "She is not in the deep sea," said Far Seer.

"Well, if she is not in the deep sea, look in the cloudy heavens."

Far Seer looked around; in the turn of an eye he surveyed the broad sky and the cloudy heavens. He saw a cocoon hanging from a thread slender as a spider-web, and hidden in that cocoon the Green Daughter of the Green King. "I have found her!" said Far Seer.

"Where is she?" asked Kiss Miklos.

"Far, far away, near the round forest, from the cloudy heavens is hanging a silk thread, slender as a spider-web, and on the end dangles a cocoon; in that she is hidden."

"Now, Far Caster, come forth!" said Miklos.

Far Caster stood like a pillar before Kiss Miklos, only waiting for command; but he had not long to wait, for Miklos said: "Listen, good friend Far Caster. Seest thou that thin silk thread hanging from the cloudy sky near the round forest?"

"I see."

"Then cast it down; but only when Swift Runner reaches the place beneath, so that it may not fall on the earth, but into his hand. Therefore, Swift Runner, move thy wheels that way; catch the cocoon and bring it to us."

Swift Runner rushed at horse-death speed to the place; Far Caster brought down the cocoon. Swift Runner caught it safely, and brought it to Miklos, who with his bright knife cut it open, and out came the princess. Then he seated her a third time in the coach; but they had arrived in the domains of the Lead Friend, so the Green Daughter of the Green King, having lost her power, could play no more tricks.

Kiss Miklos took farewell of his good friends, thanking them kindly for their aid. When they were alone the Green Daughter of the Green King fell to crying, and said: "My heart's beautiful love, I know thou art taking me to that dog of a Lead Friend, and I would rather be the bride of death than of him."

"Oh, my heart's golden bird," said Miklos, "I am taking thee for myself; but thou canst not be mine till I know where the strength of the Lead Friend lies. If we can discover that, it will be easy to destroy him."

"If that is thy grief, my heart's heart," said she, "I will soon help thee; leave that to me. Thou must know I am a woman."

With that Miklos and the princess kissed each other, and there was holy peace; they said: "I am thine, thou art mine."

They travelled and journeyed across forty-nine kingdoms, till Kiss Miklos could say, "We are at home," – for they were at the Lead Friend's mansion, – and could say to the princess, "Come out of thy coach; it won't cost thee a copper." Here the Lead Friend ran panting out of his mansion to the beautiful princess, but she turned from him. This pleased not the Lead Friend, and though one word is not much, he uttered not that much, but brought her into the lead mansion in silence.

Next day at sunrise the Lead Friend had to go to his furnace, taking Kiss Miklos with him. The young woman remained all alone. She took a lamp and started to search through the lead house. From chamber to chamber she went till she came to the cellar, but that was closed against her with seven iron doors. Now the question was to get into the cellar. Another would not have been able to pass the first door, but every iron door opened of itself before the magic of the Green Daughter of the Green King. She passed through the seven doors and entered the cellar. She saw there seven leaden vats placed in a row, and every one of them filled to the brim with gold and silver. She took off her apron and filled it with gold, went up, summoned the goldsmith, and gilded the lead threshold a hand in thickness. The Lead Friend was such a miser that he had not bread enough to eat, and every little coin he turned seven times between his teeth before he let it go once from his hand.

Well, in the evening the Lead Friend came home from his furnace, saw the housekeeping and what the young woman had done. Then, 'pon my soul! he plucked out his own lead beard and hair, trampled them like tow, and roared till the lead house was trembling.

"Who, in the name of a hundred thousand thunders, did this?" asked the Lead Friend.

"I did it," answered quite bravely the princess.

"How didst thou dare to do it without my knowledge, – without informing me?" With that the Lead Friend went to the Green Daughter of the Green King, and seized in his hand the golden hair which reached her heels. Twelve times did he drag her on the lead floor, and he wanted to take the lead flail to her. Kiss Miklos did not permit that, but took the maiden from his grasp and placed her on the silken bed. She was neither dead nor alive, but lay as a lifeless block of wood. But the Green Daughter of the Green King had no more pain than good myself; being a magic woman, seest thou, she had much in her power.

Now, what did she do? When the Lead Friend wound around his hand the golden hair reaching to her heels, she suddenly sprang out of her skin, and a devil jumped into it. And if the Lead Friend had struck him with the back of an axe, he would not have felt a dog's trouble; for the more he was beaten the more he would have laughed.

But the Lead Friend was troubled; ragged, with torn hair, crying and weeping he entered the white chamber, where the princess was lying without life. He went to her; pushed her, but she waked not; talked to her, but she heard not; cried, but she listened not. At last he found this to say: "Wake, my heart's beautiful love; I will do all that may please thee, but stop the gilding."

Then the princess spoke up to the Lead Friend, "I'll stop the gilding, but tell where thy strength lies."

"Oh, my heart's beautiful love, I would rather part with life than tell that."

Well, things remained thus. Next day at sunrise the Lead Friend went to his furnace, taking Kiss Miklos with him, for he lived in the suspicion that Miklos and the Green Daughter of the Green King would plot together and strive for his destruction.

The bride remained alone; she took the lamp and turned straight to the cellar. The great iron doors opened before her and closed behind. When she had passed the seven iron doors and entered the cellar, she spread her silk apron, and filled it with gold. Three times she returned, and three times she bore away the same amount, so that the apron was almost torn under it. Straightway she called the goldsmith and had the lead thresholds of three chambers gilded to the thickness of a hand. And as I say, the Lead Friend was so stingy that he did not eat bread enough, and every little coin he put seven times between his teeth before he let it out of his hand once.

The Lead Friend came home from his furnace towards evening, and saw the housekeeping, and saw also that now not one but three thresholds were gilded a hand's thickness. Here, 'pon my soul! the Lead Friend fell into such rage that he tore his own lead beard and hair out, and trampled them as he would tow. Then he roared so terribly that the lead house quivered, and turning to the princess he asked: "In the name of a hundred thousand devils, who did this?"

"I did it," answered the princess quite bravely.

"How didst thou dare to do this without my knowledge and consent?"

With that the Lead Friend seized the golden hair of the princess, which reached to her heels, and dragged her twelve times up and down the lead floor, twelve times did he hurl her against the floor, then he ran for the lead flail to kill her. Kiss Miklos would not let him do that, but seized the maiden from his hands, and placed her on the silken bed. The Green Daughter of the Green King was neither dead nor alive; she lay there still as a soulless block of wood. Still the princess felt no more pain than good myself. She knew witchcraft, and whatever she did or did not do, when the Lead Friend twisted her golden hair in his hand, she jumped out of her skin in a twinkle, and a devil got into it; if they had beaten him like a two-headed drum, or even more, he would have taken it as if they were fondling him.

Now the Lead Friend was terribly sorry; ragged, with torn hair, he entered the white chamber weeping; he wept a long time; pushed the princess, who waked not; spoke to her, she heard not; at last he found this to say: "Wake up, my heart's beautiful love; all thy desires will be accomplished, only stop the gilding."

"I'll stop the gilding, but tell where thy strength lies."

"Oh, my heart's beautiful love, I would rather part with my life than tell that."

Next day at sunrise the Lead Friend took Kiss Miklos to the furnace, lest while he was gone himself Miklos might go in secret and gather another man's hay. The bride was alone again, and wanted nothing better. Again she took the lamp and went straight to the cellar, where she opened her beautiful silk apron and filled it with gold, – took so much that the apron almost tore under it. She came seven times, and each time carried so much gold that her nose almost cut the earth, like the coulter of a plough. Then she called a goldsmith, and gilded to a hand's thickness the thresholds of seven rooms.

When the Lead Friend came home in the evening, he saw that not three but seven thresholds had a hand's thickness of gold on them. Then he fell into such a rage that he tore his leaden beard and hair, and trampled them as he would tow; but what good did that do him? – for he was trampling his own. Then he roared till the lead house rattled, and in his fury he asked: "A thousand million demons, who did this?"

"I did it," answered the princess all bravely.

"How didst thou dare to do this without my knowledge or command?"

With that he went in fury to the Green Daughter of the Green King, wound round his hand the golden hair which reached to her heels. Twelve times did he drag her over the leaden floor, twelve times did he dash her against it, twelve times did he raise her aloft, – and that was not enough; but he took out the lead flail, and began to thrash and beat the princess as if she were a bundle of wheat, so that she was swimming in blood. Kiss Miklos took her from his hands and placed her on the silken bed, where she lay, neither dead nor alive, still as a lifeless block.

Now the Lead Friend grew terribly sorry, and making himself squalid looking, he entered the white chamber, rushed to the princess, wept without ceasing, touched her but she woke not, spoke to her but she heard him not. At last he found this to say: "Wake up, my heart's beautiful love. I will tell where my strength lies. In the silken meadow under the seventh bush is a hare, under the tail of the hare an egg, in the egg a hornet, and in the hornet is hidden my strength, so that I live as long as the hornet lives; if the hornet dies, I die too."

The Green Daughter of the Green King heard all these words clearly, but acted as if she were neither dead nor alive, – lay there like a soulless block.

Well, 'pon my soul! what came of the affair or what did not, the princess rose from her silken bed in the night-time, quietly, in one garment; but she threw a great shawl around her neck, slipped out of the gate, found Kiss Miklos, to whom her word and speech was this: "Wake up, my heart's beautiful love, renowned Kiss Miklos, I know now where the strength of the Lead Friend lies; but listen to my word. In the silken meadow under the seventh bush lies a hare, under the hare's tail is an egg, in the egg a hornet, in the hornet is the Lead Friend's strength. If thou kill the hornet, the Lead Friend will lose his strength."

Our Miklos wanted nought else. He turned himself at once into a hound, drove the hare from the seventh bush of the silken meadow. The hare began to run, but the hound was not slow; with a long stick he struck the egg from the hare's tail. The egg broke and the hornet flew out, but the hound was not slow; with a great jump he caught the hornet, and crushed it to bits in his teeth. Then the hound shook himself and turned into Kiss Miklos again.

At daylight the Lead Friend was sick. He had lost his strength, he could not move his hands or his feet, and lay groaning on his lead couch like a man who had been pressing a straw-bed for seven years; and when the sun rose he breathed out his cursed soul.

Who was more delighted at his death than our Kiss Miklos and the Green Daughter of the Green King? Straightway they called a priest and a hangman and an iron cap. The priest joined them, the hangman thrashed around, God's arrow flashed, but no one was struck. There was soup plenty and to spare, lucky was the man who came with a spoon; the unhappy were happy; the gypsy fiddled, and the music spoke. When the feasting and the poppy week had passed, Kiss Miklos and his consort took a chariot of glass and gold, drawn by six black-haired steeds, and set out for Miklos's birthplace. Now, the shining sun had shone so sadly, and the bright moon had beamed so sadly that it could not be more so;

but the moment they beheld Miklos and his wife in the chariot of glass and gold, the bright sun shone joyously, and so did the clear moon.

"What's this? What's this?" said to himself the old king, who still rejoiced in good health. He summoned the wise men and the skilled scribes of the kingdom to his palace and gave them the following question: "Explain to me this. It is seven years since the two sons of the poor man brought back the bright moon and the shining sun; these two sons are now ruling kings, – may God keep them in health! – but the clear moon and the shining sun gave us such sorrowful light, and now all at once both are radiant."

One old man skilled in letters, and so old that his white beard almost came to the earth, and he could not stand on his feet alone, but three men supported him, spoke the following words: "Haho! High lord, there is great reason for this. The clear moon and the shining sun were sad because the man who really freed them from the claws of the dragons was pinioned in bondage; and he is no other than the renowned Kiss Miklos, the poor man's youngest son, who even at this moment is driving to the king's palace with the Green Daughter of the Green King, in a chariot drawn by six horses."

That moment Kiss Miklos and his wife entered the white chamber together. Here the lords and those great wise men all rose before them, as did even the old king himself, who advancing embraced and kissed them, led them to his own purple velvet throne, seated them thereon, and turning to the wise men and the skilled scribes, asked them, "Who really deserves the kingdom, the elder brothers or Kiss Miklos?"

The council said: "Kiss Miklos."

Then Miklos rose and said to the old king and the council: "High king and worthy council, it is true that I deserve the kingdom, and I would take it were I not the heir of the far-famed Lead Friend, and were it not that the dominions of the Green King, after his death, – which from my heart I wish not, – will come to me. This being the case the worthy council can see, and thy Highness can see also, that I may not accept the kingdom. Let it remain as it is, – let my eldest brother be king, and my second brother be viceroy; they are, I think, honourable men, and worthy."

The lords, sages, and skilled scribes present, as well as the old king, rose up and confirmed the wise speech of the youthful Kiss Miklos.

Then the two brothers of Kiss Miklos – the king and the viceroy – entered; they embraced and kissed one another, and sacred was the peace. After that, Kiss Miklos and his wife returned to the domains of the Lead Friend, and after the death of the Green King, Kiss Miklos inherited his dominions. And so he ruled two kingdoms very happily; and he and the Green Daughter of the Green King are living yet, if they are not dead.

The Orphan Boy and the Magic Stone

A CHIEF OF INDE NAMED INKITA had a son named Ayong Kita, whose mother had died at his birth.

The old chief was a hunter, and used to take his son out with him when he went into the bush. He used to do most of his hunting in the long grass which grows over nearly all the Inde country, and used to kill plenty of bush buck in the dry season.

In those days the people had no guns, so the chief had to shoot everything he got with his bow and arrows, which required a lot of skill.

When his little son was old enough, he gave him a small bow and some small arrows, and taught him how to shoot. The little boy was very quick at learning, and by continually practising at lizards and small birds, soon became expert in the use of his little bow, and could hit them almost every time he shot at them.

When the boy was ten years old his father died, and as he thus became the head of his father's house, and was in authority over all the slaves, they became very discontented, and made plans to kill him, so he ran away into the bush.

Having nothing to eat, he lived for several days on the nuts which fell from the palm trees. He was too young to kill any large animals, and only had his small bow and arrows, with which he killed a few squirrels, bush rats, and small birds, and so managed to live.

Now once at night, when he was sleeping in the hollow of a tree, he had a dream in which his father appeared, and told him where there was plenty of treasure buried in the earth, but, being a small boy, he was frightened, and did not go to the place.

One day, some time after the dream, having walked far and being very thirsty, he went to a lake, and was just going to drink, when he heard a hissing sound, and heard a voice tell him not to drink. Not seeing anyone, he was afraid, and ran away without drinking.

Early next morning, when he was out with his bow trying to shoot some small animal, he met an old woman with quite long hair. She was so ugly that he thought she must be a witch, so he tried to run, but she told him not to fear, as she wanted to help him and assist him to rule over his late father's house. She also told him that it was she who had called out to him at the lake not to drink, as there was a bad Ju Ju in the water which would have killed him. The old woman then took Ayong to a stream some little distance from the lake, and bending down, took out a small shining stone from the water, which she gave to him, at the same time telling him to go to the place which his father had advised him to visit in his dream. She then said, "When you get there you must dig, and you will find plenty of money; you must then go and buy two strong slaves, and when you have got them, you must take them into the forest, away from the town, and get them to build you a house with several rooms in it. You must then place the stone in one of the rooms, and whenever you want anything, all you have to do is to go into the room and tell the stone what you want, and your wishes will be at once gratified."

Ayong did as the old woman told him, and after much difficulty and danger bought the two slaves and built a house in the forest, taking great care of the precious stone, which he placed in an inside room. Then for some time, whenever he wanted anything, he used to go into the room and ask for a sufficient number of rods to buy what he wanted, and they were always brought at once.

This went on for many years, and Ayong grew up to be a man, and became very rich, and bought many slaves, having made friends with the Aro men, who in those days used to do a big traffic in slaves. After ten years had passed Ayong had quite a large town and many slaves, but one night the old woman appeared to him in a dream and told him that she thought that he was sufficiently wealthy, and that it was time for him to return the magic stone to the small stream from whence it came. But Ayong, although he was rich, wanted to rule his father's house and be a head chief for all the Inde country, so he sent for all the

Ju Ju men in the country and two witch men, and marched with all his slaves to his father's town. Before he started he held a big palaver, and told them to point out any slave who had a bad heart, and who might kill him when he came to rule the country. Then the Ju Ju men consulted together, and pointed out fifty of the slaves who, they said, were witches, and would try to kill Ayong. He at once had them made prisoners, and tried them by the ordeal of Esere bean to see whether they were witches or not. As none of them could vomit the beans they all died, and were declared to be witches. He then had them buried at once. When the remainder of his slaves saw what had happened, they all came to him and begged his pardon, and promised to serve him faithfully. Although the fifty men were buried they could not rest, and troubled Ayong very much, and after a time he became very sick himself, so he sent again for the Ju Ju men, who told him that it was the witch men who, although they were dead and buried, had power to come out at night and used to suck Ayong's blood, which was the cause of his sickness. They then said, "We are only three Ju Ju men; you must get seven more of us, making the magic number of ten." When they came they dug up the bodies of the fifty witches, and found they were quite fresh. Then Ayong had big fires made, and burned them one after the other, and gave the Ju Ju men a big present. He soon after became quite well again, and took possession of his father's property, and ruled over all the country.

Ever since then, whenever anyone is accused of being a witch, they are tried by the ordeal of the poisonous Esere bean, and if they can vomit they do not die, and are declared innocent, but if they cannot do so, they die in great pain.

The Thunder's Bride

THERE WAS A CERTAIN woman of Rwanda, the wife of Kwisaba. Her husband went away to the wars, and was absent for many months. One day while she was all alone in the hut she was taken ill, and found herself too weak and wretched to get up and make a fire, which would have been done for her at once had anyone been present. She cried out, talking wildly in her despair: "Oh, what shall I do? If only I had someone to split the kindling wood and build the fire! I shall die of cold if no one comes! Oh, if someone would but come – if it were the very Thunder of heaven himself!"

So the woman spoke, scarcely knowing what she said, and presently a little cloud appeared in the sky. She could not see it, but very soon it spread, other clouds collected, till the sky was quite overcast; it grew dark as night inside the hut, and she heard thunder rumbling in the distance. Then there came a flash of lightning close by, and she saw the Thunder standing before her, in the likeness of a man, with a little bright axe in his hand. He fell to, and had split all the wood in a twinkling; then he built it up and lit it, just with a touch of his hand, as if his fingers had been torches. When the blaze leapt up he turned to the woman and said, "Now, oh wife of Kwisaba, what will you give me?" She was quite paralyzed with fright, and could not utter a word. He gave her a little time to recover, and then went on: "When your baby is born, if it is a girl, will you give her to me for a wife?" Trembling all over, the poor woman could only stammer out, "Yes!" and the Thunder vanished.

Not long after this a baby girl was born, who grew into a fine, healthy child, and was given the name of Miseke. When Kwisaba came home from the wars the women met him with the news that he had a little daughter, and he was delighted, partly, perhaps, with the thought of the cattle he would get as her bride-price when she was old enough to be married. But when his wife told him about the Thunder he looked very serious, and said, "When she grows older you must never on any account let her go outside the house, or we shall have the Thunder carrying her off."

So as long as Miseke was quite little she was allowed to play out of doors with the other children, but the time came all too soon when she had to be shut up inside the hut. One day some of the other girls came running to Miseke's mother in great excitement. "Miseke is dropping beads out of her mouth! We thought she had put them in on purpose, but they come dropping out every time she laughs." Sure enough the mother found that it was so, and not only did Miseke produce beads of the kinds most valued, but beautiful brass and copper bangles. Miseke's father was greatly troubled when they told him of this. He said it must be the Thunder, who sent the beads in this extraordinary way as the presents which a man always has to send to his betrothed while she is growing up. So Miseke had always to stay indoors and amuse herself as best she could – when she was not helping in the house work – by plaiting mats and making baskets. Sometimes her old playfellows came to see her, but they too did not care to be shut up for long in a dark, stuffy hut.

One day, when Miseke was about fifteen, a number of the girls made up a party to go and dig *inkwa* (white clay) and they thought it would be good fun to take Miseke along with them. They went to her mother's hut and called her, but of course her parents would not hear of her going, and she had to stay at home. They tried again another day, but with no better success. Some time after this, however, Kwisaba and his wife both went to see to their garden, which was situated a long way off, so that they had to start at daybreak, leaving Miseke alone in the hut. Somehow the girls got to hear of this, and as they had already planned to go for *inkwa* that day they went to fetch her. The temptation was too great, and she slipped out very quietly, and went with them to the watercourse where the white clay was to be found. So many people had gone there at different times for the same purpose that quite a large pit had been dug out. The girls got into it and fell to work, laughing and chattering, when, suddenly, they became aware that it was growing dark, and, looking up, saw a great black cloud gathering overhead. And then, suddenly, they saw the figure of a man standing before them, and he called out in a great voice, "Where is Miseke, daughter of Kwisaba?" One girl came out of the hole, and said, "I am not Miseke, daughter of Kwisaba. When Miseke laughs, beads and bangles drop from her lips." The Thunder said, "Well, then, laugh, and let me see." She laughed, and nothing happened. "No, I see you are not she." So one after another was questioned and sent on her way. Miseke herself came last, and tried to pass, repeating the same words that the others had said; but the Thunder insisted on her laughing, and a shower of beads fell on the ground. The Thunder caught her up and carried her off to the sky and married her.

Of course she was terribly frightened, but the Thunder proved a kind husband, and she settled down quite happily and, in due time, had three children, two boys and a girl. When the baby girl was a few weeks old Miseke told her husband that she would like to go home and see her parents. He not only consented, but provided her with cattle and beer (as provision for the journey and presents on arrival) and carriers for her hammock, and sent her down to earth with this parting advice: "Keep to the high road; do not turn aside into any unfrequented bypath." But, being unacquainted with the country, her carriers soon strayed from the main track. After they had gone for some distance along the wrong road they found the path barred by a strange monster called an *igikoko*, a sort of ogre, who demanded something to eat. Miseke told the servants to give him the beer they were carrying: he drank all the pots dry in no time. Then he seized one of the carriers and ate him, then a second – in short, he devoured them all, as well as the cattle, till no one was left but Miseke and her children. The ogre then demanded a child. Seeing no help for it, Miseke gave him the younger boy, and then, driven to extremity, the baby she was nursing, but while he was thus engaged she contrived to send off the elder boy, whispering to him to run till he came to a house. "If you see an old man sitting on the ash-heap in the front yard that will be your grandfather; if you see some young men shooting arrows at a mark they will be your uncles; the boys herding the cows are your cousins; and you will find your grandmother inside the hut. Tell them to come and help us."

The boy set off, while his mother kept off the ogre as best she could. He arrived at his grandfather's homestead, and told them what had happened, and they started at once, having first tied the bells on their hunting dogs. The boy showed them the way as well as he could, but they nearly missed Miseke just at last; only she heard the dogs' bells and called out. Then the young men rushed in and killed the ogre with their spears. Before he died he said, "If you cut off my big toe you will get back everything belonging to you." They did so, and, behold! out came the carriers and the cattle, the servants and the children, none of them any the worse. Then, first making sure that the ogre was really dead, they set off for Miseke's old home. Her parents were overjoyed to see her and the children, and the time passed all too quickly. At the end of a month she began to think she ought to return, and the old people sent out for cattle and all sorts of presents, as is the custom when a guest is going to leave. Everything was got together outside the village, and her brothers were ready to escort her, when they saw the clouds gathering, and, behold! all of a sudden Miseke, her children, her servants, her cattle, and her porters, with their loads, were all caught up into the air and disappeared. The family were struck dumb with amazement, and they never saw Miseke on earth again. It is to be presumed that she lived happily ever after.

The Three Princesses in Whiteland

ONCE UPON A TIME there was a fisherman, who lived near the king's castle, and caught fish for the king's table. One day when he had gone fishing, he could not catch a thing. Try as he might, no matter how he baited or flung, not the tiniest fish would bite; but when this had gone on for a while, a head rose from the water and said: "If you will give me the first new thing that has come into your house, you shall catch fish a-plenty!" Then the man agreed quickly, for he could think of no new thing that might have come into the house. So he caught fish all day long, and as many as he could wish for, as may well be imagined.

But when he got home, he found that heaven had sent him a little son, the first new thing to come into the house since he had made his promise. And when he told his wife about it, she began to weep and wail, and pray to God because of the vow her husband had made. And the woman's grief was reported at the castle, and when it came to the king's ears, and he learned the reason, he promised to take the boy and see if he could not save him. And so the king took him and brought him up as though he were his own son, until he was grown. Then one day the boy asked whether he might not go out fishing with his father, he wanted to so very much, said he. The king would not hear of it; but at last he was given permission, so he went to his father, and everything went well all day long, until they came home in the evening. Then the son found he had forgotten his handkerchief, and went down to the boat to get it. But no sooner was he in the boat than it moved off with a rush, and no matter how hard the youth worked against it with the oars, it was all in vain. The boat drove on and on, all night long, and at last he came to a white strand, far, far away. He stepped ashore, and after he had gone a while he met an old man with a great, white beard. "What is this country called?" asked the youth. "Whiteland," was the man's answer, and he asked the youth where he came from, and what he wanted, and the latter told him. "If you keep right on along the shore," said the man, "you will come to three princesses, buried in the earth so that only their heads show. Then the first will call you – and she is the oldest – and beg you very hard to come to her and help her; and the next will do the same; but you must go to neither of them; walk quickly past them, and act as though you neither saw nor heard them. But go up to the third, and do what she asks of you, for then you will make your fortune."

When the youth came to the first princess, she called out to him, and begged him most earnestly to come to her; but he went on as though he had not seen her. And he passed the next one in the same manner; but went over to the third. "If you will do what I tell you to, you shall have whichever one of us you want," said she. Yes, he would do what she wanted. So she told him that three trolls had wished them into the earth where they were; but that formerly they had dwelt in the castle he saw on the edge of the forest.

"Now you must go to the castle, and let the trolls whip you one night through for each one of us," said she, "and if you can hold out, you will have delivered us." "Yes," said the youth, he could manage that. "When you go in," added the princess, "you will find two lions standing by the door; but if you pass directly between them, they will do you no harm. Go on into a dark little room and lie down, and then the troll will come and beat you; but after that you must take the bottle that hangs on the wall, and anoint yourself where he has beaten you, and you will be whole again. And take the sword that hangs beside the bottle, and kill the troll with it." He did as the princess had told him, passed between the lions as though he did not see them, and right into the little room, where he lay down. The first night a troll with three heads and three whips came, and beat the youth badly; but he held out, and when the troll had finished, he took the bottle and anointed himself, grasped the sword and killed the troll. When he came out in the morning the princesses were out of the ground up to their waists. The next night it was the same; but the troll who came this time had six heads and six whips, and beat him worse than the first one. But when he came out in the morning, the princesses were out of the ground up to their ankles. The third night came a troll who had nine heads and nine whips, and he beat and whipped the youth so severely that at last he fainted. Then the troll took him and flung him against the wall, and as he did so the bottle fell down, and its whole contents poured over the youth, and he was at once sound and whole again. Then he did not delay, but grasped the sword, killed the troll, and when he came out in the morning, the princesses were entirely out of the ground. So he chose the youngest of them to be his queen, and lived long with her in peace and happiness.

But at last he was minded to travel home, and see how his parents fared. This did not suit his queen; but since he wanted to go so badly, and finally was on the point of departure, she said to him: "One thing you must promise me, that you will only do what your father tells you to do, but not what your mother tells you to do." And this he promised. Then she gave him a ring which had the power of granting two wishes to the one who wore it. So he wished himself home, and his parents could not get over their surprise at seeing how fine and handsome he had become.

When he had been home a few days, his mother wanted him to go up to the castle and show the king what a man he had grown to be. His father said: "No, he had better not do that, for we will have to do without him in the meantime." But there was no help for it, the mother begged and pleaded until he went. When he got there he was more splendidly dressed and fitted out than the other king. This did not suit the latter, and he said: "You can see what my queen looks like, but I cannot see yours; and I do not believe yours is as beautiful as mine." "God grant she were standing here, then you would see soon enough!" said the young king, and there she stood that very minute. But she was very sad, and said to him: "Why did you not follow my advice and listen to your father? Now I must go straight home, and you have used up both of your wishes." With that she bound a ring with her name on it in his hair, and wished herself home.

Then the young king grew very sad, and went about day in, day out, with no other thought than getting back to his queen. "I must try and see whether I cannot find out where Whiteland is," thought he, and wandered forth into the wide world. After he had gone a while he came to a hill; and there he met one who was the lord of all the beasts of the forest – for they came when he blew his horn – and him the king asked where Whiteland was. "That I do not know," said he, "but I will ask my beasts." Then he called them up with his horn, and asked whether any of them knew where Whiteland might be; but none of them knew anything about it.

Then the man gave him a pair of snowshoes. "If you stand in them," said he, "you will come to my brother, who lives a hundred miles further on. He is the lord of the birds of the air. Ask him. When you have found him, turn the snowshoes around so that they point this way, and they will come back home of their own accord." When the king got there, he turned the snowshoes around, as the lord of the beasts had told him, and they ran home again. He asked about Whiteland, and the man called up all the birds with his horn, and asked whether any of them knew where Whiteland might be. But none of them knew. Long after the rest an old eagle came along; and he had been out for some ten years, but did not know either.

"Well," said the man, "I will lend you a pair of snowshoes. When you stand in them you will come to my brother, who lives a hundred miles further on. He is the lord of all the fishes in the sea. Ask him. But do not forget to turn the snowshoes around again." The king thanked him, stepped into the snowshoes, and when he came to the one who was lord of all the fishes in the sea, he turned them around, and they ran back like the others. There he once more asked about Whiteland.

The man called up his fishes with his horn, but none of them knew anything about it. At last there came an old, old carp, whom he had called with his horn only at the cost of much trouble. When he asked him, he said: "Yes, I know it well, for I was cook there for fully ten years. Tomorrow I have to go back again, because our queen, whose king has not come home again, is going to marry someone else." "If such be the case," said the man, "I'll give you a bit of advice. Out there by the wall three brothers have been standing for the last hundred years, fighting with each other about a hat, a cloak and a pair of boots. Anyone who has these three things can make himself invisible, and wish himself away as far as ever he will. You might say that you would test their possessions, and then decide their quarrel for them." Then the king thanked him, and did as he said. "Why do you stand there fighting till the end of time?" said he to the brothers. "Let me test your possessions if I am to decide your quarrel." That suited them; but when he had hat, cloak and boots, he told them: "I will give you my decision the next time we meet!" and with that he wished himself far away. While he was flying through the air he happened to meet the North Wind. "And where are you going?" asked the North Wind. "To Whiteland," said the king, and then he told him what had happened to him. "Well," said the North Wind, "you are travelling a little quicker than I am; for I must sweep and blow out every corner. But when you come to your journey's end, stand on the steps beside the door, and then I'll come roaring up as though I were going to tear down the whole castle. And when the prince who is to have the queen comes and looks out to see what it all means, I'll just take him along with me."

The king did as the North Wind told him. He stationed himself on the steps; and when the North Wind came roaring and rushing up, and laid hold of the castle walls till they fairly shook, the prince came out to see what it was all about. But that very moment the king seized him by the collar, and threw him out, and the North Wind took him and carried him off. When he had borne him away, the king went into the castle. At first the queen did not recognize him, for he had grown thin and pale because he had wandered so long in his great distress; but when he showed her the ring, she grew glad at heart, and then they had a wedding which was such a wedding that the news of it spread far and wide.

Cherry

THERE WAS ONCE A POOR LABOURER who had so many children that he was hardly able to buy food and clothing for them. For this reason, as soon as they grew old enough, they went out into the world to shift for themselves. One after another they left their home, until at last only the youngest one, Cherry by name, was left. She was the prettiest of all the children. Her hair was as black as jet, her cheeks as red as roses, and her eyes so merry and sparkling that it made one smile even to look at her.

Every few weeks one or another of the children who were out at service came back to visit their parents, and they looked so much better fed, and so much better clothed than they ever had looked while they were at home that Cherry began to long to go out in the world to seek her fortune, too.

"Just see," she said to her mother; "all my sisters have new dresses and bright ribbons, while I have nothing but the old patched frocks they have outgrown. Let me go out to service to earn something for myself."

"No, no," answered her mother. "You are our youngest, and your father would never be willing to have you go, and you would find it very different out there in the world from here, where everyone loves you and cares for you."

However, Cherry's heart was set upon going out to seek her fortune, and when she found her parents would never give their consent, she determined to go without it. She tied up the few clothes she had in a big handkerchief, put on the shoes that had in them the fewest holes, and off she stole one fine morning without saying goodbye to anyone but the old cat that was asleep upon the step.

As long as she was within sight of the house she hurried as fast as she could, for she was afraid her father or mother might see her and call her back, but when the road dipped down over a hill she walked more slowly, and took time to catch her breath and shift her bundle from one hand to the other.

At first the way she followed was well known to her, but after she had travelled on for several hours she found herself in a part of the country she had never seen before. It was bleak and desolate with great rocks, and not a house in sight, and Cherry began to feel very lonely. She longed to see her dear home again, with the smoke rising from the chimney and her mother's face at the window, and at last she grew so homesick that she sat down on a rock and began to sob aloud.

She had been sitting there and weeping for some time when she felt a hand upon her shoulder. She looked up and saw a tall and handsome gentleman standing beside her. He was richly dressed and looked like a foreigner, and there were many rings upon his fingers. It seemed so strange to see him standing there close to her, when a little time before there had been no one in sight, that Cherry forgot to sob while she stared at him. He was smiling at her in a friendly way, and his eyes sparkled and twinkled so brightly that there never was anything like it.

"What are you doing in such a lonely place as this, my child?" said he. "And why are you weeping so bitterly?"

"I am here because I started out to take service with someone," answered Cherry; "and I am weeping because it is so lonely, and I wish I were at home again"; and she began to sob.

"Listen, Cherry," said the gentleman, once more laying his hand on her shoulder. "I am looking for a kind, bright girl to take charge of my little boy. The wages are good, and if you like, you shall come with me and be his nurse."

This seemed a great piece of good luck to Cherry, for she was sure from the gentleman's looks that he must be very rich as well as kind. She quickly wiped her eyes and told him she was more than willing to go with him.

As soon as the stranger heard this he smiled again, and bidding her follow him he turned aside into a little path among the rocks that Cherry had not noticed before. At first this path was both rough and thorny, but the further they went the broader and smoother it grew, and always it led downhill. After a while instead of thorns, flowering bushes bordered the path, and later still, trees loaded with such fruit as Cherry had never seen before. It shone like jewels, and smelled so delicious that she longed to stop and taste it, but that her master would not allow. There was no sunlight now, but neither were any clouds to be seen overhead. A soft, pale light shone over everything, making the landscape seem like something seen in a dream.

The gentleman hurried her along, and when he saw she was growing tired he took her hand in his and immediately all her weariness disappeared, and her feet felt so light it seemed as though she could run to the ends of the earth.

After they had gone a long, long way they came to a gate overhung with an arch of flowering vines. The garden within was filled with fruit trees even more wonderful than those along the road, and through them she could see a beautiful house that shone like silver.

The gentleman opened the gate, and immediately a little boy came running down the path toward them. The child was very small, but his face looked so strange and wise and old that Cherry was almost afraid of him.

The gentleman stooped and kissed him and said, "This is my son," and then they all three went up the path together.

When they came near the house the door opened and a little, strange-looking old woman looked out. She was gnarled and withered and grey, and looked as though she might be a hundred.

"Aunt Prudence, this is the nurse I have brought home to look after the boy for us," said the gentleman.

The old woman scowled, and her eyes seemed to bore into Cherry like gimlets. "She'll peep and pry, and see what shouldn't be seen. Why couldn't you have been satisfied with one like ourselves for a nurse?" grumbled the old woman.

"It's best as it is," answered the gentleman in a low voice. "Many a one has sent her child to rest in a cradle there above, and they've been all the better for it."

Cherry did not know what he was talking about, but if she had been afraid of the child she was even more afraid of the old woman.

And indeed in the next few days Aunt Prudence made the girl's life very unhappy. The gentleman gave Cherry full charge of the child, and seemed very contented with her, but the old woman grumbled and scolded, and found fault with everything she did.

It was Cherry's duty to bathe the child every morning, and after she had washed him she was obliged to anoint his eyes with a certain ointment that was kept in a silver box. "And be very careful," said her master, sternly, "that you never touch the least particle of it to your own eyes, for if you do, misfortune will certainly come upon you."

Cherry promised that she would not, but she felt very curious about this ointment. She was sure it must have some very wonderful properties, for always after she had rubbed the child's eyes with it they looked stranger and brighter than ever, and she was sure he saw things that she could not see. Sometimes he would seem to join in games invisible to her, and sometimes he would suddenly leave her and run down a path to meet someone, though as far as she could see not a living soul was there. But if Cherry asked him any questions he would become quite silent, and look at her sideways in a strange way.

There were doors in the house that Cherry was forbidden to open, and she used to wonder and wonder what was behind them. Once she saw her master come out from one of the rooms beyond, but he shut the door quickly behind him, and she caught no glimpse of what was within.

However, she was very comfortable there – well-fed, well-clothed and well-paid, and she would have been quite happy if it had not been for Aunt Prudence. Instead of growing kinder to her as time went on, the old woman grew crosser and crosser. She was always scolding, and her tongue was so sharp that she often made Cherry weep bitterly, and wish she was at home again, or any place but there. Once when she was sobbing to herself in the garden, her master came to her. "Cherry," he said, "I see that you and Aunt Prudence can never live in peace together, and I am going to send her away for a while, but if I do, you must promise to do nothing that might displease me."

Cherry promised, and after that the old woman disappeared, and the girl did not know what had become of her.

Cherry was now very happy. Her master was never cross with her, and the child was very obedient, and if he did not ever laugh, neither did he ever weep. She helped her master in the garden very often, and when she had done very well he would sometimes kiss her and call her a good child and then she was happier than ever.

But one time he went away for a few days, and Cherry seemed quite alone in the house except for the child, for the other servants she had never seen. The little boy went out to play in the garden, and suddenly Cherry began to feel so curious as to what was back of the forbidden doors that it seemed as though she would die if she did not look. She tried to think of other things, and to remember how displeased her master would be if she opened the doors, but at last she could bear it no longer. She would just see what was behind one of them, and then she would look no further. But first she made sure that the little boy was still at play in the garden. He was sitting on the edge of a fountain, looking down into it, and suddenly he waved his hand and called out as though to something in the water.

Then Cherry opened the door and slipped through.

She found herself in a long hall entirely of marble. The floor, the ceilings and walls all were of blocks of marble, black and white, and ranged up and down it were many marble statues. Some were the figures of beautiful women, some were of princes with crowns upon their heads or of young men magnificently dressed. She went slowly down the hall, staring and wondering, and at the very end she came upon Aunt Prudence, but it was an Aunt Prudence turned into marble, and scowling at her with marble, unseeing eyes. When she saw that, Cherry knew that she was in fairyland, and that her master had by his magic powers turned the old woman into this shape to quiet her scolding tongue.

She was terrified, for she was afraid that, as her master was a fairy, he would know that she had disobeyed him, and she went out quickly and closed the door behind her. However, when the gentleman came home that evening he was as kind and pleasant as ever, so she made sure that he knew nothing of what she had done.

But there was one thing Cherry was even more curious about than she had been about the doors, and that was about the ointment she rubbed upon the child's eyes. Every day, more and more, she longed to rub her own eyes with it and try whether she, too, would not see invisible things. But beside her fear of disobeying her master the child's eyes were always upon her while she had the box open, and as soon as she had rubbed his eyes and closed it she was obliged to give it to him, and she never could tell what he did with it or where he put it.

One morning, however, just after she had rubbed his eyes, and before she had washed her hands, she made out she had dropped the box by accident, and when she stooped to pick it up she managed to rub one eye with a finger that had a little ointment upon it. The child did not see what she had done, but when Cherry looked about her what a wonderful change had come over the garden. Where all had seemed lonely and silent before, were crowds of little people playing around or going seriously about their business. They swung in the flower bells, they climbed the blades of grass. They spun ropes of cobweb, or sat in groups among the roots of trees, talking together and nodding their wise little heads. But when she looked down into the fountain she saw the strangest sight of all, for there was her master, dressed just as he had been when he said goodbye to her that morning, but now he was no longer than her hand, and riding a fish that he drove round and round in the water with a tiny whip. Cherry looked and looked, but her master never looked up nor noticed her. He played round with the fishes for quite a while and then suddenly disappeared. A moment after, the gate clicked, and when Cherry looked up there he was coming in, as tall as ever, and with not a hair of him wet.

He was often away after this and on one of these times Cherry determined to look into the marble room again.

She made sure that the child was outside and playing around with the other fairies, and then she stole to the forbidden door and softly opened it a crack. As soon as she did this, she heard a sound of pleasant music. She peeped in and what a wonderful sight she saw! The stone ladies and gentlemen had all come to life, and were dancing there to the music. They moved and smiled and bowed to each other, and at the head of the dance was her master with the loveliest lady of them all as his partner. While Cherry looked, the dance came to an end and he led the lady to a seat, but before she sat down he kissed her.

When Cherry saw that, she closed the door and ran away to her room, and there she began to sob and cry; she was so jealous over what she had seen that it seemed as though her heart would burst.

That afternoon her master came again as kind and smiling as ever, but Cherry would hardly look at him or answer anything he said. Presently he asked her to come out into the garden and help him with the flowers, and this she did, though she was still very moody.

They worked there for quite a while, and then when they had finished everything there was to be done, her master said, "You are a good child, Cherry," and kissed her.

Cherry pushed him away and began to sob again. "Why do you kiss me?" she cried. "You don't care for anybody but your beautiful lady. If you want to kiss anybody, go kiss her."

When her master heard that, his face changed, and he looked at her so angrily that Cherry was frightened. "So you have been prying!" he cried, "and Aunt Prudence was right when she warned me not to trust you. Now that you have seen what you have seen, you can stay here no longer."

"Oh, do not send me away," Cherry begged of him. "Let me stay and I promise that I will never disobey you again."

"I am sorry, Cherry," her master answered, and he no longer looked angry, "but after this, they would not let me keep you." With that he raised his hand and gave her a sharp box on the ears, and she lost all consciousness.

When she came to herself she was sitting on the doorstep of her own home and her mother was shaking her by the shoulder and calling her.

Cherry started up and looked about her. "Where – where is he?" she cried. "How did I come here, and what has become of my master?"

Her mother did not know what she was talking about, and when after a little, Cherry began and told her all her story, she thought the child was dreaming or had lost her wits. But when later on she found that the girl's pockets were full of fairy gold, enough to make them rich for years, she was obliged to believe that the story was true, wonderful as it was.

But for a long time after she came home, Cherry used to trudge away to the lonely heath every now and then, and sit there hoping her master would come for her. But he never did, and never again did she find a place where the wages were in gold and paid as freely as they had been in fairyland.

The Oat Cake

ONE TIME THE FARMER'S WIFE made two oat cakes. She shaped them, and patted them and put them down in front of the fire to bake. "They will do for the good man's dinner," said she.

Then said one cake to the other cake, "It is all very well for the woman to say that, but I have no wish to be eaten. I will wait until I am baked hard, and then I shall set out to see the world."

"That is a poor way to talk, brother," replied the other. "Oat cakes were made to be eaten, and you should be proud to think the master himself is to have you for dinner." "Master or no master, I have no wish to be eaten," repeated the first oat cake.

Not long after that, the farmer came home, and he was very hungry. First he ate the oat cake that wished to be eaten, and after he had finished it, he stretched out his hand for the other, but it slipped through his fingers and away it rolled, out of the door and on down the road.

It rolled along and rolled along until it came to a neat, tidy house with a thatched roof.

"This looks like a good and proper place for me to stop," said the oat cake, so it rolled on in through the doorway.

There inside were a tailor and his two apprentices, all of them sitting cross-legged and sewing away; and the tailor's wife stood by the fire, stirring the porridge.

When the tailor and the boys saw the oat cake come rolling in across the floor so boldly, they were frightened, and jumped up and hid behind the woman.

"Now out upon you! To be frightened by an oat cake!" cried the good wife. "Quick! Catch hold of it and divide it among you, and I'll give you some milk to drink with it."

When the tailor and his apprentices heard this, they took courage and ran out and tried to catch the oat cake; but it dodged them and rolled under the table and under the chairs, and while they were chasing it and the woman watching them, the porridge boiled over into the fire and was burned.

But the oat cake escaped them, and rolled out through the door, and on down the road again. "I'd better go a bit farther before I settle down for the night," it thought to itself.

Presently it came to a little small house. "I'll try how it is in here," said the oat cake, and in it rolled.

There sat a weaver at his loom, and his wife was winding some yarn.

"What's that that just came in at the door?" asked the weaver, for his eyesight was not very good.

"It's an oat cake!" said his wife staring.

"Catch it woman! Catch it, before it rolls away again!" cried the weaver.

The woman chased the oat cake up and down and round about, and the weaver left his work and joined in the chase, but the oat cake was too lively for them. Every time they thought they had it, it slipped through their fingers as though it were buttered.

"Throw your yarn over it and snare it," cried the weaver.

The woman threw her yarn over the oat cake, but the cake tangled up the yarn so that later on it took the woman a good two days to straighten it out again. But the oat cake escaped and rolled out and down the road.

"That's too lively a place for me to stay," said the oat cake to itself.

At the next place where the oat cake stopped, a woman was churning.

"Oh, the dear little, pretty little oat cake!" cried she. "I have good thick cream today, and plenty of it, and the oat cake will taste good with it."

"But first you must catch me," said the oat cake.

It rolled round and round the churn, and the woman ran after it, and in the end she fell against the churn and upset it.

While she was cleaning up the mess, the oat cake set out on further adventures.

"So far I've found no place in the world where an oat cake can rest in peace and quiet," said the cake. "But, there must be such a place somewhere, and if there is, I mean to find it."

Soon it came to a bit of a stream, with a mill beside it.

The oat cake rolled into the mill, and there stood a miller at work, and he was all white with flour. "Oat cake and a bit of cheese taste well together," said the miller. "The cheese I already have. Come in, come in and make the other half of the feast."

But the oat cake was frightened and rolled on out, and the miller never bothered his head further about it.

The next place the oat cake stopped was at a smithy. The smith was busy beating out a horseshoe, but when he saw the oat cake he laid aside the shoe.

"Welcome! Welcome! I like an oat cake and a drink of ale as well as the next man. Come in and let us feast together."

"Not I," cried the oat cake, and away it rolled in haste, and as the road was downhill now, it made good time.

The smith ran after it, and when he found the cake was going too fast for him, he threw his hammer after it, and the hammer fell into a thicket, and the smith had a great time finding it.

But the oat cake hid in a crack between two rocks, and lay there quiet until the smith had found his hammer and gone back to his smithy again grumbling. Then out it came and away it rolled, but it was getting tired now.

"Maybe it would have been better if I had gone to rest in the good man's stomach," said the oat cake, "but here we go, and I have no mind to be eaten by the first stranger who takes a fancy to me, – no, nor by the second either."

In the next house the oat cake entered, the good wife was cooking supper, and her husband sat plaiting straw rope.

"Look at that!" cried the woman. "You're always asking me for oat cake, and there is one ready to your hand. Quick! Quick! Shut the door and catch it."

The man jumped up to shut the door, but he caught his foot in the rope he was plaiting and fell flat on the floor. The woman threw her porridge stick at the cake, but away it went and off down the road.

"Now I'll have to find some place to sleep," said it to itself. "No knowing what will happen if I lay me down by the roadside."

It saw an open door, and in it rolled. The good man of the house had just taken off his breeches, and the woman was tucking the children into bed.

"Look! Look!" cried the woman. "There is an oat cake rolling in at the door, and no one coming after to claim it. Catch it before it can get away again."

The good man jumped up and threw his breeches at it. They fell on the oat cake and almost smothered it, but it managed to roll out from under them and away it went, with the man and his wife in full chase after it, and the children crying after them.

But the oat cake was too quick, even for the two of them. It outran them both, and the man and his wife had to go back home without it, the man with his bare legs, and the neighbours peeking out at him from behind their window curtains.

By this time it was dark. "I'll have to hurry if I want to find a place tonight where I can sleep in quiet," said the oat cake.

So now it rolled along more briskly, and presently it came to a pasture, and it leaped and bounded across it at a great rate, for it was all downhill, and then suddenly – plunk! – it fell down into a fox's hole.

The fox was at home and half asleep, but as soon as he saw the oat cake, he was wide awake again in a moment. The fox had had nothing to eat all day, and he did not stop to look twice at the oat cake, but bit it in half and swallowed it down in a trice and with no words about it.

So the oat cake slept quiet after all its wanderings, but it might as well have been eaten by the farmer in the first place.

The Princess of the Brazen Mountain

THERE WAS A YOUNG PRINCE, who was not only most handsome and well-grown, but also most kind-hearted and good. Now sooner or later kindness always meets its reward, though it may not seem so at first.

One summer's evening the prince was walking on the banks of a lake, when he looked up, and saw to his great surprise, in the air, against the rosy clouds of the sunset, three beautiful beings with wings – not angels, nor birds – but three beautiful damsels.

And having alighted on the ground they dropped their wings and their garments, and left them lying on the shore and leaped into the cool water, and began splashing and playing about in it, like so many waterfowl.

As soon as the prince saw this he came out from his hiding-place in the bushes, picked up one pair of wings and hid himself again.

When they had been long enough in the water, the beautiful damsels came again to land, and dressed themselves quickly.

Two of them soon had on both their white dresses and their wings; but the youngest could not find hers.

They held a short consultation, and the result was, that the two elder flew away in the shape of birds, as fast as they could, to fetch another pair of wings for their younger sister.

They soon vanished in the blue sky; but she remained alone, wringing her hands, and crying.

"What are you crying for, you lovely maiden?" asked the prince, emerging from the bushes.

"Oh! I am so unhappy!" she replied. "I am a princess of the Brazen Mountain; my sisters and I came here to bathe in the lake; and somebody has stolen my wings; so I must wait here, until they bring me another pair."

"I am a prince," he replied; "this is my father's kingdom; be my wife, and I will give you back your wings."

"Very well," she said; "I consent, only you must give me back my wings at once."

"Let us first go to church, and get married," he answered, and taking the lovely princess by the hand, he brought her to his father and mother, and asked their permission to marry her.

The king and queen were delighted with their beautiful daughter-in-law, gave them their blessing, and all was got ready for the wedding.

And directly they came back from church the prince, overcome with joy, kissed his bride, and gave her back her wings.

She took them joyfully, fastened them to her shoulders; then flew out of the window, and vanished.

All the wedding-guests were in consternation; the king looked very serious; the queen wept bitterly; but the prince so grieved after his bride, that, having obtained his parents' consent, he went out into the wide world to search for that Brazen Mountain, where he hoped to find her.

He travelled for a long time, inquiring about it of everyone he met; but nobody had ever heard of such a mountain; and he began to give up all hope of ever finding it.

Late one evening he saw a twinkling light before him, which he followed, in the hope of coming to some habitation. It led him on a long way, across level plains, through deep defiles, and at length some way into a dark forest. But at last he came to whence the light proceeded – from a solitary hermitage.

He went in; but found the hermit lying dead, with six wax candles burning around him. He had evidently been dead for some time. Yet there seemed to be nobody near him, nor any inhabitants at all in this desolate region.

The prince's first thought was how to get him buried, and with proper rites, when there was no priest – nor indeed any people at all – to be found in the neighbourhood.

While he was thinking over this, something fell from a peg in the wall, close beside him; it was a leather whip.

The prince took it up, and read on the handle these words:

'The Magic Whip.'

As he knew its virtue, he called out:

"Ho! Magical Whip!
To right and left skip!
And do what I will!"

The whip jumped from his hand, became invisible, and flew away.

In a short time there was the hum of a multitude through the forest; and the head forester entered, breathless, followed by a crowd of under-keepers, and many more people with them.

Some set about making a coffin, others began digging a grave, and the head-keeper rode off to fetch a priest.

And as soon as it was dawn mass was said; the bells began ringing from several far-distant churches; and at sunrise the corpse was decently buried. When the funeral was over all the people dispersed to their homes, and the Magical Whip returned of itself to the prince's hand.

He stuck it into his girdle, and went on, till after an hour or two he came to a clearing in the forest, where twelve men were fighting desperately among themselves.

"Stop, you fellows!" exclaimed the prince. "Who are you? And what are you fighting about?"

"We are robbers," they replied, "and we are fighting for these boots, which were the property of our deceased leader. Whoever has them can go seven leagues at one step; and he who gets them will be our leader. As you are a stranger we will abide by your decision, as to whom this pair of boots shall belong, and give you a heap of gold into the bargain for your trouble."

The prince drew on the boots, took the Magical Whip from his girdle, and said:

"Ho! Magical Whip!
To right and left skip!
And do what I will!"

The whip jumped from his hand, became invisible, and well thrashed the robbers. In the midst of the confusion the prince made his escape, and having the boots on he went seven miles at every step, and was soon far enough away from the robbers' den.

But as he was no nearer to finding out where the Brazen Mountain was, he had no need to go quite so fast; so he took off the seven-league boots, put them under his arm, and the Magic Whip in his girdle, and went at his ordinary pace, till he came to a narrow path between some rocks, where again he came upon twelve men fighting.

They explained that they were fighting for an invisible cap, which had belonged to their late leader; and asked him, as a stranger, to decide who should have it.

So he set the Magical Whip, as before, to work; and there was a nice confusion among these robbers, for not seeing where the blows came from they fell upon one another; and at last, frightened out of their senses, they took flight, and scattered in all directions. The prince, having put on the invisible cap, was able to walk among them, and talk to them; and they all heard, though they could not see him.

He now began to consider whether he could not use all these treasures to help him to find the Brazen Mountain. So he drew on the seven-league boots, settled the invisible cap on his forehead, and taking the Magical Whip from his girdle, said:

"Oh! Thou wondrous Magic Whip!
Lead me on; I'll follow thee!
Onward to the Brazen Mountain
Lead me, where I fain would be!"

The whip sprang from his hand. It did not become invisible this time, but glided rapidly a little above the ground, like a boat over a calm sea. Though it flew like a bird, the prince was quite able to keep pace with it, because he had on the seven-league boots. He was scarcely aware of the fact, when in less than a quarter of an hour they came to a standstill – at the Brazen Mountain.

At first the prince was overjoyed at having reached the goal of his wishes; but when he looked more closely at its smooth perpendicular sides, hard as adamant – its summit lost in the clouds – he was in despair; for how was he ever to get to the top of it?

However, he thought there must be some way up after all; so taking off his boots and cap, he set off to walk round the base of the mountain.

In half an hour he came to a mill, with twelve millstones. The miller was an old wizard, with a long beard down to the ground. He stood beside a stove – whereupon a kettle was boiling – stirring the contents with a long iron spoon, and piling wood on the fire.

The prince looked into the kettle.

"Good morning to you, gaffer. What are you doing there?"

"That's my own business," replied the miller gruffly.

"What mill is this?" the prince next asked.

"That's no business of yours," replied the miller.

The prince was not going to be satisfied with this; so he gave his usual orders to the Magical Whip, which forthwith became invisible, and began to lash the miller soundly. He tried to run away; but it was no use; till the prince took pity on him, and called the whip back again. He put it up, and then said:

"Whose mill is this?"

"It belongs to the three princesses of the Brazen Mountain," replied the miller. "They let down a rope here every day, and draw up all the flour they want by the rope."

As he said this a thick silken rope came down, with a loop at the end, which struck the threshold of the mill.

The prince made ready; and when the usual sack of wheat flour was bound fast in the loop, he climbed upon it, having first put on his invisible cap, and was thus drawn up to the top of the Brazen Mountain.

The three princesses, having drawn up their supply of flour, put it into their storehouse, and went back to their dwelling.

Their palace was most beautiful, all silver without, and all gold within. All the windows were of crystal; the chairs and tables were made of diamonds, and the floors of looking-glass. The ceilings were like the sky, with mimic stars and moon shining therein; and in the principal saloon there was a sun, with rays all round; beautiful birds were singing, monkeys were telling fairy tales; and in their midst amongst all this sat three most beautiful princesses.

The two eldest were weaving golden threads in their looms; but the youngest, the prince's wife, sat silently apart from her sisters, listening to the murmur of a fountain, her head leaning on her hand, in deep thought. And as she sat there two pearly tears coursed down her lovely face.

"What are you thinking of, sister?" asked the two elder princesses.

"I am thinking of the prince, my husband. I love to think of him, and I am so sorry for him, poor fellow! To think I left him for no fault at all; and when we loved one another so dearly! Oh! Sisters! I shall have to leave you, and go back to him; only I fear he will never forgive me, however I entreat him, for having behaved so unkindly to him."

"I forgive you, I forgive you everything, darling!" exclaimed the prince throwing off the invisible cap, and embracing her rapturously.

Then she gave him wings like her own, and they flew away together. In an hour or two they arrived in his father's kingdom.

The king and queen welcomed them joyfully, and all was greatest joy and happiness henceforward.

Little Brother Primrose and Sister Lavender

I

THE STRONGHOLD OF A WISE AND NOBLE PRINCESS was attacked by her enemies. The princess could not gather together her large and faithful army quickly enough to defend her castle, but had to fly by night with her little prince in her arms.

So she fled all through the night, and at daybreak they reached the foot of grisly Mount Kitesh, which was on the border of the principality.

At that time there were no more dragons anywhere in the world, nor fairies, nor witches, nor any monsters. The Holy Cross and human reason had driven them forth. But in the fastnesses of Mount Kitesh the last of the Fiery Dragons had found a refuge, and seven Votaress Fairies attended upon him. That is why Mount Kitesh was so grisly. But at the foot of the mountain lay a quiet valley. There dwelt the shepherdess Miloika in her little willow cabin, and tended her flock.

To that very valley came the princess at dawn with her baby, and when she saw Miloika sitting outside her cabin she went up to her and begged: "Hide me and the little prince in your cabin through the day. At nightfall I will continue my flight with the prince." Miloika made the fugitives welcome, gave them ewes' milk to drink, and hid them in her cabin.

As evening approached, the kind and noble princess said: "I must go on now with the prince. But will you take my Golden Girdle and the prince's little Gold Cross on a red ribbon? If our enemies should chance to find us they would know us by the Girdle and the Cross. Put these two things by and take good care of them in your little cabin. When my faithful captains have gathered together an army and driven out the enemy, I shall return to my castle and there you shall be my dear friend and companion."

"Your companion I cannot be, noble princess," said Miloika, "for I am not your equal either by birth or understanding. But I will take care of your Girdle and your Cross, because in time of real sorrow and trouble even the heart of a beggar can be companion to the heart of a king."

As she said this, Miloika received the Girdle and the Cross from the princess for safe keeping, and the princess took up the little prince and went out and away with him into the night, which was so dark that you could not tell grass from stone, nor field from sea.

II

Many years passed, but the princess did not return to her lands nor to her castle.

Her great army and her illustrious captains were so disloyal that they all immediately went over to her enemies. And so the enemy conquered the lands of the good and noble princess, and settled down in her castle.

No one knew or could discover what had become of the princess and the little prince. Most probably her escape on that dark night had ended by her falling into the sea, or over a precipice, or perishing in some other way with her baby.

But Miloika the shepherdess faithfully kept the Golden Girdle of the princess and the prince's little Gold Cross.

The smartest and wealthiest swains of the village came to ask Miloika to marry them, because the Golden Girdle and the little Gold Cross on the red ribbon were worth as much as ten villages. But Miloika would have none of them for her husband, saying: "You come because of the Golden Girdle and the little Cross; but they are not mine, and I must take better care of them than of my sheep or my cabin."

So said Miloika, and chose a penniless and gentle youth to be her husband, who cared nothing about the Girdle and Cross of Gold.

They lived in great poverty, and at times there was neither bread nor meal in the house, but they never thought of selling either Girdle or Cross.

Within a few years Miloika's husband fell ill and died; and not long afterwards a sore sickness came upon Miloika, and she knew that she too must die. So she called her two children, her little daughter Lavender and her still smaller son Primrose, and gave them each a keepsake. Round Lavender's waist she bound the Golden Girdle, and round Primrose's neck she hung the Gold Cross on the red ribbon. And Miloika said:

"Farewell, my children! You will be left alone in this world, and I have taught you but little craft or skill; but with God's help, what I have taught you will just suffice for your childish needs. Cleave to one another, and guard as a sacred trust what your mother gave into your keeping, and then I shall always remain with you." Thus spoke the mother, and died.

Lavender and Primrose were so little that they did not know how their mother had come by the Girdle and Cross, and still less did they understand the meaning of their mother's words. But they just sat side by side by their dead mother like two poor little orphans and waited to see what would become of them.

Presently the good folk of the village came along and said that Miloika would have to be buried next day.

III

But that was not the only thing that happened next day. For when the people came back from the funeral, they all went into the house to gossip, and only Lavender and Primrose remained outside, because they still fancied that their mother would yet somehow come back to them.

Suddenly a huge Eagle pounced down upon them from the sky, knocked Lavender down, caught her by the Girdle with his talons, and carried her off into the clouds.

The Eagle flew away with Lavender to his eyrie, high up on Mount Kitesh.

It did not hurt Lavender at all to fly along like that, hanging by her Gold Girdle. She was only sorry at being parted from her only brother, and kept on thinking: "Why didn't the Eagle take Primrose too?"

So they flew over Mount Kitesh, and there, all of a sudden, Lavender saw what neither she nor anyone else of the inhabitants of the valley had ever seen; for everyone avoided the grisly mountains, and of those who had happened to stray into them not one had ever returned. What Lavender saw was this: all the seven Votaress Fairies who waited upon the

Fiery Dragon assembled together upon a rock. They called themselves *Votaresses* because they had vowed, as the last of the fairy kin, to take vengeance upon the human race.

The Fairies looked up, and there was the Eagle carrying a little girl. Now the Fairies and the Eagles had made a bargain between them that each should bring his prey to that rock, and there hold a prizecourt upon the rock to settle what was to be done with the prey and who was to have it. And for that reason the rock was called *Share-spoil*.

So the Fairies called out to the Eagle:

"Ho, brother Klickoon! Come and alight on Share-spoil!"

But luckily the bargain was no sounder than the parties to it.

The Eagle Klickoon had taken a fancy to Lavender, so he did not keep to the bargain, nor would he alight on Share-spoil, but carried Lavender on to his eyrie for his Eaglets to play with.

But he had to fly right across the summit of the Mountain, because his eyrie was on the far side.

Now, on the top of the Mountain there was a Lake, and in the Lake there was an island, and on the island there was a little old chapel. Around the Lake was a tiny meadow, and all round the meadow ran a furrow ploughed in days of old. Across this furrow neither the Dragon, nor the Fairies, nor any monster of the Mountain could pass. About the Lake bloomed flowers, and spread their perfume; there doves took refuge, and nightingales, and all gentle creatures from the mountains.

Neither clouds nor mist hung over the holy furrow-surrounded Lake; but evermore the sun and moon in turn shed their light upon it.

As Klickoon flew over the Lake with Lavender, she caught sight of the chapel. And as she caught sight of the chapel, she remembered her mother; and as she remembered her mother, she pressed her hand to her heart; and as she pressed her hand to her heart, her mother's trust, the Golden Girdle, came undone upon Lavender.

The Girdle came undone; Lavender dropped from the Eagle's talons straight into the Lake, and the Girdle after her. Lavender caught hold of the Golden Girdle and stepped over the reeds, and the water-lilies, and the water-weeds, and the rushes to the island. There she sat down on a stone outside the chapel. But Klickoon flew on like a whirlwind in a rage, because he could not come near the Holy Lake.

Lavender was safe enough now, for nothing evil could reach her across the furrow. But what was the good of that, when the poor little child was all alone on the top of the grisly Mount Kitesh, and none could come to her, and she could not get away?

IV

Meantime the people who had buried Miloika noticed that the Eagle had carried off Lavender. At first they all burst out lamenting, but then one of them said:

"Good people, it is really as well that the Eagle carried off Lavender. It would have been hard to find someone in the village who could take charge of the *two* children. But for Primrose alone we shall easily find someone who will look after him."

"Yes, yes," the others all immediately agreed, "it is better so. We can easily look after Primrose."

They stood yet a while outside the cabin gazing in the direction towards which the Eagle had disappeared with Lavender into the skies, and then they went back indoors to drink and to talk, repeating all the time:

"There's not one of us but will be glad to take Primrose."

So they said. But not one of them troubled so much about Primrose as to offer him a drink of water, although it was very hot. Now Primrose was thirsty and went in to ask for water. But he was so tiny that not one of those people could understand what he said. Primrose wanted someone to get him his little wooden mug; but not one of those people knew that Primrose's little wooden mug was behind the beam.

When Primrose saw all this, he looked round the room for a moment, and then the child thought: "This is no good to me. I am left all alone in the world." So he leaned over the pitcher that stood on the floor, drank as much water as he could, and then set out to see if he could find his little sister Lavender.

He went out of the house and set off towards the sun – the direction in which he had seen the Eagle fly away with Lavender.

V

The sun was setting beyond Mount Kitesh, and so Primrose, always looking at the sun, presently came to Mount Kitesh, too. There was no one beside Primrose to say to him: "Don't go up the Mountain, child! The Mountain is full of terrors." And so he went on, poor, foolish baby, and began to climb up the Mountain.

But Primrose did not know what fear was. His mother had kept him safe like a flower before the altar, so that no harm, not even the smallest, had ever befallen him; he had never been pricked by a thorn, nor scared by a harsh word.

And so no fear could enter Primrose's heart, no matter what his eyes beheld or his ears heard.

Meantime, Primrose had got well up into the Mountain and already reached the first rocks and crags.

And there, below Share-spoil, the Votaress Fairies were all assembled and still discussing how Klickoon had cheated them. Suddenly they saw a child coming towards them, climbing up the Mountain. The Votaresses were delighted; it would be easy to deal with such a little child!

As Primrose came nearer, the Votaresses went down to meet him. In less than no time they had surrounded him. Primrose only wondered when he suddenly saw so many ladies coming towards him, each with a great pair of wings! One of the Votaresses went close up to the child to take him by the hand.

Now Primrose was wearing the little Cross round his neck. When the Fairy saw the Cross, she screamed and started away from Primrose, for she could not touch him because of the Cross.

But the Fairies had no intention of letting the child off so easily. They hovered about him in a wide circle and conferred softly about what was to be done with him.

Little Primrose's heart was untroubled within him. The Fairies conferred, and their thoughts were so black that they came out in a cloud of black forest wasps buzzing round their heads. But Primrose just looked at them, and as he could see no harm in them, how was he to be frightened? On the contrary, the wings of one of the Votaresses took his fancy, flapping like that, and so he toddled up to her to see what she was really like.

"That will do nicely," thought the Votaress. "I cannot touch him, but I will entice him into the Wolf's Pit."

For nearby there was a pit all covered over with boughs, so that you could not see it; and the bottom of the pit was full of horrible stakes and spikes. Whoever stepped on the boughs was bound to fall through and kill himself on the spikes.

So the Votaress Fairy enticed Primrose to the Wolf's Pit, always slipping away from him, and he always following to see what her wings really were. And so they came to the Pit. The Fairy flew over the Pit; but poor little misguided Primrose stepped on the boughs and fell down the hole.

The Votaresses shrieked for joy, and hurried up to see the child perish on the spikes.

But what do Fairies know about a baby!

Primrose was light as a chicken. Some of the boughs and branches fell down with him, the branches covered the spikes, and Primrose was so small and light that he came to rest upon the leaves as if they had been a bed.

When Primrose found himself lying down upon something soft, he thought: "I suppose I had better go to sleep!" So he tucked his little hand under his head and went sound asleep, never thinking that he was caught in a deep hole and could not get out.

Round him there were still many bare spikes, and the wicked Fairies were bending over the Pit. But Primrose slept peacefully and quietly, as though he were bedded on sweet basil. Primrose never moved. His mother had taught him: "When you are in your bed, darling, shut your little eyes and lie quite still, so as not to frighten your guardian angel."

So the Fairies stood round the Pit, and saw the baby falling asleep like a little duke in his golden crib. "That child is not so easy to deal with, after all," said the Votaresses. So they flew off to Share-spoil, and took counsel as to how they might kill him, since they could not touch him because of the little Cross.

They argued and argued, and at last one of the Votaresses had an idea. "We will raise a storm," said she; "we will cause a terrific rain. A torrent will pour down the Mountain, and the child will be drowned in the Pit."

"Whoo-ee, whoo-ee!" howled the Votaresses. They flapped their wings for joy, and at once rose up into the air and above the Mountain to roll up the clouds and raise a storm.

VI

Little Lavender was sitting on the top of the Mountain on her island in the Holy Lake. Round her fluttered lovely butterflies, even settling on her shoulders; and the grey dove guided her young to her lap to let her feed them with seeds. A wild raspberry-cane bent over Lavender, and Lavender ate the crimson fruit, and wanted for nothing.

But she was all alone, poor child! And sad at heart, because she believed she was parted for ever from Primrose, her only brother; and, moreover, she thought: "Did anyone, I wonder, remember to give him a drink or to put him to bed?"

In the midst of these sad thoughts Lavender looked up at the sky and saw a mist, black as night, rolling up round the Mountain. Over Lavender and over the holy furrow-surrounded Lake the sun shone brightly; but all around the mist was gathering and rising, inky clouds drifted and whirled, rose and fell like a pall of smoke, and every now and again fiery flashes darted from the gloom.

It was the Votaresses, flapping their great wings, who had piled up those black clouds upon the Mountain, and it was from their eyes that the fiery flashes shot across the darkness. And then suddenly it began to thunder most terribly within the clouds; heavy rain beat down all around upon the Mountain, and the Votaresses howled and darted to and fro through the thunder and the rain.

When Lavender saw that, she considered: "Over my head there is sunshine, and no harm can come to me. But perhaps there is someone abroad on the Mountain in need of help in this storm."

And although Lavender thought there was never a Christian soul on the Mountain, yet she did as her mother had taught her to do in a storm: she crossed herself and prayed. And as there was still a bell in the ruined chapel, Lavender took hold of the rope and began to toll the bell against the storm. Lavender did not know for whom she was praying or for whom she was tolling, but she tolled for a help to anyone who might be in distress.

When the bell on the island began to ring so unexpectedly, after having been silent for a hundred years, the Votaresses took fright up there in the clouds; they got worried and confused; they left off making a storm; they fled in terror in all directions, and hid under the rocks, under the crags, in hollow trees, or in the ferns.

In a little while the Mountain was clear, and the sun shone on the Mountain, where there had been no sunshine for a hundred years.

The sun shone; the rain stopped suddenly. But for poor little Primrose the danger was not yet over.

That first great downpour had formed a big torrent in the Mountain, and the wild water was rushing fast towards the very Pit where Primrose was sleeping.

Primrose had heard neither the storm nor the thunder, and now he did not hear the torrent either as it came rushing and roaring with frightful swiftness towards him to drown him.

The water poured into the Pit, poured in, and in a moment it had overwhelmed the child.

It covered him, overwhelmed him in a moment. There was not a thing to be seen, neither Pit, nor spikes, nor Primrose, nothing but the wild water foaming down the Mountain.

But as the flood rushed into the pit, it eddied at the bottom, surged round and up and back upon itself, and then suddenly the water lifted up the boughs and branches, and little Primrose, too, upon the boughs. It lifted him up, clean out of the Pit, and carried him downhill on a bough.

The torrent was so strong that it carried away great stones and ancient oaks, rolling them along, and nothing could stop them, because they were heavy and stout, and the torrent very fierce.

But tiny Primrose on his bough floated lightly down the flood, as lightly as a white rosebud, so that any bush could stop him.

And indeed, there was a bush in the way, and the bough with Primrose caught in its branches. Primrose woke up with a start, caught hold of the branch with his little hands, climbed up into the bush, and there he sat on the top of the bush, just like a little bird.

Above Primrose the sun shone clear and sweet; below Primrose foamed the dreadful water; and he sat in the bush in his little white shirt, and rubbed his eyes in wonder, because he could not make out what had happened and what had waked him up so suddenly.

By the time he had finished rubbing his eyes the water had all run away downhill; the torrent was gone. Primrose watched the mud squelching and writhing round the bush, and then Primrose climbed down, because he thought:

"I suppose I ought to go on now, since they have waked me up."

And so he went on up the hill. And he had slept so sweetly that he felt quite happy, and thought: "Now I shall find Lavender."

VII

No sooner had the bell stopped ringing than the Votaresses recovered their strength. They took courage and crept out of their hidey-holes. When they got out, lo! the sun was shining on the Mountain, and there is nothing in the world the wicked Fairies fear more than the sunlight. And as they could not wrap the whole Mountain in mist all in a hurry, each one quickly rolled herself up in a bit of fog, and off they flew to the Pit to make sure that Primrose was drowned.

But when they got there and looked into the Pit, the Pit was empty; Primrose was gone!

The Fairies cried aloud with vexation, and looked all over the Mountain to see whether the water had not dashed him against a stone. But as the Votaresses looked, why, this is what they saw: Primrose going blithely on his way; the sun was drying his little shirt for him on his back, and he was crooning away to himself as little children will.

"That child will escape us at this rate," sobbed one of the Votaresses. "The child is stronger than we are. Hadn't we better ask the Fiery Dragon to help us?"

"Don't disgrace yourselves, my sisters," said another Votaress. "Surely we can get the better of a feeble infant by ourselves."

So said the Fairy, but she did not know that Primrose in his simplicity was stronger than all the evil and all the cunning in Mount Kitesh.

"We will send the She-bear to kill the child for us," suggested a Votaress. "Dumb animals do not fear the Cross." And she flew off at once to the bears' den.

There lay the She-bear, a-playing with her cub.

"Run along, Bruineen, down that path. There is a child coming up the path. Wait for him and kill him, Bruineen dear," said the Votaress.

"I can't leave my cub," answered Bruineen.

"I'll amuse him for you," said the Votaress, and straightway began to play with the little bear.

Bruineen went away down the path, and there was Primrose already in sight.

The great She-bear rose up on her hind legs, stretched out her front paws, and so went forwards towards Primrose to kill him.

The She-bear was terrible to see, but Primrose saw nothing terrible in her, and could only think:

"Here's somebody coming and offering me his hand, so I must give him mine."

So Primrose raised both his little hands and held them out to the She-bear, and went straight up to her, as though his mother had called him to her arms.

Well, another moment, and the dreadful She-bear would seize him. She had come up to him, and would have caught and killed him at once had he offered to run. But she saw that she had time to consider how she had best take hold of him. So she drew herself right up, looked at Primrose from the right and from the left, and now she was going to pounce.

But at that very moment the little bear cub in the den began to squeal. One of the black wasps that always buzzed round the Votaress's head had stung him. The cub howled lustily, because, although the Bruins are a spiteful folk themselves, they won't stand spite from anybody else. So the cub squealed at the top of his voice, and when Bruineen heard her baby crying she forgot about Primrose and the Mountain! Bruineen dropped on all fours and trundled away like fury to her den.

The angry She-bear caught the Votaress by the hair with her great paw. They fought, they rolled, they tore at each other, and left Primrose in peace.

Primrose followed the She-bear and looked on for a bit while they fought and scuffled; he looked, and then he laughed aloud, silly baby! And went on up the Mountain, and never knew what a narrow escape he had had!

VIII

Once more the Votaresses assembled on Share-spoil to discuss what was to be done about Primrose. They saw that they were weaker than he.

Moreover, they were getting tired of flying to Share-spoil and back and conferring about Primrose, and so they were very angry.

"Well, we will poison the child. Neither spells nor cunning shall help him now," they resolved. And straightaway one of them took a wooden platter and hurried off to a certain meadow on the Mountain to gather poison berries.

But Primrose, never dreaming that anybody should be talking about him or worrying their brains about him, walked gaily over the Mountain, cooing softly to himself like a little dove.

Presently he came to the poison meadow. The path led through the middle of it. On one side of the path the meadow was covered with red berries and on the other side with black. Both were poisonous, and whoever ate of either the one or the other was sure to die.

But how was Primrose to know that there was such a thing as poison in the world, when he had never known any food but what his mother gave him?

Primrose was hungry, and he liked the look of the red berries in the meadow. But he saw someone over there in front of him on the red side picking berries and seemingly in a great hurry, for she never raised her head. It was the Votaress, and she was gathering red berries to poison Primrose.

"That is her side," thought Primrose, and went over to the black berries, because he had never been taught to take what belonged to another. So he sat down among the black berries and began to eat; and the Fairy wandered far away among the red berries and never noticed that Primrose had already come up and was eating black ones.

When Primrose had eaten enough he got up to go on. But, oh dear! A mist rose before his eyes; his head began to ache most dreadfully, and the earth seemed to rock beneath his feet.

That was because of the black poison.

Poor little Primrose! Indeed you know neither spells nor cunning, and how are you going to save yourself from this new danger?

But Primrose struggled on all the same, because he thought it was nothing that a mist should rise before his eyes and the ground rock beneath his feet!

And so he came up with the Fairy where she was picking berries. The Votaress caught sight of Primrose, and at once she ran on to the path in front of him with her plateful of red berries. She laid down the platter before him and invited him by signs to eat.

The Votaress did not know that Primrose had already eaten of the black berries; and if she had known, she would never have offered him red ones, but would have let him die of the black poison.

Primrose did not care for any more berries, because his head ached cruelly; but his mother used to say to him: "Eat, darling, when I offer you something, and don't grieve your mother."

Now this was neither spell nor cunning what Primrose had been taught by his mother. But it was in a good hour that Primrose did as his mother had taught him.

He took the plate and ate of the red berries; and as he ate, the mist cleared before his eyes, his head and his heart stopped aching, and the ground no longer rocked beneath his feet.

The red poison killed the black in Primrose's veins. He merrily clapped his hands and went on his way as sound as a bell and as happy as a grig.

And now he could see the top of the Mountain ahead of him, and Primrose thought:

"This is the end of the world. There is nothing beyond the top. There I shall find Lavender."

IX

The Votaress would not believe her eyes; she stared after Primrose, and there was he toddling along and the dreadful poison doing him no harm!

She looked and she looked – and then she shrieked with rage. She could not imagine by what miracle Primrose had escaped. All she could see was that the child would slip through her hands and reach the Lake, for he was getting near the top.

The Votaress had no time to fly to Share-spoil and confer with her sisters. In time of real trouble people don't hold conferences. But she flew straight to her brother, the thunder-voiced bird Belleroo.

Belleroo's nest was in a little bog on the Mountain, close to the furrow which ran round the Holy Lake. As he was an ill-tempered bird, he too could not cross the furrow, but the evil Things of the Mountain had appointed his place here on the boundary, so that he might trouble the peace of the Lake with his booming.

"Kinsman, brother, Belleroo," the Votaress cried out to Belleroo, "there is a child coming up the path. Delay him here at the furrow with your booming, so that he may not escape me across the farrow to the Lake. I am going for the Fiery Dragon."

No sooner had the Votaress said this than she flew like an arrow down the Mountain to fetch the Fiery Dragon, who was lying asleep in a deep gully.

As for Belleroo, he was always all impatience to be told to boom, because he was horribly proud of his loud voice.

Dusk was beginning to fall. It was evening. Nearer and nearer to the furrow came Primrose. Beyond the furrow he could see the Lake, and the chapel looming white on the Lake.

"Here I am at the end of the world; I have only to cross that furrow," thought Primrose.

Suddenly the Mountain rang with the most awful noise, so that the branches swayed and the leaves trembled on the trees, and the rocks and cliffs re-echoed down to the deepest cavern. It was Belleroo roaring.

His boom was terrible. It would have scared the great Skanderbeg himself, for it would have reminded Skanderbeg of the boom of the Turkish guns.

But it did not in the least frighten the little innocent Primrose, who had never yet been shouted at in grief or anger.

Primrose heard something making such a noise that the very Mountain shook, and so he went up to see what great thing it might be. When he got there, lo! it was a bird no bigger than a hen!

The bird dipped its beak in a pool, then threw up its head and puffed out its throat like a pair of bellows, and boomed – heavens, it boomed so that Primrose's sleeves fluttered on him! This new wonder took Primrose's fancy so much that he sat down so as to see from nearby how Belleroo boomed.

Primrose sat down just below the holy furrow beside Belleroo, and peered under his throat – because by now it was dark – the better to see how Belleroo puffed out his throat.

Had Primrose been wiser he would not have lingered there on the Mountain just below the furrow, where every evil Thing could hurt him, but he would have taken that one step across the furrow so as to be safe where the evil Things could not come.

But Primrose was just a little simpleton, and might easily have come to grief just there, within sight of safety.

Primrose was much amused by Belleroo.

He was amused; he was beguiled.

And while he was amusing himself in this fashion, the Fairy went and roused the Fiery Dragon where he slept in a deep gully.

She roused him and led him up the Mountain. On came the fearsome Fiery Dragon, spouting flame out of both nostrils and crushing firs and pine-trees as he went. There wasn't room enough for him, you see, in the forest and the Mountain.

Why don't you run, little Primrose? One jump across the furrow, and you will be safe and happy!

But Primrose did not think of running away. He went on sitting quite calmly below the furrow, and when he saw the flames from the Dragon flaring up in the darkness, he thought to himself: "What is making that pretty light on the Mountain?"

It was a cruel fire coming along to devour Primrose, and he, foolish baby! sat looking at it, all pleased and wondering: "What is making that pretty light on the Mountain?"

The Votaress caught sight of Primrose, and said to the Fiery Dragon:

"There is the child. Fiery Dragon! Get your best fire ready!"

But the Dragon was panting with the stiff climb.

"Wait a moment, sister, while I get my breath," answered the Dragon.

So the Dragon took a deep breath, once, twice, three times!

But that is just where the Dragon made a mistake.

Because his mighty breath caused an equally great wind on the Mountain. The wind blew, and bowled Primrose over the furrow and right up to the Holy Lake!

The Votaress gave one shriek, threw herself down on the ground, rolled herself up in her black wings, and sobbed and cried like mad.

The angry Dragon snorted and puffed; he belched fire as from ten red-hot furnaces. But the flames could not cross the furrow; when they reached the furrow they just rose straight upwards as if they had come up against a marble wall.

Sparks and flame crackled and spurted and returned upon Mount Kitesh. Half the Mountain did the Dragon set on fire, but he lost little Primrose!

When the wind bowled Primrose over like that, Primrose only laughed at being carried away so fast. He laughed once; he laughed twice....

X

On the island in the Lake, beside the little chapel, sat Lavender.

It was evening, but Lavender could not go to sleep because of the hurly-burly on the Mountain. Lavender heard the Votaresses howling and shrieking and Bruineen growling. She heard the Dragon come snorting up from his lair, and saw him spout fire all over the Mountain.

And now she saw the blazing flames shooting upwards to the skies.

But then she heard something – good gracious! What was it she heard? A laugh, like a little silver bell. Lavender's heart throbbed within her.

The tiny voice laughed again.

Then Lavender could bear it no longer, but called from the Island:

"Who is that laughing in the Mountain?" asked Lavender gently, and all a-tremble at the thought of who might answer.

"Who is that calling me from the Island?" answered little Primrose.

And Lavender recognized Primrose's baby-talk.

"Primrose! my own only Brother!" cried Lavender, and stood up white in the moonlight.

"Lavender, little sister!" cried Primrose; and, light as a moth, he stepped over the reeds and the rushes and the water-weeds to the Island. They hugged and they kissed; they sat down side by side in the moonlight by the little chapel. A little did they talk, but they were not clever at making a long story. They clasped each other's little hands and went to sleep.

XI

That was how they began to live day after day on the Holy Lake. Primrose was quite happy and desired nothing better.

There was clear water in the Lake, and there were sweet raspberries. There were plenty of flowers and butterflies in the meadow, and fireflies and dew by night. Nightingales and doves nested in the trees.

Every evening Lavender would make Primrose a bed of leaves, and in the morning she bathed him in the Lake and tied up his little shoes. And Primrose thought: "What do we want with a wider world than this within the furrow?"

Primrose was well off; he was only a baby!

And Lavender was happy, but she was troubled about Primrose, how she should look after him and get him food. Because God has so ordered it that the young folk can never get food without the old folk having to think about it.

That is so all the world over, and couldn't be otherwise even on the Holy Lake.

So Lavender was worried. "Tomorrow will be St. Peter's Day. Will the raspberries be over when St. Peter's is past? Will the water grow cold and the sun fail when autumn comes? How shall we get through the winter all alone? Will our cottage in the valley go to rack and ruin?"

So Lavender worried, and wherever there is worry, there temptation comes most easily.

One day she sat and mused: "Oh dear! What luck it would be if only we could get back to our cottage!" Just then she heard somebody calling from the Mountain. Lavender looked, and there in the wood on the far side of the furrow stood the youngest of the Votaresses.

She was prettier than the other Votaresses, and loved finery. She had noticed the Golden Girdle on Lavender, and now she wanted that Golden Girdle above anything else in the world.

"Little girl, sister, throw me your Girdle," called the fairy across the furrow.

"I can't do that, Fairy; I had that Girdle from my mother," answered Lavender.

"Little girl, sister, it wasn't your mother's Girdle; it belonged to the princess, and the princess has been dead long ago. Throw me the Girdle," said the Fairy, who remembered the princess.

"I can't, Fairy; the Girdle is from my mother," repeated Lavender.

"Little girl, sister, I will carry you and your brother down to the valley, and no harm shall come to you; throw me the Girdle," cried the Fairy once more.

This was a sad temptation for Lavender, who so longed to get away from the Mountain! But all the same she would not sacrifice her mother's keepsake to the greedy Fairy, but answered:

"I cannot, Fairy; I had the Girdle from my mother."

The Fairy went away quite sadly, but next day she came back and began again:

"Throw me the Girdle, and I will take you down the Mountain."

"I cannot, Fairy; I had the Girdle from my mother," Lavender answered once more, but with a very heavy heart.

For seven days did the Fairy come, and for seven days she tempted Lavender. Temptation is worse than the sharpest care, and poor little Lavender pined away, so great was her wish to get down to the valley. Yet all the same she would not give up the Girdle.

For seven days did the Fairy call, and for seven days did Lavender answer her:

"I cannot, Fairy; the Girdle is from my mother."

And when she answered thus on the seventh day, the Fairy saw that there was no help for it.

The Fairy went down the Mountain; she sat down on the last, lowest stone, shook down her hair and cried bitterly, so great was her desire for the Golden Girdle of the princess.

XII

Meantime the good and noble princess was not dead, but had lived for many a year in a far country with her son, the prince.

The princess never told anybody how high-born a lady she was, and her son was too young at the time of their flight for him to remember.

And so in that country not a soul knew – not even the prince – that they came of royal blood. But how could anybody tell that she was a princess, when she had neither crown nor Golden Girdle? And though she was good, gentle, and noble, that did not prove that she was a princess.

The princess lived in the house of a worthy peasant, and there she span and wove for his household.

In this way she earned enough to keep herself and her son.

The boy had grown up into a tall and handsome youth of unusual strength and power, and the princess taught him nothing that was not good and right.

But one thing was bad. The prince had a very hasty and fierce temper. So the people called him *Rowfoot Relya*, because he was so rough and strong – and so poor withal.

One day Rowfoot Relya was mowing his master's meadow, and lay down at noon in the shade to rest. And a young squire came riding by, and called to Relya:

"Hi, young man! Jump up and run back along the road and find me my silver spur; it fell off somewhere on the way."

When Relya heard that, his princely blood, his hot and hasty blood, was roused to evil within him because the other had disturbed him in his rest and would send him out to find his spur.

"Won't I, by heaven!" cried Relya, "and you can lie here and rest instead of me!" And with that he sprang at the young squire, pulled him off his horse, and flung him down in the shade, so that he lay there for dead.

But Rowfoot Relya, still furious, rushed home to his Mother, and cried out upon her:

"Wretched Mother! why was I born a rowfoot churl, for others to send me out to find their spurs for them in the dust?"

Relya's face was quite distorted with rage as he said this.

The Mother looked at her son, and her heart grieved sorely. She saw that there would be no more peace for her and her son, because she would have to tell him what she had so far kept secret.

"You are not a rowfoot churl, my son," replied the princess, "but an unfortunate prince." And she told Relya all about herself and him.

Relya listened; his eyes blazed with a strange fire, and he clenched his hands in bitter anger. Then he asked:

"Is there nothing left, then, Mother, of our lands?"

"Nothing, my son, save a little Cross on a red ribbon and a Golden Girdle," answered his Mother.

When Relya heard that, he cried:

"I am going, Mother, and I shall bring back that Cross and Girdle, wherever they may be! Threefold will the sight of them increase my princely strength!"

And then he asked:

"And where did you leave the Cross and the Girdle, Mother? Did you leave them with the chief of your captains for him and your great army to guard?"

"No, my son," replied the princess, "and it is a good thing that I did not, for my captains and my great army went over to the enemy, and are now feasting and drinking with the enemy and wasting my lands."

"Did you perhaps leave them in the lowest room of your castle, in the seventh vault, under seven locks?"

"No, my son, and it is a good thing that I did not, because the enemy got into my castle, broke open and ransacked its secret chambers, searched its nine vaults, and fed his horses upon pearls out of my treasure hoards," replied the princess.

"But where did you leave the Golden Girdle and the Cross on the red ribbon?" asked Relya, with flashing eyes.

"I left them with a young shepherdess in a willow cabin, where there are neither locks nor strong boxes. Go, my son, perchance you will find them there still."

Relya would not believe that the Girdle and Cross might be safe in a willow cabin when the noble princess's pearls had not been safe even in the ninth vault under her castle.

But his princely blood, so proud and masterful, was roused yet more to evil in Relya's veins, and he roughly said to his Mother:

"Farewell, then, Mother! I shall find the Cross and Girdle wherever they may be, and it shall be no jesting matter for those who would refuse to let me have them! I shall bring you back your Girdle and Cross, by the princely blood in my veins."

As Prince Relya said this, he took the blade of the scythe, fitted it with a mighty hilt at the forge, and then hurried out into the world to find his heritage. The earth rang beneath his feet; his hair streamed in the wind, so swiftly did he stride; and his murderous blade shone in the sun as though it were plated with flame.

XIII

So Relya went on without stopping. He strode on by day, and by night he did not rest; both great and small got out of his way.

It is far to Mount Kitesh, but Relya had no difficulty in finding out the way, because Mount Kitesh was known throughout seven kingdoms for its terrors.

On St. John's Day Relya bade farewell to his Mother, and on St. Peter's Day he reached the foot of the Mountain.

When he reached the foot of the Mountain, he inquired after the willow cabin, the shepherdess Miloika, and the Golden Girdle and Cross.

"There is the cabin in the valley. Miloika we buried the first Sunday after Easter, and her children have the Girdle and Cross. As for the children, the Fairies have carried them off to Mount Kitesh," replied the villagers.

Very wroth was Relya when he heard that the Girdle and Cross had been carried off to Mount Kitesh. He was so angry that he could not make up his mind which to do first – hasten up the Mountain or find out about the castle, since that was uppermost in his desires.

"And where is the princess's castle?" shouted Relya.

"Over there, a day's journey from here," answered the villagers.

"And how stands it with the castle?" asked Relya, and his hand played with his sword. "Tell me all you know about it!"

"None of us has been in the castle, because the lords of it are hard of heart. Round the castle they have placed mutes for guards and savage bloodhounds. We cannot force our way past the bloodhounds, and we do not know how to persuade the guards," answered the villagers. "And within the castle are fine lords, drinking red wine in the halls, playing upon silver lutes, and tossing golden balls to each other over a silken carpet. In the outer hall are two hundred workmen cutting hearts out of mother-o'-pearl for targets for the lords. And when the lords make a great feast, they load their guns with precious stones and shoot at the hearts of mother-o'-pearl."

When the villagers told him this, a mist swam before Relya's eyes, so furious was he when he heard how wantonly the treasure in his Mother's vaults was being squandered.

For a while Relya hesitated, and then he cried:

"I am going up the Mountain to win the Cross and Girdle, and then I shall return to thee, O my castle."

Thus cried Relya; he made the sword sing through the air above his head, and then strode swiftly up into Mount Kitesh. There he found the great Dragon asleep in the deep gully. You see, the Dragon had tired himself out with belching so much fire at Primrose, and now he had gone fast asleep to gather fresh strength.

But Relya was all impatience to fight someone so as to cool his anger and to prove his strength. He was tired of seeing everybody, both great and small, get out of his way all the time, so now he rushed up to the Fiery Dragon to rouse and dare him to mortal combat.

Relya was a Doughty Hero, and the Fiery Dragon was a Terrible Monster, and so their combat must be sung in verse, beginning where Relya rushed up to the Dragon:

Childe Relya smote the Dragon on the side
With the flat blade, to rouse him from his sleep.
The Beast looked up, raising his grisly head,
Beheld the hero Relya standing by.
Up leapt the Dragon, with a rending blow
O'erturns the cliff and widens out the gap
To make a fitting space wherein to fight!
Anon unto the clouds he rears him up;
Anon on Relya pounces from the clouds,
And so with Relya joins in mortal fray.
Now groans the earth and splits the solid rock.
With tooth and flame the Dragon turns to bay,
And thrusts at Relya with his fiery head.
But Relya waits him with a ready sword,
And meets the onslaught with a ready sword;
And with his weapon beating down the flame

Seeks for the sword an undefended spot,
Where he may smite the Dragon on the head.
Deep bites the brand – so mighty was the shock
That brand and bone no more will come apart.
From dawn till noontide did the battle rage,
And weaker grew the Dragon all the while,
With brooding on the shame that galled his heart,
Because the babe, young Primrose, had escaped.
And stronger grew Childe Relya all the while,
For he did battle for his heritage.
When at high noon the sun burned overhead,
Childe Relya swung his gleaming brand aloft
Towards the sun, and called on Heaven for aid.
Down fell the sword betwixt the Dragon's eyes –
Full swiftly fell, yet lightly struck the blade,
Yet with such force, it cleft the Beast in twain.
Into the hollow falls the Dragon, slain,
And as stretched him in his dying spasm,
The monstrous limbs block up the ancient chasm.

Thus did the doughty Relya overcome the Fiery Dragon. But his brave arms and shoulders ached terribly. So Relya said to himself: "I shall never get over the Mountain at this rate. I must consider what I had better do." And Relya went back to the foot of the Mountain, and there the hero sat down on a stone and considered how he was to get across the Mountain, and how he was to overcome the monsters, and where he might find Miloika's children and with them the Golden Girdle and Cross.

Relya was deep in thought, but all of a sudden he heard somebody weeping and sobbing near him. Relya turned, and there was a Fairy sitting on a stone, her hair all unbound, and crying her heart out.

"What ails you, pretty maiden? Why do you weep?" asked Relya.

"I weep, O hero, because I cannot get the Golden Girdle from the child on the Lake," answered the Fairy.

When Relya heard that he was overjoyed.

"Tell me, maiden, how can I get to that Lake?" asked Relya.

"And who may you be, unknown hero?" returned the Fairy.

"I am Prince Relya, and I seek a Golden Girdle and a Cross on a red ribbon," replied Relya.

When the Fairy heard that, she thought within her evil heart: "How lucky for me! Let Relya get the Girdle away from the Lake and on to the Mountain, and I will soon destroy Relya and keep the Girdle for myself."

So the cunning Fairy spoke these honeyed words to Relya:

"Let us go, noble Prince! I will guide you across the Mountain. No harm will come to you, and I will show you where the children are. Why should you not have what is yours by inheritance?"

Thus sweetly did the Fairy speak, but in her heart she thought otherwise. Relya, however, was mightily pleased, and at once agreed to go with the Fairy.

So they went across the Mountain. Neither Fairies nor monsters touched Relya, because he was being guided by the young Votaress Fairy.

On the way the Fairy advised Relya and tried to fill his heart with anger.

"You should but see, noble Prince, how insolent these children are! Not even to you will they give the Girdle. But you are a hero above all heroes, Relya, so do not let them put you to shame."

Relya laughed at the idea that two children should withstand him – *him* who had cleft in twain the Fiery Dragon!

The Fairy then went on to tell him how the children had come up into the Mountain, and how they did not know how to get away from it again.

In her joy at the prospect of getting the Girdle, the Fairy talked so much that her cunning deserted her, and she chattered to Relya and boasted to him of her knowledge.

"They are silly children, without any cunning. Yet if they knew what *we* know they would have escaped us already. There is a taper in the chapel and a censer. If they would start the fire that is not lit with hands, and then light the taper and censer, they could go with taper and censer across the whole Mountain as if it were a church. Paths would open before them and trees bow down as they passed. But for us this would be the worst thing possible, because all we Fairies and Goblins in Mount Kitesh would perish wherever the smoke from the taper and censer spread. But what do these silly, insolent children know?"

If the Votaress had not been so overjoyed, she would surely never have told Relya about the taper and censer, but would have kept the secret of the Votaresses.

So they came to the furrow, and there was the Holy Lake before them.

XIV

The Prince peered cautiously from behind a tree, and the Fairy pointed out the children to him. Relya saw the little chapel on the island. Before the chapel sat a little girl, pale as a white rose. She neither sang nor crooned, but sat still with her hands clasped in her lap and her eyes raised to Heaven.

On the sand beside the chapel played a little boy, baby Primrose, and round his neck hung a little Gold Cross.

He played on the sand, built castles and pulled them down again with his tiny hands, and then laughed at his handiwork.

Relya watched, and as he watched he began to think. But the Votaress had no time to wait while the Prince finished thinking things out, so she softly prompted Relya.

"I will call to the little girl, noble Prince, and you shall see that she will not give up the Girdle; then do you draw your burnished sword, go up and take what is yours, and then come back to me to the Mountain, and I will guide you back down the Mountain so that my sisters shall not hurt you."

As the Fairy said this, she secretly rejoiced, thinking how easily she would kill Relya and get the Girdle for herself, so long as Relya would bring it from the Lake. But Relya only listened with half an ear to what the Votaress was saying, for he was lost in looking at the girl.

The Fairy called to Lavender:

"Little girl, sister, throw me the Girdle, and I will take you and your brother down the Mountain."

When Lavender heard this, her face grew yet paler, and she clasped her little hands yet more tightly. She was so sad that she could scarcely speak. She would so gladly have left the Mountain; her little heart was bursting with longing.

But all the same she would not part with her Mother's Girdle.

Tears flowed down Lavender's face; she wept softly, but through her tears she answered: "Go away, Fairy, and do not come back again, because you will not get the Girdle."

When Relya saw and heard this, his princely blood, his noble blood, was roused within him, but to a good purpose.

He was filled with pity for these two poor orphans in the midst of the grisly Mount Kitesh, defending themselves all alone against monsters and temptations, death and destruction. "Great Heavens!" thought he, "the princess trusted in her armed warriors and her strongholds to defend her lands, and the lands were lost; but these babes are left alone in the world, they have fallen among Fairies and Dragons, yet neither Fairies nor Dragons can rob them of what their Mother gave them." All Relya's face changed as his heart went out with pity to the children. Thus changed, he turned towards the Votaress.

The Votaress looked at Relya. Why did he raise his sword? Was it to cut down those insolent children? No; Relya raised the sword aloft and threatened the wicked Fairy with it.

"Fairy, avaunt! As if you had never been! If you had not been my guide across the Mountain, I would strike your fair head from off your shoulders. I was not born a prince, nor did I forge this mighty sword that I might roam the world a spoiler of the fatherless!"

The poor Votaress was quite frightened. She started, and then fled to the hills. And Relya shouted after her:

"Go, Fairy! Call your Fairies and monsters! Prince Relya does not fear them!"

When the Fairy had run off to the hills, Relya crossed the furrow and went towards the children on the island.

How happy was Lavender when she saw a human being coming towards them and looking at them kindly! She sprang to her feet and stretched out both her arms, as a captive bird spreads its wings when you open your hand and let it go free.

Lavender was quite certain that Relya had come up only to bring them safe back from the Mountain. She ran to Primrose, took him by the hand, and both crossed over to Relya by the little bridge which they had fashioned with their own tiny hands across the reeds.

XV

A doughty hero was Relya, and he felt strange talking to children. But the children did not feel in the least strange talking to a hero, because they thought kindly of everybody, and there was no guile in their hearts.

Primrose took hold of Relya's hand and looked at his great sword. The sword was twice as big as Primrose! Primrose reached up with his little hand; he stood on tiptoe, and yet he could scarcely touch the hilt of it. Relya looked, and never had he seen such tiny hands beside his own. Relya was now in a sad quandary; he forgot all about the Girdle and Cross as he thought: "What shall I say to these poor orphan babes? They are little and foolish, and they do not understand."

Just then Lavender asked Relya:

"And how shall we get out of the mountains, my lord?"

"Well, that is quite a sensible little girl," considered Relya. "Here am I, marvelling how small and foolish they are, and never thinking that, after all, we have to get out of the mountains."

Then Relya remembered what the Votaress had told him about the taper and censer.

"Listen to me, little girl! The Votaress has gone to call her sisters to help her, and I am going on to the Mountain to meet them. Please God, I shall overcome the Votaress Fairies, return to you by the Holy Lake, and lead you away from the Mountain. But if the Fairies should overcome me, if I perish on the Mountain, then do you start the fire that is not lit with hands, light the taper and censer, and you will pass over the Mountain as though it were a church."

When Lavender heard this, she was sadly grieved, and said to Prince Relya:

"You must not do that, my lord! What shall we poor orphans do if you perish on the Mountain? You have only just come to be our protector, and if you were to leave us straightway and get killed what should we do? Let us rather set to at once and start the fire, so as to light taper and censer, and do you, my lord, go forth with us over the Mountain."

But at that Relya became very angry, and said:

"Don't talk foolishness, you silly child! I was not born a hero for taper and censer to lead me while yet I wear a sword by my side."

"Not taper and censer will lead you, but God's will and commandment," replied Lavender.

"Don't talk foolishness, you silly child! My sword would rust were I to be led by taper and censer."

"Your sword will not rust when you go a-mowing in field and meadow."

Relya was troubled. It was not so much Lavender's words as the sweet, serious look in the little girl's eyes that troubled him. He knew well enough that he would scarcely overcome the fairies and monsters, and that he would most probably perish if he were to go out to fight on the Mountain.

Little Primrose flung his arms round Relya's knees and looked at him coaxingly. And Relya's princely heart beat quick in his bosom, so that he forgot about Cross and Girdle and fight and castle, and all he could think was: "Well, I have to protect and save these faithful little orphans."

So he said:

"I will not throw away my life out of sheer wilfulness. Come, children, start the fire, light taper and censer; your little hands shall lead me."

XVI

A few moments later, and there was a wondrous marvel to be seen on Mount Kitesh.

A wide path opened all the way down the Mountain, and on the path grew turf as soft as silk. On the right-hand side walked little Primrose, still in his little white shirt, and in his hand he held an ancient wax taper, burning serenely and crackling softly, as though it were talking with the sun. On the left walked Lavender, wearing the Golden Girdle and swinging a silver censer, from which rose a cloud of white smoke. Between the two children strode Relya, tall and strong. It seemed strange to him, in his strength and valour, that taper and censer should thus guide him and not his own good sword. But he smiled gently at the children. His great sword hung over his shoulder, and as he strode on he said to the sword:

"Do not fear, my faithful friend. We shall go a-mowing in field and meadow; we shall clear scrub and forest; we shall hew rafters and build steadings. The sun will gild thee a thousand times while thou art winning bread for these two orphan babes."

So they went across the Mountain as though it were a church. A thin wraith of smoke rose from the taper, and sacred odours spread from the censer.

But woe and alas for the Votaresses on Mount Kitesh! Wherever the smoke and the odour of incense spread upon the Mountain, there the Votaresses perished and died. They made an end, each one as it seemed most beautiful and fitting to her.

One turned herself into a grey stone, and then hurled herself down the rocks into a chasm, where the stone broke into a thousand splinters.

The second changed into a crimson flame, and then at once went out, puff! into the air.

The third dissolved into fine coloured dust, scattering herself over rock and fern. And so each of them chose what seemed to her the most beautiful way to die.

But it really didn't matter in the least. One way or another, they all had to leave this world, and even the most beautiful ways of dying could not make up for that!

In this way all the seven Votaress Fairies perished, and that is why there are no Fairies, nor Dragons, nor Monsters now on Mount Kitesh or anywhere else in the world.

But Relya and the children reached the valley in safety, and Lavender took them to their cottage. And only then did Relya remember why he had gone up Mount Kitesh.

XVII

They went into the cottage and rested a little. Lavender, who knew where was her Mother's modest store cupboard, brought out a little dry cheese, and they refreshed themselves.

But now Relya was puzzled what to do about those two orphans. Ever since they had come down into the valley, Relya's mind had begun to run once more upon the castle and upon his promise to his Mother that he would bring her back the Cross and Girdle.

Therefore Relya said to Lavender:

"Listen to me, little girl: you will have to give me the Golden Girdle and Cross now, you and your brother, because they belong to me."

"But we belong to you too, my lord," said Lavender, and looked at Relya quite astonished, because he had not grasped that before.

Relya laughed, and then he said:

"But I must take the Girdle and Cross to my Mother."

When Lavender heard that, she cried out overjoyed:

"Oh, sir, if you have a Mother, do go and bring her here to us, because we have no Mother now."

A stone would have wept to hear little Lavender speak of her Mother in that poor and bare little cottage! A stone would have wept at the thought that so lovely a child should be left all alone in the world, when she turned to Prince Relya and begged him to bring them a Mother because their Mother was dead.

Again Relya was filled with pity, so that he almost wept. Therefore he bade the children goodbye and went away to fetch his Mother.

XVIII

It took Relya seven days to return to his Mother. She was waiting for him by the window, and when she saw him coming, lo, there was Relya coming home without sword, Cross, or Girdle. Relya never gave her time to ask questions, but called to her in a gentle voice:

"Make ready, Mother, and come with me, that we may guard what is ours."

So they set out together. And on the way the princess asked Relya whether he had found the Cross and the Girdle, whether he had raised an army and had reconquered their castle and lands?

"I found the Girdle and Cross, Mother; but I raised no army, neither have I reconquered our lands. We shall do better without an army, Mother, for you shall see what is left to us of our heritage," said Relya.

After seven days' travel they reached the cabin where Lavender and Primrose were waiting for them.

Oh, my dear! But there is great joy when kind hearts foregather! The princess hugged Lavender and Primrose; she kissed their cheeks, eyes, hands, and lips, and would scarcely let them go, so dear were they to her, those orphan children from her lost lands!

XIX

And so they lived together in the valley, although the little cabin was rather too small for them. But Relya had strong hands, and he built them a little house of stone. Their lives were uneventful, but there was a blessing upon them. Primrose tended the ewes and lambs, Lavender looked after the house and garden, the princess span and sewed, and Relya worked in the fields.

The people of the village got to know the wisdom of the princess and Relya's strength. Presently they remarked how well the Golden Girdle became the princess, and, although none of them had ever seen the princess before, they said:

"She must be our noble princess." And so they gave Relya and the princess a great piece of land in the valley, and begged Relya to be their leader in all things and the princess to be their counsellor.

God's blessing was with Relya's strength and the princess's wisdom. Their fields and meadows increased; other villages joined them; gardens and cottages sprang up in the villages.

Meantime the fine lords in the castle went on drinking and feasting as before. Now this had gone on far too long, and although the vaults and cellars of the castle had been the richest in seven kingdoms, yet after so many years of waste there began to be a lack of precious stones.

First of all the gems gave out in the treasure vaults, and then the mother-o'-pearl in the passages. Yet a little while, and there was no more bread for the servants, who had grown lazy. At last there was not even meat for the bloodhounds and guards. The faithless servants rebelled, the hounds ran away, and the guards left their posts.

But all this did not trouble the fine lords, because they had dulled their wits with drinking and feasting. But one fine day the wine gave out. *Then* they decided to hold a council! They met in the great hall and debated upon where they should get wine, because round about the castle all was desolate: the inhabitants had left, and the vines had run wild in the vineyards.

So the fine lords debated. But their vengeful and rebellious servants had cut through the rafters of the great hall, and when the lords were in the midst of their conference the roof fell in upon them. They were buried under the ruins of the great tower of the castle and all of them killed.

When the servants heard the tower crashing and falling, they too deserted the castle.

And so the castle was left without hounds, servants, or fine lords, ruinous and deserted, and dead.

Soon the news of this spread through the land, but not a soul troubled to go and see what had happened in the dead castle. From all sides they flocked together and went to the foot of Mount Kitesh to beg Relya to be their prince, because they had heard of his strength and courage and of the wisdom of the noble princess. Wherefore the people promised with their own hands to build them a new castle, all fair and stately.

Relya accepted the people's offer, because he rightly judged that God had given him such great strength and courage, and had delivered him from his hot and cruel temper, so that he might be of use to his country.

So Relya became a prince; and the princess, who was getting old by now, yet lived to see great happiness in her old age. And when the princess and Relya, with Lavender and Primrose, entered their new and stately castle for the first time, the village children scattered evergreens and sweet basil on their path, men and women pressed round the princess, seized the hem of her robe and kissed it.

But the princess, radiant with joy, remembered that but for the loyalty of Lavender and Primrose none of this would ever have come to pass. She clasped the children to her breast and said:

"Happy the land whose treasure is not guarded by mighty armies or strong cities, but by the mothers and children in shepherds' cots. Such a land will never perish!"

* * *

Later on Prince Relya married Lavender, and never in the world was there a princess sweeter and more lovely than Princess Lavender.

Primrose grew up into a brave and handsome youth. He rode a fiery dapple grey, and he would often ride over Mount Kitesh, upon whose summit men were building a new chapel by the Holy Lake.

How Quest Sought the Truth

I

ONCE UPON A TIME very long ago there lived an old man in a glade in the midst of an ancient forest. His name was Witting, and he lived there with his three grandsons. Now this old man was all alone in the world save for these three grandsons, and he had been father and mother to them from the time when they were quite little. But now they were full-grown lads, so tall that they came up to their grandfather's shoulder, and even taller. Their names were Bluster, Careful and Quest.

One spring morning old Witting got up early, before the sun had risen, called his three grandsons and told them to go into the wood where they had gathered honey last year; to see how the little bees had come through the winter, and whether they had waked up yet from their winter sleep. Careful, Bluster and Quest got up, dressed, and went out.

It was a good way to the place where the bees lived. Now all three brothers knew every pathway in the woods, and so they strode cheerily and boldly along through the great forest. All the same it was somewhat dark and eerie under the trees, for the sun was not yet up and neither bird nor beast stirring. Presently the lads began to feel a little scared in that great silence, because just at dawn, before sunrise, the wicked Rampogusto, King of Forest Goblins, loves to range the forest, gliding softly from tree to tree in the gloom.

So the brothers started to ask one another about all the wonderful things there might be in the world. But as not one of them had ever been outside the forest, none could tell the others anything about the world; and so they only became more and more depressed. At last, to keep up their courage a bit, they began to sing and call upon All-Rosy to bring out the Sun:

Little lord All-Rosy bright.
Bring golden Sun to give us light;
Show thyself, All-Rosy bright,
Loora-la, Loora-la lay!

Singing at the top of their voices, the lads walked through the woods towards a spot from where they could see a second range of mountains. As they neared the spot they saw a light above those mountains brighter than they had ever seen before, and it fluttered like a golden banner.

The lads were dumbfounded with amazement, when all of a sudden the light vanished from off the mountain and reappeared above a great rock nearer at hand, then still nearer, above an old limetree, and at last shone like burnished gold right in front of them. And then they saw that it was a lovely youth in glittering raiment, and that it was his golden cloak which fluttered like a golden banner. They could not bear to look upon the face of the youth, but covered their eyes with their hands for very fear.

"Why do you call me, if you are afraid of me, you silly fellows?" laughed the golden youth – for he was All-Rosy. "You call on All-Rosy, and then you are afraid of All-Rosy. You talk about the wide world, but you do not know the wide world. Come along with me and I will show you the world, both earth and heaven, and tell you what is in store for you."

Thus spoke All-Rosy, and twirled his golden cloak so that he caught up Bluster, Careful and Quest, all three in its shimmering folds. Round went All-Rosy and round went the cloak, and the brothers, clinging to the hem of the cloak, spun round with it, round and round and round again, and all the world passed before their eyes. First they saw all the treasure and all the lands and all the possessions and the riches that were then in the world. And they went on whirling round and round and round again, and saw all the armies, and all spears and all arrows and all the captains and all plunder which were then in the world. And the cloak twirled yet more quickly, round and round and round again, and all of a sudden they saw all the stars, great and small, and the moon and the Seven Sisters and the winds and all the clouds. The brothers were quite dazed with so many sights, and still the cloak went on twirling and whirling with a rustling, rushing sound like a golden banner. At last the golden hem fluttered down; and Bluster, Careful and Quest stood once more on the turf. Before them stood the golden youth All-Rosy as before, and said to them:

"There, my lads, now you have seen all there is to see in the world. Listen to what is in store for you and what you must do to be lucky."

At that the brothers became more scared than ever, yet they pricked up their ears and paid good heed, so as to remember everything very carefully. But All-Rosy went on at once:

"There! This is what you must do. Stay in the glade, and don't leave your grandfather until he leaves you; and do not go into the world, neither for good nor for evil, until you have repaid your grandfather for all his love to you." And as All-Rosy said this, he twirled his cloak round and vanished, as though he had never been; and lo, it was day in the forest.

But Rampogusto, King of the Forest Goblins, had seen and heard everything. Like a wraith of mist he had slipped from tree to tree and kept himself hidden from the brothers among the branches of an old beech-tree.

Rampogusto had always hated old Witting. He hated him as a mean scoundrel hates an upright man, and above all things he hated him because the old man had brought the sacred fire to the glade so that it might never go out, and the smoke of that fire made Rampogusto cough most horribly.

So Rampogusto wasn't pleased with the idea that the brothers should obey All-Rosy, and stay beside their grandfather and look after him; but he bethought himself how he could harm old Witting, and somehow turn his grandsons against him.

Therefore, no sooner had Bluster, Careful and Quest recovered from their amazement and turned to go home than Rampogusto slipped swiftly, like a cloud before the wind, to a wooded glen where there was a big osier clump, which was chock-full of goblins – tiny, ugly, humpy, grubby, boss-eyed, and what not, all playing about like mad creatures. They squeaked and they squawked, they jumped and they romped; they were a pack of harum-scarum imps, no good to anybody and no harm either, so long as a man did not take them into his company. But Rampogusto knew how to manage that.

So he picked out three of them, and told them to jump each on one of the brothers, and see how they might harm old Witting through his grandsons.

Now while Rampogusto was busy choosing his goblins, Bluster, Careful and Quest went on their way; and so scared were they that they clean forgot all they had seen during their flight and everything that All-Rosy had told them.

So they came back to the cabin, and sat down on a stone outside and told their grandfather what had happened to them.

"And what did you see as you were flying round, and what did All-Rosy tell you?" Witting asked Careful, his eldest grandson. Now Careful was in a real fix, because he had clean forgotten, neither could he remember what All-Rosy had told him. But from under the stone where they were sitting crept a wee hobgoblin – ugly and horned and grey as a mouse.

The goblin tweaked Careful's shirt from behind and whispered: "Say: I have seen great riches, hundreds of beehives, a house of carved wood and heaps of fine furs. And All-Rosy said to me: 'Thou shalt be the richest of all the three brothers.'"

Careful never bothered to think whether this was the truth that the imp was suggesting, but just turned and repeated it word for word to his grandfather. No sooner had he spoken than the goblin hopped into his pouch, curled himself up in a corner of the pouch – and there stopped!

Then Witting asked Bluster, the second grandson, what he might have seen in his flight, and what All-Rosy might have told him? And Bluster, too, had noticed nothing and remembered nothing. But from under the stone crept the second hobgoblin, quite small, ill-favoured, horned and smutty as a polecat. The goblin plucked Bluster by the shirt and whispered: "Say: I saw lots of armed men, many bows and arrows and slaves galore in chains. And All-Rosy said to me: 'Thou shalt be the mightiest of the brothers.'"

Bluster considered no more than Careful had done, but was very pleased, and lied to his grandfather even as the goblin had prompted him. And the goblin at once jumped on his neck and crawled down his shirt, hid in his bosom, and stopped there.

Now the grandfather asked the youngest grandson, Quest, but he, too, could recall nothing. And from under the stone crept the third hobgoblin, the youngest, the ugliest, horned with big horns, and black as a mole.

The hobgoblin tugged Quest by the shirt and whispered: "Say: I have seen all the heavens and all the stars and all clouds. And All-Rosy said to me: 'Thou shalt be the wisest among men and know what the winds say and the stars tell.'"

But Quest loved the truth, and so he would not listen to the goblin nor lie to his grandfather, but kicked the goblin and said to his grandfather:

"I don't know, grandfather, what I saw or what I heard."

The goblin gave a squeal, bit Quest's foot, and then scuttled away under the stone like a lizard. But Quest gathered potent herbs and bound up his foot with them, so that it might heal quickly.

II

Now the goblin whom Quest had kicked first scooted away under the stone, and then wriggled into the grass, and hopped off through the grass into the woods, and through the woods into the osier clump.

He went up to Rampogusto all shaking with fright and said: "Rampogusto, dread sovereign, I wasn't able to jump on that youth whom you gave into my care."

Then Rampogusto fell into a frightful rage, because he knew those three brothers well, and most of all he feared Quest, lest he should remember the truth. For if Quest were to remember the truth, why, then Rampogusto would never be able to get rid of old Witting nor the sacred fire.

So he seized the little goblin by the horns, picked him up and dusted him soundly with a big birchrod.

"Go back!" he roared – "go back to the young man, and it will be a black day for you if ever he remembers the truth!"

With these words Rampogusto let the goblin go; and the goblin, scared half out of his wits, squatted for three days in the osier clump and considered and considered how he might fulfil his difficult task. "I shall have as much trouble with Quest, for sure, as Quest with me," reflected the goblin. For he was a scatterbrained little silly, and did not care at all for a tiresome job.

But while he squatted in the osier clump those other two imps were already at work, the one in Careful's pouch and the other in Bluster's bosom. From that day forth Careful and Bluster began to rove over hill and dale, and even slept but little at home – and all because of the goblins!

There was the goblin curled up in the bottom of Careful's pouch, and that goblin loved riches better than the horn over his right eye.

So all day long he butted Careful in the ribs, teasing and goading him on: "Hurry up, get on! We must seek, we must find! Let's look for bees, let's gather honey, and then we will keep a tally with rows and rows of scores!"

So said the goblin, because in those days they reckoned up a man's possessions with tallies.

Now a tally is only a long wooden stick with a notch cut in it for every sum that is owing to a man!

But Bluster's goblin butted him in the breast, and that goblin wanted to be the strongest of all and lord of all the earth. So he worried and worried Bluster, and urged him to roam through the woods looking for young ash plants and slender maple saplings to make a warrior's outfit and weapons. "Hurry up, get on!" teased the goblin. "You must seek, you must find! Spears, bows and arrows to suit a hero's mind, so that man and beast may tremble before us."

And both Bluster and Careful listened to their goblins, and went off after their own concerns as the goblins led them.

But Quest stayed with his grandfather that day and yet other three days, and all the time he puzzled and puzzled over whatever it was that All-Rosy might have told him; because Quest wanted to tell his grandfather the truth; but, alas! he could not remember it at all!

So that day went by, and the next, and so three days; and on the third day Quest said to his grandfather:

"Goodbye, grandfather. I am going to the hills, and shall not come back until I remember the truth, if it should take me ten years."

Now Witting's hair was grey, and there was little he cared for in this world except his grandson Quest, and him he loved and cherished as a withered leaf cherishes a drop of dew. So the old man started sadly and said:

"What good will the truth be to me, my boy, when I may be dead and gone long before you remember it?"

This he said, and in his heart he grieved far more even than he showed in his words; and he thought: "How could the boy leave me!"

But Quest replied:

"I must go, grandfather, because I have thought it out, and that seems the right thing to me."

Witting was a wise old man, and considered: "Perhaps there is more wisdom in a young head than in an old one; only if the poor lad is doing wrong it's a sad weird he will have to dree – because he is so gentle and upright." And as Witting thought of that he grew sadder than ever, but said nothing more. He just kissed his grandson goodbye and bade him go where he wished.

But Quest's heart sadly misgave him because of his grandfather, and he very, very nearly changed his mind on the threshold and stayed beside him. But he forced himself to do as he had made up his mind to, and went out and away into the hills.

Just as Quest parted from his grandfather his imp thought he might as well get out of the osier clump and tackle that tiresome job; and he reached the clearing just as Quest was hurrying away.

So Quest went off to the hills, very downcast and sad; and when he came to the first rock, lo and behold, there was the goblin, gibbering.

"Why," thought Quest, "it's the very same one – quite small, misshapen, black as a mole and with big horns."

The goblin stood right in Quest's way, and would not let him pass. So Quest got angry with the little monster for hindering him like this; he picked up a stone, threw it at the goblin, and hit him squarely between the horns. "Now I've killed him," thought Quest.

But when he looked again there was the goblin as spry as ever, and two more horns had sprouted where the stone had hit him!

"Well, evidently stones won't drive him off," said Quest. So he went round the goblin and forward on his way. But the imp scuttled on in front of him, to the right and to the left, and then straight in front, for all the world like a rabbit.

At last they came to a little level spot between cliffs – a very stony place; and on one side of it there was a deep well-spring. "Here will I stay," said Quest; and he at once spread out his sheepskin coat under a crabtree and sat down, so that he might reflect in peace and remember what All-Rosy had verily and truly told him.

But when the imp saw that, he squatted down straight in front of Quest under the tree, played silly tricks on him, and worried him horribly. He chased lizards under Quest's feet, threw burrs at his shirt, and slipped grasshoppers up his sleeves.

"Oh dear, this is most annoying!" thought Quest, when it had gone on for some little time. "I have left my wise old grandfather, my brothers and my home, so that I might be in quiet and remember the truth – and here am I wasting my time with this horned imp of mischief!"

But as he had come out in a good cause, he nevertheless thought it the right thing to stay where he was.

III

So Quest and the goblin lived together on that lone ledge between the cliffs, and each day was like the first. The goblin worried Quest so that he couldn't get on with his thinking.

On a clear morning Quest would rise from sleep and feel happy. "How still it is, how lovely! Surely today I shall remember the truth!" And lo, from the branch overhead a handful of crabs would come tumbling about his ears, so that his head buzzed and his thoughts all got mixed. And there was the little monster mocking him from the crabtree and laughing fit to burst. Or Quest would be lying in the shade, thinking most beautifully, till he felt like saying: "There, there now, *now* it will come back to me, *now* I shall puzzle out the truth!" And then the goblin would squirt him all over with ice-cold water from the spring through a hollow elder twig – and again Quest would clean forget what he had already thought out.

There was no silly trick nor idle joke that the goblin did not play on Quest on the ledge there. And yet all might have been well, if Quest hadn't found it just a tiny bit amusing to watch these tomfooleries; and though he was thinking hard about his task, yet his eyes *would* wander and look round to see what the imp might be doing next.

Quest was angry with himself over this, because he was wearying more and more for his grandfather, and he saw full well that he would never remember the truth while the goblin was about.

"I must get rid of him," said Quest.

Well, one fine morning the goblin invented a new game. He climbed up the cliff where there was a steep water-course in the face of the rock, got astride a smooth bit of wood as if it had been a hobby-horse, and then scooted down the water-course like a streak of lightning! This prank pleased the little wretch so mightily that he must needs have company to enjoy it the better! So he whistled on a blade of grass till it rang over hill and dale, and lo, from scrub and rock and osier clump the goblins came scuttling along, all tiny like himself. He gave orders, and every man-jack of them took a stick and shinned up the cliff with it. My word! How they got astride their hobby-horses and hurtled down the water-course! There were all sorts and sizes and kinds of goblins – red as a robin's breast, green as greenfinches, woolly as lambs, naked as frogs, horned as snails, bald as mice. They careered down the water-course like a crazy company on crazy horses. Down they flew, each close at the other's heels, never stopping till they came to the middle of the ledge; and there was a great stone all overgrown with moss. There they were brought up short, and what with the bump of stopping so suddenly and sheer high spirits they tumbled and scrambled about all atop of one another in the moss!

Shrieking with glee, the silly crew had made the trip some two or three times already, and poor Quest was hard put to it between two thoughts. For one thing, he wanted to watch the imps and be amused by them, and for another he was angry with them for making such a hullabaloo that he could not remember the truth. So he shilly-shallied a while, and at last he said: "Well, this is past a joke. I must get rid of these good-for-nothing loons, because while they are here I might as well have stopped at home."

And as Quest considered the matter, he noticed that as they rushed down the water-course they made straight for the spring, and that, but for the big stone, they would all have toppled into it head foremost. So Quest crouched behind the stone, and when the imps came dashing down again guffawing and chuckling as before, he quickly rolled the stone aside, and the whole mad party rushed straight on to the well-spring – right on to it and then into it, head first, each on top of the other – red as robin's breasts, green as greenfinches, woolly as lambs, naked as frogs, horned as snails, bald-headed as mice – and first of all the one who had fastened himself on to Quest...

And then Quest tipped a big flat stone over the well, and all the goblins were caught inside like flies in a pitcher.

Quest was ever so pleased to have got rid of the goblins, sat down and made sure he would now recollect the truth in good earnest.

But he had no luck, because down in the well the goblins began to wriggle and to ramp as never before. Through every gap and chink shot up tiny flames which the goblins gave out in their fright and distress. The flames danced and wavered round the spring till Quest's head was all in a whirl. He closed his eyes, so that their flashing should not make him giddy.

But then there arose from the pit such a noise, hubbub, knocking and banging, barking and yowling, such yelling and shrieking for help, that Quest's ears were like to burst; and how could he even try to think through it? He stopped his ears so as not to hear.

Then a smell of brimstone and sulphur drifted over to him. Through every crack and crevice oozed thick sooty smoke which the imps belched forth in their extremity. Smoke and sulphur fumes writhed round Quest; they choked and smothered him.

So Quest saw there was no help for it. "Goblins shut up," said he, "are a hundred times worse than goblins at large. So I'll just go and let them out, since I can't get rid of them anyhow. After all, I am better off with their tomfooleries than with all that yammering."

So he went and lifted off the stone; and the terrified goblins scuttled away in all directions like so many wild cats, and ran away into the woods and never came back to the ledge any more.

None stayed behind, but only the one black as a mole and with big horns, because he did not dare to leave Quest for fear of Rampogusto.

But even he sobered down a little from that day forward, and had more respect for Quest than before.

And so these two came to a sort of arrangement between them; they got used to one another and lived side by side on the stony ledge.

In that way close on to a year slipped by, and Quest was no nearer remembering what All-Rosy had really truly told him.

When the year was almost gone the goblin began to be most horribly bored.

"How much longer have I got to stick here?" thought he. So one evening, just as Quest was about to fall asleep, the imp wriggled up to him and said:

"Well, my friend, here you've been sitting for close on a year and a day, and what's the good of it? Who knows but perhaps in the meantime your old granddad has died all alone in his cabin."

A pang shot through Quest's heart as if he had been struck with a knife, but he said: "There, I have made up my mind not to budge from here until I remember the truth, because truth comes before all things." Thus said Quest, because he was upright and of good parts.

But all the same he was deeply troubled by what the goblin had said about his grandfather. He never slept a wink all night, but racked his brains and thought: "How is it with the old man, my dear grandfather?"

IV

Now all this time the grandfather went on living with Careful and Bluster in the glade – only life had taken a very sad turn for the old man. His grandsons ceased to trouble about him, nor would they stay near him. They bade him neither "Good morning" nor "Good night," and only went about their own affairs and listened to the goblins they harboured, the one in his pouch and the other in his bosom.

Every day Careful brought more bees from the forest, felled timber, shaped rafters, and gradually built a new cabin. He carved himself ten tallies, and every day he counted and reckoned over and over again when these tallies would be filled up.

As for Bluster, he went hunting and reiving, bringing home game and furs, plunder and treasure; and one day he even brought along two slaves whom he had taken, so that they might work for the brothers and wait upon them.

All this was very hard and disagreeable for the old man, and harder and more disagreeable still were the looks he got from his grandsons. What use had they for an old man who would not be served by the slaves, but disgraced his grandsons by cutting wood and drawing water from the well for himself? At last there wasn't a thing about the old man that didn't annoy his grandsons, even this, that every day he would put a log on the sacred fire.

Old Witting saw very well whither all this would lead, and that very soon they would be thinking of getting rid of him altogether. He did not care so much about his life, because life was not much use to him, but he was sorry to die before seeing Quest once more, the dear lad who was the joy of his old age.

One evening – and it was the very evening when Quest was so troubled in his mind thinking of his grandfather – Careful said to Bluster: "Come along, brother, let's get rid of grandfather. You have weapons. Wait for him by the well and kill him."

Now Careful said this because he specially wanted the old cabin at all costs, so as to put up beehives on that spot. "I can't," replied Bluster, whose heart had not grown so hard, amidst bloodshed and robbery, as Careful's among his riches and his tallies.

But Careful would not give over, because the imp in his bag went on whispering and nagging. The imp in his pouch knew very well that Careful would be the first to put the old man away, and so gain him great credit with Rampogusto.

Careful tried hard to talk over Bluster, but Bluster could not bring himself to kill his grandfather with his own hand. So at last they agreed and arranged that they would that very night burn down the old man's hut – burn it down with the old man inside!

When all was quiet in the glade, they sent out the slaves to watch the traps in the woods that night. But the brothers crept up softly to Witting's cabin, shut the outer door tight with a thick wedge, so that the old man might not escape from the flames, and then set fire to the four corners of the house…

When all was done they went away and away into the hills so as not to hear their poor old grandfather crying out for help. They made up their minds to go over the whole of the mountain as far as they could, and not to come back until next day, when all would be over, and their grandfather and the cabin would be burnt up together.

So they went, and the flames began to lick upwards slowly round the corners. But the rafters were of seasoned walnut, hard as stone, and though the fire licked and crept all round them it could not catch properly, and so it was late at night before the flames took hold of the roof.

Old Witting awoke, opened his eyes and saw that the roof was ablaze over his head. He got up and went to the door, and when he found that it was fastened with a heavy wedge he knew at once whose doing it was.

"Oh, my children! My poor darlings!" said the old man, "you have taken from your hearts to add to your wretched tallies; and behold, your tallies are not even full, and there are many notches still lacking; but your hearts are empty to the bottom already, since you could burn your own grandfather and the cabin where you were born."

That was all the thought that Father Witting gave to Careful and Bluster. After that he thought neither good nor bad about them, nor did he grieve over them further, but went and sat down quietly to wait for death.

He sat on the oak chest and meditated upon his long life; and whatever there had been in it, there was nothing he was sorry for save only this, that Quest was not with him in his last hour – Quest, his darling child, for whom he had grieved so much.

So he sat still, while the roof was already blazing away like a torch.

The rafters burned and burned, the ceiling began to crack. It blazed, cracked, then gave way on either side of the old man, and rafters and ceiling crashed down amid the flames into the cabin. The flames billowed round Witting, the roof gaped above his head. Already he saw the dawn pale in the sky before sunrise. Old Witting rose to his feet, raised his hands to heaven, and so waited for the flames to carry him away from this world, the old man and his old homestead together.

V

Quest worried terribly that night, and when morning broke he went to the spring to cool his burning face.

The sun was just up in the sky when Quest reached the spring, and when he came there he saw a light shining in the water. It shone, it rose, and lo! beside the spring and before Quest stood a lovely youth in golden raiment. It was All-Rosy.

Quest started with joy, and said:

"My little lord All-Rosy bright, how I have longed for you! Do tell me what you told me then that I must do? Here I have been racking my brains and tormenting myself and calling on all my wits for a year and a day – and I cannot remember the truth!"

As Quest said this, All-Rosy rather crossly shook his head and his golden curls.

"Eh, boy, boy! I told you to stay with your grandfather till you had rendered him the love you owe him, and not to leave him till he left you," said All-Rosy.

And then he went on:

"I thought you were wiser than your brothers, and there you are the most foolish of the three. Here you have been racking your brains and calling on your wits to help you for a year and a day so that you might remember the truth; and if you had listened to your heart when it told you on the threshold of your cabin to turn back and not to leave your old grandfather – why then, you silly boy, you would have had the truth, even without wits!"

Thus spoke All-Rosy. Once more he crossly shook his head with the golden curls; then he took his golden cloak about him and vanished.

Shamed and troubled, Quest remained alone beside the spring, and from between the stones he heard the imp giggling – the hobgoblin, quite small, misshapen, and horned with big horns. The little wretch was pleased because All-Rosy had shamed Quest, who always gave himself such righteous airs; but when Quest roused himself from his first amazement he called out joyfully:

"Now I'll just wash quickly and then fly to my dear old grandfather." This he said and knelt by the spring to wash. Quest leaned down to reach the water, leaned down too far, lost his balance, and fell into the spring.

Fell into the spring and was drowned....

VI

The hobgoblin jumped up from among the stones, leaped to the edge of the spring, and looked down to see with his own eyes whether it was really true.

Yes, Quest was really truly drowned. There he lay at the bottom of the water, white as wax.

"Yoho, yoho, yo hey!" yelled the goblin, who was only a poor silly. "Yoho, yoho, yo hey! My friend, we're off today!"

The imp yelled so that all the rocks round the ledge rang with the noise. Then he heaved up the stone that lay by the edge of the spring, and the stone toppled over and covered the spring like a lid. Next the imp flung Quest's skin-coat on the top of the stone; last of all he went and sat on the coat, and then he began to skip and to frolic.

"Yoho, yoho! My job is done!" yelled the goblin.

But it wasn't for long that he skipped on the skin; it wasn't for long that he yelled.

For when the goblin had tired himself out, he looked round the ledge, and a queer feeling came over him.

You see, the goblin had got used to Quest. Never before had he had such an easy time as with that good youth. He had been allowed to fool about as he chose, without anybody scolding him or telling him to stop; and now that he came to think of it, he would have to go back to the osier clump, to the mire, to his angry King Rampogusto, and go on repeating the old goblin chatter among five hundred other goblins – all of them just as he used to be himself.

He had lost the habit of it. He began to think – to *think* a very little. He began to feel sad – just a little sad, then more and more miserable; and at last he was wringing and beating his hands, and the silly, thoughtless goblin, who a minute ago had been yelling with glee, was now weeping and wailing with grief and rolling about on the coat all crazy with distress.

He wept and he howled till all his former yelling was clean nothing in comparison. For a goblin is always a goblin. Once he starts wailing he wails with a vengeance. And he pulled the fur out of the skin-coat in handfuls, and rolled about on it as if he had taken leave of his senses.

Now just at that moment Bluster and Careful came to the lone ledge.

They had wandered all over the mountain, and were now on their way home to the glade to see if their grandfather and the cabin were quite burnt up. On the way back they came to a lone ledge where they had never been before.

Bluster and Careful heard something wailing, and caught sight of Quest's skin-coat; and they thought at once that Quest must have come to grief somehow.

Not that they felt sorry for their brother because they could not grieve for anybody while the goblins were about them.

But at that moment their goblins began to wriggle, because they could hear that one of their own kind was in trouble. Now there is no sort that sticks more closely together and none more faithful in trouble than the hobgoblins were. In the osier clump they would fight and squabble all day; but if there was trouble each would give the skin off his shins for the other!

So they wriggled and they worried; they pricked up their ears, and then peered out, the one from the pouch and the other from the shirt. And as they peered they at once saw a brother of theirs rolling about with somebody or something – rolling and writhing, and nothing to be seen but the fur flying.

"A wild beast is worrying him!" cried the terrified goblins. They jumped out, one out of Careful's pouch and the other out of Bluster's bosom, and scuttled off to help their friend.

But when they reached him, he would still do nothing but roll about on the skin and howl:

"The boy is dead! – The boy is dead!" The other two goblins tried to quiet him, and thought: "Maybe a thorn has got into his paw, or a midge into his ear" – because they had never lived with a righteous man, and did not know what it means to lament for others.

But the first goblin went on wailing so that you couldn't hear yourself speak, and he wouldn't be comforted either.

So the other goblins were in a fine taking as to what they were to do with him. Nor could they leave him there in his sore trouble. At last they had an idea. Each laid hold of the sheep-skin coat by one sleeve, and so they dragged along the coat with their brother inside, scuttled away into the woods, and out of the woods into the osier clump and home to Rampogusto.

So for the first time for a year and a day Bluster and Careful were quit of their goblins. When the imps hopped away from them, the brothers felt as though they had walked the world like blind men for a year and a day, and were seeing it plainly again now for the first time there on the rocky ledge.

First they looked at each other in amazement, and then they knew at once what a terrible wrong they had done their grandfather.

"Brother! Kinsman!" each cried to the other, "let us fly and save our grandfather." And they flew as if they had falcon's wings, home to the clearing.

When they came to the glade the cabin was roofless. Flames were rising like a column from the hut. Only the walls and the door were still standing, and the door was still tightly wedged.

The brothers hurried up, tore out the wedge, rushed into the cabin, and carried out the old man in their arms from amid the flames, which were just going to take hold on his feet.

They carried him out and laid him on the cool green turf, and then they stood beside him and neither dared speak a word.

After a while old Witting opened his eyes, and as he saw them he asked nothing about them. The only question he put was:

"Did you find Quest anywhere in the mountain?"

"No, grandfather," answered the brothers. "Quest is dead. He was drowned this morning in the well-spring. But, grandfather, forgive us, and we will serve you and wait upon you like slaves."

As they were speaking thus, old Witting arose and stood upon his feet.

"I see that you are already forgiven, my children," said he, "since you are standing here alive. But he who was the most upright of you three had to pay with his life for his fault. Come, children, take me to the place where he died."

Humbly penitent, Careful and Bluster supported their grandfather as they led him to the ledge.

But when they had walked a little while they saw that they had gone astray, and had never been that way before. They told their grandfather; but he just bade them keep on in that path.

So they came to a steep slope, and the road led up the slope right to the crest of the mountain.

"Our grandfather will die," whispered the brothers, "with him so feeble and the hillside so steep."

But old Witting only said: "On, children, on – follow the path."

So they began to climb up the track, and the old man grew ever more grey and pallid in the face. And on the mountain's crest there was something fair that rustled and crooned and sparkled and shone.

And when they reached the crest, they stood silent and stone still for very wonder and awe.

For before them was neither hill nor dale, nor mountain nor plain, nor anything at all, but only a great white cloud stretched out before them like a great white sea – a white cloud, and on the white cloud a pink cloud. Upon the pink cloud stood a glass mountain, and on the glass mountain a golden castle with wide steps leading up to the gates.

That was the Golden Castle of All-Rosy. A soft light streamed from the Castle – some of it from the pink cloud, some from the glass mountain, and some from the pure gold walls; but most of all from the windows of the Castle itself. For there sit the guests of All-Rosy, drinking from golden goblets health and welcome to each newcomer.

But All-Rosy does not enjoy the company of such as harbour any guilt in their souls, nor will he let them into his Castle. Therefore it is a noble and chosen company that is assembled in his courts, and from them streams the light through the windows.

Upon the ridge stood old Witting with his grandsons, all speechless as they gazed at the marvel. They looked – and of a sudden they saw someone sitting on the steps that led to the Castle. His face was hidden in his hands and he wept.

The old man looked and knew him – knew him for Quest.

The old man's soul was shaken within him. He roused himself and called out across the cloud:

"What ails you, my child?"

"I am here, grandfather," answered Quest. "A great light lifted me up out of the well-spring and brought me here. So far have I come; but they won't let me into the Castle, because I have sinned against you."

Tears ran down the old man's cheeks. His hands and heart went out to caress his dear child, to comfort him, to help him, to set his darling free.

Careful and Bluster looked at their grandfather, but his face was altogether changed. It was ashen, it was haggard, and not at all like the face of a living man.

"The old man will die of these terrors," whispered the brothers to each other.

But the old man drew himself up to his full height, and already he was moving away from them, when he looked back once more and said:

"Go home, children, back to the glade, since you are forgiven. Live and enjoy in all righteousness what shall fall to your part. But I go to help him to whom has been given the best part at the greatest cost."

Old Witting's voice was quite faint, but he stood before them upright as a dart.

Bluster and Careful looked at one another. Had their grandfather gone crazy, that he thought of walking across the clouds when he had no breath even for speech?

But already the old man had left them. He left them, went on and stepped out upon the cloud as though it were a meadow. And as he stepped out he went forward. On he walked, the old man, and his feet carried him as though he were a feather, and his cloak fluttered in the wind as if it were a cloud upon that cloud. Thus he came to the pink cloud, and to the glass mountain, and to the broad steps. He flew up the steps to his grandson. Oh the joy of it, when the old man clasped his grandson! He hugged him and he held him close as if he would never let him go. And Careful and Bluster heard it all. Across the cloud they could hear the old man and his grandchild weeping in each other's arms for pure joy!

Then the old man took Quest by the hand and led him up to the Castle gates. With his left hand he led his grandson, and with his right he knocked at the gate.

And lo, a wonder! At once the great gates flew open, all the splendour of the Castle was thrown open, and the company within, the noble guests, welcomed grandfather Witting and grandson Quest upon the threshold.

They welcomed them, held out their hands to them, and led them in.

Careful and Bluster just saw them pass by the window, and saw where they were placed at the table. The first place of all was given to old Witting, and beside him sat Quest, where All-Rosy, the golden youth, drinks welcome to his guests from a goblet of gold.

A great fear fell upon Bluster and Careful when they were left alone with these awesome sights.

"Come away, brother, to our clearing," whispered Careful; and they turned and went. Bewildered by many marvels, they got back to their clearing, and never again could they find either the path or the slope that led to the mountain's crest.

VII

Thus it was and thus it befell.

Careful and Bluster went on living in the glade. They lived long as valiant men and true, and brought up goodly families, sons and grandsons. All good parts went down from father to son, and, of course, also the sacred fire, which was fed with a fresh log every day so that it might never go out.

So, you see, Rampogusto was right in being afraid of Quest, because if Quest had not died in his search for truth those goblins would never have left Careful and Bluster, and in the glade there would have been neither righteous men nor sacred fire.

But so everything fell out. To the great shame and discomfiture of Rampogusto and all his crew.

When those two goblins dragged Quest's sheep-skin before Rampogusto, and inside it the third goblin, who was still yammering and carrying on like one demented, Rampogusto flew into a furious rage, for he knew that all three youths had escaped him. In his great wrath he gave orders that all three goblins should have their horns cropped close, and so run about for everyone to make fun of!

But the worst of Rampogusto's discomfiture was this: Every day the sacred smoke gets into his throat and makes him cough most horribly. Moreover, he never dares venture out into the woods for fear of meeting someone of the valiant people.

So Rampogusto got nothing out of it but Quest's cast-off sheep-skin; and I'm sure he is welcome to that, for Quest doesn't want a sheep-skin coat anyhow in All-Rosy's Golden Halls.

The Seven Golden Peahens

THERE WAS ONCE A KING who had three sons, and he had also a golden apple tree, that bore nothing but golden apples, and this tree he loved as though it had been his daughter. The king was never able, however, to have any of the fruit it bore, for no sooner were the apples ripe than they would disappear in the night, and this in spite of a guard being set around the garden to watch it and see that no one entered in.

One time the eldest prince came to the king and asked to be allowed to keep watch over the tree that night. "And if I do," said he, "I promise you that nothing shall be allowed to approach it, not even the smallest sparrow."

The king consented to this, so that evening the prince took his sword, and went out into the garden to mount guard over the tree. Scarcely had it become dark when he heard a sound of wings beating through the air, and this sound made him so drowsy that his eyelids weighed like lead, and he fell into a deep sleep. When he awoke it was morning, and all the apples were gone from the tree.

The prince returned to the palace, and was obliged to confess to the king that he had slept all the night through.

The king was very angry, but the second son said, "My father, allow me to keep watch over the tree the next time, and I promise you I will do better than my brother, for I will not so much as close my eyes until daybreak."

The king was willing, so when evening came the second son took his sword and went into the garden to watch the tree as his brother had done before him.

Hardly was it dark before he heard the sound of wings, and then in spite of himself his eyes closed and he fell into a deep sleep. He never stirred until daylight, and when he sat up and looked about him every apple was gone.

After this it was the turn of the third son to watch the tree, but he was a very wise prince. He had listened to all his brothers had to say about the sound of wings they had heard, and how the sound had put them to sleep, and before he went into the garden he stuffed his ears with cotton so that he could hear nothing. Then he placed himself near the tree and began his watch.

As soon as it was dark the sound of beating wings began, and the sound drew nearer and nearer, but the prince did not hear it because of the cotton in his ears. Then a light appeared in the sky, and seven golden peahens flew into the garden. They shone so that all the place was lit up as though by the light of day. Six of the peahens settled on the branches of the apple tree and began to shake down the apples, but the seventh changed into the most beautiful princess the prince had ever seen in all his life. Her hair was like a golden cloud about her; her eyes were as blue as the sky, and from head to foot she was dressed all in cloth of gold. She began to gather up the fruit that the others shook down to her, and for a while the prince could neither stir nor speak for wonder of her beauty. Then he took the cotton from his ears, and went over to her, and began to talk to her and ask her who she was.

At first when the princess saw him she was frightened, but presently she told him that she and the six peahens were the daughters of a king who lived far away, and that they had flown over seven mountains and over seven seas, all for the love of the golden apples. She also told him that by day she and her sisters lived in a beautiful pleasure palace their father had built for them, but when night came they changed themselves into peahens, and flew about the world wherever they chose.

After a while the day began to break, and then the princess changed herself into a peahen again, and she and her sisters flew away, but she left with the prince three of the golden apples she had gathered.

The prince returned to the palace and gave the apples to his father, and the king was delighted at the sight of them. "And did you find out who it is that steals them?" he asked.

Instead of answering him, the prince managed to put him off, and the next night he said he would watch in the garden again. Then the same thing happened. He stopped his ears with cotton, the seven peahens arrived and six alighted in the tree, but the seventh became a beautiful princess, and came across the garden to him. Then the prince unstopped his ears and they talked together until daybreak, when she flew away with her sisters, and this time, as before, she left three of the apples with him.

As soon as it was morning the prince carried the apples to his father, and now, whether or no, the king would have him say who it was who came into the garden every night to steal the fruit.

The prince was obliged to tell his story, but when he said it was seven golden peahens that stole the apples, and that they were the daughters of a great king his father would scarcely believe him. The brothers, too, laughed him to scorn, for they were very jealous of him. "This is a strange story," they cried, "and it certainly cannot be true. Either you are trying to deceive us, or you fell asleep and dreamed it all."

"It is all certainly true," answered the youngest brother, "and there are the three golden apples to prove it."

"They are no proof," answered the others. "If you would have us believe you, keep watch in the garden again tonight, and when the princess comes cut a lock of her golden hair and keep it to show to us. When we see that then we will believe you."

At first the prince would not consent to do this, but they were so urgent that he finally agreed, and when he went into the garden he took a pair of sharp scissors with him.

After a time the golden peahens flew into the garden, and after the youngest sister had changed into a princess, she and the prince talked together all night. When she was about to go the prince managed, without being seen, to take hold of a lock of her hair and cut it off.

No sooner had he done this, however, than the princess gave a sorrowful cry. "Alas, alas!" said she, "If you had only been patient for a little while longer all would have gone well. Now I must go away forever, and you will never see me again unless you journey over the seven seas and over the seven mountains to seek me." Then she changed into a peahen, and flew away with the others.

The prince was filled with despair at the thought that he had lost her, for he loved her so well that he did not know how he could live without her.

In the morning his father and his brothers came to seek him in the garden, and when they saw the lock of golden hair they were obliged to believe him, and they could not wonder enough.

But the young prince saddled his horse and set out in search of his princess. On he went and on he went, and everywhere he rode he asked those he met whether they had seen seven golden peahens, but no one could tell him anything about them.

At last after he had journeyed over seven mountains, and over seven seas, he came to a palace that stood beside a Lake, and in this palace lived an enchantress queen and her daughter. He knocked at the door and when the queen came to see who was there he once more asked whether she could tell him anything of the seven golden peahens who were the daughters of a king.

"Oh, yes, that I can," answered the queen, "and if you are in search of them you have not much further to go. Every morning they come to bathe in this Lake, and anyone who watches them can see them."

When the prince heard this he was filled with joy and would have set out for the lake at once, but the queen, seeing how young and handsome he was, begged him to come in and rest for awhile. "Why do you follow after these seven princesses?" she asked. "My daughter is a princess, too, and a beautiful girl. If you can take a fancy to her you shall marry her and live here and after I die this palace and all that is in it shall be yours."

The prince, however, would not listen to this, for he loved the golden peahen princess with all his heart, and her alone would he marry.

When the queen found that he was not to be persuaded she pretended to fall in with his wishes. "Very well," said she, "it shall be as you desire, but let me send someone with you to show you the way to the lake."

The prince thanked her, and she called a servant to go with him, but before they set out she took the servant aside and gave him privately a small pair of bellows. "When you reach the lake," said she, "take an opportunity to get behind the prince and blow upon the back of his neck with these bellows. If you do this I will reward you well."

The servant promised to obey her and then he and the prince set out together.

When they reached the shore the prince sat down on some rocks to watch for the peahens, but the servant got back of him and blew upon his neck with the bellows and immediately the prince fell asleep.

Presently there was a light in the sky and the seven golden peahens came flying and alighted upon the borders of the lake. Six of them began to bathe themselves in its waters but the seventh one changed into a princess. She came over to the prince and began to call to him and caress him, but she could not awaken him from his sleep.

After a time the peahens came up from the water, and the princess said to the servant, "Tell your master when he awakens twice more will I come but never again." Then she and the others all flew away together.

When the prince awoke and found that the princess had been there and had tried in vain to awaken him, he was ready to die with grief and disappointment. However, she would return the next day, and he determined he would be there watching for her and that this time he would not by any means allow himself to fall asleep.

So the next morning he hurried down to the lake again, and the servant went with him, but before they left the castle the queen gave the servant the pair of bellows, and bade him blow upon the back of the prince's neck when he was not aware of it.

They reached the lake, and the prince would not sit down for he feared he might fall asleep again, but the servant managed to get back of him and blow upon his neck with the bellows. Then, in spite of himself the prince sank down in a deep sleep.

Presently the peahens came flying, and as before the youngest sister came over to the prince and began to call and caress him, but he still slept on in spite of her. Then she turned to the servant and said to him, "Tell your master when he awakens that once more will I come and never again, but unless he cuts the head of the nail from the body he will never see me."

When the prince awoke and heard the message the princess had left he understood that the servant had deceived him, and that the princess meant unless he destroyed the servant he would never find her. So the next day when they started out together the prince took a sharp sword with him. He waited until they were out of sight of the castle, and then he turned and cut the servant's head from his shoulders and went on down, alone, to the lake.

He had not been there long when he saw a light, and heard the seven peahens coming. No sooner had they alighted than the seventh one changed into the beautiful princess. When she saw that the prince was awake and watching for her, she was overcome with joy. "Now we shall never be parted again," she said, "but you shall go to our palace with me and be my own dear husband."

Then she changed him into a golden peacock, and the six peahens came up from the water and they all flew away together. On and on they went until they came to the pleasure palace the king had built for his daughters, and there the golden peacock was changed back into a prince, and the peahens became seven princesses. The prince was married to the youngest one, amidst great rejoicings and they all lived there happily together.

Everything went joyfully for seven months, and then the princess came to the prince and said, "My dear husband, the time has now come when my sisters and I must go to pay a visit to the king our father. You cannot go with us, but if you will obey what I am about to tell you all will go well. We will be away for three days, and during that time the palace and all that is in it will be yours. You may go where you please except into the third cellar that is over beyond the others. There you must not go, for if you do some terrible misfortune will certainly come upon both of us."

The prince promised that all should be as she wished, and then she and her sisters flew away together leaving him alone.

For the first day the prince did not go near the cellar and scarcely thought of it. The second day he looked to see where it was, and when he came to the door it was so heavily chained and bolted that he could not but wonder what was back of it, and the third day he could think of nothing but the cellar and what was in it. At last he felt that come what might he must see what treasure it was that was kept locked away behind that door. He went down to it again and began to unfasten the bolts and bars; the last one fell and he opened the door and stepped inside and looked about him. There was nothing there to see but a great chest with holes bored in the lid, and bound about with nine bands of iron.

The prince stared and wondered, and while he still stood there he heard a groaning sound from within the chest, and a voice cried, "Brother, for the love of mercy give me some water to wet my poor mouth."

The prince was always pitiful toward those in trouble, and as soon as he heard this, without stopping to inquire what was inside of the chest he ran and fetched a cup of water and poured it through one of the holes.

Scarcely had he done this before there was a straining sound, and three of the iron bands burst asunder.

"Brother, that was scarcely enough to wet my mouth," said the voice inside. "For the love of mercy give me another cup of water to cool my throat."

The prince ran and fetched the water and poured it through the hole in the lid, and now three more of the iron bands burst asunder.

"More water, brother; more, for the love of mercy," cried the voice. "That still is not enough to quench my thirst."

The prince fetched a third cup of water and poured it into the chest, and now with a sound like thunder the last of the iron bands were broken, and out from the chest flew a great green dragon. It flew up through the cellars and out of the castle, and the prince ran after it.

The seven princesses were just coming home, and without even stopping for a moment the dragon caught up the youngest one in his claws and flew away with her, and the prince still ran after them shouting like one distracted. Even after the dragon had disappeared over the mountains the prince ran on, and when he could no longer run he walked.

On and on he went, and after a while he came to a stream, and in a hole near it lay a small fish gasping for breath.

"Brother," it cried, "for the love of mercy put me back in the water; but first take one of my scales, and if you are ever in need rub it and call upon me, and I may be able to help you."

The prince stooped and took up the fish, but before he put it back in the water he took from it a tiny scale as it had bade him. This scale he wrapped carefully in his handkerchief, and journeyed on again, leaving the fish happy at being again in the stream.

Later on he came to a forest, and under some bushes lay a fox whining to itself with its paw caught in a trap. "Brother," it called to the prince as soon as it saw him, "for the love of mercy open this trap and let me go free. It may be that I may succour you in a time of need."

The prince was sorry for the poor animal, and managed to pry open the trap.

The fox thanked him, and before it ran away it told him to pull three hairs from its tail. "If you are ever in need, rub those hairs and call upon me," it said, "and wherever I am I will hear and come to help you."

The prince thanked him and journeyed on, and in the depths of the forest he came upon a wolf which was caught by a rock that had fallen on its paw.

"Help, brother, for the love of mercy," cried the wolf.

The prince managed to roll away the rock, and when the wolf found it was free it gave him three hairs from its tail. "If you are ever in need, rub these hairs and call upon me," he said, "and wherever I am I will come and help you."

The prince thanked him and journeyed on, and before long he came out of the forest and saw before him a great castle that stood upon a mountain. While he stood there looking at it the gate opened and out rode the dragon on a great coal-black horse. Then the prince knew that this was the place he was in search of. He waited until the dragon had disappeared, and then he went up to the castle and entered in, and the very first person he saw was his own dear wife sitting alone and weeping. As soon as she saw him she jumped up and ran into his arms, and after they had kissed and caressed each other they began to plan how they could escape.

Out in the stable was another horse, and this the prince saddled. He mounted upon it and took the princess up before him, and then they rode down the mountain and away as fast as they could go.

It was not until evening that the dragon returned to the castle, but as soon as he came in and found the princess was gone he knew what had happened, and that she had ridden away with the prince.

Then he took counsel with his coal-black horse, and asked it, "Shall we ride after them at once, or shall we eat and drink first?"

"Let us eat and drink first," answered the horse, "for even after that we can easily catch up with them."

So the dragon sat down and ate and drank, and then he mounted his steed and rode after the runaways. He soon caught up with them, and took the princess from the prince, and set her on his own horse in front of him. "This one time I will spare you," he said to the prince, "because you had mercy upon me when I was a prisoner in the cellar, but if you ever come to my castle again I will certainly destroy you." Then he rode back home again faster than the wind, carrying the princess with him.

The prince waited until he was out of sight, and then he turned the horse loose and started back toward the castle, for even the dragon's threat could not keep him away from his dear princess.

When he had come within sight of the castle again he hid himself and waited until the next day when the dragon had ridden away. Then he went up to the castle and hunted through the rooms until he found the princess.

When she saw him she began to tremble with fear and wring her hands. "Why have you returned?" she cried. "Do you not remember that if the dragon finds you here he will tear you to pieces?"

"Listen, dear one," said the prince. "I will hide myself behind the curtains, and when the dragon comes home you must find out from him where he got his coal-black steed, for I can easily see that unless we find a match to it we will never be able to escape from him."

This the princess agreed to do, and they talked together until they heard the dragon returning, and then the prince hid himself back of the curtains.

When the dragon came in the princess pretended to be very glad to see him, and at this he was delighted, for always before she had met him with tears and reproaches.

After a time she said, "That is a very wonderful horse that you have. Do you suppose there is another one like it in all the world?"

"Yes," said the dragon, "there is one and only one, and that is the brother of my steed."

The princess asked him where this wonderful steed was to be found, and the dragon told her it belonged to the old grey woman who had but one eye and lived at such and such a place. "She has twelve beautiful horses standing in her stable," the dragon went on, "but this steed is none of them. It is the lean and sorry nag that is crowded away in the furthest stall, and no one to look at it would think it worth anything, but all the same it is the brother of my horse, and to the full as good as he is."

"And would it be possible for anyone to get that horse?" asked the princess.

"Possible but difficult. If anyone serves the old grey woman for three days, and during that time is able to fulfill her bidding he will be able to ask his own reward and she cannot refuse him; in that way can he gain possession of that horse and in no other."

The prince heard all this behind the curtain where he was hidden, and after a time, when the dragon had gone to sleep he stole out and set forth in search of the old grey woman who had but one eye.

He went on and on, and after a while he came to the house and there was the old grey woman herself looking out of the window.

He knocked at the door, and when she opened it he asked whether he might take service with her.

"Yes, you may," answered the old grey woman, "for I am in need of a stout lad to drive my black mare out to the pasture and keep her from running away. If you can do this for three days you may ask what reward you choose and it shall be yours, but if you are not able to bring her home every evening your head shall be cut from your shoulders and set upon a stake."

The prince agreed to this bargain, and the next morning, as soon as it was light, he drove the black mare out to the pasture. Before they started however the old woman went to the black mare's stall and whispered in her ear, "Today you must change yourself into a fish and hide down in the stream for there the lad will never be able to find you."

When the prince reached the pasture with the mare he determined to sit upon her back all day, for if he did that he was sure she could never escape from him. He sat there for a long time, but he grew drowsier and drowsier, and at last he fell fast asleep. When he awoke he was seated on a log of wood with the halter still in his hand, and the mare was gone.

The prince was in despair, but suddenly he remembered the promise the little fish had made him. He took out the scale which he had been carrying all this time, and rubbing it gently he cried:

"Little fish, if friend indeed,
Help me in my time of need."

Immediately the little fish stuck its head up from a stream nearby. "What can I do to help you, brother?" it asked.

"Can you tell me where the black mare has gone?" asked the prince.

"Yes; she has changed herself into a fish and is hiding down in the stream with us. But do not trouble yourself about that. Just strike the halter upon the ground and call out, 'Black mare, black mare, come out from among the fishes for it is time to go home.'"

The prince did as the fish bade him and as soon as the black mare down in the stream heard those words it was obliged to come out and take its natural shape again. The prince then mounted upon it and rode it home.

When they reached the stable the old grey woman was on the watch, and she could scarcely hide her rage and disappointment at finding the serving lad had managed to bring the black mare home. However, she bade him go to the kitchen and get his supper, and she followed the black mare to the stall. "You fool," she cried, and she was ready to beat it in her rage, "why did you not hide among the fishes as I bade you?"

"Mistress, I did," answered the mare, "but the fishes are friends of the lad, and told him where I was, so I was obliged to come forth."

"Tomorrow, change yourself into a fox and hide among the pack. There he will certainly be unable to find you."

After that she went into the kitchen where the lad was eating his supper.

"Well," she said, "you have done very well so far, but tomorrow is still another day, and we will see how things go then."

On the morrow the prince rode the black mare out to pasture, and again he sat on her back so that she should not escape him. After awhile he fell asleep in spite of himself, and when he awoke he was sitting astride of a branch with the halter in his hand.

At first the prince did not know what to do; he was in despair. Then he remembered the promise the fox had made him. He took the hairs and rubbed them between his fingers.

"Little fox, if friend indeed,
Help me in my time of need,"

he said.

Immediately the little red fox came running out of the wood. "What would you have of me, brother?" he asked.

"Can you tell me where the grey woman's black mare has gone?"

"That is easily answered. She has changed herself into a fox and is hiding with the pack. Strike the halter on the ground and call out: 'Black mare, black mare, come from among the foxes; it is time to go home.'"

The prince did as he was told and as soon as the mare heard him calling to her in this way she was obliged to come out from the pack and take her real shape, and the prince mounted upon her back and rode her home.

When the witch saw him riding back to the house she ground her teeth with rage. As soon as she had sent him to the kitchen she went out to the black mare's stall to beat it. "To the foxes! To the foxes! That was what I told you," she cried.

"Mistress, I did hide among them as you bade me," answered the mare, "but this lad is a friend of the foxes too, and they told him where I was."

"Then tomorrow hide among the wolves," said the old woman. "He will certainly never look for you there."

The next day it was the same thing over again. The prince sat on the mare's back so that she should not escape him. After while he went to sleep, and the mare slipped away from him, but this time it was into a wolf she changed herself.

When the prince awoke he was in despair, until he remembered that he had still one friend to help him. He gently rubbed the hairs the wolf had given him, and said,

"Kind grey wolf, if friend indeed,
Help me in my time of need."

Immediately the wolf came galloping out of the wood and asked the prince what he could do for him.

The prince told him how he had been set to watch the black mare and had gone to sleep and lost her; "And now," said he, "I fear there is nothing for me but to lose my head and have it set upon a post."

"That will not happen yet," answered the wolf. "The mare has changed herself to a wolf and is hiding with the pack. Strike the halter on the ground and call to her and she will be obliged to come."

The prince did as he was told and called to the mare to come, and she was obliged to take her real shape and come out to him.

The prince slipped the halter over her head, sprang upon her back and rode her home.

When the old grey woman saw him coming in this way instead of upon his feet, she almost burst with rage. However, there was no help for it. The lad had earned his wages, and have them he must.

"And what is it you will choose?" asked the old grey woman.

"Give me the poor nag that stands in the furthest stall," said the prince. "It is but a sorry looking beast, but I will be content with that," answered the prince.

When the old woman heard that she turned green in the face. She offered him first one and then another of the handsome horses in her stable, but the lad would have none of them. The sorry nag was his choice and it alone would he take, and in the end the old woman was obliged to give it to him. He rode away on it, and it was not the old grey mother's blessing that went with him.

When they were well out of sight of the house and in the depths of the forest, the prince alighted and taking out a curry comb he had brought with him he began to rub and curry the horse, and when he had done that it shone like burnished silver.

Then he mounted again and rode on until he came to the dragon's castle. As soon as he drew near, the princess came running down to meet him, for the dragon was away, and she had been watching from a high tower and had seen him coming.

He took her up on the saddle before him and turned his horse's head and rode away from the castle even faster than he had ridden toward it, and they had journeyed far before the dragon returned home.

As soon as he reached there and found the princess gone he knew what had happened. Then he said to his horse, "Shall we follow after them now, or shall we eat and drink first?"

"We have no time for meat or drink now," answered the black horse, "and it will be all I can do to overtake them, for now they ride my own brother."

Then the dragon leaped upon his horse, and off they flew, faster than the wind, in pursuit of the prince and princess. They went on and on, and after a while the dragon came within sight of them, for though the white horse was swifter than the wind, too, he carried double and so could not go at his highest speed.

Nearer and nearer came the dragon and his steed, and the prince began to beg and plead with his steed to go faster, but it answered, "There is no need of that, master; only leave everything to me and all will go well."

Then the black horse came near enough to speak, and he called after the other, "For mercy's sake go slower, brother. I shall kill myself running after you."

"There is no need of your doing that," answered the white horse. "Throw up your heels and rid yourself of the monster that sits upon your back. You have been his servant too long as it is."

When the black horse heard this he began to plunge and kick up his heels so that the dragon was thrown from his back and falling upon a rock he was broken to pieces.

But the black horse came up to his brother, and the prince set the princess upon his back, while he himself kept the white horse to ride. So they all journeyed back to the pleasure palace together, and when the six sisters saw them there were great rejoicings, and they all lived together happily in the palace forever after.

The Evil Eye of Sani

ONCE UPON A TIME SANI, or Saturn, the god of bad luck, and Lakshmi, the goddess of good luck, fell out with each other in heaven. Sani said he was higher in rank than Lakshmi, and Lakshmi said she was higher in rank than Sani. As all the gods and goddesses of heaven were equally ranged on either side, the contending deities agreed to refer the matter to some human being who had a name for wisdom and justice. Now, there lived at that time upon earth a man of the name of Sribatsa, who was as wise and just as he was rich. Him, therefore, both the god and the goddess chose as the settler of their dispute. One day, accordingly, Sribatsa was told that Sani and Lakshmi were wishing to pay him a visit to get their dispute settled. Sribatsa was in a fix. If he said Sani was higher in rank than Lakshmi, she would be angry with him and forsake him. If he said Lakshmi was higher in rank than Sani, Sani would cast his evil eye upon him. Hence he made up his mind not to say anything directly, but to leave the god and the goddess to gather his opinion from his action. He got two stools made, the one of gold and the other of silver, and placed them beside him. When Sani and Lakshmi came to Sribatsa, he told Sani to sit upon the silver stool, and Lakshmi upon the gold stool. Sani became mad with rage, and said in an angry tone to Sribatsa, "Well, as you consider me lower in rank than Lakshmi, I will cast my eye on you for three years; and I should like to see how you fare at the end of that period." The god then went away in high dudgeon. Lakshmi, before going away, said to Sribatsa, "My child, do not fear. I'll befriend you." The god and the goddess then went away.

Sribatsa said to his wife, whose name was Chintamani, "Dearest, as the evil eye of Sani will be upon me at once, I had better go away from the house; for if I remain in the house with you, evil will befall you and me; but if I go away, it will overtake me only." Chintamani said, "That cannot be; wherever you go, I will go, your lot shall be my lot." The husband tried hard to persuade his wife to remain at home; but it was of no use. She would go with her husband. Sribatsa accordingly told his wife to make an opening in their mattress, and to stow away in it all the money and jewels they had. On the eve of leaving their house, Sribatsa invoked Lakshmi, who forthwith appeared. He then said to her, "Mother Lakshmi! As the evil eye of Sani is upon us, we are going away into exile; but do thou befriend us, and take care of our house and property." The goddess of good luck answered, "Do not fear; I'll befriend you; all will be right at last." They then set out on their journey. Sribatsa rolled up the mattress and put it on his head. They had not gone many miles when they saw a river before them. It was not fordable; but there was a canoe there with a man sitting in it. The travellers requested the ferryman to take them across. The ferryman said, "I can take only one at a time; but you are three – yourself, your wife, and the mattress." Sribatsa proposed that first his wife and the mattress should be taken across, and then he; but the ferryman would not hear of it. "Only one at a time," repeated he; "first let me take across the mattress." When the canoe with the mattress was in the middle of the stream, a fierce gale arose, and carried away the mattress, the canoe, and the ferryman, no one knows whither. And it was strange the stream also disappeared, for the place, where they saw a few minutes since the rush of waters, had now become firm ground. Sribatsa then knew that this was nothing but the evil eye of Sani.

Sribatsa and his wife, without a pice in their pocket, went to a village which was hard by. It was dwelt in for the most part by woodcutters, who used to go at sunrise to the forest to cut wood, which they sold in a town not far from the village. Sribatsa proposed to the woodcutters that he should go along with them to cut wood. They agreed. So he began to fell trees as well as the best of them; but there was this difference between Sribatsa and the other woodcutters, that whereas the latter cut any and every sort of wood, the former cut only precious wood like sandal-wood. The woodcutters used to bring to market large loads of common wood, and Sribatsa only a few pieces of sandal-wood, for which he got a great deal more money than the others. As this was going on day after day, the woodcutters through envy plotted together, and drove away from the village Sribatsa and his wife.

The next place they went to was a village of weavers, or rather cotton-spinners. Here Chintamani, the wife of Sribatsa, made herself useful by spinning cotton. And as she was an intelligent and skilful woman, she spun finer thread than the other women; and she got more money. This roused the envy of the native women of the village. But this was not all. Sribatsa, in order to gain the good grace of the weavers, asked them to a feast, the dishes of which were all cooked by his wife. As Chintamani excelled in cooking, the barbarous weavers of the village were quite charmed by the delicacies set before them. When the men went to their homes, they reproached their wives for not being able to cook so well as the wife of Sribatsa, and called them good-for-nothing women. This thing made the women of the village hate Chintamani the more. One day Chintamani went to the riverside to bathe along with the other women of the village. A boat had been lying on the bank stranded on the sand for many days; they had tried to move it, but in vain. It so happened that as Chintamani by accident touched the boat, it moved off to the river. The boatmen, astonished at the event, thought that the woman had uncommon power, and might be useful on similar occasions in future. They therefore caught hold of her, put her in the boat, and rowed off. The women of the village, who were present, did not offer any resistance as they hated Chintamani. When Sribatsa heard how his wife had been carried away by boatmen, he became mad with grief. He left the village, went to the riverside, and resolved to follow the course of the stream till he should meet the boat where his wife was a prisoner. He travelled on and on, along the side of the river, till it became dark. As there were no huts to be seen, he climbed into a tree for the night. Next morning as he got down from the tree he saw at the foot of it a cow called a Kapila-cow, which never calves, but which gives milk at all hours of the day whenever it is milked. Sribatsa milked the cow, and drank its milk to his heart's content. He was astonished to find that the cow-dung which lay on the ground was of a bright yellow colour; indeed, he found it was pure gold. While it was in a soft state he wrote his own name upon it, and when in the course of the day it became hardened, it looked like a brick of gold – and so it was. As the tree grew on the riverside, and as the Kapila-cow came morning and evening to supply him with milk, Sribatsa resolved to stay there till he should meet the boat. In the meantime the gold bricks were increasing in number every day, for the cow both morning and evening deposited there the precious article. He put the gold bricks, upon all of which his name was engraved, one upon another in rows, so that from a distance they looked like a hillock of gold.

Leaving Sribatsa to arrange his gold bricks under the tree on the riverside we must follow the fortunes of his wife. Chintamani was a woman of great beauty; and thinking that her beauty might be her ruin, she, when seized by the boatmen, offered to Lakshmi the following prayer – "O Mother Lakshmi! have pity upon me. Thou hast made me beautiful, but now my beauty will undoubtedly prove my ruin by the loss of honour and chastity. I therefore beseech thee, gracious Mother, to make me ugly, and to cover my body with some loathsome disease, that the boatmen may not touch me." Lakshmi heard Chintamani's prayer; and in the twinkling of an eye, while she was in the arms of the boatmen, her naturally beautiful form was turned into a vile carcase. The boatmen, on putting her down in the boat, found her body covered with loathsome sores which were giving out a disgusting stench. They therefore threw her into the hold of the boat amongst the cargo, where they used morning and evening to send her a little boiled rice and some water. In that hold Chintamani had a miserable life of it; but she greatly preferred that misery to the loss of chastity. The boatmen went to some port, sold the cargo, and were returning to their country when the sight of what seemed a hillock of gold, not far from the river-side, attracted their attention. Sribatsa, whose eyes were ever directed towards the river, was delighted when he saw a boat turn towards the bank, as he fondly imagined his wife might be in it. The boatmen went to the hillock of gold, when Sribatsa said that the gold was his. They put all the gold bricks on board their vessel, took Sribatsa prisoner, and put him into the hold not far from the woman covered with sores. They of course immediately recognized each other, in spite of the change Chintamani had undergone, but thought it prudent not to speak to each other. They communicated their ideas, therefore, by signs and gestures. Now, the boatmen were fond of playing at dice, and as Sribatsa appeared to them from his looks to be a respectable man, they always asked him to join in the game. As he was an expert player, he almost always won the game, on which the boatmen, envying his superior skill, threw him overboard. Chintamani had the presence of mind, at that moment, to throw into the water a pillow which she had for resting her head upon. Sribatsa took hold of the pillow, by means of which he floated down the stream till he was carried at nightfall to what seemed a garden on the water's edge. There he stuck among the trees, where he remained the whole night, wet and shivering. Now, the garden belonged to an old widow who was in former years the chief flower-supplier to the king of that country. Through some cause or other a blight seemed to have come over her garden, as almost all the trees and plants ceased flowering; she had therefore given up her place as the flower-supplier of the royal household. On the morning following the night on which Sribatsa had stuck among the trees, however, the old woman on getting up from her bed could scarcely believe her eyes when she saw the whole garden ablaze with flowers. There was not a single tree or plant which was not begemmed with flowers. Not understanding the cause of such a miraculous sight, she took a walk through the garden, and found on the river's brink, stuck among the trees, a man shivering and almost dying with cold. She brought him to her cottage, lighted a fire to give him warmth, and showed him every attention, as she ascribed the wonderful flowering of her trees to his presence. After making him as comfortable as she could, she ran to the king's palace, and told his chief servants that she was again in a position to supply the palace with flowers; so she was restored to her former office as the flower-woman of the royal household. Sribatsa, who stopped a few days with the woman, requested her to recommend him to one of the king's ministers for a berth. He was accordingly sent for to the palace, and as he was at once found to be a man of intelligence, the king's minister asked him what post he would like to have. Agreeably to his wish he was appointed collector of tolls on the river. While discharging his duties as river toll-gatherer, in the course of a few days he saw the very boat in which his wife was a prisoner. He detained the boat, and charged the boatmen with the theft of gold bricks which he claimed as his own. At the mention of gold bricks the king himself came to the river-side, and was astonished beyond measure to see bricks made of gold, every one of which had the inscription – Sribatsa. At the same time Sribatsa rescued from the boatmen his wife, who, the moment she came out of the vessel, became as lovely as before. The king heard the story of Sribatsa's misfortunes from his lips, entertained him in a princely style for many days, and at last sent him and his wife to their own country with presents of horses and elephants. The evil eye of Sani was now turned away from Sribatsa, and he again became what he formerly was, the Child of Fortune.

The Bell of Dōjōji

THE MONK ANCHIN WAS YOUNG IN YEARS but old in scholarship. Every day for many hours he read the Great Books of the Good Law and never wearied, and hard characters were not hard to him.

The monk Anchin was young in years but old in holiness; he kept his body under by fastings and watchings and long prayers. He was acquainted with the blessedness of sublime meditations. His countenance was white as ivory and as smooth; his eyes were deep as a brown pool in autumn; his smile was that of a Buddha; his voice was like an angel's. He dwelt with a score of holy men in a monastery of the mountains, where he learned the mystic 'Way of the Gods.' He was bound to his order by the strictest vows, but was content, rejoicing in the shade of the great pine trees and the sound of the running water of the streams.

Now it happened that on a day in springtime, the old man, his Abbot, sent the young monk Anchin upon an errand of mercy. And he said, "My son, bind your sandals fast and tie spare sandals to your girdle, take your hat and your staff and your rosary and begging bowl, for you have far to go, over mountain and stream, and across the great plain."

So the monk Anchin made him ready.

"My son," the Abbot said, "if any wayfarer do you a kindness, forget not to commend him to the gods for the space of nine existences."

"I will remember," said the monk, and so he set forth upon his way.

Over mountain and stream he passed, and as he went his spirit was wrapped in contemplation, and he recited the Holy Sutras aloud in a singing voice. And the Wise Birds called and twittered from branch to branch of the tall trees, the birds that are beloved of Buddha. One bird chanted the grand Scripture of the Nicheten, the Praise of the Sutra of the Lotus, of the Good Law, and the other bird called upon his Master's name, for he cried:

"O thou Compassionate Mind! O thou Compassionate Mind!"

The monk smiled. "Sweet and happy bird," he said.

And the bird answered, "O thou Compassionate Mind! … O thou Compassionate Mind!"

When the monk Anchin came to the great plain, the sun was high in the heavens, and all the blue and golden flowers of the plain languished in the noontide heat. The monk likewise became very weary, and when he beheld the Marshy Mere, where were bulrush and sedge that cooled their feet in the water, he laid him down to rest under a sycamore tree that grew by the Marshy Mere.

Over the mere and upon the farther side of it there hung a glittering haze.

Long did the monk Anchin lie; and as he lay he looked through the glittering haze, and as he looked the haze quivered and moved and grew and gathered upon the farther side of the mere. At the last it drew into a slender column of vapour, and out of the vapour there came forth a very dazzling lady. She wore a robe of green and gold, interwoven, and golden sandals on her slender feet. In her hands were jewels – in each hand one bright jewel like a star. Her hair was tied with a braid of scarlet, and she had a crown of scarlet flowers. She came, skirting the Marshy Mere. She came, gliding in and out of the bulrush and the sedge. In the silence there could be heard the rustle of her green skirt upon the green grass.

The monk Anchin stumbled to his feet and, trembling, he leaned against the sycamore tree.

Nearer and nearer came the lady, till she stood before Anchin and looked into his eyes. With the jewel that was in her right hand she touched his forehead and his lips. With the jewel that was in her left hand she touched his rice-straw hat and his staff and his rosary and his begging bowl. After this she had him safe in thrall. Then the wind blew a tress of her hair across his face, and when he felt it he gave one sob.

For the rest of his journey the monk went as a man in a dream. Once a rich traveller riding on horseback threw a silver coin into Anchin's begging bowl; once a woman gave him a piece of cake made of millet; and once a little boy knelt down and tied the fastening of his sandal that had become loose. But each time the monk passed on without a word, for he forgot to commend the souls of these compassionate ones for the space of nine existences. In the tree-tops the Wise Birds of Buddha sang for him no more, only from the thicket was heard the cry of the *Hototogisu*, the bird lovelorn and forsaken.

Nevertheless, well or ill, he performed his errand of mercy and returned to the monastery by another way.

Howbeit, sweet peace left him from the hour in which he had seen the lady of the Marshy Mere. The Great Books of the Good Law sufficed him no longer; no more was he acquainted with the blessedness of divine meditations. His heart was hot within him; his eyes burned and his soul longed after the lady of the green and golden robe.

She had told him her name, and he murmured it in his sleep. "Kiohimé – Kiohimé!" Waking, he repeated it instead of his prayers – to the great scandal of the brethren, who whispered together and said, "Is our brother mad?"

At length Anchin went to the good Abbot, and in his ear poured forth all his tale in a passion of mingled love and grief, humbly asking what he must do.

The Abbot said, "Alack, my son, now you suffer for sin committed in a former life, for Karma must needs be worked out."

Anchin asked him, "Then is it past help?"

"Not that," said the Abbot, "but you are in a very great strait."

"Are you angry with me?" said Anchin.

"Nay, Heaven forbid, my poor son."

"Then what must I do?"

"Fast and pray, and for a penance stand in the ice-cold water of our mountain torrent an hour at sunrise and an hour at sunset. Thus shall you be purged from carnal affection and escape the perils of illusion."

So Anchin fasted and prayed, he scourged his body, and hour after hour he did penance in the ice-cold water of the torrent. Wan as a ghost he grew, and his eyes were like flames. His trouble would not leave him. A battle raged in his breast. He could not be faithful to his vows and faithful to his love.

The brethren wondered, "What can ail the monk Anchin, who was so learned and so holy – is he bewitched by a fox or a badger, or can he have a devil?"

But the Abbot said, "Let be."

Now on a hot night of summer, the monk being sleepless in his cell, he was visited by Kiohimé, the magic lady of the mere. The moonlight was on her hands and her long sleeves. Her robe was green and gold, interwoven; golden were her sandals. Her hair was braided with scarlet and adorned with scarlet flowers.

"Long, long have I waited for thee on the plains," she said. "The night wind sighs in the sedge – the frogs sing by the Marshy Mere. Come, lord...."

But he cried, "My vows that I have vowed – alas! The love that I love. I keep faith and loyalty, the bird in my bosom ... I may not come."

She smiled. "*May not*?" she said, and with that she lifted the monk Anchin in her arms.

But he, gathering all his strength together, tore himself from her and fled from the place. Barefooted and bareheaded he went, his white robe flying, through the dark halls of the monastery, where the air was heavy with incense and sweet with prayers, where the golden Amida rested upon her lotus, ineffably smiling. He leaped the grey stone steps that led down from her shrine and gained the pine trees and the mountain path. Down, down he fled on the rough way, the nymph Kiohimé pursuing. As for her, her feet never touched the ground, and she spread her green sleeves like wings. Down, down they fled together, and so close was she behind him that the monk felt her breath upon his neck.

"As a young goddess, she is fleet of foot..." he moaned.

At last they came to the famed temple of Dōjōji, which was upon the plains. By this Anchin sobbed and staggered as he ran; his knees failed him and his head swam.

"I am lost," he cried, "for a hundred existences." But with that he saw the great temple bell of Dōjōji that hung but a little way from the ground. He cast himself down and crept beneath it, and so deemed himself sheltered and secure.

Then came Kiohimé, the Merciless Lady, and the moonlight shone upon her long sleeves. She did not sigh, nor cry, nor call upon her love. She stood still for a little space and smiled. Then lightly she sprang to the top of the great bronze bell of Dōjōji, and with her sharp teeth she bit through the ropes that held it, so that the bell came to the ground and the monk was a prisoner. And Kiohimé embraced the bell with her arms. She crept about it, she crawled about it and her green robe flowed over it. Her green robe glittered with a thousand golden scales; long flames burst from her lips and from her eyes; a huge and fearsome Dragon, she wound and coiled herself about the bell of Dōjōji. With her Dragon's tail she lashed the bell, and lashed it till its bronze was red hot.

Still she lashed the bell, while the monk called piteously for mercy. And when he was very quiet she did not stop. All the night long the frogs sang by the Marshy Mere and the wind sighed in the sedges. But the Dragon Lady was upon the bell of Dōjōji, and she lashed it furiously with her tail till dawn.

The Flute

LONG SINCE, THERE LIVED IN YEDO a gentleman of good lineage and very honest conversation. His wife was a gentle and loving lady. To his secret grief, she bore him no sons. But a daughter she did give him, whom they called O'Yoné, which, being interpreted, is 'Rice in the Ear.' Each of them loved this child more than life, and guarded her as the apple of their eye. And the child grew up red and white, and long-eyed, straight and slender as the green bamboo.

When O'Yoné was twelve years old, her mother drooped with the fall of the year, sickened, and pined, and ere the red had faded from the leaves of the maples she was dead and shrouded and laid in the earth. The husband was wild in his grief. He cried aloud, he beat his breast, he lay upon the ground and refused comfort, and for days he neither broke his fast nor slept. The child was quite silent.

Time passed by. The man perforce went about his business. The snows of winter fell and covered his wife's grave. The beaten pathway from his house to the dwelling of the dead was snow also, undisturbed save for the faint prints of a child's sandalled feet. In the springtime he girded up his robe and went forth to see the cherry blossom, making merry enough, and writing a poem upon gilded paper, which he hung to a cherry-tree branch to flutter in the wind. The poem was in praise of the spring and of *saké*. Later, he planted the orange lily of forgetfulness, and thought of his wife no more. But the child remembered.

Before the year was out he brought a new bride home, a woman with a fair face and a black heart. But the man, poor fool, was happy, and commended his child to her, and believed that all was well.

Now because her father loved O'Yoné, her stepmother hated her with a jealous and deadly hatred, and every day she dealt cruelly by the child, whose gentle ways and patience only angered her the more. But because of her father's presence she did not dare to do O'Yoné any great ill; therefore she waited, biding her time. The poor child passed her days and her nights in torment and horrible fear. But of these things she said not a word to her father. Such is the manner of children.

Now, after some time, it chanced that the man was called away by his business to a distant city. Kyoto was the name of the city, and from Yedo it is many days' journey on foot or on horseback. Howbeit, go the man needs must, and stay there three moons or more. Therefore he made ready, and equipped himself, and his servants that were to go with him, with all things needful; and so came to the last night before his departure, which was to be very early in the morning.

He called O'Yoné to him and said: "Come here, then, my dear little daughter." So O'Yoné went and knelt before him.

"What gift shall I bring you home from Kyoto?" he said.

But she hung her head and did not answer.

"Answer, then, rude little one," he bade her. "Shall it be a golden fan, or a roll of silk, or a new *obi* of red brocade, or a great battledore with images upon it and many light-feathered shuttlecocks?"

Then she burst into bitter weeping, and he took her upon his knees to soothe her. But she hid her face with her sleeves and cried as if her heart would break. And, "O father, father, father," she said, "do not go away – do not go away!"

"But, my sweet, I needs must," he answered, "and soon I shall be back – so soon, scarcely it will seem that I am gone, when I shall be here again with fair gifts in my hand."

"Father, take me with you," she said.

"Alas, what a great way for a little girl! Will you walk on your feet, my little pilgrim, or mount a pack-horse? And how would you fare in the inns of Kyoto? Nay, my dear, stay; it is but for a little time, and your kind mother will be with you."

She shuddered in his arms.

"Father, if you go, you will never see me more."

Then the father felt a sudden chill about his heart, that gave him pause. But he would not heed it. What! Must he, a strong man grown, be swayed by a child's fancies? He put O'Yoné gently from him, and she slipped away as silently as a shadow.

But in the morning she came to him before sunrise with a little flute in her hand, fashioned of bamboo and smoothly polished. "I made it myself," she said, "from a bamboo in the grove that is behind our garden. I made it for you. As you cannot take me with you, take the little flute, honourable father. Play on it sometimes, if you will, and think of me." Then she wrapped it in a handkerchief of white silk, lined with scarlet, and wound a scarlet cord about it, and gave it to her father, who put it in his sleeve. After this he departed and went his way, taking the road to Kyoto. As he went he looked back thrice, and beheld his child, standing at the gate, looking after him. Then the road turned and he saw her no more.

The city of Kyoto was passing great and beautiful, and so the father of O'Yoné found it. And what with his business during the day, which sped very well, and his pleasure in the evening, and his sound sleep at night, the time passed merrily, and small thought he gave to Yedo, to his home, or to his child. Two moons passed, and three, and he made no plans for return.

One evening he was making ready to go forth to a great supper of his friends, and as he searched in his chest for certain brave silken *hakama* which he intended to wear as an honour to the feast, he came upon the little flute, which had lain hidden all this time in the sleeve of his travelling dress. He drew it forth from its red and white handkerchief, and as he did so, felt strangely cold with an icy chill that crept about his heart. He hung over the live charcoal of the *hibachi* as one in a dream. He put the flute to his lips, when there came from it a long-drawn wail.

He dropped it hastily upon the mats and clapped his hands for his servant, and told him he would not go forth that night. He was not well, he would be alone. After a long time he reached out his hand for the flute. Again that long, melancholy cry. He shook from head to foot, but he blew into the flute. "Come back to Yedo …come back to Yedo … Father! Father!" The quavering childish voice rose to a shriek and then broke.

A horrible foreboding now took possession of the man, and he was as one beside himself. He flung himself from the house and from the city, and journeyed day and night, denying himself sleep and food. So pale was he and wild that the people deemed him a madman and fled from him, or pitied him as the afflicted of the gods. At last he came to his journey's end, travel-stained from head to heel, with bleeding feet and half-dead of weariness.

His wife met him in the gate.

He said: "Where is the child?"

"The child…?" she answered.

"Ay, the child – my child … where is she?" he cried in an agony.

The woman laughed: "Nay, my lord, how should I know? She is within at her books, or she is in the garden, or she is asleep, or mayhap she has gone forth with her playmates, or…"

He said: "Enough; no more of this. Come, where is my child?"

Then she was afraid. And, "In the Bamboo Grove," she said, looking at him with wide eyes.

There the man ran, and sought O'Yoné among the green stems of the bamboos. But he did not find her. He called, "Yoné! Yoné!" and again, "Yoné! Yoné!" But he had no answer; only the wind sighed in the dry bamboo leaves. Then he felt in his sleeve and brought forth the little flute, and very tenderly put it to his lips. There was a faint sighing sound. Then a voice spoke, thin and pitiful:

"Father, dear father, my wicked stepmother killed me. Three moons since she killed me. She buried me in the clearing of the Bamboo Grove. You may find my bones. As for me, you will never see me any more – you will never see me more…."

* * *

With his own two-handed sword the man did justice, and slew his wicked wife, avenging the death of his innocent child. Then he dressed himself in coarse white raiment, with a great rice-straw hat that shadowed his face. And he took a staff and a straw raincoat and bound sandals on his feet, and thus he set forth upon a pilgrimage to the holy places of Japan.

And he carried the little flute with him, in a fold of his garment, upon his breast.

The Land of Yomi

FROM THE GLORIOUS CLOUDS OF HIGH HEAVEN, from the divine ether, the vital essence, and the great concourse of eternal deities, there issued forth the heavenly pair – Izanagi, His Augustness, the Lord of Invitation, and with him, Izanami, Her Augustness, the Lady of Invitation.

Together they stood upon the Floating Bridge of High Heaven, and they looked down to where the mists swirled in confusion beneath their feet. For to them had been given power and commandment to make, consolidate and give birth to the drifting lands. And to this end the august powers had granted them a heavenly jewelled spear. And the two deities, standing upon the Floating Bridge of High Heaven, lowered the jewelled spear head-first into chaos, so that the mists were divided. And, as they waited, the brine dripped from the jewels upon the spear-head, and there was formed an island. This is the island of Onogoro.

And His Augustness, the Lord of Invitation, took by the hand Her Augustness, the Lady of Invitation, his lovely Younger Sister, and together they descended to the island that was created. And they made the islands of Japan; the land of Iyo, which is called Lovely

Princess; the land of Toyo, which is called Luxuriant Sun Youth; the land of Sanuki, which is called Good Prince Boiled Rice; and Great Yamato, the Luxuriant Island of the Dragon Fly; and many more, of which to tell were weariness.

Furthermore, they gave birth to many myriads of deities to rule over the earth, and the air, and the deep sea; and for every season there were deities, and every place was sacred, for the deities were like the needles of the pine trees in number.

Now, when the time came for the Fire God, Kagu-Tsuchi, to be born, his mother, the Lady Izanami, was burned, and suffered a change; and she laid herself upon the ground. Then Izanagi, the Prince who Invites, asked, "What is it that has come to thee, my lovely Younger Sister?"

And she answered, weeping, "The time of my departure draws near … I go to the land of Yomi."

And His Augustness Izanagi wept aloud, dropping his tears upon her feet and upon her pillow. And all his tears fell down and became deities. Nevertheless, the Lady Izanami departed.

Then His Augustness, the Prince who Invites, was wroth, and lifted his face to High Heaven, and cried, "O Thine Augustness, my lovely Younger Sister, that I should have given thee in exchange for this single child!"

And, drawing the ten-grasp sword that was girded upon him, he slew the Fire God, his child; and binding up his long hair, he followed the Lady Izanami to the entrance of Yomi, the world of the dead. And she, the Princess who Invites, appearing as lovely as she was when alive, came forth to greet him. And she lifted up the curtain of the Palace of Hades that they might speak together.

And the Lord Izanagi said, "I weary for thee, my lovely Younger Sister, and the lands that thou and I created together are not finished making. Therefore come back."

Then the Lady made answer, saying, "My sweet lord, and my spouse, it is very lamentable that thou camest not sooner unto me, for I have eaten of the baked meats of Yomi. Nevertheless, as thou hast dearly honoured me in thy coming here, Thine Augustness, my lovely Elder Brother, if it may be, I will return with thee. I go to lay my desire before the Gods of Yomi. Wait thou here until I come again, and, if thou love me, seek not to look upon me till the time." And so she spoke and left him.

Izanagi sat upon a stone at the entrance of the Palace of Hades until the sun set, and he was weary of that valley of gloom. And because she tarried long, he arose and plucked a comb from the left tress of his hair, and broke off a tooth from one end of the comb, and lighting it to be a torch, he drew back the curtain of the Palace of Yomi. But he saw his beloved lying in corruption, and round about her were the eight deities of Thunder. They are the Fire Thunder, and the Black Thunder, and the Cleaving Thunder, and the Earth Thunder, and the Roaring Thunder, and the Couchant Thunder, and the Young Thunder. And by her terrible head was the Great Thunder.

And Izanagi, being overawed, turned to flee away, but Izanami arose and cried, "Thou hast put me to shame, for thou hast seen my defilement. Now I will see thine also."

And she called to her the Hideous Females of Yomi, and bade them take and slay His Augustness, the Lord who Invites. But he ran for his life, in the gloom stumbling upon the rocks of the valley of Yomi. And tearing the vine wreath from his long hair he flung it behind him, and it fell to the ground and became many bunches of grapes, which the Hideous Females stayed to devour. And he fled on. But the Females of Yomi still pursued him; so then he took a multitudinous and close-toothed comb from the right tresses of his long hair, and cast it behind him. When it touched the ground it became a groove of bamboo shoots, and again the females stayed to devour; and Izanagi fled on, panting.

But, in her wrath and despair, his Younger Sister sent after him the Eight Thunders, together with a thousand and five hundred warriors of Hades; yet he, the Prince of Invitation, drew the ten-grasp sword that was augustly girded upon him, and brandishing it behind him gained at last the base of the Even Pass of Hades, the black mouth of Yomi. And he plucked there three peaches that grew upon a tree, and smote his enemies that they all fled back; and the peaches were called Their Augustnesses, Great Divine Fruit.

Then, last of all, his Younger Sister, the Princess who Invites, herself came out to pursue. So Izanagi took a rock which could not have been lifted by a thousand men, and placed it between them in the Even Pass of Hades. And standing behind the rock, he pronounced a leave-taking and words of separation. But, from the farther side of the rock, Izanami called to him, "My lovely Elder Brother, Thine Augustness, of small avail shall be thy making of lands, and thy creating of deities, for I, with my powers, shall strangle every day a thousand of thy people."

So she cried, taunting him.

But he answered her, "My lovely Younger Sister, Thine Augustness, if thou dost so, I shall cause, in one day, fifteen hundred to be born. Farewell."

So Her Augustness, the Lady who Invites, is called the Queen of the Dead.

But the great lord, His Highness, the Prince who Invites, departed, crying, "Horror! Horror! Horror! I have come to a hideous and polluted land." And he lay still by the riverside, until such time as he should recover strength to perform purification.

The Donkey's Revenge

CHUNG CH'ING-YÜ was a scholar of some reputation, who lived in Manchuria. When he went up for his master's degree, he heard that there was a Taoist priest at the capital who would tell people's fortunes, and was very anxious to see him; and at the conclusion of the second part of the examination, he accidentally met him at Pao-t'u-ch'üan. The priest was over sixty years of age, and had the usual white beard, flowing down over his breast. Around him stood a perfect wall of people inquiring their future fortunes, and to each the old man made a brief reply: but when he saw Chung among the crowd, he was overjoyed, and, seizing him by the hand, said, "Sir, your virtuous intentions command my esteem." He then led him up behind a screen, and asked if he did not wish to know what was to come; and when Chung replied in the affirmative, the priest informed him that his prospects were bad. "You may succeed in passing this examination," continued he, "but on returning covered with honour to your home, I fear that your mother will be no longer there." Now Chung was a very filial son; and as soon as he heard these words, his tears began to flow, and he declared that he would go back without competing any further. The priest observed that if he let this chance slip, he could never hope for success; to which Chung replied that, on the other hand, if his mother were to die he could never hope to have her back again, and that even the rank of Viceroy would not repay him for her loss. "Well," said the priest, "you and I were connected in a former existence, and I must do my best to help you now." So he took out a pill which he gave to Chung, and told him that if he sent it post-haste by someone to his mother, it would prolong her life for seven days, and thus he would be able to see her once again after the examination was over. Chung took the pill, and went off in very low spirits; but he soon reflected that the span of human life is a matter of destiny, and that every day he could spend at home would be one more day devoted to the service of his mother. Accordingly, he got ready to start at once, and, hiring a donkey, actually set out on his way back. When he had gone about half a mile, the donkey turned round and ran home; and when he used his whip, the animal threw itself down on the ground. Chung got into a great perspiration, and his servant recommended him to remain where he was; but this he would not hear of, and hired another donkey, which served him exactly the same trick as the other one. The sun was now sinking behind the hills, and his servant advised his master to stay and finish his examination while he himself went back home before him. Chung had no alternative but to assent, and the next day he hurried through with his papers, starting immediately afterwards, and not stopping at all on the way either to eat or to sleep. All night long he went on, and arrived to find his mother in a very critical state; however, when he gave her the pill she so far recovered that he was able to go in and see her. Grasping his hand, she begged him not to weep, telling him that she had just dreamt she had been down to the Infernal Regions, where the King of Hell had informed her with a gracious smile that her record was fairly clean, and that in view of the filial piety of her son she was to have twelve years more of life. Chung was rejoiced at this, and his mother was soon restored to her former health.

Before long the news arrived that Chung had passed his examination; upon which he bade adieu to his mother, and went off to the capital, where he bribed the eunuchs of the palace to communicate with his friend the Taoist priest. The latter was very much pleased, and came out to see him, whereupon Chung prostrated himself at his feet. "Ah," said the priest, "this success of yours, and the prolongation of your good mother's life, is all a reward for your virtuous conduct. What have I done in the matter?" Chung was very much astonished that the priest should already know what had happened; however, he now inquired as to his own future. "You will never rise to high rank," replied the priest, "but you will attain the years of an octogenarian. In a former state of existence you and I were once travelling together, when you threw a stone at a dog, and accidentally killed a frog. Now that frog has re-appeared in life as a donkey, and according to all principles of destiny you ought to suffer for what you did; but your filial piety has touched the gods, a protecting star-influence has passed into your nativity sheet, and you will come to no harm. On the other hand, there is your wife; in her former state she was not as virtuous as she might have been, and her punishment in this life was to be widowed quite young; you, however, have secured the prolongation of your own term of years, and therefore I fear that before long your wife will pay the penalty of death." Chung was much grieved at hearing this; but after a while he asked the priest where his second wife to be was living. "At Chung-chou," replied the latter; "she is now fourteen years old." The priest then bade him adieu, telling him that if any mischance should befall him he was to hurry off towards the south-east

About a year after this, Chung's wife did die; and his mother then desiring him to go and visit his uncle, who was a magistrate in Kiangsi, on which journey he would have to pass through Chung-chou, it seemed like a fulfilment of the old priest's prophecy. As he went along, he came to a village on the banks of a river, where a large crowd of people was gathered together round a theatrical performance which was going on there. Chung would have passed quietly by, had not a stray donkey followed so close behind him that he turned round and hit it over the ears. This startled the donkey so much that it ran off full gallop, and knocked a rich gentleman's child, who was sitting with its nurse on the bank, right into the water, before anyone of the servants could lend a hand to save it. Immediately there was a great outcry against Chung, who gave his mule the rein and dashed away, mindful of the priest's warning, towards the south-east. After riding about seven miles, he reached a mountain village, where he saw an old man standing at the door of a house, and, jumping off his mule, made him a low bow. The old man asked him in, and inquired his name and whence he came; to which Chung replied by telling him the whole adventure. "Never fear," said the old man; "you can stay here, while I send out to learn the position of affairs." By the evening his messenger had returned, and then they knew for the first time that the child belonged to a wealthy family. The old man looked grave and said, "Had it been anybody else's child, I might have helped you; as it is I can do nothing." Chung was greatly alarmed at this; however, the old man told him to remain quietly there for the night, and see what turn matters might take. Chung was overwhelmed with anxiety, and did not sleep a wink; and next morning he heard that the constables were after him, and that it was death to anyone who should conceal him. The old man changed countenance at this, and went inside, leaving Chung to his own reflections; but towards the middle of the night he came and knocked at Chung's door, and, sitting down, began to ask how old his wife was. Chung replied that he was a widower; at which the old man seemed rather pleased, and declared that in such case help would be forthcoming; "for," said he, "my sister's husband has taken the vows and become a priest, and my sister herself has died, leaving an orphan girl who has now no home; and if you would only marry her...." Chung was delighted, more especially as this would be both the fulfilment of the Taoist priest's prophecy, and a means of extricating himself from his present difficulty; at the same time, he declared he should be sorry to implicate his future father-in-law. "Never fear about that," replied the old man; "my sister's husband is pretty skilful in the black art. He has not mixed much with the world of late; but when you are married, you can discuss the matter with my niece." So Chung married the young lady, who was sixteen years of age, and very beautiful; but whenever he looked at her he took occasion to sigh. At last she said, "I may be ugly; but you needn't be in such a hurry to let me know it;" whereupon Chung begged her pardon, and said he felt himself only too lucky to have met with such a divine creature; adding that he sighed because he feared some misfortune was coming on them which would separate them for ever. He then told her his story, and the young lady was very angry that she should have been drawn into such a difficulty without a word of warning. Chung fell on his knees, and said he had already consulted with her uncle, who was unable himself to do anything, much as he wished it. He continued that he was aware of her power; and then, pointing out that his alliance was not altogether beneath her, made all kinds of promises if she would only help him out of this trouble. The young lady was no longer able to refuse, but informed him that to apply to her father would entail certain disagreeable consequences, as he had retired from the world, and did not any more recognize her as his daughter. That night they did not attempt to sleep, spending the interval in padding their knees with thick felt concealed beneath their clothes; and then they got into chairs and were carried off to the hills. After journeying some distance, they were compelled by the nature of the road to alight and walk; and it was only by a great effort that Chung succeeded at last in getting his wife to the top. At the door of the temple they sat down to rest, the powder and paint on the young lady's face having all mixed with the perspiration trickling down; but when Chung began to apologize for bringing her to this pass, she replied that it was a mere trifle compared with what was to come. By-and-by, they went inside; and threading their way to the wall beyond, found the young lady's father sitting in contemplation, his eyes closed, and a servant-boy standing by with a chowry. Everything was beautifully clean and nice, but before the dais were sharp stones scattered about as thick as the stars in the sky. The young lady did not venture to select a favourable spot; she fell on her knees at once, and Chung did likewise behind her. Then her father opened his eyes, shutting them again almost instantaneously; whereupon the young lady said, "For a long time I have not paid my respects to you. I am now married, and I have brought my husband to see you." A long time passed away, and then her father opened his eyes and said, "You're giving a great deal of trouble," immediately relapsing into silence again. There the husband and wife remained until the stones seemed to pierce into their very bones; but after a while the father cried out, "Have you brought the donkey?" His daughter replied that they had not; whereupon they were told to go and fetch it at once, which they did, not knowing what the meaning of this order was. After a few more days' kneeling, they suddenly heard that the murderer of the child had been caught and beheaded, and were just congratulating each other on the success of their scheme, when a servant came in with a stick in his hand, the top of which had been chopped off. "This stick," said the servant, "died instead of you. Bury it reverently, that the wrong done to the tree may be somewhat atoned for." Then Chung saw that at the place where the top of the stick had been chopped off there were traces of blood; he therefore buried it with the usual ceremony, and immediately set off with his wife, and returned to his own home.

The Magic Path

IN THE PROVINCE OF KUANGTUNG there lived a scholar named Kuo, who was one evening on his way home from a friend's, when he lost his way among the hills. He got into a thick jungle, where, after about an hour's wandering, he suddenly heard the sound of laughing and talking on the top of the hill. Hurrying up in the direction of the sound, he beheld some ten or a dozen persons sitting on the ground engaged in drinking. No sooner had they caught sight of Kuo than they all cried out, "Come along! Just room for one more; you're in the nick of time." So Kuo sat down with the company, most of whom, he noticed, belonged to the literati, and began by asking them to direct him on his way home; but one of them cried out, "A nice sort of fellow you are, to be bothering about your way home, and paying no attention to the fine moon we have got tonight." The speaker then presented him with a goblet of wine of exquisite bouquet, which Kuo drank off at a draught, and another gentleman filled up again for him at once. Now, Kuo was pretty good in that line, and being very thirsty withal from his long walk, tossed off bumper after bumper, to the great delight of his hosts, who were unanimous in voting him a jolly good fellow. He was, moreover, full of fun, and could imitate exactly the note of any kind of bird;

so all of a sudden he began on the sly to twitter like a swallow, to the great astonishment of the others, who wondered how it was a swallow could be out so late. He then changed his note to that of a cuckoo, sitting there laughing and saying nothing, while his hosts were discussing the extraordinary sounds they had just heard. After a while he imitated a parrot, and cried, "Mr. Kuo is very drunk: you'd better see him home;" and then the sounds ceased, beginning again by-and-by, when at last the others found out who it was, and all burst out laughing. They screwed up their mouths and tried to whistle like Kuo, but none of them could do so; and soon one of them observed, "What a pity Madam Ch'ing isn't with us: we must rendezvous here again at mid-autumn, and you, Mr. Kuo, must be sure and come." Kuo said he would, whereupon another of his hosts got up and remarked that, as he had given them such an amusing entertainment, they would try to shew him a few acrobatic feats. They all arose, and one of them planting his feet firmly, a second jumped up on to his shoulders, a third on to the second's shoulders, and a fourth on to his, until it was too high for the rest to jump up, and accordingly they began to climb as though it had been a ladder. When they were all up, and the topmost head seemed to touch the clouds, the whole column bent gradually down until it lay along the ground transformed into a path. Kuo remained for some time in a state of considerable alarm, and then, setting out along this path, ultimately reached his own home. Some days afterwards he revisited the spot, and saw the remains of a feast lying about on the ground, with dense bushes on all sides, but no sign of a path. At mid-autumn he thought of keeping his engagement; however, his friends persuaded him not to go.

Bokwewa, the Humpback

BOKWEWA AND HIS BROTHER lived in a far-off part of the country. By such as had knowledge of them, Bokwewa, the elder, although deformed and feeble of person, was considered a manito, who had assumed the mortal shape; while his younger brother, Kwasynd, manly in appearance, active, and strong, partook of the nature of the present race of beings.

They lived off the path, in a wild, lonesome place, far retired from neighbours, and, undisturbed by cares, they passed their time, content and happy. The days glided by serenely as the river that flowed by their lodge.

Owing to his lack of strength, Bokwewa never engaged in the chase, but gave his attention entirely to the affairs of the lodge. In the long winter evenings he passed the time in telling his brother stories of the giants, spirits, weendigoes, and fairies of the elder age, when they had the exclusive charge of the world. He also at times taught his brother the manner in which game should be pursued, pointed out to him the ways of the different beasts and birds of the chase, and assigned the seasons at which they could be hunted with most success.

For a while the brother was eager to learn, and keenly attended to his duties as the provider of the lodge; but at length he grew weary of their tranquil life, and began to have a desire to show himself among men. He became restive in their retirement, and was seized with a longing to visit remote places.

One day, Kwasynd told his brother that he should leave him; that he wished to visit the habitations of men, and to procure a wife.

Bokwewa objected; but his brother overruled all that he said, and in spite of every remonstrance, he departed on his travels.

He travelled for a long time. At length he fell in with the footsteps of men. They were moving by encampments, for he saw, at several spots, the poles where they had passed. It was winter; and coming to a place where one of their company had died, he found upon a scaffold, lying at length in the cold blue air, the body of a beautiful young woman. "She shall be my wife!" exclaimed Kwasynd.

He lifted her up, and bearing her in his arms, he returned to his brother. "Brother," he said, "can not you restore her to life? Oh, do me that favour!"

He looked upon the beautiful female with a longing gaze; but she lay as cold and silent as when he had found her upon the scaffold.

"I will try," said Bokwewa.

These words had been scarcely breathed, when the young woman rose up, opened her eyes, and looked upon Bokwewa with a smile, as if she had known him before.

To Kwasynd she paid no heed whatever; but presently Bokwewa, seeing how she lingered in her gaze upon himself, said to her, "Sister, that is your husband," pointing to Kwasynd.

She listened to his voice, and crossing the lodge, she sat by Kwasynd, and they were man and wife.

For a long time they all lived contentedly together. Bokwewa was very kind to his brother, and sought to render his days happy. He was ever within the lodge, seeking to have it in readiness against the return of Kwasynd from the hunt. And by following his directions, which were those of one deeply skilled in the chase, Kwasynd always succeeded in returning with a good store of meat.

But the charge of the two brothers was greatly lightened by the presence of the spirit-wife; for without labour of the hand, she ordered the lodge, and as she willed, everything took its place, and was at once in proper array. The wish of her heart seemed to control whatever she looked upon, and it obeyed her desire.

But it was still more to the surprise of her husband Kwasynd that she never partook of food, nor shared in any way the longings and appetites of a mortal creature. She had never been seen arranging her hair, like other females, or at work upon her garments, and yet they were ever seemly, and without blemish or disorder.

Behold her at any hour, she was ever beautiful, and she seemed to need no ornament, nor nourishment, nor other aid, to give grace or strength to her looks.

Kwasynd, when the first wonder of her ways had passed, payed little heed to her discourse; he was engrossed with the hunt, and chose rather to be abroad, pursuing the wild game, or in the lodge, enjoying its savoury spoil, than the society of his spirit-wife.

But Bokwewa watched closely every word that fell from her lips, and often forgot, like her, all mortal appetite and care of the body, in conferring with her, and noting what she had to say of spirits and fairies, of stars, and streams that never ceased to flow, and the delight of the happy hunting-grounds, and the groves of the blessed.

One day Kwasynd had gone out as usual, and Bokwewa was sitting in the lodge, on the opposite side to his brother's wife, when she suddenly exclaimed:

"I must leave you," as a tall young man, whose face was like the sun in its brightness, entered, and taking her by the hand he led her to the door.

She made no resistance, but turning as she left the lodge, she cast upon Bokwewa a smile of kind regard, and was at once, with her companion, gone from his view.

He ran to the door and glanced about. He saw nothing; but looking far off in the sky, he thought that he could discover, at a great distance, a shining track, and the dim figures of two who were vanishing in heaven.

When his brother returned, Bokwewa related all to him exactly as it had happened.

The face of Kwasynd changed, and was dark as the night. For several days he would not taste food. Sometimes he would fall to weeping for a long time, and now only it seemed that he remembered how gentle and beautiful had been the ways of her who was lost. At last he said that he would go in search of her.

Bokwewa tried to dissuade him from it; but he would not be turned aside from his purpose.

"Since you are resolved," said Bokwewa, "listen to my advice. You will have to go south. It is a long distance to the present abiding-place of your wife, and there are so many charms and temptations by the way that I fear you will be led astray and forget your errand. For the people whom you will see in the country through which you have to pass, do nothing but amuse themselves. They are very idle, gay and effeminate, and I fear that they will lead you astray. Your path is beset with dangers. I will mention one or two things which you must be on your guard against.

"In the course of your journey you will come to a large grapevine lying across your path. You must not even taste its fruit, for it is poisonous. Step over it. It is a snake. You will next come to something that looks like bear's fat, of which you are so fond. Touch it not, or you will be overcome by the soft habits of the idle people. It is frog's eggs. These are snares laid by the way for you."

Kwasynd promised that he would observe the advice and bidding his brother farewell, he set out. After travelling a long time he came to the enchanted grapevine. It looked so tempting, with its swelling purple clusters, that he forgot his brother's warning, and tasted the fruit. He went on till he came to the frog's eggs. They so much resembled delicious bear's fat that Kwasynd tasted them. He still went on.

At length he came to a wide plain. As he emerged from the forest the sun was falling in the west, and it cast its scarlet and golden shades far over the country. The air was perfectly calm, and the whole prospect had the air of an enchanted land. Fruits and flowers, and delicate blossoms, lured the eye and delighted the senses.

At a distance he beheld a large village, swarming with people, and as he drew near he discovered women beating corn in silver mortars.

When they saw Kwasynd approaching, they cried out:

"Bokwewa's brother has come to see us."

Throngs of men and women, in bright apparel, hurried out to meet him.

He was soon, having already yielded to temptation by the way, overcome by their fair looks and soft speeches, and he was not long afterward seen beating corn with the women, having entirely abandoned all further quest for his lost wife.

Meantime, Bokwewa, alone in the lodge, often musing upon the discourse of the spirit-wife, who was gone, waited patiently his brother's return. After the lapse of several years, when no tidings could be had, he set out in search of him, and he arrived in safety among the soft and idle people of the south. He met the same allurements by the way, and they gathered around him on his coming as they had around his brother Kwasynd; but Bokwewa was proof against their flattery. He only grieved in his heart that any should yield.

He shed tears of pity to see that his brother had laid aside the arms of a hunter, and that he was beating corn with the women, indifferent to the fate and the fortune of his lost wife.

Bokwewa ascertained that his brother's wife had passed on to a country beyond.

After deliberating for a time, and spending several days in a severe fast, he set out in the direction where he saw that a light shone from the sky.

It was far off, but Bokwewa had a stout heart; and strong in the faith that he was now on the broad path toward the happy land, he pressed forward. For many days he travelled without encountering anything unusual. And now plains of vast extent, and rich in waving grass, began to pass before his eyes. He saw many beautiful groves, and heard the songs of countless birds.

At length he began to fail in strength for lack of food; when he suddenly reached a high ground. From this he caught the first glimpse of the other land. But it appeared to be still far off, and all the country between, partly veiled in silvery mists, glittered with lakes and streams of water. As he pressed on, Bokwewa came in sight of innumerable herds of stately deer, moose, and other animals which walked near his path, and they appeared to have no fear of man.

And now again as he wound about in his course, and faced the north once more, he beheld, coming toward him, an immense number of men, women, and children, pressing forward in the direction of the shining land.

In this vast throng Bokwewa beheld persons of every age, from the little infant, the sweet and lovely penaisee, or younger son, to the feeble, grey old man, stooping under the burden of his years.

All whom Bokwewa met, of every name and degree, were heavily laden with pipes, weapons, bows, arrows, kettles and other wares and implements.

One man stopped him, and complained of the weary load he was carrying. Another offered him a kettle; another his bow and arrows; but he declined all, and, free of foot, hastened on.

And now he met women who were carrying their basket-work, and painted paddles, and little boys, with their embellished war-clubs and bows and arrows, the gifts of their friends.

With this mighty throng, Bokwewa was borne along for two days and nights, when he arrived at a country so still and shining, and so beautiful in its woods and groves and plains, that he knew it was here that he should find the lost spirit-wife.

He had scarcely entered this fair country, with a sense of home and the return to things familiar strong upon him, when there appeared before him the lost spirit-wife herself, who, taking him by the hand, gave him welcome, saying, "My brother, I am glad to see you. Welcome! Welcome! You are now in your native land!"

The Crane that Crossed the River

A FAMOUS HUNTER who lived in a remote part of the north had a fair wife and two sons, who were left in the lodge every day while he went out in quest of the animals whose flesh was their principal support.

Game was very abundant in those days, and his labours in the chase were well rewarded. They lived a long distance from any other lodge, and it was seldom that they saw any other faces than those of their own household.

The two sons were still too young to follow their father in the hunt, and they were in the habit of diverting themselves within reach of the lodge.

While thus engaged, they began to take note that a young man visited the lodge during their father's absence, and that these visits were constantly renewed.

At length the elder of the two said to his mother:

"My mother, who is this tall young man that comes here so often during our father's absence? Does he wish to see him? Shall I tell him when he comes back this evening?"

"Naubesah, you little fool," said the mother, "mind your bow and arrows, and do not be afraid to enter the forest in search of birds and squirrels, with your little brother. It is not manly to be ever about the lodge. Nor will you become a warrior if you tell all the little things that you see and hear to your father. Say not a word to him."

The boys obeyed, but as they grew older and still noticed the visits of the stranger, they resolved to speak again to their mother.

They now told her that they meant to make known to their father all that they had witnessed, for they frequently saw this young man passing through the woods, and he did not walk in the path, nor did he carry any thing to eat. If he had any message to deliver at their lodge, why did he not give it to their father? For they had observed that messages were always addressed to men, and not to women.

When her sons spoke thus to her, the mother was greatly vexed.

"I will kill you," she said, "if you speak of it."

In fear they for a time held their peace, but still taking note that the stranger came so often and by stealth to the lodge, they resolved at last to speak with their father.

Accordingly one day, when they were out in the woods, learning to follow the chase, they told him all that they had seen.

The face of the father grew dark. He was still for a while, and when at length he looked up –

"It is done!" he said. "Do you, my children, tarry here until the hour of the falling of the sun, then come to the lodge and you will find me."

The father left them at a slow pace, and they remained sporting away their time till the hour for their return had come.

When they reached the lodge the mother was not there. They dared not to ask their father whither she had gone, and from that day forth her name was never spoken again in the lodge.

In course of time the two boys had grown to be men, and although the mother was never more seen in the lodge, in charge of her household tasks, nor on the path in the forest, nor by the river side, she still lingered, ever and ever, near the lodge.

Changed, but the same, with ghastly looks and arms that were withered, she appeared to her sons as they returned from the hunt, in the twilight, in the close of the day.

At night she darkly unlatched the lodge-door and glided in, and bent over them as they sought to sleep. Oftenest it was her bare brow, white, and bony, and bodiless, that they saw floating in the air, and making a mock of them in the wild paths of the forest, or in the midnight darkness of the lodge.

She was a terror to all their lives, and she made every spot where they had seen her, hideous to the living eye; so that after being long buffeted and beset, they at last resolved, together with their father, now stricken in years, to leave the country.

They began a journey toward the south. After travelling many days along the shore of a great lake, they passed around a craggy bluff, and came upon a scene where there was a rough fall of waters, and a river issuing forth from the lake.

They had no sooner come in sight of this fall of water, than they heard a rolling sound behind them, and looking back, they beheld the skull of a woman rolling along the beach. It seemed to be pursuing them, and it came on with great speed; when, behold, from out of the woods hard by, appeared a headless body, which made for the beach with the utmost dispatch.

The skull too advanced toward it, and when they looked again, lo! they had united, and were making all haste to come up with the hunter and his two sons. They now might well be in extreme fear, for they knew not how to escape her.

At this moment, one of them looked out and saw a stately crane sitting on a rock in the middle of the rapids. They called out to the bird, "See, grandfather, we are persecuted. Come and take us across the falls that we may escape her."

The crane so addressed was of extraordinary size, and had arrived at a great old age, and, as might be expected, he sat, when first descried by the two sons, in a state of profound thought, revolving his long experience of life there in the midst of the most violent eddies.

When he heard himself appealed to, the crane stretched forth his neck with great deliberation, and lifting himself slowly by his wings, he flew across to their assistance.

"Be careful," said the old crane, "that you do not touch the crown of my head. I am bald from age and long service, and very tender at that spot. Should you be so unlucky as to lay a hand upon it, I shall not be able to avoid throwing you both in the rapids."

They paid strict heed to his directions, and were soon safely landed on the other shore of the river. He returned and carried the father in the same way; and then took his place once more where he had been first seen in the very midst of the eddies of the stream.

But the woman, who had by this time reached the shore, cried out, "Come, my grandfather, and carry me over, for I have lost my children, and I am sorely distressed."

The aged bird obeyed her summons, and flew to her side. He carefully repeated the warning that she was not to touch the crown of his head; and he was so anxious that she should take it to heart, that he went over it a second and a third time, word by word. He begged her to bear in mind that she should respect his old age, if there was any sense of virtue left in her.

She promised to obey; but they were no sooner fairly embarked in the stream, than she stealthily sought to disregard the warning she had received. Instantly the crane cast her into the rapids, and shook his wings as if to free himself of all acquaintance with her.

"There," said he, as she sunk in the stream, "you would ever do what was forbidden. In life, as you sought those you should have avoided, so now you shall be avoided by those who should seek you. Go, and be henceforth Addum Kum Maig!"

The woman disappeared, was straightway carried by the rapid currents far out into the waters, and in the wide wilderness of shoreless depths, without companion or solace, was lost forever.

The family of the hunter, grateful for his generous help, adopted the bird as their family emblem or mark, and under the guardianship of the Crane that Crossed the River, they prospered, with days of plenty and nights of peace.

A Visit to the King of Ghosts

WHEN ANY PERSON LAY IN AN UNCONSCIOUS STATE, it was supposed by the ancient Hawaiians that death had taken possession of the body and opened the door for the spirit to depart. Sometimes if the body lay like one asleep the spirit was supposed to return to its old home. One of the Hawaiian legends weaves their deep-rooted faith in the spirit-world into the expressions of one who seemed to be permitted to visit that ghost-land and its king. This legend belonged to the island of Maui and the region near the village Lahaina. Thus was the story told:

Ka-ilio-hae (the wild dog) had been sick for days and at last sank into a state of unconsciousness. The spirit of life crept out of the body and finally departed from the left eye into a corner of the house, buzzing like an insect. Then he stopped and looked back over the body he had left. It appeared to him like a massive mountain. The eyes were deep caves, into which the ghost looked. Then the spirit became afraid and went outside and rested on the roof of the house. The people began to wail loudly and the ghost fled from the noise to a cocoanut-tree and perched like a bird in the branches. Soon he felt the impulse of the spirit-land moving him away from his old home. So he leaped from tree to tree and flew from place to place wandering toward Kekaa, the place from which the ghosts leave the island of Maui for their home in the permanent spirit-land – the Under-world.

As he came near this doorway to the spirit-world he met the ghost of a sister who had died long before, and to whom was given the power of sometimes turning a ghost back to its body again. She was an aumakua-ho-ola (a spirit making alive). She called to Ka-ilio-hae and told him to come to her house and dwell for a time. But she warned him that when her husband was at home he must not yield to any invitation from him to enter their house, nor could he partake of any of the food which her husband might urge him to eat. The home and the food would be only the shadows of real things, and would destroy his power of becoming alive again.

The sister said, "When my husband comes to eat the food of the spirits and to sleep the sleep of ghosts, then I will go with you and you shall see all the spirit-land of our island and see the king of ghosts."

The ghost-sister led Ka-ilio-hae into the place of whirlwinds, a hill where he heard the voices of many spirits planning to enjoy all the sports of their former life. He listened with delight and drew near to the multitude of happy spirits. Some were making ready to go down to the sea for the hee-nalu (surf-riding). Others were already rolling the ulu-maika (the round stone discs for rolling along the ground). Some were engaged in the mokomoko, or umauma (boxing), and the kulakulai (wrestling), and the honuhonu (pulling with hands), and the loulou (pulling with hooked fingers), and other athletic sports.

Some of the spirits were already grouped in the shade of trees, playing the gambling games in which they had delighted when alive. There was the stone konane-board (somewhat like checkers), and the puepue-one (a small sand mound in which was concealed some object), and the puhenehene (the hidden stone under piles of kapa), and the many other trials of skill which permitted betting.

Then in another place crowds were gathered around the hulas (the many forms of dancing). These sports were all in the open air and seemed to be full of interest.

There was a strange quality which fettered every new-born ghost: he could only go in the direction into which he was pushed by the hand of some stronger power. If the guardian of a ghost struck it on one side, it would move off in the direction indicated by the blow or the push until spirit strength and experience came and he could go alone. The newcomer desired to join in these games and started to go, but the sister slapped him on the breast and drove him away. These were shadow games into which those who entered could never go back to the substantial things of life.

Then there was a large grass house inside which many ghosts were making merry. The visitor wanted to join this great company, but the sister knew that, if he once was engulfed by this crowd of spirits in this shadow-land, her brother could never escape. The crowds of players would seize him like a whirlwind and he would be unable to know the way he came in or the way out. Ka-ilio-hae tried to slip away from his sister, but he could not turn readily. He was still a very awkward ghost, and his sister slapped him back in the way in which she wanted him to go.

An island which was supposed to float on the ocean as one of the homes of the aumakuas (the ghosts of the ancestors) had the same characteristics. The ghosts (aumakuas) lived on the shadows of all that belonged to the earth-life. It was said that a canoe with a party of young people landed on this island of dreams and for some time enjoyed the food and fruits and sports, but after returning to their homes could not receive the nourishment of the food of their former lives, and soon died. The legends taught that no ghost passing out of the body could return unless it made the life of the aumakuas tabu to itself.

Soon the sister led her brother to a great field, stone walled, in which were such fine grass houses as were built only for chiefs of the highest rank. There she pointed to a narrow passage-way into which she told her brother he must enter by himself.

"This," she said, "is the home of Walia, the high chief of the ghosts living in this place. You must go to him. Listen to all he says to you. Say little. Return quickly. There will be three watchmen guarding this passage. The first will ask you, 'What is the fruit [desire] of your heart?' You will answer, 'Walia.' Then he will let you enter the passage.

"Inside the walls of the narrow way will be the second watchman. He will ask why you come; again answer, 'Walia,' and pass by him.

"At the end of the entrance the third guardian stands holding a raised spear ready to strike. Call to him, 'Ka-make-loa' [The Great Death]. This is the name of his spear. Then he will ask what you want, and you must reply, 'To see the chief,' and he will let you pass.

"Then again when you stand at the door of the great house you will see two heads bending together in the way so that you cannot enter or see the king and his queen. If these heads can catch a spirit coming to see the king without knowing the proper incantations, they will throw that ghost into the Po-Milu [The Dark Spirit-world]. Watch therefore and remember all that is told you.

"When you see these heads, point your hands straight before you between them and open your arms, pushing these guards off on each side, then the ala-nui [the great way] will be open for you – and you can enter.

"You will see kahilis [soft long feather fans] moving over the chiefs. The king will awake and call, 'Why does this traveller come?' You will reply quickly, 'He comes to see the Divine One.' When this is said no injury will come to you. Listen and remember and you will be alive again."

Ka-ilio-hae did as he was told with the three watchmen, and each one stepped back, saying, "Noa" (the tabu is lifted), and he pushed by. At the door he shoved the two heads to the side and entered the chief's house to the Ka-ikuwai (the middle), falling on his hands and knees. The servants were waving the kahilis this way and that. There was motion, but no noise.

The chief awoke, looked at Ka-ilio-hae, and said: "Aloha, stranger, come near. Who is the high chief of your land?"

Then Ka-ilio-hae gave the name of his king, and the genealogy from ancient times of the chiefs dead and in the spirit-world.

The queen of ghosts arose, and the kneeling spirit saw one more beautiful than any woman in all the island, and he fell on his face before her.

The king told him to go back and enter his body and tell his people about troubles near at hand.

While he was before the king twice he heard messengers call to the people that the sports were all over; anyone not heeding would be thrown into the darkest place of the home of the ghosts when the third call had been sounded.

The sister was troubled, for she knew that at the third call the stone walls around the king's houses would close and her brother would be held fast forever in the spirit-land, so she uttered her incantations and passed the guard. Softly she called. Her brother reluctantly came. She seized him and pushed him outside. Then they heard the third call, and met the multitude of ghosts coming inland from their sports in the sea, and other multitudes hastening homeward from their work and sports on the land.

They met a beautiful young woman who called to them to come to her home, and pointed to a point of rock where many birds were resting. The sister struck her brother and forced him down to the seaside where she had her home and her responsibility, for she was one of the guardians of the entrance to the spirit-world.

She knew well what must be done to restore the spirit to the body, so she told her brother they must at once obey the command of the king; but the brother had seen the delights of the life of the aumakuas and wanted to stay. He tried to slip away and hide, but his sister held him fast and compelled him to go along the beach to his old home and his waiting body.

When they came to the place where the body lay she found a hole in the corner of the house and pushed the spirit through. When he saw the body he was very much afraid and tried to escape, but the sister caught him and pushed him inside the foot up to the knee. He did not like the smell of the body and tried to rush back, but she pushed him inside again and held the foot fast and shook him and made him go to the head.

The family heard a little sound in the mouth and saw breath moving the breast, then they knew that he was alive again. They warmed the body and gave a little food. When strength returned he told his family all about his wonderful journey into the land of ghosts.

Maui Seeking Immortality

Climb up, climb up,
To the highest surface of heaven,
To all the sides of heaven.

Climb then to thy ancestor,
The sacred bird in the sky,
To thy ancestor Rehua
In the heavens.

– New Zealand kite incantation

THE STORY OF MAUI SEEKING IMMORTALITY for the human race is one of the finest myths in the world. For pure imagination and pathos it is difficult to find any tale from Grecian or Latin literature to compare with it. In Greek and Roman fables gods suffered for other gods, and yet none were surrounded with such absolutely mythical experiences as those through which the demi-god Maui of the Pacific Ocean passed when he entered the gates of death with the hope of winning immortality for mankind. The really remarkable group of legends which cluster around Maui is well concluded by the story of his unselfish and heroic battle with death.

The different islands of the Pacific have their Hades, or abode of dead. It is, with very few exceptions, down in the interior of the earth. Sometimes the tunnels left by currents of melted lava are the passages into the home of departed spirits. In Samoa there are two circular holes among the rocks at the west end of the island Savaii. These are the entrances to the underworld for chiefs and people. The spirits of those who die on the other islands leap into the sea and swim around the land from island to island until they reach Savaii. Then they plunge down into their heaven or their hades.

The Tongans had a spirit island for the home of the dead. They said that some natives once sailed far away in a canoe and found this island. It was covered with all manner of beautiful fruits, among which rare birds sported. They landed, but the trees were shadows. They grasped but could not hold them. The fruits and the birds were shadows. The men ate, but swallowed nothing substantial. It was shadow-land. They walked through all the delights their eyes looked upon, but found no substance. They returned home, but ever seemed to listen to spirits calling them back to the island. In a short time all the voyagers were dead.

There is no escape from death. The natives of New Zealand say: "Man may have descendants, but the daughters of the night strangle his offspring"; and again: "Men make heroes, but death carries them away."

There are very few legends among the Polynesians concerning the death of Maui. And these are usually fragmentary, except among the Maoris of New Zealand.

The Hawaiian legend of the death of Maui is to the effect that he offended some of the greater gods living in Waipio valley on the Island of Hawaii. Kanaloa, one of the four greatest gods of Hawaii, seized him and dashed him against the rocks. His blood burst from the body and coloured the earth red in the upper part of the valley. The Hawaiians in another legend say that Maui was chasing a boy and girl in Honolii gulch, Hawaii. The girl climbed a breadfruit tree. Maui changed himself into an eel and stretched himself along the side of the trunk of the tree. The tree stretched itself upward and Maui failed to reach the girl. A priest came along and struck the eel and killed it, and so Maui died. This is evidently a changed form of the legend of Maui and the long eel. Another Hawaiian fragment approaches very near to the beautiful New Zealand myth. The Hawaiians said that Maui attempted to tear a mountain apart. He wrenched a great hole in the side. Then the elepaio bird sang and the charm was broken. The cleft in the mountain could not be enlarged. If the story could be completed it would not be strange if the death of Maui came with this failure to open the path through the mountain.

The Hervey Islands say that after Maui fished up the islands his hook was thrown into the heavens and became the curved tail of the constellation of stars which we know as 'The Scorpion.' Then the people became angry with Maui and threw him up into the sky and his body is still thought to be hanging among the stars of the scorpion.

The Samoans, according to Turner, say that Maui went fishing and tried to catch the land under the seas and pull it to the surface. Finally an island appeared, but the people living on it were angry with Maui and drove him away into the heavens.

As he leaped from the island it separated into two parts. Thus the Samoans account for the origin of two of their islands and also for the passing away of Maui from the earth.

The natives of New Zealand have many myths concerning the death of Maui. Each tribe tells the story with such variations as would be expected when the fact is noted that these tribes have preserved their individuality through many generations. The substance of the myth, however, is the same.

In Maui's last days he longed for the victory over death. His innate love of life led him to face the possibility of escaping and overcoming the relentless enemy of mankind and thus bestow the boon of deathlessness upon his fellow-men. He had been successful over and over again in his contests with both gods and men. When man was created, he stood erect, but, according to an Hawaiian myth, had jointless arms and limbs. A web of skin connected and fastened tightly the arms to the body and the legs to each other. 'Maui was angry at this motionless statue and took him and broke his legs at ankle, knee and hip and then, tearing them and the arms from the body, destroyed the web. Then he broke the arms at the elbow and shoulder. Then man could move from place to place, but he had neither fingers or toes.' Here comes the most ancient Polynesian statement of the theory of evolution: 'Hunger impelled man to seek his food in the mountains, where his toes were cut out by the brambles in climbing, and his fingers were also formed by the sharp splinters of the bamboo while searching with his arms for food in the ground.'

It was not strange that Maui should feel self-confident when considering the struggle for immortality as a gift to be bestowed upon mankind. And yet his father warned him that his time of failure would surely come.

Mr. John White, who has collected many of the myths and legends of New Zealand, states that after Maui had ill-treated Mahu-ika, his grandmother, the goddess and guardian of fire in the underworld, his father and mother tried to teach him to do differently. But he refused to listen. Then the father said:

"You heard our instructions, but please yourself and persist for life or death."

Maui replied: "What do I care? Do you think I shall cease? Rather I will persist forever and ever."

Then his father said: "There is one so powerful that no tricks can be of any avail."

Maui asked: "By what shall I be overcome?" The answer was that one of his ancestors, Hine-nui-te-po (Great Hine of the night), the guardian of life, would overcome him.

When Maui fished islands out of the deep seas, it was said that Hine made her home on the outer edge of one of the outermost islands. There the glow of the setting sun lighted the thatch of her house and covered it with glorious colours. There Great Hine herself stood flashing and sparkling on the edge of the horizon.

Maui, in these last days of his life, looked toward the west and said: "et us investigate this matter and learn whether life or death shall follow."

The father replied: "There is evil hanging over you. When I chanted the invocation of your childhood, when you were made sacred and guarded by charms, I forgot a part of the ceremony. And for this you are to die."

Then Maui said, "Will this be by Hine-nui-te-po? What is she like?"

The father said that the flashing eyes they could see in the distance were dark as greenstone, the teeth were as sharp as volcanic glass, her mouth was large like a fish, and her hair was floating in the air like sea-weed.

One of the legends of New Zealand says that Maui and his brothers went toward the west, to the edge of the horizon, where they saw the goddess of the night. Light was flashing from her body. Here they found a great pit – the home of night. Maui entered the pit – telling his brothers not to laugh. He passed through and turning about started to return. The brothers laughed and the walls of night closed in around him and held him till he died.

The longer legend tells how Maui after his conversation with his father, remembered his conflict with the moon. He had tied her so that she could not escape, but was compelled to bathe in the waters of life and return night after night lest men should be in darkness when evening came.

Maui said to the goddess of the moon: "Let death be short. As the moon dies and returns with new strength, so let men die and revive again."

But she replied: "Let death be very long, that man may sigh and sorrow. When man dies, let him go into darkness, become like earth, that those he leaves behind may weep and wail and mourn."

Maui did not lay aside his purpose, but, according to the New Zealand story, "did not wish men to die, but to live forever. Death appeared degrading and an insult to the dignity of man. Man ought to die like the moon, which dips in the life-giving waters of Kane and is renewed again, or like the sun, which daily sinks into the pit of night and with renewed strength rises in the morning."

Maui sought the home of Hine-nui-te-po – the guardian of life. He heard her order her attendants to watch for anyone approaching and capture all who came walking upright as a man. He crept past the attendants on hands and feet, found the place of life, stole some of the food of the goddess and returned home. He showed the food to his brothers and persuaded them to go with him into the darkness of the night of death. On the way he changed them into the form of birds. In the evening they came to the house of the goddess on the island long before fished up from the seas.

Maui warned the birds to refrain from making any noise while he made the supreme effort of his life. He was about to enter upon his struggle for immortality. He said to the birds: "If I go into the stomach of this woman, do not laugh until I have gone through her, and come out again at her mouth; then you can laugh at me."

His friends said: "You will be killed." Maui replied: "If you laugh at me when I have only entered her stomach I shall be killed, but if I have passed through her and come out of her mouth I shall escape and Hine-nui-te-po will die."

His friends called out to him: "Go then. The decision is with you."

Hine was sleeping soundly. The flashes of lightning had all ceased. The sunlight had almost passed away and the house lay in quiet gloom. Maui came near to the sleeping goddess. Her large, fish-like mouth was open wide. He put off his clothing and prepared to pass through the ordeal of going to the hidden source of life, to tear it out of the body of its guardian and carry it back with him to mankind. He stood in all the glory of savage manhood. His body was splendidly marked by the tattoo-bones, and now well oiled shone and sparkled in the last rays of the setting sun.

He leaped through the mouth of the enchanted one and entered her stomach, weapon in hand, to take out her heart, the vital principle which he knew had its home somewhere within her being. He found immortality on the other side of death. He turned to come back again into life when suddenly a little bird (the Pata-tai) laughed in a clear, shrill tone, and Great Hine, through whose mouth Maui was passing, awoke. Her sharp, obsidian teeth closed with a snap upon Maui, cutting his body in the centre. Thus Maui entered the gates of death, but was unable to return, and death has ever since been victor over rebellious men. The natives have the saying:

"If Maui had not died, he could have restored to life all who had gone before him, and thus succeeded in destroying death."

Maui's brothers took the dismembered body and buried it in a cave called Te-ana-i-hana, 'The cave dug out,' possibly a prepared burial place.

Maui's wife made war upon the spirits, the gods, and killed as many as she could to avenge her husband's death. One of the old native poets of New Zealand, in chanting the story to Mr. White, said: "But though Maui was killed, his offspring survived. Some of these are at Hawa-i-i-ki and some at Aotea-roa (New Zealand), but the greater part of them remained at Hawa-i-ki. This history was handed down by the generations of our ancestors of ancient times, and we continue to rehearse it to our children, with our incantations and genealogies, and all other matters relating to our race."

"But death is nothing new,
Death is, and has been ever since old Maui died.
Then Pata-tai laughed loud
And woke the goblin-god,
Who severed him in two, and shut him in,
So dusk of eve came on."

– Maori death chant, New Zealand

Biographies & Text Sources

The stories in this book derive from a multitude of original sources, often from the nineteenth century and often based on the writer's first-hand accounts of tales narrated to them by natives, while others are their own retellings of traditional tales. Authors, works and contributors to this book include:

R. Nisbet Bain
The Horse-Devil and the Witch; The Magic Turban, the Magic Whip, and the Magic Carpet
R. Nisbet Bain (1854–1909) was born in London, England. As a historian and linguist with the ability to read over twenty languages, Bain was a prolific translator, especially of folklore and fairy tales. Bain worked often with folklore from Ukraine, Russia and Turkey. He is known for his translation of *Weird Tales from Northern Seas* (1893), a Norwegian classic by Jonas Lie, and *Turkish Fairy Tales* (1901), by Ignácz Kúnos. Bain also contributed frequently to the *Encyclopaedia Britannica* and worked for the British Museum.

Ivana Brlić-Mažuranić
Little Brother Primrose and Sister Lavender; How Quest Sought the Truth
Ivana Brlić-Mažuranić (1874–1938) was a Croatian author. She was born in Ogulin to a well-known family of writers and politicians. Writing initially in French, she kept diaries and composed poetry and essays. By the early twentieth century, her work was being published frequently by journals and magazines. Her most popular work today remains her short story collection entitled *Croatian Tales of Long Ago* (1916), translated by F.S. Copeland.

Samuel Butler
The Odyssey: Books IX–XII (Extract)
Samuel Butler (1835–1902) was born in Nottinghamshire, England. He was a novelist, essayist and critic. His most famous works include *The Way of All Flesh*, an autobiographical novel largely considered his magnum opus; and *Erewhon*, a utopian satire of the mentality and lifestyles embraced by Victorian England. The chapters of *Erewhon* which comprise 'The Book of the Machines' were adapted from articles he submitted to *The Press*, which posited that machines might undergo evolution in a similar way to humans.

Matt Cardin
Foreword
Matt Cardin is the author of *To Rouse Leviathan* and *What the Daemon Said* and the editor of *Mummies around the World*, *Horror Literature through History*, and *Born to Fear: Interviews with Thomas Ligotti*. A former professor of English and religion, he has a Ph.D. in leadership and a master's degree in religious studies. His work has been nominated for the World Fantasy Award and praised by *Publishers Weekly*, *Kirkus Reviews*, *Booklist*, *Library Journal*, *Asimov's Science Fiction* and more.

Padraig Colum
The Winning of the Golden Fleece; How Orpheus the Minstrel Went Down to the World of the Dead
Padraic Colum (1881–1972) was born in County Longford, Ireland. He wrote prolifically as a

poet, biographer, novelist, playwright, dramatist, children's book author and folklore collector. A prominent figure in the late nineteenth-century Irish Literary Revival, Colum developed connections with numerous well-known Irish writers, including James Joyce and W.B. Yeats. His first book, a poetry collection entitled *Wild Earth*, was published in 1907. Later living in the US, Colum ventured into prose fiction and children's books, and taught at Columbia University and the City College of New York.

F.S. Copeland

Little Brother Primrose and Sister Lavender; How Quest Sought the Truth

Fanny Susan Copeland (1872–1970) was an Irish translator, journalist, linguist and mountaineer. Born in Birr, in County Offaly, Ireland, Copeland spent her childhood in numerous cities across Europe, and spent much of her adult life in Slovenia. She published numerous articles in various journals, and worked at the University of the Kingdom of Serbs, Croats and Slovenes in Ljubljana, in the Faculty of Arts' English department. She was the translator for Ivana Brlić-Mažuranić's story collection *Croatian Tales of Long Ago* (1916).

Jeremiah Curtin

The Three Kingdoms: The Copper, the Silver and the Golden; The Enchanted Princess; The Poor Man and the King of the Crows; Kiss Miklos and the Green Daughter of the Green King

Jeremiah Curtin (1835–1906) was a Detroit-born ethnographer and folklorist. While much of his work focused on collecting myths and folktales from around the world, Curtin was also renowned for his translations of works by Polish author Henryk Sienkiewicz. Between 1883 and 1891 Curtin's interests would focus closer to home, when he worked as a field researcher recording the myths and customs of Native American people, which would later result in the publication of the book *Creation Myths of Primitive America* (1898).

Elphinstone Dayrell

The Orphan Boy and the Magic Stone

Elphinstone Dayrell (1869–1917) collected his tales after hearing many first-hand from the Efik and Ibibio peoples of south-eastern Nigeria when he was District Commissioner of South Nigeria. His collections of folklore include *Folk Stories from Southern Nigeria* (1910) and *Ikom Folk Stories from Southern Nigeria*, the latter published by the Royal Anthropological Institute of Great Britain and Ireland in 1913.

Lal Behari Dey

The Evil Eye of Sani; The Boy with the Moon on His Forehead

Lal Behari Dey (1824–1892) was born in the Bengal Presidency but spent much of his life in Calcutta. Converting to Christianity in 1843, Dey became a missionary and minister, as well as a journalist. He later worked as a professor of English at various government-administered colleges in Berhampore and Hooghly. He is known for his short story collection *Folk-Tales of Bengal* (1912) and *Govinda Samanta, or The History of Bengal Ráiyat* (1874).

Herbert Allen Giles

The Magic Path; Ta-Nan in Search of His Father; The Donkey's Revenge

Herbert Allen Giles (1845–1935) was a British diplomat and sinologist, working in Mawei, Shanghai, Tamsui and finally as British Consul at Ningpo. In 1897 he became professor of Chinese language at Cambridge University, a post that lasted for 35 years. He published many writings on Chinese language, as well as literature and religion, such as his *Chinese-English Dictionary* (1891), and several translations of classic Chinese tales, including *Pu Songling's Strange Stories from a Chinese Studio* (1880).

A.J. Glinski

The Eagles; The Princess of the Brazen Mountain

A.J. Glinski (1817–1866) was a Polish author and collector of folklore. He is considered the Polish equivalent to the Brothers Grimm, having collected, recorded and preserved a wealth of fairy tales and traditional stories from Polish oral tradition. He achieved this by travelling across the countryside and speaking with a range of ordinary people. These stories were published in his popular collection *Polish Fairy Tales* (1862).

Sir George Grey

The Discovery of New Zealand; The Voyage to New Zealand

Sir George Grey (1812–1898) was a British author, explorer, soldier and colonial administrator, and served in a series of governing positions in Australia, South Africa and New Zealand. He was heavily involved in the colonization of New Zealand, playing a key role in purchasing and annexing Māori land. He studied Māori culture, became fluent in the language and produced a work on the culture and mythology of the Māori entitled *Polynesian Mythology and Ancient Traditional History.*

William Elliot Griffis

The Sky Bridge of Birds

Born in Philadelphia in 1843, William Elliot Griffis served as a corporal in the American Civil War, and later graduated from Rutgers University in 1869. In 1870, Griffis went to Japan and became Superintendent of Education in the province of Echizen. Throughout the 1870s, Griffis taught at several subsequent institutions and wrote for numerous newspapers and magazines. His works include the collections *Japanese Fairy Tales*, *Korean Fairy Tales*, *Belgian Fairy Tales*, and *Swiss Fairy Tales*. He died in Florida in 1928.

Homer

The Odyssey

Little is known for certain about the life of Homer, the Greek poet credited as the author of the great epics *The Iliad* and *The Odyssey*, although he is believed to have been born sometime between the twelfth and eighth centuries BC. *The Odyssey* describes the trials of the hero Odysseus on his journey home to Ithaca following the Trojan War. It has had a huge influence on Western literature, inspiring extensive translations, poems, plays and novels.

Joseph Jacobs

The Greek Princess and the Young Gardener

Joseph Jacobs (1854–1916) was born in Australia and settled in New York. He is most famous for his collections of English folklore and fairy tales, including 'Jack and the Beanstalk' and 'The Three Little Pigs'. He also published Celtic, Jewish and Indian fairy tales during his career. Jacobs was an editor for books and journals centred on folklore, and he was a member of The Folklore Society in England.

Grace James

Green Willow; The Flute; The Black Bowl; Horaizan; The Bell of Dōjōji

Grace James (1882–1965) was born in Tokyo to English parents. Growing up in Japan until the age of 12 when her family moved back to England, James was fascinated with Japanese culture and became a Japanese folklorist. She published retellings of traditional stories in her collection *Japanese Fairy Tales* (1910) and wrote about her experiences of Japan in her memoir *Japan: Recollections and Impressions* (1936). She was also an author of children's fiction, including the *John and Mary* series.

Ignácz Kúnos

The Horse-Devil and the Witch; The Magic Turban, the Magic Whip, and the Magic Carpet

Ignácz Kúnos (1860–1945) was a Hungarian linguist, author and Turkologist. He was a prominent scholar of Turkish folk literature and dialectology. Having studied linguistics at Budapest University and spending five years studying the Turkish language and culture in Constantinople (now Istanbul), he became professor of Turkish philology at Budapest University in 1890. He later worked as a professor at various other institutions and established the Department of Folkloristics at Istanbul University in 1925. His folktale collections include *Turkish Fairy Tales and Folk Tales* (1896) and *Forty-Four Turkish Fairy Tales* (1914).

Andrew Lang

The Dragon of the North; The Flower Queen's Daughter; The Flying Ship; The Cat's Elopement; How the Dragon Was Tricked; Catherine and Her Destiny; Esben and the Witch

Poet, novelist and anthropologist Andrew Lang (1844–1912) was born in Selkirk, Scotland. He is now best known for his collections of fairy stories and publications on folklore, mythology and religion. Inspired by the traditional folklore tales of his home on the English-Scottish border, Lang compiled twelve fairy books of different colours which collected 798 stories from French, Danish, Russian and Romanian sources, amongst others. This series was hugely popular and had a wide influence on increasing the popularity of fairy tales in children's literature. His fairy tale collections include *The Red Fairy Book* (1890), *The Lilac Fairy Book* (1910) and *The Book of Dreams and Ghosts* (1897).

Edmund Leamy

Princess Finola and the Dwarf; The Little White Cat

Edmund Leamy (1848–1904) was an Irish journalist, barrister, author of fairy tales and nationalist politician. Born in Waterford, Ireland, he became a Member of Parliament in the House of Commons of the United Kingdom of Great Britain and Northern Ireland, in which he represented various Irish seats from 1880 until his death in 1904. During his life, he wrote several fairy tales, such as "Princess Finola and the Dwarf" and "The Little White Cat". After they gained popularity, they were reprinted several times throughout Britain and Ireland. His main collection of stories was called *Irish Fairy Tales* (1890).

Frederick H. Martens

The Isle of Udröst; The Three Princesses in Whiteland; East of the Sun and West of the Moon; Silverwhite and Lillwacker; Faithful and Unfaithful

Frederick H. Martens (1874–1932) was an American translator and music journalist. His translation work mainly consisted of books for children, and he worked several times with the author Clara Stroebe to translate her collections of stories and fairy tales into English. Martens was the translator of Stroebe's *The Norwegian Fairy Book* (1922) and *The Swedish Fairy Book* (1921). He also translated Elsie Spicer Eells' *The Brazilian Fairy Book* (1926) and R. Wilhelm's *The Chinese Fairy Book* (1921). His original works include *Violin Mastery* (1919) and a number of newspaper and magazine articles.

Minnie Martin

Morongoe the Snake

Minnie Martin was the wife of a government official, who arrived in South Africa in 1891 and settled in

Lesotho (at that time Basutoland). In her preface to *Basutoland: Its Legends and Customs* (1903), she explains that "We both liked the country from the first, and I soon became interested in the people. To enable myself to understand them better, I began to study the language, which I can now speak fairly well." And thus she wrote this work, at the suggestion of a friend. Despite the inaccuracies pointed out by E. Sidney Hartland in his review of her book, he deemed the work "an unpretentious, popular account of a most interesting branch of the Southern Bantus and the country they live in."

Cornelius Mathews

Gray Eagle and His Five Brothers

Cornelius Mathews (1817–1899) was an American author. After attending Columbia College, Mathews went on to study at New York University, where he graduated in 1834, and then proceeded on to law school. Mathews rebelled against the literary status quo of the time, which had viewed American literature as inferior to British literature. He pursued the development of a new, distinctly American literary style. He is best known for helping to form the literary group Young America in the 1830s. He wrote for and co-edited the Young Americans' journal, *Arcturus*, from 1840 to 1842. Throughout the 1840s and 1850s, Mathews was involved in a number of American journals and magazines, either as a contributor or editor, including the *New Yorker*, the *Comic World* and the *New York Dramatic Mirror*.

Elodie L. Mijatovich

Gray Eagle and His Five Brothers

Elodie L. Mijatovich (1825–1908) was a British author. During the 1850s she lived in Boston, Massachusetts, where she advocated for the abolitionist movement. Following her marriage to a Serbian politician, she moved to Belgrade, and then to London. She was the translator of several Serbian literary works, including *Serbian Folk-Lore* (1874), *Serbian Fairy Tales* (published posthumously in 1918) and *The History of Modern Serbia* (1872). She also translated numerous Serbian national songs of the Kosovo cycle into English.

Katharine Pyle

Long, Broad and Sharpsight; The Dwarf with the Golden Beard; The Great White Bear and the Trolls; The Stones of Plouvinec; The Princes and the Friendly Animals; The Oat Cake; The Dreamer; Schippeitaro; The Three Silver Citrons; The Triumph of Truth; The Seven Golden Peahens; Haamdaanee and the Wise Gazelle; The Feather of the Zhar Bird; The Beautiful Maria di Legno; Buttercup; Cherry

Katharine Pyle (1863–1938) was an American author and illustrator. She primarily wrote books for young adults, as well as works on the colonial history of her home state of Delaware. She became interested in writing and art as a child, and later attended the Philadelphia School of Design for Women. Pyle initially published poems in *St. Nicholas Magazine* and *Harper's Bazaar*, and she co-wrote the book *The Wonder Clock* (1887) with her brother Howard Pyle. She contributed to America's Golden Age of Illustration and collaborated with fellow creatives on many books as both a writer and an illustrator.

Lewis Spence

The Quest of Gilgamesh

James Lewis Thomas Chalmers Spence (1874–1955) was a scholar of Scottish, Mexican and Central American folklore, as well as that of Brittany, Spain and the Rhine. He was also a poet, journalist, author, editor and nationalist who founded the party that would become the Scottish National Party. He was a Fellow of the Royal Anthropological Institute of Great Britain and Ireland, and Vice President of the Scottish Anthropological and Folklore Society.

Henry M. Stanley

The City of the Elephants ; King Gumbi and His Lost Daughter

"Dr Livingstone, I presume?" Welshman Sir Henry Morton Stanley (1841–1904) is probably most famous for a line he may or may not have uttered on encountering the missionary and explorer he had been sent to locate in Africa. He was also an ex-soldier who fought for the Confederate Army, the Union Army and the Union Navy before becoming a journalist and explorer of Central Africa. He joined Livingstone in the search for the source of the Nile and worked for King Leopold II of Belgium in the latter's mission to conquer the Congo basin. His works include *How I Found Livingstone* (1872), *Through the Dark Continent* (1878) *The Congo and the Founding of Its Free State* (1885), and *My Dark Companions* (1893).

Clara Stroebe

The Isle of Udröst; The Three Princesses in Whiteland; East of the Sun and West of the Moon; Silverwhite and Lillwacker; Faithful and Unfaithful

Clara Stroebe (1887–1932) was a German author, born in Freiburg im Breisgau. She attended Heidelberg University in 1907, followed by Ludwig Maximillian University of Munich from 1909 to 1910. Stroebe gathered and edited a number of fairy tale collections, including *The Swedish Fairy Book* (1921) and *The Norwegian Fairy Book* (1922), among several others. These books were published as part of the *Fairy Book* series produced by the Frederick A. Stokes Company. She is also often credited as Klara Stroebe.

Alice Werner

The Thunder's Bride; The Tale of Murile

Alice Werner (1859–1935) was a writer, poet and professor of Swahili and Bantu languages. She travelled widely in her early life, but by 1894 she had focused her writing on African culture and language, and later joined the School of Oriental Studies, working her way up from lecturer to professor. *Myths and Legends of the Bantu* (1933) was her last main work, but others on African topics include *The Language Families of Africa* (1915), *Introductory Sketch of the Bantu Languages* (1919), *The Swahili Saga of Liongo Fumo* (1926) and *Swahili Tales* (1929).

W.D. Westervelt

A Visit to the King of Ghosts; Maui Seeking Immortality

W.D. Westervelt (1849–1939) was an American author and pastor. He settled in Hawaii in 1899 and served as the Corresponding Secretary for the Hawaiian Historical Society beginning in 1908. His enormous interest in Hawaiian mythology and culture led him to publish numerous articles and books on the subject. His best-known works include *Legends of Gods and Ghosts (Hawaiian Mythology)* (1915), *Legends of Old Honolulu* (1915) and *Hawaiian Legends of Volcanoes* (1916). He is considered one of the foremost authorities on Hawaiian folklore in English.

GOTHIC FANTASY